THE
FINANCIER

A NOVEL

BY
THEODORE DREISER

AUTHOR OF
"JENNIE GERHARDT" "SISTER CARRIE"

HARPER & BROTHERS PUBLISHERS
NEW YORK AND LONDON
M - C - M - X - I - I

K-M

THE FINANCIER

THE FINANCIER

CHAPTER I

"I came into the world feet first and was born with teeth.
The nurse did prophesy that I should snarl and bite."
—RICHARD III.

THE Philadelphia into which Frank Algernon Cowperwood was born was at his very birth already a city of
two hundred and fifty thousand and more. It was set
with handsome parks, notable buildings, and crowded
with historic memories. Many of the things that we and
he knew later were not then in existence—the telegraph,
telephone, express company, ocean steamer, or city delivery of mails. There were no postage-stamps or regis-
tered letters. The street-car had not arrived, and in its
place were hosts of omnibuses, and for longer travel,
the slowly developing railroad system still largely connected with canals. Young Cowperwood's father was a
bank clerk at his birth, and ten years later, when young
Cowperwood was turning a very sensible, vigorous eye
on the world, his father was still a clerk, although he was
a much more trusted and desired one, and was so near
a tellership that there was not the least doubt in the world
that he would get it. The next year, because the president died and the vice-president became president, the
cashier was made vice-president, and Mr. Henry Worthington Cowperwood was moved into the place vacated by
the promoted teller. He was a happy man. It meant

I

the munificent sum of thirty-five hundred dollars a year, and he decided, as he told his wife joyously the night he heard it, that he, or they, rather, would now move from Number 21 Buttonwood Street to Number 124 New Market, where there was a nice brick house of three stories in height, as opposed to the one of two stories which they now occupied. Buttonwood Street, at the point which they were now located, was rapidly being surrounded by business conditions which were unbearable; and New Market at the point he had picked on was removed, at least a score of blocks, from the region which was once so nice but was now becoming so sorrowfully defiled. There was the probability that some day they would come into something even much better than this, but for the present this was sufficient. He was exceedingly grateful.

Mr. Henry Worthington Cowperwood was at this time a significant figure—tall, lean, inquisitorial, clerkly, the pink of perfection in the niceties of commercial conduct, absolutely practical — a man who believed only what he saw, was not at all disturbed about those silly fancies which might trouble the less rational brains of this world, and content to be what he was—a banker, or prospective one. He looked upon life as a business situation or deal, with everybody born as more or less capable machines to take a part in it. It was surprising to him to see how many incapable or unsatisfactory machines there were; but, thank heaven, now that he was getting along fairly well, this was no affair of his. At first, when he was much younger—he was now thirty-six—life had seemed just a little unsatisfactorily organized. But now—well now it didn't look so bad. He had nice, smooth, closely cropped side-whiskers coming to almost the lower lobe of his ears, and his upper lip was smooth and curiously long. He had a straight nose of a somewhat longish length and a chin that tended to be pointed. His manner might have been called severe, though really it was more of a cultivated manner than anything else.

THE FINANCIER

His eyebrows were bushy, emphasizing vague grayish-green eyes, and his hair was short and smooth and nicely parted. He wore a frock-coat always—it was quite the financial thing in these days—and a high hat. And he kept his hands and nails immaculately clean. Being ambitious to get somewhere socially and financially without falling, he was very careful of whom or with whom he talked; and he was as much afraid of expressing a rabid or unpopular political or social opinion as he was of being seen with an evil character, though he had no opinion of great political significance to express. He was neither anti nor pro slavery, though the air was stormy with abolition sentiment and its opposition. He believed sincerely that vast fortunes were to be made out of railroads if one only had the capital and that curious thing, a magnetic personality—the ability to win the confidence of others. He was sure that Andrew Jackson was all wrong in his opposition to Nicholas Biddle and the United States Bank, one of the great issues of the day; and he was worried, as he might well be, by the perfect storm of wildcat money which was floating about and which was constantly coming to his bank—discounted, of course—and handed out again to anxious borrowers at a profit, you may be sure. His bank was the Third National of Philadelphia, located in that center of all Philadelphia, and indeed almost, at that time, of all national finance, Third Street; and its owners did a brokerage business on the side. As a broker's clerk, Mr. Cowperwood had to know all sorts of banks here and elsewhere, for immense quantities of uncurrent bank-notes were to be handled, distributed, and mailed each day. There was a perfect plague of State banks, great and little, in those days, issuing notes practically without regulation upon insecure and unknown assets and failing and suspending with unheard-of rapidity; and these Mr. Cowperwood had to know about. He was convinced after a short experience that life was a ticklish business,

3

and he had become the soul of caution. Unfortunately for him, he lacked in a great measure the two things that are necessary for distinction in any field-magnetism and vision. He was not destined to be a great financier, though he was marked out to be a moderately successful one.

Mr. Cowperwood's home was in Buttonwood Street for the time being, and a pleasant little home it was, to be sure. Mrs. Cowperwood was of a Christian, saving disposition—Episcopalians, they were. She was a small woman, very attractive in her day, with light-brown hair and clear brown eyes. Later in life she became rather prim and matter-of-fact, and when Frank Cowperwood was ten she was the watchful mother of three boys and one girl. The former, captained by the eldest, Frank, were a source of considerable annoyance to her, for they were forever making expeditions to different parts of the city, getting in with bad boys probably, and seeing and hearing things they should neither see nor hear. Mr. Henry Cowperwood, with his future opportunities shining clear before him, hit upon the private school and tutor method as a happy solution, and so these boys for some years afterward were carefully watched. Nevertheless, boys would be boys, and these were no exceptions.

During all these years that Frank was growing up he was a natural-born leader. At the day school, and later at the Central High School, where he was finally educated, he was looked upon as one whose common sense could unquestionably be trusted in all cases, and he never disappointed this belief. He was a sturdy youth, courageous and defiant. After he was ten years old his mother learned to know that Joseph and Edward, the two younger brothers, were perfectly safe in his care, and if they asked to go anywhere it was customary for her to ask if Frank were going. If so, well and good. If not, not. If they wanted to do anything when he was with them and he objected, he was most emphatic in a quiet way.

"Can't we go down to the old market and jump on the cars?" Joseph used to ask. They were a great sight in those days—the railroad yards. The tracks came into Market Street, and many of the cars being locally switched about were hauled by horses. The boys were fond of riding, stealing as much as they could in this way; and Joseph and Edward were no exceptions.

"Why not?" Edward might ask.

"Because it isn't good for you, that's why. You keep off those things."

"Aw, the Collinses go down there."

"Well, we're not the Collinses. Don't you ever go down there alone."

Having the parental confidence and backing as well as his own natural force, Frank's word was law; and yet he was a liberal interpreter of the law. He liked to play "one old cat," the new baseball game coming into vogue at that time, and he was fond of football as played by his Central High School team. He liked visiting the museums in Chestnut Street—there were several—a menagerie, a museum of anatomy, and another of curious fish and birds; and he liked the theater, and would gladly take his brothers to a minstrel show or a pirate melodrama, paying the expense himself when he had the money. From the very first he was a good leader, but also a splendid second to those older than himself whom he sincerely admired. There was a certain "Red" Gilligan, a tall, shambling, and yet rather brilliant and pyrotechnic rowdy, who took a great fancy to young Cowperwood for a time. He used to see him at first, when he was a ten-year-old boy, passing the corner of Arch and Second, where Gilligan with the members of what was known as the "River gang" used to "hang out." Gilligan had another young protégé, "Spat" McGlathery, who received a terrible drubbing one afternoon from young Cowperwood a year or two later for spitting on his shoes. It came about in this way. He was passing innocently by, carrying his books, when the former, wishing to evince his contempt for all the refinements of this world—particularly those that were manifested by boys of his own age—spat sneeringly and contemptuously at the latter's feet and landed a nice spatter of tobacco-juice on his toes. This enraged Cowperwood greatly. Like a flash, though naturally calm, he dropped his books and went for his opponent. He wore a silver ring on his right hand which his mother had given him, and curiously it flashed into his mind in a lightning calculation to take it off, but he did not. Instead, he planted his right fist swift and straight on young McGlathery's jaw, then his left in the same place, then his right on the latter's mouth, then his left square between the latter's mouth and nose.

It was a terrific onslaught, quick and ugly, to which his opponent returned with enthusiasm, but he was no match for his new adversary. The latter forced him back steadily, and as he retreated Frank followed him. There was a crowd in a moment, for Spat was considered a star fighter of the gang; but Cowperwood drove him by sheer force and swiftness all about the sidewalk. He was not thinking of the crowd. He was thinking how thoroughly he could "lick" this bully and in how short a time. Red Gilligan, who was standing amazedly by, was delighted. He did not know that this nice-looking "mama's boy," as they called all the refined youths of the neighborhood, could do anything of the sort. To see Spat McGlathery, whom he greatly admired as a "scrapper," being drubbed in this way, and to realize yet as he did that Spat would scorn assistance, even though licked, and that therefore this was one of those admirable contests which one could judge on its merits, was inspiring. He followed them around, pushing the other "hickeys," as the bad boys of the gang were called, aside, and seeing that what he called fair play was had. He had on a red shirt, a brown coat, much too short for him, a baggy pair of trousers, fastened about his waist by a belt; and his pugnacious but quizzical and intelligent face was surmounted by a small, close-fitting cloth cap with a vizor pulled over his eyes. He was so interested that he was closely over the fighters all the time.

"Police!" yelled the neighbors from stores and windows.

"Let 'em alone," he yelled to his compatriots, fearing interruption. "Hands off! I'll smack your jaw!" (This to some youth interfering.) "If he can lick him, let him lick him."

The gang stood by.

It was a swift and rapid fight for all of four minutes, all over the red-brick sidewalk and into the gutter. Young Spat, recovering from his surprise and realizing that he had a terrible adversary, clinched. Frank manœuvered the former's head under his arm by sheer, hard force and punched him vigorously.

"Huh! Huh! Huh!" he grunted, as he struck him.

Mr. McGlathery was bleeding profusely.

"Aw! call him off," Spat's friends yelled.

"Let him alone," yelled Gilligan. "Spat 'll say when he's had enough."

Cowperwood forced him to the pavement, punching him and sitting astride of him. After a time he pushed his head against the bricks and punched some more.

"I quit," yelled McGlathery, after a time. He was bleeding and almost crying, in spite of himself, and he could not get up nor loosen Cowperwood's hold.

Young Cowperwood got up. He began brushing his clothes and looking about for some friendly face.

"Say, kid," called Gilligan, grabbing his arm, "say, you're a wonder! What's your name?"

"Cowperwood," replied Frank, kneading the dirt off his coat and trousers and feeling for his handkerchief.

"Kick the stuffing out of him," some other youth called, approaching and chafing to avenge McGlathery.

"Yah do, and I'll kick your head off, you flannel mouth. Git back!" It was Red Gilligan talking.

Cowperwood realized he had a friend.

"Where's my books?" he asked.

"Where's his books?" called Gilligan, authoritatively. An obsequious underling sought and found them.

"Say, kid," said his new protector, "I'm Red Gilligan. You're all right. You can fight. Don't you worry. They're not goin' to jump on you."

Cowperwood was looking apprehensively about.

Gilligan walked down the street with him the while a part of the gang stayed to console Spat McGlathery, while another part followed to witness the triumph of the victor. They could scarcely believe their senses— one of their bravest members licked! A policeman, attracted by the cries of shopkeepers and women, shortly hove into view and scattered the crowd. Red Gilligan, drawn by the charm of Cowperwood's personality, put his arm over the latter's shoulder—he was at least nine inches taller, spare and bony—and leered down joyfully in his new discovery's face. "Say, I'll be d—d!" he said. "You're all right! You're fine. Cowperwood, eh? Well, you know me from now on. You can have anything I got. I like you."

"I didn't want to fight him," said Cowperwood, conservatively. He was not sure whether he welcomed the attentions of this new friend or not. Still he did not mind them so much. They were pleasant.

"I know you didn't. Don't you be afraid. You didn't do any more than you ought to. He spit on your shoes. That's all right; you ought to lick him. You did just what you ought to do. That gang's goin' to do all right by you. They're goin' to be fair. Don't you let any of 'em give you any lip. If they do, soak 'em. I'll see that you git fair play. You can come around where I am any time you want to. Just come and tell me." He patted Frank's shoulder.

THE FINANCIER

Frank realized he was talking to a leader. Gilligan looked it. He was so raw, so uncouth, so strange; still he was fine and strong and brave, and Frank liked him.

"I don't want to have any trouble," he suggested, quietly. "I didn't start it. I really didn't mean to hit him as hard as I did at first."

"Don't you worry. He can take care of himself. You're in with me. I'm your friend. You and I are pards. I live over here in Vine Street."

Cowperwood smiled gladly. "All right," he said. "I'm afraid they'll jump on me if you don't head 'em off."

"No, they won't. If any one of 'em says a word you let me know. They won't do it again."

He accompanied Frank to his door. Gilligan shook hands with him.

"Say, Cowperwood," he said, "you're fine. Come around some Saturday. I'm always over there about one or two o'clock."

Frank smiled. "All right!" he said.

He went in, and Mr. Gilligan strolled away.

"Say," he chuckled to himself, as he strolled, "that was a real fight, that was. Gee, he's got a punch! That's the end of Spat McGlathery, all right. He got all that was comin' to him—say!"

Meanwhile Mr. Spat McGlathery had returned to his home in Topper's Alley, a region that swarmed with low-caste laboring life, and there meditated on the fortunes of those who encounter unexpected and untoward forces. It was a sad afternoon for him. Still he did not despair. He had simply found some one at last who could thoroughly "lick" him.

For a time thereafter Mr. Cowperwood was patronized by Mr. Gilligan, but only in an admiring, friendly way. Mr. Gilligan wanted to attach him to his retinue of stars; but that could not be done very well. Mr. Cowperwood's home ties were too exacting. They did explore certain

9

sections of the city together. Mr. Gilligan did "sic" him "on to" certain boastful persons whose colors, in his estimation, needed to be lowered; but Frank was in a way ashamed to do useless and pointless fighting. He liked Mr. Gilligan—his spirit—but his connections were rather reprehensible. So, after a time, he judiciously cut him, giving suave excuses, and Mr. Gilligan really took no offense. Frank made him see how it was. Out of friendship he gradually let him go. But the street-corner gang at Second and Arch never molested him after that one encounter.

From the very start of his life Frank wanted to know about economics and politics. He cared nothing for books. He was a clean, stocky, shapely boy with a bright, clean-cut, incisive face; large, clear gray eyes; a wide forehead; short, bristly, dark-brown hair. He had an incisive, quick-motioned, self-sufficient manner, and was forever asking questions with a keen desire for a brief and intelligent reply. He did not know what sickness was, never had an ache or pain, ate his food with gusto, and ruled his brothers with a rod of iron. "Come on, Joe! Hurry, Ed!" These commands were issued in no rough, but always a sure way; and Joe and Ed came. They looked up to Frank from the first as a master; and what he had to say, or what he saw or encountered, was listened to eagerly. He himself was pondering, pondering, pondering—one fact astonishing him quite as much as another, for he could not figure out how this thing he had come into—this life—was organized. How did all these people get into the world? What were they doing here? Who started things, anyhow? His mother told him the story of Adam and Eve; but he didn't believe it. There was a fish-market not so very far from his own home; and there, when he went to see his father at the bank, or when he took his brothers on after-school expeditions for mail or errands for his father, he liked to look at a certain tank in front of one store where they kept odd specimens of sea-life which the Delaware Bay fishermen would bring in. He saw once there a sea-horse—just a queer little sea-animal that looked somewhat like a horse—and another time he saw an electric eel which Franklin's discovery had explained. One day he saw a jelly-fish put in, and then a squid, and then a lobster. The lobster and the squid came well along in his fish experiences; he was witness of a familiar tragedy in connection with these two, which stayed with him all his life and cleared things up considerably intellectually. The squid, it appeared from the talk of the idle bystanders who were always loafing about this market, was considered the rightful prey of the lobster; and the latter had no other food offered him. The lobster lay at the bottom of the clear glass tank on the yellow sand, apparently seeing nothing—you could not tell in which way his beady, black buttons of eyes were looking—but apparently they were never off the body of the squid. The latter, pale and waxy in texture, looking very much like pork fat or jade, was moving about in torpedo fashion; but his movements were apparently never out of the eyes of his enemy, for by degrees small portions of his body began to disappear, snapped off by the relentless claws of his pursuer. The latter, as young Cowperwood was one day a witness, would leap like a catapult to where the squid was apparently idly dreaming, and the squid, very alert, would dart away, shooting out at the same time a cloud of ink, behind which it would disappear. It was not always completely successful, however. Some small portions of its body or its tail were frequently left in the claws of the monster below. Days passed, and, now fascinated by the drama, young Cowperwood came daily.

"Say, pa," he said to his father, one night, "did you ever see that tank in front of Joralemon's?"

"Yes, I know where it is," said his father.

"Did you ever see the squid and lobster they got in there?"

"I don't know. Why?"

"Well, that lobster's going to eat that squid. I can see more and more of him gone every day."

"How's that?" asked his father, indifferently.

"Why, that old lobster he just lies down there on the bottom of the tank, and he keeps his eyes fixed on that squid; and every now and then he jumps up with a bang, and he almost gets him. Sometimes he does get him— a little; but the squid pulls away. He's nipped off almost half his tail by now. And you know that ink-bag he carries—that stuff he shoots out to make a cloud?"

"Yes."

"Well, that's almost empty now. He's shot out so much he ain't got any more, or hardly any more."

"He hasn't any more," corrected his father.

"Well," went on his son, ignoring the correction, "you see, he's getting tired. I can see it. I've been watching him every day now for a week, and he's getting weaker all the time. That lobster won't give him any rest. I can see him looking at him all the time. He's goin' to get him. That squid's a goner. He's goin' to get him, sure!"

He paused, his eye alight, his whole body keyed up. He was interested—not pityingly so much as dramatically interested. His young face was keen and hungry for further information.

"Well, what of that?" asked his father, curiously.

"Oh, nothing. Only I'm going by there in the morning. I want to see whether he's got him."

In the morning he went, his young pantalooned legs squared out solidly in front of the tank. The squid was not gone, but a piece of him; and his ink-bag was emptier than ever. In the corner of the tank sat the lobster, poised apparently for action.

Young Cowperwood put his nose to the glass. He looked solemnly at the lobster. He stayed as long as he could, the bitter struggle fascinating him. He liked to study the rough claw with which the lobster did his deadly work. He liked to stare at the squid and think how fateful was his doom. Now, maybe, or in an hour or a day, he might die, slain by the lobster, and the lobster would eat him. He looked again at the greenish-copperish engine of destruction in the corner and wondered when this would be. To-night, maybe. He would come back to-night.

He returned one night, and lo! to his grief and astonishment, his wish was granted. There was a little crowd around the tank. The lobster was in the corner. Before him was the squid cut in two and partially devoured.

"He got him at last," observed one bystander. "I was standing right here an hour ago, and up he leaped and grabbed him. The squid was too tired. He wasn't quick enough. He did back up, but that lobster he calculated on his doing that. He's been figuring on his movements for a long time now. He got him to-day."

"Well, I swan!" somebody observed.

Cowperwood Junior only stared. He had missed this. It was too bad. He wanted to see it. The least touch of sorrow came to him for the squid as he stared at it slain. Then he stared at the victor.

"That's the way it has to be, I guess," he commented to himself. "That squid wasn't quick enough. He didn't have anything to feed on." He figured it out. The squid couldn't kill the lobster—he had no weapon. The lobster could kill the squid—he was heavily armed. There was nothing for the squid to feed on; the lobster had the squid as prey. What was the result to be? What else could it be? "He didn't have a chance," he said, finally, tucking his books under his arm and trotting on.

It made a great impression on him. It answered in a rough way that riddle which had been annoying him so much in the past: "How is life organized?" Things lived on each other—that was it. Lobsters lived on squids and other things. What lived on lobsters? Men, of course! Sure, that was it! And what lived on men? he asked himself. Was it other men? Wild animals lived on men. And there were Indians and cannibals. And some men were killed by storms and accidents. He wasn't so sure about men living on men yet; but men did kill each other. How about wars and street fights and mobs? He had seen a mob once. It attacked the *Public Ledger* building as he was coming home from school. His father had explained what for, too. There was great excitement. It was about the slaves. That was it! Sure, men lived on men. Look at the slaves. They were men. That's what all this excitement was about these days. Men killing other men—negroes.

He went on home quite pleased with himself at his solution.

"Say," he said to his mother, that night, "he got him, mother!"

"Got who? What got what? Go wash your hands."

"Why, that lobster got that squid I was telling you and pa about."

"Well, that's all right. It's too bad. What makes you take any interest in such things? Run, wash your hands."

"Well, it's interesting. You don't often see anything like that. I never did."

He went out in the back yard, where there was a hydrant and a post with a little table on it, and on that a cleanly tin-pan and a bucket of water. Here he washed his face and hands.

"Say, papa," he said to his father, later, "you know that squid?"

"Yes."

"Well, he's dead. The lobster got him."

The father stared at his paper. "Well, that's too bad," he said, indifferently.

For days and weeks Frank thought of this and of the life

he was tossed into, for he was already thinking of what he should be in this world, and how he should get along. From seeing his father count money, he was sure that he would like banking; and Third Street, where his father's office was, seemed to him the cleanest, brightest, most fascinating street in the world.

CHAPTER II

THE growth of young Frank Algernon Cowperwood was through years of what might be called a comfortable and happy family existence, for, although the first ten years of his life had been spent in Buttonwood Street, he was, of course, very young and knew little of those social distinctions which afterward became so marked in his consciousness. Buttonwood Street was a lovely place to live for a boy. It contained mostly small two and three story brick houses—red, of course—with small, white-marble steps leading up to the front door, and thin, white-marble trimmings outlining the front door and windows. There were trees in the street—plenty of them. The road pavement was of big, round cobblestones made bright and clean by the rains; and the sidewalks were of brick—red, of course—and, always damp and cool. In the windows, in summer-time, were sometimes flowers; and in the rear always was a yard with trees and flowers and grass, for the lots were almost always one hundred feet deep, and the house-fronts, crowding close to the pavement in front, left a comfortable space in the rear. The Cowperwoods, father and mother, were not so lean and narrow that they could not enter into the natural tendency to be happy and joyous with their children; and so this family, which increased at the rate of a child every two or three years after Frank's birth, was quite an interesting affair when he was ten, and they were ready to move into the New Market Street home. Henry Worthington Cowperwood's connections were increased as his position grew more responsible, and gradually he was becoming quite a personage. He already knew a number of the more prosperous merchants who dealt with his bank, and because, as a clerk, during banking hours he frequently had to hurry about to other banking-houses and brokers making exchanges, verifying accounts and checks, he had come to be familiar with and favorably known in the Bank of the United States, the Drexels, the Edwardses, and others. The brokers knew him as representing a very sound organization and being particularly reliable and trustworthy. He was not brilliant, but apparently honest and worthy of confidence in many things.

"Hey, Hy!" they sometimes called to him. (Hy Cowperwood he was known as in his earlier days.) "How are things over in your place?" And they secured advice as to the looseness or tightness of money as he would hear of it, and how credits were running. When his tellership arrived he was not so familiarly greeted, except by those who were much superior to him financially.

In this progress of his father, once he was ten years old and the former had become teller, young Cowperwood definitely shared. It was not uncommon for Cowperwood Senior to let his boy come to the bank on Saturdays, when he was not at school, and witness the deft exchange of bills at the brokerage end of the business, at the counting of which, and the calculations in connection with which, his father was an expert. Young Cowperwood was vastly interested in this process—wanted to know where all the types of money came from, why discounts of from ten to fifteen per cent. were demanded and received, what the men did with all the money they received. His father was glad to explain, pleased at his interest; and Frank was eager to learn. Even at this early age—from ten to fifteen—he gained a wide knowledge of the condition of the country financially—what a State bank was, and what a national one; what brokers did; what stocks were, and bonds, and why they fluctuated in value, and why they were quoted in the papers.

He began to see clearly what was meant by money as a medium of exchange, and how all values were calculated according to one primary value, that of gold. If gold were high or scarce, money was said to be tight, and times were bad. If gold was plentiful, money was easy, credits were large, and business was flourishing. Young Cowperwood finally studied all this out for himself, coming to a clear understanding of banking as a machine for doing business. It facilitated, as he saw it, the exchange of this general medium, gold, or its certificates of presence and deposit and ownership. Finance fascinated him much as art might fascinate another boy, or literature another. He was a financier by instinct, and all the knowledge that pertained to that great art was as natural to him as the emotions and subleties of life are to a poet. This medium of exchange, *gold*, interested him intensely. He asked his father where it came from, and when told that it was mined, dreamed that he owned a gold-mine and waked to wish that he did. Even what gold was made of—its chemical constituents—interested and held his attention. He marveled that it ever came to be, and how it was finally selected as the medium or standard of exchange. So all those piles of bills on his father's desk—those yellow and green papers—represented gold deposited somewhere, or claimed to be deposited. If they were worth their face value, the gold was where the certificate said it was; if the certificate was not worth its face value, the presence of the gold was in question, or hard to get at, just so much as the certificate was discounted. He was interested in stocks and bonds, too, which were constantly being deposited as collateral; and he learned that some stocks and bonds were not worth the paper they were written on, and that others were worth much more than their face value indicated.

"There, my son," said his father to him, one day, "you won't often see a bundle of those around this neighborhood."

They were a series of shares in the British East India Company deposited as collateral, at two-thirds of their face value, for a loan of one hundred thousand dollars. Some Philadelphia magnate of the day owned them, and had hypothecated them for the use of the ready cash which he needed. Young Cowperwood looked at them curiously.

"Say, they're plain-looking, aren't they?" he commented, curiously.

"They are worth just four times their face value," said his father, archly.

Frank Cowperwood re-examined them. "The British East. India Company," he read. "Ten pounds—that's pretty near fifty dollars."

"Forty-eight thirty-five," commented his father, dryly. "Well, if we had a bundle of those we wouldn't need to work very hard. You'll notice there are scarcely any pin-marks on these. They aren't hauled around very much. I don't suppose these have ever been used as collateral before."

Young Cowperwood gave them back after a time, but not without a keen sense of the vast ramifications of finance. What was the East India Company? What did it do? His father told him. These shares in companies interested him. They made him think that he would handle shares of his own some day.

At the Cowperwood home also, as young Frank grew older, there was considerable talk at one time and another of this and that financial investment and adventure. He heard, for one thing, of a curious character by the name of Steemberger, who was a great beef speculator from Virginia at the time, and who was attracted to Philadelphia in those days by the hope of large and easy credits. Steemberger, so his father said, had formerly been close to Nicholas Biddle, Lardner, and others of the United States Bank, or at least friendly with them, and seemed to be able to obtain from that organization nearly all that he asked for. His operations in the purchase of cattle in Virginia, Ohio, and other States were vast, amounting, in fact, to an entire monopoly of the business of supplying beef to Eastern cities. He was a big man, enormous, with a face, his father said, something like that of a pig; and he wore a high beaver hat and a long frock-coat which hung loosely about his big chest and stomach. He had managed to force the price of beef up to thirty cents a pound at this time, causing all the retailers and consumers to rebel, and this was what made him so conspicuous. He used to come to the elder Cowperwood's bank, or, rather, the brokerage end of it, with as much as one hundred thousand or two hundred thousand dollars in twelve months—post-notes of the United States Bank in denominations of one thousand, five thousand, and ten thousand dollars. These he would cash at from ten to twelve per cent. under their face value, having previously given the United States Bank his own note at four months for the entire amount. He would take his pay from the Third National brokerage counter in packages of Virginia, Ohio, and western Pennsylvania bank-notes at par, because he made his disbursements principally in those States. The Third National would in the first place realize a profit of from four to five per cent. on the original transaction; and as it took the Western bank-notes at a discount, it also made a profit on those. Young Frank listened to the story of these transactions with a greedy ear. They seemed wonderful to him; but this whole world of money was like a fairyland, full of delight. Why, in Third Street there was nothing but money, great piles of it.

There was another man his father told him about—or rather told his mother and he overheard—who was known as "Francis J. Grund." He was apparently a famous newspaper correspondent and lobbyist at Washington, and possessed the faculty of getting at and developing secrets of every kind, especially if they related to financial legislation. The secrets of the President and the Cabinet, as well as of the Senate and the House of Representatives, seemed to be open to him. Grund had been about, years before, purchasing through one or two brokers large amounts of the various kinds of Texas debt certificates and bonds, which, as Frank's father observed, other government officials of that time were also doing. The Republic of Texas, in its struggle for independence from Mexico, had issued bonds and certificates in great variety, amounting in value to ten or fifteen million dollars. A scheme had been on foot to make Texas a State of the Union, and a bill was finally passed providing a contribution on the part of the United States of five million dollars, to be applied to the extinguishment of this old debt. Grund knew of this, and also of the fact that some of this debt, owing to the peculiar conditions of issue, was to be paid in full, while other portions were to be scaled down, and there was to be a false or prearranged failure to pass the bill appropriating the five million dollars at one session, in order to frighten off the outsiders who might have heard and begun to buy the old certificates for their own profit. Grund knew of this. The Third National knew of Grund's knowledge through him; and Cowperwood, as teller, was also informed in some way. He told his wife about it afterward; and so his son, in this roundabout way, heard it, and his clear, big eyes glistened. He wondered why his father did not take advantage of it and buy some Texas certificates himself, but the latter was too honest, too careful. So this was the way money was made. Men schemed and planned, and then they reaped big profits. Grund, so his father said, and possibly three or four others, had made over a hundred thousand dollars apiece. It wasn't exactly legitimate, he seemed to think, and yet it was, too. Why shouldn't such inside information be rewarded? Somehow, Frank realized that his father had never been involved in any way in these, to him, wonderful operations. Why? Why didn't his father make a hundred thousand dollars out of something? Look at Steemberger, with a hundred thousand dollars in notes in his hat, and this man Grund, and others! When he grew up, Frank told himself, he was going to be a broker, or a financier, or a banker, and do some of these things. It was so easy for him to see how they were done. You had to get in with people—that was how: you had to know what was going on. His father was nice, but he was slow—surely he was. If *he* were his father, now.

He walked to school each day thinking of these things; but he was sick of school and books. What did his teachers know about money? Nothing. What did these other boys know of what was going on in Third Street? Not a thing. Why, a man might get down in there and get rich before anybody knew anything about anything. He wondered that the street was not crowded with people like Steemberger and Grund. It was so easy. He could see how it was. He could see how he could do it. Wait. He would be a broker, that's what he would be; and that just as quick as he was out of school, if not sooner. He would work and coin some money, and then he would become a broker, and then he would become rich.

There was an uncle who came to the Cowperwoods' house about this time—the one in New Market Street—when they became well located there, who had not previously appeared in the life of young Cowperwood and his brothers and sister. He was rather a fascinating type of man, solid and unctuous, say five feet ten in height, with a big, round body, a round, smooth head rather bald, a clear, ruddy complexion, blue eyes, and what little hair he had of a sandy hue. He was exceedingly well dressed for men of those days, indulging in flowered waistcoats, long, light-colored frock-coats, and the invariable (for a fairly prosperous man) high hat. Frank was fascinated by him, because he had been a planter in Cuba and still owned a big ranch there, and could tell him tales of Cuban life—

rebellions, ambuscades, hand-to-hand fighting with machetes on his own plantation, and things of that sort. He was a brother of Mrs. Cowperwood, Seneca Davis by name; and he brought from Cuba, where he had been for ten years, a collection of Indian curios, to say nothing of an independent fortune and several slaves. He had one slave, named Manuel, a tall, raw-boned black, who was his constant attendant, a body-servant as it were. He still had his sugar-plantation, and at this day shipped raw sugar in boat-loads to the Southwark wharves in Philadelphia. Frank liked him because he took life in a hearty, jovial way, rather rough and offhand for this somewhat quiet and reserved household.

"Why, Nancy Arabella," he said to Mrs. Cowperwood, on arriving one Sunday afternoon, when the household was thrown into joyous astonishment at his unexpected and unheralded appearance, "you haven't grown an inch! I thought when you married old Brother Hy here that you were going to fatten up and grow tall, something like your brother. Look at you! I swear to Heaven you don't weigh five pound." And he jounced her up and down by the waist, much to the perturbation of the children, who had never before seen their mother so familiarly handled. Henry Cowperwood was exceedingly interested in and pleased at the arrival of this rather prosperous relative; for, twelve years before, when he was married, Seneca Davis had not taken much notice of him. He was a man of his own age, but a much more forceful type of character.

"Look at all these little putty-faced Philadelphians. They ought to come down to my ranch in Cuba and get tanned up. That would take away this waxy look." And he pinched the cheek of Anna Adelaide, the only girl, now five years old. "I tell you, Henry, you have a rather nice place here." And he looked at the main room of the rather conventional three-story house with a critical eye.

It was nice. This particular room was twenty by twenty-four, and finished in imitation cherry, with a set of new and shapely Sheraton parlor furniture. Since Henry, the father, had become teller of the Third National the family had indulged in a piano—a decided luxury in those days—brought from Europe; and it was intended that Anna Adelaide, when she was old enough, should learn to play. There were a few uncommon ornaments in the room—a gas-chandelier for one thing, a glass bowl with goldfish in it, some rare and highly polished shells, and a marble Cupid bearing a basket of flowers, which Cowperwood had picked up somewhere at a sale. It was summer-time, the windows were open, and the trees outside, with their softly extended green branches, were pleasantly visible shading the brick sidewalk. Uncle Seneca strolled out into the back yard to see if they had a hammock.

"Well, this is pleasant enough," he observed, noting a large elm and seeing that the yard was partially paved with brick and inclosed within brick walls, up the sides of which vines were clambering. "Where's your hammock? Don't you string a hammock here in summer? Down on my verandas at San Pedro I have six or seven."

He noted Edward, the youngest boy, at his side, with Frank in the distance, looking at him. Mr. and Mrs. Cowperwood were conservatively located in the doorway.

"We hadn't thought of putting one up because of the neighbors; but it would be nice. Henry will have to get one."

"I have two or three in my trunks over at the hotel. I thought you mightn't have any. My niggers make 'em down there. I'll send Manuel over with them in the morning."

He plucked at the vines, tweaked Edward's ear, told Joseph, the second boy, he would bring him an Indian tomahawk, and went back into the house.

"This is the lad that interests me," he said, after a

time, laying his hand on the shoulder of Frank. "What did you name him in full, Henry?"

"Frank Algernon."

"Well, you might have named him after me. There's something to this boy. He's got something in his eye. How would you like to come down to Cuba and be a planter, my boy?"

"I'm not so sure that I'd like to," replied the eldest.

"Well, that's straight-spoken. What have you against it?"

"Nothing, except that I don't know anything about it."

"What do you know?"

The boy smiled wisely. "Not so very much, I guess."

"Well, what are you interested in?"

"Money!"

"Aha! What's bred in the bone, eh! Get something of that from your father, eh? Well, that's a good trait. And spoken like a man, too! We'll hear more about that later. Nancy, you're breeding a financier here, I think. He talks like one."

He looked at this boy carefully now, and he was impressed. There was real force in that sturdy young body—no doubt of it. Those large, clear gray eyes indicated much, and revealed nothing. They seemed full of intelligence and light without speaking of anything apparently that they knew.

"A smart boy," he said to Henry, his brother-in-law. "I like his get-up. You have a bright family."

Henry Cowperwood smiled dryly. None knew better than he Frank's bent. And this man, if he liked him, might do much for him. He might eventually leave him some of his fortune. He was wealthy and single.

Uncle Seneca became a frequent visitor to the house— he and his negro body-guard, Manuel, who spoke both English and Spanish, much to the astonishment of the children; and he took an increasing interest in Frank.

"When that boy gets old enough to find out what he wants to do, I think I'll help him to do it," he observed to his sister one day; and she told him she was very grateful. He talked to Frank about his studies, and found that what he said was true—he cared little for books or most of the study he was compelled to pursue. Grammar was an abomination. Literature silly. Latin was of no use. History—well, it was fairly interesting.

"I like bookkeeping and arithmetic," he observed. "I want to get out and get to work, though. That's what I want to do."

"You're pretty young, my son," observed his uncle. "You're only how old now? Fourteen?"

"Thirteen."

"Well, you can't leave school much before sixteen. You'll do better if you stay until seventeen or eighteen. It can't do you any harm. You won't be a boy again."

"I don't want to be a boy. I want to get to work."

"Don't go too fast, son. You'll be a man soon enough. Be quiet. Study now. When the time comes you'll get a good start. You want to be a banker, do you?"

"Yes, sir!"

"Well, when the time comes, if everything is all right and you've behaved yourself and you still want to, I'll help you get a start in business. If I were you and were going to be a banker, I'd first spend a year or so in some good grain and commission house. There's good training to be had there. You'll learn a lot that you ought to know. When the time comes you do that. And, meantime, keep your health and learn all you can. Wherever I am, you let me know, and I'll write and find out how you've been conducting yourself."

He brought some great cannon-crackers out on the evening of July the Fourth, and he and Frank helped entertain and disturb the neighborhood by setting them off. He gave the boy a handsome purse and a ten-dollar gold piece, which he got from Henry Cowperwood by exchange, to start a bank-account with.

"That boy is a bright boy," he said to the father. "He's a real man already. There's something to him. He's going to make his mark."

And, not strange to say, he liked the whole Cowperwood household much better for this dynamic, self-sufficient, sterling youth who was an integral part of it.

CHAPTER III

THE years that passed between the time that young Cowperwood was fully decided that he wanted to be a banker and the time that he actually achieved this result were filled with curious interests. It was in his thirteenth year that he made his first business venture and it was decidedly profitable from his point of view. Near his home in New Market Street was a grocer where his mother traded; and here he was wont to see great piles of things displayed for sale at one time and another—boxes of soap, for instance, jars of fruit—not cans, for the tinning industry had not developed in those days to the proportions it later assumed—papers of coffee and the like. These things took his eye and interested him in the ramifications of the grocery business—where these things came from, principally. He knew from his geography now that many things were imported to this land —coffee, sugar (his uncle Seneca did that), rice, tea; and he wondered from time to time whether there was much money in the buying and selling of these things. In far-off China, practically unknown to the world commercially, they grew and fired tea, and his geography showed him a picture of that. In Front Street were spice houses which imported spices from Java and the Dutch East Indies; their signs said so. There was one man who sold tropical birds, brought by boat, and monkeys; and there was another man who offered, from time to time, invoices of silks and mattings. The good tailoring-houses brought all their fine weaves from England; and cutlery came from the same place.

But to return. One day he was walking in Front Street,

and he saw an auctioneer's flag hanging out before a store, a wholesale grocery store, and inside the contents were being disposed of, the owner having decided to wind up his business.

"What am I bid for this exceptional lot of Java coffee, twenty-two bags all told, which is now selling in the market for seven dollars and thirty-two cents a bag wholesale? What am I bid? What am I bid? The whole lot must go as one. What am I bid?"

"Eighteen dollars," suggested one trader, who was standing near the door, indifferently, more to start the bidding than anything else, for he was not vastly interested in coffee. Frank, who was passing, paused.

"Twenty-two!" called another.

"Thirty!" a third. "Thirty-five!" a fourth; and so on up to seventy-five, less than half of what it was worth.

"I'm bid seventy-five! I'm bid seventy-five! I'm bid seventy-five!" called the auctioneer, loudly. "Any other offers? Going once at seventy-five; am I offered eighty? Going twice at seventy-five, and"—he paused, one hand raised dramatically. Then he brought it down with a slap in the palm of the other—"sold to Mr. Silas Gregory for seventy-five. Make a note of that, Jerry," he called to his red-headed, freckle-faced clerk beside him. Then he turned to another lot of grocery staples —this time starch, eleven barrels of it.

Young Cowperwood was making a rapid calculation. If, as the auctioneer said, coffee was worth seven dollars and thirty-two cents a bag in the open market, and this buyer was getting this coffee for seventy-five dollars, he was making then and there eighty-six dollars and four cents, to say nothing of what his profit would be if he sold it at retail as Frank's mother's grocer did.

As Frank recalled, his mother was paying twenty-eight cents a pound. He drew nearer, his books tucked under his arm, and watched these operations closely. The starch, as he soon heard, was valued at ten dollars a barrel, and it only brought six. Some kegs of vinegar were knocked down at one-third their value, and so on. He began to wish he could bid; but he had no money, just a little pocket change. The auctioneer noticed him standing almost directly under his nose, and was curious at his interest. He was also impressed with the stolidity—solidarity—of the boy's expression.

"I am going to offer you now a fine lot of Castile soap—seven cases, no less, which, as you know, if you know anything about soap, is now selling at fourteen cents a bar. This soap is worth anywhere at this moment eleven dollars and seventy-five cents a case. What am I bid? What am I bid? What am I bid?" He was talking fast in the usual style of auctioneers, with much unnecessary emphasis; but Cowperwood was not unduly impressed. He was already rapidly calculating for himself. Seven cases at eleven dollars and seventy-five cents would be worth just eighty-two dollars and twenty-five cents; and if it went at half—if it went at half—

"Twelve dollars," commented one bidder.

"Fifteen," bid another.

"Twenty," called a third.

"Twenty-five," a fourth.

Then it came to dollar raises, for Castile soap was not such a vital commodity. "Twenty-six." "Twenty-seven." "Twenty-eight." "Twenty-nine." There was a pause.

"Thirty," observed young Cowperwood, decisively.

The auctioneer, a short, lean-faced, spare man with bushy hair and an incisive eye, looked at him curiously—without pausing, however. He had, somehow, in spite of himself, been impressed by the boy's peculiar eye; and now he felt, without knowing why, that the offer was probably legitimate enough, and that the boy had the money. . He might be the son of a grocer.

"I'm bid thirty! I'm bid thirty! I'm bid thirty for this fine lot of Castile soap. It's a fine lot. It's worth fourteen cents a bar. Will any one bid thirty-one? Will any one bid thirty-one? Will any one bid thirty-one?"

"Thirty-one," said a voice.

"Thirty-two," replied Cowperwood.

The same process was repeated.

"I'm bid thirty-two! I'm bid thirty-two! I'm bid thirty-two! Will anybody bid thirty-three? It's fine soap. Seven cases of fine Castile soap. Will anybody bid thirty-three?"

Young Cowperwood's mind was working. He had no money with him; but his father was teller of the Third National Bank, and he could quote him as references. His uncle was Seneca Davis. He could sell all of his soap to his grocer, surely; or, if not, to other grocers. Other people were anxious to get this soap at this price. Why not he?

The auctioneer paused.

"Thirty-two once! Am I bid thirty-three? Thirty-two twice! Am I bid thirty-three? Thirty-two three times! Seven fine cases of soap. Am I bid anything more? Once, twice! Three times! Am I bid anything more?"—his hand was up again—"and sold to Mr.—?" He leaned over and looked curiously into the face of his young bidder.

"Frank Cowperwood, son of the teller of the Third National Bank," replied the boy, decisively.

"Oh yes," said the man, fixed by his glance.

"Will you wait while I run up to the bank and get the money?"

"Yes. Don't be gone long. If you're not here in an hour I'll sell it again."

Young Cowperwood made no reply. He hurried out and ran fast; first, not to his father, but to his grocer, which was within a block of his home.

Thirty feet from the door he slowed up, put on a nonchalant air, and, strolling in, looked about for Castile soap.

THE FINANCIER

There it was, the same kind, displayed in a box and looking just as his soap looked.

"How much is this a bar, Mr. Dalrymple?" he inquired.

"Sixteen cents," replied that worthy.

"If I could sell you seven boxes for sixty-two dollars just like this would you take them?"

"The same soap?"

"Yes, sir."

Mr. Dalrymple calculated a moment.

"Yes, I think I would," he replied, cautiously.

"Would you pay me to-day?"

"I'd give you my note for it. Where is the soap?"

He was perplexed and somewhat astonished by this unexpected proposition on the part of his neighbor's son. He knew Mr. Cowperwood well—and Frank also.

"Will you take it if I bring it to you to-day?"

"Yes, I will," he replied. "Are you going into the soap business?"

"No. But I know where I can get some of that soap cheap."

He hurried out again and ran to his father's bank. It was after banking hours; but he knew how to get in, and he knew that his father would be glad to see him make thirty dollars. He only wanted to borrow the money for a day.

"What's the trouble, Frank?" asked his father, looking up from his desk when he appeared, breathless and red-faced.

"I want you to loan me thirty-two dollars! Will you?"

"Why, yes, I might. What do you want to do with it?"

"I want to buy some soap—seven boxes of Castile soap. I know where I can get it and sell it. Mr. Dalrymple will take it. He's already offered me sixty-two for it. I can get it for thirty-two. Will you let me have the money? I've got to run back and pay the auctioneer."

32

His father smiled. This was the most business-like attitude he had, as yet, seen his son manifest. He was so keen, so alert for a boy of thirteen.

"Why, Frank," he said, going over to a drawer where some bills were, "are you going to become a financier already? You're sure you're not going to lose on this? You know what you're doing, do you?"

"You let me have the money, father, will you?" he pleaded. "I'll show you in a little bit. Just let me have it."

He was like a young hound on the scent of game. His father could not resist his appeal, it was so fascinating.

"Why, certainly, Frank," he replied. "I'll trust you." And he counted out six five-dollar certificates of the Third National's own issue and two ones. "There you are."

Frank ran out of the building with a briefly spoken thanks. He returned to the auction-room as fast as his legs would carry him. When he came in, sugar was being auctioned, but he paid no attention to that. He made his way to the auctioneer's clerk.

"I want to pay for that soap," he suggested.

"Now?" asked the boy.

"Yes. Will you give me a receipt?"

"Yep."

"Do you deliver this?"

"No. No delivery. You have to take it away in twenty-four hours."

That difficulty did not trouble him. He had some change.

"All right," he said, and pocketed his paper testimony of purchase.

The auctioneer watched him as he went out. In half an hour he was back with a drayman—an idle levee-wharf hanger-on who was waiting for a job.

Frank had bargained with him to deliver the soap for sixty cents. In still another half-hour he was before the door of the astonished Mr. Dalrymple, and he had him come out and look at the boxes before attempting to remove them. His plan was to have them carried on to his own home if the operation for any reason failed to go through. Though it was his first great venture, he was now as cool as a cucumber.

"Yes," said Mr. Dalrymple, scratching his gray head reflectively. He was a tall man, spare, stoop-shouldered, rather near-sighted, and wore steel-rimmed spectacles. "Yes, that's the same soap. I'l' take it. I'll be as good as my word. Where'd you get it, Frank?"

"At Bixom's auction up here," the latter replied, frankly and blandly.

It did not strike Mr. Dalrymple as so strange that this boy should attend an auction in his own neighborhood and buy soap cheaper than he could, but it was strange just the same. He had the drayman bring in the soap; and after some formality—more because the agent in this case was a boy than anything else—he made out his note at thirty days and gave it to him.

Frank thanked him and pocketed the note. He decided to go back to his father's bank and discount it, as he had seen others doing, thereby paying his father back and getting his own profit in ready money. It couldn't be done ordinarily on any day after business hours; but his father would make an exception in his case. Most note-brokers kept open until nine o'clock at night in Third Street.

He hurried back, whistling; and his father glanced up smiling when he came in.

"Well, Frank, how'd you make out?" he asked.

"Here's a note at thirty days," he said, producing the paper Dalrymple had give him. "Do you want to discount that for me? You can take your thirty-two out of that."

His father examined it closely. "Sixty-two dollars!" he observed. "Mr. Dalrymple! That's good paper!

Yes, I can. It will cost you ten per cent.," he added, jestingly. "Why don't you just hold it, though? I'll let you have the thirty-two dollars until the end of the month."

"Oh no," said his son. "You discount it and take your money. I may want mine." He had an air of business.

His father smiled. "All right," he said, "I'll fix it to-morrow. Tell me just how you did this." And his son told him.

His senior listened with keen interest. This, he thought, was a remarkable thing for a boy of Frank's age to have done—clearing thirty dollars at one clip. He wanted to go home and tell his wife, and later his brother-in-law, Seneca Davis, when he should see him again. Frank was a remarkable boy. At this rate he would certainly make his mark some day.

At seven o'clock that night his wife heard about it, and in due time Uncle Seneca. Frank had indulged in no other exciting deeds until that time. Uncle Seneca was pleased.

"What 'd I tell you, Cowperwood?" he asked. "He has stuff in him, that youngster. Look out for him."

Mrs. Cowperwood looked at her boy curiously at dinner. Was this the son she had nursed at her bosom not so very long before? Surely he was developing rapidly. As for the financier, he was bland and calm, radiant but inscrutable, and without any desire to talk or boast.

"Yes, I made thirty dollars," he answered his father, when the latter told it in the presence of his mother; but he neither blushed nor was he nervous nor manifested excitement in any way.

"Well, Frank, I hope you can do that often," said his mother, happily.

"I hope so, too, ma," was his rather non-committal reply.

CHAPTER IV

FROM the very first young Cowperwood knew how to make money. He was an adept at turning all sorts of practical tricks, such as taking subscriptions for a boys' paper, taking the agency for the sale of a new kind of ice-skate from an ice-skate company, and once organizing a band of neighborhood youths into a union for the purpose of purchasing their summer straw hats at wholesale. There were only twelve of them, but he secured the wholesale rate for that number, and took a commission of two dollars on the total purchases. There was nothing small or cheap in his ideas. He was not doing this in a picayune way. It was not his idea that he could get rich by saving. From the first he had the notion that liberal spending was better, and that somehow he would get along. He did this more to be doing it and to exercise his talent for financiering. No one ever dreamed of thinking of him as stingy. He was not wasteful; but he paid naturally, easily, and unconcernedly as he went.

The soap transaction, coming as it did at the end of his thirteenth year, broadened his horizon greatly. It showed him clearly what trade was, and how transactions, even on a small scale, could be made exceedingly profitable. Auction sales were not to be discovered every day. His home grocer was only open to one such transaction in a reasonable period of time. But there were other things which could be done, and he remembered, to his great dissatisfaction, that all the staples in the auction-room had been auctioned off at such bargain prices. If he had been able to buy them all and dispose of them all as readily as he had his soap, he would have made a small fortune. As it was, he realized that he must get money first—considerable money in a small way—before he could do these things. It set his mind to running on money chances, and thereafter he was keenly on the alert for anything which might show a quick, clear, easy profit. A quick, clear, easy profit—that was the thing he wanted. And how was he to get it?

It was in this year, or a little earlier, that he began to take a keen interest in girls. He had from the first showed a shrewd eye for the beautiful; and, being good-looking and magnetic himself, it was not hard for him to attract the sympathetic interest of those in whom he was interested. A ten-year-old girl, Patience Barlow, who lived a number of doors from him up the street, was the first to attract his attention or to be attracted by him. Black hair and snapping black eyes were her portion, with pretty pigtails down her back, and dainty feet and ankles to match a dainty figure. She was a Quakeress, the daughter of Quaker parents, wearing a demure little bonnet; but that made no odds. Her disposition was vivacious; and she liked this self-reliant, self-sufficient, straight-spoken boy who lived in her street. He had such clear, non-committal, and yet dancing eyes. Their first encounter was lost in a maze of mere passings to and fro—he could not have said when; but one day, after an exchange of glances from time to time, he said, with a smile and the courage that was innate in him (she was passing him in the same direction at the time):

"You live up my way, don't you?"

"Yes," she replied, a little flustered—this last manifested in a nervous swinging of her school-book bag— "I live at number one forty-one."

"I know the house," he said. "I've seen you go in there. You go to the same school my sister does, don't you? Aren't you Patience Barlow?"

He had heard some of the boys speak her name.

"Yes. How do you know?"

"Oh, I've heard," he smiled. "I've seen you. Do you like licorice?"

He fished in his coat and pulled out some of the fresh wooden sticks that were then sold.

"Thank you," she said, sweetly, taking one.

"It isn't very good. I've been carrying it a long time. I had some taffy the other day."

"Oh, it's all right," she replied, chewing the end of hers.

"Don't you know my sister, Anna Cowperwood?" he recurred, by way of self-introduction. "She just began school last year. She's in a lower grade than you are, of course. I thought maybe you might have seen her."

"I think I know who she is. I've seen her coming home from school."

"I live right over there," he confided, pointing to his own home as he drew near to it, as if she didn't know. "I'll see you around here now, I guess."

"Do you know Ruth Merriam?" she asked, when he was about ready to turn off into the cobblestone road to reach his own door.

"No, why?"

"She's giving a party next Tuesday," she volunteered, seemingly pointlessly, but with great point.

"Where does she live?"

"There in twenty-eight."

"I wish I might go," he suggested, sweetly, as he swung away from her.

"Maybe she'll ask you," she called back, growing more courageous as the distance between them widened. "I'll ask her."

"Thanks," he smiled.

And she began to run gaily onward.

He looked after her with a smiling face. She was very pretty. He felt a keen desire to kiss her, and what might transpire at Miss Merriam's party rose vividly before his eyes.

This was just one of the early love affairs, or puppy

loves, that held his mind from time to time in the mixture of after events. Patience Barlow was kissed by him in secret ways many and many a time before he found another girl. She and others of the street, which was highly respectable, ran out to play in the snow of a winter's night, or lingered after dusk before her own door when the days grew dark early. It was so easy to catch and kiss her then, and to talk to her foolishly at parties. Then came Dora Fitler, when he was sixteen years old and she was twelve; and Marjorie Stafford, when he was seventeen and she was fifteen. Dora Fitler was a brunette, but much lighter-complexioned than Patience Barlow; and Marjorie Stafford was as fair as the morning, with bright-red cheeks, bluish-gray eyes, and flaxen hair, and as plump as a partridge.

Shall the story of Marjorie be told? It isn't as innocent as the others. But, no, let it go. There will be more than sufficient without it.

It was at seventeen that, having endured all he could of the so-called educative processes of the time, he decided to leave school. He had not graduated. He had only finished the third year in high school; but he had had enough. Ever since his thirteenth year his mind had been on finance, and that only in the form in which he saw it manifested in Third Street. There had been odd things that he had been able to do to earn a little money now and then. His Uncle Seneca had allowed him to act as assistant weigher at the sugar-docks in Southwark, where three-hundred-pound bags were weighed into the government bonded warehouses under the eyes of United States inspectors. In certain emergencies he was called to assist his father, and paid for it. He even made an arrangement with Mr. Dalrymple to assist him on Saturdays; but his father became cashier of his bank shortly after his son had reached his fifteenth year, and, receiving an income of four thousand dollars a year, it was self-evident that Frank assisting a grocer on Saturdays was out of order. All that was left after that was weighing at the sugar-docks and helping his father, which he did as times and conditions warranted.

It should be said of Cowperwood, Jr., that during all these years he was exceedingly democratic. He appeared at times a little bit removed and superior or distant, but solely because he was thinking. He had a cheerful, hearty way of greeting people which was in the main entirely disconnected from what he thought of them. Even at this early age he was a keen judge of men, and he saw at once without much philosophic or sociologic knowledge just how the world was arranged. There were the weak and the strong, physically and mentally. Some men were destined for success by their temperament—that he could see; others were cut out for failure by the same token. You could not expect a weak, spindling, half-constructed figure of a man with no brain and no force to cut a figure in the world, and you could not possibly expect a great dynamic soul like Steemberger not to be heard of. Men, as he saw them, were starred by fortune to succeed or fail, or be middle-class; and really in so far as he was concerned he was neither very sorry nor very glad. Now and then—even at this age—some poor fool of a creature, some boy of his own age or man much older, who "cut up" silly tricks, or did aimless, wandering things, moved him to scorn or pity; but if he began with scorn he always came back to the thought, "Well, they cannot help it." Why should he judge? Time and chance happened to all men. Look at the squid he had seen. Was it its fault that it had been put in the tank with the lobster with no chance ultimately of saving its life? Some great, curious force was at work here throwing vast masses of people into life; and they could not all succeed. Some had to fail—many. Only a few could lead. He wondered about himself—whether he was born to lead. He had strength, health, joy in life. Would he make good?

A great desire to hurry, and yet to go cautiously, always followed in the train of the former thought. He must succeed; he must work; he mustn't be a spindling figure like some of these poor things about him. Never!

It was when he turned seventeen, and it was nearing the end of his current school-year, that his Uncle Seneca, who happened to be back in Philadelphia at the time, stouter and more domineering than ever, said to him one day:

"Now, Frank, if you're ready for it, I think I know where there's a good opening for you. There won't be any salary in it for the first year, but if you mind your p's and q's, they'll probably give you something as a gift at the end of that time. Do you know of Henry Waterman and Company down in Second Street?"

"I've seen their place."

"Well, they tell me they might make a place for you as a bookkeeper. They're brokers in a way—grain and commission men. You say you want to get in that line. When school's out you go down and see Mr. Waterman— tell him I sent you, and he'll make a place for you, I think. Let me know how you come out."

Uncle Seneca was married now, having, because of his wealth, attracted the attention of a poor but ambitious Philadelphia society matron; and because of this the general connections of the Cowperwoods were considered much better. Henry Cowperwood, the father, was planning to move with his family rather far out on North Front Street, which commanded at that time a beautiful view of the river and was witnessing the construction of some charming dwellings. His four thousand dollars a year in these before-the-war times was considerable. He was making what he considered judicious and conservative investments—some little money in a railroad company in which he was a joint organizer; some few thousands more in a real-estate venture in the western part of the city, in which direction it was generally thought the city

THE FINANCIER

would eventually grow. Because of his cautious, conservative, clock-like conduct, it was thought he might reasonably expect to be vice-president, and possibly president, some day, of his bank. He knew what the financial relations of the city, the State, and the government were, what the trade needs were in various directions. He made it his business to find out, by every possible method, what the means, resources, and intelligence of every business house and bank were; what people said and thought of them; what the constituent members were doing. He was keen to know, as was his duty, what the various financial ventures of the day were—the large ones—what chance they had of success. People were running into his bank constantly asking the president and the vice-president for loans. As cashier now, the man who was in actual touch with debits and credits—who met the depositors largely face to face, and who was expected to know instantly the condition of every account in the bank—he was advised with constantly. Now and then the president and the vice-president were kind enough to give him a financial tip—namely, that this or that stock, for this or that sound reason, was expected to advance. He was never expected or permitted, theoretically, to gamble on margins; but if he had any money to invest in a legitimate way, here and there were estimable chances. So the father, now nearing the age of forty-five, was becoming quite a factor in local life; and young Cowperwood had considerable reason to look up to him.

Still young Cowperwood, outside of a strong natural affection, was not so sure that his father was in any way an exceptional man. He expected to be much further along at his father's age than the latter was now. This offer of Uncle Seneca to get him in with Waterman & Co. was a god-send, just the thing to start him off right; for he was heartily sick of school, and this would give his mind its natural free play. He reported to that

42

organization at 74 South Second one day in June, and was cordially received by Mr. Henry Waterman, Sr. There was, as he soon learned, a Henry Waterman, Jr., a young man of twenty-five; and a George Waterman, a brother, aged fifty, who was the confidential inside man. Henry Waterman, Sr., a man of fifty-five years of age, was the general head of the organization, inside and out— traveling about the near-by territory to see customers when that was necessary, coming into final counsel in cases where his brother could not adjust matters, suggesting and advising new ventures which his associates and hirelings carried out. He was, to look at, a phlegmatic type of man—short, stout, wrinkled about the eyes, rather protuberant as to stomach, red-necked, red-faced, the least bit pop-eyed, but shrewd, kindly, good-natured, and witty. He had, because of his naturally common-sense ideas and rather pleasing disposition, built up a sound and successful business here. Merchants, farmers, and warehouse men in various sections of eastern Pennsylvania, southern New Jersey, Delaware, and Maryland made large consignments of grain, flour, and occasionally produce, to his house, which handled them for the Philadelphia and New York markets, sometimes reshipping, but nearly always disposing of them locally. From long years of dealing with local interests, wholesale and retail grocers, flour-mills, and produce-dispensing organizations generally, the Watermans had built up a steady demand which came to them naturally, and had to be supplied. Their daily morning orders were large, sometimes so large in certain directions that they could not be supplied. On the other hand, their daily offer of shipments was sometimes out of proportion to what they could easily dispose of. Flour might pour in when there was a glut of flour. It was quite the same with grain and vegetables. The problem of preserving the more perishable fruits and vegetables was a great one. Because the icing and telegraph industries were in their infancy, it was not possible to handle large consignments of any perishable fruit or vegetable. Attempts were made in this direction now and again, but without much success. The cost was too great. Early morning or late night calls were made on other houses offering to take over or transfer, at a loss sometimes, shipments which, if their own market had been larger or smaller, could have been handled to a nicety. In the main, this was Mr. Henry Waterman's business; but he was getting along in years, and would gladly have welcomed the hearty co-operation of his son, if the latter had been entirely suited to the business.

He was not, however. The latter was not as democratic, as quick-witted, or as pleased with the work in hand as was his father. To a certain extent the business offended him, and if the trade had been eventually left to his care it would have rapidly disappeared. His father saw the point, was grieved, was hoping some young man would eventuate who would be interested in the business, who would handle it in the same spirit in which it had been handled, and who would not crowd his son out—would, in other words, be content to take an interest in the business and work for the latter.

Then came young Cowperwood, spoken of to him by Seneca Davis. He looked him over critically. Yes, this boy might do, he thought. There was something full, easy, and sufficient about him. He did not appear to be in the least flustered or disturbed. Mr. Davis had sent him, he said. He knew how to keep books. He knew nothing of the details of the grain and commission business. It was interesting to him. He would like to try.

The boy's eye was so bright, and yet so inscrutable, Henry Waterman took to him at once. "I like that fellow," he said to his brother, the moment Frank had gone, having been told to report the following morning. "There's something to him. He's the cleanest, briskest, most alive thing that's walked in here in many a day."

THE FINANCIER

He was sitting beside his battered flat-top desk looking out into the rout of Second Street through the open
window, which, when closed, was composed of many
small six-by-six window-panes. The rear of the store—
indeed, all but the first thirty feet—was quite shadowy
and cool because of the lack of side windows. Little of
the stock of the company was kept here, because most of
the transfers were made from cars in Market Street, and
from boats at the water-front or on the Schuylkill.

"Yes," said George, a much leaner and slightly taller
man with dark, blurry, reflective eyes and a thin, largely
vanished growth of black, or brownish-black, hair, which
contrasted strangely with the egg-shaped whiteness of
his bald head. George was milder, less vigorous, less
sanguine than his brother. He was more sicklied o'er
with the pale cast of thought, and given to pulling a very
neat, small, black mustache. "Yes, I like him. He's
a nice young man. It's a wonder his father don't take
him in his bank up there."

"Well, he may not be able to," said his brother. "He's
only the cashier there."

"That's right."

"We'll give that fellow a trial. I bet anything he makes
good. He's a likely-looking youth."

"This fellow we have is nothing," said George, gloomily.
"When I ask him to look up a credit it takes him a month
to find it. He won't do. He's always talking about an
uncle that runs a dry-goods store in New York, Harry
tells me."

Harry was another clerk and general factotum, and
George reported this as though it were in some way a
notable offense.

"Well, let him go and work for his uncle," observed
Henry, sterterously. This warm June weather made
him breathe heavily.

He got up and walked out into the main entrance looking into Second Street. The cool, cobble pavements,

shaded by the wall of buildings on the east—of which his was a part—from the eastern sun, the noisy trucks and drays, the busy crowds hurrying to and fro, pleased him. He looked at the buildings over the way—all three and four stories, and largely of graystone and crowded with life— and thanked his stars that he had originally located in so prosperous a neighborhood. They really couldn't be better off. Here was the center of things—this and the street above. Here property had advanced tremendously in the last twenty years. He had a score of clerks, bookkeepers, runners, and general helpers. If he had only bought more property at the time he bought this!

"Eddie, you go down and see if those potatoes have come in yet," he said to a clerk who happened to be hurrying in with a bill of lading.

"Yes, sir. I'll go right away."

"I wish that Cowperwood boy would turn out to be the kind of man I want," he observed to himself, meditatively. "He could save me a lot of running these days."

Curiously, after only three or four minutes of conversation with the boy, he had this marked sense of efficiency. Something told him that this boy would do well—excellently so.

CHAPTER V

THE appearance of young Cowperwood at this time was, to say the least, prepossessing and satisfactory. His hair was rather a neutral shade, dark brown, as crisp as it had been years before, and thicker. His head was large, shapely, notably commercial in its aspect, and fixed on a square pair of shoulders and a stocky body. Nature had destined him to be about five feet ten inches tall. His eyes already had the look that subtle years of thought bring, but they were more inscrutable than ever. Absolutely you could tell nothing by his eyes. He walked with a light, confident, springy step. Life had given him no severe shocks nor rude awakenings. He had not been compelled to complain of illness or pain or deprivation of any kind. He saw people richer than himself, but he hoped to be rich. His family was respected, his father well placed. He owed no man anything. Once he had let a small note of his become overdue at the bank; but his father raised such a row that he never forgot it. "I would rather crawl on my hands and knees than let my paper go to protest," the old gentleman observed; and this fixed in his mind what scarcely needed to be so sharply emphasized—the significance of credit. No paper of his ever went to protest or became overdue after that through any negligence of his.

Young Cowperwood turned out to be the most efficient clerk that the house of Waterman & Co. had ever known. They put him on the books at first as assistant bookkeeper, vice Mr. Thomas Trixler, dismissed, and in two weeks George said: "Why don't we make Cowperwood head bookkeeper? He knows more in a minute than that fellow Sampson will ever know. I saw him (Sampson) sitting in there the other day looking at his fingers for fully fourteen minutes—I timed him—as though he had something very serious on his mind. What's he got so serious to think about?"

"Make the transfer, George, but don't fuss so. You're the darndest man to sit around and watch people I ever saw. You're as good as a detective. A man's got a right to look at his fingers. He might have been trying to solve a problem."

"Oh, nothing of the sort! I've seen him do it before."

"We'll put in Cowperwood. He belongs there. He won't be a bookkeeper long, though. I want to see if he can't handle some of these transfers for me after a bit. The more he knows about the books the better."

The books of Messrs. Waterman & Co., fairly complicated as they were, were child's play to Frank. He went through them with an ease and rapidity which surprised his erstwhile superior, Mr. Sampson. The latter could not understand why Mr. Cowperwood—this young upstart—was so nonchalant about some things, so abstract at times, and why he could so easily and so quickly run over long-standing accounts and say, "Yes, yes," without seeming to pay attention. He couldn't hope to succeed that way. He would surely fail.

"Why, that fellow," Mr. Sampson told his friend, William Woodruff, another clerk in the employ of Waterman & Co., on the first day he had seen Cowperwood work, "he's too brisk. He's going to make a bad break. I know that kind. Wait a little bit until we get one of those rush credit and transfer days."

Somehow the bad break Mr. Sampson anticipated did not materialize. Mr. Cowperwood went through the books with so much ease and speed that in less than a week he knew the financial condition of Messrs. Waterman & Co. as well as they did—better, to a dollar. He knew how their accounts were distributed; from what section they drew the most business; who sent poor produce and good—the varying prices for a year told that. To satisfy himself he ran back over certain accounts in the ledger, verifying his suspicions. Bookkeeping did not interest him except as a record, a demonstration of a firm's life; and when he knew that, the day-to-day work of entering credits and debits, making out bills, O. K.-ing vouchers, transferring accounts, and maintaining the bank balances, was drudgery. He knew he would not want to do this long; he knew that he would not do it. Something else would happen; but he saw instantly what the grain and commission business was—every detail of it. He saw where, for want of greater activity in offering the goods consigned, quicker communication with shippers and buyers, a better working agreement with surrounding commission men, this house, or, rather, its customers, for it had nothing, endured severe losses. A man would ship a tow-boat or a car-load of fruit or vegetables against a supposedly rising or stable market; but if ten other men did the same thing at the same time, or other commission men were flooded with fruit or vegetables, and there was no way of disposing of them within a reasonable time, the price had to fall. Every day was bringing its special consignments. It instantly occurred to him that he would be of much more use to the house as an outside man disposing of heavy shipments, but he hesitated to say anything so soon. More than likely, things would adjust themselves shortly.

Nevertheless, the Watermans, Henry and George, were greatly pleased with the way he handled their accounts. There was a sense of security in his very presence. It was only a few days before Cowperwood began to call Brother George's attention to the condition of certain accounts, making suggestions as to their possible liquidation or discontinuance, which pleased that individual greatly. He was doing this himself constantly to his brother Henry; but this young man saw further, pointed flaws in

49

their methods which even George did not see, and all in a way which gave no offense, but seemed rather to emanate from the general wisdom of the concern. George saw a way of lightening his own labors through the intelligence of this youth, while at the same time developing a sense of pleasant companionship with him.

Brother Henry was for trying him on the outside. It was not always possible to fill the orders with the stock on hand, and somebody had to go into the street, exchange or buy — usually he did this. One morning, when way-bills indicated a probable glut of flour and a shortage of grain—Frank saw it first—the elder Waterman called him into his office and said:

"Frank, I wish you would see what you can do with this condition that confronts us on the street. By tomorrow we're going to be overcrowded with flour. We can't be paying storage charges, and our orders won't eat it up. We're short on grain. Maybe you could trade out the flour to some of those brokers and get me enough grain to fill these orders."

"I'd like to try," said his employee.

He knew from his books where the various commission-houses were. He knew what the local merchants' exchange, and the various commission-merchants who dealt in these things, had to offer. This was the thing he liked to do—adjust a trade difficulty of this nature. It was pleasant to be out in the air again, to be going from door to door. He objected to desk work and pen work and poring over books. As he said in later years, his brain was his office. He hurried to the principal commission-merchants, learning what the state of the flour market was, and offering his surplus at the very rate he would have expected to get for it if there had been no prospective glut. Did they want to buy for immediate delivery (forty-eight hours being immediate) six hundred barrels of prime flour? He would offer it at nine dollars straight, in the barrel. They did not. He offered it in fractions, and some agreed to take one portion, and some another. In about an hour he was all secure on this save one lot of two hundred barrels, which he decided to offer in one lump to a famous operator with which his firm did no business. The latter, a big man with curly gray hair, a gnarled and yet pudgy face, and little eyes that peeked out shrewdly through fat eyelids, looked at Cowperwood curiously when he came in. His hands and feet were large—the former bristling, as to their backs, with sandy hair. His name was Genderman.

"What's your name, young man?" he asked, leaning back in his four-legged wooden chair, when Frank appealed to him.

"Cowperwood."

"So you work for Waterman and Company? You want to make a record, no doubt. That's why you came to me?"

He scarcely knew what he said. He was inclined to think poorly of any proposition which came to him outside his regular channels of exchange, but this young agent's appearance pleased him.

Cowperwood merely smiled.

"Well, I'll take your flour. I need it. Bill it to me."

Cowperwood hurried out. He went direct to a firm of brokers in Walnut Street, with whom his firm dealt, and had them bid in the grain he needed at prevailing rates. This, George had told him, was the custom of the company. Then he returned to Mr. Waterman.

"Well," said the latter, when he reported, "you did that quick. Sold old Genderman two hundred barrels direct, did you? That's doing pretty well. He isn't on our books, is he?"

"No, sir."

"I thought not. Well, if you can do that sort of work on the street you won't be on the books long."

He consulted with his brother George as to the rather remarkable showing the boy had made.

"We can use him to good advantage on the outside. Whenever we're short or glutted, and I'm not here, you'd better let him see what he can do on the street. He can let Sampson do that work under him. If he wants any extra help, give it to him."

Thereafter, in the course of time, Frank became a familiar figure in the commission district and on 'change (the Produce Exchange), striking balances for his employer, picking up odd lots of things they needed, soliciting new customers, breaking gluts by disposing of odd lots in unexpected quarters. The Watermans were astonished at his facility in this respect. He had an uncanny faculty for getting appreciative hearings, making friends, being introduced into new realms. New life began to flow through the old channels of the Waterman company. Their customers were better satisfied. George was for sending him out into the rural districts to drum up trade, and this was eventually done. There were certain big shippers in near-by places whose accounts they desired, and they fancied Frank could get them. Henry had not troubled to do this soliciting work in some years.

Near Christmas-time Henry said to George: "We'll have to make Cowperwood a liberal present. He hasn't any salary. How would five hundred dollars do?"

"That's pretty much, seeing the way times are, but I guess he's worth it. He's certainly done everything we've expected, and more. He's cut out for this business."

"What does he say about it? Do you ever hear him say whether he's satisfied?"

"Oh, he likes it pretty much, I guess. You see him as much as I do."

"Well, we'll make it five hundred. That fellow wouldn't make a bad partner in this business some day. He has the real knack for it when he comes to understand it thoroughly. You see that he gets the five hundred dollars with a word from both of us."

So the night before Christmas, as Cowperwood was

looking over some way-bills and certificates of consign-
ment preparatory to leaving all in order for the interven-
ing holiday, George Waterman came to his desk.

"Hard at it," he said, standing under the flaring gas-
light and looking at his brisk employee with great satisfaction.

It was early night, and the snow was making a speckled
pattern through the windows in front.

"Just a few points before I wind up," smiled the latter.

"My brother and I have been especially pleased with
the way you have handled the work here during the past
six months. We wanted to make some acknowledgment,
and we thought about five hundred dollars would be right.
Beginning January first we'll give you a regular salary of
twenty dollars a week."

"I'm certainly much obliged to you," said Frank. "I
didn't expect that much. It's a good deal. I've learned
considerable here that I'm glad to know."

"Oh, don't mention it. We know you've earned it.
You can stay with us as long as you like. We're glad to
have you with us."

Cowperwood smiled his hearty, genial smile. He was
feeling very comfortable under the evidence of approval.
He looked bright and cheery in his well-made clothes of
English tweed.

He closed up his desk after a time and went home.
On the way he speculated as to the nature of this business.
He knew he wasn't going to stay there so long, even in
spite of this gift and promise of salary. They were grateful, of course; but why shouldn't they be? He was efficient,
he knew that; under him things transpired rapidly wherever he went. He had an air of deliberation, and certi-
tude combined with speed. Order came out of chaos;
difficulties dwindled away—there weren't any. He did
business quickly and surely, looking a long way ahead
and forewarning his patrons time and again of things that
needed to be prepared for, in order that everything might

go smoothly. It never occurred to him that he belonged in the realm of clerkdom. Those people were the kind of beings who ought to work for him, and who would. There was nothing savage in his attitude, no rage against fate, no dark fear of failure. These two men he worked for were already nothing more than characters in his eyes —their business significated itself. He could see their weaknesses and their shortcomings as a much older man might have viewed a boy's.

He went on home, and at the house, after dinner, and before leaving to call on his girl, Marjorie Stafford, he told his father of the change—of the gift of five hundred and the promised salary.

"That's splendid," said the older man. "You're doing better than I thought. I suppose you'll stay there."

"No, I won't. I think I'll quit sometime next year."

"Why?"

"Well, it isn't exactly what I want to do. It's interesting enough, but I'd rather try my hand at brokerage, I think. That appeals to me."

"Don't you think you are doing them an injustice not to tell them?"

"Not at all. They need me."

He surveyed himself in a fine mirror that had been introduced into the new house, straightening his tie and adjusting his coat.

"Have you told your mother?"

"No. I'm going to do it now."

He went out into the dining-room, where his mother was still straightening things around.

"Mammy," he said, slipping his arms around her little body, "what do you think?"

"Well, what?" she asked, looking affectionately into his eyes.

"I got five hundred to-night, and I get twenty a week next year. What do you want for Christmas?"

"You don't say! Isn't that nice! Isn't that fine! They must like you. You're getting to be quite a man, aren't you?"

"What do you want for Christmas?"

"Nothing. I don't want anything. I have my children."

He smiled. "All right. Then nothing it is."

She knew he would buy her something.

He went out, chucking his sister in the waist at the door, and saying that he'd be back about midnight. He hurried to his girl's house, in a poorer neighborhood, because he had promised to take her to a show—his fifteen-year-old girl—and kissed her in the hall.

"Anything you want now for Christmas this year, Margy?" he asked, confiding to her. "I got five hundred to-night."

She was an innocent little thing, no guile, no shrewdness.

"Oh, you needn't get me anything."

"Don't I?" he asked, squeezing her waist and kissing her mouth.

It was fine to be getting on this way in the world and having such a good time.

"No," he said to himself, even as he talked to her about silly things, "he would not stay in the commission business. There was no real money in it. Pshaw! it was too slow. Dealing in flour, grain, and occasionally odd lots of staples, even though done in large quantities, was too much like petty trade. It wasn't mental enough. Money was the thing—plain money, discounted, loaned, cornered, represented by stocks and bonds—that interested him. He could never get men like Francis J. Grund and Steemberger off his mind. With money you were free of all these messy dealings and with people who, after all, say what you might, weren't as clever as the bankers and the brokers. Those were the people. They sustained these latter; they made it possible, through the machinery of finance, for these people to do business. No, George and Henry Waterman were all right; but when he was a little further along, just a little bit older, he was going to start in for himself."

CHAPTER VI

IN the mean time he worked on with the Waterman company until the following October, when, having passed his eighteenth year by nearly six months, and feeling sure that he should never want anything to do with the grain and commission business as conducted by them, he decided to sever his relations with them. Great was the grief of Mr. George Waterman; and Mr. Henry Waterman was actually chagrined as well as disappointed by this defection.

"Why, I thought," he exclaimed, vigorously, when informed by Cowperwood, "that you liked the business. Is it a matter of salary?"

"No, not at all, Mr. Waterman. I hope you won't feel badly about this thing. I have been thinking it all over, and I've decided that I've made a mistake in coming into this line at all. I don't like it as well as I do the straight-out brokerage business. I want to get into that. I thought so a little while after I came in here; but I didn't want to say anything so long as you were satisfied."

"No one else has made you a better offer?"

"I wouldn't take one in this line."

"Well, that certainly is too bad. I'm sorry. I don't want to urge you against your own best interests. You know what you are doing. But George and I had about agreed to offer you an interest in this thing after a bit. Now you're picking up and leaving. Why, damn it, man, there's good money in this business."

"I know it," smiled Cowperwood; "but I don't like it. I have other plans in view. I'll never be a grain and commission man."

"Going in with your father?"

"No, I'm going to work for Tighe and Company."

"Oh, that's the lay, eh? Well, they're clever people. I know Ed Tighe."

The old commission man was greatly depressed. He had fancied, through the presence of Frank, that he was fixed in ease and surety for the rest of his days. Now here was that prop knocked square from under him. And his son was no good. It was too bad.

Brother George came in after a time and heard the news. He was much more excitable than his brother, much more nervous.

"Well, now, what do you think of that?" he asked. "Here we were, you and me, just getting ready to give him an interest, and now he picks up and walks off. I never noticed that he was dissatisfied before. What does he say?"

"He hasn't any complaint," said Henry. "He says he don't like this business. I don't believe him, sometimes. He wants to get in the money game, like his father—wants to be a broker. He's going over with Tighe and Company."

"Oh, that's it," said Brother George. "Well, now, I wonder who we'll get to take his place?"

"You can't get any one to take his place," replied Henry, sourly. "He's a natural-born financier. He's an organizer. We might have known we couldn't expect to hold him. He won't stay long with Tighe. That fellow's going to go it alone pretty soon. Can't you see it in his eye? He isn't going to work for anybody. Neither you nor I nor any one can keep him."

He switched around in his chair and looked gloomily out of the window. "Now," he said to himself, "I have got to get up and hustle around the street myself. If that boy of mine were any good—" His thoughts trailed off into oblivion.

George returned to the little coop where he kept his

papers. "That means I have to watch all these accounts myself," he groaned, internally. And he had just been coming to the place where his Saturdays and Sundays and some other half-holidays were a delight to him.

The firm of Tighe & Co., unlike that of Waterman & Co., was located in a handsome green-gray stone building at 66 South Third Street, in what was then, and for a number of years afterward, the heart of the financial district. Great institutions of national and international import and repute were near at hand—Drexel & Co., Edward Clark & Co., the Third National Bank, the First National Bank, the Stock Exchange, and similar institutions. Almost a score of smaller banks and brokerage firms were also in the vicinity. Edward Tighe, the head and brains of this concern, was a Boston Irishman, the son of an emigrant to this country who had flourished and done well in that conservative city. Young Tighe had come to Philadelphia to interest himself in the speculative life there, because he considered there was a good opening to be had for himself. "Sure, it's a right good place for those of us who are awake," he told his friends, with a slight Irish accent, and he considered himself very much awake. He was a medium-tall man, not very stout, slightly and prematurely gray, and with a manner which was as lively and good-natured as it was combative and self-reliant. His upper lip was ornamented by a short, gray mustache.

"May heaven preserve me," he said, not long after he came there, "these Pennsylvanians never pay for anything they can issue bonds for." It was the period when Pennsylvania's credit, and for that matter Philadelphia's, was so bad in spite of its great wealth. "If there's ever a war there'll be battalions of Pennsylvanians marching around offering notes for their meals. If I could just live long enough I could get rich buyin' up Pennsylvania notes and bonds. I think they'll pay some time; but, my God, they're mortal slow! I'll be dead before the State government will ever catch up on the interest they owe me now."

It was true. The condition of the finances of the State and city were most reprehensible. Both State and city were rich enough; but there were so many schemes for looting the treasury in both instances that when any new work had to be undertaken bonds were issued to raise the money. These bonds, or warrants, as they were called, were made out to bear six per cent. interest; but when the interest fell due, instead of paying it, the city or State treasurer, as the case might be, stamped the same with the date of presentation, and the warrant then bore interest for not only its original face value, but the amount then due in interest. In other words, it was being slowly compounded. But this did not help the man who wanted to raise money very much, for as security they could not be hypothecated for more than seventy per cent. of their market value, and they were not selling at par, but at ninety. A man might buy or accept them in foreclosure, but he had a long wait. Also, in the final payment of most of them favoritism ruled, for it was only when the treasurer knew that certain warrants were in the hands of "a friend" that he would advertise that such and such warrants—those particular ones that he knew about—would be paid.

What was more, the money system of the United States was only now beginning slowly to emerge from something approximating chaos to something approaching order. The United States Bank, of which Nicholas Biddle was the progenitor, had gone completely in 1841, and the United States Treasury with its sub-treasury system had come in 1846; but still there were many, many wildcat banks, and they were sufficient in number to make the average exchange-counter broker a walking encyclopedia of solvent and insolvent institutions. Still, things were slowly improving, for the telegraph had facilitated stock-

THE FINANCIER

market quotations, not only between New York, Boston, and Philadelphia, but between a local broker's office in Philadelphia and his stock exchange. In other words, the short private wire had been introduced. Communication was quicker and freer, and daily grew better. Railroads had been built to the South, East, North, and West. There was as yet no stock-ticker and no telephone, and the clearing-house had only recently been thought of in New York, and had not yet been introduced in Philadelphia. Instead of a clearing-house service, messengers ran daily between banks and brokerage firms, balancing accounts on pass-books, exchanging bills, and, once a week, transferring the gold coin, which was the only thing that could be accepted for balances due, seeing that there was no stable national currency. "On 'change," when the gong struck announcing the close of the day's business, a company of young men, known as "settlement clerks," after a system borrowed from London, gathered in the center of the room and compared or gathered the various trades of the day in a ring, thus eliminating all those sales and resales between certain firms which naturally canceled each other. They carried long account-books, and called out the transactions— "Delaware and Maryland sold to Beaumont and Company," "Delaware and Maryland sold to Tighe and Company," and so on. This simplified the bookkeeping of the various firms, and made for quicker and more stirring commercial transactions.

Seats "on 'change" sold for two thousand dollars each. The members of the latter had just passed rules limiting the trading to the hours lying between ten and three (before this they had been any time between morning and midnight), and had fixed the rates at which brokers could do business, in the face of cutthroat schemes which had previously held. Severe penalties were fixed for those who failed to obey. In other words, things were shaping up for a great 'change business, and Mr. Tighe, as did many another broker, felt that, all in all, he had a worth-while future before him.

His manner of meeting young Cowperwood was ordinary enough. The latter had frequently entered Mr. Tighe's office in his capacity as outside man for Waterman & Co. Their relations with brokers were not large; but now and then paper came into their hands which had to be discounted—the banks, their particular banks, refusing to take it. Cowperwood had presented notes from fairly responsible out-of-town firms which Tighe & Co., who also had a note-brokerage share or end connected with their business, had discounted for him; and in the process they had come to exchange friendly greetings. From the first Mr. Tighe took a keen interest in this subtle young emissary — he could not have said why.

"How's business with you people?" he would ask, genially, or, "Find that you're getting many I. O. U.'s these days?"

There were prospects of hard times soon, because of the unsettled condition of the country, the over-inflation of securities, the slavery agitation, and so forth. Somehow—he could not have told you why—this young man struck him as some one who was worth while talking to on these matters. He was not really old enough to know, and yet he did know.

"Oh, things are going pretty well with us, thank you, Mr. Tighe," Cowperwood would answer.

"I tell you," he said to Cowperwood, one morning, "this slavery agitation, if it doesn't stop, is going to cause trouble."

A negro slave belonging to a visitor from Cuba had just been abducted and set free, because the laws of Pennsylvania made freedom the right of any negro brought into the State, even to the extent of uninterrupted transit to another portion of the country, and there was great excitement over the matter. Several persons had been arrested, and the newspapers were discussing it roundly.

"I don't think the South is going to stand for this thing. It's making trouble in our business, and it must be doing the same thing for others. We'll have secession here, sure as fate, one of these days." He talked with the vaguest suggestion of a brogue.

"It's coming, I think," said Cowperwood, quietly. "It can't be healed, in my judgment. The negro isn't worth all this excitement; but they'll go on agitating for him—emotional people always do this. They haven't anything else to do. It's hurting our Southern trade."

"I thought so. That's what the people tell me."

He turned to a new customer as young Cowperwood went out the door; but again the boy struck him as being inexpressibly sound and deep-thinking financially. "If that young fellow wanted a place I'd give it to him," he thought.

Finally, one day he said to him: "How would you like to try your hand at being a floor-man for me in 'change? I need a young man here. One of my clerks is leaving."

"I'd like it," replied Cowperwood, smiling and looking intensely gratified. "I had thought of speaking to you myself some time."

"Well, if you're ready and can make the 'change, the place is open. Come any time you like."

"I'll have to give a reasonable notice at the other place," Cowperwood said, quietly. "Would you mind waiting a week or two?"

"Not at all. It isn't as important as that. I thought you might like to move in here, and we need a man. But I can wait. Come as soon as you can straighten things out. I don't want to inconvenience your employers."

It was after that that Frank had his talk with Waterman, and two weeks later he took his departure.

CHAPTER VII

IT was some time before this change had occurred that Henry Cowperwood, Sr., having lived for years in the comfortable New Market Street home, had removed to a still better, or, rather, larger house in North Front Street facing the river, and had furnished it in even better style than the one he had previously occupied. The rage of the day in the matter of furniture was for a modified Chippendale, and this now, in regard to some room-sets, was introduced. The house was four instead of three stories tall, and stood twenty-five feet on the street-front, without a yard.

Here now the family began to entertain in a small way, and there came to see them, now and then, representatives of the various interests that Mr. Henry Cowperwood had encountered in his upward climb to the position of cashier. It was not a very distinguished company as yet, seeing that he was still a cashier; but it included a number of people who were about as successful as himself, heads of small businesses who traded at his bank—dealers in dry-goods, leather, groceries (wholesale), and grain. His daughter, Anna, now twelve years of age, was blessed with a small company of girl friends of her own age, who gathered here frequently; and Frank, Joseph, and Edward had come to have intimates of their own—school chums, girls, commercial acquaintances, and the like. Now and then, because of church connections, Mrs. Cowperwood ventured to hold an afternoon tea or reception, and gathered around her the wives and daughters of those whom her husband knew, and toward whom he was friendly. Even Cowperwood attempted the gallant in so far as to stand about in a genially foolish way and greet those whom his wife had invited. It was a very painful procedure to him, unless he could maintain his gravity in a very solemn way and be greeted without being required to say much.

Among those who came to the house were Mrs. Seneca Davis, for an occasional brief visit, and the wife of one of the curates of Christ Church, which the Cowperwoods had always attended, together with a number of the wives and daughters of Mr. Cowperwood's business connections. Singing was indulged in at times, a little dancing on occasion; and there was considerably more "company to dinner," in an informal way, than had previously been. Frank met here a certain Mrs. Semple, the wife of a retail shoe-dealer who was by way of becoming a manufacturer of importance, who interested him greatly. Her husband had a handsome shoe store in Chestnut Street, near Third, and was planning to open a second one farther out on the same street.

The occasion of this meeting was an evening call on their part, Mr. Semple being desirous of talking with Henry Cowperwood concerning a new transportation feature which was then entering the world—namely, street-cars. A tentative line, incorporated by the North Pennsylvania Railway Company, had been put in operation on a mile and a half of tracks extending from Willow Street along Front to Germantown Road, and thence by various streets to what was then known as the Cohocksink Depot; and it was thought that in time this mode of locomotion might drive out the hundreds and hundreds of omnibuses which now crowded and made impassable the down-town streets. Young Cowperwood had been greatly interested from the start. The whole thought of railway transportation interested him, anyway; but this particular phase was most fascinating. It was already creating so much interest, and he, with others, had gone to see it. A strange but interesting new type of car, running on small iron car-wheels and being fourteen feet long, seven feet wide, and nearly the same height, was giving great satisfaction as being quieter and easier-riding than omnibuses; and Alfred Semple, Mrs. Semple's husband, was privately considering investing in another proposed line which, if it could secure a franchise from the legislature, was to run on Fifth and Sixth streets.

Mr. Cowperwood, Sr., was greatly interested in this discussion. He had seen the line in question, had ridden on it time and time again, and was satisfied that this type was destined to suspend the omnibus entirely. In his mind's eye he saw a great future for this thing; but he did not see as yet how the capital was to be raised for it. Frank believed that Tighe & Co. should attempt to become the selling agents of this new stock of the Fifth and Sixth Street Company in case they succeeded in getting a franchise. He understood that a company was already formed, that a large amount of stock was to be issued against the prospective franchise on its being secured, and that these shares were to be sold at five dollars, as against an ultimate par value of one hundred. He wished he had sufficient money to take a large block of them. Meanwhile, he studied Lillian Semple, who was in the room a part of the time, and who, with Mrs. Cowperwood, occasionally appeared and disappeared.

Just what it was about Lillian Semple that attracted him at this age it would be hard to say, for she was really not suited to him emotionally, intellectually, or otherwise. He was not without some experience with women or girls, as has been indicated, and still held a tentative relationship with Marjorie Stafford; but Mrs. Semple, in spite of the fact that she was married and that he could have no legitimate interest in her, seemed not wiser and saner, but more worth while. Her husband was not so very rich—say forty to fifty thousand dollars—and there

was no certainty that he was worth so much. Frank heard
his father say that Semple had had some bad years at
one time and another. He was a man of George Waterman's type or style—medium tall, spare, dark-eyed, dark-
haired, with a sharp, clean-cut, albeit pasty-white face,
and a dapper, supple, well-thought-out and pleasant
manner. Having had no early advantages, he was a
little uncertain of himself, and did not appear to have
much to say at any time. He talked with Cowperwood
and his son of trade, slavery, the growth of Philadelphia
—which was now over four hundred thousand—the prosperity of their church, and so on.

Mrs. Semple was an interesting type in her way—not
as young as Frank Cowperwood, for he was but nineteen,
while she was twenty-four; but still young enough in her
thought and looks to appear of his own age. She was
slightly taller than he was—though he was now nearly
his full height (five feet ten and one-half inches)—and,
despite her height, shapely, artistic in form and feature,
and with a certain unconscious placidity of soul, which
came more from lack of understanding than from force
of character. Her hair was the color of a dried English
walnut, rich and plentiful, and her complexion waxen—
cream wax—with lips of faint pink, and eyes that varied
from gray to blue and from gray to brown, according to
the light in which you saw them. Her hands were thin
and shapely, her nose straight, her face artistically narrow. She was not brilliant, not active, but rather peaceful and statuesque without knowing it. Young Cowperwood looked at her the first time he saw her, and, without
knowing anything about her, or grasping the nature of
her disposition, was carried away by her appearance.
Somehow this placidity matched his own. Her beauty
measured up to his present sense of the artistic. She was
lovely, he thought—gracious, dignified. If he could have
his choice of a wife, this was the kind of girl he would
like to have. She looked at him several times dreamily,

not thinking much of anything, and smiled in a conventional, social way. Frank Cowperwood thought her smile and her mouth beautiful. Thereafter he never forgot Mrs. Semple for a moment. She seemed to him to be a beautiful woman, and he wished he had met her before she married Mr. Semple.

Cowperwood's judgment of women was largely from the artistic standpoint from the beginning. Powerfully passionate in a material way, not only in his desire for wealth, prestige, and dominance, but in his desire for women and beauty, he saw them from the artistic side only. The homely woman meant nothing to him. His mother, it is true, was no longer so startlingly attractive; but, then, she was his mother. His sister, now thirteen, gave promise of being clever if not physically attractive, and for that reason more than anything else appealed to him. She could retort, even at this age, with ideas and observation which fixed themselves in his mind. But women, by and large, the vast mass, merely seemed so much dead wood to him, a mass which he could not understand. He heard family discussions of this and that sacrificial soul among women, as well as among men—women who toiled and slaved for their husbands or children or both, who gave way to relatives or friends in crises or crucial moments, because it was right or kind to do so; but somehow these stories did not appeal to him. He could not have told you why. People seemed foolish, or at the best very unfortunate not to know what to do in all circumstances, and how to protect themselves. There was also great talk along the line of current morality, much praise of virtue and decency, and much lifting of hands in righteous horror at people who broke or were even rumored to have broken the Seventh Commandment. He did not take this talk seriously. Already he had broken it secretly many times. Other young men did. He was a little sick of the plain women of the streets or

the bagnio. There were too many coarse, evil features
in connection with them. For a little while the false
tinsel-glitter of the house of ill repute appealed to him,
for there was a certain force and luxury to it—rich, as a
rule, with red-plush furniture, showy red hangings, some
coarse but showily framed pictures, and, above all, the
strong-bodied or sensuously lymphatic women who dwelt
there, as his mother phrased it, to prey on men. The
strength of their bodies, the lust of their souls, the fact
that they could, with a show of affection or good-nature,
receive man after man, astonished and later disgusted
him. It is true that their often shapely bodies, bright
belladonnaed eyes, and scarlet lips appealed to him—he
was no trembling novice quailing at every thought of the
moral law; but after a while the beauty and luxury of
some of their clothing, the manner in which they indulged
themselves in cosmetics, subtle and sensuous perfumes,
incense and other aids to the creation of the lure that
stirs the passion of man, cloyed on him. They were not
smart. There was no vivacity of thought there. All
that they could do in the main, he fancied, was this one
thing. He pictured to himself the dreariness of the
mornings after, the stale dregs of things when only sleep
and the thought of gain could aid in the least; and more
than once, even at this age, he shook his head. These
women were in a physical hell from which all women
fled—and yet were they? Other women, girls and worn
mothers, were in a state of unrest and unhappiness not
so much better mentally than this. He had heard his
father and other men talk of employment conditions in
certain quarters which were horrible. As for that matter,
he had his own eyes and could see. Life was before him.
Philadelphia, with its miles of red-brick streets and sidewalks, was quite as much an open book to him as to any
one else—more so, for he was more plenteously endowed
with that subtle thing called understanding. He could
see how things were going. Still, the inartistic absence

of refinement in these women of the houses stayed him. He wanted contact which was more intimate, subtle, individual, personal.

Well, on top of this came Mrs. Semple—Lillian Semple, who was nothing to him save an ideal; but she cleared up certain of his ideas in regard to women. She was not forceful and vigorous like these other women—raw, brutal contraveners of accepted theories and notions; but for that very reason, because she was artistic and nothing more, he liked her. She was not subtle, quick, or daring; but because he was possessed of these things himself in a secret, unsuggested way, he could afford to favor the beauty that was not subtle or remarkably efficient. Just quiet, refined beauty was fascinating, and in Mrs. Semple he thought he saw this.

The home of Mr. and Mrs. Semple was fortunately, or, perhaps it would be better to say, curiously, located not so very far from his own, on North Front Street, in the neighborhood of what is now No. 956. It was a pretty two-story brick house, and, unlike so many of the older houses in the down-town section, was set in a yard. It had, in summer, quite a wealth of green leaves and vines. The little side porch which ornamented its south wall commanded a charming view of the river, and all the windows and doors were topped with round arches and set with lunettes of small-paned glass. The interior of the house was not so very artistic. It was about what the interior of a house owned by a manufacturing and a retail merchant would ordinarily be. There was no sense of artistic harmony to the furniture, though it was new and good. The pictures were—well, simply pictures. There were no books to speak of—the Bible, a few current novels, some of the more significant histories, and a collection of antiquated odds and ends in the way of books inherited from relatives. The china was nice—of a delicate pattern. The carpets and wall-paper were too high in key. So it went. Still, the personality of Lillian Semple was worth something, for she was really artistic to look at, making a picture wherever she stood or sat.

There were no children—a dispensation of sex conditions which had nothing to do with her, for she longed to have them. She was without any notable experience in social life, except such as had come to the Wiggin family, of which she was a member—relatives and a few neighborhood friends visiting. Lillian Wiggin—that was her maiden name—had two brothers and one sister, all living in Philadelphia, and all married at this time. They thought she had done very well in her marriage.

It could not be said that she had wildly loved Mr. Semple at any time. Although she had cheerfully married him, he was not the kind of man who would arouse a notable passion in any woman. He was practical, methodic, orderly. His shoe store was a model of cleanliness, and what one might term pleasing brightness. He loved to talk, when he talked at all, of shoe-manufacturing companies, the price of leather, the development of shoe machinery, the development of lasts and styles. The ready-made shoe—machine-made to a certain extent —was just coming into its own slowly, and outside of these, supplies of which he kept, there were many bench-making shoemakers whom he employed himself, satisfying his customers with personal measurements, and making the shoes to order.

Mrs. Semple read a little—not much. She had a habit of sitting and apparently brooding reflectively at times, but it was not based on any deep thought. She had this curious beauty of body, though, that made her somewhat like a figure on an antique vase or out of a Greek chorus. It was in this light, unquestionably, that young Cowperwood saw her, for from the beginning he could not keep his eyes off of her. He would study her secretly, and in a way she was aware that he was doing so; but she did not attach any significance to it. Thoroughly conventional, satisfied now that her life was bound permanently and inexorably with that of Mr. Semple, she had settled down to a staid and quiet existence. She interested herself in charitable and church work to a certain extent, called on her husband's friends and many of the church families who were of her faith, and went to market and to the shops for herself and her husband with methodic regularity. Frank Cowperwood ran in her mind in a way, at times, as being a rising, forceful, interesting young man. She thought he would make some woman a splendid husband.

But Frank Cowperwood was interested in her. Unusual though it was in him, he followed her up. He was not without some little experience with women, a certain kind; but he soon found that the coarse, unrefined, abandoned type found in a certain quarter did not appeal to him. He early learned of the terrors of disease, and, anyhow, he was not interested that way—in that offhand manner. He wanted personal reaction of thought and feelings, a certain kinship of soul or understanding in any woman he drew near to, and if he could not have that he was not interested. There was great talk in his family, always had been, of the solidarity of marriage—in a way its divine authorization. The Bible was taken literally. Some people fought and had a great deal of trouble in their married state; but that was nothing. Separation was never to be thought of. It was their duty to fight on. Practically he paid little attention to these opinions one way or the other, for the simple reason that they, or rather the state they represented, was not before him for solution. If he had been in an unhappy state—but then it scarcely occurred to him that he would be.

In the mean time he worked at his new situation, learning many things which he had not previously known. This stock-exchange world, primitive as it would seem to-day, was most fascinating to him. The room that he went to in Third Street at Dock, where the brokers or their agents and clerks gathered one hundred and fifty strong, was nothing to speak of artistically—a square chamber sixty by sixty, reaching from the second floor to the roof of a four-story building; but it was striking to him. The windows were high and narrow; a large-faced clock faced the west entrance of the room where you came in from the stairs; a collection of telegraph instruments, with their accompanying desks and chairs, occupied the northeast corner. On the floor, in the early days of the exchange, were rows of chairs where the brokers sat while various lots of stocks were offered to them. Later in the history of the exchange the chairs were removed and at different points posts or floor-signs indicating where certain stocks were traded in were introduced. Around these the men who were interested in these lines of securities gathered to do their trading. From a hall on the third floor a door gave entrance to a visitors' gallery, small and poorly furnished; and on the west wall, where no windows were—the latter were only present on the east and north and south—a large blackboard carried current quotations in stocks as telegraphed from New York and Boston. A wicket-like fence in the center of the room surrounded the desk and chair of the official recorder; and a very small gallery opening from the third floor on the west gave place for the secretary of the board, when he had any special announcement to make. There was a room off the southwest corner, where reports and annual compendiums of various kinds were kept and were available for the use of members.

Young Cowperwood would not have been admitted at all, as either a broker or broker's agent or assistant, except that Tighe, feeling that he needed him and believing that he would be very useful, bought him a seat on 'change—holding the two thousand dollars it cost as a debt over Cowperwood—and ostensibly took him into partnership. It was against the rules of the exchange to sham a partnership in this way in order to put a man on the floor; but brokers did it. These men who were known to be minor partners and floor assistants were derisively called "eighth chasers" and "two-dollar brokers," because they were always seeking small orders and were willing to buy or sell for anybody on their commission, accounting, of course, to their firms for their work. Cowperwood was of their number, and he was put under the direction of Mr. Arthur Rivers, Tighe & Co.'s regular floor-man, who had charge of all their large operations. The latter was an exceedingly forceful man of thirty-five, well-dressed, well-shaped, with a hard, smooth, evenly chiseled face which was ornamented, as to the upper lip, by a short, black mustache, and, as to the eyes, by fine, black, clearly penciled eyebrows. His hair came to an odd point at the middle of his forehead, where he divided it, and his chin was faintly and attractively cleft. He had a quiet, conservative manner, a soft voice, and both in and out of this brokerage and trading world was controlled by good form. The impression that young Cowperwood immediately gained was that he was polite, indifferent, self-sufficient, socially well placed, cold, cool in action, shrewd, but not wide in his views of life. He knew what his social world was and what it was worth to him; he knew that outside of it there was a great mess of life which he did not care very much about; he knew that most of these men around him were exceedingly clever, some of them as well placed as himself, but that a very large number of them were socially impossible. In business, outside of trades—and even in them, except under great stress—he was charming. He had an even, curiously ingratiating mouth, which parted pleasantly and affably when he talked. His eyes spoke his intended and prearranged courtesy. His hands rarely aided his voice or expression, but when they did they were artistically controlled—poised, weighed, withdrawn. He had not much to say to young Cowperwood at first beyond explaining the fact that certain stocks in which Tighe & Co. were interested were very treacherous, and that certain people on the floor were suspicious of him and his assistants. He was suspected always of having a *beat* of some kind in view, and there was a subtle conspiracy on among a few traders to prevent him from obtaining the price he might have fixed on as his harvesting-point.

Cowperwood studied Rivers as he did everything else with which he came in contact. He wondered at first why Rivers should work for Tighe—he appeared almost as able—but afterward learned that he was in the company. Tighe was the organizer and general hand-shaker, Rivers the floor and outside man.

This company of men with whom Cowperwood was thrown here were nondescript. They ranged from "eighth chasers" and "two-dollar" assistants like himself—nineteen to twenty-five years of age—to men of thirty, forty, fifty, and more. Some had been successful manipulators for years, owning their own "seats on 'change" and representing only themselves; and others had been successful and individual operators, but were now failures and hirelings. Others were able men like Arthur Rivers— secret partners or the private representatives of rich men who owned or controlled big industries, and who, because of their loans at banks, secured by certain kinds of stocks given as collateral, were anxious that the market price of the stocks should be watched and sustained in order that their loans might not be unexpectedly called. There were men who represented half-baked, fly-by-night, poorly organized brokerage concerns dealing with country customers and small adventurers who had a hard time to meet their margins and were always leaving to their brokers the responsibility for small but disastrous trades. It was useless, as Frank soon found, to try to figure out exactly why stocks rose and fell. Some general reasons there were, of course, as he was told by Tighe, who liked him much from the first, but they could not always be depended on.

"Sure, anything can make or break a market"—Tighe's delicate brogue will have to be imagined—"from the failure of a bank to the rumor that your second cousin's grandmother has a cold. It's a most unusual world, Cowperwood. No man can explain it. I've seen breaks in stocks that you could never explain at all—no one could. It wouldn't be possible to find out why they broke. I've seen rises the same way. My God, the rumors of the stock exchange! They beat the devil. If they're going down in ordinary times some one is unloading, or they're rigging the market. If they're going up—God knows times must be good or somebody must be buying—that's sure. Beyond that—well, ask Rivers to show you the ropes. Don't you ever lose for me, though. That's the cardinal sin in this office."

He grinned maliciously, even if kindly, at that.

Cowperwood understood—none better. This subtle world appealed to him. It answered to his temperament. He used to stand about when he had the time to spare, and there were many times when he could do nothing at all, studying out this curious crowd on the 'change floor. He liked to watch them drift in in the morning: first a few brisk clerks like himself (the janitor was always there ahead of everybody else to open up), and after that this broker and that trader, the telegraph-operator, the messenger-boys calling names, an old woman who stood at the foot of the 'change stairs in a green-and-gray shawl selling apples, and so on. In spring or warm weather some of the men, particularly the telegraph-operators and floor-men, took off their street coats and put on linen floor coats. Some lounged and studied the early quotations on the blackboard, or those that were left from the day before. Others stood in groups of twos and threes and conversed in low tones. There was considerable tom-foolery and idle good-nature displayed, as when a man would take another's hat and stick a feather in it, or slap a fellow-broker on the back with a "Hi! You old aboli-

tionist! Who you buyin' all that P. and A. for?" There
were rumors, rumors, rumors of great railway and street-
car undertakings, land developments, government revision of the tariff, war between France and Turkey,
famine in Russia or Ireland, and so on. The first Atlantic cable had not been laid as yet, and news of any kind
from abroad was slow and meager. Still there were great
financial figures in the field, men who, like Cyrus Field,
or William H. Vanderbilt, or F. X. Drexel, were doing
marvelous things, and their activities and the rumors
concerning them counted for much. There was one old
broker, Hosea Whitney, a little insect of a man with a
face like Punch, of "Punch and Judy" fame, who was
convinced that the current slavery agitation was going
to depress all stock and destroy values. Each fresh kid-
napping outrage, each "underground" uproar which
followed the escape of some slave, caused the old man
to trot about, his hands crossed behind his back, croak-
ing like a raven. He did not come to know Cowperwood
at once, but Frank used to see him talking to Arthur
Rivers and others.

"I tell you, Arthur," he would exclaim, screwing up
one eye most ominously, "if this stealing of niggers don't
stop, you and I are going to find it hard to make a living
after a while. It's going to cause trouble! I can feel it!
Something's going to happen to this country. Things
aren't right."

Amusedly Rivers would survey him, keeping all the
while a considerate manner.

"I wouldn't worry, Hosea; we'll probably be all right.
You're naturally bearish in your mood."

"Bearish be damned! I'm not any more bearish than
you are. Facts are facts. Look at that case again this
morning! What d'ye think o' that?"

"Well, it's pretty bad; but we'll never have any trouble
about that. The country is growing too fast."

"Country be damned! I tell you we're going to have

trouble. These abolitionists are going to be sorry some-time. I'm not down on the nigger, but the business of the country can't stand this sort of thing. It's stirring up sectional feeling."

Rivers, or whoever else he talked to, would rub their chins, stare up at the clock to see if it was time for the gong to strike, or look about for an excuse to move. As a rule Rivers would make no comment concerning Hosea to any one else: but some of the less considerate would exclaim: "Here comes old Hosea again!" or "There he goes. It's those abolitionists again. George, but they do stir up poor old Uncle Hosea's blood!"

"Sixty-five and one-eighth for any part of three hun-dred P. and A.," Uncle Hosea would call, scuttling crab-like to his favorite post as the gong struck and trading began. He was not at all weak physically, and quite able to take care of himself in even the severest crushes. He had the broker's habit of holding up as many fingers of his brown, skinny hand as he had lots to buy or sell. He was not a large trader; but he owned his own seat and made a good living.

There was another curious character, Andrew Pohlhemus, a German of the second or third generation, who had a face which somebody said was like that of a "wooden Indian which had been hit by a hatchet." His nose was broken, which gave his face a concave angle, and his form was like that of a pouter-pigeon.

Every morning he would, on arrival, take out his big silver watch and compare it with the 'change clock, which he seemed to think was in danger of going astray. In summer he wore a prodigious straw hat which was ridiculous, and in winter a furry beaver cap which made him still more marvelous. His face was a healthy red, and his hands and feet were fat.

"Pohlhemus regulating the universe," somebody called one day, striking an attitude and throwing out his chest.

"Ach, du lieber Pohlhemus," some one else called.

THE FINANCIER

The brokers, in idle moments, liked to pin pieces of paper or ribbon, or anything else voluminous they could find, to the ends of his coat-tails and see him stroll unwittingly about.

"You make me sick," he would call, if he caught any one at this; but, as a rule, he did not, and when informed would grunt, "Oh yes, more damn foolishness."

He was not disliked; and he never lost or won very much, for he never gambled very freely.

CHAPTER VIII

IT was while Cowperwood was working under Rivers for Tighe that he learned all those subtleties of the stock-market system which afterward stood him in such good stead. By degrees he picked up all the technicalities of the situation, and all the terminology, though the latter was not more than an hour's lesson the first day, given him succinctly by Rivers. A "bull," he learned, was one who bought in anticipation of a higher price to come; and if he was "loaded up" with a "line" of stocks he was said to be "long." He sold to "realize" his profit, or if his margins were exhausted he was "wiped out." A "bear" was one who sold stocks which most frequently he did not have, in anticipation of a lower price, at which he could buy and satisfy his previous sales. He was "short" when he had sold what he did not own, and he "covered" when he bought to satisfy his sales and to realize his profits or to protect himself against further loss in case prices advanced instead of declining. He was caught in a "corner" when he found that he could not buy in order to make good the stock he had borrowed for delivery and the return of which had been demanded. He was then obliged to settle practically at a price fixed by those to whom he and other "shorts" had sold.

Tighe, Cowperwood learned from Rivers, carried a certain line of stocks for certain people for whom he bought and sold. The latter did not take this boy into his confidence very much at first; but he gave him some interesting bits of information. Certain houses were handling certain stocks, certain others were buying certain others. He was to watch their men. The general run of things

THE FINANCIER

outside of these particular specialties which he was handling need not trouble him.

"Watch what they're doing. Take their offers. I want all I can get up to five thousand of A. and C. If you hear of any Morse Telegraph offered under sixty take it—all you can get. Buy me sixty Fifth and Sixth Street. I want a hundred New York and Harlem at eighty—no more, do you hear?"

"Yes, I hear," said Frank, submissively.

Cowperwood was a fine, live floor operator, and soon convinced Rivers that he had an ideal man as an assistant.

After the first few days spent in studying this noble community of souls Frank soon learned of what cheap, mortal clay they were, and at the same time what a shrewd, hungry lot of fish, and what a vast subtle world they represented. You could never tell what any particular individual was "up to." You could never guess what stock was being "nursed" or "washed" or being handled by a specialist. Rumor was the breath of life of this chamber, and suspicion its blood. He smiled at first at the air of great secrecy and wisdom on the part of the younger men. They were so heartily and foolishly suspicious. The older men, in the large majority of cases, were inscrutable. They pretended great innocence, uncertainty, indifference. They were like certain fish after a certain kind of bait, however. Snap! and the opportunity was gone. Somebody else had picked up what you wanted. All had their little note-books. All had their peculiar squint of eye or position or motion which meant "Done! I take you!" Sometimes they seemed scarcely to confirm their sales and purchases—they knew each other so well—but they did. If the market was for any reason active, the brokers and their agents were apt to be more numerous than if it were dull and the trading indifferent. A gong sounded the call to trading at 10 A.M.; and if there was a noticeable rise or decline in a stock or a group of stocks, you were apt to witness a quite spirited scene. Fifty to a hundred men would shout, gesticulate, shove here and there in an apparently aimless manner, endeavoring to take advantage of the stock offered or called for.

"Five-eighths for five hundred P. and W.," some one would call—Rivers or Cowperwood, or any other broker.

"Five hundred at three-fourths," would come the reply from some one else, who either had an order to sell the stock at that price or who was willing to sell it short, hoping to pick up enough of the stock at a lower figure later to fill his order and make a little something besides. If the supply of stock at that figure was large Rivers would probably continue to bid five-eighths. If, on the other hand, he noticed an increasing demand, he would probably pay three-fourths for it. If the professional traders believed Rivers had a large buying order, they would probably try to buy the stock before he could at three-fourths, believing they could sell it out to him at a slightly higher price. The professional traders were, of course, keen students of psychology; and their success depended on their ability to guess whether or not a broker representing a big manipulator, like Tighe, had an order large enough to affect the market sufficiently to give them an opportunity to "get in and out," as they termed it, at a profit before he had completed the execution of his order. All their days were spent in just this thought and effort. They were like hawks watching for an opportunity to snatch their prey from under the very claws of their opponents.

Four, five, ten, fifteen, twenty, thirty, forty, fifty, and sometimes the whole company, would attempt to take advantage of the given rise of a given stock by either selling or offering to buy, in which case the activity and the noise would become deafening. Given groups might be trading in different things; but the large majority of them would abandon what they were doing in order to take advantage of a specialty. The eagerness of certain young brokers or clerks to discover all that was going on, and to take advantage of any given rise or fall, made for quick physical action, darting to and fro, the excited elevation of explanatory fingers. Distorted faces were shoved over shoulders or under arms. Grimaces the most ridiculous were purposely or unconsciously indulged in. At times there were situations in which some individual was fairly smothered with arms, faces, shoulders, crowded toward him when he manifested any intention of either buying or selling at a profitable rate. At first it seemed quite a wonderful thing to young Cowperwood—the very physical face of the thing—for he liked human presence and activity; but a little later the sense of the thing as a pic-ture or a dramatic situation, of which he was a part, faded, and he came down to a clearer sense of the in-tricacies of the problem before him. Buying and selling stocks, as he soon learned, was an art, a subtlety, almost a psychic emotion. Suspicion, intention, feeling—these were the things to be "long" on. You had to know what a certain man was thinking of—why, you could not say— and suspect that he was going to buy or unload a given amount—why, you could not say. If you had a big buy-ing or a big selling order, it was vitally important that your emotions, feeling, or subtlest thought should, by no trick of thought transference, telepathy, facial expression, or unguarded mood on your part be conveyed to any other person. Some men, Rivers informed him, were psychic— clairvoyant was the word in use then. They could tell— "how, God bless me," he exclaimed, "I don't know."

"Keep away from Targool over there. He's particu-larly good at that. When you see him hanging around you, avoid him."

Cowperwood studied the man curiously. He had no fear that any one would get away any of his subtle thought from him; but this small, thin, gray-headed broker— say forty-five years of age—with smooth red cheeks, keen gray eyes, gray eyebrows, gray mustache, and the most exquisite nicety of manner and clothing, interested him. So he was clairvoyant, eh?—Newton Targool. He watched him, and in spite of his personal confidence gave him a wide berth when he had any heavy buying or selling orders. Rapidly he came to be a trusted and forceful 'change man, forcing his way quickly to the center of any situation, suspecting readily what his rivals were up to, knowing the nature, character, and substance of all the stocks offered, knowing, as much as any one on 'change could know, by whom and for what purpose they were being manipulated. His mind began naturally to study out combinations, tricks that could be played, ways of "bulling" and "bearing" in the same hour to effect a profit. At first he loved the idea of it—the chance and drama; but after a little while he grew tired of it as a personal medium of gain, for the simple reason that it was so vastly uncertain.

Who was it, he asked himself, who made the real money —the stock-brokers? Not at all. Some of them were making money; but they were, as he quickly saw, like a lot of gulls or stormy petrels, hanging on the lee of the wind, hungry and anxious to snap up any unwary fish. There were all these stocks to be handled, to be sure. The handling of them represented a legitimate need for people, as he saw it—financiers who had to have some place where they could realize quickly on assets in time of stress; but who were the people who made the real money? They were not the brokers. The latter were agents, messengers, hirelings working for a fixed commission. Back of them were other men, men with shrewd ideas, subtle resources, abundant cash. Better yet, they were men of immense means whose enterprise and holdings these stocks represented, the men who schemed out and built the railroads, opened the mines, organized trading enterprises, and built up immense manufactories. Where were they? Not here. They might use brokers or other agents to buy and sell on 'change; but this buying and selling must be, and always so, incidental to the actual fact, the mine, the railroad, the wheat crop, the flour-mill, and so on. Anything less than straight-out sales to realize quickly on assets, or buying to hold as an investment, was gambling pure and simple; and these men were gamblers. He was nothing more than a gambler's agent—that was all. He said nothing about it. It was not troubling him any just at this moment; but it was not at all a mystery now, what he was. As in the case of Waterman & Co., he sized up these men shrewdly, judging some to be weak, some foolish, some clever, some slow; but, in the main, all small-minded or deficient because they were agents, tools, or gamblers. A man, a real man, must never be an agent, a tool, or a gambler—acting for himself or for others—he must employ such. A real man—a financier—was never a tool. He used tools. He created. He led.

Clearly, very clearly, at nineteen, twenty, and twenty-one years of age, he saw all this; but he was not quite ready yet to do anything about it. He was certain, however, that his day would come later.

It was while he was working for Tighe & Co., in the capacity of a "two-dollar broker," which phrase not infrequently made him smile, that his interest in Mrs. Semple was secretly and strangely growing. Because the latter had been at first so informally nice to him, and because the families knew each other slightly, when he received a casual invitation to call he did so. It was with a curious feeling of satisfaction that he approached, the first time, the place where this quiet couple resided, for the thought of seeing Mrs. Semple, without any idea of ever possessing her, was delightful. Their home, as he practically noted, was not as nice in some respects as his father's. In others it was better. The yard and trees were an advantage which his father's place did not possess. At first Mrs. Semple—Lillian Semple—did not have so much to say. She was gracious when he called;

but the burden of conversation fell on her husband. Cowperwood would sit and look at her while he talked to her husband, watching the varying expressions of her face; and if she had been at all psychic, she must have felt something. Fortunately she was not. Mr. Semple talked to him pleasantly because, in the first place, Frank was becoming financially significant—was suave and ingratiating—and, in the next place, Mr. Semple was anxious to get richer, and somehow Frank represented progress to him in that line. One spring evening they sat on the porch and talked—nothing very important: slavery, street-cars, the panic—it was on then, that of 1857—the development of the West. Mr. Semple wanted to know all about the stock exchange. Frank told him. He asked about the ramification of the shoe business, though he really did not care. All the while, inoffensively, he watched Mrs. Semple. Her manner, he thought, was soothing, attractive, delightful. She served tea and cake for them. They went inside after a time to avoid the mosquitoes. She played a little. At ten o'clock he left.

Thereafter, for a year or so, Mr. Cowperwood bought his shoes of Mr. Semple. He occasionally stopped in his Chestnut Street store to exchange the time of the day. Mr. Semple wanted his opinion as to the advisability of buying some shares in the Fifth and Sixth Street line, which, having secured a franchise, was creating great excitement. Mr. Cowperwood gave him his best judgment. It was sure to be profitable. He had purchased one hundred shares at five dollars a share, and so urged Mr. Semple to do so. Did he like him? Not particularly. He was not in any especial way interested in him personally. No, he liked Mrs. Semple, and he did not see her very often, either. She did not know that he liked her. She thought he was merely a friend of her husband's.

The time came, about a year later, when Mr. Semple died. It was an untimely death, one of those fortuitous and in a way undramatic episodes which are, nevertheless, dramatic in a dull way. He was seized with a cold in the chest late in the fall—one of those seizures ordinarily attributed to wet feet, or going out on a damp day without an overcoat—and because he paid little or no attention to it, insisted on going to business when Mrs. Semple urged him to stay at home and recuperate, after the third or fourth day he was very much worse. Mr. Semple was in his way a very determined person, not obstreperously so, but quietly and under the surface. Business was a great urge. Wealth, that thing he hoped for, lay, he thought, in his giving unbroken attention to business early and late. He saw himself soon worth about fifty thousand dollars. Then this cold—nine more days of pneumonia—and he was dead. The shoe store was closed for a few days; the house was full of sympathetic friends and church people. There was a funeral, with burial service in the Callowhill Presbyterian Church, to which they belonged, and then Mr. Semple was buried. Mrs. Semple cried bitterly. The shock of death affected her greatly and left her for a time in a depressed state. A brother of hers, David Wiggin, undertook for the time being to run the shoe business for her. There was no will, but in the final adjustment, which included the sale of the shoe business, there being no desire on anybody's part to contest her right to all the property, she received over eighteen thousand dollars. She continued to reside in the Front Street house, and was at once considered a charming and interesting widow.

Through this procedure young Cowperwood, only twenty years of age, was quietly manifest. He called through the illness. He attended the funeral. He helped her brother, David Wiggin, dispose of the shoe situation by volunteering to go and talk to certain shoe dealers as to the advisability of their taking over this stock. He called once or twice after the funeral, then stayed away for a considerable time. In five months he reappeared, and thereafter he was a periodic caller at stated intervals—periods of a week or ten days.

Again, it would be hard to say what he saw in Mrs. Semple. Her prettiness, wax-like in its quality, fascinated him; her indifference aroused perhaps his combative soul; he could not have explained why, but he wanted her in an urgent, passionate way. He could not think of her reasonably, and he did not talk of her much to any one. His family knew that he knew her. They knew that he went to see her; but there had grown up in the Cowperwood family a deep respect for the mental force of Frank. He was genial, cheerful, gay at most times, without being talkative; and he was decidedly successful. Everybody knew he was making money now. His salary was fifty dollars a week, and he was certain soon to get more. Some lots of his in West Philadelphia, bought three years before, had increased notably in value. His street-car holdings, augmented by still additional lots of fifty and one hundred and one hundred and fifty shares in new lines incorporated, were slowly rising, in spite of hard times, from the initiative five dollars in each case to ten, fifteen, and twenty-five dollars a share—all destined to go to par. He was learning constantly a great many things about the financial life of Philadelphia—its banks, brokers, financial speculators, schemes on foot, and schemes possible to be put on foot. He was liked in the financial district, and he was sure that he had a successful future. Because of his analysis of the brokerage situation he had come to the conclusion that he did not want to be a stock gambler at all; but a side line which he had observed to be very profitable, which involved no risk and where one was always right so long as one had capital, was that of bill-brokering. This appealed to him much more. It was a sounder proposition. People had bills to discount. There were many who were glad to take a reasonable risk. You were dealing in securities, behind which there was a tangible value not subject to aimless fluctuations and stock-jobbing tricks. Through his work and his father's connections he had met many people— merchants, bankers, traders. He could get their business, or a part of it, he knew. People in Drexel & Co. and Clark & Co. were friendly to him. Jay Cooke, a rising banking personality, was a personal friend of his. He thought it over.

Meanwhile he called on Mrs. Semple, and the more he called the better he liked her. There was no exchange of brilliant ideas between them; but he had a way of being comforting and social when he wished. He asked her aimless questions which seemed sound enough to her. He advised her about her business affairs in so intelligent a way that even her relatives approved of it. He appeared absolutely disinterested as far as her financial affairs were concerned, except that he was anxious to see her come out perfectly sound in the matter. On more than one evening he sat beside her, calculating her assets, explaining their advantageous investment, suggesting ways and means. She came to like him, because he was so considerate, quiet, reassuring, and so ready to explain over and over until everything was quite plain to her. She could see that he was looking on her affairs quite as if they were his own, trying to make them safe and secure.

"You're so very kind, Frank," she said to him, one night. "I'm awfully grateful. I don't know what I would have done if it hadn't been for you."

She looked at his handsome face, which was turned to hers with child-like simplicity.

"Not at all. Not at all. I want to do it. I wouldn't have been happy if I couldn't."

His eyes had a peculiar, subtle ray in them—not a gleam. She felt warm toward him, sympathetic, quite satisfied that she could lean on him.

"Well, I am very grateful just the same. You've been so good. Come out Sunday again, if you want to, or any evening. I'll be home."

She didn't think of him as anything save a remarkably talented young man, able, forceful, direct, incisive, and yet gentle—to her. He took his hat, held her hand, looked into her eyes, and went away. After he had gone she paused a moment, coming out of something that seemed like a warm, cheering vapor. He enveloped her completely with the charm of his personality. She could not have said why; but he did.

It was while he was calling on her in this way in her widowhood that his Uncle Seneca died in Cuba and left him fifteen thousand dollars outright. Davis had originally intended to leave him more; but Mrs. Davis's two children by him came in for later consideration, and he had to revise his will. This money, at this age, made Frank worth nearly twenty-five thousand dollars in his own right, and he knew exactly what to do with it. A panic had come since Mr. Semple had died, which had illustrated to him very clearly what an uncertain thing the brokerage business was. It was really a severe business depression. Money was so scarce that it could fairly be said not to exist at all. Capital, frightened by uncertain trade and money conditions everywhere, retired to its hiding-places in banks, vaults, tea-kettles, and stockings. The country seemed to be going to the dogs. War with the South or secession was vaguely looming up in the distance. The temper of the whole nation was nervous. People dumped their holdings which they had purchased in all sorts of enterprises on the market in order to get money—of course, from those who had money. They were purchased for a song; but these purchases were not many. Tighe, forced by the situation, discharged three of his clerks. He cut down his expenses in every possible way, and used up all his private savings to protect his private holdings. He had many shares of stock in this, that, and the other sound organization; but he had hypothecated them all for loans, and these, in many instances, were being called. He mortgaged his house, his land holdings — everything; and in many cases young Cowperwood was his intermediary, carrying blocks of shares to different banks with the suggestion to get what he could.

"See if your father's bank won't loan me fifteen thousand on these," he said to Frank, one day, producing a bundle of Philadelphia & Wilmington shares. The latter had heard his father speak of them in times past as excellent. Now he carried them, fifty thousand dollars' worth, and showed them to his father.

"They ought to be good," the elder Cowperwood said, dubiously. "At any other time they would be. But money is so tight. We find it awfully hard these days to meet our own obligations. I'll talk to Mr. Kugel." The latter was the president.

There was a long conversation—a long wait. His father came back to say it was doubtful whether they could. Eight per cent., then being secured for money, was a small rate of interest, considering its need. For ten per cent. Mr. Kugel might make a call-loan. Frank went back to his employer.

"For Heaven's sake, is there no money at all in the town?" he asked, contentiously, his commercial choler rising. "Why, the interest they want is ruinous! I can't stand that. Well, take 'em back and bring me the money. Good God, this 'll never do at all, at all!"

Frank went back. "He'll pay ten per cent.," he said, quietly.

His father conferred again. After a while Mr. Tighe was credited with a deposit of fifteen thousand dollars, with privilege to draw against it at once. He made out a check for the total fifteen thousand at once to the Girard National Bank to cover a shrinkage there. So it went.

During all these days young Cowperwood was following these financial complications with interest. He was not disturbed by the cause of slavery, or the talk of secession, or the general progress or decline of the country, except in so far as it affected his immediate interests. He wished he were a stable financier; but, now that he saw the inside of the brokerage business, he was not so sure that he wanted to stay in it. Gambling in stocks, according to conditions produced by this panic, seemed very hazardous. A number of brokers failed. He saw them rush into Tighe with anguished faces and ask that certain trades be canceled. Their very homes were in danger, they said. They would be wiped out, their wives and children put out on the street.

"Why, man alive, I can't do it!" he heard Tighe exclaim, one day. "Don't you know I can't? I'm on the ragged edge myself. I'm hanging on by the skin of my teeth as it is now. You know I can't do it. Good God, man, be reasonable! I know you're hard put to it—but so am I. So is everybody. I'd be doing this every fifteen minutes in the day if I did it for you. It can't be done."

Cowperwood knew this was so. It was hard logic, sad, cruel; but what else could Tighe or any other man do? He couldn't reasonably jeopardize himself. He saw a man one day—a big, strong, strapping fellow whom he knew as having a brisk office on the street, and who had been mentioned to him as one of the coming men—put his face in his hands in Tighe's little walled-off private office and begin to sob vigorously.

"Why, man, come to," said his employer, inexorably, but at the same time sympathetically standing over him. "I'd help you if I could. As God is my judge I would. But I can't. You won't die! I've been wiped out myself. When this thing is over, some of us 'll help you to get on your feet. I'll be glad to."

"I know, I know," sobbed the man, the tears trickling between his fingers. "If it wasn't for Bessie and the kids—"

"There, there, now," soothed Tighe, with his slightly Irish brogue.

Suddenly the broker leaped up.

"Damn the brokerage business, anyhow!" he exclaimed. "I've never had a day's peace since I entered this street. I'll quit this hole for good. I'll dig in a ditch first."

His face was red, his eyes flaring and tempestuous. Cowperwood noticed that his hair was of a peculiarly rich, flaxen hue, and that his finger-nails were particularly shiny from having been long polished.

"Don't say that, now," said Tighe. "You'll feel better after a while. You'll come back. We all do."

The man strode out.

"There you have it, Cowperwood," observed Tighe, meditatively. "That's the way. This is the worst run I've been through yet. I don't know where we're going to end. I may have to close myself yet."

Cowperwood looked out at the street through the window at the time. Surely life was grim. And you couldn't blame anybody. This panic was somewhat like a storm blowing from nowhere. No particular person was to blame; but, nevertheless, he felt as though he had had enough of the brokerage business, and decided, now that he had this free money, to leave Tighe and go into business for himself. Tighe, like Waterman & Co., had decided that he could use Cowperwood best as a minor partner; but the latter was not to be tempted.

"I think you have a nice business," he explained, in refusing; "but I want to get in the note-brokerage business for myself. I don't trust this stock game. I don't believe I'm a good gambler at heart. I'd rather have a little business of my own than all the floor work in this world."

"But you're pretty young, Frank," argued his employer. "You have lots of time to work for yourself."

In the end he parted friends with both Tighe and

Rivers. They said they would be glad to help him, which they did; but they were sorry.

"That's a smart young fellow," observed Tighe, ruefully.

"He'll make his mark," rejoined Rivers. "Surely he will. He's the shrewdest boy of his age I ever saw."

CHAPTER IX

LIFE takes on a peculiar and curious light when love enters. Ordinarily it is sicklied o'er by the pale cast of reflection, wearisome and drab; but when love enters, it is as though the sun rose after a dreary stretch of weather—the world becomes roseate once more. Young Cowperwood, facing his new venture, was cheered by this radiance of a new morning, in which for him love was. He had some free money now—considerable, he thought— in addition to his investments; and long since he had learned the art of hypothecating securities. He could take his street-car stocks, which were steadily enhancing in value, and raise seventy per cent. of their market price by paying the current rate of interest. He could put a mortgage on his lots and get money there, if he could use it to any greater advantage. He could borrow on his credit, his personality, from his father and others —Tighe for one, or Waterman—and so he was getting on. He had established financial relations with the Girard National Bank, a man by the name of Davison being president there and taking a fancy to him, and he proposed to borrow from that institution some day. All he wanted was suitable investments—things in which he could realize surely, quickly, and greatly—and his eye was constantly set for things of that kind. One of the things outside of the note-brokerage business in which he saw fine prospective profits was the street-car business, which was rapidly growing in its local ramifications.

However, the thing that interested him most at this time was the personality of Mrs. Semple, who, as he saw her more and more regularly, following up the lead his

THE FINANCIER

interest in her affairs had given him, came to look upon
him not so much as a boy as a man—in a way a shrewder
man than her late husband. It has been said that the
latter had not made much of an impression on her. It
is true. She was really not of a very impressionable
nature; but there was a tang or sting to the personality
of young Cowperwood which could not be indifferently
passed over by any one. He was memorable in his
quality. She talked to him about commonplace things;
he helped her set the table one night in the absence of
the maid, and brought her, at other times, her wraps or
lace mantilla from some near-by dressing-case when she
was cold; but she felt an intangible something which
had nothing to do with words or actions. Atmosphere it
was—the atmosphere or aroma or vibration of his particular personality. It was grateful.

One night, when she was going to bed, she stopped in
front of her dressing-table and looked at her face and
neck and arms, which were bare. They were pretty and
shapely. A subtle something came over her as she surveyed her long, peculiarly shaded hair. She thought of
young Cowperwood; and then, the vision of the late Mr.
Semple returning, and the force and quality of public
opinion, she chilled and was ashamed. It frightened her,
this thought, as being something antic, evil, impossible.
She went to bed, tucking the covers up about her nose;
but somehow the personality of Mr. Cowperwood would
not down.

The latter looked at her always, when he was with her,
in such a peculiar way. He came in with such a brisk,
healthy, vigorous air. His smile was like a dash of cold
salt water, awakening her, and his eyes—you could not
explain the force of his eyes. He purchased a horse and
buggy about this time, the most attractive-looking animal
and vehicle he could find—the combination cost him five
hundred dollars—and invited Mrs. Semple to drive with
him. She refused at first, but later consented. From

96

him, during many visits, she had heard of his success, his prospects, his windfall of fifteen thousand dollars, his intention of going into the note-brokerage business. She knew his father was likely to succeed to the position of vice-president in the Third National Bank, and she liked the Cowperwoods. At her husband's death they had called, and there had been visits since. Now she began to realize that there was something more than friendship here. This erstwhile boy was a man, and he was calling on her. It was almost ridiculous in the face of things—her seniority, her widowhood, her placid, retiring disposition—but it wasn't. The sheer, quiet, determined force of the young man made it not so, and in a cool, determined way he was not ready to be balked by her fear or her sense of convention.

In spite of her fears and her uncertainty, Mrs. Semple accepted his attentions and his interest because, equally in spite of herself, she was drawn to him. He had a direct, offhand, apparently unconsidered manner. Though Mrs. Semple was five years his senior in the things that concerned her world, mentally he was ten years hers. Her little financial affairs were as nothing to him. He was not eager for her money, though he was well aware of it. He felt that he could use it to her advantage. He wanted her physically—he wanted to shock this peculiarly interesting, torpid beauty into something different, and he felt a keen preliminary interest in the children they would have. He wanted to know if he could make her love him vigorously, and could rout out the memory of the other life. Strange ambition. Strange perversion, one might almost say.

In these latter days, after her first keen sense of widowhood had worn off, he would call and talk to her, and she would listen to his general observations with an assumption of a kindly interest.

"Why do you come to see me so often?" she asked him, once.

"Oh, don't you know?" he replied, looking at her in an inscrutable way.

"No."

"Sure you don't?"

"Well, I know you liked Mr. Semple, and I always thought you liked me as his wife. He's gone, though, now."

"And you're here," he replied.

"And I'm here?"

"Yes. I like you. I like to be with you. Don't you like me that way?"

"Why, I've never thought of it. You're so much younger. I'm five years older than you are."

"In years," he said, "certainly. That's nothing. I'm fifteen years older than you are in other ways. I know more about life in some ways than you can ever hope to learn—don't you think so?" he added, softly, persuasively.

"Well, that's true. But I know a lot of things you don't know." She laughed softly, showing her pretty teeth.

It was evening. They were on the side porch. The river was before them.

"Yes, but that's only because you're a woman. A man can't hope to get a woman's point of view exactly. I'm talking about you as far as the management of the affairs of this world is concerned. You're not as old as I am mentally."

"Well, what of it?"

"Nothing. You asked why I came to see you. That's why. Partially."

He relapsed into silence and stared at the water.

She thought of him, looking at him from the difficult ground of the late union. His handsome body, slowly broadening, was nearly full grown. His face, because of its full, clear, big, inscrutable eyes, had an expression which was almost babyish. She could not have guessed the depths it veiled. His cheeks were pink, his hands not large, but sinewy and strong. Her pale, uncertain, lymphatic body extracted a form of dynamic energy from him even at this range. She looked her name—a lily—to him. He looked like a young warrior to her, with his even teeth, his square jaw, his lip that could part into an always enigmatic but heavenly smile.

"I don't think you ought to come to see me so often. People won't think well of it." She ventured to take a distant, matronly air—the air she had originally held toward him.

"People," he said, "don't worry about people. People think what you want them to think. I wish you wouldn't take that distant air toward me."

"Why?"

"Because I like you."

"But you mustn't like me. It's wrong. I can't ever marry you. You're too young. I'm too old."

"Hush that," he said, imperiously, "there's nothing to it. I want you to marry me. You know I do. Now, when will it be?"

"Why, how silly! I never heard of such a thing!" she exclaimed. "It will never be, Frank. It can't be!"

"Why can't it?" he asked.

"Because—well, because I'm older. People would think it strange. I'm not long enough free."

"Oh, long enough nothing!" he exclaimed, irritably. "That's the one thing I have against you—you are so worried about what people think. They don't make your life. They certainly don't make mine. Think of yourself first. You have your own life to make. Are you going to let what other people think stand in the way of what you want to do?"

"But I don't want to," she smiled.

He arose and came over to her, looking into her eyes.

"Well?" she asked, nervously, quizzically.

He merely looked at her.

"Well?" she queried, more flustered.

He stooped down to take her arms, but she got up.

"Now you must not come near me," she pleaded, determinedly. "I'll go in the house, and I'll not let you come any more. It's terrible! You're silly! You mustn't interest yourself in me."

She did show a good deal of moral determination, and he desisted. He went away that night unsatisfied as to a caress he wanted to take again, and again, and again. Then one night, when they had gone inside because of the mosquitoes, and when she had insisted that he could not come any more, that his attentions were noticeable to others, and that she would be disgraced, he caught her, under desperate protest, in his arms.

"Now, see here!" she exclaimed. "I told you! It's silly! You mustn't kiss me! How dare you! Oh! oh! oh!—"

She broke away and ran up the near-by stairway to her room. Cowperwood followed her swiftly. As she pushed the door to he forced it open and recaptured her. He lifted her bodily from her feet and held her crosswise, lying in his arms.

"Oh, how could you!" she exclaimed. "I will never speak to you any more. I will never let you come here any more if you don't put me down this minute. Put me down!"

"I'll put you down, sweet," he said. "I'll take you down," at the same time pulling her face to him and kissing her. He was very much aroused, excited.

While she was twisting and protesting, pleading to be put on the floor, he carried her down the stairs again into the living-room, and seated himself in the great armchair, still holding her tight in his arms.

"Oh!" she sighed, falling limp on his shoulder when he refused to let her go. Then, because of the set determination of his face, some intense pull in him, she smiled. "How would I ever explain if I did marry you?" she asked, weakly. "Your father! Your mother!"

"You don't need to explain. I'll do that. And you needn't worry about my family. They won't care."

THE FINANCIER

"But mine," she recoiled.

"Don't worry about yours. I'm not marrying your family. I'm marrying you. We have independent means."

She relapsed into additional protests; but he kissed her the more. There was a deadly persuasion to his caresses. Mr. Semple had never displayed any such fire. He aroused a force of feeling in her which had not previously been there. She was afraid of it and ashamed.

"Will you marry me in a month?" he asked, cheerfully, when she paused.

"You know I won't!" she exclaimed, nervously. "The idea! Why do you ask?"

"What difference does it make? You're entitled to marry me. We're going to get married, eventually. Just as soon as you want." He was thinking how attractive he could make her look in other surroundings. Neither she nor his family knew how to live.

"Well, not in a month. Wait a little while. I will marry you after a while—after you see whether you want me."

He caught her tight. "I'll show you," he said.

"Please stop. You hurt me."

"How about us? Two months?"

"Certainly not."

"Three?"

"Well, maybe."

"No maybe in that case. We marry."

"But you're only a boy."

"Don't worry about me. You'll find out how much of a boy I am."

He seemed of a sudden to open up a new world to her, and she realized that she had never really lived before. This man represented something bigger and stronger than ever her husband had dreamed of. In his young way he was terrible, irresistible.

"Well, in three months then," she whispered, when he rocked her cozily in his arms.

CHAPTER X

THE moral nature of Frank Cowperwood may, at this juncture, be said to have had no material or spiritual existence. He had never had, so far as he had reasoned at all, a fixed attitude in regard to anything except preserving himself intact and succeeding. His father talked, or had in earlier years, of business honor, commercial integrity, and so forth. Frank thought of this a long time at odd moments. What was honor? He had never been able to define it. Men seemed to think it referred to some state of mind which would not allow a man to take undue advantage of another; but life, experience, taught and were teaching him something different. Honor was almost, he thought, a figment of the brain. If it referred to anything, it referred to force, generosity, power; but these were not rules of conduct, but terms of temperament and condition. A man might be generous at times, and at such times be honorable; but he might not, on the face of things, be able at other times to be generous. Then he would not be honorable. Or, there were times, such as in the days of panic, when honor would ultimately accrue most to him who held his own. There was no honor for the failure. Like Tighe, when appealed to, a man had better say "I can't" or "I won't" firmly and let it go at that. You couldn't be generous or kind in times of stress. Look at the conditions on the stock exchange.

Here men came down to the basic facts of life—the necessity of self care and protection. There was no talk, or very little there, of honor. There were rules of conduct which men observed because they had to. So far as he could see, force governed this world—hard, cold force and quickness of brain. If one had force, plenty of it, quickness of wit and subtlety, there was no need for anything else. Some people might be pretending to be guided by other principles—ethical and religious, for instance; they might actually be so guided—he could not tell. If they were, they were following false or silly standards. In those directions lay failure. To get what you could and hold it fast, without being too cruel, certainly not to individuals—that was the thing to do, and he genially ignored or secretly pitied those who believed otherwise.

It is not possible to say how a boy of twenty-one should come by such subtle thoughts; but he had. Religion was nothing to him—a lot of visionary speculations which had no basis in fact. Why should people get excited about religion? He smiled at hearing his father tell how only a few years before a regulation of the city council had permitted the fastening of chains across the streets in front of churches in Philadelphia, in order to prevent traffic from annoying the worshipers. And even now there was a terrific agitation against any infraction of the Sunday quiet and rest. For instance, they would not allow the new street-car lines to run on Sunday. Religious people struck him as being caught by some emotion or illusion which had no relation to life, and his thought was not to rebel, but to get some method of ignoring or humoring them without suffering for it.

"Go through the motions," he said to his brother Joseph, one day when the latter was complaining of the necessity of going to hear a dry sermon. "It won't hurt you. Father has a business to look after."

But he would not even do that himself. He preferred to substitute the reality for the seeming. When he was better acquainted with Mr. Rivers, and could call on him on Sunday morning to talk things over, he did that, saying that he was going to church with Miss Emily Rivers, the broker's sister, which he sometimes did. He called on his Uncle Seneca's widow on Sunday, and at other houses where he had been introduced—the Watermans, George and Henry, the Leighs—the head of this house, Walter, being an assistant teller in Drexel & Co.—and similar individuals. He had a curious feeling that certain types of men would be useful to him, and he could be charmingly civil. All these older people liked him—they enjoyed his quiet, sensible, non-committal observations.

When it came to his attitude toward Mrs. Semple he did not delude himself with any noble theories of conduct in regard to her. He liked her. She was beautiful, peculiar, with a mental and physical lure for him that was irresistible, and that was all he desired to know. No other woman was holding him like that. It never occurred to him that he could not like other women at the same time. He did so—Marjorie Stafford, in a lessening way. There was a great deal of palaver about the sanctity of the home. It rolled off his mental sphere like water off the feathers of a duck. Here again he was not fixed or held by anything. Homes were nice. His father and most of his acquaintances had one—individual homes. There were children in many cases, much talk of purity and chastity, and cleaving only to one woman. He was not so sure about that. One woman might fascinate him. He fancied he could live with Mrs. Semple all his days, and not desire any other woman; but other men might not be able to live with their wives. For all the rules of conduct prevalent in the air, married men and women did fall out. He heard that his Uncle Seneca and his wife had begun to quarrel before the former had died. George Waterman's wife was supposed to be very sickly and peevish, and one of the clerks at Waterman & Co. had once confided to him that he had heard George tell Henry that he wished his wife was dead. George had been angry about something. In Frank's own neighborhood and social circle there were rumors and facts. Men and women did separate. Some men and some women ran away. Others fought terribly. There were storms of ill-feeling and brutality reported. He knew of a number of cases where the husband and wife were permanently separated. His own father and mother got along nicely; but his mother was of a quiet, peaceful, sympathetic, and religious temperament, and his father was cautious. They quarreled now and then. There were little strains of feeling over trivial things. Unquestionably both harbored regrets of various kinds. Nearly every one did. He had no regrets as yet, but he might have. The saddest thing to him was to see the defeated man—the man who had failed because he could not think quick enough. He wanted to make himself so secure financially that even lack of quick thinking later on would not subject him to distress and regret.

As may be imagined, the family was greatly disturbed at the announcement of his coming marriage to Mrs. Semple. She was too old, his mother and father thought; and then Frank could have done so much better with his prospects. Young Anna fancied that Mrs. Semple was designing, which was, of course, not true at all. His brothers, Joseph and Edward, were interested, but not certain as to what they actually thought, seeing that Mrs. Semple was good-looking and had some money. Frank seemed to know what he was about, but could have done better if he had waited, of course. His friends and the family's friends were surprised when told; but young Cowperwood was getting along, and, from a worldly point of view, it was all right. Mrs. Semple had a right to remarry after two years, if she wished. There was no moral or ethical law binding a woman so young to single blessedness.

The time drifted by, and meanwhile Frank, who had resigned his position with Tighe & Co.,, had opened a little note-broker's office at No. 64 South Third Street. He had various excellent connections which

THE FINANCIER

served him in good stead. For one thing, he was well and favorably known in the street. All the men on 'change had observed him, and finally became friendly with him. Like Rivers, he was considered able and uniformly courteous, but not nearly so cold or hard seeming. He breathed out, quite in spite of himself, and without any shabby intention of making friends, an atmosphere of humanness. Everybody seemed to understand and take for granted that, no matter what their motives or tricks, Cowperwood understood and took no umbrage. He made no great show of hurry, and yet without giving offense he succeeded in doing business quickly. In the stock-exchange deals he had been as quick as a flash at times, always on the spot snapping bargains right from under the teeth of his rivals, and yet he had a bland smile which allayed chagrin and anger.

"Sold!" It was something to hear his quick, cool voice.

"Seventy-three for any part of five hundred 'Green and Coates'" (a street-car stock).

"Sold!"

Cowperwood would be under the seller's very nose. He had the faculty which he had envied in Targool—clairvoyance. He could fairly see and feel in advance what was coming. Sometimes he missed. Not often. His trades were not tremendous; but he had come to the place where soon he would have succeeded Rivers on the floor. Now, in this new note-brokerage business, these men remembered him. He would go to one house, where he suspected ready money would be desirable, and offer to negotiate their notes or any paper they might issue bearing six per cent. interest for a commission, and then he would take the paper to some man who he knew had idle money and would welcome a secure investment, and sell him the paper for a small commission. Sometimes his father, sometimes other people helped him with suggestions as to when and how. Between the two ends he might make

four and five per cent. on the total transaction himself.
It wasn't much; but since he was doing this all the time,
and people were friendly to him, more and more so all
the time, it can be seen how it was that in the first
year he cleared six thousand dollars over and above
all expenses. That wasn't much; but he was augment-
ing it in another way which meant great profit in the
future.

This was in the new street-car stocks which were being
issued, and in which, the future of which, he believed
firmly. Before the first line, which was a shambling
affair, had been laid in Front Street, the streets of Philadelphia had been crowded with hundreds of rough,
springless omnibuses rattling over rough, hard cobblestones. Now, thanks to the idea of John Stephenson, in
New York, the double-rail-track idea had come, and besides the line in Fifth and Sixth streets (the cars running
out one street and back another), which had paid splendidly from the start, there were many other lines proposed or under way. The city was as crazy to see
street-cars replace omnibuses as it was to see railroads
replace canals. There was opposition, of course. There
always is. The cry of probable monopoly was raised.
Disgruntled and defeated omnibus owners and drivers
groaned aloud.

Cowperwood, like his father, was one of those who believed in the future of the street-railway. The latter was
timid; but Frank, believing, risked all he could spare on
new issues of stock shares in new companies. He was
not one of those who, like the average rank outsider, seize
unwittingly whatever is thrown them by an inside ring.
If possible, he wanted to be on the inside himself; but in
this matter of the street-railways, having been so young
when they started, and not having arranged his financial
connections to any great degree, it was difficult to manage. Still, he knew that they were going to pay, and pay
largely. The Fifth and Sixth Street line, which had been

but recently started, was paying six hundred dollars a day. A project for a West Philadelphia line (Walnut and Chestnut) was on foot, as were lines to occupy Second and Third streets, Race and Vine, Spruce and Pine, Green and Coates, Tenth and Eleventh, and so forth. They were engineered and backed by some big capitalists who had influence with the State legislature, and could, in spite of a great public protest which was now raised, obtain franchises. Charges of corruption were in the air. It was argued that the streets were valuable, and that the companies should pay a road tax of a thousand dollars a mile. Somehow these splendid grants were gotten through without much protest, however; and the public, hearing of the Fifth and Sixth Street line profits, was eager to invest. Cowperwood was one of these. The whole incident had renewed his contempt for public opinion, but it did not lessen his interest in street-railways; rather strengthened it. He had taken all the stock he could afford in the Fifth and Sixth Street line. Now, when the Second and Third Street line was engineered, he invested in that and in the Walnut and Chestnut Street line. He began to have vague dreams of controlling or engineering a line himself some time; but as yet he did not see how it was to be done. His father was helping him with suggestions as to where negotiable paper could be disposed of; but his business was as yet far removed from a financial bonanza.

In the midst of this early work he married Mrs. Semple, and there was no vast to-do about it. He did not want any. His bride-to-be was nervous, fearsome of public opinion, disturbed as to what her closest friends might be thinking. Frank was so young—five years younger— she was a widow. Still, he forced her to yearn for him, dominated her completely; and now in these later days she was as eager to have him as he was to have her. One of her sisters had come to live with her. Her two brothers were frequent visitors. Frank would call there of an evening and hold her in his arms, whispering dreams of the future. They were going to refurnish this house and live in it for a while. He was going to arrange his affairs so that he could take at least two weeks off. After the first shock of announcement his mother warmed to Mrs. Semple, and helped to arrange things. Even Anna assisted—Joseph and Edward called often socially. Then, one warm October day, he and Lillian were married in the First Presbyterian Church, of Callowhill Street, because she wished it so; and together they visited New York and Boston—practically her first journey. His bride, he was satisfied, looked exquisite in a trailing gown of cream lace—a creation of months and much labor. Mr. and Mrs. Cowperwood, his parents; Mrs. Seneca Davis; the Wiggin family, brothers and sisters, and some friends were present. He was a little opposed to this idea; but Lillian wanted it. He stood up straight and correct in black broadcloth for the wedding ceremony—because she wished it, but later changed to a smart business suit for traveling. They took an afternoon train for New York, which required five hours to reach. When they were finally alone in the Astor House, New York, after hours of make-believe and public pretense of indifference, he gathered her stoutly in his arms.

"Oh, it's delicious," he exclaimed, "to have you all to myself."

She met his eagerness with that beautiful, smiling passivity which he had so much admired, but which this time was tinged strongly with a communicated desire. He thought he should never have enough of her, her beautiful face, her lovely, shapely arms, her smooth, lymphatic body. They were like two children billing and cooing, driving, dining, seeing the sights. He was curious to visit the financial sections of both cities and look at the great banks and financial offices. New York and Boston appealed to him as commercially solid. He wondered, as he observed the former, whether he should ever leave

Philadelphia. He was going to be very happy there now, he thought, with Lillian, and possibly a young brood of Cowperwoods. He was going to work hard and make money. With his means and hers now at his command he might become, very readily, notably wealthy.

CHAPTER XI

THE home atmosphere which they established when they returned from their honeymoon was more artistic than that which had characterized the earlier life of Mrs. Cowperwood as Mrs. Semple. Cowperwood, aggressive in his current artistic mood, had objected at once after they were engaged to the spirit of the furniture and decorations, or lack of them, and had suggested that he be allowed to have it brought more in keeping with his idea of what was appropriate. During these years in which he had been growing into manhood he had come instinctively into sound notions of what was artistic and refined. He had seen so much of homes that were more distinguished and harmonious than his own. One could not walk or drive about Philadelphia without seeing and being impressed with the general tendency toward a more refined and cultivated social life. There were many excellent and expensive houses going up in the west. The front lawn, with some attempt at floral gardening, was coming into local popularity. In the homes of the Tighes, the Leighs, Mr. Arthur Rivers, and others, were art objects of some distinction, which he had seen—bronzes, marbles, hangings, pictures, clocks, rugs better than any his family had ever possessed. He had meditated on these things at odd moments, drawn to them mightily. Now, when he was thinking of setting up his own home, these thoughts for the time being became uppermost.

The previous condition of the Semple home had not appealed to him at all. Mr. Semple appeared dull; Mrs. Semple indifferent but beautiful. Her setting was not right, and she, of her own volition and resources, could not make it right. He admitted to himself that in all likelihood she did not have the taste; but that did not make any difference. His was the active disposition, taking great joy in doing things. He could take this comparatively commonplace house, and with very little money make it into something charming. The dining-room, for instance, which, through two plain windows set in a flat side wall back of the veranda, looked south over a stretch of grass and several trees and bushes to a dividing fence where the Semple property ended and a neighbor's began, could be made into something so much more attractive. That fence—sharp-pointed, gray palings—was an abomination. It could be torn away and a hedge put in its place. The wall which divided the present dining-room from the parlor should be knocked through, and a hanging of some pleasing character put in its place. A bay-window could be built to replace the two oblong ones now present—a bay which would come down to the floor and open out on the lawn *via* swiveled, diamond-shaped, lead-paned frames which would be so much more attractive. All this shabby, nondescript furniture, collected from heaven knows where—partly inherited from the Semples and the Wiggins, and partly bought—could be thrown out or sold, and something better and more harmonious introduced. He had heard vaguely of styles of furniture—Louis XIV., Louis XV., Louis XVI., the Empire, Sheraton, Chippendale, Colonial, Old English. Any of these, or some modification of them, something simple, would do. He knew a young man by the name of Ellsworth, an architect newly graduated from a local school, whom he had met at the bachelor home of Arthur Rivers. With him he had struck up an interesting friendship—one of those inexplicable inclinations of temperament—which pleased him greatly. Ellsworth, Wilton Ellsworth, was an artist in spirit, quiet, meditative, refined. Cowperwood had liked his looks on sight. From discussing the quality of a certain building in Chestnut Street, which was then being done, and which Ellsworth pronounced atrocious, they fell to discussing art in general, or the lack of it in America. "We are so very far away from anything at all as yet, I know, unless it is Colonial architecture," Ellsworth remarked. "I haven't been abroad; but I want to go."

Cowperwood felt a keen kinship with this thought. He wanted to travel also some time.

They met again on the street accidentally and talked; and so now, when Cowperwood thought of this house and what was the matter with it, he thought of Ellsworth. It occurred to him that Ellsworth would carry out his decorative views to a nicety. It seemed to him that the Semple home would be much more endurable if its parlor and sitting-room were knocked together into one big room, which could be used as a combined living-room and library, and a certain fireplace, which was now too small for one room, were enlarged to make it at once effective and artistic. The walls ought to be papered or decorated in corresponding colors—probably dark—and the furniture all thrown out and something new, correlative, and soothing be introduced. He did not feel that as yet he could afford many expensive objects of art, but in so far as his means permitted he wanted his proposed home to be artistic. He interested Mrs. Cowperwood in young Ellsworth, and then in his own ideas of how the house could be revised.

Mrs. Cowperwood was not an intellectual leader. Her young lover appeared to be a man of infinite tact and discrimination. She could understand well enough, though not vitally, the significance of most of his thoughts when presented to her, and these concerning the revision of the house appealed to her very much. She wanted to live nicely — to be significant in her circle. His idea of changing the dining-room and parlor was particularly grateful.

"Oh yes, let's do that," she exclaimed, when he told her. "Wouldn't that be pretty? Can Mr. Ellsworth carry out your ideas exactly?"

"I think so. It may cost a little something; but we will want to live in it for some time, maybe, and, anyhow, if you should want to sell it, it would bring more changed as I say."

"I want to sell it!" she commented. "Say we, dear."

"Very well then, we."

He smiled and smoothed her chin and cheek with his hand.

So while they were gone on their honeymoon Mr. Ellsworth began the revision on an estimated cost of three thousand dollars for the furniture and all. It was not completed for nearly three weeks after they returned; but when done it was a comparatively new house. The dining-room bay hung low over the grass, as Frank wished, and the windows were diamond-paned and leaded, swiveled on brass rods. The opening between the living-room and the dining-room had noiseless rolling doors; but the intention was to use only a light-blue, brown, and green silk hanging, which represented a wedding scene in Normandy, in the square space. Delicately cut Old English oak was used in the dining-room, an American imitation of Chippendale and Sheraton for the sitting-room and the bedrooms. There were a few simple water-colors hung here and there, some bronzes of Hosmer and Powers, a marble Venus by Potter, a now forgotten sculptor, and other objects of art—nothing of any distinction. Pleasing, appropriately colored rugs covered the floor. Mrs. Cowperwood was shocked by the nudity of the Venus which conveyed an atmosphere of European freedom not common to America; but she said nothing. It was all harmonious and soothing, and she did not feel herself capable to judge. Frank knew about these things so much better than she did. Instantly a maid and a man of all work were installed, and that process of entertaining which young married couples so much enjoy was begun on a small scale.

Those who recall the early years of their married life can best realize the subtle changes which this new condition brought to Frank, for, like all who accept the hymeneal yoke, he was influenced to a certain extent by the things with which he surrounded himself. Primarily, from certain traits of his character, one would have imagined him called to be a citizen of eminent respectability and worth. He appeared to be an ideal home man. He liked horses moderately—the vehicular object of them more than the horse itself. He liked a yard, the idea of a home, the thought of decorating and arranging it individually. This thought of his wife's cottage, and her in it, cheered him greatly. She was so nice in it. He delighted to fondle her body evenings; and, leaving the crowded down-town section where traffic clamored and men hurried in a great stress of effort, he would come out through the dusk of the evening to this spot where were vines, in season, and a charming view of the river spreading wide and gray in dark weather, or leaden blue and silver in bright, and feel that he was well stationed and physically happy in life. The thought of the dinner-table with candles upon it (his idea); the thought of Lillian in a trailing gown of pale-blue or green silk—he liked her in those colors; the thought of a big fireplace flaming with solid lengths of cord-wood, and Lillian snuggling in his arms, gripped his forceful imagination. As has been said before, he cared nothing for books; but life, pictures, physical contact, trees—these, in spite of his shrewd and already gripping financial calculations, held him. To live richly, joyously, fulsomely—his whole nature craved that.

And Mrs. Cowperwood, in spite of the difference in their years, appeared to be a fit mate for him at this time. She was, once awakened, and for the time being, clinging, responsive, dreamy. His mood and hers was for a baby, and in a little while that happy expectation was whispered

to him by her. She had half fancied that her previous
barrenness was due to herself, and was rather surprised
and delighted at the proof that it was not so. It opened
new possibilities—a seemingly glorious future of which
she was not afraid. He liked it, the idea of self-duplica-
tion. It was almost acquisitive, this thought. For days
and weeks and months and years, at least the first four
or five, he took a keen satisfaction in coming home evenings, strolling about the yard, driving with his wife,
having friends in to dinner, talking over with her in an
explanatory way the things he intended to do. She did
not understand his financial abstrusities, and he did not
trouble to make them clear. A suggestion was enough.
But love, her pretty body, her lips, her quiet manner—
the lure of all these combined, and his two children, when
they came—two in four years—held him. He was really
a very comfortable and home-interested young man.
He would dandle Frank, Jr., who was the first to arrive,
on his knee, looking at his chubby feet, his kindling
eyes, his almost formless yet bud-like mouth, and wonder
at the process by which children came into the world.
There was so much to think of in this connection—the
spermatozoic beginning, the strange period of gestation
in women, the danger of disease and delivery. He had
gone through a real period of strain when Frank, Jr.,
was born, for Mrs. Cowperwood was frightened. She
had heard that it might be very trying. He cared for
the beauty of her body—the danger of losing her; and he
actually endured his first worry when he stood outside
the door the day the child came. Not much—he was too
self-sufficient, too resourceful; and yet he worried, con-
juring up thoughts of death and the end of their present
state. Then word came, after certain piercing, harrowing
cries, that all was well, and he was permitted to look at
the new arrival. The experience broadened his concep-
tion of things, made him more solid in his judgment of
life. That old conviction of tragedy underlying the sur-

face of things, like wood under its veneer, was emphasized. He knew that he had gifts and powers not vouchsafed him because of any effort on his part, and he knew that he must exercise them sanely and continuously in order to obtain and maintain what he wished to be. Little Frank, and later Lillian, blue-eyed and golden-haired, touched his imagination for a while. There was a good deal to this home idea, after all. That was the way life was organized, and properly so—on the theory or corner-stone of the home. The world must have homes. Children must be raised within their sheltering walls, safe-guarded, nurtured, trained, given a point of view. He had been so reared. Now he was handing on this tradi-tion, this principle unmodified. That was the way things should be, no doubt.

It would be impossible to indicate fully how subtle were the material changes which these years involved— changes so gradual that they were, like the lap of soft waters, unnoticeable. Considerable—a great deal, con-sidering how little he had to begin with—of wealth was added in the next five years. He came, in his financial world, to know fairly intimately, as commercial relation-ships go, some of the subtlest characters of the steadily enlarging financial world. In the old days, at Tighe's and on 'change, many curious figures had been pointed out to him—the State and city officials of one grade and another who were "making something out of politics," and some of the national figures who came from Washington to Philadelphia at times to see Drexel & Co., Clark & Co., and even Tighe & Co. These men, as he learned and as his father often told him, had something "up their sleeve." They had tips or advance news of legislative or economic changes which were sure to affect certain stocks or trade opportunities. Various brokers represented them, and they "came over" for consultation. A young clerk, Satterlee by name, had once pulled his sleeve at Tighe's.

"See that man going in to see Tighe?"

"Yes."

"That's Murtagh, the city treasurer. Say, he don't do anything but play a fine game. All that money to invest, and he don't have to account for anything except the principal. The interest goes to him."

Young Cowperwood smiled subtly, without comment, but bidding by his smile for more.

"You know that Baltimore and Washington stock?"

"Yes."

"It's all being carried for him. Tighe draws on the Treasury for whatever he needs to buy with. He's put one hundred thousand in B. and W. for Murtagh in the last sixty days."

Cowperwood understood. All these city and State officials speculated. They had a habit of depositing city and State funds with certain bankers and brokers as authorized agents or designated State depositories. The banks paid no interest—save to the officials personally. They loaned it to certain brokers on the officials' secret order, and the latter invested it in "sure winners." The bankers got the free use of the money a part of the time, the brokers another part; the officials made money, and the brokers received a fat commission. There was a political ring in Philadelphia in which the mayor, certain members of the council, the treasurer, the chief of police, the commissioner of public works, and others shared. It was a case generally of "You scratch my back and I'll scratch yours." Young Cowperwood did not know the exact details of this ring and its operation at this time; but there were so many evidences of its presence that he could not fail to see how subtle and powerful it was. The public was being beautifully hoodwinked. City money and city privileges were being hawked about and traded upon. He thought it rather shabby work at first; but many men were rapidly getting rich, and no one seemed to care. The newspapers were always talking about civic patriotism and pride, but never a word about these things. And the men who did them were powerful and respected.

Still, although in no position to make any large connections as yet, he himself was doing very well, and so these things did not trouble him as yet. There were many houses, a constantly widening circle, that found him a very trustworthy agent in disposing of note issues or note payment. He seemed to know so quickly where to go to get the money. From the first he made it a principle to keep twenty thousand dollars in cash on hand in order to be able to take up a proposition instantly and without discussion. So, often he was able to say, "Why, certainly, I can do that," when otherwise, on the face of things, he would not have been able to do so. His versatile mind told him where he could find men and means, and moneyed men liked him. He was asked if he would not handle certain stock transactions on 'change. He had no seat, and he intended not to take any at first; but now he changed his mind and bought one, not only in Philadelphia, but in New York also. A certain Joseph Zimmerman, a dry-goods man for whom he had handled various note issues, suggested that he undertake operating in street-railway shares for him, and this was the beginning of his return to the floor.

In the meanwhile his family life was changing—growing, one might have said, finer and more secure. Mrs. Cowperwood had, for instance, been compelled from time to time to make a subtle readjustment of her personal relationship with people, as he had with his. When Mr. Semple was alive she had been socially connected with tradesmen principally—retailers and small wholesalers—a very few. Some of the women of her own church, the First Presbyterian, were friendly with her. There had been church teas and sociables which she and Mr. Semple attended, and dull visits to his relatives and hers. The Cowperwoods, the Watermans, and a few families of that caliber, had been the notable exceptions. Now all this was changed. Young Cowperwood did not care very much for her relatives, and the Semples, bag and baggage, had been alienated by her second, and to them outrageous, marriage. His own family was closely interested by ties of affection and mutual prosperity; but, better than this, Cowperwood was drawing to himself some really significant personalities. When he went through Third Street in the morning—he came down to Arch Street on a car and then walked—he was nodded to by many presidents, vice-presidents, treasurers, and other officials of banks and organizations, by whom he was well and favorably known. His little office on the ground floor in No. 64 now boasted a 'change "floor-man," a cashier, a bookkeeper, and several clerks. His brothers were coming in with him shortly as associates. He brought home with him, socially—not to talk business, for he disliked that idea rather thoroughly—bankers, investors, customers, and prospective customers. He could not avoid a certain amount of discussion at first; but he preferred to entertain merely and be a good fellow. Out on the Schuylkill, the Wissahickon, and elsewhere, were popular dining-places where one could drive on Sunday. He and Mrs. Cowperwood frequently drove out to Mrs. Seneca Davis's; to Judge Kitchen's; to the home of Andrew Sharpless, a lawyer whom he knew; to the home of Harper Steger, his own lawyer, and others. Cowperwood had the art of being genial. None of these men or women suspected the depth of his nature—he was thinking, thinking, thinking; but enjoyed life as he went.

One of his earliest and steadily growing traits was his penchant for pictures. Art from the very first fascinated him. He admired nature; but, somehow, without knowing why, he fancied one must see it best through some personality or interpreter, just as we gain our ideas of law and politics through individuals. Mrs. Cowperwood cared not a whit one way or the other; but she accompanied him, thinking all the while that Frank was a little peculiar, as he had always been. He tried, because he loved her, to interest her in these things intelligently; but while she pretended slightly, she could not really see or care, and it was very plain that she could not.

The children, after they came, took up a great deal of her time; and she settled into a quiet home life, which she wanted to make ideally conservative and respectable for his sake. She was not as strong as she had been before these sieges of childbirth, and it made some difference in her looks. However, Cowperwood was not troubled about this at this time. It struck him as delightful and exceedingly worth while that she should be so devoted. A little later it was not quite so remarkable or notable, for he was used to her attitude by now; and the children, after the first three or four years, bored him a little. He was used also to her manner, her vague smile, her sometimes seeming indifference which sprang largely from a sense of absolute security. She took her second marriage quite as she had taken her first—a solemn fact which contained no possibility of mental alteration or change. He was bustling about in a world which, financially at least, seemed all alteration—there were so many sudden and almost unheard-of changes. He began to look at her at times with a speculative eye—not very critically, for he liked her—but with a solid attempt to weigh up her personality. He had known her five years and more now. What did he know about her? The vigor of desire in youth—these first years—had made up for so many things; but now that he had her safely—

There were odd things that came in this period—things that would have affected some men's lives radically. For one thing, there was the slow approach, and, finally, the declaration, of war between the North and the South, which had been attended with so much excitement that almost all current minds were notably colored by it. It was terrific. There were many meetings, public and stirring, and riots; the arrival of John Brown's body; the arrival of Lincoln, the great commoner, on his way from Springfield, Illinois, to Washington *via* Philadelphia, to take the oath of office; the battle of Bull Run; the battle of Vicksburg; the battle of Gettysburg, and so on. Cowperwood saw Lincoln. One day the great war President spoke at Independence Hall before his inauguration—a tall, shambling man, bony, gawky, but tremendously impressive. He (Cowperwood) was only twenty-five at the time, a cool, determined youth, who thought the slave agitation might be well founded in human rights—no doubt was—but exceedingly dangerous to trade. He hoped they would win; but it might go hard with him personally and other financiers. He did not care to fight. That seemed silly for the individual man to do. Others might go—there were many poor, thin-minded, half-baked creatures who would put themselves up to be shot; but they were only fit to be commanded or shot down. As for him, his life was sacred to himself and his family and his personal interests. He recalled seeing, one day, in one of the quiet side streets, as the working-men were coming home from their work, a small enlisting squad of soldiers in blue marching enthusiastically along, the Union flag flying, the drummers drumming, the fifes blowing, the idea being, of course, to so impress the hitherto indifferent or wavering citizen, to exalt him to such a pitch, that he would lose his sense of proportion, or self-interest, and, forgetting all—wife, parents, home, and children—and seeing the great need of the country, fall in behind and enlist. He saw one working-man swinging his pail, and evidently not contemplating any such dénouement to his day's work, pause, listen as the squad approached, hesitate as it drew close, and as it passed, with a peculiar look of uncertainty or wonder in his eyes, fall in behind and march solemnly away to the enlisting quarters. What was it that had caught this man? Frank asked himself.

How was he overcome so easily? He had not intended to go. His face was streaked with the grease and dirt of his work—he looked like a foundry man or machinist, say twenty-five years of age. Frank watched the little squad disappear at the end of the street round the corner under the trees. Other people were staring. Windows had opened, residents had come out. There were other men who had fallen in. There were expressions of patriotic devotion here and there.

"The South 'll have enough of this thing before it's through," one quiet-looking citizen, a man with a Michelangelo expression—the full-bearded face and solemn eyes—observed to him—that intensity of spirit that comes only with a great emotion shining in his eyes.

"Yes, I think so," replied Cowperwood, conservatively.

He drew away still pondering. This current war-spirit was strange. The people seemed to him to want to hear nothing but the sound of the drum and fife, to see nothing but troops, of which there were thousands now passing through on their way to the front, carrying cold steel in the shape of guns at their shoulders, to hear of war and the rumors of war. It was a noble sentiment, no doubt, great but unprofitable. It meant self-sacrifice, and he could not see that. If he went he might be shot, and what would his noble emotion amount to then? No doubt, this war was a great thing; but he was not a soldier. He would rather make money, regulate current political, social, and financial affairs. The poor fool who fell in behind the enlisting squad—no, not fool, he would not call him that—the poor overwrought working-man—well, Heaven pity him! Heaven pity all of them! They really did not know what they were doing.

It was a raw, slushy morning of a late February day; Lincoln, the great war President, was just through with his solemn pronunciamento in regard to the bonds that might have been strained but must not be broken. His face, as he issued from the doorway of the famous birthplace of liberty, in spite of the applause and enthusiasm created by his presence, was set in a sad, meditative calm. Cowperwood, passing by on the other side of the street, detained temporarily by the crowd and the curiosity in himself that the occasion prompted, saw the great, tall, shambling figure, and was interested in spite of himself. He looked at him fixedly as he issued from the doorway surrounded by chiefs of staff, local dignitaries, detectives, and the curious, sympathetic faces of the public. As he studied the strangely rough-hewn countenance a sense of great worth and dignity came over him.

"A real man, that," he thought; "a wonderful temperament." He could not explain why the singular appearance of the statesman appealed to him so, but his every gesture came upon him with great force. He watched him enter his carriage, thinking "So that is the rail-splitter, the country lawyer. Well, fate has picked a great man for this crisis."

For days the face of the man haunted him, and then, through all the years of the war until Lincoln's assassination, he had nothing but good to think of this singular figure. It seemed to him unquestionable that fortuitously he had been permitted to look upon one of the world's really great men. War and statesmanship were not for him; but now he knew how important those things were—at times.

CHAPTER XII

IT was while the war was on, and after it was perfectly plain that it was not to be of a few days' duration, that his first great financial opportunity came to him. There was a strong demand for money at this time on the part of the nation, the State, and the city. In July, 1861, Congress had authorized a loan of fifty million dollars, to be secured by twenty-year bonds with interest not to exceed seven per cent., and the State authorized a loan of three millions on much the same security, the first being handled by financiers of Boston, New York, and Philadelphia, the second by Philadelphia financiers alone. Cowperwood had no hand in this. He was not big enough. He read in the papers of gatherings of men whom he knew personally or by reputation, "to consider the best way to aid the nation or the State"; but he was not included. He was as yet a mere financial spectator. And yet his soul yearned to be of them. These great financiers who worked in the street, how he envied their reputations! They walked so defiantly, so freely. The papers spoke of them so respectfully, fawning. He was a mere note and stock broker; but he knew how these tricks were turned. Money was the first thing to have—a lot of it. Then the reputation of handling it wisely would treble, quadruple, aye, increase its significance a hundred and a thousand fold. First you secured the money. Then you secured the reputation. The two things were like two legs on which you walked. Then your mere word was as good as money, or better. It would unlock the doors to endless treasures. He noticed how often a rich man's word sufficed—no money, no

certificates, no collateral, no anything—just his word.
If Drexel & Co., or Jay Cooke & Co., or Gould &
Fiske were rumored to be behind anything, how secure it
was! The thought in these cases was as good as the deed.
Jay Cooke, a young man in Philadelphia, had made a
great strike taking this State loan in company with
Drexel & Co., and selling it at par. The general opinion
was that it ought to be and could only be sold at ninety.
Cooke did not believe this. He believed that State pride
and State patriotism would warrant offering the loan
to small banks and private citizens, and that they would
subscribe it fully and more. Cowperwood, reading of the
situation in the financial column of the papers, had
fancied that Cooke was right; but he was not sure.
Events justified Cooke magnificently, and his public reputation was assured. Cowperwood wished he could make
some such strike; but he was too practical to worry over
anything save the facts and conditions that were before him.

His chance came about six months later, when it was
found that the State would have to have much more
money. The State's quota of troops would have to be
equipped and paid. There were measures of defense to
be taken, the treasury to be replenished. A call for a
loan of twenty-three million dollars was finally authorized by the legislature and issued. There was great talk
in the street as to who was to get it, handle it—Drexel &
Co. and Jay Cooke & Co., of course.

Cowperwood pondered over this. He had thought
much over this matter of disposing of loans. It was not
so much of a trick. His note-brokerage business was
quite the same thing in a smaller way. A firm or small
corporation (sound, of course) needed money. It issued
its promise to pay in the shape of notes bearing six per
cent. interest, and he sold or placed them with other
people for cash and pocketed his commission. There was
no difference between this and the larger transaction. If

he could handle a fraction of this great loan now—he could not possibly handle the whole of it, for he had not the necessary connections—he could add considerably to his reputation as a broker while making a tidy sum. How much could he handle? That was the question. Who would take portions of it? His father's bank? Probably. Waterman & Co.? A little. Judge Kitchen? A small fraction. The Mills-David Company? Yes. He thought of different individuals and concerns who, for one reason and another—personal friendship, good-nature, gratitude for past favors, and so on—would take a percentage of the seven-per-cent. bonds through him. He totaled up his possibilities, and discovered that in all likelihood, with a little preliminary missionary work, he could dispose of one million dollars if personal influence, through local political figures, could bring this much of the loan his way. He had learned, as Tighe had learned, that personal connections were almost the be-all and the end-all in finance. Some time since he had begun to give great attention to this matter, and now he had some significant connections—councilmen, city officers, contractors, who knew of him, and who sometimes came to him with stock-jobbing propositions.

One man in particular had grown strong in his estimation as having some subtle political connection not visible on the surface, and this was Edward Malia Butler, a contractor by business or profession, who drifted across Cowperwood's path in a peculiar way. Butler was a contractor, undertaking the construction of sewers, water-mains, foundations for buildings, street-paving, and the like. In the early days, long before Cowperwood had known him, he had been a slop-contractor or dealer on his own account. That sounds strange, perhaps. The city had no extended street-cleaning service, particularly in its outlying sections and some of the older, poorer regions. A slop-man, a man who could come with a great wagon filled with barrels and haul away the slops from your back door, was absolutely essential. Edward Butler, having a few cows and pigs, and being a poor Irishman, had originally, when he was twenty-five years of age, collected slops, in a tumble-down wagon filled with barrels to hold them, from his neighbors, and had fed the slops to his pigs and cattle, charging at first nothing for the service. Later he discovered that not only the profitable selling of milk and pigs' meat resulted from this, but that some people—the better-to-do, who had the most slops—were willing to pay a small charge. Then a local political character, a councilman living in his vicinity and a friend of his—they were both Catholics—saw a new point in the whole thing. Butler could be made official swill-collector. The council could vote an annual appropriation for this service. Butler could employ many more wagons than he did now —dozens of them, scores. (He had only six, and had gone into the soap business in a small way, because the rendering of some slops, as he had found, yielded soap-fat.) Not only that, but no other slop-collector would be allowed. There were others, but the official contract awarded him would also, officially, end the life of any and every disturbing rival. Councilman Comiskey—Patrick Gavin Comiskey—undertook through a group of associates with whom he worked to bring this about. He and Butler were to go into the slop-contracting business together. A certain amount of the profitable proceeds would have to be set aside to assuage the feelings of those who were not contractors. Funds would have to be loaned at election time to certain individuals and organizations; but no matter. The amount would be small. Mr. Butler saw a light. He and Mr. Comiskey (the latter silently) entered into business relations. Mr. Butler gave up driving a wagon himself. He was no longer seen carrying buckets of slops around the sides of houses from their back doors in his once conspicuous and, in a way, flaunted red shirt. He hired a young man, a smart Irish boy of his neighborhood, Jimmy Sheehan, to be his assistant, superintendent, stableman, bookkeeper, and what not. Since he began to make between four and five thousand a year, where before he made two thousand, he moved into a nice brick house in an outlying section of the south side, and sent his children to school. Mrs. Butler gave up making soap and feeding pigs for housework. And since then times had been exceedingly good with Edward Butler.

He could neither read nor write at first; but now he knew how, of course. He had learned from association with Mr. Comiskey that there were other forms of contracting. The slop-contracting business could not endure; it had to give way to sewers, water-mains, gasmains, street-paving, and the like. Who better than Edward Butler to do it? He knew the councilmen, many of them. He had met them in the back rooms of saloons, on Sundays and Saturdays at political picnics, at election councils and conferences, for as a beneficiary of the city's largess he was expected to contribute not only money, but advice. Curiously he had developed a strange political wisdom. He knew a successful man or a coming man when he saw one. So many of his bookkeepers, superintendents, time-keepers, and so on graduated into councilmen and State legislators. His nominees—suggested to political conferences—were so often known to make good. They were never silly or light-headed, but cautious and conservative; and he could, on occasion, talk to them like a Dutch uncle. If a man went wrong (against the local political wisdom of the hour) or proved ungrateful, it was usually thought that Butler's men had nothing to do with it, and they had not. First he came to have influence in his councilman's ward, then in his legislative district, then in the city councils of his party—Whig, of course—and then he was supposed to have an organization.

Mysterious forces worked for him in council. He was

awarded significant contracts, and he always bid. The slop business was now a thing of the past. His eldest boy, Owen, was a member of the State legislature, and a partner in his business affairs. His second son, Callum, was a clerk in the city water department, and an assistant to his father also. Aileen, his eldest daughter, fifteen years of age, was still in a convent school, St. Agatha's, at Germantown. Norah, his second daughter and youngest child, thirteen years of age, was in attendance at a local private school conducted by a Catholic sisterhood. The Butler family had moved away from South Philadelphia into Girard Avenue, near the twelve hundreds, where a new, expensive, and rather interesting social life was beginning. They were not of it; but Edward Butler, contractor, now sixty years of age, worth, say, five hundred thousand dollars, had many political and financial friends. He was not a "rough-neck" any more. He was a solid, reddish-faced man, slightly tanned, with broad shoulders, a solid chest, gray eyes, gray hair, a typically Irish face made wise and calm and undecipherable by much experience. His big hands and feet showed a day when he did not wear the best English cloth suits and tanned leather; but his presence was not in any way offensive—rather the other way about. Though still possessed of a brogue, he was soft-spoken, winning, and persuasive.

The presence of Edward Malia Butler in Third Street was due to street-cars. Years before, when he was a slop-collector, he had thought of some day becoming a 'bus owner and driver, but other and more brilliant things had intervened. Since then—but comparatively recently at that—he had watched the development of this street-car business and had come to the conclusion, as had Cowperwood and many others, that it was going to be a great thing. The money returns on the stocks or shares he had been induced to buy had been ample evidence of that. He had dealt through one broker and another, having failed, because of his other interests, to get in on the original corporate organizations. He wanted to pick up such stock as he could in one organization and another, for he believed that they all had a future; and most of all, he wanted to get control of a line or two. Both Owen and Callum were evincing considerable executive ability in his private schemes. They were not ne'er-do-wells, but they were too young. His contracting business, he could see, depended very largely on his political tact and wisdom, on making under-the-surface deals; but neither Owen nor Callum was such a politician as he. A street-railway or two, well managed, would give them a fixed position in life. The business was young. They could be respectively president and vice-president or general manager. He could see them safely placed before he died. He did not want any shrewd broker in his affairs, running from one concern to another making deals and altering plans at his expense. He wanted to find some reliable young man, honest and capable, who would work under his direction and do what he said. By dint of visiting and asking in a roundabout way he learned of Cowperwood, and one day sent for him and asked him to call at his house. Cowperwood responded quickly, for he knew of Butler, his rise, his connections, his force. He welcomed this idea of working for him, however it might be, for he surmised at once that it might mean political connections. Tighe had them. Many of the big bankers and brokers had them. There were lots of politicians drifting through the street for one purpose and another. He called as Mr. Butler directed, one cold, crisp February morning, at his house. He remembered the appearance of the street afterward — broad, brick-paved as to sidewalks, macadamized as to roadway, powdered over with a light, cold snow and set with young, leafless, scrubby trees and lamp-posts. Mr. Butler's house was not new—he had bought and repaired it—but it was not an unsatisfactory specimen of the architecture of the time. It was fifty feet wide, four stories tall, of graystone, and with four wide, white stone steps leading up to the door. The window arches, framed in white, had U-shaped keystones. He noticed the curtains of lace and a glimpse of red plush through the windows, which gleamed warm against the cold and snow outside. A trim Irish maid came to the door.

"Is Mr. Butler here?"

"I'm not sure, sir. I'll find out. He may have gone out. Who shall I say?"

Mr. Cowperwood had his card ready, and gave it to her.

She invited him in and disappeared. In a little while he was asked to come up-stairs, where he found Mr. Butler in a somewhat commercial-looking front room. It had a desk, an office chair, some leather furnishings, and a book-case, but no completeness or symmetry as either an office or a home room. There were several pictures on the wall—an impossible oil-painting for one thing, dark and gloomy; a canal and barge scene in pink and nile green for another; some daguerreotypes of relatives and friends which were not half had. Cowperwood noticed one of two girls, one with reddish-gold hair, another with what appeared to be silky brown. The beautiful silver effect of the daguerreotype had been tinted. They were pretty girls, healthy, smiling, Celtic, their young heads close together, their eyes looking straight out at you. He admired them casually, and fancied they must be Butler's daughters.

"Mr. Cowperwood?" spoke Mr. Butler, turning his round, solid face on him and uttering the name fully with a peculiar accent on the vowels (he was a slow-moving man, solemn and deliberate). Cowperwood noticed that his body was hale and strong like seasoned hickory, tanned by wind and rain. The flesh of his cheeks was pulled taut, and there was nothing either soft or flabby about him.

"I'm that man."

"I have a little matter of stocks to talk over with you" (the "matter" almost sounded like "mather"), "and I thought you'd better come here rather than that I should come down to your office. We can be more private-like, and, besides, I'm not as young as I used to be."

He allowed a semi-twinkle to rest in his eye as he looked his visitor over.

Cowperwood smiled.

"Well, I hope I can be of service to you," he said, genially.

"I happen to be interested just at present in pickin' up certain street-railway stocks on 'change. I'll tell you about them later. Won't you have somethin' to drink? It's a cold morning."

"No, thanks; I never drink."

"Never? That's a hard word when it comes to whisky. Well, no matter. It's a good rule. My boys don't touch anything, and I'm glad of it. As I say, I'm interested in pickin' up a few stocks on 'change; but, to tell you the truth, I'm more interested in findin' some clever young felly like yourself through whom I can work. One thing leads to another, you know, in this world." And he looked at his visitor non-committally, and yet with a genial show of interest.

"Quite so," replied Cowperwood, with a friendly gleam, in return.

"Well," Butler meditated, half to himself, half to Cowperwood, whose presence for the moment he ignored, "there are a number of things that a bright young man could do for me in the street if he were so minded. I have two bright boys of my own, but I don't want them to become stock-gamblers, and I don't know that they would or could if I wanted them to. But this isn't a matter of stock-gambling. I'm pretty busy as it is, and, as I said awhile ago, I'm getting along. I'm not as light on my toes as I once was. But if I had the right sort of

THE FINANCIER

a young man—I've been looking into your record, by the way, never fear—he might handle a number of little things—investments and loans—which might bring us each a little somethin'. Sometimes the young men around town ask advice of me in one way and another— they have a little somethin' to invest, and so—"

He paused and looked tantalizingly out of the window, knowing full well Cowperwood was greatly interested, and that this talk of political influence and connections could only whet his appetite. Butler wanted him to see clearly that fidelity was the point in this case—fidelity, tact, subtlety, and concealment. A young man with real tact and fidelity would be well rewarded. Another without it would not get so much as a moment's consideration.

"Well, if you have been looking into my record," observed Cowperwood, with his own elusive smile, leaving the thought suspended.

Mr. Butler felt the force of the temperament and the argument. He liked the young man's poise and balance. A number of people had spoken of Cowperwood to him. It was now Cowperwood & Co. The company was fiction purely. He asked him something about the street; how the market was running; what he knew about street-railways. Finally he outlined his plan of buying all he could of the stock of the two given lines—the Ninth and Tenth and the Fifteenth and Sixteenth — without attracting any attention, if possible. It was to be done slowly, part on 'change, part from individual holders. He did not tell him that there was certain legislative pressure he hoped to bring to bear to give him franchises for extensions in the regions beyond where the lines now ended, in order that when the time came for them to extend their facilities they would have to see him or his sons, who might be large minority stockholders in these very concerns. It was a far-sighted plan, and meant that the lines would eventually drop in his or his sons' basket.

"I'll be delighted to work with you, Mr. Butler, in any way that you may suggest," observed Cowperwood. "I can't say that I have so much of a business as yet—merely prospects. My connections are good. I have had experience on 'change. I am now a member of the New York and Philadelphia exchanges. Those who have dealt with me seem to like the results I get. You can take any set of men among those who know me you choose and look me up. I'd rather you would."

"I know a little something about you already," reiterated Butler, wisely.

"Very well, then; whenever you have a commission you can call at my office or write, or I will call here. I will give you my secret operating code, so that anything you say will be strictly confidential."

"Well, we'll not say anything more now. In a few days I'll have somethin' for you. When I do, you can draw on my bank for what you need, up to a certain amount."

He got up and looked out into the street, and Cowperwood also arose.

"It's a fine day now, isn't it?"

"It surely is."

"Well, we'll know each other better."

He held out his hand.

"I hope so."

Cowperwood went out, and Butler accompanied him to the door. As he did so a young girl bounded in from the street, red-cheeked, blue-eyed, wearing a scarlet cape with the peaked hood thrown over her red-gold hair.

"Oh, daddy, I almost knocked you down."

She gave her father, and incidentally Cowperwood, a gleaming, radiant, inclusive smile. Her teeth were bright and small, and her lips bud-red.

"You're home early. I thought you were going to stay all day?"

"I was, but I changed my mind."

She passed on in swinging her arms.

"Yes, well—" Butler continued, when she had gone. "Then how will later do? We'll leave it for a day or two. Good day."

"Good day."

Cowperwood, warm with this enhancing of his financial prospects, went down the steps; but incidentally he spared a passing thought for the gay spirit of youth that had manifested itself in this red-cheeked maiden. What a bright, healthy, bounding girl! Her voice had the subtle, vigorous ring of fifteen or sixteen. She was all vitality. Some young fellow would make a fine catch of her some day, and her father would make him rich, no doubt, or help to.

CHAPTER XIII

IT was to Edward Malia Butler that Cowperwood's thoughts turned now, some nineteen months later, when he was thinking of the influence that might bring him an award of a portion of the State issue of bonds. Butler would probably be interested to take some of those himself, or could help him place some. He had come to like Cowperwood very much, and to trust him, which was better yet. Butler was now being carried on Cowperwood's books as a prospective purchaser of large blocks of three different stocks, and Cowperwood had only to send a certificate of purchase to Butler's personal bank in order to get the money for what he had agreed to buy. The stocks would then be delivered at leisure. In addition, there were a number of city officials who were now beginning to come to him, advised or lured by some subtle suggestion dropped by Butler. Cowperwood had been visited by the county sheriff, who had a little money to invest on margin, and who knew, per advice of others, what stock he was to buy. There came, also, the assessor of taxes, Orville Clark, large sums of whose collections were deposited in various city banks without interest, and who was using some money—possibly his own, but not probably—to carry certain stocks for a rise. In due time arrived Councilmen Dale and Semperich, fine specimens of the genus councilman, eager to make a little money in stocks, and not very scrupulous as to how they made it. Councilman Thomas Dale was lean, slit-eyed, forked as to mustache, a little suspicious of every-body, black-haired, narrow-minded, and single-minded. He had but one idea, and that was to get up in the world *via* money. Jacob Semperich was a stout, rosy German, a butcher originally, not very clever in anything, but let in on certain deals because of his councilmanic vote and his rubber-stamp-like subserviency. They came with tips of their own, recommended by Sheriff Pohlmann and Assessor Clark. Cowperwood was a little chary of some phases of his new clientele; but, seeing to what circle they belonged, it was not possible to ignore them. He had to be nice. He refrained from giving any save the safest advice to this small fry; but if they had tips and wished him to carry out instructions, he could not do less than act faithfully in the matter. Brother Joseph was now his floor-man at sixty dollars a week. Brother Edward was his inside office-man and alter-ego. Both were as faithful as it was possible for men to be. Their admiration for Brother Frank was unbounded. It was rather an unusual combination; but Cowperwood was an unusual man, and he felt that he could trust his brothers. He was sympathetic toward them without being in any way partial or unfair to others. He had always dominated them as boys; and now, as a man, he put them into the traces of his vehicle of success, without much thought that they were ever to be anything more than assistants. All these years he had felt that they were not going to be as strong as he was, and he felt sorry for them. At the same time he felt that this was as good a way as any for them to get their preliminary training. His father, who, by the way, was now vice-president of his bank, might find something better for them later on.

This "political gang," as Brother Joe described them to Brother Ed, looked suspicious to both; but Frank was a strong man, and master of his affairs. He kept a most tactful attitude, a cross between keen interest and severe impartiality, which at once won and kept in their place this uncertain and hungry crew. Such men as Assessor Clark, Sheriff Pohlmann, State Senator Donovan, and others, to say nothing of Contractor Butler, he was only

too anxious to keep. They represented to him something
—he could scarcely say what—vast possibilities, principally. Something seemed to tell him that these men
might be tremendously useful to him at some time; and,
while not infringing in any way on his fixed principles of
business, he went as far as he could in being gracious
socially and commercially. The others, though, he ignored,
using them only as business opportunities in a small way
—pretending an interest he did not feel.

It was to Contractor Butler that he turned now; and in
this hour of desire and hope the latter did not fail him.

"So you wanted a portion of those State bonds to sell,
is that it?" the latter asked, genially, when Cowperwood,
in response to permission requested, called to see him concerning this matter. It was in the evening. Spring was
coming on, but it was early and cool. A grate-fire was
burning in Mr. Butler's improvised private office, and he
was ensconced in a large, comfortable leather chair.
"Well now, that isn't so easy. You ought to know more
about that than I do. I'm not a financier, as you well
know." And he grinned apologetically.

Cowperwood smiled.

"It's a matter of influence. I don't know the political
ropes well enough to know how this is managed. It's
largely a matter of favoritism, that I know. Drexel and
Company and Cooke and Company have connections at
Harrisburg. They have men of their own looking after
their interests. The attorney-general and the State
treasurer are hand in glove with them. Even if I put in
a bid, and can demonstrate that I can handle the loan,
it won't help me to get it. Other people have done that.
I have to have friends—influence. You know how it is."

"Them things," Butler said, solemnly, "is easy enough
if you know the right parties to approach. Now there's
Jimmy Oliver, he ought to know something about that."
Jimmy Oliver was the whilom district attorney serving
at this time, and incidentally free adviser to Mr. Butler

in many ways. He was also, accidentally, a warm personal friend of the State treasurer.

"How much of the loan do you want?"

"Five million."

"Five million!" Mr. Butler sat up. "Man, what are you talking about? Five million! That's a good deal of money. Where are you going to sell all that?"

"I want to bid for five million," assuaged Cowperwood, softly. "I only want one million; but I want the prestige of putting in a bona-fide bid for five million. It will do me good on the street."

Mr. Butler sank back somewhat relieved.

"Five million! Prestige! You want one million. Well, now that's different. That's not such a bad idea. We ought to be able to get that."

He rubbed his chin some more and stared into the fire. Cowperwood liked his comforting, helpful "we."

Cowperwood liked this great, solid Irishman. He liked his history. He was just democratic enough and practical-minded enough to like to see such men get along. He had met Mrs. Butler, a rather fat and phlegmatic Irish woman, who cared nothing at all for show, and still liked to go into the kitchen and superintend the cooking, but who was not without a world of hard sense. She had told her husband that Cowperwood was a shrewd, forceful young man. He had met Owen and Callum Butler, the boys, and Aileen and Norah, the girls. Aileen was the one who bounded up the steps the first day he had called on Mr. Butler several seasons before. He recalled her red cape and rosy cheeks. Since then he had seen more of her—a remarkable girl temperamentally, who could play showily and, in a way, brilliantly on the piano, and sing charmingly. She was seventeen now, just verging into long dresses, with a figure which was subtly provocative. Her manner was boyish, hoidenish at times; but there was a softness lurking somewhere back in the blue eyes that was not hoidenish entirely, but sympathetic and human. She was terribly young, though, and, although convent-trained, which usually veneers so nicely, inclined to refuse all thought of restraint. Her brothers quarreled with her, and her father and mother gave her sage advice. She was subtle, though, in the bargain, thinking her own thoughts and wondering hourly what she should do with herself.

Norah, the youngest, was two years younger than her sister, and promised to be interesting in another way. She was more quiet and reserved; not so daring as her sister. Cowperwood had studied them at odd moments on his visits. He had once met Aileen in Third Street shopping with her mother. She was alone at the time, and he paused to pass the time of the day with her.

"Good morning," he said, smilingly. "It's nice to see you. Isn't this a lovely day?"

It was bright and clear and crisp. The windows of the offices and banks were water-clear in the shade— bright and refreshing. The trucks and vehicles were numerous, crackling and brisk.

"It's fine," she replied, with a toss of her head. "I'm just down with mother looking for some birthday presents."

She reminded him of a high-stepping horse without a check-rein.

"Your birthday?" he inquired, archly, with a show of complimentary interest.

"No, a cousin of mine. We have so many relatives."

Her voice had that affected, bored tone which young girls love to assume when they think they are making an impression—the "Oh, dear! Oh, dear! life is so tiresome, don't you know" tone, when as a matter of fact every moment and every incident is of thrilling interest to them.

Cowperwood understood her exactly. He had before now taken her mental measure as he had that of every

man and every woman he had ever encountered. A girl
with a high sense of life in her, romantic, full of the thought
of love—the possibilities of joy. As he looked at her
quickly now—her very shapely young body, robust and
powerful, clothed in a full skirt of large, bright, black-
and-white check below a smooth-fitting pelisse of green
velvet, her little feet smoothly incased in jaunty Balmoral
boots of patent leather, her hands pulled tight in bright
lemon-colored gloves and tucked into a tiny ermine muff
just large enough to hold them—he had the sense of seeing
the best that Nature can do when she attempts to produce
physical perfection. Her throat was circled with a stiff
linen collar, her pocket decorated with a small gold watch,
and her red-gold hair surmounted by a "jockey hat"
with a rolling brim and a long, metallic-green rooster
feather. This girl was alive, he thought, fiery. Already she was nearing the danger age. Old Butler and
his wife had better look out for her and marry her off.
He recalled hearing a shrewd comment by Councilman
Dale, talking to several politicians about some other girl
in his office one afternoon, which seemed to apply in this
case. It came back to Cowperwood now. "When a
high-stepping girl that ought to be wearing a check-rein
and a Mexican bit gets so she thinks she can drink booze
with the fellow that is keeping her company, she needs
her mother, a spanking, and a life-preserver. The first
glass of wine for that kind of a girl, whether she's up in
G or only a working-man's daughter, is right at the top
of a toboggan-chute that has hell at the bottom."

Councilman Dale was a coarse man, shanty-bred,
socially impossible, and his phraseology was vile in a
way; but it struck Cowperwood as being intensely true,
nevertheless, and Aileen was just this kind of a girl. Her
father had hauled slops. He was rich now, and she was
convent-trained; but—

"Well, I suppose when your birthday comes around
some one else does the shopping, eh?"

"Oh, they don't think very much of me. They don't buy me very much of anything."

Her lips parted in an arch, superior, indifferent smile. She was fishing for a compliment, and Cowperwood indulged her.

"Fie! I know your room looks like a flower-garden, then. When is your birthday?"

"I'm a winter baby. I was born in December on the shortest day—the twenty-first. Isn't that too bad?"

"Why, no; I think that rather nice. It's distinctive. You aren't as dark and gloomy as that day usually is. You probably came to brighten it."

Her eyes snapped. This man in front of her had the nimbleness of mind, the subtlety of gaze, the force, looks, fascination that she thought a real man ought to have. He was strong. And she heard her father and her mother say he was able. And her father knew. She had come to think that her father was one of the most wonderful men in the world—so many compliments were paid her for being his daughter.

"Now you're teasing me. I must be going. Good morning."

She held out her smooth little hand, so tightly gloved in yellow leather.

"Give my regards to your father and mother," he said.

He looked after her as she walked away—just a glance. She was striding briskly, with a force, an incisiveness, a vigor which fascinated him in spite of himself. She carried her head so high, with so much hauteur.

"Vain little piece," he said; and yet he thought how really charming she was—delightful.

Well, he had his own wife and children now. Lillian was a different type of woman. She wouldn't know how to take Aileen Butler if she knew her—she hadn't met her as yet, and if she did she wouldn't approve of her. Lillian was too conservative and hourly becoming more so. She wasn't as good-looking as she had formerly been. Her face was thinner, less artistic. He wondered, in his direct way, whether he should always be faithful to her. So far he had been. But these young women like Aileen! Every now and then he saw one who took his fancy, and they were always gracious to him. He was good-looking, and he had a full intellectuality, which they could not well resist. More than once in dancing at different places a girl had squeezed his hand or said sweet, complimentary things to him, but he had waved the matter aside. His business interests, his two children, his affection for his wife, deterred him. But this Aileen—well, she was Butler's daughter, and some lucky young dog would marry her pretty soon and carry her away. But whoever secured her would have to hold her by affection and subtle flattery and attention if he held her at all.

CHAPTER XIV

THE days passed, and the influence of Mr. Butler proved sufficient to get Mr. Cowperwood the award he desired, for after considerable private conversation between one person and another here and there he was introduced to City Treasurer Julian Bode, who promised to introduce him to State Treasurer Van Nostrand (Frederick), and to see that Mr. Cowperwood's claims to consideration were put right before the people. "Of course, you know," he said to Cowperwood, in the presence of Butler, for it was at the latter's home that the conference took place, "this banking crowd is very powerful. You know who they are. They don't want any interference in this bond-issue business. I was talking to Terrence Relihan, who represents them up there"—meaning Harrisburg, the State capital—"and he says they won't stand for it at all. You may have trouble right here in Philadelphia after you get it—they're pretty powerful, you know. Are you sure just where you can place it?"

"Yes, I'm sure," replied Cowperwood.

"Well, the best thing in my judgment is not to say anything at all. Just put in your bid. Van Nostrand, with the governor's approval, will make the award. We can fix the governor, I think. After you get it they may talk to you personally; but that's your business."

Cowperwood smiled his inscrutable smile. There were so many ins and outs to this financial life. It was an endless network of underground holes, along which all sorts of influences were moving. A little wit, a little nimbleness, a little luck—time and opportunity—these sometimes availed. Here he was, through his ambition to get on, and nothing else, coming into contact with the State treasurer and the governor. They were going to consider his case personally, because he demanded that it be considered—nothing more. Others more influential than himself had quite as much right to a share, but they didn't take it. Nerve, ideas, aggressiveness, how these counted when one had luck! He went away thinking how surprised Drexel & Co. and Cooke & Co. would be to see him appearing in the field as a competitor, and he was not a distinguished financier as yet at all. He went home to his wife and children—for the conference had been held in the evening, and in a little office on the second floor next his bedroom, which he had fixed up as a really-truly office with a desk, a safe, and a leather chair, he consulted his resources. There were so many things to think of. He went over again the list of people whom he had seen and whom he could count on to subscribe, and in so far as that was concerned—the award of one million dollars—he was safe. He figured to make two per cent. on the total transaction, or twenty thousand dollars. If he did he was going to buy a house out on Girard Avenue beyond the Butlers', or, better yet, buy a piece of ground and erect one. His father was prospering nicely. He might want to build a house next to him, and they could live side by side. His own business, aside from this deal, would yield him ten thousand dollars this year. His street-car investments, aggregating fifty thousand, were paying six per cent. His wife's property, represented by this house, some government bonds, and some real estate in West Philadelphia, was worth forty thousand more. Between them they were rich; but he expected to be much richer. All he needed now was to keep cool. If he succeeded in this bond-issue matter, he could do it again and on a larger scale. There would be more issues. He turned out his light after a while and went into his wife's boudoir, where she was sleeping. The nurse and the children were in a room beyond.

"Well, Lillian," he observed, when she woke up and turned over toward him, hearing the noise, "I think I have that bond matter that I was telling you about arranged at last. I think I'll get a million of it, anyhow. That 'll mean twenty thousand. If I do we'll build out on Girard Avenue. That's going to be the street. The college is making that neighborhood."

"That 'll be nice, won't it, Frank?" she observed, and rubbed his arm as he sat on the side of the bed.

Her remark was vaguely speculative.

"We'll have to show the Butlers some attention. He's been very nice to me. He asked me to bring you over some time. We must go. Be nice to his wife. He can do a lot for me if he wants to. He has two daughters, too. We'll have to have them over here."

"I'll have them to dinner right afterward," she agreed, "and I'll stop and take Mrs. Butler driving if she'll go, or she can take me."

She had already learned that the Butlers were rather showy—the younger generation, that they were sensitive as to their lineage, and that money (what they could do financially) was supposed to make up for everything else. "Butler himself is a very conservative man," Cowperwood had once remarked to her; "but Mrs. Butler—well, she's all right, but she's a little commonplace. She's a fine woman, though, I think, good-natured and good-hearted." He cautioned her not to overlook Aileen and Norah, because the Butlers, mother and father, were very proud of them. "We'll have to have them over here now and again."

At this time the Cowperwoods had not moved from North Front Street, and because of the superior size of Butler's house and the newer character of their street, to say nothing of Mr. Butler's wealth, the girls, as well as their mother, conceived themselves to be much superior to the Cowperwoods. Mrs. Cowperwood was nearing that time of life when women become exceedingly sensitive as to the outward and material character of their surroundings. She was no longer young. Cowperwood was twenty-seven, and she was thirty-two. The birth and care of two children had made even more difference in her looks than he had noted at first. She was no longer as softly pleasing, for all of her height, but more angular. Her face was artistically hollow-cheeked, like so many of Rossetti's and Burne-Jones's women. Her health was really not quite so good; she was a little run down nervously, and she suffered from fits of depression. Cowperwood had noticed this. It made some difference in her attractiveness and her charm. He tried to be gentle and considerate; but he was too much of a utilitarian and practical-minded observer not to realize that he was likely to have a sickly wife on his hands later, who would not be so pleasing to him. Sympathy and affection were great things; but desire and charm must endure, or one was compelled to be sadly conscious of their loss. So often now he saw young girls, six, seven, eight, and even nine years younger than himself, who were quite in his mood, and who were exceedingly robust and joyous. It was fine, advisable, practical, to adhere to the virtues as laid down in the modern lexicon of happiness; but if you had a sickly wife— Besides, Lillian was narrow. Her greatest charm had been her artistic appearance. Life to her meant meeting conventionally with conventional people, talking over future clothes, trips, homes, marriages, deaths, etc., all within a strict pale of thought. Outside of this was sounding a brilliant world which had nothing, or little or nothing, to do with these things. It was a dangerous world, anything but monogamous. And anyhow, was a man entitled to only one wife? Must he never look at any other woman? Supposing he found some one? He pondered those things between hours of labor, and he concluded that it did not make so much difference. If a man could, and not be exposed, it was all right. He had to be careful, though. To-night, as he

sat on the side of his wife's bed, he was thinking somewhat of this, for he had seen Aileen again, playing and
singing at her piano as he passed the parlor door. She
was like a bright luminary radiating health and enthusiasm—a reminder of youth in general.

"It's a strange world," he thought; but his thoughts
were his own, and he didn't propose to tell any one about
them.

The bond issue, when it came, was a curious compromise; for, although it netted him his twenty thousand
dollars and more and served to introduce him to the
financial notice of Philadelphia and the State of Pennsylvania, it did not permit him to manipulate the subscriptions as he had planned. The State treasurer was seen
by him at the office of a local lawyer of great repute,
where he worked when in the city. He was gracious to
Cowperwood, because, seeing that Butler and others were
behind him, he had to be. He fancied that Butler or
some one else might be planning to make something out
of it. He explained to him just how things were regu-
lated at Harrisburg. The big financiers were looked to
for campaign funds. They were represented by henchmen in the State assembly and senate. The governor
and the treasurer were foot-free; but there were other
influences — prestige, friendship, social power, political
ambition, etc. The big men might constitute a close
corporation, which in itself was unfair; but, after all,
they were the legitimate sponsors for big money loans
of this kind. The State had to keep on good terms with
them, especially in times like these. Seeing that Mr.
Cowperwood was so well able to dispose of the million
he expected to get, it would be perfectly all right to award
it to him; but Van Nostrand had a counter-proposition
to make. Would Cowperwood, in case the financial
crowd now handling the matter so desired, turn over his
award to them for a consideration—a sum equal to what
he expected to make—in case the award was made to him?

Certain financiers desired this. It was dangerous to him to oppose them. They were perfectly willing he should put in a bid for five million and get the prestige of that; to have him awarded one million and get the prestige of that was well enough also; but, nevertheless, they desired to handle the twenty-three million dollars in an unbroken lot. It looked better. He need not be advertised as having withdrawn. They would be content to have him achieve the glory of having done what he started out to do. But the example was so bad. Others might imitate him. If it were known in the street privately that he had been coerced, for a consideration, into giving up, others would be deterred from imitating him in the future. Besides, if he refused, they could cause him trouble. His loans might be called. Various banks might not be so friendly in the future. His constituents might be warned against him in one way or another.

The State treasurer was perfectly friendly. He wanted Cowperwood to succeed. Now that he saw him he liked him. He might do a little business with him in the future. The State treasurer often had money to put out on deposit. Still, this was a ticklish business.

Cowperwood saw the point. He acquiesced. It was something with just the plain decision to "get in on this," to have brought so many high and mighties to their knees. So they knew of him now! They were quite well aware of him! Well and good. He would take the award and twenty thousand or thereabouts and withdraw. The State treasurer was delighted. It solved a ticklish proposition for him.

"I'm glad to have seen you," he said. "I'm glad we've met. I'll drop in and talk with you some time when I'm down this way. We'll have lunch together."

The State treasurer, for some odd reason, felt that Mr. Cowperwood was a man who could make him some money. His eye was so keen; his expression was so alert, and yet so subtle. He appeared to be a man who could work wonderfully well in the dark. He thought this whole thing over, and decided that it was a remarkable thing for Cowperwood to have done; and he told the governor and some other of his associates so. Terrence Relihan heard of him.

"You want to go in and see him some time," Van Nostrand told Relihan. "He's a coming man. You can feel it. That young fellow's going to get along."

So the award was finally made; Cowperwood, after some private negotiations in which he met the officers of Drexel & Co. and Cooke & Co., was paid his twenty thousand dollars, and turned his share of the award over to them. His name was mentioned in the papers, and his prestige grew rapidly. He was a man to be reckoned with—a banker, a broker, a man with strong connections.

New faces showed up in his office now from time to time, faces not hitherto seen there, that of Mr. Van Nostrand and of Mr. Relihan. He was introduced to the governor one day at lunch, and he began working on plans with young Ellsworth for his new house. He was going to build something exceptional this time, he told Lillian. They were going to have to do some entertaining—entertaining on a larger scale than ever. North Front Street was becoming too tame. He put the house up for sale, consulted with his father as to the plans, and found that he was willing to move. The old gentleman was prospering mightily. Between his own prosperity and his son's—their joint consultations—they were doing exceedingly well. His son's prosperity had redounded to the credit of the father. The directors of his bank, he told his son, were becoming much more friendly to him. Next year President Kugel was going to retire. Because of Frank's noted coup, as well as his own long service, he was going to be made president. They had already signified as much. Frank was a great borrower from his father's bank. By the same token he was a large depositor. His connection with Edward Butler was significant. He sent his father's bank certain accounts which it otherwise could not have secured. The city treasurer became interested in it, and the State treasurer. Cowperwood, Sr., stood to earn twenty thousand a year as president, and he owed much of it to his son. The two families were now on the best of terms. Anna, now twenty-one, and Edward and Joseph frequently spent the night at Frank's house. Lillian called almost daily at his mother's. There was much interchange of family gossip, and it was thought well to build side by side. So Cowperwood, Sr., bought fifty feet of ground next to his son's thirty-five, and together they commenced the erection of two charming, commodious homes, which were to be connected by a covered passageway, or pergola, which could be inclosed with glass in winter.

The most popular stone, granite, was chosen; but Mr. Ellsworth promised to present it in such a way that it would be especially pleasing. Cowperwood, Sr., decided that he could afford to spend seventy-five thousand dollars—he was now worth two hundred and fifty thousand; and Frank decided that he could risk fifty, seeing that he could raise money on a mortgage. The two of them agreed that, considering their prospects, it was advisable. Other men of less financial significance were better located than they. Frank decided that he would at the same time remove his office farther south on Third Street and occupy a building of his own. He knew where an option was to be had on a twenty-five-foot building, which, though old, could be given a new brownstone front and made very significant. He saw in his mind's eye a handsome building, fitted with an immense plate-glass window; inside his hardwood fixtures visible; and over the door, or to one side of it, set in bronze letters, Cowperwood & Co. His trading accounts on 'change had grown so that they would net him fifteen thousand dollars this coming year, and they were still growing.

THE FINANCIER

Vaguely but surely he began to see looming before him, like a lovely, fleecy cloud on the horizon, his future fortune. He was to be rich, very rich, because he was strong, young, healthy, shrewd, subtle. And he did not dream.

6

CHAPTER XV

DURING all this time that Cowperwood had been building himself up so thoroughly in his financial affairs the great war of the rebellion had been fought almost to its close. It was now October, 1864. The capture of Mobile and the battle of the Wilderness were fresh memories. Grant was now before Petersburg; and the great general of the South was giving that last brilliant and hopeless display of his ability as a strategist and a soldier. During all these years Cowperwood had been compelled by the curiosities, the terrors, and the fortune of the war to give great mental attention to it. There had been times—as, for instance, during the long, dreary period in which the country was waiting for Vicksburg to fall, for the Army of the Potomac to prove victorious, when Pennsylvania was invaded by Lee—when stocks fell and commercial conditions were very bad generally. In times like these Cowperwood's own manipulative ability was taxed to the utmost, and he had to watch every hour to see that his fortunes were not destroyed by some unexpected and destructive piece of intelligence.

The boy's attitude toward the war—for he was still a boy in years if not in judgment — aside from his patriotic feeling that the Union ought to be maintained, was that it was destructive and wasteful. He was not so wanting in national emotion and passion but what he could feel that the Union, as it had now come to be, spreading its great length from the Atlantic to the Pacific, and from the snows of Canada to the Gulf, was worth while. Since his birth, in 1837, he had seen the nation reach that physical perfection—barring Alaska—which it

154

finally retained. Not so much earlier than his youth
Florida had been added to the Union by purchase from
Spain; Mexico, after the unjust war of 1848, had ceded
Texas and the territory to the West. The boundary dis-
putes between England and the United States in the far
Northwest had been finally adjusted. To a man with
great social and financial imagination, these facts could
not help but be significant; and if they did nothing more,
they gave him a sense of the boundless commercial
possibilities which existed potentially in so vast a realm.
He was not of that order of speculative financial enthusiasm which, in the type known as the "promoter,"
sees endless possibilities for gain in every unexplored
rivulet and prairie reach; but the very vastness of the
country suggested possibilities which he hoped might
remain undisturbed. As a territory covering the length
of a whole zone and between two seas, it seemed to him
to possess an individuality which it would not retain if
the States of the South were lost.

Nevertheless, the freedom of the negro was not a significant point with him. He had observed their race from
his boyhood and with considerable interest, and had been
struck with virtues and defects which seemed inherent
and conditioned by their experiences.

He was not at all sure, for instance, that the negroes
could be made into anything much more significant than
they were. At any rate, it was a long uphill struggle
for them, of which many future generations would not
witness the conclusion. He had no particular quarrel
with the theory that they should be free; he saw no
particular reason why the South should not protest
vigorously against the destruction of their property and
their system. It was too bad that the negroes as slaves
should be abused in some instances. He felt sure that
that ought to be adjusted in some way; but beyond that
he could not see that there was a great ethical basis for
the contentions of either side. The vast majority of

men and women, as he could see, were not essentially
above slavery, even when they had all the guarantees of
a constitution formulated to prevent it. There was mental
slavery, the slavery of the weak mind and the weak body.
He followed the contentions of such men as Sumner,
Garrison, Phillips, and Beecher with considerable interest; but at no time could he see that the problem was
a vital one for him. He did not care to be a soldier or an
officer of soldiers; he had no gift of polemics; his mind
was not of the disputatious order—not even in the realm
of finance. He was concerned only to see what was of
vast advantage to him, and to devote all his attention to
that. This fratricidal war in the nation could not help
him. It really delayed, he thought, the true commercial
and financial advancement of the country, and he hoped
that it would soon end. He was not of those who complained bitterly of the excessive war taxes, though he knew
them to be trying to many. Some of the stories of death
and disaster moved him greatly; but, alas, they were
among the unaccountable fortunes of life, and could not
be remedied by him. So he had gone his way day by
day, watching the coming in and the departing of troops,
seeing the bands of dirty, disheveled, gaunt, sickly men
returning from the fields and hospitals; and all he could
do was to feel sorry. This war was not for him. He
had taken no part in it, and he felt sure that he could
only rejoice in its conclusion—not as a patriot, but as a
financier. It was wasteful, pathetic, unfortunate.

The months proceeded apace. A local election intervened
and there was a new city treasurer, a new assessor of taxes,
and a new mayor; but Edward Malia Butler continued
to have apparently the same influence as before. The
Butlers and the Cowperwoods, although the latter had
not moved, had become quite friendly. Mrs. Butler
rather liked Lillian, though they were of different religious
beliefs; and they went driving or shopping together, as
the case might be, the younger woman a little critical and

ashamed of the elder because of her poor grammar, her Irish accent, her plebeian tastes—as though the Wiggins had not been plebeian as any. The old lady was good-natured, however, and good-hearted. She loved to give, since she had plenty, and sent presents here and there to Lillian, the children, and others. "Now youse must come over and take dinner with us"—the Butlers had arrived at the evening-dinner period—or "Youse must come drive with me to-morrow."

"Aileen, God bless her, is such a foine girl," or "Norah, the darlin', is sick the day."

It astonished Mrs. Cowperwood how Mr. Butler could have attained to such wealth and distinction; but Frank told her he was tremendously able and powerful, both he and his boys.

It was well known to her, through Frank, that Mrs. Butler could neither read nor write; but that made no difference. But Aileen, her airs, her aggressive disposition, her love of attention, her vanity, irritated and at times disgusted Mrs. Cowperwood.

"The little snip"—she was not little at all, but on the contrary quite sizable—"she thinks the sun rises and sets in her father's pocket," Lillian observed, one day, to her husband. "To hear her talk you'd think they were descended from Irish kings. Her pretended interest in art and music amuses me."

"But I think she *is* rather artistic," observed Cowperwood, persuasively. He liked Aileen very much as a personality. "She plays very well, and she has a good voice."

"Yes, I know; but she has no real refinement. How could she have? Look at her father and mother. 'Youse must come over now, soon.'" Mrs. Cowperwood was imitating Mrs. Butler. The latter's red face and hands and her use of "youse" were most offensive to her. She admired the manners and appearance of the other significant personages they had met so much more.

"I don't see anything much the matter with her," insisted Cowperwood. "She's bright and good-looking. Of course she's only a girl; but she'll come out of that. She has real sense and force, at that."

Aileen was most friendly to him. In spite of the presence of his wife and children, she liked him individually, separately, apart from them. She used to play the piano brilliantly in his home, and sing for him, and she sang only when he was there. There was something about his steady, even gait, his stocky body and handsome head which attracted her. In spite of her own vanity and egotism she felt a little overawed before him at times—keyed up. When he came where she was she seemed to be exalted in her mood, to grow gayer and more brilliant. All her thoughts, feelings, emotions vibrated rapidly, and yet she did not think of him as anything save a most charming and likable man.

The most futile thing in this world is to attempt exact definitions of character. All individuals are a bundle of contrarieties—none more so than the most capable. In the latter subtlety enters to conceal so that we cannot —always—see. Policy surrounds the great like a mystic veil. We cannot know, because it is not expedient for us to know. Power identifies a man or a woman with great consequences, and the result of exposure is most carefully guarded against by all.

In the case of Aileen Butler it would be quite impossible to give an exact definition. Talent of a raw, crude order was certainly present—a native force which had been somewhat polished, as granite may be, by the feelings, opinions, and conventions of current society, but which still showed through in an elemental and yet attractive way. At this time she was only eighteen years of age, goodly to look at—decidedly so from the point of view of a man of Frank Cowperwood's temperament—but beneath his social opportunities, as Mrs. Semple had been. Already

it has been indicated that he was physically urgent. It
has also been shown that he was artistically minded.
Aileen Butler supplied something which he had not previously known or consciously craved. No other woman
or girl whom he had known had ever possessed so much
innate force as this one possessed, none so much vitality
and vivacity. Her red-gold hair—it was not so much
red as decidedly golden, with a suggestion of red in it—
was rich and plentiful. It looped itself in heavy folds
about her forehead, and sagged at the base of her neck.
She had a beautiful nose, not sensitive, but straight-cut
with small nostril openings, and eyes that were big, and
while forceful, were still sensuous. They were such a nice
shade of blue—gray-blue. Her clothes, for some strange
reason, seemed to suggest undue luxury. They hinted at
the bangles, anklets, ear-rings, and breast-plates of the oda-
lisque, and yet, of course, these were not there. She confessed to him years afterward that she would love to
have stained her nails and painted the center of the palms
of her hands with madder-red. Yet she was as vigorous,
as healthy, and as normal seeming as any girl could be.
She was intensely interested in life, men, what they would
think of her, and how she compared with other women.
The fact that she could ride in a carriage, live in a fine
home in Girard Avenue, visit such homes as those of the
Cowperwoods and others, was of great weight; and yet,
even at this age, she realized that life was more than
these things. Many did not have them and lived. But
these facts of wealth and advantage gripped her; and
when she sat at the piano and played or rode in her carriage or walked or stood before her mirror, she was conscious of her figure, her charms, what they meant to men,
how women envied her. Sometimes she looked at poor,
hollow-chested or homely-faced girls and felt sorry for
them; at other times she flared into inexplicable opposition to some handsome girl or woman who dared to
brazen her socially or physically. There were such girls

of the better families, who, in Chestnut Street, in the expensive shops, or on the drive, on horseback or in carriages, tossed their heads and indicated as well as human motions can that they were better bred and knew it. She flared instantly with a terrible hate. Her blood boiled and chilled. "I would have you know," her mind declared, vehemently, to herself, thinking of her charms, and she would sit bolt upright on her horse or in her father's brougham, looking as queenly as the best. She knew well enough that it was against her and her sister and her brothers that her father was once a ——; but to that she never referred, even mentally, to herself. She hated the thought, and she wanted ever so much to get up in the world; and yet namby-pamby men of better social station than herself did not attract her at all. She wanted a man. Now and then there was one "something like," but not entirely, who appealed to her; but most of them were politicians or legislators—socially nothing at all, and so they wearied or disappointed her. Her father did not know the truly élite. But Mr. Cowperwood—he seemed so refined, so exquisite, so forceful, and so reserved. She often looked at Mrs. Cowperwood and thought how fortunate she was.

The development of Mr. Frank Algernon Cowperwood's financial significance—his significance as Cowperwood & Co.—finally brought him into relationship with one man who proved of the utmost significance to him, morally, financially, and in other ways, and because he did this he must be dealt with here at length. This was George W. Stener, the new city treasurer-elect, who, to begin with, was a puppet in the hands of other men; but who, also, in spite of this fact, became a personage of considerable significance, for the simple fact that he was weak. Stener had been a real-estate dealer and insurance man in a small way before he was made city treasurer. He was one of those men, of whom there are so many thousands in every large community, who have no breadth of vision, no real subtlety, no craft, no great skill in anything. He was not a bad real-estate dealer. He could follow up small trades with avidity, talk a blacksmith, a mechanic, a grocer, or a moderate professional man into taking out a life-insurance policy—if the latter was so inclined—or into buying a lot; but he had no idea of any of the superior affairs of the world. You would never hear a new idea emanating from Stener. He never had one in his life. Now and then some one would drop a real thought which seemed quite wonderful to him, or he would hear of something which he could make use of in his business. He was not a bad fellow. He had a stodgy, dusty, commonplace look to him which was more a matter of his mind than his body. His eye was of vague gray-blue; his hair a dusty light-brown and thin. His mouth—there was nothing impressive there. He was quite tall, nearly six feet, with moderately broad shoulders; but his figure was anything but shapely—not at all satisfactory. He seemed to stoop a little, his stomach was the least bit protuberant, and he talked commonplaces—the small change of newspaper and social (street and business) gossip. People liked him in his own neighborhood. He was thought to be honest and kindly; and he was, in so far as he knew. His wife and four children were as average and insignificant as the wives and children of such men usually are. A really intelligent, artistically minded individual would have been bored to extinction by George W. Stener; and his family had no social life whatsoever—at least before he was made treasurer. They went to a Methodist church Sundays because it was the largest in their vicinity. They knew their neighbors "next door," and for a few doors away. They went in to see people who were sick or dying, and they lived fairly comfortably on, say, twenty-five hundred a year, putting a little by for a rainy day, at that.

George W. Stener was brought into temporary public notice by the same political methods which have existed in Philadelphia, practically unmodified, for the last half hundred years and more.

He was known first to the local councilman and ward-leader; because he was of the same political faith as the dominant local political party he was used in one or two political campaigns to drum up votes. He was absolutely without value as a speaker, for he had no ideas; but as a vote-chaser—a political bookkeeper—he was excellent. You could send him from door to door, asking the grocer and the blacksmith and the butcher how he felt about things. You could dole him out a few platitudes, and he would repeat them. The Republican party, which was the new-born party then, but dominant in Philadelphia, needed your vote; it was necessary to keep the rascally Democrats out—he could scarcely have said why. They had been for slavery. They were for free trade. It never once occurred to him that these things had nothing to do with the local executive and financial administration of Philadelphia. The reputation and secret political standing of such men as Senator Mark Simpson, Edward Malia Butler, and Henry A. Mollenhauer, who were supposed jointly to control the political destiny of Philadelphia, was a wonderful thing to him, a curiosity. There were all sorts of men prominent politically, and he often wondered how they came to be so. By degrees he learned how politics were worked in his ward, then in the city generally; but, having no personal magnetism, he still could not understand it. Men controlling other men, being looked up to—that was a strange thing.

In no other city save such a one as this, where the inhabitants were of a deadly average in so far as being commonplace was concerned, could such a man have been elected city treasurer. But the people of Philadelphia, the rank and file, did not, except in a few rare instances, make up their political programme, and never had. An inside ring had this matter in charge. Certain positions were allowed to such and such men or to such and such factions of the party for such and such services rendered —but who does not know politics?

One year George W. Stener became *persona grata* to Edward Strobik, a quondam councilman who afterward became ward leader and still later president of council, and who was in private life a stone-dealer and owner of a brickyard. Strobik was a henchman of Henry A. Mollenhauer, ostensibly a coal merchant, the hardest and coldest of all three of the political leaders. The latter had things to get from council, and Strobik was his tool. Strobik had Stener elected in his place; and because he was faithful in voting as he was told Stener was later made an assistant superintendent of the highways department.

Here he came into the eyes of Edward Malia Butler, and was slightly useful to him. He came to have a little influence in his ward—to be, so to speak, in charge of it. Then the central political committee, which was composed of Butler, Mollenhauer, and Simpson, decided that some nice, docile man who would at the same time be absolutely faithful was needed for city treasurer, and so Stener was put on the ticket. He knew little of finance, but was an excellent bookkeeper; and, anyhow, Corporation Counsel Regan was there to advise him at all times. It was a very simple matter. Being put on the ticket was equivalent to being elected, and so, after a few weeks of exceedingly trying platform experiences, in which he stammered through platitudinous declarations that the city needed to be honestly administered, he was inducted into office; and there you were.

Now it wouldn't have made so much difference what George W. Stener's executive and financial qualifications for the position in question were, but the city of Philadelphia was still hobbling along under the financial system, or lack of it, previously outlined—namely, that of allowing the assessor and the treasurer to collect and hold

moneys outside of the city's private vaults without expecting that they invest them for interest for the city's
benefit, or do more than restore the principal intact which
was with them when they entered or left office. It was
not understood or publicly demanded that the moneys so
collected, or drawn from any source, be maintained intact in the vaults of the city treasury. They could be
loaned out, deposited in banks, used to further private
interests, so long as the principal was returned, and no
one was the wiser. Of course, this theory of finance was
not publicly sanctioned. People did not agree that State
and city treasurers and assessors should do this; but it
was politically and journalistically, and, in high finance,
socially known that they could and did do it, and that
was all there was to it. How were you going to stop it?
A certain group of gentlemen, including Messrs. Butler,
Mollenhauer, Simpson, certain bankers, brokers, journa-
lists, and others directly or indirectly profited by this
sort of thing, but said nothing, winked their eyes, let
things go as they were and were happy. They constituted,
as it were, an inside ring, a notable hierarchy of power
which used this money to their own advantage. Edward
Malia Butler was one of those; but he was only one.
These organizations are never dominated by one man
alone. They grow like a rank growth of weeds in a small
community. They fatten and are added to until, if
you attempt to trace them out, you reach by wider and
ever-widening circles the very body and blood of the people themselves. We are all sinners, either directly or
indirectly, if no more than by the fact that we do not
protest. If we do not protest, it is evident that this idea
is not so very shocking to us, certainly not enough to
irritate us to the point of protesting.

We plead the difficulty of life, the necessity; life is so
hard to regulate; the individual man is so weak, and so
on. All of us are too busy grasping at immediate gains
to trouble about far-off evils and errors. So— Any-

how, the city treasurers and assessors did not need to account for more than the principal of the sums intrusted to them; and from this sprang all the hurry and enthusiasm of private speculation, which was so profitable and satisfactory to so many individuals.

how the city treasurer and assessor did not wish to provide for taxation the redemption of the sum indicated to them, and that the carrying off the many were con thousands of public speculation, which was profitable and satisfactory to a great individuals

CHAPTER XVI

MR. FRANK ALGERNON COWPERWOOD, in approaching Mr. Edward Malia Butler, had been unconsciously let in on this atmosphere of erratic and unsatisfactory speculation without really knowing it. When he had left the office of Tighe & Co., seven years before, it was with the idea that henceforth and forever he would have nothing to do with the stock-brokerage proposition; but now behold him back in it again, with more vim than he had ever displayed in the first place, for now he was working for himself, the firm of Cowperwood & Co., and he was eager to satisfy the world of new and powerful individuals who by degrees were drifting to him. From many sections of this political world they came. All had a little money. All had tips, and they wanted him to carry certain lines of stocks on margin for them, because he was known to other political men, and because he was safe. He was not a speculator or a gambler on his own account. He soothed himself with the thought that in all these years he had never gambled for himself, but had always acted strictly for others instead. Now Mr. George W. Stener had another proposition to offer him, which was not quite the same thing as stock-gambling for himself, and yet it was. How will be explained.

During a long period of years preceding the Civil War, and through it, the city of Philadelphia had been in the habit, as a corporation, when there were no available funds in the treasury, of issuing what were known as city warrants, which were nothing more than notes or I. O. U.'s bearing six per cent. interest, and payable some-

times in thirty days, sometimes in three months, sometimes in six months, and sometimes much longer—all
depending on the amount and how soon the city treasurer
thought there would be sufficient money in the treasury
to take them up and cancel them. Small tradesmen and
large contractors were frequently paid in this way; the
small tradesman who sold supplies to the city institutions,
for instance, being compelled to discount his notes at
the bank if he needed ready money, usually for ninety
cents on the dollar, while the large contractor could afford
to hold his and wait. It can readily be seen that this
might be a system quite to the disadvantage of the small
dealer and merchant, and quite a fine thing for a large
contractor or note-broker; for the city was sure to pay
the warrants some time, and six per cent. interest was a
nice rate, considering the absolute security. A banker or
broker who gathered these things up from small tradesmen at ninety cents on the dollar made a fine thing of it
all around if he could wait.

Originally, in all probability, there was no intention
on the part of the city treasurer to do any one an injustice,
and it is likely that there really were no funds to pay with
at the time. However that may have been, there was
later no excuse for issuing the warrants at all, seeing
that the city might have been economically managed.
But these warrants, as can be readily imagined, had come
to be a fine source of profit for note-brokers, bankers,
political financiers, and inside political manipulators
generally. It was so easy for the "right" city treasurer
to issue a large number of these warrants. It was so
easy for him to refuse payment within any reasonable
period, merely stamping the amount of interest due
on the face of the note and letting the holder keep it.
The small tradesman then, because of his necessities, had
to discount his notes. The large banker said to himself,
"Where can I get a better or safer investment than this?
Let the city pay me with interest as long as it pleases.

When the time comes when these things must be taken up, it will pay me one hundred cents on the dollar where I only paid ninety." There was just one drawback to all this, and that was, in order to get the full advantage of this condition, the large banker holding them must be an "inside banker," one close to the political forces of the city, for in case he was not and he needed money (must have it), and he carried his warrants to the city treasurer, he would find that he could not get cash for them. But if he transferred them to some banker or note-broker who was close to the political force of the city, it was quite another matter. Then the warrants were in the right hands. The treasury would find means to pay. Or, if the note-broker or banker—the right one—wished, notes which were intended to be met in three months, and should have been settled at that time, would be allowed to run on years and years, drawing interest at six per cent., even when the city had ample funds wherewith to meet them. This meant an illegal interest drain on the city, but that was all right also. "No funds" could cover that. The general public did not know. It could not find out. The newspapers were not at all vigilant, being pro-political. There were no persistent, enthusiastic reformers who obtained any political credence. During the war these warrants outstanding in this manner rose in amount to much over two million dollars, all drawing six per cent. interest; and then, of course, it began to get a little scandalous. Besides, the investors began to want their money back.

In order to clear up this outstanding indebtedness, and make everything shipshape again, it was decided that the city must issue a loan, say, for two million dollars— no need to be exact about the amount. And this loan must take the shape of interest-bearing certificates of a par value of one hundred dollars, redeemable in six, twelve, or eighteen months, as the case may be. These certificates of loan were then ostensibly to be sold on the open market, a sinking-fund set aside for their redemption, and the money so obtained used to take up the long-outstanding warrants which were now such a subject of public comment.

It is obvious that this was merely a case of robbing Peter to pay Paul. There was no real clearing up of the outstanding debt. It was the intention of the schemers to make it possible for the financial politicians on the inside to reap the same old harvest by allowing the certificates to be sold to the right parties for ninety or less, setting up the claim that there was no market for them, the credit of the city being bad. To a certain extent this was true. Times had changed. The war was just over. Money was high. Investors could get more than six per cent. elsewhere unless the loan was sold at ninety. But there were a few watchful politicians not in the administration, and some newspapers and non-political financiers who, because of the high strain of patriotism existing at the time, insisted that the loan should be sold at par. Because of the recent patriotic war-feeling it was assumed that this could be done, and it was not easy to avoid this vaunted call to honesty. A clause had to be inserted in the enabling ordinance providing that the loan certificate must be sold at par.

This destroyed the politicians' little scheme to get it at ninety. Nevertheless they desired that the money tied up in the old warrants and now not redeemable because of lack of funds should be paid them. The only way this could be done would be to have some broker who knew the subtleties of the stock market handle this new city loan on 'change in such a way that it would be made to seem worth one hundred and so would be sold to outsiders at that figure. Afterward, if it fell below that, the politicians could buy as much of it as they pleased, and eventually have the city redeem it at par. Meanwhile they would receive the money tied up in the old city warrants.

Mr. George W. Stener, entering as city treasurer at this time, and bringing no special financial intelligence to the proposition, was really troubled. Mr. Henry A. Mollenhauer, one of the men who had gathered up a large amount of the old city warrants, and who now wanted his money, in order to invest it in bonanza offers in the West, called on Mr. Stener, and also on the mayor. He was one of the big three, of whom Simpson and Butler were the others.

"I think something ought to be done about these warrants that are outstanding," he explained. "I am carrying a large amount of them, and there are others. We have helped the city a long time by saying nothing; but now I think that something ought to be done. Mr. Butler and Mr. Simpson feel the same way. Couldn't these new loan certificates be listed on the stock exchange and the money raised that way? Some clever broker could bring them to par."

Mr. Stener was greatly flattered by the visit from Mr. Mollenhauer. The latter, a large-bodied, broad-chested, broad-faced man, of still, impressive countenance, who said little, looked fixedly at anything before him, and read his victims much as a cat reads a bird, was a great power in the city. He knew much of what was being done politically in large and small ways; but henchmen, as a rule, executed his orders. Rarely, and then only in cases of this kind, where several hundred thousand dollars of his money was involved, did he trouble to put in a personal appearance, and then only for the weight and effect his presence would have. He called on the mayor and the president of council, much as he called on Mr. Stener, with a lofty, distant, inscrutable air. They were as office-boys to him. They were not deep in the secrets of political and social finance such as he knew. Mr. Stener was notably impressed.

In order to understand exactly the motive of Mr. Mollenhauer's interest in Stener, and the significance of this visit and Stener's subsequent action in regard to it, it will be necessary to scan the political horizon for some little distance back. Although George W. Stener was in a way a political henchman and appointee of Mollenhauer's, the latter was only vaguely acquainted with him. He had seen him before; knew of him; had agreed that his name should be put on the local slate largely because he had been assured by those who were closest to him and who did his bidding that Stener was "all right," that he would do as he was told, that he would cause no one any trouble, etc. During several administrations, of which that of Mr. Bode, Mr. Stener's immediate predecessor, was one, Mr. Mollenhauer had maintained a subsurface connection with the treasury which was very profitable to him, as it was in a way, though not so directly, to both Butler and Simpson. The two latter had more or less large private interests of their own. Mollenhauer was too large a man politically and financially to risk a close working connection with the treasury which might readily be traced; but he was not above a plan which was not known in all its details to either of his associates, Messrs. Simpson and Butler, but which was nevertheless profitable to them in one way and another, namely, that of using political and commercial stool-pigeons to bleed the city treasury as much as possible without creating a scandal. Various agents were employed—Mr. Edward Strobik, president of council; Mr. Asa Conklin, the then incumbent of the mayor's chair; Mr. Thomas Wycroft, alderman; Mr. Jacob Harmon, alderman, and others. These men were used to organize dummy companies under various names, whose business it was to deal in those things which the city needed and was compelled to have. It saved the city the trouble of looking far and wide for honest and reasonable dealers.

Since the action of three of these men will have something to do with the development of Frank Cowperwood's story they may be briefly described. Mr. Edward

Strobik, the chief of them, and the one most useful to Mr. Mollenhauer, in a minor way, although not generally known to be so, was a very spry person of about thirty-five at this time—raised and educated in Philadelphia, lean and forceful in a narrow way, with black hair, black eyes, and an inordinately large black mustache. He was, all in all, rather dapper, inclined to noticeable clothing— a pair of striped trousers, a white vest, a black cutaway coat, and a high silk hat. His markedly ornamental shoes were always polished to perfection, and his immaculate appearance gave him the nickname of "The Dude" among some. Nevertheless he was quite able in a mediocre way, and was well liked by many. He was valued by Mr. Mollenhauer, who kept him where he was.

His two closest associates, Messrs. Thomas Wycroft and Jacob Harmon, were in a way less attractive and less brilliant. Jacob Harmon was a rather stuffy person of about the mental caliber of Mr. Andrew Pohlhemus, whom Cowperwood had known in his earlier days on 'change, a thick wit of a person socially, but no fool financially. He was big and rather doleful to look upon, with sandy brown hair and brown eyes, but fairly intelligent, and absolutely willing to approve anything which was not too broad in its crookedness and which would afford him sufficient protection to keep him out of the clutches of the law. He was really not so much cunning as dull and anxious to get along.

Mr. Thomas Wycroft, the last of this useful but minor triumvirate, was a tall, lean man, candle-waxy, hollow-eyed, gaunt of face, pathetic to look at physically, but rather shrewd. He was an iron-molder by profession or training; had gotten into politics much as Stener had— because in a way he was useful; and he had managed to make some money *via* this triumvirate of which Strobik was the ringleader, and who were engaged in various peculiar businesses which will now be indicated.

The companies which these several henchmen were

supposed to organize, or had organized under previous administrations, such as Bode's, consisted of organizations dealing in meat, building material, lamp-posts, highway supplies, anything you will, which the city departments or its institutions needed. A city contract once awarded, say to supply beef to the city's institutions, or lamp-posts and other iron equipments to the highways department, was irrevocable, but certain councilmen had to be fixed in advance and it took money to do that. The company so organized need not do any actual business. It need not slaughter any cattle or mold lamp - posts. All it had to do was to organize to do that, obtain a charter, secure a contract for supplying such material to the city from the city council (which Mr. Strobik, Mr. Harmon, and Mr. Wycroft would attend to), and then sublet this to some actual beef-slaughterer or iron-founder, who would supply the material and allow them to pocket their profit. It was so easy and in a way so legitimate. The particular beef-slaughterer or iron-founder thus favored could not hope of his own ability thus to obtain a contract. He ought to be glad to obtain it under any circumstances from Messrs. Strobik, Harmon, and Wycroft. Mr. Stener, or whoever was in charge of the city treasury at the time, for his services in loaning money at a low rate of interest to be used as surety for the proper performance of contract, and to aid in some instances the beef-killer or iron-founder to carry out his end, was to be allowed not only the one or two per cent. which he might pocket (other treasurers had), but a fair proportion of the profits. A complacent, confidential chief clerk who was all right would be recommended to him. It did not concern Mr. Stener that Mr. Strobik, Mr. Harmon, and Mr. Wycroft acting for Mr. Mollenhauer were incidentally planning to use a little of the money loaned for purposes quite outside that indicated. It was his business to loan it. And anyhow that is another story. But it indicates the subtleties and ramifications of these political-financial-commercial arrangements which occur in every American city, and that is what this particular paragraph is intended to illustrate.

Stener, before his induction into office and in fact some time before he was even nominated, had learned from Mr. Strobik, who, by the way, was one of his sureties as treasurer (which suretyship was against the law, as were those of Councilmen Wycroft and Harmon, the law of Pennsylvania stipulating that one political servant might not become surety for another), that they would not ask him to do anything which it was not perfectly legal for him to do, but that he must be complacent and not stand in the way of big municipal perquisites nor bite the hands that fed him. They did not and never had. Not only did Strobik, Wycroft, and Harmon make this perfectly plain to him, but also that once he was well in office a little money for himself was to be made. As has been indicated, Mr. Stener had always been a poor man. He had seen all those who had dabbled in politics to any extent about him heretofore do very well financially indeed, while he pegged along as an insurance and real-estate agent. He had worked hard as a small political henchman. Other politicians were building themselves nice homes in newer portions of the city. They were going off to New York or Harrisburg or Washington on jaunting parties. They were seen in happy converse at road-houses or country hotels in season with their wives or their women favorites, and he was not, as yet, of this happy throng. He was promised something. What would he get?

When it came to this visit from Mr. Mollenhauer, with its suggestion in regard to bringing city loan to par, although it bore no obvious relation to Mollenhauer's distant connection with Stener, or his control of Strobik and the others, yet Stener dimly recognized it to be such, and hurried to the latter for information.

"Just what would you do about this?" he asked of

Strobik, who knew of Mollenhauer's visit before Stener told him, and was waiting for Stener to speak to him. "Mr. Mollenhauer talks about having this new loan listed on 'change and brought to par so that it will sell for one hundred."

Neither Strobik, Harmon, nor Wycroft knew how the certificates of city loan which were only worth ninety on the open market were to be made to sell for one hundred on 'change; but a certain Mr. Sengstack, who was Mollenhauer's secretary, had suggested to Strobik, acting as Mollenhauer's go-between, that since Butler was dealing with young Cowperwood and Mollenhauer did not care particularly for his private broker in this instance it might be as well to try Cowperwood. Mollenhauer knew little of him save that he was clever. So Strobik and Harmon and Wycroft, who all knew, so advised Stener.

"Why don't you try that young fellow Cowperwood?" suggested Strobik. "They tell me he is very clever. Mollenhauer knows of him. He can tell you what can be done. I guess the old man" (he was referring to Mollenhauer) "has got something new up his sleeve if he wants you to redeem those warrants."

So Cowperwood, who was by this time strong in the confidence of Butler, was sent for and he took this as another evidence that he was growing in power and popularity in political headquarters, and that he would soon be decidedly prosperous. In his days as a servitor for Tighe & Co. he had seen one city treasurer visit there, and since then there had been another, Mr. Bode, who had dealt with the same firm. Now this was coming to him. He fancied that Mr. Stener wanted to dabble in certain stocks—street-railways very likely, which were very active—rising. Well, it was none of Mr. Cowperwood's business what money he used. He had long ago settled for himself that he did not propose to trouble himself about people's motives. He was a practical man. Finance was a practical world. It contained nothing which related to motives. So long as he was free and clear of any legal complicity, any intention to defraud, what did it concern him where his customers came from, who they were, or how they obtained their money?

The air, at this time, was redolent of speculation. The exuberance of the average American in regard to the future of the United States made him sanguine, dramatic, almost dangerous. "This political world is a great world," Cowperwood said to himself. "These fellows have access to ready money. I must go slow; but I can go slow, and they will make me rich." He journeyed to Mr. Stener's office and was introduced to him at once. He looked at the peculiarly shambling, heavy-cheeked, middle-class man before him without either interest or sympathy, and realized at once that he had a financial baby to deal with. Stener knew nothing. If he could act as adviser to this man—be his sole counsel for four years!

"How do you do, Mr. Stener?" he said, in his soft, ingratiating voice, as the latter held out his hand. "I am glad to meet you. I have heard of you before, of course."

Mr. Stener was not long in explaining to Mr. Cowperwood just what his difficulty was. He went at it in a club-footed fashion, stumbling through the difficulties of the situation he was to meet.

"The main thing is to make these certificates sell at par. I can issue them in any sized lots you like, and as often as you like. I want to get enough now to clear away two hundred thousand dollars' worth of the outstanding warrants, and as much more as I can get later."

Cowperwood felt like a physician feeling a patient's pulse—a patient who is not really sick at all, but the reassurance of whom would mean a fat fee for him. The abstrusities of the stock exchange were as his A B C's to him. He knew if he could have this loan put in his hands—all of it; if he could have it kept dark that he was acting for the city, and that if Mr. Stener would allow him to buy as a "bull" for the sinking-fund while selling judiciously for a rise, he could do wonders even with a big issue. It was silly to suppose that these certificates, bearing six per cent. interest, could not be brought to par. He had to have all of it, though, had to have agents under him. Looming up in his mind there was a scheme whereby he could make a lot of the unwary speculators about 'change go short of this stock or loan, in the idea that it was scattered freely in various people's hands, and that they could buy as much of it as they wanted. Then they would wake to find that they could not get it; that he had it all. Only he would not risk his secret that far. He would drive the city loan to par and then sell.

"I tell you what I'd like to do, Mr. Stener," he said, after he had listened to his explanation, and asked how much of the city loan he would like to sell during the coming year. "I'd like to take this under advisement for a day or two. It can be done. I'll be glad to undertake it. But I'd like to have a day or two in which to think it over. Then you can see what you think."

"Why, certainly, certainly, Mr. Cowperwood," replied Mr. Stener, genially. "That's all right. Take your time. If you know how it can be done, just show me when you're ready. By the way, what do you charge?"

"Well, the stock exchange has a regular scale of charges which we brokers are compelled to observe. It's one-fourth of one per cent. on the par value of bonds and loans. Of course I may have to do a lot of fictitious selling—I'll explain that to you later—but I won't charge you anything for that so long as it is a secret between us. I'll give just the best service I can, Mr. Stener. You can depend on that. Let me have a day or two to think it over, though."

He shook hands with Mr. Stener, and they parted. Cowperwood was satisfied that he was on the verge of a significant combination, and Stener that he had found some one on whom he could lean. Cowperwood was so much younger, but he was so forceful, so intelligent. Now, if Mr. Cowperwood were nice he might show him, Mr. Stener, how to make a little money on the stock exchange. He had heard of city officials doing this. And it was all between him and Mr. Cowperwood—quite a secret. He liked him very much.

The plan Mr. Cowperwood developed after a few days' meditation would be plain enough to any one who knew anything of commercial and financial manipulation, but a dark secret to those who do not. In the first place, the city treasurer was to use his (Cowperwood's) office as a bank of deposit. He was to turn over to him, actually, or set over to his credit on the city's books, subject to his order, certain amounts of city loans—two hundred thousand dollars at first, since that was the amount it was desired to raise quickly—and he would then go into the market and see what could be done to have it brought to par. The city treasurer was to ask leave of the stock exchange at once to have it listed as a security. Cowperwood would use his influence to have this application acted upon quickly. Mr. Stener was to dispose of all city loan certificates through him, and him only. He was to allow him to buy for the sinking-fund, supposedly, such amounts as he might have to buy in order to keep the price up to par. To do this, once a considerable number of the loan certificates had been unloaded on the public, it might be necessary to buy back a great deal. However, these would be sold again. The law concerning selling only at par would have to be abrogated to this extent—*i. e.*, that the wash sales and preliminary sales would have to be considered no sales until par was reached. There was a subtle advantage here, Cowperwood pointed out to Mr. Stener. In the first place, since the certificates were going ultimately to reach par anyway, there was no objection to Mr. Stener or any one else buying low at the opening price and holding for a rise. Cowperwood would be glad to carry him on his books for any amount, and he would settle at the end of each month. He would not be asked to buy the certificates outright. He could be carried on the books for a certain reasonable margin, say ten points. The money was as good as made for Mr. Stener now. In the next place, in buying for the sinking-fund it would be possible to buy these certificates very cheap, for, having the new and reserve issue entirely in his hands, Cowperwood could throw such amounts as he wished into the market at such times as he wished to buy, and consequently depress the market. Then he could buy, and, later, up would go the price. Having the issues totally in his hands to boost or depress the market as he wished, there was no reason why the city should not ultimately get par for all its issues, and yet why considerable should not be made out of the manufactured fluctuations. He, Cowperwood, would be glad to make most of his profit that way. The city should allow him his normal percentage on all his actual sales of certificates for the city at par (he would have to have that in order to keep straight with the stock exchange); but beyond that, and for all the other necessary manipulative sales, of which there would be many, he would depend on his knowledge of the stock market to reimburse him. And if Mr. Stener wanted to speculate with him—well.

Dark as this transaction may seem to the uninitiated, it will appear quite clear to those who know. Manipulative tricks have always been worked in connection with stocks of which one man or one set of men has had complete control. It was no different from what has since been done with Erie, Standard Oil, Copper, Sugar, Wheat, and what not. Cowperwood was one of the earliest and one of the youngest to see how it could be done. When he first talked to Stener he was twenty-eight years of age. When he last talked to him, or did business with him, he was thirty-four. Stener put himself in his hands as a child confides itself to a nurse. He could not see how this subtle young man looked upon him. He only knew that Cowperwood had worked out a successful plan for the solution of his difficulties, and that he was delighted to have the privilege of trying it.

CHAPTER XVII

THE houses and the bank-front of Cowperwood & Co. had been proceeding apace. The latter was a thought of Cowperwood's modified by Ellsworth. It was early Florentine in its decorations, reserved and refined, with windows which grew narrower as they approached the roof, and a door of wrought iron set between delicately carved posts, and a straight lintel of brownstone. It was low in height and distinguished. In the center panel had been hammered a hand, delicately wrought, thin and artistic, holding aloft a flaming brand. The latter, Ellsworth informed him, had formerly been a money-changer's sign used by a small and successful group of usurers in Venice, but long since fallen into the limbo of nothingness. Here it would look quaint. Cowperwood approved, for, in spite of his financial subtlety and money tendency generally, this idea of the refining influence of art appealed to him greatly. He sympathized with the artistic spirit, believed that after wealth and feminine beauty it was the one great thing. Perhaps wealth and beauty and material art forms—the arts and crafts of the world—were indissolubly linked. Sometimes, as he looked at life—the mere current, visible scene—it seemed intensely artistic. A snow-storm outside his window, a crowd of men on 'change, the full-sailed boats coming up the Delaware—he had not much time for these things, he was so busy, but they were beautiful. Once he saw a great, disheveled, dusty, and blood-stained company of men returning from Gettysburg, their knapsacks awry, their blankets dirty, their arms or foreheads or legs roughly bandaged in several instances, and he thought this would make a great battle picture. If he were an artist, now! But he wasn't, and so, after a few minutes, he put the thought briskly aside. But these things were haunting him at odd moments, and he thought, once he was indestructibly rich, he would probably come to live in a very notable manner, not grandiose, but beautiful.

So the new bank building was done over in a very simple and yet impressive way, with an interior quite different from anything else in the street, for it was all highly polished hardwood stained in imitation of the gray lichens which infest trees, but in a somewhat lower key. Large sheets of clear, beveled glass were used, some oval, some oblong, some square, and some circular, following a given theory of eye movement. The fixtures for the gas-jets were modeled after the early Roman flame-brackets, and the office safe was made an ornament, raised on a marble platform at the back of the office and lacquered a silver-gray, with Cowperwood & Co. lettered on it in gold. One had a sense of great reserve, taste, and beauty pervading this place, and yet it was also inestimably prosperous, solid, and assuring. Cowperwood, when he viewed it at its completion, complimented Ellsworth cheerily. "This is really beautiful," he said. "It's delightful. It will be a pleasure to work here. If those houses are going to be anything like this, they will be perfect."

"Wait till you see them. I think you should be pleased, Mr. Cowperwood. I am taking especial pains with yours because it is smaller. It is really easier to treat your father's. But yours—" He went off into a description of the entrance-hall, reception-room, and parlor, which he was arranging and decorating in such a way as to give an effect of size and dignity not really conformable to the actual space.

Cowperwood looked at this young man, who frequently drove to the office to consult him, or met him at the spot where the houses were in process of erection, and felt a warm, kindly feeling for him. He was following a line of work which seemed delightfully dignified, worth while, and essential. Art must have its devotees. If this boy were so beautifully minded as to be important and successful in his field, he ought to be well paid for his taste. It was pleasant to have such men to deal with. As in his youth, he had no thought of stinting money. His idea of making money was not by saving. One had to think of large, productive things to do and then pay liberally for their execution.

When the houses were finished they were really charming. things to look upon. They were quite different from the conventional residences of the street. The architect had borrowed a note from the Gothic, or rather Tudor, theory of art, not so elaborated as the style later became, in many of the residences in Philadelphia and elsewhere; but still ornate and picturesque. His idea was to have the façades of the two residences blend as one. The most striking features in each instance were rather deep-recessed doorways under wide, low, slightly floreated arches, and three projecting windows of rich form, one on the second floor of Frank's house, two on the façade of his father's. There were six gables showing on the front of the two houses, two on Frank's and four on his father's. In the front of each house on the ground floor was a recessed window unconnected with the recessed doorways, formed by setting the inner external wall back from the outer face of the building. This window looked out through an arched opening to the street, and was protected by a dwarf parapet or balustrading. It was possible to set potted vines and flowers here, which was later done, giving a pleasant sense of greenery from the street, and to place about a few chairs, which were reached *via* heavily barred French casements.

Ellsworth, because Frank's house was the smaller of the two, advised that it be placed on the corner—for these were corner lots on which they were building. He pointed out that Frank's father would have the advantage of the west light (the building faced south), because the two houses were to be separated by a space of twenty feet laid out as a greensward. He extended a glass window twenty-four inches outside of Frank's west wall, which commanded the side street for a distance of twenty feet on the second floor, and placed within a library and reading-room, making it habitable by stained glass of a low, soothing key. On the ground floor of each house he placed a conservatory for flowers facing each other, and in the yard, which was jointly used, he placed a pool of white marble eight feet in diameter, with a marble Cupid upon which jets of water played from concealed pipes, gurgling for joy. The yard, which was inclosed by a high but pierced wall of green-gray brick, especially burnt for this purpose the same color as the granite of the house and surmounted by a white marble coping, was sown to grass, and had a lovely, smooth, velvety appearance. The two houses, as originally planned, were connected by a low, green-columned pergola which could be inclosed in winter in glass. The interior was decorated after periods, or styles, and much attention was given to this matter.

These rooms, which were now slowly being decorated and furnished for the arrival of the Cowperwoods, particularly for the arrival of the son, though the father was important also, were very significant in that they enlarged and strengthened Frank Cowperwood's idea of the art of the world in general. It was a comforting experience to Frank Cowperwood, and one which made for artistic and intellectual growth, to hear Ellsworth explain at length the styles and types of architecture and furniture, the nature of woods and ornaments employed, the qualities and peculiarities of hangings, draperies, furniture panels, and floor coverings. Ellsworth was a student of decoration as well as of architecture, and interested in the artistic taste of the American people, which he fancied some time would have a splendid outcome. He was wearied to death of the prevalent Romanesque composite combinations of country and suburban villa, so called, which were plentiful. The time was ripe for something new. He scarcely knew what it would be; but this that he had figured out for Cowperwood and his father was different, while at the same time being pleasing, simple, and reserved. It was in marked contrast to the rest of the architecture of the street. Cowperwood's dining-room, reception-room, conservatory, and butler's pantry he had put on the first floor, together with the general entry-hall, staircase, and coat-room under the stairs. For the second floor he had reserved the library, general living-room, parlor, and a small office for Cowperwood, together with a boudoir for madame, connected with a dressing-room and bath. On the third floor, neatly divided and accommodated with baths and dressing-rooms, were the nursery, the servants' quarters, and several guest-chambers. Ellsworth showed Cowperwood books of designs containing furniture, hangings, étagères, cabinets, pedestals, and some exquisite piano forms. He discussed woods with him—rosewood, mahogany, walnut, English oak, bird's-eye maple, and the manufactured effects such as ormolu, marquetry, and Boule, or buhl. He explained the latter—how difficult it was to produce, how unsuitable it was in some respects for this climate, the brass and tortoise-shell inlay coming to swell with the heat or damp, and so bulging or breaking. He told of the difficulties and disadvantages of certain finishes, but finally recommended ormolu furniture for the reception-room, medallion tapestry for the parlor, French renaissance for the dining-room and library, and bird's-eye maple (dyed blue in one instance, and left its natural color in another) and a rather lightly constructed but daintily carved walnut for the other rooms. The hangings, wall-paper, and floor coverings were to harmonize—not match—and the piano and music-cabinet for the parlor, as well as the étagère, cabinets, and pedestals for the reception-rooms, were to be of buhl or marquetry, if Frank cared to stand the expense. Ellsworth advised him to obtain a triangular piano if he could afford it—the square shapes were so inexpressibly wearisome to the initiated. Cowperwood listened fascinated, for this architect appealed to him in his every instinct, and he foresaw a home which would be chaste, soothing, and delightful to look upon. If he hung pictures, gilt frames were to be the setting, large and deep; and if he wished a picture-gallery, the library could be turned into that, and the general living-room, which lay between the library and the parlor on the second floor, could be turned into a combination library and living-room. This was eventually done; but not until his taste for pictures had considerably advanced.

It was now that Cowperwood began to take a keen interest in objects of art, pictures, bronzes, little carvings and figurines, which by degrees he began to hear of and which he now needed, a few for his cabinets, pedestals, tables, and étagères. During the few years he had been living in North Front Street he had learned a little—not much. Now, however, the size and quality of this house and his father's emphasized the point, and he began to look about him. Philadelphia did not hold much that was distinguished in this realm—certainly not in the open market. There were many private houses which were enriched by private travel; but his connection with the best families was as yet small. He had connections which were gradually leading to them, if he but chose to follow carefully; but he was not sure that he cared to. The finely veneered social type was rather foreign to his mood. He was not at all interested in books, feeling life to be so much more worth while; but he filled his handsome case with recommended sets of the masters. He helped his father hunt for things with which to soften and decorate his much larger rooms, and in so doing learned many things concerning furniture, decorations, pictures, and art objects which he had not previously known. There were then two famous American sculptors, Powers and Hosmer, of whose work he had examples; but Ellsworth told him that they were not the last word in sculpture, and that he should look into the merits of the ancients. He began to wish that he were the possessor of art figures by them. His black Italian pedestals were as yet empty. He finally secured a head of David, by Thorwaldsen, which delighted him, and some landscapes, by Hunt, Sully, and Hart, which seemed somewhat in the spirit of his new world.

It is curious what the effect of a house of this character will be on a man. We think we are individual, separate, above houses and material objects generally; but there is a subtle connection which makes them reflect us quite as much as we reflect them, and vice versa. A man in a way is the shadow of his possessions and deeds, quite as much as they are a projection or reflection of him. The twain are indissolubly linked. They grow as a tree and its shade. The man is stronger for his possessions, and his possessions are stronger for the man. They lend dignity, subtlety, force, each to the other, and what beauty, or lack of it, there is is shot back and forth from one to the other as a shuttle in a loom, weaving, weaving. Cut the thread, separate a man from that which is rightfully his own, characteristic of him, and you have a peculiar figure, half success, half failure, much as a spider without its web, which will never be its whole self again until all its dignities and emoluments (those things in which it believes and rejoices) are restored.

Of course there are those highly spiritualized characters, just as at the other extreme there are those grossly material ones, which by their over-emphasis of polar phases establish, while seeming to discountenance, the rule. Of Isaiah and Jeremiah it might be predicated that they do not require the eternal hills as witness of

THE FINANCIER

the loftiness of their souls, but they, nevertheless, require them. Be he ever so innately callous and brutal, the butcher or the executioner, separated from his ax and the atmosphere of blood and grime surrounding him, loses much of his savage identity.

CHAPTER XVIII

IT was not long after the significant arrangement between Treasurer Stener and Cowperwood had been made that the machinery for the carrying out of that political-financial relationship was put in motion. The sum of two hundred and ten thousand dollars in six per cent. interest-bearing certificates, payable in ten years, was set over to the credit of Cowperwood & Co. on the books of the city, subject to his order. He waited until it was properly listed on 'change. Then through several brokers who were in his employ he began to offer small amounts at more than ninety, and at the same time, by those subtle methods known to the stock-jobbing world—rumors, wash sales, the use of the financial column *via* the financial reporters, and so on—attempted to create the impression that it was going to be a prosperous investment. Various people were supposed to have purchased large amounts from the city, but were not willing to let go. Whenever one of these small lots was offered by him one of his agents picked it up, offering it sometimes for a still higher price. The certificates gradually rose and were unloaded in rising amounts until one hundred was reached, when all the two hundred thousand dollars' worth—two thousand certificates in all—were fed out in small lots. It was ticklish business, requiring frequent repurchases at the current market rate. He saw how easy it would be to slump the market and drive the certificates down to eighty or less, if he wished, but he refrained with a clear idea of bigger things to come in the future. Stener was satisfied. Two hundred shares had been carried for him and sold at one hundred, which netted him two thousand dollars. It was illegitimate gain, unethical; but his conscience was not very much troubled by that. He saw visions of a halcyon future.

It is difficult to make perfectly clear what a subtle and significant power this suddenly placed in the hands of Cowperwood. Consider that he was only twenty-eight —nearing twenty-nine. Imagine yourself by nature versed in the arts of finance, capable of playing with sums of money in the forms of stocks, certificates, bonds, and cash, as the ordinary man plays with checkers or chess. Or, better yet, imagine yourself one of those subtle masters of the mysteries of the higher forms of chess—the type of mind so well illustrated by the famous and historic chess-players, who could sit with their backs to a group of rivals playing fourteen men at once, calling out all the moves in turn, remembering all the positions of all the men on all the boards, and winning. This, of course, would be an overstatement of the subtlety of Frank Cowperwood at this time, and yet it would not be wholly out of key. He knew instinctively what could be done with a given sum of money—how as cash it could be deposited in one place, and yet as credit and the basis of moving checks, used in not one but many other places at the same time. When properly watched and followed this manipulation gave one the constructive and purchasing power of ten and a dozen times as much as the original sum might have represented. He knew instinctively the principles of "pyramiding" and "kiting." He could see exactly not only how he could raise and lower the value of these certificates of loan, day after day and year after year, if he were so fortunate as to retain his hold on the city treasurer; but, seeing that he was to have, ultimately, all of the issue of two million, and that he was to be able to call for the delivery of fifty, seventy-five, one hundred, one hundred and fifty, or two hundred thousand dollars' worth of city loan at one time, to be deposited in his care or held subject to his order, it

gave him a credit with the banks hitherto beyond his
wildest dreams. His father's bank was one of the first
to profit by this and to extend him loans. The various
politicians—Mollenhauer, Butler, Simpson, and others—
seeing the success of his efforts in this direction, speculated
in city loan. He became known to Mr. Mollenhauer and
Mr. Simpson, by reputation if not personally, as the man
who was carrying this city loan proposition to a successful
issue. Stener was supposed to have done a clever thing
in finding him. The stock exchange stipulated that all
trades were to be compared the same day and settled
before the close of the next; but this working arrangement
with the new city treasurer gave Cowperwood much more
latitude, and now he had always until the first of the
month, or practically thirty days at times, in which to
render an accounting for all deals connected with the
loan issue.

And, moreover, this was really not an accounting in the
sense of removing anything from his hands. Since the
issue was to be so large, the sum at his disposal would
always be large, and so-called transfers and balancing at
the end of the month would be a mere matter of bookkeeping. He could take these city loan certificates deposited with him for manipulative purposes and deposit
them at any bank as collateral for a loan, quite as if they
were his own, thus raising seventy per cent. of their actual
value in cash, and he did not hesitate to do so. He could
take this cash, which need not be accounted for until the
end of the month, and cover other stock transactions,
on which he could borrow again. There was no limit
to the resources of which he now found himself possessed,
except the resources of his own energy, ingenuity, and the
limits of time in which he had to work. The politicians
did not realize what a bonanza he was making of it all
for himself, because they could not understand the subtlety of his mind. When Mr. Stener told him, after talking the matter over with the mayor, Strobik, and others

who were advised by Butler, Simpson, and Mollenhauer, that he would formally, during the course of the year, set over on the city's books all of the two millions in city loan, Cowperwood was delighted. It meant enormous transactions to and fro between himself and others. It was not exactly a legitimate matter. Certain officials expected to make money out of these manipulated rises and falls. But it was legal, anyhow. No criminal intention attached to him, and it certainly was not his money. He had been called in as a financial adviser, and he had given his advice. Cowperwood was not a man who inherently was troubled with conscientious scruples. He believed he was financially honest. He was no sharper or shrewder than any other financier—certainly no sharper than any other one would be if he could. On the day he received word from Stener that he was to be given manipulative control of the full amount of city loan, he sent a note down the street to his father asking him to drive home with him, and on the way they discussed his wonderful future. The old gentleman had not heard any of the details of this before, and was dazzled. He looked upon his son as a very remarkable person—extraordinary. He tried to be impartial, hoped he would be, but somehow his son seemed to know more and see farther.

"What do you think of that, father?" Frank asked, his own conclusions reached long before.

The old gentleman weighed all the facts judicially, thinking that his own opinion was exceedingly important. He sat bolt upright as he drove, his hands incased in new leather driving-gloves, his body tightly fitted into a frock-coat. He wore a high silk hat, and his side-whiskers—mutton-chops they were derisively termed— were brushed out in little fluffy gray tufts. His eyebrows were heavy and shaded, and marked his eyes in a distinctive way. He had always a smoothly shaven face, the bare upper lip of which seemed long.

"Why, it seems all right to me, Frank. You know

what money is bringing; it's a good risk, I think; it looks to me that that ought to work out."

Frank was constantly running to his father's bank for money, and he would usually warn him the day before when he was going to draw heavily. "I'm coming down on you to-morrow for fifty thousand. Do you think you can let me have so much?"

"Oh, that's all right," the old gentleman replied. "I guess you're good for it."

He was so proud of this sturdy youth, the only one of his sons who had real financial talent, that his good judgment was in danger. Ed and Joe were good boys, but not brilliant like Frank.

One night Frank said to his father: "If you want to carry a little 'city loan' now I can show you how to make some money."

Frank would never have invited his father except that he felt so sure. Besides, every buyer holding for a rise was a valuable adjunct at this time.

"I oughtn't to speculate. I never have," his father said to him; "but at the same time I cannot help but feel that this is all right—quite another thing from ordinary speculation. You have made such an advantageous arrangement here." It was notorious that the "city deals" were profitable. Others had made thousands and hundreds of thousands out of inside combinations with the city.

"I haven't ever done it before; but if you want to put me down for five or six hundred shares, it's all right. Is that enough?"

"Say five hundred. The money's as good as in your pocket."

Frank did not want to hold his father out long, and after listing him on his books closed him out at a profit of three points. It netted the old gentleman fifteen hundred dollars. It tickled him immensely; but Frank was unkind in that he ever dragged his father into his affairs at all.

THE FINANCIER

Young Cowperwood was one of those men whom incoming possessions were widening and hourly making more significant. The sight of his new house going up made him feel of more weight in the world, and the possession of his suddenly achieved connection with the city treasurer was as though a wide door had been thrown open to the Elysian fields of opportunity. He rode about the city those days behind a spirited team of bays, whose glossy hides and shining metaled harness bespoke the watchful care of hostler and coachman. Ellsworth was building him and his father an attractive stable in the little side street back of the house, which they were to occupy jointly. He told Mrs. Cowperwood that he intended to buy her a victoria—as the low, open, four-wheeled coach was then known—as soon as they were well settled in their new home, and that they were to go out more. There was some plain talk about entertaining—the value of it—and that he would have to reach out socially for certain individuals who were not now known to him. He found, as he said, that there had to be give-and-take in these matters, and that if they were entertained by people of distinction they had to return these entertainments in the same spirit and on the same scale. All these years for one so young he had been holding exceedingly close to his financial affairs; but, now that things were beginning to broaden out so rapidly, it was to be somewhat different. He and his wife would enjoy life a little more. Together with Anna, his sister, and his two brothers, Joseph and Edward, they would use the two houses jointly. There was no reason why Anna might not make a splendid match. Joe and Ed might marry well, since they were not destined to set the world on fire in commerce. At least it would not hurt them to try. He and Lillian were destined to go out more—he could see it coming—but, alas! he could also see that she would not make the figure he had once thought she would. She was charming to look at, but not brilliant; and the chil-

dren—well, the children detained her more than they
would some women.

"Don't you think you will like that?" he asked her
once, curiously.

She smiled wanly. "I suppose so," she said. She
took a dignified, peaceful interest in her home which—he
felt sure—would not bear the strain of great social endeavor.

It is curious how a thought like this weakens the interest of the average ambitious man in a woman. Ambition mounts as a great strain in some hearts. Usually
it is the feminine in so far as social distinction is concerned;
but ever and anon, in the American social cosmos, the
social, commercial, and artistic type combines in some
forceful male who does not require the social ambition
of a woman to egg him on. It may be quite the other way
about, and the very lack of a helpmeet suitable to the
varied dreams of advancement which germinate and swim
in a temperament of this kind may cause friction of a
violent and sometimes disastrous character. Cowperwood was not of a violent strain, however. He merely
perceived, as he went forward financially, that there was
a social face to this problem—that men who hobnobbed
with each other socially as well as financially were in some
ways stronger, securer, more "in on things" than those
who did not. There was a financial ring in Philadelphia,
which had its social counterpart in the west end of the
city and in the suburbs. Great financiers were in many
cases very close to each other in their home relations;
there were balls, parties, marriages, christenings, and summer and winter hegiras in which the same people, closely
related socially and financially, took part. Cowperwood
saw the names of various sons and daughters of men he
knew to be prominent in Third Street, together with their
wives and relatives, listed as participants in this and that
function over and over. His father, because of his presidency of the Third National Bank, was already gingerly

admitted to certain commonplace and private evenings at certain of these well-to-do homes; but this was nothing. It was too late. His father was already too old—past fifty, and it did not interest him any more. His principal interest in the new home was the social and financial prestige it would give his sons and daughter. This was equally true of Frank's mother. But in his own case it was somewhat different. He was twenty-nine. Now that he was beginning to live in his new home, and to do business in his new banking office, he might expect some notable results. Money was now coming to him rather swiftly. In the last six months he had made over thirty thousand dollars, and he believed he saw his way to making over a hundred thousand in the year, or certainly in the next two. Stener, at the instigation of others behind him, had already approached him with a plan whereby he might be willing to loan him a certain amount of city funds entirely apart from the city loan, which he already controlled—ready cash at, say, two per cent.—wherewith they might endeavor to get control of certain railway stocks. Frank did not know who was back of Stener in this; but he did know it could not be the city treasurer alone. He had no courage.

It should be said here that this proposition of Stener's in regard to city money, very veiled at first and bearing apparently no relationship to city funds, bore no connection with the attitude of the principal leaders in local politics, in regard to this same subject, unscrupulous as this attitude was. As has been said, they themselves had been using city money to make big loans to favorite banks, using the subterfuge of designating them as depositories for city funds; but Cowperwood's was not one of these. Messrs. Mollenhauer, Butler, and Simpson were interested in street-railways separately, on their own account. There was no understanding between them on this score. If they had thought at all on the matter they would have decided that they did not want any outsider to interfere. As a matter of fact the street-railway business in Philadelphia was not sufficiently developed at this time to suggest to any one the grand scheme of union which came later. This proposition of Stener's was due entirely to Strobik, who, seeing how things were going generally, but without the capacity of a Mollenhauer or a Simpson, was anxious to further his own affairs. Nevertheless, he did not care to appear in the matter. Like Cowperwood he thought it was a good idea to use Stener as a catspaw. He did not realize the subtlety of the man to whom he was sending Stener. His plan was to get Stener to buy, through Cowperwood, sufficient street-railway shares in any given line to control it, and then, if he could, by efforts of his own, to get the city council to set aside certain streets for its extension. This had to be done very carefully, because naturally his superiors were watchful, and if they found him dabbling in affairs of this kind to his own advantage, they might make it impossible for him to continue politically in a position where he could help himself. Any outside organization such as a street-railway company already in existence had a right to appeal to the city council for privileges which would naturally further the growth, and, other things being equal, these could not be refused. It would not do, however, for him as a recognized shareholder and president of council to appear in the matter. But with Cowperwood acting privately for Stener it would be another thing. Because of what he could do in the future politically, and because Stener needed some one on whom he could lean before he could be induced to act at all, Strobik knew that he could induce Stener to give him a share in anything which the use of city money in this way would bring about. Hence the proposition which Stener made to Cowperwood.

The interesting thing about this proposition of Mr. Stener's was that it raised, without appearing to do so, the whole question of Cowperwood's attitude toward the city administration. Although he was dealing privately for Edward Butler as an agent, and although he had never met either Mollenhauer or Simpson, the rumored controlling powers of the city, he nevertheless felt that in so far as the manipulation of the city loan was concerned he was acting for them. That is, they were making money from the tips and information which were constantly issuing from his office. In this matter of the private street-railway purchase which Stener now brought to him he realized from the very beginning, by Stener's attitude, that there was something untoward in it, that Stener felt he was doing something which he ought not to do.

"Cowperwood," he said to him the first morning he ever broached this matter—it was in Stener's office, at the old city hall at Sixth and Chestnut, and Stener was feeling very good indeed in view of his oncoming prosperity—"isn't there some street-railway property around town here that a man could buy in on and get control of if he had sufficient money?"

This was exactly the way that Edward Strobik had addressed Stener on the subject some three weeks before, when he had begun with Machiavellian subtlety to suggest the deed.

Cowperwood knew that there were such properties. His very alert mind had long since sensed the general opportunities here. The omnibuses were slowly disappearing. The best routes were already pre-empted. Still, as Cowperwood was quick to perceive and point out, there were other streets, and the city was growing. The incoming population would make great business in the future. One could afford to pay almost any price for the short lines already built if one could wait and extend the lines into larger and better areas later. Anyhow, he had already conceived in his own mind the theory of the "endless chain," or "agreeable formula," as some one has called it—namely, that of buying a certain property on a long-time payment and issuing stocks or bonds sufficient not only to pay your seller, but to reimburse you for your trouble, to say nothing of giving you a margin wherewith to invest in other things—allied properties, for instance, against which more bonds could be issued, and so on, *ad infinitum*. It is an old story now, but it was new then, and he kept the thought closely to himself. He was glad to have Stener speak of this matter, though, for street-railways were his hobby, and he was convinced from looking at them that he would be a great master of them if he ever had an opportunity to control them.

"Why, yes, George," he said, non-committally, "there are two or three that offer a good chance if a man had money enough. It would take a good deal of money unless you wanted to go rather slow. I notice blocks of stock being offered on 'change now and then by one person and another. It would be good policy to pick these things up as they're offered, and then to see later if some of the other stockholders won't want to sell out. Green and Coates, now, looks like a good proposition to me. If I had three or four hundred thousand dollars that I thought I could put into that by degrees I would follow it up. It only takes about thirty per cent. of the stock of any railroad to control it. Most of the shares are scattered around so far and wide that they never vote, and I think two or three hundred thousand dollars would control this road." He spoke of one or two other lines that might possibly be secured in the same way in the course of time.

Stener meditated. "That's a good deal of money," he said, thoughtfully. "I'll talk to you about that some more later."

Cowperwood knew that Stener did not have any two or three hundred thousand dollars to invest in anything. There was only one way that he could get it—and that was to loan it out of the city treasury and forego the interest. This thought did not trouble Cowperwood any at the moment. He knew that the larger politicians were using the treasury, only in a more subtle way. Stener had never interested him as an individual. He was merely an opportunity to him. He was thinking now, though, of his own attitude in regard to the use of this money. No harm could come to him, Cowperwood, if Stener's ventures were successful; and there was no reason why they should not be. Even if they were not, he would be merely acting as an agent. In addition, he saw how in the manipulation of this money for Stener he could probably eventually control certain lines for himself.

There was one line being laid out to within a few blocks of his new home—the Seventeenth and Nineteenth Street line it was called—which interested him greatly. He rode on it occasionally when he was delayed or did not wish to trouble about a vehicle. It ran through two thriving streets of red-brick houses, and was destined to have a great future once the city grew large enough. As yet it was really not long enough. If he could get that, for instance, and combine it with Butler's lines, once they were secured—or Mollenhauer's or Simpson's, the legislature could be induced to give them additional franchises. He even dreamed of a combination between Butler, Mollenhauer, Simpson, and himself. Between them, politically, they could get anything. But Butler was not a philanthropist. He would have to be approached with a very sizable bird in hand. The combination must be obviously advisable. Besides, Frank was dealing for Butler in street-railway stocks as it was, and if this particular line were such a good thing Butler might wonder why it had not been brought to him in the first place, seeing that he was in the field to buy. It would be better, Frank thought, to wait until he actually had it as his own, in which case it would be a different matter. Then he could talk as a capitalist. He began to dream of a city-wide street-railway system controlled by a few men, or preferably him alone.

At the same time, he reflected that this plain proposition of handling stolen money—even though it were not admitted that it was stolen—was something that ought not to be undertaken unadvisedly. It was a long road he had traveled since the days he had worked for Waterman & Co. and Tighe & Co. He was a much harder, colder, shrewder person. Stener talked about others, whom he represented as wanting to invest, but Cowperwood knew that this was mere talk. The money was coming from the treasury direct and nowhere else. The matter was really not up for final consideration as yet. In a general way he fancied that if Stener wanted to do this it was all right. He would keep his own skirts as clear as possible. Nevertheless, because of his crafty attitude toward life, his judgment troubled him a little. Why should he do this when he knew that the money was being taken without the knowledge of the superior leaders of the city and when he really need not do it? It was just possible that this transaction might cause him a little trouble at some time or other, if it were ever found out. The other deal in regard to city loan was so much more normal commercially. The loan was ordered by city council and sanctioned by all the powers that were. This thing which Stener proposed was something else. Still it was no worse than a score of other tricks that were played in the financial world and which were quite satisfactory in their result. Why not in this case?

The days that had been passing had brought him and Aileen Butler somewhat closer together in spirit. It will shock the conventionally sensitive to have a fact so subversive of social order so plainly stated; but it is really better so. This girl, whom he had first seen at the age of fifteen, when he called at Butler's house, and who had first begun to show herself at his own home in North Front Street when she was seventeen, was now nineteen, and she had grown into some subtle thoughts of her own.

Because of the pressure of his growing affairs Cowperwood had not paid so much attention to her as he might have; but he had seen her often this last year, in and out of his home in North Front Street—he had not moved as yet—and occasionally at her father's house, where he frequently called. The Butler home, for all the old gentleman's wealth, was not in the least what it should have been, was commonplace and dull—almost dingy in comparison with the Cowperwoods' old home. Its interior was so badly done that it was really not worth talking about.

There was no attempt at true, artistic harmony, though notable prices had been paid for many objects. Such atrocities as exceedingly heavy leather-upholstered furniture for the library, salon-sized chairs and hangings of extra heavy plush for the parlor, a reception-room not simply set with a few curio cases which might entertain, but overfull of heavy oak furniture after the fashion of a club lobby, were instances in point. The pictures were impossible, and the furniture in some instances was unmatched. It was really not Butler's fault entirely. He had asked for advice in the beginning, but had fallen into the hands of a bad architect. Since then he had strayed into odd purchases of his own—things that he liked. At first Aileen, the older of the two girls, had not noticed, being so young; but now these idiosyncrasies and homely variations had begun to irritate. She was beginning to see what the difference between good taste and bad taste was. Even the modest little home of the Cowperwoods on North Front Street was much superior in the point of sweetness and harmony. There was something elusively delicate about it. And their new home, which was building in Girard Avenue quite near the Butlers', was obviously distinguished.

"Papa, why do we stay in this old barn?" she asked her father one evening at dinner, when there were gathered the usual members of the Butler family—Owen, Callum, Norah, and their mother.

"What's the matter with this house, I'd like to know?" demanded Butler, who was drawn up close to the table, his napkin tucked comfortably under his chin, for he insisted on this when company was not present. "I don't see anything the matter with this house. Your mother and I manage to live in it well enough."

"Oh, it's awful, papa. You know it," supplemented Norah, who was seventeen and quite as bright as her sister, though a little less experienced. "Everybody says so. Look at all the nice houses that are being built everywhere about here."

"Everybody! Everybody! Who is 'everybody,' I'd like to know?" demanded Butler, with the faintest touch of choler and much humor. "I'm somebody, and I like it. Those that don't like it don't have to live in it. Who are they? What's the matter with it, I'd like to know?"

The question in just this form had been up a number of times before, and had been handled in just this manner, or passed over entirely with a healthy Irish grin. To-night, however, it was destined for a little more extended thought.

"You know it's bad, papa," corrected Aileen, firmly. "Now what's the use getting mad about it? It's old and cheap and dingy. The furniture is all worn out. That old piano in there ought to be given away. I won't play on it any more. The Cowperwoods——"

"Old, is it!" exclaimed Butler, his accent growing with a somewhat self-induced rage. He almost pronounced it "owled." "Dingy, hi! Where do you get that? At your convent, I suppose. And where is it worn? Show me where it's worn."

He was coming to her reference to Cowperwood, but he hadn't reached that when Mrs. Butler interfered. She was a stout, broad-faced, smiling-mouthed woman most of the time, with blurry, gray Irish eyes, and a touch of red in her hair, now modified by grayness. Her left cheek, below the mouth, was considerably accented by a large wen.

"Children! children!" (Mr. Butler, for all his commercial and political responsibility, was as much a child to her as any.) "Youse mustn't quarrel now. Come now. Give your father the tomatoes."

There was an Irish maid serving at table; but plates were passed from one to the other just the same. A heavily ornamented chandelier, holding sixteen imitation candles in white porcelain, hung low over the table and was brightly lighted, another offense to Aileen.

"Mama, how often have I told you not to say 'youse'?" pleaded Norah, very much disheartened by her mother's grammatical errors. "You know you said you wouldn't."

"And who's to tell your mother what she should say?" called Butler, more incensed than ever at this sudden and unwarranted rebellion and assault. "Your mother talked before ever you was born, I'd have you know. If it weren't for her workin' and slavin' you wouldn't have any fine manners to be paradin' before her. I'd have you know that. She's a better woman nor any you'll be runnin' with this day, you little baggage, you!"

"Mama, do you hear what he's calling me?" complained Norah, hugging close to her mother's arm and pretending fear and dissatisfaction.

"Eddie! Eddie!" cautioned Mrs. Butler, pleading with her husband. "You know he doesn't mean that, Norah. Don't you know he doesn't?"

She was stroking her baby's head. The reference to her grammar had not touched her at all.

Butler was sorry that he had called his youngest a baggage; but these children—God bless his soul—were a great annoyance. Why, in the name of all the saints, wasn't this house good enough for them?"

"Why don't you people quit fussing at the table?" observed Callum, a likely youth in bright tweed, his black hair laid smoothly over his forehead in a long, distinguished layer reaching close to his right ear, and his upper lip carrying a short, crisp mustache. His nose was short and retroussé, and his ears were rather prominent; but he was bright and attractive. He and Owen both realized that the house was old and poorly arranged; but Mr. and Mrs. Butler liked it, and business sense and family peace dictated silence on this score. Butler, *père*, expected conservatism and social support from his two sons.

"Well, I think it's mean to have to live in this old place when every one else—people not one-fourth as good as we are—are living in better ones. The Cowperwoods —why, even the Cowperwoods—"

"Yes, the Cowperwoods! What about the Cowperwoods?" demanded Butler, turning squarely to Aileen— she was sitting beside him—his big, red face glowing.

"Why, even they have a better house than we have, and he's merely an agent of yours."

"The Cowperwoods! The Cowperwoods! I'll not have any talk about the Cowperwoods. I'm not takin' my rules from the Cowperwoods. Suppose they have a fine house, what of it? My house is my house. I want to live here. I've lived here too long to be pickin' up and movin' away. If you don't like it you know what else you can do. Move if you want to. I'll not move."

It was Butler's habit when he became involved in these family quarrels, which were as shallow as rain water, to wave his hands rather antagonistically under his wife's or his children's noses. He was doing it now to Aileen, quite forgetful of how bad-mannered and shocking it seemed to her.

"Oh, well, I will get out one of these days," she replied. "Thank heaven I won't have to live here always."

There flashed across her mind the beautiful reception-room, library, parlor, and boudoirs of the Cowperwoods, which were now being arranged preparatory to moving and about which Anna Cowperwood talked to her so much

—their dainty, lovely triangular grand piano in gold and painted pink-and-blue. Why couldn't they have things like that? Her father was unquestionably a dozen times as wealthy. But no, her father, whom she loved dearly, was of the old school. He was just what people charged him with being, a rough Irish contractor. He might be rich. She flared up a little at the injustice of things—why couldn't he have been rich and refined, too? Then they could have—but, oh, what was the use complaining? They would never get anywhere with her father and mother in charge. She would just have to wait. Marriage was the answer—the right marriage. But who was she to marry?

"You surely are not going to go on fighting about that now," pleaded Mrs. Butler, as strong and patient as fate itself. She knew where Aileen's trouble lay.

"But, anyhow, we might have the house done over," whispered Norah to her mother.

"Hush, now. In good time. Wait. We'll fix it all up some day, sure. You run to your lessons now. You've had enough."

Norah arose and left.

Aileen subsided. What was the use? Her father was simply stubborn and impossible. And yet he was nice, too.

"Come now," he said, after they had left the table, "play me somethin' on the piano, somethin' nice." He wanted showy, clattery things which exhibited his daughter's skill and muscular ability and left him wondering how she did it. That was what education was for—to enable her to play these very difficult things quickly and forcefully. The significance of it? Well, there wasn't any to him, and Aileen knew that also. Her taste was so much better. "And you can have a new piano any time you like. Go and see about it. This looks pretty good to me; but if you don't want it, all right."

Aileen squeezed his arm. What was the use of arguing

with her father? What good would a lone new piano do, when the whole house and the whole family atmosphere ought to be disposed of? But she played Schumann, Schubert, Offenbach, Chopin, and the old gentleman strolled to and fro and stared, smiling. There was real feeling and a thoughtful interpretation given to some of these things, for Aileen was not without sentiment, though she was so strong, vigorous, and withal so defiant; but it was all lost on him. He looked on her, his bright, healthy, enticingly beautiful daughter, and wondered what was going to become of her. Some rich man was going to marry her—some fine, rich young man with good business instincts—and he, her father, would leave her a lot of money.

CHAPTER XIX

THERE was a reception and a dance to be given to celebrate the opening of the two Cowperwood homes — the reception to be held in Frank Cowperwood's residence, and the dance later in the evening at Henry's, his father's. The Henry Cowperwood domicile, although it has not been described, was much more pretentious, the reception - room, parlor, music-room, and conservatory being in this case all on the ground floor and much larger. Ellsworth had arranged it so that those rooms, on occasion, could be thrown into one, leaving excellent space for promenade, auditorium, dancing—anything, in fact, that a large company might require. It had been the intention all along of the two men to use these houses jointly. There was, to begin with, a combination use of the various servants, the butler, gardener, laundress, and maids. Frank Cowperwood employed a governess for his children. The butler was really not a butler in the best sense. He was Henry Cowperwood's private servitor. But he could carve and preside, and he could be used in either house as occasion warranted. There was also a hostler and a coachman for the joint stable. When two carriages were required at once, both drove. It made a very agreeable and satis-factory working arrangement.

The preparation of this reception had been quite a matter of importance with the Cowperwoods, father and son, for it was necessary for financial reasons to make it as extensive as possible, and for social reasons as exclusive. The matter was rather neatly solved in this way, that the afternoon reception at Frank's house, with its natural overflow into Henry W.'s, was to be for all—the Tighes, Steners, Butlers, Mollenhauers, as well as the more select groups to which, for instance, belonged Arthur Rivers, Mrs. Seneca Davis, Mr. and Mrs. Trenor Drake, and some of the younger Drexels and Clarks, whom Frank had met. It was not likely that the latter would condescend, but cards had to be sent. Later in the evening the more purely social list was to be entertained, which included the friends of Anna, Mrs. Cowperwood, Edward, and Joseph, and any list which Frank might personally have in mind. This was to be *the* list. The best that could be persuaded, commanded, or influenced of the young and socially elect were to be invited here.

It was not possible not to invite the Butlers, parents and children, particularly the children, though the presence of the parents, if they should by any chance take it into their heads to stay, would be most unsatisfactory. Even Aileen and Norah were a little unsatisfactory to Anna Cowperwood and Mrs. Frank; and these two, when they were together supervising the list of invitations, often talked about it.

"She's so hoidenish," observed Anna, to her sister-in-law, when they came to the name of Aileen. "She thinks she knows so much, and she isn't a bit refined. Her father! Well, if I had her father I wouldn't talk so smart."

Mrs. Cowperwood, who was before her secretaire in her new boudoir, lifted her eyebrows.

"You know, Anna, I sometimes wish that Frank's business did not compel me to have to do with them. Mrs. Butler is such a bore. She means well enough, but she doesn't know anything. And Aileen is too rough. She's too forward, I think. She comes over here and plays upon the piano, particularly when Frank's here. I wouldn't mind so much for myself, but I know it must annoy him. All her pieces are so noisy. She never plays anything really delicate and refined."

"I don't like the way she dresses," observed Anna, sympathetically. "She gets herself up too conspicuously. Now, the other day I saw her out driving, and oh, dear! you should have seen her! She had on a crimson Zouave jacket heavily braided with black about the edges, and a turban with a huge crimson feather, and crimson ribbons reaching nearly to her waist. Imagine that kind of a hat to drive in. And her hands! You should have seen the way she held her hands—oh—just—so—self-consciously. They were curved just so"—and she showed how. "She had on yellow gauntlets, and she held the reins in one hand and the whip in the other. She fairly drives like mad when she drives, anyhow, and William, the footman, was up behind her. You should just have seen her look. Oh, dear! oh, dear! she does think she is so much!" And Anna giggled half in reproach, half in amusement.

"I suppose we'll have to invite her; I don't see how we can get out of it. I know just how she'll do, though. She'll walk about and pose and hold her nose up."

"Really, I don't see how she can," commented Anna. "Now, I like Norah. She's much nicer. She doesn't think she's so much."

"I like Norah, too," added Mrs. Cowperwood. "She's really very sweet, and to me she's prettier in a quiet way."

"Oh, much so. Oh, indeed, I think so, too."

It was curious, though, that it was Aileen who commanded nearly all their attention, held their thought, and fixed their minds on her so-called idiosyncrasies. It is true that all they said was in its peculiar way true; but in addition the girl was really beautiful and much above the average in intelligence and force. She was running high with a great ambition, and it was all the more conspicuous, and in a way irritating to some, because it reflected her own consciousness of her social defects, against which she was inwardly fighting. She resented the fact that people could justly consider her parents ineligible, and her also for that reason. To bedlam with them!

She was intrinsically as worth while as any one. Cowperwood, so able, and rapidly becoming so distinguished, seemed to realize it. He was nice to her, and liked to talk to her. Whenever he was at her house now, or she was at his and he was present, he managed somehow to say a word. He would come over quite near and look at her in a warm, friendly way.

"Well, Aileen,"—she could see his genial, significant eyes—"how is it with you? How are your father and mother? Been out driving? That's fine. I saw you to-day. You looked beautiful."

"Oh, Mr. Cowperwood!"

"You did. You looked stunning. A black riding-habit becomes you. I can tell your gold hair a long way off."

"Oh, now, you mustn't say that to me. You'll make me vain! My mother and father tell me I'm too vain as it is."

"Never mind your mother and father. I say you looked stunning, and you did. You always do."

"Oh!"

She almost gave a little gasp of delight. The color mounted to her cheeks and up to her temples. Mr. Cowperwood was the kind of man to know. He was so intensely forceful. His own quiet intensity matched her restless force. He was the one man whose force did seem to be equal to hers. He knew what good looks were. He knew what style was. No one else had ever told her this in the same forceful, dramatic way. It made her like him better; and yet, perhaps—she wasn't sure—perhaps he ought not to talk to her in that way. But oh! he was so strong and so successful to be so young. Her own forceful father had said—she had heard him say it more than once—that he was one of the most able young men he had ever met. A coming man!

On the night of the reception, then, among many others, and principally because she could not be reasonably eliminated, Aileen Butler and her sister were coming, and there had been much intermediate discussion of this fact. The Butlers, *mère* and *père*, had to be eliminated, and Cowperwood himself was quite well aware that it ought to be attended to. After his wife had asked him what he intended to do about it, or whether he thought they'd really come, he approached Aileen at the piano one evening in his own home. Norah and Anna were discussing things in general in the living-room before a grate-fire. Mrs. Cowperwood was teaching Frank Cowperwood, Jr., to spell beside the table lamp. Aileen was meditatively strumming in an effort to match a mood.

He leaned over her, watching her hands.

"Do your father and mother understand that the dance afterward is principally for young people?"

It was rather a hard thing to ask; but he dressed it out in a nonchalant air, and gave it with a sweetness that was full of real sympathy, consideration, and something more.

Aileen nodded her head. She knew what the point was. They did not want her father and mother; but neither did she, truly. She had been planning to obviate this all along. Still, if any one else save he had said it, if he had asked it in any other way than this, with much of appeal and much of sympathy and understanding thrown in, it would have been very different. But, as it was, she understood, and between them they understood. He wanted to help her, and she him.

"You have pretty hands," he said, softly.

She pursed her lips reproachfully.

"You mustn't tell me that."

He went away, not at all hurt, but because he was cautious. He was playing a subtle rôle, and it was dangerous. Still, this girl held him in spite of any of these difficulties which might intervene. Caution—plenty of it—and he might be as nice to her as he pleased.

This dance was coming—the very night, at last—and

with it a crowd of the smartest young people that the Cowperwoods had ever welcomed beneath their roof. Their lives were broadening. Cowperwood could feel that. In answer to the one hundred and fifty carefully chosen invitations one hundred and twenty-five, or thereabouts, had answered. Some of the really smart people, girls and boys, men and women, would be present. Arthur Rivers was coming with Mrs. Simmons, a noted beauty. The daughter of Henry Waterman and the two sons of George were to be on hand, notably good-looking children all, and of some social prestige. Mrs. Seneca Davis, Mrs. Schuyler Evans, Mr. and Mrs. Simeon Jones, Mary and Ethel Clark, Roberta and Alice Cadwalader, Henry and Dorothea Willing, of a minor branch of that family, and so on. There was some curiosity as to the quality and charm of the two houses the Cowperwoods had erected, and some interest as to the basis of their social pretensions. Who were the Cowperwoods, anyhow? It was recalled that several branches of this family were in excellent standing, and had been since the Revolution, though they had no money. Would they do? Mrs. Seneca Davis was charming; Henry W. Cowperwood was sufficiently conservative—being a bank president—and useful, too. This young Frank—well, people said he was a genius. He was likely to become very, very rich. A little early friendship would not do any harm. Young Ellsworth, who went about a great deal socially in the best circles, sang his praises to the skies. A great young man, if ever there was one—tactful, discriminating, grave, subtle, able. The world would surely hear of him. And he was rich already—much richer than his father.

So the rumor of this thing went, and it brought a throng.

But to deal with the reception itself—the actual event. During the afternoon there was a stream of people—the carriages of the Butlers, the Mollenhauers, the Simpsons, the Davises, the Watermans—all after four o'clock, and Henry W. and Frank were in the reception-room of

Frank's house, which gave off into the dining-room. There
were wine, cigars, liqueurs for the gentlemen; flowers,
sweets, cake and tea, sandwiches, and salad for the ladies,
or for both ladies and gentlemen, as the case might be.
There was music. There were many, very many introductions. There were tactful descriptions of little
effects Mr. Ellsworth had achieved under rather trying
circumstances; walks under the pergola; viewings of
Mr. Cowperwood's home; introductions of Mrs. Cowperwood, Sr., Mrs. Cowperwood, Jr., Anna, and the boys.
Many of the guests were old friends. They gathered in
the libraries and dining-rooms and talked. There was
much jesting, some slapping of shoulders, some good
story-telling, and so the afternoon waned into evening,
and they went away. The Cowperwoods dined hastily
alone between seven and eight.

At nine the evening guests began to arrive, and now
the throng was of a different complexion. There were
young people—many of them handsome, well-bred, spick-
and-span youths in evening dress, their necks and cheeks
powdered above their white collars and ties, their feet
incased in soft, black leather, their hair parted to a
nicety. They threw their coats and hats to servitors and
strolled idly about, seeming scarcely to note the newness
and elegance of all things, though they did. Outside in
the cold—for it was late fall—the carriage doors were
slamming, and new guests were arriving constantly.
Mrs. Lillian Cowperwood stood with her husband and
Anna in the main entrance to the reception-room, while
Joseph and Edward Cowperwood and Mr. and Mrs.
Henry W. Cowperwood lingered in the background.
Mrs. Lillian Cowperwood looked charming in a train
gown of old rose, with a low, square neck and bell sleeves,
showing a delicate chemisette of fine lace. Her beauty
of figure still was a notable thing, though her face was
not as smoothly sweet as it had been years before when
Cowperwood had first met her. Anna Cowperwood was

not so pretty, though she could not be said to be homely. She was small and dark, with a turned-up nose, snapping black eyes, a pert, inquisitive, intelligent, and, alas, somewhat critical air. She had considerable tact in the matter of dressing, and knew the few things that became her very well. Black, in spite of her darkness, with shining beads or sequins on it, helped her complexion greatly, as did a red rose in her hair. She had smooth, white, well-rounded arms and shoulders, so these were used to their full advantage. Bright eyes, a pert manner, clever remarks—these assisted to create an illusion of charm, though, as she often said, it was all of little use. "The men want the dolly things."

Aileen Butler was anything but the "dolly" type. She had been here once before during the afternoon with her father and mother, Callum and Norah—for Owen could not come—and she had created an impression in a street costume of dark-blue silk with velvet pelisse to match, and trimmed only with elaborate pleatings and shirrings of the same materials. A toque of blue velvet, with high crown and one large dark-red imitation orchid, had given her a jaunty, dashing air. Beneath the toque her red-gold hair was arranged in an enormous chignon, with one long curl escaping over her collar. She was not exactly as daring as she seemed; but she loved to give the impression of it.

"The bold thing," Anna had commented. "Just as I thought."

"You look stunning," Cowperwood said, as she passed.

"I'll look different to-night," was her only answer.

"Tst! Tst! Tst!" Mrs. Lillian Cowperwood had commented to herself. "Well, they had better look after her."

She had swung with a slight, swaggering stride into the dining-room and disappeared. Norah and her mother stayed to chatter.

"Well, it's lovely now, isn't it?" breathed Mrs. Butler. "It's charming, altogether. Sure you'll be happy here.

Sure you will. When Eddie fixed the house we're in now, says I, 'Eddie, it's almost too fine for us altogether—surely it is,' and says 'e, 'Norah, nothin' this side o' heavin or beyond is too good for ye'—and he kissed me. Now what d'ye think of that fer a big, hulkin' gossoon?"

"It's perfectly lovely, I think, Mrs. Butler," commented Mrs. Cowperwood, a little bit nervous because of others.

"Mama does love to talk so. Come on, mama. Let's look at the dining-room." It was Norah talking.

"Well, may ye always be happy in it. I wish ye that. I've always been happy in mine. May ye always be happy." And Mrs. Butler waddled good-naturedly along.

But in this later inpouring throng of young men and women—girls in mauve and cream-white and salmon-pink and silver-gray, laying aside lace shawls and loose dolmans, a form of opera cape, the men in smooth black helping them—came Aileen and Norah, without their father and mother. Mrs. Cowperwood and Anna and the Henry Cowperwoods and Frank had been inestimably pleased by the showing they were making. Frank, particularly, was charmed; for in this fair-spoken, tastefully garbed company, which was passing in review before him, he saw a reflection, the first dawning rays of the sun of his prosperity striking against life. It was true that he had been prospering financially before this; but it was only as a tree prospers whose roots are working in the dark, gathering force for the leaves and blossoms overhead. That fine tint of the May-time in leaf and bud—this was it. In a way this was what force and constructive ability were for—to blossom forth in material splendor. To be sure, this was not much material splendor, perhaps one hundred and fifty thousand dollars all told for him and his father; but it was something, a beginning. It might, probably would, lead to other things. These people could be useful to him, some of them. They would spread his repute—Ellsworth here, whom he was clasping hands with, and Traynor Fox, now bowing to him. Suddenly, as he thought, out of the cold, where gusty winds were and the flicker of gas-lamps, came Aileen and Norah, the former throwing off a thin net veil of black lace and a dolman of black silk, which her brother Owen was taking. Callum was with Norah, a straight, erect, smiling young Irishman who looked as though he might carve a notable career for himself. Norah was in a short, girlish dress that came to a little below her shoe-tops, a pale-figured lavender-and-white silk, with a fluffy hoop-skirt of dainty lace-edged ruffles, against which tiny bows of lavender stood out in odd places. There was a great sash of lavender about her waist, and in her hair a rosette of the same material. She had an incurving nose, small and sweet, and looked exceedingly girlish and winsome—quite eager and bright-eyed. Cowperwood thought of her heavy, stolid father and mother. How much of their primary unworkable clay was in her?

But behind her was her sister in ravishing black satin, scaled as a fish with glistening crimsoned-silver sequins, her round, smooth arms bare to the shoulders, her corsage cut as low in the front and back as her daring, in relation to her sense of the proprieties, permitted. She was naturally of exquisite figure—Diana-formed, erect, full-breasted, with somewhat more than gently swelling hips; which, nevertheless, sunk away in lovely, harmonious lines; and this low-cut corsage, receding back and front into a deep V, above a short, gracefully draped overskirt of black tulle and silver tissue, set her off to perfection. It was only the intense vigor of her personality which seemed to emphasize, and, in a way, over-emphasize the significance of all her lines and features. Her full, smooth, roundly modeled neck was enhanced in its cream-pink whiteness by an inch-wide necklet of black jet cut in many faceted black squares. Her complexion, naturally high in tone because of the pink of health, was enhanced by the tiniest speck of black court-plaster laid upon her cheek-

8

bone; and her hair, heightened in its reddish-gold by her dress, was fluffed loosely and adroitly about the eyes. The main mass of this treasure was done in two loose, massy braids caught up in a black spangled net at the back of her neck; and her eyebrows had been emphasized by a pencil into something almost as significant as her hair. She was, for the occasion, a little too emphatic, perhaps, and yet more because of her burning vitality than of her costume. Art for her should have meant subduing her physical and spiritual significance. Life for her meant emphasizing them.

"Lillian!" Anna nudged her sister-in-law. She was grieved to think that Aileen was wearing black and looked so much better.

"I see," Lillian replied, in a subdued tone.

"So you're back again." She was addressing Aileen. "It's chilly out, isn't it?"

"I don't mind. Don't the rooms look lovely, now?"

She was gazing at the softly lighted chambers and the throng before her.

Norah began to babble to Anna. "You know, I just thought I never would get this old thing on." She was speaking of her dress. "Aileen wouldn't help me—the mean thing!"

Aileen had swept on to Cowperwood and his mother, who was near him. She had removed the black satin ribbon which held her train from her arm, and kicked the skirts loose and free. Her eyes gleamed almost pleadingly for all her hauteur, like a spirited collie's, and her even teeth showed beautifully.

Cowperwood understood her precisely, as he did any fine, spirited animal. His wife, his mother, many people would not know how to take her at all.

"I can't tell you how nice you look," he whispered to her, familiarly, as though there were an old understanding between them. "You're like fire and a song."

He did not know why he said this. He was not especially poetic, he imagined. He had not formulated the phrase beforehand. Since his first glimpse of her in the hall his feelings and ideas had been leaping and plunging like spirited horses. And in the grip of his super-self were the reins of control checking them. This girl made him set his teeth and narrow his eyes. He involuntarily squared himself, looking more defiant, forceful, efficient as she drew near. His equivocal smile, the best phase of it, so useful in his commercial and social relations with men, was on his lips. He drew a deep, essential breath.

"Oh, how nice!" she answered, tossing her head; but she, too, was excited. Because he was so, she was, and she knew it.

"We thought we'd walk over once," she explained to his mother, who was close by. "It's so near."

"I'm afraid you have caught cold, my dear," replied Mrs. Henry W. "It's quite chilly out to-night."

She was wondering what the other guests would think of Aileen, she was so—well, so over-impressive. Cowperwood was thinking so, also; but a radiant, fulsome blonde, Mrs. Martyn Walker, in snowy silk and bursting from her corsets, confronted him, a red rose in her flaxen hair, and he said to himself she would do as a foil. Would there were many more.

Aileen and Norah were surrounded shortly by young men to be introduced, and to write their names on their dance-cards, and for the time being she was lost to view.

CHAPTER XX

THE subtle, metaphysical seeds of change are rooted deeply. From the first mention of the dance by Mrs. Cowperwood and Anna, with the light description of the surroundings which were to attend it, Aileen had been conscious of an effective presentation of herself which would transpire as a result—a better presentation to a more distinguished group of people than she as yet, for all her father's money, had been able to achieve.

The difference between the Cowperwood standard of life and that of her parents was obvious. There was less money to be charged to the former's credit in the practical American way; but there was so much more of what one might call freedom of thought, art understanding, social, and even financial possibility and probability than was inherent in her own family group and circle. Frank Cowperwood was so dynamic. He was the Cowperwood family to her—father, mother, wife, sister, brothers, children, and all. He was never in the foreground—appeared always to shun the conspicuous position, and yet where he was there was the position. No one else in all this group counted in her incisive intuitions. Her family was Catholic, and went to mass on Sundays in the family conveyance—a handsome carryall—but the Catholic religion was a curious and mystical thing to her. She had learned a great deal at home and at her convent school about the theory and forms of its ritual; but she could not understand them.

"Who gave St. Peter the power to forgive sins?" she once asked her father, when she was a little girl of ten; and he had answered, promptly, "Jesus Christ."

"Thou art Peter," he quoted, for he was fairly well up on Church dogma, and accepted it literally, "and upon this rock I will build my church, and the gates of hell shall not prevail against it. And I will give unto thee the keys of the kingdom of heaven, and whatsoever thou shalt bind on earth shall be bound in heaven; and whatsoever thou shalt loose on earth shall be loosed in heaven."

This was a most significant point with Catholics, apt to be assailed by non-Catholics, and he knew the exact phraseology, for he had read it often and heard it pronounced from the pulpit.

"What is the rock?" she asked, not connecting the apostle with the spiritual significance of his name.

"Peter is the rock. The Church is built on him. There now, be off with you." Mr. Butler was busy thinking of something else at the time.

She had gone away; but it was with a vague idea of a tomb or grave in which Peter was lying, and over which was built a material church not unlike their own, St. Timothy's. It had never become any clearer, to speak of, for as she grew older she paid less and less attention to it.

St. Timothy's and the convent school at Germantown, where she was educated, were peculiar institutions to her. She had been taken to the church, year in and year out, until she was twelve, and then she had been packed off to the quiet retreat of the Sisters of the Holy Childhood, at St. Agatha's, and there she stayed, barring periodic visits to her home, until she was seventeen. The church, with its tall, dimly radiant windows, its high, white altar, its figures of St. Joseph on one side and St. Mary on the other, clothed in golden-starred robes of blue, and wearing halos or carrying scepters, had impressed her greatly. The church as a whole—any Catholic church —was beautiful to look at—soothing. The altar, during high mass, lit with a half-hundred candles or more, and dignified and made impressive by the rich, lacy vestments of the priests and the acolytes, the impressive needle-work and gorgeous colorings of the amice, chasuble, cope, stole, and maniple, took her fancy and held her eye. Let us say there was always lurking in her a sense of grandeur coupled with a love of color and a love of love. From the first she was somewhat sex-conscious. She had no desire for accuracy—those so organized rarely do—no desire for precise information. Innate sensuousness rarely has. It basks in sunshine, bathes in color, dwells in a sense of the impressive and the gorgeous, and rests there. Activity is not necessary except in the case of aggressive, acquisitive natures when it manifests itself as a desire to seize. Sensuousness can be so manifested in the most active dispositions, and apparently only in such.

There is need of guarding such statements in their application to Aileen. It would hardly do to speak of her nature as being definitely sensual at this time. It was too rudimentary. Any harvest is of long gathering. The confessional, dim on Friday and Saturday nights, when the church was lighted but by few lamps, and the priest's warnings, penances, and ecclesiastical forgiveness whispered through narrow lattices, moved her as something subtly pleasing. She was not afraid of her sins. Hell, so definitely set forth, did not frighten her. Really, it had not laid hold on her conscience. The old women and men hobbling into church, bowed in prayer, murmuring over their beads, were objects of curious interest like the wood-carvings in the peculiar array of wood-reliefs emphasizing the stations of the Cross. She herself liked to confess, particularly when she was fourteen and fifteen, and to listen to the priest's voice as he admonished her with, "Now, my dear child." A particularly old priest, a French father, who came to hear their confessions at St. Agatha's, interested her as being kind and sweet. He was old and bent, with a narrow, sallow face and large, kindly eyes. They were sad, and she felt sorry for him—a little—because he was old and the sunshine of life could mean little to him. His forgiveness and blessing seemed sincere—better than her prayers which she went through perfunctorily. And then there was a young priest at St. Timothy's, Father David, hale and rosy, with a curl of black hair over his forehead, and an almost jaunty way of wearing his priestly hat, who came down the aisle Sundays sprinkling holy water with a definite, distinguished sweep of the hand, while the acolytes held back the sleeves of his amice. It would not be fair to say that it was more than the idle, wandering moods of a girl with which this particular priest had nothing to do. He was quite unconscious of her. She did not always think of him as an impersonal figure. There were moments when she looked upon him as she looked upon herself, as some one who must be young, eager, full of life, and she was not willing to accept that he had been set apart, and to think that he could never marry. She looked at him at times quite appealingly, but he was religious and sealed to his vows.

At St. Agatha's she was rather a difficult person to deal with. She was, as the good sisters of the school readily perceived, too full of life, too active, to be easily controlled. "That Miss Butler," observed Sister Constantia, the Mother Superior, to Sister Sempronia, Aileen's immediate mentor, "is a very spirited girl. You may have a great deal of trouble with her unless you use a good deal of tact. You may have to coax her with little gifts. You will get on better." So Sister Sempronia sought to find what Aileen was most interested in, and bribe her therewith. Being intensely conscious of her father's competence, and vain of her personal superiority, it was not so easy to do. She wanted to go home occasionally, though; she wanted to be allowed to wear the sister's rosary of large beads with its pendent cross of ebony and its silver Christ, and this was held up as a great privilege. For keeping quiet in class, walking softly, and speaking softly—as much as it was in her to do—for not stealing into other girls' rooms after lights were out, and for abandoning *crushes* on this and that sympathetic sister, these awards and others, such as walking out in the grounds on Saturday afternoons, being allowed to have all the flowers she wanted, some extra dresses, jewels, etc., were offered. She liked music and the idea of painting, though she could not paint; and books, novels, interested her, but she could not get them. The rest— grammar, spelling, sewing, church and general history— she loathed them. Deportment—well, there was something in that. She liked the rather exaggerated courtesies they taught her, and she often reflected on how she would use them when she reached home.

When she came out into life the little social distinctions which have been indicated began to impress themselves on her, and she wished sincerely that her father would build a better home—a mansion—such as those she could see elsewhere, and launch her properly in society. Failing in that, she could think of nothing save clothes, jewels, riding-horses, carriages, and the appropriate changes of costume which were allowed her for these. Her family could not entertain in any distinguished way where they were, and so already, at nineteen, she was beginning to feel the sting of a blighted ambition. She was eager for life. How was she to get it?

Her room was a study in the foibles of an eager and ambitious mind. It was full of clothes, beautiful things for all occasions, which she had small opportunity to wear. Her shoes, stockings, lingerie, laces, rings, and pins were legion. She had a dozen necklaces. In a crude way she had made a study of perfumes and cosmetics, though she needed the latter not at all, and these were present in abundance. She was not very orderly, rather the other way about, and she loved lavishness of display; and so her curtains, hangings, table ornaments, and pictures inclined to gorgeousness, which did not go well with the rest of the house. One might have said she was giving early evidences of a sybaritic temperament; but time and opportunity might have corrected many things.

This approaching occasion of the Cowperwood ball had foreshadowed something better than she had known socially, and it gave her a sense of possible rivalry with girls of equal or better station whom she had never seen. She was conscious there would be a number of strange young men there, dandies of the class she had, in a way, been dreaming of, young men of sufficient refinement and force and station to suit her ideas of a matrimonial possibility; but since she had been meditating these things Cowperwood had appeared as something more definite in her mind than he had been before, and to save herself she could not get him out of her consciousness. The things that he said and did interested her; the fact that his wife was older and not so fascinatingly good-looking was a point well taken. His commercial connections with her father; his handsome bank building, which she had noticed in Third Street; his new house, executed with so much taste by Mr. Ellsworth, stayed with her as impressive facts. She could recall, and did often without knowing why, his peculiarities of manner—a certain rigidity of eye, a certain elasticity of step, a lightness of curl to his hair; and he was growing a mustache. It became him, a fine, dark, bristly mustache. He was always so definite. He said exactly what he meant, and his soft, low, even voice had a sting in it. She could tell where he was in the room without looking for him or hearing him.

To-night, when she was dressing in her boudoir, a vision of him had come to her. She had dressed in a way for him. She was never forgetful of the times he had looked at her in an interested way, the times he had said directly and forcefully that she looked "stunning" or "beautiful." He had commented on her hands once. To-day, when she had worn her rather subdued street costume, he had said that she looked "stunning," and she had thought how easy it would be to impress him to-night—to show him how truly beautiful she was, how *really stunning* she could look. Why? He was a married man! She had no idea that he was going to desert his good-looking wife and his beautiful home and take up with her—marry her—and that was what any interest like this should normally mean. She really had no business to be dressing for him; but there was, nevertheless, little thought of the other young men, some of them decidedly eligible, who were sure to be there. She stood before her mirror between eight and nine—it was nine-fifteen before she was really ready—and pondered over what she would wear. The matter of the selection of a gown did not come up immediately, for there was undressing and underdressing to do, and in the selection of stockings, shoes, lingerie, and a corset she was oddly finicky. There were two tall pier mirrors in her wardrobe—an unduly large piece of furniture—and one in her closet door. She stood before the latter looking at her bare arms and shoulders, her shapely figure, thinking of the prettiness of her smooth black-silk-stockinged legs, of the fact that her left shoulder had a dimple, and that she had selected garnet garters garnished with heart-shaped silver buckles. She had discovered them in one of the jewelry stores recently and purchased them. The corset could not be made quite tight enough at first, and she chided her maid, Kathleen Kelly. It was at this time she was studying how to fix her hair, and there was much ado about that before it was finally adjusted. Before her mirror she penciled her eyebrows and plucked at her hair about her forehead to make it loose and shadowy. She cut the black court-plaster with her nail-shears, and tried different-sized pieces in different places. Finally she found one size and one place that suited her. She turned her head from side to side, looking at the combined effect of her hair, her penciled brows, her dimpled shoulder, and the black beauty-spot. She stood up straight in all her proud beauty and admired herself. If some one man could see her as she was now, some time. Which man? That thought scurried back like a frightened rat into its hole. She was, for all her strength, afraid of the thought of the one—the very deadly—*the* man.

And then she came to the matter of a train-gown. Kathleen laid out five, for Aileen had come into the joy and honor of these things recently, and she had, with the permission of her mother and father, indulged herself to the full. She studied a golden-yellow silk, with cream-lace shoulder-braces, and some gussets of garnet beads in the train that shimmered delightfully, but set it aside. She took and considered favorably a black-and-white striped silk of odd gray effect, and, though she was sorely tempted to wear it, finally let it go. There was a maroon dress, with basque and overskirt over white silk; a rich cream-colored satin; and then this black sequined gown, which she finally chose. She tried on the cream-colored satin first, however, being in much doubt about it; but her penciled eyes and beauty-spot did not seem to endure it very well. Then she put on the black silk with its glistening crimsoned-silver sequins, and, lo, it touched her. She liked its coquettish drapery of tulle and silver about the hips. The "overskirt," in all its varying forms, was at that time just coming into fashion, and was avoided by the more conservative; but Aileen had adopted it at once with enthusiasm. She thrilled a little at the rustle of this black dress, and thrust her chin and nose forward to make it set right, and had it undone after it was buttoned to have Kathleen tighten her corsets the more; and then when she was buttoned again, she gathered the train over her arm by its train-band and looked again. Something was wanting. Oh yes, her neck! What to wear—red coral? It did not look right. A string of pearls? She had a beautiful necklace. It would not do. There was a necklace made of small cameos set in silver which her mother had purchased, and another of diamonds which belonged to her mother; but they were not right. Finally her jet necklet, which she did not value very highly, came into her mind, and, oh, how it looked! How soft and smooth and glistening her chin looked above it. She caressed her neck affectionately, called for her black-lace mantilla, her long black-silk dolman lined with red, and she was ready.

"Oh, Aileen, aren't you ever coming?" had sounded a dozen times on the stairs. It was Norah's complaining but sisterly and affectionate voice.

"Aileen!"

That was her father.

"Aren't youse soon ready, now?"

That was the affectionate voice of her dear, darling mother, who wanted to get her off in reasonable time.

"Yes, I'm coming now," she finally declared, and she swept out.

The ball-room, as she entered, was lovely enough. The young men and women she saw there were interesting; and, being so much of a gorgeous picture, she was not wanting for admirers. Stalwart youths craved introductions of her brothers, or of those who had been introduced, and she was permitted to nod smilingly to many girls of her own age and women older than herself, to whom she was led by charmed brothers and somewhat too eager sons. The most aggressive and liberal of these youths— the most forceful in their opinions—recognized in this maiden a fillip to life, a sting to existence. She was rather as a honey-jar surrounded by too hungry flies.

"Oh, are all your dances gone? No? Then you won't mind giving me one."

They showed even, ingratiating teeth and smiling eyes. It had not been known that Edward Butler's daughter was so charming. And he was rich and powerful, too.

But it occurred to her, as her dance-list was filling up, that there was not much left for, say, Mr. Cowperwood, if he should care to dance with her at all. He had not come near her as yet. She had not seen him since she left the reception-room. He was probably there, and he might not want to dance at all.

"Have you a spare dance left?"

It was a shining cavalier in immaculate linen—Mr. Arthur Rivers, no less—who was asking.

"I'm sorry." Her head was up, her eyes level. "They are all gone." It was a lie. There were three left; and he was so nice, too.

With ruthless, instinctive artifice it occurred to her that she could claim confusion and misunderstanding as to numbers if it came to—if it came to the necessity of making a place for any one at any time. Where was he, anyhow?

"Won't you take me to see the flowers?" she asked ingratiatingly of a lad who was near her. "I haven't seen them yet."

"Why, certainly. I'm charmed." And off they strutted.

Cowperwood was meditating, as he received the last of the guests, how subtle this matter of sex arrangement in life really was. He was not at all sure that there was any law governing the matter. By comparison now with Aileen Butler, his wife looked rather dull, quite too old; and when he was ten years older she would look very much older.

"Oh yes, Ellsworth has made quite an attractive arrangement out of these two houses—better than we ever thought he could do." He was talking to Henry Hale Sanderson, a young banker of considerable promise, who had strolled up. "He had the advantage of combining two into one, and I think he's done more with my little one, considering the limitations of space, than he has with this big one. Father's has the advantage of size. I tell the old gentleman he's simply built a lean-to for me."

He smiled as he thought of his father's good-nature, in so far as he was concerned.

"I like the way he harmonized and connected these rooms. George, I do! Clever chap, that. Is he here?"

"He's somewhere around here, I think. Do you know him?"

"Surely."

"Then you'll meet him."

But this matter of building oneself up. It forced itself inconsequently but persistently upon Cowperwood as the flattering crowd filed past. There was a curious circumstance about it. Prejudice had so much to do with it. Prejudice? Life, so far as he could make out, was woven of mistaken ideas. Religion certainly was one. How plain it was that people with religious notions were not necessarily in accord with high religious ideas! And commercial honor! Write in its place commercial necessity, and you had the warp and woof of its fabric. Men defended their children—the honor of them; but the children cared nothing for the defenses as a rule, had to be constrained in order that they might observe them. He himself was a very excellent example. He had two children. It would be quite the same with them. And then take all of those who might have been good but couldn't—

"Yes, yes, indeed, it's lovely. We're very pleased. I'm certainly glad to see you here."

Yes, there were thousands who never had any chance at all. On 'change it was live and let live only, up to the point where self-interest began. Then— And in the banking and commercial world. God, what a struggle! The fights! The cries of the sinking! Strength was the thing. A strong, tactful man could do anything if he could scheme it out well enough beforehand; but one had to plan subtly, very subtly. There was so much danger, so much rank accident; and then what was it Burns said? "The best laid schemes o' mice an' men gang aft a-gley." Surely, surely.

"Oh, I say, Rivers. Have you seen De Morgan? He wants to see you. I'm going in now. Quite a crowd, isn't it?"

Anna and Mrs. Cowperwood had gone somewhere long before. His father and a number of his old cronies were over in the dining-room of his house, glad to get away from the crowd. He would have to stay, and, besides, he wanted to. Had he better dance with Aileen? Mrs. Cowperwood would dance, once probably, anyhow. She cared little for it. And Anna—to be sure. He would have to dance with Anna. There was Mrs. Seneca Davis smiling at him and Aileen. George, how wonderful! What a girl! She was smiling at him now.

"I suppose your dance-list is full to overflowing. Let me see." He was standing before her, and she was holding out the little blue-bordered, gold-monogrammed booklet. An orchestra of stringed instruments was playing a serenade in the music-room. The dance would begin shortly. There was plenitude of delicately constructed, gold-tinted chairs about the walls and behind the palms.

He looked down into her eyes—those excited, life-loving, eager eyes.

"You're quite full up. Let me see. Nine, ten, eleven. Well, that will be well enough. I don't suppose I shall want to dance very much. It's nice to be popular."

"I'm not so sure about number three. I think that's a mistake. You might have that if you wish."

She was falsifying. Her arms were beautiful. That little beauty-spot! And the dimple! He could see it.

"It doesn't matter so much about him, does it?"

His cheeks flushed a little.

"No."

Her own flamed.

"Well, I'll see where you are when it's called. You look so lovely I'm afraid of you."

He shot a level, interested glance at her, then at Mrs. Davis, who was walking near—then left her. Aileen's bosom heaved. It was almost hard to breathe sometimes in this warm air.

CHAPTER XXI

MRS. COWPERWOOD had passed the time of pleasure in dancing. It never had been more than a mild exhilaration—that left-over suggestion of ancient sensuous emotion. She had always been too phlegmatic and conservative in her feelings—her movements in it were not particularly graceful—and since the two children had come she was less inclined than ever to, as she would have phrased it, "waste her time in that." Mrs. Cowperwood, although she had yielded to the strong magnetic attraction of Cowperwood at twenty-one—it could not be called "fiery impetuosity"—might well be described as a natural conservator of public morals. Many women have this, what might be called duality of temperament—the cold purity of the snow-drift in so far as the world may see, combined with at times the murky flame of the wanton. They are ashamed of their humanity, however—ashamed of the passions that at times sweep in and dominate them. Cowperwood had been aware of this subtle duality in his wife's temperament. It had irritated him as it would almost always irritate any strong, acquisitive, direct-seeing temperament gifted with a scientific and at the same time a philosophic point of view. He objected to seeing life being shadowed at its meridian. Not that he wished her to let the whole world know what she thought. He had no keen desire to let the world in on his own private reflections —quite the contrary. But this was a matter the most intimate between him and her. In love, where the farthest reaches of emotion and revelation prevail, why should there be concealment, or, if not quite that, at least mental evasion of a fact which physically she subscribed to? Why do one thing and think another? The religionist will call Cowperwood's attitude evil; the cowardly life lover, hiding behind the bulwarks of convention, like a clam shut in its shell, will say that he was too brutal—too unnecessarily frank. Cowperwood merely noticed the fact of his wife's attitude as a sign of mental weakness—of a spirit too frail to front the truths of life. When he was younger—when he had first married her—there had been a kind of charm in her shyness and her unwillingness or inability to see life as it was; but, now that he was growing into deeper and sterner things, it seemed anything but worth while. Compulsion to face hard, brutal facts had made him at times long for a wife who would face them with him. Why was it that so often he could not tell her the things that he thought, that he felt he could tell Aileen, for instance? He was not afraid to do so, yet he did not. Not so much for his sake as for hers. He hated to lacerate that shell of belief with which she clothed the world. She covered it over, as it were, with a soft-tinted seeming, woven of her own ideas solely, like an oyster pearling its hard and chalky home.

But the necessity of dancing at least two or three times this evening was quite obvious, and Lillian led the cotillon, which was the opening feature, with her husband. Later she danced once with Arthur Rivers, who was an old family acquaintance by now, and once with a younger friend of Cowperwood's, Shelley Brooks. Ellsworth asked her to dance, but she felt tired and a little bored, and asked to be excused. While she and Cowperwood were dancing he noticed the languid manner in which she laid her arm on his.

"You don't care for this much, do you?" he observed.

"Not at all. I never did. I'm a little tired to-night, anyhow."

He had observed how she had shirked her music of

late years—really given it up—and how she strolled about as a rule in a meditative dream. He felt no such indifference to life. As a matter of fact, it was just beginning to take on real significance to him. Because of his money-making proclivities, and his success therein, he was just beginning to feel that sense of freedom which the possession of ample capital conveys. Some natures, the weaker ones, attain this sense of freedom with the possession of a very little money—it depends on their understanding of life. Those with larger ambitions and perceptions require a great deal. Your money-genius knows no sense of wealth as it is ordinarily understood. His total perception is of power—the more world-wide the better. Cowperwood was in his way a money-genius in embryo. He did not recognize his own possibilities. His thought was that he might get to be worth a million, and that when he did he would retire. Curiously, thirty-five was the age at which he fancied he might be worth that sum if nothing happened. He was progressing rapidly. The other day, in an idle mood, he had tabulated his assets and liabilities. He balanced the former at five hundred thousand dollars, and the latter at three hundred thousand dollars, which left him two hundred thousand dollars clear almost, at a forced sale. If he had time to liquidate slowly, which as a shrewd business man he never expected to have, he would come out much better. And this next year—this next year—surely it would yield him one hundred thousand dollars more. With each additional dollar stored up he had greater realizing facilities—larger ability to take advantage of larger opportunities. When he was thirty-five—yes, in six years from now—he might well be worth a million, and then he could buy a yacht and build himself a large mansion and travel and see the world. The world! The world! It called alluringly to Frank Cowperwood. Back of that solid, corrective brain, which stood like a mailed knight at the drawbridge of his fortune, was a vague,

cloudy realm of beauty as sensuous as a summer land-
scape, as alluring as a tinted sea. He often thought,
when he was through fighting what would he do? Where
would he live? With whom would he dwell? Mrs.
Cowperwood? He was not so very sure of that. The
world was very wide and very strange and very beautiful. He would wait and see. He would work and see.

While he was dancing, first with Mrs. Cowperwood,
and later with Mrs. Seneca Davis, and still later with Mrs.
Martyn Walker, he had occasion to look at Aileen often;
and each time that he did so there swept over him a sense
of great vigor there, a content of raw, dynamic energy,
which came upon him with great force. She was beautiful, this girl, in spite of his wife's repeated derogatory
comments; and he felt also that she was nearer to his
clear, aggressive, unblinking attitude than any one whom
he had yet seen in the form of woman. She was unsophisticated, in a way, that was plain; and yet in another
way it would take so little to make her understand so
much. Largeness was the sense he had of her—not
physically, though she was nearly as tall as himself, but
emotionally. She seemed so intensely alive. Now, as
he watched her whirling about, running backward at times
as her partner ran forward after her, the clean, clicking
strength of a blooded horse was all that he could think
of. Her arms were so beautiful, undulating through
endless motions; and her neck—how the movements of
her head set it off! She passed close to him a number of
times, her eyes wide and smiling, her lips parted, her teeth
agleam; and he felt a stirring of sympathy and companionship for her which he had not previously experienced.
She was lovely, all of her—delightful.

"I'm wondering if that dance is open now?" he said to
her, as he drew near toward the beginning of the third
set. She was seated with her last admirer in a far corner
of the general living-room, a clear floor now waxed to
perfection. A few palms here and there made em-

brasured parapets of green. "I hope you'll excuse me," he added, in a deferential way, to her companion.

"Surely," the latter, a young blood, replied, rising.

"Yes, indeed," she replied. "And you'd better stay here with me. It's going to begin soon. You won't mind," she added, to her companion, giving him a radiant smile.

"Not at all. I've had a lovely waltz." He strolled off.

Cowperwood sat down. "That's young Ledoux, isn't it? I thought so. I saw you dancing. You like it, don't you?"

"I'm crazy about it."

"Well, I can't say that myself. It's fascinating, though. Your partner makes such a difference. Mrs. Cowperwood doesn't care as much as I do."

His mention of Mrs. Cowperwood made her think of Lillian in a faintly derogatory way for the moment. She did not exactly like her, and yet she called here and had at the other house, because it had always, somehow, seemed a worth-while thing to do. Mrs. Cowperwood had always been nice to her, largely because of Cowperwood's connection with her father, and Frank had been especially genial. She had been able to talk a good deal of herself and her affairs, and Lillian had always listened genially and placidly. Now, though—well—

"I think you dance very well."

"I watched you, too."

"Oh, did you?"

"Yes."

He was a little keyed up because of her—slightly cloudy in his thoughts, because she was generating a problem in his life, or would if he would let her; and so his talk was a little tame. He was thinking of something to say —some word which would bring them a little nearer together. But for the moment he could not think of it. Truth to tell, he wanted to say a great deal.

"Well, that was nice of you," he added, after a moment. "What made you do it?"

He turned with a mock air of inquiry. The music was sounding. The dancers were rising. He arose.

He had not intended to give this particular remark a serious turn; but, now that she was so near him, he looked into her eyes steadily but with a soft appeal and said, "Yes, why?"

They had come out from behind the palms. He had put his hand to her waist. His right arm held her left extended arm to arm, palm to palm. Her right hand was on his shoulder, and she was close to him, looking into his eyes. As they began the gay undulations of the waltz she looked away and then down without answering. She put a strange force into her movements, which were as light and airy as those of a butterfly. He felt a sudden lightness himself, communicated as by an invisible current. He wanted to match the suppleness of her body with his own, and did. Her arms, the flash and glint of the crimson sequins against the smooth, black silk of her closely fitting dress, her neck, her glowing, radiant hair, all combined to provoke a slight intellectual intoxication. She was so vigorously young, so, to him, truly beautiful.

"But you didn't answer," he continued.

"Isn't that lovely music?" she said.

He pressed her fingers.

She lifted shy eyes to him, for, in spite of her gay, aggressive force, she was a little afraid of him. His personality was obviously so superior. Now that he was so close to her, dancing, she conceived of him as something quite wonderful, and yet she experienced a nervous reaction—a momentary desire to run away.

"Very well, if you won't tell me," he smiled, mockingly.

He thought she wanted him to talk to her so, to tease her with suggestions of this concealed feeling of his—this strong liking. He wondered if he could love her if he wanted to. There was his wife, his two children. What could come of any such an understanding as this, anyhow?

"Oh, I just wanted to see how you danced," she said, tamely, the force of her original feeling having been weakened by a thought of what she was doing. He noted the change and smiled; it gave him pause for the moment, but a few seconds later the same exalted mood had returned. It was a lovely thing to be dancing with her. He had not thought mere dancing could hold such charm.

"You like me?" he said, suddenly, as the music drew to its close.

She thrilled from head to toe at the phrase. A piece of ice dropped down her back could not have startled her more. It was apparently tactless, and yet it was anything but tactless. It was well within the range of his subtle understanding. She looked up quickly, directly; but his strong eyes were too much.

"Why, yes," she answered, as the music stopped, trying to keep an even tone to her voice. She was shaken, though, as by a strong blow. She was glad they were walking toward a chair.

"I like you so much," he said, relaxing his cruel definiteness, "that I wondered if you really did like me." There was an appeal in his voice, soft and gentle. His manner was almost sad.

"Why, yes," she replied, instantly returning to her earlier mood toward him. "You know I do."

"I need some one like you to like me," he continued, in the same vein. "I need some one like you to talk to. Oh, you dance beautifully. You are beautiful—wonderful."

"We mustn't," she said. "I mustn't. I don't know what I'm doing."

She looked at a young man strolling toward her. "I have to explain to him. He's the one I had this with."

Cowperwood strolled away. It was quite clear to him that he had just done a very treacherous thing. Under the current law of life he had no right to do it. It was against the rules, as they were understood by everybody. However much breaking of the rules under the surface of things there might be, the rules were still there. As he had heard one young man remark once at school, when some story had been told of a boy leading a girl astray and to a disastrous end, "That isn't the way at all."

Still, now that he had said this, strong thoughts of her were in his mind. It is curious how we grow on what we eat. We seem at times to work the bellows that heighten the flames of our desires; we feed the fire that ultimately consumes us—and how deliberately and resourcefully! Our conscience, as some one has said, may be as the shell is of the sea, murmurous of morality; but it avails nothing. There appears to exist an age-old fight between spirit and the flesh, God and the devil, idealism and materialism, heat and cold, wealth and poverty, strength and weakness, and so on—a struggle without evidence of victory or failure on either hand. "From everlasting to everlasting" may as well have been spoken of evil as of good. Or there is no evil, nor any good, as we understand them.

Aileen's thoughts were interrupted the least moment by her apologies for having evaded her prospective partner and given the dance to some one else. As she had planned to prevaricate, so she did. She returned to her chair, weary for the time being of other attentions, for this sudden definite suggestion of Cowperwood's gave her so much to think of. She toyed aimlessly with her fan as a black-haired, thin-faced young law student talked to her, one of the scions of the better families; and, seeing Norah in the distance through the hangings separating this from the music-room, she asked to be allowed to run and talk to her. Mrs. Drake interrupted her flight, but delineated upon the fair, plump body and face—she saw Cowperwood. He had set a strange tingling in her veins. What was this? Did she love him? Why was it that his straight-looking gray eyes fascinated her? His shoulders were so wide, so level. He held himself so erect; and there was something about his walk, the definite and poised way in which he walked, that caught her fancy. He was so good-looking, so clean. His clear, tinted skin betokened such an abundance of health and vitality.

"Oh, Aileen," called Norah, "I've been looking for you everywhere. Where have you been?"

"Dancing, of course. Where do you suppose I've been? Didn't you see me on the floor?"

"No, I didn't," complained Norah, as though it were most essential that she should. "How late are you going to stay to-night?"

"Until it's over, I suppose. I don't know."

"Owen says he's going at twelve."

"Well, that doesn't matter. Some one will take me home. Are you having a good time?"

"Fine. Oh, let me tell you. I stepped on a lady's dress over there, last dance. She was terribly angry. She gave me such a look."

"Well, never mind, honey. She won't hurt you. Where are you going now?"

Aileen always maintained a most affectionate attitude toward her sister.

"I want to find Callum. He has to dance with me next time. I know what he's trying to do. He's trying to get away from me. But he won't."

Aileen smiled. Norah looked very sweet. And she was so bright. What would she think of her if she knew. She turned back, and her fourth partner sought her. She began talking gaily, for she felt that she had to make a show of composure; but all the while there was ringing in her ears that definite question of his, "You like me, don't you?" and her later uncertain but not less truthful answer, "Yes, of course I do."

CHAPTER XXII

THE growth of a passion is a very peculiar thing. In the highly organized intellectual and artistic types it is so often apt to begin with keen appreciation of certain qualities, modified by many, many mental reservations. The egoist, the intellectual, gives but little of himself and asks much. Nevertheless, the lover of life, male or female, finding himself or herself in sympathetic accord with such a nature, is apt to gain much.

Cowperwood was innately and primarily your egoist and intellectual, though blended strongly therewith was a humane and democratic spirit. We think of egoism and intellectualism as closely confined to the arts. Finance is an art. And it presents the operations of the subtlest of the intellectuals and of the egoists. Your true prince is primarily a financier as well as a statesman. It were not possible, otherwise, to live in the memory of the world.

Cowperwood was a financier. Instead of dwelling on the works of nature, its beauty and subtlety, to his material disadvantage, he found a happy mean, owing to the swiftness of his intellectual operations, whereby he could intellectually and emotionally rejoice in the beauty of life without interfering with his perpetual material and financial calculations. And when it came to women and morals, which involved so much which related to beauty, happiness, a sense of distinction and variety in living, he was just now beginning to think clearly that there was no basis, outside of convention and theory, for the one-life, one-love idea. How had it come about that so many people agreed on this single point, that it was good and necessary to marry one woman and cleave to her until

242

death? He did not know. It was not for him to bother about the subtleties of evolution, which even then was being noised abroad, or to ferret out the curiosities of history in connection with this matter. He had no time. Suffice it that the vagaries of temperament and conditions with which he came into immediate contact proved to him that there was great dissatisfaction, and over and under surface variability in connection with the rule. People did not cleave to each other until death; and in thousands of cases where they did, they did not want to. Quickness of mind, subtlety of idea, fortuitousness of opportunity, made it possible for some people to right their matrimonial and social infelicities; whereas for others, because of dullness of wit, thickness of comprehension, poverty, and lack of charm, there was no escape from the slough of their despond. They were compelled by some devilish accident of birth to stew in their own juice of wretchedness, or to shuffle off this mortal coil—which under other circumstances had such glittering possibilities—*via* the rope, the knife, the bullet, or the cup of poison.

"I would die, too," he thought to himself, one day, reading of a man who, confined by disease and poverty, had lived for twelve years alone in a back bedroom attended by an old and probably decrepit housekeeper. A darning-needle forced into his heart had ended his earthly woes. "To the devil with such a life! Why twelve years? Why not at the end of the second or third?" And if this smiling fate, which now turned to him such a radiant face and seemed to be bending over him with outstretched and protecting wings, should turn away and reveal only hate or indifference, he would quit also. He would not want to live like that. He did not know, however, how much he really did love life.

Again, it was so very evident, in so many ways, that force was the answer—great mental and physical force. Why, these giants of commerce and money could do as they pleased in this life. The little guardians of so-called law and morality, the newspapers, the preachers, the police, and the public moralists generally, so loud in their denunciation of evil in humble places, were cowards all when it came to corruption in high ones. They did not dare to utter even a feeble squeak until some giant had accidentally fallen and they could do so without danger to themselves. Then, O heavens, what a palaver! What beatings of tom-toms! Run now, good people, for you may see clearly how evil is dealt with in high places! It made him smile. Such hypocrisy! Such cant! Still, so the world was organized, and it was not for him to set it right. Let it wag as it would. The thing for him to do was to get rich and hold his own—to build up a seeming of virtue and dignity which would pass muster for the genuine thing. Force would do that. Quickness of wit. And he had these. Let the world wag. "I satisfy myself," was his motto; and it might well have been emblazoned upon any coat of arms which he could have contrived to set forth his claim to intellectual and social nobility.

But this matter of Aileen, which had come to a definite point, was up for consideration and solution at this present moment, and because of his forceful, determined character he was not at all disturbed by the problem it presented. It was a problem, like some of those knotty financial complications which presented themselves daily; but it was not insoluble. What did he want to do? He couldn't leave his wife and fly with Aileen, that was certain. He had too many connections. He had too many subtle things to bind him. Besides, he was not at all sure that he wanted to. He did not intend to leave his growing interests, and at the same time he did not intend to give up Aileen immediately. The unheralded manifestation of interest on her part was too attractive. Mrs. Cowperwood was no longer what she should be physically and mentally, in so far as he was concerned. To be sure, she was devoted to him in her quiet way, not passionately (as he looked back he could not say that she had ever been that), but intellectually. Duty, as she understood it, played a great part in this. She was dutiful. And then what people thought, what the time-spirit demanded —these were the great things. Aileen, on the contrary, was probably not dutiful, and it was obvious that she had no temperamental connection with current convention. No doubt she had been as well instructed as many another girl, but look at her. She was not obeying her instructions. She was flirting with him, and she was as charming a bit of modeling as the laboratory of nature had ever produced. He had never seen a more striking-looking girl than she was this night. He had never seen any one more beautiful; and she was so full of that passionate will to live. Why, here was a piece of fleshly fire, and she was drawing to him out of pure temperamental affiliation.

There were a few more words between them during another dance this evening, but he was afraid to say too much. She was excited, and then people might be looking. Because of her costume, and the astonishing force it lent to her charms, she was the cynosure of many eyes, and not unenvious ones. She had made herself a little too conspicuous. One remark, though, Cowperwood did make which added much to all that had gone before. It was when they were passing near his wife, seated in a corner with Mrs. Davis.

"I'm not so sure Lillian would like our talking if she knew."

"I'm very sure she wouldn't."

She lifted her eyes, and they glided gracefully out of the reach of a swirl of figures.

So she was thinking of that, too. The difficulty of complications was not out of her mind. He admired her for her direct, incisive fronting of her moods.

"What would your father think?"

He was suffering from a brief, feverish choking of the throat.

"I've been thinking of that."

He felt a keen desire to kiss her, something that had not formulated itself so definitely before. And she would let him, that he knew, after, perhaps, a deadly nervous strain which might be slightly antagonistic.

"I'm a little dizzy to-night," he said. "You're like a dose of poison in my veins."

"Poison?"

"Love-poison."

The music stopped, and after a while he saw her going out, her black-silk dolman wrapped loosely about her body. Owen was with her.

"Good night, Mrs. Cowperwood," she said to his wife. "I've had such a delightful time. And, Mr. Cowperwood, your new homes are beautiful."

She extended her hand.

He pressed the warm, smooth fingers gently.

"I hope you enjoyed yourself."

"I did. I surely did."

She swung away, followed by Owen, and Cowperwood followed her with his eyes.

"A beautiful creature," he thought, "and absolutely irresponsible, self-willed, and wonderful."

In the next three months this relationship took on a more flagrant form. Aileen, knowing full well what her parents would think, how unspeakable in the mind of the current world were the thoughts she was thinking, persisted, nevertheless, in so thinking and longing. Cowperwood, now that she had gone thus far and compromised herself in intention, if not in deed, took on a peculiar charm for her. It was not his body—great passion is never that, exactly. The flavor of his spirit was what attracted and compelled, like the glow of a flame to a moth. There was a light of romance in his eye which, however, was so governed and controlled that he seemed all-powerful. Her father was a wonderful man to her, with his rugged frame and face; but this youth, so much smaller, comparatively speaking, was even more so. When he touched her hand at parting, it was as though she had received an electric shock, and she recalled that it was very difficult for her to look him straight in the eye. Something akin to a destructive force seemed to issue from them at times. Other people, men particularly, found it difficult to look into Cowperwood's glazed stare persistently. It was as though there were another pair of eyes behind watching through thin, impenetrable curtains. You could not tell what they were like—what he was thinking.

It could not be said that she was going outside of her temperament to do evil. And was that temperament evil? It is so easy in this world to divide the sheep and the goats in a superficial way. The slogan of the moralist is that we can all do right if we want to. The answer is that the spirit of man is clothed over with a fleshly envelope which has moods and subtleties of its own. The spirit of man may, as the idealistic metaphysicians have it, be a reflection of a perfect unity which governs the universe, or it may not. It depends on how one conceives the governing spirit of the universe. But of the mold into which this spirit is born, who shall say? There are time moods, and nation moods, and climate moods, and they bring forth great clouds of individuals curiously minded. Our particular national temperament appears to be conservative, at least in so far as conforming outwardly to a fixed social code is concerned. Underneath, what are we? You might as well have said to a thistle, "Be a grapevine, or we will destroy you," as to have said to Aileen Butler, "Be a calm, placid, virtuous girl, or society will cast you out." Aileen Butler might well have answered, if she could have reasoned so far, "How can I?" Even in the face of the threatening force of society it would have been difficult for her at any time. There were strange, unconventional moods stirring in her, and strange longings. She was seeking some wondrous, peculiar, individual destiny, just as a thistle is unquestionably seeking to perfect a red, thorny blossom. Root it out? Precisely. Society does precisely that when it finds something that does not agree with its current mood. The "murmurous morality" of the universe has its representatives everywhere, and they are actually fighting the representatives of what they conceive to be the unrighteous. So Aileen would fare badly if she were discovered even in her secret longings. But she was not discovered as yet.

And during these three months she was coming closer and closer to Cowperwood, for, being at his house one evening, seated at the piano, and no one being present at the moment, he leaned over and kissed her. She was the least bit pensive at the time, as the sensualistic temperament is apt to be. There was a cold, snowy street visible through the interstices of the hangings of the windows, and gas-lamps flickering outside. She had not betaken her way to her own home yet for dinner, because Norah was next door at the Henry Cowperwoods' home talking with Anna. Norah had become Anna's pet. Cowperwood had come in early. He was in his wife's boudoir for a little while, and then, hearing Aileen, he came to where she was seated at the piano. Her attractive body was set off by a rough, gray-wool cloth, jauntily suggestive of her temperament. It was ornately banded with a fringed Oriental embroidery in inch-deep blue and burnt orange, and her beauty was further enhanced by a gray hat planned to match her dress, with a plume of shaded orange and blue. On her fingers were four or five rings, far too many—an opal, an emerald, a ruby, and a diamond—flashing visibly upon her hands as she played. He watched her from the fireplace in the living-room, looking through the great opening into the parlor, and then approached.

She knew who it was without turning. He came beside her and she looked up smiling, not interrupting the reverie she was attempting to recall from Schubert. Suddenly he bent over and pressed his lips firmly to hers. His mustache thrilled her with its silky touch. She stopped playing and tried to catch her breath, for, strong as she was, it affected her breathing. Her heart was beating like a trip-hammer. She did not say "oh," or "you mustn't," but rose and walked over near a window less visible than the piano from the living-room, and lifted the curtain, pretending to look out. She felt as though she might faint, so intensely happy was she.

Cowperwood followed her quickly. Slipping his arms about her waist, he pulled her head back, looking at her flushed cheeks, her clear, moist eyes, her red mouth.

"You love me?" he whispered, rather grim with desire.

"Yes; yes! You know I do."

He crushed her face to his, and she put up her hands and stroked his hair.

A terrible feeling of possession, mastery, happiness, and understanding, love of her and of her body, suddenly overwhelmed him.

"I love you," he said, as though he were surprised to hear himself say it. "I didn't think I did; but I do. You're beautiful. I'm wild about you now."

"And I love you," she answered. "I can't help it. I know I shouldn't, but—oh—" Her hands closed tight over his ears and temples. She put her lips to his and dreamed into his eyes. Then she stepped away quickly, looking out into the street, and he walked back into the sitting-room. No one had come. They were quite alone. He was debating whether he should risk anything further when Norah appeared, and not long afterward Mrs. Cowperwood. Then Aileen and Norah left.

CHAPTER XXIII

THIS definite and final understanding having been reached, it was but natural that this liaison should proceed to a closer and closer relationship. It is useless to speculate on the horror of it as those, conventionally minded, will surely do. There is or has been much theorizing in this world concerning the need of following the inward light or leading which all are supposed to possess. That there may be superimposed upon the mass a social conscience which has nothing to do with the normal bent or chemical nature of the individual occurs to few. A Christian ideal had been poured out upon the world like a sea of air, and those who live in it, who are many, draw their convictions as their breath from that. It is not necessarily native to them. Something underneath—the flesh, for instance, and material pleasure—wars against it; but it is almost a part of their blood, so long has the world moved in it. Still the native materiality of man will not down any more than his ideality. Perhaps the two go hand in hand. Before Christianity was man, and after it he will also be. A metaphysical idealism will always tell him that it is better to preserve a cleanly balance, and the storms of circumstance will teach him a noble stoicism. Beyond this there is nothing which can reasonably be imposed upon the conscience of man.

Aileen, despite her religious training, was decidedly a victim of her temperament. Current religious feeling and belief could not control her. During all these years, for at least nine or ten, there had been slowly forming in her mind a notion of what her lover should be like. He should be strong, handsome, direct, successful, with clear eyes, a ruddy glow of health, and a certain native understanding and sympathy—a love of life which matched her own. Many young men had approached her. Perhaps the nearest realization of her ideal was Father David, of St. Timothy's; and he was, of course, a priest, and sworn to celibacy. No word had ever passed between them. Then came Frank Cowperwood; and by degrees, because of his presence and contact, he had been slowly built up in her mind as the ideal person. From the time she had first seen him, as he stood talking to her father on their own doorstep—the time she dashed past him in red cape and hood—until now, there had been a strong pull from him to her. She was drawn as some planets are drawn by the sun. Moral speculations really had nothing to do with it. They were of no service one way or the other. Her family training was of no value. This emotion rose quickly, like a swelling tide, and drowned thoughts of family training and everything else. The passions are never concerned with rules of life, anyhow. Beauty of dress, beauty of appearance, some one to love her, some man like this man—*the man*—to tell her that she was sweet and lovely and beautiful—to fondle her as Cowperwood was now beginning to do—that was what she wanted. After she had left him this night, going home with Norah, she would have given anything to have been able to run back, unimpeded in any way, and fling herself in his arms. She wanted to be held on his lap, to feel his arms around her, his cheek against hers, his lips against her lips. Oh, the bliss of that! If she could only be with him now, just after he had told her that he loved her so. The blood of her heart buzzed in her brain. There was a murmurous rumbling in her ears. Her eyes swam with visions. The guiding light within was quite submerged. If it ever had any force, it was quite non-existent at this moment. Love! Love! That was the greatest thing in the world. And Frank Cowperwood was the loveliest, most wonderful, most beautiful man that ever was.

THE FINANCIER

It is a question what would have happened if antagonistic forces could have been introduced just at this time. Emotions and liaisons of this character can, of course, occasionally be broken up and destroyed. The characters of the individuals can be modified or changed to a certain extent, but the force must be quite sufficient. Fear is a great deterrent—fear of material loss where there is no spiritual dread; but wealth and position so often tend to destroy this dread. It is so easy to scheme with means.

Aileen had no spiritual dread whatever. Cowperwood had no spiritual, or, perhaps better, no religious thought whatsoever. Religion meant nothing to him. He looked at this girl, and his one thought was how could he so deceive the world that he could enjoy her love and leave his present state undisturbed. Love her he did surely.

He called at Butler's house on business on several occasions, and on each occasion he saw Aileen. She managed to slip forward and squeeze his hand the first time he came—to steal a quick, vivid kiss; and another time, as he was going out, she suddenly appeared from behind the curtains hanging at the parlor door.

"Honey!"

The voice was soft and coaxing. He turned, giving her a warning nod in the direction of her father's room up-stairs.

She stood there, holding out one hand, and he stepped forward for a second. Instantly her arms were about his neck, as he slipped his about her waist.

"I long to see you so."

"I, too. I'll fix some way. I'm thinking."

He released her arms, and went out; and she slipped to the window and looked out after him. He was walking west on the street, for his house was only a few blocks away; and she looked at the shape of his body, the breadth of his shoulders, the balance of his form. He stepped so briskly, so incisively. Ah, that was a man! That was her

Frank. She thought of him in that light already. And now he was gone. If she could only be with him. She sat down at the piano and played pensively until dinner, then went to her room and read. She had found a book recently—*Carmen*—which fascinated her.

It was so easy for the resourceful mind of Frank Cowperwood to suggest ways and means. In his younger gallivantings about places of ill repute, and his subsequent occasional variations from the straight and narrow path, he had learned much of the curious resources of immorality. Being a city of five hundred thousand and more at this time, Philadelphia had its nondescript hotels, where one might go, cautiously and fairly protected from observation; and there were houses of a conservative, residential character, where appointments might be made, for a consideration. Once the scruples of innocence were overcome, it was easy enough to make those arrangements for hours of happiness which were so desirable. And as for safeguards against the production of new life—they were not mysteries to Cowperwood any longer. He knew all about them. Care was the point—caution. He had to be cautious, for he was so rapidly coming to be an influential and a distinguished man. But Aileen, of course, was not conscious, except in a vague way, of the drift of her passion; the ultimate destiny to which this affection might lead was not clear to her. Her craving was for love—to be fondled and caressed—and she really did not think so much further. Further thoughts along this line were like rats that showed their heads out of dark holes in shadowy corners and scuttled back at the least sound. They did not ever come out into the clear light of day. And, anyhow, all that was to be connected with Cowperwood would be beautiful. He was so nice, so definitely interested in her. She really did not think that he loved her yet as he should; but he would. Mrs. Cowperwood had strong claims on him. She did not know that she wanted to interfere with those.

She did not think she did. But it would not hurt Mrs. Cowperwood if Frank loved her—Aileen—also.

How shall we explain these subtleties of temperament and logic? Life has to deal with them at every turn. No man nor any woman is safe from them. We might as well look the facts in the face. They will not down, and the large, placid movements of nature outside of man's little organism would indicate that she is not greatly concerned. We see much punishment in the form of jails, diseases, failures, and wrecks; but we also see that the old tendency is not visibly lessened. Is there no law outside of the subtle will and the power to achieve? If not, it is surely high time that we knew it—one and all. We might then agree to do as we do; but there would be no silly illusion as to divine regulation. *Vox populi, vox Dei.*

There were other meetings, lovely hours which they soon began to spend the moment her passion waxed warm enough to assure compliance, without great fear and without thought of the deadly risk involved. These matters are almost always of slow growth or development. From odd moments in his own home, stolen when there was no one about to see, they advanced to clandestine meetings beyond the confines of the city. Cowperwood was not one who was temperamentally inclined to lose his head and neglect his business. As a matter of fact, the more he thought of this rather unexpected affectional development, the more certain he was that he must not let it interfere with his business time and judgment. His office required his full attention from nine until three, anyhow. He could give it until five-thirty with profit; but he could take several afternoons off, from three-thirty until five-thirty or six, and no one would be the wiser. It was customary for Aileen to drive alone almost every afternoon a spirited pair of bays, or to ride a mount, bought by her father for her from a noted horse-dealer in Baltimore. Since Cowperwood drove and rode himself, it was no difficulty to arrange meeting-places far out on the Wissahickon or the Schuylkill road. There were many places, largely spots in the newly laid-out park, which were as free from interruption for hours at a time as the depths of a forest. It was always possible that they might encounter some one; but it was always possible to make a rather plausible explanation, or none at all, since even in case of such an encounter nothing, ordinarily, would be suspected.

So, for the time being, there was love-making, the ordinary billing and cooing of lovers in a simple and much less than final fashion; and the lovely rides under the green trees of the approaching spring—they both confined themselves to saddle-horses—were idyllic. Cowperwood did not want to shock her. He had awaked to a sense of joy in life, such as he fancied in the blush of this new desire, he had never experienced before, and he wished to bring her finally to him by degrees. He was in no mood to hurry. Lillian had been lovely in those early days in which he had first called on her in North Front Street, and he had fancied himself unspeakably happy at that time; but that was nearly ten years since, and he had forgotten how it was. Since then he had had no great passion, no notable liaison; and then, all at once, in the midst of business prosperity appeared Aileen. Her young body and soul, her passionate illusions—how lovely they were! He could see always, for all her daring, that she knew so little of the hard, brutal world with which he was connected. Her father had given her all the toys she wanted without stint; her mother and brothers had coddled her, particularly her mother. Her young sister thought she was adorable, and old Butler found an echo of his own hardy youth in her ruddy temperament. No one imagined for one moment that Aileen would ever do anything wrong. She was too sensible, after all, too eager to get up in the world. Why should she, when her life lay open and happy before her—a delightful love-

match, some day soon, with some very eligible and satisfactory lover?

"When you marry, Aileen," her mother used to say to
her, "we'll have a grand time here. Sure we'll do the
house over then, if we don't do it before. Eddie will have
to fix it up, or I'll do it meself. Never fear."

"Yes—well, I'd rather you'd fix it now," was her reply.

Butler himself used to strike her jovially on the shoulder in a rough, loving way, and ask, "Well, have you
found him yet?" or "Is he hanging around the outside
watchin' for ye?"

If she said "No," he would reply: "Well, he will be,
never fear—worse luck. I'll hate to see ye go, girlie!
You can stay here as long as ye want to, and ye want to
remember that you can always come back."

Aileen paid very little attention to these caressings.
She loved her father, but it was all such a matter of
course. She always had. It was the commonplace of
her existence, and not so very significant, though delightful enough.

But how eagerly she yielded herself to Cowperwood
under the spring trees these days! She had no sense of
that ultimate yielding that was coming, for now he merely caressed and talked to her. He was a little doubtful
about himself. His growing liberties seemed natural
enough, however, and in a sense of fairness he began to
talk to her about what their love involved. Would she?
Did she understand? This phase of it puzzled and frightened her a little at first. She looked at him, standing before him one afternoon in her black riding-habit and high
silk riding-hat perched so jauntily on her pretty head; and
striking her riding-skirt with her short whip, pondered
doubtfully as she listened. He was so fascinating. He
had asked her whether she knew what she was doing?
Whither they were drifting? If she loved him truly
enough? The two horses were tethered in a thicket a
score of yards away, and from the bank of the tumbling

stream, which they had approached, she was trying to make out if she could see them. It was pretense. There was no interest in her glance. She was thinking of him and the niceness of his habit, and the exquisite condition of his mount. He had such a charming calico pony. The leaves were just far enough out to make a diaphanous lace-work of green. It was like looking through a soft, netted curtain of pale, olive-hued lace to look into the woods beyond or behind. The gray stones were already faintly mossy where the water rippled and sparkled, and early birds were calling—robins and blackbirds and wrens.

"Baby mine," he said, "do you understand all about it? Do you know exactly what you're doing when you come with me this way?"

"I think I do."

She struck her boot and looked at the ground, and then up through the trees at the blue sky.

"Look at me, honey."

"I don't want to."

"But look at me, sweet. I want to ask you something."

"Don't make me, Frank, please. I can't."

"Oh yes, you can look at me."

"No."

She backed away as he took her hands, but came forward again, easily enough.

"Now look in my eyes."

"I can't."

"See here."

"I can't. Don't ask me. I'll answer you, but don't make me look at you."

His hand stole to her cheek and fondled it. He petted her shoulder, and she leaned her head against him.

"Sweet, you're so beautiful," he said, finally, "I can't give you up. I know what I ought to do. You know, too, I suppose; but I can't. I must have you. If any exposure should come of this for you or for me, it would be quite bad for you. Do you understand?"

"Yes."

"I don't know your brothers very well; but from looking at them I judge they're pretty determined people. They think a great deal of you."

"Indeed, they do." Her vanity brightened slightly at this.

"They would probably want to kill me, and very promptly, for just this much. What do you think they would want to do if—well, if anything should happen, some time?"

He waited, watching her pretty face.

"But nothing need happen. We needn't go any further."

"Aileen!"

"I won't look at you. You needn't ask. I can't."

"Aileen! Do you mean that?"

"I don't know. Don't ask me, Frank."

"You know it can't stop this way, don't you? You know it. This isn't the end. Now, if—" He explained the whole theory of illicit meetings calmly, dispassionately. "You are perfectly safe, except for one thing, chance exposure. It might just so happen; and then, of course, there would be a great deal to settle for. Mrs. Cowperwood would never give me a divorce; she has no reason to. If I should clear in the way I hope to—if I should make a million—I would not mind knocking off now. I don't expect to work all my days. I have always planned to knock off at thirty-five. I'll have enough by that time. Then I want to travel. It will only be a few more years now. If you were free—if your father and mother were dead"—curiously she did not wince at this practical reference—"it would be a different matter. We could leave, anyhow, I suppose."

He paused. She still gazed thoughtfully at the water below, her mind running out to a yacht on the sea with him, a palace somewhere—just they two. Her eyes, half closed, saw this happy world; and her ears, listening, were fascinated.

"Hanged if I see the way out of this, exactly. But I love you!" He caught her to him. "I love you—love you!"

"Oh yes," she replied; "I want you to. I'm not afraid."

"I've taken a house in North Tenth Street," he said, finally, as they walked out to the horses. "It isn't furnished yet; but it will be, soon. I have a woman who will be in charge."

"Who is she?"

"An interesting widow of nearly fifty. Very intelligent—she is attractive, and knows a good deal of life. I found her through an advertisement. You might call on her some afternoon when things are arranged, and look the place over. You needn't meet her except in a casual way. Will you?"

She rode on, thinking, making no reply. He was so direct and practical in his calculations.

"Will you? It will be all right. You might know her. She isn't objectionable in any way. Will you?"

"Let me know when it is ready," was all she said, finally.

CHAPTER XXIV

THE vagaries of passion! What subtleties, what risk, what sacrifices are not laid wilfully upon its altar? In a little while this more than average residence to which Cowperwood had referred was prepared solely to effect a satisfactory method of concealment. Aileen had still to be allured. The house was governed by a seemingly recently bereaved widow, and it was possible for Aileen to call without seeming strangely out of place. It was a little while after this before this dénouement was eventually brought about. Yet it was not more difficult to persuade Aileen, governed as she was by her wild and unreasoning affection and passion, than it would have been to lead an innocent maiden to the altar. In a way, there was a saving element of love, for truly, above all others, she wanted this man. She had no thought or feeling toward any other. All her mind ran toward visions of the future, when, somehow, she and he might be together alone. Mrs. Cowperwood might die, or he might run away with her at thirty-five when he had a million. Some adjustment would be made, somehow. Nature had given her this man. She relied on him implicitly. When he told her that he would take care of her so that nothing evil should befall, she believed him fully. She was not exactly bad at heart, as one may readily see. Such sins as these are the commonplaces of the confessional.

It is a curious fact that, by some subtlety of logic in the Christian world, it has come to be believed that there can be no love outside of the conventional process of courtship and marriage. One life, one love, is the Christian idea; and into this sluice, channel, or mold it has been endeavoring to compress the whole world. Pagan thought held no such belief. A writing of divorce for trivial causes was the theory of the elders; and in the primeval world nature apparently held no scheme for the unity of two beyond the temporary care of the young. That the modern home is the most beautiful of schemes, when based upon mutual sympathy and understanding between two, need not be questioned. And yet this fact should not necessarily carry with it a condemnation of all love not so fortunate as to find so happy a dénouement. Life cannot be put in any mold, and the attempt might as well be abandoned at once. Those so fortunate as to find harmonious companionship for life should congratulate themselves and strive to be worthy of it. Those not so blessed, though they be written down as pariahs, have yet some justification. And, besides, whether we will or no, theory or no theory, the large basic facts of chemistry and physics remain. Like is drawn to like. Changes in temperament bring changes in relationship. Dogma may bind some minds; fear, others. But there are always those in whom the chemistry and physics of life are large, and in whom neither dogma nor fear is operative. Society lifts its hands in horror; but from age to age the Helens, the Messalinas, the Du Barrys, the Pompadours, the Maintenons, and the Nell Gwyns flourish and point a subtler basis of relationship than we have yet been able to square with our lives.

When all was arranged, the happy event took place, much as a marriage might have. There was infinite delight, and these two felt unutterably bound to each other. Cowperwood, once he came to understand her, fancied that he had found the one person with whom he could live happily the rest of his life. She was so young, so confident, so hopeful, so undismayed. All these months since they had first begun to reach out to each other Cowperwood had been hourly contrasting her with his wife. He had not been vastly dissatisfied before. As a matter of fact, his dissatisfaction, though it may be said to have been faintly growing, and was surely tending to become real enough in its substance, in so far as it had gone, was decidedly nebulous. His children were pleasing to him; his home beautiful. Mrs. Cowperwood, phlegmatic and now thin, was still not homely. All these years he had found her satisfactory enough; but now, as his passion began to grow for Aileen, his dissatisfaction with his wife began to increase. He was not one who was inclined to be querulous, and yet on occasion he could be. He began to ask questions concerning her appearance— those irritating little whys which are so trivial and yet so exasperating and discouraging to a woman. Why didn't she get a mauve hat nearer the shade of her dress? Why didn't she go out more? Exercise would do her good. Why didn't she do this, and why didn't she do that? He scarcely noticed that he was doing this; but she did, and she felt the undertone—the real significance —and took umbrage.

"Oh, why—why?" she retorted, one day, curtly. "Why do you ask so many questions? You don't care so much for me any more; that's why. I can tell."

He leaned back startled by the thrust. It was not based on any evidence of anything save his recent remarks; but he was not absolutely sure. He was just the least bit sorry that he had irritated her, and he said so.

"Oh, it's all right," she replied. "I don't care. But I notice that you don't pay as much attention to me as you used to. It's your business now, first, last, and all the time. You can't get your mind off of that."

He breathed a sigh of relief. She didn't suspect, then. Very well, everything was lovely.

But after a little time, as he grew more and more in sympathy with Aileen, he was not so disturbed as to whether his wife might suspect or not. He began to think on occasion, as his mind followed the various ramifications of the situation, that it would be better if she did. She was really not of the contentious, fighting sort. He fancied she would make no great resistance to some ultimate rearrangement. She might even divorce him. But the rub was not there nearly so much as it was in connection with the Butler family. His relations with Edward Malia Butler had become very intimate—too much so. The latter knew and thought of him only as a very practical business man. He advised with him constantly in regard to the handling of his securities, which were numerous. Mr. Butler had stocks in such things as the Pennsylvania Coal Company, the Delaware and Hudson Canal, the Morris and Essex Canal, the Reading Railroad, and things of that kind. Some of these stocks were active, others inactive. As the old gentleman's mind broadened to the significance of the local street-railway problem in Philadelphia, he decided to close out his other securities at such advantageous terms as he could, and reinvest the money in local lines. He knew that Mollenhauer and Simpson were doing this, and they were excellent judges of the significance of local affairs. Like Cowperwood, he had the idea that if he controlled sufficient of the local situation in this field, he could at last effect a joint relationship with Mollenhauer and Simpson. Political legislation, advantageous to the combined lines, could then be so easily secured. Franchises and necessary extensions to existing franchises could be added. This conversion of his outstanding stocks in other fields, and the picking up of odd lots in the local street-railway, was the business of Cowperwood. Butler, through his sons, Owen and Callum, was busy planning a new line and obtaining a franchise, sacrificing, of course, great blocks of stock and actual cash to others, in order to obtain sufficient influence to have the necessary legislation passed. It was no easy matter, seeing that others knew what the general advantages of the situation were. Cowperwood, for instance, seeing the great source of profit here, was not as eager to serve Mr. Butler, or any one else, as he was to serve himself if he could.

The scheme which Mr. George W. Stener had brought forward, representing actually in the background Mr. Strobik, Mr. Wycroft, Mr. Harmon, was a way in. This was to loan him money out of the city treasury at two per cent., or, if he would waive all commissions, for nothing (an agent for self-protective purposes was absolutely necessary), and with it take over the North Pennsylvania Company's line on Front Street, which, because of the shortness of its length, one mile and a half, and the brevity of the duration of its franchise, was neither doing very well nor being rated very high. Cowperwood in return for his manipulative skill was to have a fair proportion of the stock—twenty per cent. Mr. Strobik and Mr. Wycroft knew the parties from whom the bulk of the stock could be secured if engineered properly. Their plan was then, with this borrowed treasury money, to extend the line, extend its franchise, and then, by issuing a great block of stock and hypothecating it with a favored bank, return the principal to the city treasury and pocket their profits from the line as it earned them. There was no trouble in this, in so far as Cowperwood was concerned, except that it divided the stock very badly among these various individuals, and left him but a comparatively small share—a fifth—for his thought and pains.

Those who have been drawing preliminary conclusions as to Mr. Cowperwood's financial honesty are, perhaps, asking themselves how he viewed these rather peculiar relationships. The answer is that Mr. Cowperwood was an opportunist. At this time his financial morality was special and local in its character. He did not think it was wise for any one to steal anything from anybody where the act of taking or profiting was directly and plainly considered stealing. That was immoral. There were so many situations wherein what one might do in the way of taking or profiting was open to discussion and doubt. Morality varies with climates and traditions. Here in Philadelphia the tradition was (politically— mind you—not generally) that the city treasurer might use the money of the city without interest so long as he returned the principal intact. The city treasury and the city treasurer were like a honey-laden hive and a queen bee around which the politicians swarmed in the hope of profit. The one disagreeable thing in connection with this transaction with Stener was that neither Butler, Mollenhauer, nor Simpson, who were the actual superiors of Stener and Strobik, knew anything about it. Stener and those behind him were, through him, acting for themselves. If the larger powers heard of this it might alienate them—Butler, for instance; and Cowperwood was close to him. He had to think of this. Still, if he refused to make any advantageous deals with Mr. George W. Stener, or any other man influential in local affairs, he was cutting off his nose to spite his face, for other bankers and brokers would, and gladly. And besides it was not at all certain that Butler, Mollenhauer, and Simpson would ever hear. What business was it of his where the money came from? Why should he concern himself with the traditions of the city—whether they were honest or not? He knew this scheme of the city politicians was not honest. He knew the public at large were being hoodwinked and outdone. But was he responsible for the public? Had not the people, the rank and file, always been fools more or less? Could you do anything but manage their affairs fairly well for them and take a large profit for yourself? Capital, he saw, was very chary. It wanted large security. And men in any walk of life—wise men—would never work for nothing. They wanted great gains. If you wanted to see improvements of any kind made, you would have to expect a large spilling-over of profits—this was so in connection with anything which was being done in Philadelphia, hence—

There was another line, however, which he rode on

THE FINANCIER

occasionally, the Seventeenth and Nineteenth Street line,
which he felt was a much more interesting thing for him
to think about, if he could raise the money. It had
been originally capitalized for five hundred thousand dollars; but there had been a series of bonds to the value of
two hundred and fifty thousand dollars additional added
for improvements, and the company was finding great
difficulties in meeting the interest. The bulk of the stock
was scattered about among small investors, and it would
require all of two hundred and fifty thousand dollars to
collect it and have himself elected president or chairman
of the board of directors. Once in, however, he could
vote this stock as he pleased, hypothecating it meanwhile
at his father's bank for as much as he could get, and issuing more stocks with which to bribe legislators in the
matter of extending the line, and in taking up other opportunities to either add to it by purchase or supplement
it by working agreements. The word "bribe" is used
here in this matter-of-fact American way, because bribery
was what was in every one's mind in connection with the
State legislature. Terrence Relihan—a small, dark-faced
Irishman, a dandy in dress and manners—who represented the financial interest at Harrisburg, had told him
that nothing could be done at the capital without money,
or its equivalent, negotiable securities. Each significant
legislator, if he yielded his vote or his influence, must be
looked after. Cowperwood had met Relihan through
Frederick Van Nostrand, the State treasurer, at the time
of the bond issue, and had seen him often since. He was
frequently in town talking to Butler, Simpson, Mollenhauer, and the financial stars of Third Street. If he,
Cowperwood, had any scheme which he wanted handled
at any time, Relihan had intimated to him that he would
be glad to talk with him. He had influence, because of
those he represented, and could crack the whip at times;
but it required money. Cowperwood had figured on
this Seventeenth and Nineteenth Street line scheme

266

more than once, but he had never felt quite sure that
he was willing to undertake it. His obligations in other
directions were so large. But the lure was there, and he
pondered and pondered.

Stener's scheme of loaning him money wherewith to
manipulate the North Pennsylvania line deal put another idea in his mind. Although he was constantly
watching the certificates of loan issue, buying large quantities when the market was falling to protect it and selling
heavily though cautiously when he saw it rising, he had
to have a great deal of free money to permit him to do
it. He was constantly fearful of some break in the
market which would affect the value of all his securities
and result in the calling of his loans. There was no
storm in sight. He did not see that anything could happen in reason; but he did not want to spread himself
out too thin. If he took one hundred and fifty thousand
dollars and went after this Seventeenth and Nineteenth
Street matter it would mean that he was spread out very
thin. And if anything should happen—

"Frank," said Stener, strolling into his office one
afternoon after four o'clock when the main rush of the
day's work was over—the relationship between Cowperwood and Stener had long since reached the "Frank"
and "George" period—"Strobik thinks he has that North
Pennsylvania deal arranged so that we can take it up
if we want to. The principal stockholder, we find, is
a man by the name of Colton—not Ike Colton, but Fer-
dinand. How's that for a name?" Mr. Stener beamed
fatly and genially.

Things had changed considerably for George W.
Stener since the days when he had been fortuitously and
almost indifferently made city treasurer. He was such
an easy-going soul in the hands of others—such a comfortable tool to work with—that he had been allowed to
prosper. He was not so self-sufficient that he could not
take advice from a number of sources, and for some in-

describable reason he evoked a kind of sympathy and friendly interest in those who were drawn to him at all. They liked to "jolly" him, as an expression which went into use later had it; and, while they would not have known that he existed if he had not been made city treasurer, since he was so, it made all the difference in the world. His method of dressing had so much improved since he had been inducted into office, and his manner expressed so much more good feeling, confidence, aplomb, that he would not have recognized himself if he had been permitted to see himself as had those who had known him before. An old, nervous shifting of the eyes had almost ceased, and a feeling of restfulness, which had previously been restlessness, and had sprung from a sense of necessity, had taken its place. His large feet were incased in good, square-toed, soft-leather shoes; his stocky chest and fat legs were made somewhat agreeable to the eye by a well-cut suit of brownish - gray cloth; and his neck was now surrounded by a low, wing-point white collar and brown-silk tie—the collar low enough not to irritate his stout neck, which somehow spoke of peace and comfort and prosperity. His ample chest, which spread out a little lower in a round and constantly enlarging stomach, was ornamented by a heavy-link gold chain, and his white cuffs had large gold cuff-buttons set with rubies of a very notable size. He was rosy and decidedly well fed. In fact, he was doing very well indeed.

His family had been moved from the shabby two-story frame house in South Ninth Street—very far south —which they had formerly occupied, to a very comfortable brick one three stories in height, and three times as large, on Spring Garden Street. His wife had a few acquaintances—the wives of other politicians. His children were attending the high school, a thing he had hardly hoped for in earlier days. He was now the owner of fourteen or fifteen pieces of cheap real estate in different portions of the city, which might eventually become very valuable, and he was a silent partner in the South Philadelphia Foundry Company and the American Beef and Pork Company, two corporations on paper, whose principal business was subletting contracts secured from the city to the humble butchers and foundrymen who would carry out orders as given and not talk too much or ask questions. Needless to say, Messrs. Strobik, Wycroft, and Harmon were the leaders in these things. Needless to say, also, that George W. Stener had but small advice to offer outside of furnishing the original capital. He was doing very well, though, and Strobik and Harmon and Wycroft liked him. So did Cowperwood, after a fashion. He was a little sorry for him.

"Well, that is an odd name," said Cowperwood, blandly. "So he has it? I never thought that road would pay, as it was laid out. It's too short. It ought to run about three miles farther out into the Kensington section."

"Yes, I think you're right," said Stener, dully.

"Did Strobik say what Colton wants for his shares?"

"Sixty-eight, I think."

"The current market rate. He doesn't want much, does he? Well, George, at that rate it will take about"— he calculated quickly on the basis of the number of shares Colton was holding—"one hundred and twenty thousand to get him out alone. That isn't all. There's Judge Kitchen and Joseph Zimmerman and Senator Donovan"—he was referring to the State senator of that name. "You'll be paying a pretty fair price for that stuff when you get it. It will cost considerable more to extend the line. It's too much, I think."

Cowperwood was thinking how easy it would be to combine this line with his dreamed-of Seventeenth and Nineteenth Street line, if he could get that. If he had that he could say to Stener and his friends, once they had this line, "Here now, why not let me run this line, of which I am part owner with you, in connection with my own?" After that so many things could be done. Book-keeping is such a subtle thing. Suddenly an idea occurred to him.

"Say, George," he said, "why do you work all your schemes through Strobik and Harmon and Wycroft? Couldn't you manage some of these things alone or with just one person, instead of three or four? It seems to me that plan would be much more profitable to you."

"It would, it would!" exclaimed Stener, his round eyes fixed on Cowperwood in a rather helpless, appealing way. "I've thought of that. But these fellows have had more experience in these matters than I have had, Frank. They've been longer at the game. I don't know as much about these things as they do."

Cowperwood smiled in his soul, though his face remained passive.

"Take this railroad deal you're in on, George; you and I could manipulate this just as well and better than it can be done with Wycroft, Strobik, and Harmon in on it. They're not adding anything to the wisdom of the situation. They're not putting up any money. You're doing that. All they're doing is agreeing to see it through the legislature and the council, and as far as the legislature is concerned, they can't do any more with that than any one else could—than I could, for instance. It is a question of arranging things with Relihan and putting up a certain amount of money for him to work with. Here in town there are other people who can reach the council just as well as Strobik. I'm not asking you to change your plans on this North Pennsylvania deal. You couldn't do that very well. But there are other things. In the future why not let's see if you and I can't work some of them together? You'll be much better off, and so will I. We've done pretty well on the city-loan proposition so far."

The truth was, they had done exceedingly well. Aside from what the higher powers had made, Mr. Stener's new house, his lots, his bank-account, his good clothes, and his changed and comfortable sense of life were largely due to Cowperwood's successful manipulation of these city-loan certificates. Already there had been four issues of two hundred thousand dollars each. Cowperwood had bought and sold nearly three million dollars' worth of these certificates, acting one time as a "bull" and another as a "bear." Mr. Stener was now worth all of one hundred and fifty thousand dollars.

"There's a line that I know of here in the city which could be made into a splendidly paying property," said Cowperwood, meditatively, after a while, "if the right things could be done with it. Just like this North Pennsylvania line, it isn't long enough. The territory it serves isn't big enough. It ought to be extended; and if you and I could get it, it might eventually be worked with this North Pennsylvania Company as one company. That would save officers and offices and a lot of things. There is always money to be made out of a larger purchasing power."

He paused and looked out the window of his handsome little hardwood office, speculating upon the future. The window gave nowhere save into a back yard behind another office building which had formerly been a residence. Some grass grew feebly there. The red wall and old-fashioned brick fence which divided it from the next lot reminded him somehow of his old home in New Market Street, where his Uncle Seneca used to come as a Cuban trader followed by a black Portuguese servitor. He could see him now as he sat here looking at the yard.

"Well," asked Stener, ambitiously, taking the bait, "why don't we get hold of that—you and me? I suppose I could fix it so far as the money is concerned. How much would it take?"

Cowperwood smiled inwardly again.

"I don't know exactly," he said, after a time. "I want to look into it more carefully. The one trouble is that

I'm carrying a good deal of the city's money as it is. You see, I have that two hundred thousand dollars against your city-loan deals. And this new scheme will take two or three hundred thousand more. If that were out of the way—"

He was thinking of one of those inexplicable stock panics—those strange American depressions which have so much to do with the temperament of the people, and so little to do with the basic conditions of the country. "If this North Pennsylvania deal were through and done with—"

He rubbed his chin and pulled at his handsome silky mustache.

"Don't ask me any more about it, George," he said, finally, as he saw that the latter was beginning to think as to which line it might be. "Don't say anything at all about it. I want to get my facts exactly right, and then I'll talk to you. I think you and I can do this thing a little later, when we get the North Pennsylvania scheme under way. I'm so rushed just now I'm not sure that I want to undertake it at once; but you keep quiet and we'll see." He turned toward his desk, and Stener got up.

"I'll make any sized deposit with you that you wish, the moment you think you're ready to act. Just notify Stires, and he'll send you a check. Strobik thought we ought to act pretty soon."

Stener was speaking of city money to be deposited with Cowperwood acting as a banker, in order to finance the proposed North Pennsylvania project, for which he was broker and prospective part owner.

"I'll tend to it, George," replied Cowperwood, confidently. "It will come out all right. Leave it to me."

Stener kicked his stout legs to straighten his trousers, and extended his hand. He strolled out in the street thinking of Cowperwood and this new scheme. If he could get in with Cowperwood right he would surely be

a rich man, for Cowperwood was so successful and so
cautious. His new house, this beautiful banking office,
his growing fame, and his subtle connections with Butler
and others put Stener in considerable awe of him. Another line! They would control it and the North Pennsylvania! Why, if this went on, he might become a
magnate—he really might—he, George W. Stener, once a
cheap real-estate and insurance agent. He strolled up
the street thinking, with no more idea of the importance
of the civic duties and the nature of the social ethics
against which he was offending than if they had never
existed.

CHAPTER XXV

THE connections which Cowperwood made during
the ensuing year and a half with Stener, Strobik,
Butler, State Treasurer Van Nostrand, State Senator
Relihan, representative of "the interests," so-called, at
Harrisburg, ex-City Treasurer Julian Bode, and various
banks and concerns which were friendly to these gentlemen and others of their ilk were numerous and confidential. For Stener, Strobik, Wycroft, Harmon, and
himself he executed the North Pennsylvania deal, by
which he became a holder of a fifth of the controlling
stock which they knew of, and as much more of smaller
scattered holdings as he could possibly secure. He had
advised them that all they needed to buy was a bare
majority, if so much, of the stock, which they could hold
jointly; for, as he informed them in a friendly way, the
rank and file of stockholders never vote. Their interests
are as a rule too small, their other duties too large. They
haven't the time. Privately, he believed that a man
with a sixth interest in a very large corporation, where
the stock was widely scattered, and where the individual
holdings were small, could, if he chose, and had the manipulative and executive faculties, control the entire situation; but he did not say so. He thought it would be a
very easy matter for him to control this North Pennsylvania line once these stock transactions were settled, for
he knew more about it than any one else. He was drawing up plans for the issue of a new block of stock, to pay
for the extension of the line, once this sought control had
been secured and the legislature had granted a franchise.
He wanted Stener to lay down money for the purchase

274

and improvement of a subsidiary line, which this North Pennsylvania line would eventually have to have; and he wanted himself and Stener to control it privately, he carrying the largest holding, of course. This eventually would give him personally absolute control of the whole road, and the others would have to wait on him. He and Stener went in together on the purchase of the Seventeenth and Nineteenth Street line and in the gambling in stocks which ensued as an incident. State Treasurer Van Nostrand, State Senator Relihan, ex-Treasurer Bode, and others deposited large sums of money with him to carry these stocks on margin also. By the summer of 1871, when Cowperwood was nearly thirty-four years of age, he had a banking business estimated at nearly two million dollars, personal holdings aggregating nearly half a million, and prospects which looked forward along a straight line to wealth which might rival that of any American if he continued. The city, through its treasurer —still Mr. Stener—was a depositor with him to the extent of nearly five hundred thousand dollars. The State, through its State treasurer, Mr. Van Nostrand, carried two hundred thousand dollars on his books. Mr. Bode was speculating in street-railway stocks to the extent of fifty thousand dollars, Mr. Relihan to the same amount. A small army of politicians and political hangers-on were on his books for various sums. For Edward Malia Butler he occasionally carried as high as one hundred thousand dollars in margins, and his own loans at the banks, varying from day to day on variously hypothecated securities, were as high as seven and eight hundred thousand dollars. He had surrounded and entangled himself in a splendid, glittering network of connections, like a spider in a spangled net, every thread of which he knew, had laid, had tested; and he was watching all the details.

Nothing in the form of a collapse or failure could reasonably have come to Cowperwood at any time, barring some unforeseen, incalculable calamity, because, in spite

THE FINANCIER

of the far-reaching nature of his ambitions, he was not
spreading himself out so thin but that he was still exceedingly cautious as to how he was going in, bracing
his natural resources and power to withstand shock. His
one pet idea, the thing he put more faith in than anything else, was his street-railway holdings, and particularly his actual control of the Seventeenth and Nineteenth
Street line. Through an advance to him, or deposit,
made in his bank by Stener at a time when the stock of
the Seventeenth and Nineteenth Street was at a low ebb,
he had managed to pick it up—fifty-one per cent. of it—
for himself and Stener, by virtue of which he was able to
do as he pleased with the road. He had resorted to very
"peculiar" methods, as they afterward came to be termed
in financial circles, to get this stock at his own valuation,
for through agents he had caused suits for damages to be
brought against the company for non-payment of interest due. A little stock in the hands of a hireling, a
request made to a court of record to examine the books
of the company in order to determine whether a receivership were not advisable, a simultaneous attack in the
stock market, selling at three, five, seven, and ten points
off, brought the frightened stockholders into the market
with their holdings. The banks considered the line a
poor risk, and called their loans in connection with it.
His father's bank had made one loan to one of the principal stockholders, and that was promptly called, of course.
Then, through an agent, the several heaviest share-
holders were approached and an offer was made to help
them out. The stocks would be taken off their hands
at forty. They had not really been able to discover the
source of all their woes; but they realized that the road
was in bad condition. Better let it go. The money was
immediately forthcoming, and Mr. Frank Cowperwood
and Mr. George W. Stener jointly controlled fifty-one per
cent. But, as in the case of the North Pennsylvania line,
Cowperwood had been quietly buying all of the small

minority holdings, so that he had in reality fifty-one per cent. of the stock, and Stener twenty-five per cent. more.

This did not satisfy, but intoxicated him, for in his success in this matter he immediately saw the opportunity of fulfilling his long-contemplated dream—that of reorganizing the company in conjunction with the North Pennsylvania line, issuing three shares where one had been before and starting to unload all but a control on the general public. In these early manipulations he was really not as daring as other American financiers later became, but he was daring enough. His plan was to spread rumors of the coming consolidation of the two lines, to appeal to the legislature for privileges of extension, to get up notable prospectuses and annual reports, and to boom the stock on the stock exchange as well as his various resources would permit. The trouble is that when you are trying to make a market for a stock—to unload a large issue such as his was (over five hundred thousand dollars' worth)—while retaining five hundred thousand for yourself, it requires large capital to handle it. The owner in these cases is compelled to be able not only to go on the market and do large amounts of fictitious buyings, thus creating a fictitious demand, but once this fictitious demand has deceived the public and he has been able to unload a considerable quantity of his wares, he is, unless he rids himself of all his stock, compelled to stand behind it. If, for instance, he sells five thousand shares, as was done in this instance, and retains five thousand, he must see that the public price of the outstanding five thousand shares does not fall below a certain point, because the value of his private shares falls with them. And if, as is almost always the case, the private shares have been hypothecated with banks and trust companies for money wherewith to conduct other enterprises, the falling of their value in the open market merely means that the banks will call for large margins to protect their loans or call their loans entirely. This would mean that his work was a failure, and he might readily fail. He was already conducting one such difficult campaign in connection with this city-loan deal, the price of which varied from day to day, and which he was only too anxious to have vary, for in the main he profited by these changes. But this second burden, interesting enough as it was, meant that the necessity for watchfulness was increased, and that he had to be doubly careful. To him it was the crowning effort in a long series of ventures. Once the stock was sold at a high price, the money borrowed from the city treasurer could be returned; his own holdings, created out of foresight, by capitalizing the future, by writing the shrewd prospectuses and reports, would be worth their face value, or a little less. He would have money to invest in other lines. He could talk of a combination with Butler, Simpson, Mollenhauer, and others. He might obtain the financial direction of the whole, in which case he would be worth millions. One shrewd thing he did which indicated the foresight and subtlety of the man was to make a separate organization or company of any extension which he made to his line. Thus, if he had two or three miles of track on a street, and he wanted to extend it two or three miles farther on the same street, instead of including this extension in the existing corporation, he would make a second corporation to control the additional two or three miles of right of way. The corporation he would capitalize at so much, and issue stocks and bonds for its construction, equipment, and manipulation. This corporation he would then take over into the parent concern, issuing more stocks and bonds wherewith to do it. In writing a prospectus or a report of the conditions and prospects of the City Street Railway Company, which he finally called all his holdings, it looked so much better to write in that the City Street Railway Company was composed of the Seventeenth and Nineteenth Street line, operating so many miles of tracks and controlling such and such property; the Union Passenger Railway—which was merely an extension, perhaps—controlling so many more miles and having such and such outstanding liabilities and resources; the North Pennsylvania Street Railway Company, having so many more miles, and so on. It meant more bookkeeping; but a large amount of bookkeeping, as he very originally and very early saw, was not at all a bad thing. It was like a maze or net in which one might wander blindly unless he knew or was shown how to go. Bookkeepers and assistants generally were never to be trusted with more than a small portion of the general facts. His brothers, for instance, did not know the various ramifications of his numerous deals, and executed his orders blindly. Sometimes Joseph said to Edward, in a puzzled way, "Well, Frank knows what he is about." He would transfer balances and claims from one organization to another to suit himself, since it was all a part of his property, anyhow, and no one but himself knew exactly how he stood.

On the other hand, he was most careful to see that every current obligation was instantly met, and even anticipated, for he wanted to make a great show of regularity. Nothing was so precious as reputation and standing. He would call upon or write his bankers and trust companies weeks before an obligation was drawing to maturity, and say: "Now that matter of Union Street Railway sixes. That's coming to a head pretty soon. Do you want me to settle in full, or shall we go on? Or do you want me to give you some other stock in its place?"

His forethought, caution, and promptness pleased the bankers. They thought he was one of the sanest, shrewdest men they had ever met. His reputation and standing were so obviously precious to him. And he was so quick to take advantage of any opportunity.

"Oh, that's all right, Frank," Walter Leigh, the then

treasurer of Drexel & Co., used to say to him. "We know these things are all right. It depends on the market. If they don't drop off we won't bother. Let them stand. How's business?"

So they would fall into a pleasant social talk, and that was the way he did business.

However, by the spring and summer of 1871 Cowperwood had actually, without being in any conceivable danger from any source, spread himself out pretty thin. With his growing financial opportunities he had grown very liberal in what might be termed his understanding of living. Certain young art-dealers in Philadelphia, learning of his artistic inclinations and his growing wealth, had followed him up with suggestions as to what might be had in the lines in which they knew he was beginning to take an intelligent interest—furniture, tapestries, rugs, objects of art, and paintings—at first the American, and later the foreign masters exclusively. Even yet he did not deem that he was sufficiently wealthy to indulge in these to any notable extent; but they were growing on him, and he was buying more liberally than he had deemed it possible for him to do several years before. Pictures at three hundred, five hundred, a thousand, and even two thousand dollars were now nothing extraordinary. He was beginning to see if he wished to do anything exceptional in art—the collection of worth-while paintings, for instance—he would have to pay much more than this. The real collectors of distinguished art were paying ten, twenty, and thirty thousand dollars each for rare examples, and some even still more. There were rugs, objects of art, furniture, tapestries which he saw and heard of which were most alluring in their beauty, and which, because of his growing wisdom in these matters, he desired greatly to possess. His own and his father's house had not been furnished fully in these matters; and there was that other house in North Tenth Street, which, for reasons which many might desire to be nameless, he desired to make ex-

ceptionally beautiful. Aileen had always objected to the
condition of her father's house. As their intimacy increased it was so easy to see what had been troubling her
most in her life. Love of distinguished surroundings was
a basic longing with her, though she could never have
interpreted her longings into perfect facts. She had not
the discrimination. But this place where they were secretly meeting must be beautiful, and she was no keener
for that than was he. It became a second treasure-trove,
more distinguished on the interior than some rooms of his
own home. He began to gather here some rare examples
of altar cloths, rugs, and tapestries of the middle ages.
He bought furniture after the Georgian theory, which is
a combination of Chippendale, Sheraton, and Hepple-
white modified by the Italian Renaissance and the French
Louis. He needed handsome examples of porcelain,
statuary, Greek vase forms; and he learned of lovely collections of Japanese ivories and netzkes, if one wanted
to go to the expense, which could be displayed in handsome curio-cases or upon étagères. As a matter of fact,
as his money began to come in, and he had Aileen to love
him and secretly approve of his conduct, he felt that he
was just beginning to live. Her beauty—as is always the
case with passions of this character—grew upon him, and
he lavished presents of silver and gold and jewels, which
were secretly kept here and here secretly worn for him.
The hours when they could be together were not numerous; but she used music-lessons, visits to the art-gallery,
riding, visits to friends, and so forth, as excuses, all of
which passed muster for a period of nearly three years.

But in other ways—in his own family life and that of
his father—he was easier, more liberal. By degrees, and
largely because of his own confidence, he induced his
father to enter upon his street-car speculations, to use
the resources of the Third National to carry a part of his
loans and to furnish capital at such times as quick resources were necessary. In the beginning the old gentle-

man was a little bit nervous and skeptical, but as time wore on and nothing but profit eventuated, he grew bolder and more confident.

"Frank," he would say, looking up over his spectacles, "aren't you afraid you're going a little too fast in these matters? You're carrying a lot of loans these days."

"No more than I ever did, father, considering my resources. I'm keeping sharp books on that. You can't turn large deals without large loans. You know that as well as I do."

"Yes, I know; but—now that Green and Coates— aren't you going it pretty strong there?"

"Not at all. I know the inside conditions there. The stock is bound to go up eventually. I'll bull it up. I'll combine it with my other lines, if necessary."

Cowperwood stared at his boy over his glasses. Never was there such a defiant, daring manipulator.

"You needn't worry about me, father. If you are going to do that, call my loans. Other banks will loan on my stocks. I'd like to see your bank have the interest."

Cowperwood, Sr., was convinced. There was no gainsaying this argument. His bank, like many another, was loaning Frank heavily, but no more so than any other. And he was carrying great blocks of stocks in his son's companies, solely because they were safe and he would be told when to get out if ever that were necessary. Frank's brothers were being aided in the same way to make some money on the side; and their interests, like his father's, were now bound up indissolubly with his own.

But this matter of art was the most singular thing which had come into his life so far. Where some people have a passion for nature—the beauty of scenery and its passionate moods—and others for books or music or personal adornment, Cowperwood's growing mood was for pictures and objects of art generally. To begin with, as we have seen, he had not known so very much about them. The furnishings in the first home in North Front Street were a slight development, mild as he now saw it, and based on a very moderate income. Later he had been coming by actual purchase into the understanding of so many things. Fletcher Gray, a partner in Cable & Gray, a local firm of importers of art objects, had called on him once in connection with a tapestry of the fourteenth century weaving which he had to sell. Mr. Gray, a young man of twenty-six, was not exactly an expert in the matter, but an enthusiastic student, and almost instantly he conveyed some of his suppressed and yet fiery love of the beautiful to Cowperwood. He was a comparatively slender person, with fluffy chestnut hair that uncontrollably insisted on falling wavily over his white forehead and shading his dark walnut-colored eyes. His face in its totality suggested a carefully modeled medallion of Hermes or Mercury. Cowperwood listened to him talk of an evening and thought what a splendid thing it would be, as Gray pointed out in speaking of great men's homes generally, to have a perfect collection of blue porcelains or Japanese netzkes or sword-hilts, or Oriental rugs, or Gobelin or Flemish tapestries.

"There are fifty periods of one shade of blue porcelain alone, Mr. Cowperwood," Gray had informed him, one night. "I'm a mere novice in these things. These periods are to be detected by the slight differences in the decorations, and you can trace the changes from period to period. There are at least seven distinct schools or periods of rugs—Persian, Armenian, Arabian, Flemish, Modern Polish, Hungarian, and so on. If you ever went into that, it would be a distinguished thing to get a complete—I mean a representative—collection of some one period, or of all these periods. They are beautiful. I have seen some of them, others I've read about."

He stopped and looked at Cowperwood, who felt quite clearly that this youth for some reason expected him to take an intense interest in art. He talked as though Cowperwood would, of course, become a great collector of something.

"I tell you, Mr. Cowperwood," he said, another night, during one of their friendly chats, "there is nothing like this business to me. I love it. There's money in it, I confess that, but there is so much more to me. The study of it never wearies me. I can't get down to my place too early nor stay too late. I know that I know nothing at all comparatively, but I know also that I know a little, at that."

"You're in the right business," observed Cowperwood, sympathetically. "Any one can see that."

"It's beautiful," the latter observed, and looked lovingly at a splendid Grecian amphora unearthed somewhere in Asia Minor, which he had brought to Cowperwood's home in order to induce him to buy it. It was of a unique form, full-bodied, wide-legged, wide-based, with one of its delicious handles, that had been firmly baked to its side, gone, and the decorations done in a dull lead-blue wash against the original light umber of the burnt clay. He had the history of the excavated house in which it had been discovered, and meditated as to the art of the life that had passed. His love for its beauty was so genuine that it moved Cowperwood.

"You'll make a convert of me yet," he said. "Art will be the ruin of me. I'm inclined that way temperamentally as it is, I think, and between you and Ellsworth and Gordon Strake"—he mentioned another young man who was intensely interested in the best examples of painting—"you'll complete my downfall. Strake has a splendid idea. He wants me to begin right now—I'm using that word 'right' in the sense of 'properly,'" he commented—"and get what examples I can of just the few rare things in each school or period of art which would illustrate each properly and fully. He says the great pictures are going to increase in value, and what I could get for a few hundred thousand now will be worth millions later on. He doesn't want me to bother with American art."

"He's right," exclaimed Gray, "although it isn't good business for me to praise another art man. And I think Strake knows what he's talking about. Paintings aren't as much a specialty with us as some other things; but they are, too. I think of them most as connected with decoration. But if you did want to make a great collection, you couldn't do better than follow that idea. I've never seen or heard of anything like it outside of the great museums, but it would be splendid if it were done right. It would take a great deal of money, though, I should think."

"Not so very much. At least, not all at once. It would be a matter of years, of course. Strake thinks that some excellent examples of different periods could be picked up now and later replaced if anything better in the same field showed up."

"That's an idea, also. We all do that more or less."

Gray stirred meditatively in his chair and ran his hand through his fluffy hair. His eyes brooded great, deep things concerning the illimitable realm of refinement in which he was working. Cowperwood caught the significance and intensity of his idea clearly. What could be greater, more distinguished than to make a splendid, authentic collection of something? He was making money now. Why not begin now? What he bought could be sold later if necessary. Both Strake and Gray assured him that the rare, genuine things of art rose in value, and he knew it must be so. His common sense told him that judgment and discrimination and effort put in this realm, as in any other, must of necessity result in value as well as distinction. What was a rich man without a great distinction of presence and artistic background? The really great men had it. There were some here in Philadelphia who tried to have it, but what he had seen thus far had been woefully insufficient. If he should go on now accumulating wealth, was not this business of making a great collection just the thing to do? Surely it was. And it suited the texture and fiber of his being as it was steadily unfolding. He wanted to be at last artistically as well as financially distinguished.

CHAPTER XXVI

THINGS would have gone exceedingly well in the face of any ordinary drift or turn of fortune had it been that Cowperwood's life and career depended upon any such conventional thing as an ordinary drift of events. Some lives seem fated for the dramatic and the spectacular. There seems no such thing as peace in the stars that govern at their birth. All is unrest and turmoil, great activity and great thought.

This boy, for he was scarcely more than that, was peculiarly marked by and for this spirit of unrest. His mind, in spite of his outward placidity, was tinged by a great seeking. Wealth, in the beginning, had seemed the only goal, to which was shortly added the beauty of women. And now art, for art's sake—the first, faint radiance of a rosy dawn—had begun to shine in upon him, and to the beauty of womanhood he was beginning to see how necessary it was to add the beauty of life—the beauty of material background—how, in fact, the only background for great beauty was great art. This girl, this Aileen Butler, in her raw youth and radiance, was nevertheless creating in him a sense of the distinguished, and a need for it which had never existed in him before to the same degree. It is impossible to define these subtleties of reaction, temperament on temperament, for no one knows to what degree we are marked by the things which attract us. A love affair such as this had proved to be was quite as a drop of coloring added to a glass of clear water, or a foreign chemical agent introduced into a delicate chemical formula.

287

A definite change had taken place, and never again could things be as they had been before.

Aileen Butler, for all her crudeness, was a definite force personally. Her nature was, in a way, a protest against the clumsy conditions by which she found herself surrounded. Her father's local reputation as a quondam garbage contractor ("slop-collector," was the unfeeling comment of the vulgarian cognoscenti); her own unavailing efforts to right a condition of material vulgarity or artistic anarchy in her own home; the hopelessness of ever being admitted to those distinguished portals which she recognized afar off as the last *sancta sanctorum* of established respectability and social distinction, had bred in her, even at this early age, a feeling of deadly opposition to conditions as they were. Through the Cowperwoods at first she had hoped to meet a few people, young men and women—and particularly men—who were above the station in which she found herself, and to whom her beauty and prospective fortune (significant, but not great) would commend her; but this had not been the case. The Cowperwoods themselves, in spite of Frank Cowperwood's artistic proclivities and growing wealth, were not in yet. In fact, aside from the subtle, preliminary consideration which they were receiving, they were a long way off.

"Mrs. Cowperwood, my dear! She's charming to look at, don't you know, but essentially middle-class. He is an able man—any one can see that. If it weren't for her now—but—"

Up go the eyebrows. We assume a bored look. If we were less refined we would lift our hands vulgarly in protest. And so there you are. Frank Cowperwood, shrewd observer that he was, was beginning to see where the rub was. He knew.

But Aileen, foiled in her ambitions by a certain insouciance of manner expressed in her presence by the daughters of those superior families who deigned to come once or twice to the Cowperwood home and elsewhere where she went, and offended by the passionate interest youth may display without admitting social equality, had turned in thought to the strongest, most artistic, most distinguished personality of them all—Cowperwood himself. In him instinctively she recognized a way out—a door—and by the same token a subtle, impending artistic future of great magnificence. (That Cowperwood saw the same in her need not be assumed.) This man would make a name for himself; he would rise beyond anything he now dreamed of—she felt it. There was here in him, in some nebulous, unrecognizable form, a great artistic reality which was finer than anything she could plan for herself. She wanted luxury, magnificence, social station. Well, if she could get this man they would come to her. There were, apparently, insuperable barriers in the way; but hers was no weakling nature, and neither was his. They ran together temperamentally from the first like two leopards. Her own thoughts—crude, half formulated, half spoken— nevertheless matched his to a degree in the quality of their force and their raw directness.

"I don't think papa knows how to do," she said to him, one day. "It isn't his fault. He can't help it. He knows that he can't. And he knows that I know it. For years I wanted him to move out of that old house there. He knows that he ought to. But even that wouldn't do much good."

She paused, looking at him with a straight, clear, vigorous glance. He liked the medallion sharpness of her features—their smooth, vigorous modeling.

"Never mind, pet," he replied. They were in the North Tenth Street house at the time; and he had been more than ever impressed with the force and fire of her disposition and the essential largeness of a mind which would never be perfect for want of some subtle strain of refinement—he could not tell what. "We will arrange

all these things later, you and I. I don't see my way
out of this now; but I think the best thing to do is to
confess to Lillian some day, and see if some other plan
can't be arranged. She doesn't want to injure the children any more than I do. I want to fix it so they won't
be injured. But if she's being neglected, as she certainly is in this case, and I'm not satisfied, the best thing
to do is to separate. I can provide for her amply.
I wouldn't be at all surprised if she would be willing
to let me go. She certainly wouldn't want any publicity."

He was counting practically, and man-fashion, on her
love for her children.

Aileen looked at him with clear, questioning, uncertain eyes. She was not wholly without sympathy, but
in a way this situation did not appeal to her as needing
much. Mrs. Cowperwood was not friendly in her mood
toward her. It was not based on anything save a difference in their point of view. Mrs. Cowperwood could never
understand how a girl could carry her head so high and
"put on such airs," and Aileen could not understand how
any one could be so lymphatic and lackadaisical as her
hostess. That was no way to live. Life was made for
riding, driving, dancing, going. It was made for airs
and banter and persiflage and coquetry. To see this
woman, the wife of a young, forceful man like Cowperwood, acting, even though she were five years older and
the mother of two children, as though life on its romantic
and enthusiastic pleasurable side were all over was too
much for her. Of course Lillian was unsuited to Frank;
of course he needed a young woman like herself, and fate
would surely give him to her. Then what a delicious life
they would lead!

"Oh, Frank," she exclaimed to him, over and over,
"if we could only manage it. Do you think we can?"

"Do I think we can? Certainly I do. It's only a
matter of time. I think if I were to put the matter to

her clearly, she wouldn't expect me to stay. You look out how you conduct your affairs. If your father or your brother should ever suspect me there'd be an explosion in this town, if nothing worse. They'd fight me in all my money deals, if they didn't kill me. Are you thinking carefully of what you are doing?"

"All the time. If anything happens I'll deny everything. They can't prove it if I deny it. I'll come to you in the long run, just the same."

She stroked his cheeks with the loving fingers of the wildly enamoured woman.

"I'll do anything for you, sweetheart," she declared. "I'd die for you if I had to. I love you so."

"Well, pet, no danger. You wouldn't have to do anything like that. But be careful."

Then, after several years of this secret relationship, in which the ties of sympathy and understanding grew stronger instead of weaker, came the storm. It burst unexpectedly and out of a clear sky, and bore no relation to the intention or volition of any individual. It was nothing more than a fire, a distant one, the great Chicago fire, October 7th, 1871, which burned that city—its vast commercial section—to the ground, and instantly and incidentally produced a financial panic, vicious, though of short duration. The fire began on Saturday, October 7th, and continued apparently unabated until the following Wednesday. It destroyed the banks, the commercial houses, the shipping conveniences, and vast stretches of property—millions upon millions—of the Western city. The heaviest loss fell naturally upon the insurance companies, which instantly, in many cases—the majority—closed their doors. This threw the loss back on the merchants—New York and New England principally—who had sold goods to the Western dealers on credit, and who now could not expect to be paid for even a very small percentage of their claims. Again, very grievous losses were borne by the host of Eastern capitalists who had for years past partly owned, or who held heavy mortgages on, the magnificent buildings for business purposes and residences in which Chicago was already rivaling every city on the continent. Transportation was disturbed, and the keen scent of Wall Street, and Third Street in Philadelphia, and State Street in Boston, instantly perceived in the early reports the gravity of the situation. Nothing could be done on Saturday or Sunday after the exchange closed, for the opening reports came too late. On Monday, though, the facts were pouring in thick and fast; and the owners of railroad securities, government securities, street-car securities, and, indeed, all other forms of stocks and bonds, began to throw them on the market in order to raise cash. The banks naturally were calling their loans, and the result was a stock stampede which equaled the Black Friday of Wall Street of two years before.

Cowperwood and his father were out of town at the time the fire began. They had gone with several friends —bankers—to look at a proposed route of extension of a local steam-railroad, on which a loan was desired. In buggies they had driven over a good portion of the route, and were returning to Philadelphia late Sunday evening when the cries of newsboys hawking an "extra" reached their ears.

"Ho! Extra! Extra! All about the big Chicago fire!"

"Ho! Extra! Extra! Chicago burning down! Extra! Extra!"

The cries were long-drawn-out, ominous, pathetic. In the dusk of a dreary Sunday afternoon, when the city had apparently retired to Sabbath meditation and prayer, with that tinge of the dying year in the foliage and in the air, one caught a sense of something grim and gloomy.

"Hey, boy!" called Cowperwood, listening, seeing a shabbily clothed misfit of a boy with a bundle of papers under his arm turning a corner. "What's that? Chicago burning!"

He looked at his father and the other men in a significant way as he reached for the paper, and then, glancing at the headlines, realized the worst.

ALL CHICAGO BURNING

FIRE RAGES UNCHECKED IN COMMERCIAL SECTION SINCE YESTERDAY
EVENING. BANKS, COMMERCIAL HOUSES, PUBLIC BUILDINGS
IN RUINS. DIRECT TELEGRAPHIC COMMUNICATION
SUSPENDED SINCE THREE O'CLOCK TO-
DAY. NO END TO PROGRESS
OF DISASTER IN SIGHT

"That looks rather serious," said Cowperwood, calmly, to his companions, a cold, commanding force coming into his eyes and voice. To his father he said a little while afterward, "It's panic, unless the majority of the banks and brokerage firms stand together."

He was thinking quickly, brilliantly, resourcefully of his own outstanding obligations. His father's bank was carrying one hundred thousand dollars' worth of his street-railway securities at sixty, and fifty thousand dollars' worth of city loan at seventy. His father had "up with him" (Cowperwood) over forty thousand dollars in cash covering market manipulations in these stocks. The banking house of Drexel & Co. was on his books as a creditor for one hundred thousand, and that loan would be called unless they were especially merciful, which was not likely. Jay Cooke & Co. were his creditors for another one hundred and fifty thousand. They would want their money. At four smaller banks and three brokerage companies he was debtor for sums ranging from sixty and fifty thousand dollars down. The city treasurer was involved with him to the extent of nearly five hundred thousand dollars, and exposure of that would create a scandal; the State treasurer for two hundred thousand. There were small accounts, hundreds of them, ranging from one hundred dollars up to five and ten thousand. A panic would mean not only a withdrawal of deposits and a calling of loans, but a heavy depression of securities. How could he realize on his securities?—that was the question—how, without selling so many points off that his fortune would be swept away and he would be ruined?

CHAPTER XXVII

IT was early evening when these cries of "extra" had sounded in Cowperwood's ears. They were, in a way, like a death-knell, for never in all the upbuilding of his affairs had his lines of interests been so extended. His investment in local street-railway stocks for himself and Stener represented fully half of all his interests. And the deposit of city loan, which he manipulated for the city treasurer, represented a fourth more. If this were a temporary depression which would affect only a few houses, he might be able to borrow heavily from others; but it was not a temporary depression in that sense. All houses would be affected—all business. New York, Chicago, Boston, Philadelphia—it was all the same now. No banking house, insurance company, trust company, or other commercial organization would be loaning much of anything on anything for some time to come. They would be calling their loans. And those investors who had deposited money with him for speculative purposes would now, on the morrow, cancel their orders and withdraw their deposits, or sell short. Where would he raise the money to meet these cancellations, withdrawals, calls, and shrinkages in values? He had, perhaps, between four and five hundred thousand dollars in quick assets; but to-morrow's complications might necessitate a million or more—in all likelihood would. To-morrow would see a great shrinkage. At the sound of the gong on the floor of the stock exchange, announcing the opening of the day's business, there would be a general crash, a rush to sell. These stocks of his companies which he valued at eighty and ninety cents on the dollar, and which he had hypothecated with banks at these figures for sixty and seventy per cent. of their total value, would drop ten, fifteen, or twenty points in the hour. It was probable that even at these figures they could not be disposed of in sufficient quantities to aid him; and, anyhow, it was his business to support the market—not sell. But that would not retard the banks from demanding that additional collateral be furnished to cover the shrinkage, if they did not demand the total of his loans. Where was he to get it? He was sorry now that he was so badly involved with the city treasury. Something ill might come of that. He figured briskly the while he waved adieu to his financial friends, who hurried away, struck with their own predicament; and he and his father waited to take a car for Girard Avenue.

"You had better go on out to the house, father, and I'll stop and send some telegrams." The 'phone had not been invented then. "I'll be right out, and we'll go into this thing together. It looks like black weather to me. I wouldn't, if I were you, say anything to any one until after we have had our talk; then we can decide what to do."

Old Cowperwood was plucking at his side-whiskers in his mackerel-like way. He was cogitating as to what might happen to him in case his son failed, for he was deeply involved with him. He was a little gray in his complexion now, frightened; for he had strained a point in his affairs to accommodate his son. If Frank should not be able promptly on the morrow to meet the call which the bank might have to make for one hundred and fifty thousand dollars, the onus and scandal of the situation would be on him. Why had he favored his son so largely, and that on stocks which were liable to shrink so notably? would be the first question that would be asked. The subtle eyes of Adam Davi, the first vice-president of the bank, would have to be met—a man who was obviously waiting to step into his shoes. He was a shrewder man than Cowperwood, *père*, as the latter knew; and he held secret relations with some of the directors— was on friendly outside terms with several—and might gladly comment on this situation, if it proved unfavorable to the powers in charge. It was ticklish business, and had to be solved by an immediate return of the cash on call, if at all.

On the other hand, Cowperwood, the son, was meditating on the tangled relation he now found himself in in connection with the city treasurer and the fact that it was not possible for him to support the market alone. Those who should have been in a position to help him were now as bad off as himself. There were many unfavorable points in the whole situation. Drexel & Co. had been booming railway stocks—loaning heavily on them. Jay Cooke & Co. had been backing Northern Pacific—were practically doing their best to build that immense transcontinental system alone. Naturally, they were long on that. At the first word they would throw over their surest securities—government bonds, and the like—in order to protect their more speculative holdings. The bears would see the point. They would hammer and hammer, selling short all along the line. But he did not dare to do that. He would be breaking his own back quickly, and what he needed was time. If he could only get time—three days, a week, ten days—this storm would surely blow over.

The thing that was troubling him most was the matter of the half-million invested with him by Stener. A fall election was drawing near. Stener, although he had served two terms, was slated for re-election. A scandal in connection with the city treasury would be a very bad thing. It would end Stener's career as an official— would very likely send him to the penitentiary, and would seriously damage his own reputation as a banker. It might wreck the Republican party's chances to win. It would certainly involve him as having much to do with it. If that happened, he would have the politicians to reckon with. For, if he were hard pressed, as he would be, and failed, the fact that he had been trying to invade the city street-railway preserves which they held sacred to themselves, with borrowed city money, and that this borrowing was liable to cost them the city election, would all come out. They could not view all that with a kindly eye. It would be useless to say, as he could, that he had borrowed the money at two per cent. (most of it, to save himself, had been covered by a protective clause of that kind), or that he had merely acted as an agent for Stener. That might go down with the unsophisticated of the outer world, but it would never be swallowed by the politicians. They knew better than that. His failure at this time would be peculiarly disastrous. What was he to do?

There was another phase to this situation, however, that encouraged him, and that was his knowledge of how city politics were going in general. It was useless for any politician, however lofty, to take a high and mighty tone in a crisis like this. All of them, great and small, were profiting in one way and another through city privileges. Butler, Mollenhauer, and Simpson, he knew, made money out of contracts—legal enough, though they might be looked upon as rank favoritism—and also out of vast sums of money collected in the shape of taxes—land taxes, water taxes, etc.—which were deposited in the various banks that these men and the others had had designated as legal depositories for city money. The banks supposedly carried the city's money in their vaults as a favor, without paying interest of any kind, and then reinvested it—for whom? Cowperwood had no complaint to make, for he was being well treated, but these men could scarcely expect to monopolize all the city's benefits. He did not know either Mollenhauer or Simpson personally—he often wished he had been introduced to them—but he knew they as well as Butler had made money out of his own manipulation of city loan. Also, Butler, whom he did know, was most friendly to him. It was not unreasonable for him to think, in a crisis like this, that if worst came to worst, he could make a clean breast of it to Butler and receive aid. In case he could not get through secretly with Stener's help, Cowperwood made up his mind that he would do this.

His first move, however, would be to go at once to Stener's house and demand the loan of an additional three or four hundred thousand dollars. Stener had always been very tractable, and in this instance would see how important it was that his shortage of half a million should not be made public. This additional loan would go far toward seeing him (Cowperwood) through. But he must get as much more as possible. Where to get it? Presidents of banks and trust companies, large stock jobbers, and the like, would have to be seen. Then there was a loan of one hundred thousand dollars he was carrying for Butler. The old contractor might be induced to leave that. He hurried to his own house, secured his runabout, and drove rapidly to Stener's.

As it turned out, however, much to his distress and confusion, Stener was out of town—down on the Chesapeake with several friends of Strobik's and Harmon's shooting ducks and fishing, and was not expected back for several days. Mrs. Stener, all unconscious of calamity impending, informed Cowperwood that she was not certain whether her husband could be reached quickly by telegraph or not. He was in the marshes back of some small town. Cowperwood sent an urgent wire to the nearest point and then, to make assurance doubly sure, to several other points in the same neighborhood, asking him to return immediately. He was not at all sure, however, that Stener would return in time and was greatly nonplussed and uncertain for the moment as to what his next step would be. Aid must be forthcoming from somewhere and at once.

Suddenly a helpful thought occurred to him. Butler and Mollenhauer and Simpson were long on local street-railways. They must combine to support the situation and protect their interests. They could see the big bankers, Drexel & Co. and Cooke & Co., and others and urge them to sustain the market. They could strengthen things generally by organizing a buying ring, and under cover of their support, if they would, he might sell enough to let him out, and even permit him to go short and make something—a whole lot. It was a brilliant thought, worthy of a greater situation, and its only weakness was that it was not absolutely certain of fulfilment.

He decided to go to Butler at once, the only disturbing thought being that he would now be compelled to reveal his own and Stener's affairs. But delay might be fatal. He might not be able to connect with Stener before he would be compelled to close his doors as a banker—unless the politicians, ignorant of his true predicament, were able and willing to do much more for him than he could safely count upon their doing—in which case the facts in connection with the treasury defalcation would become quite plain anyhow, and he and Stener would be hopelessly compromised. Twenty-four hours could make a felon out of Stener, a bankrupt out of himself. He had been through panics before. The first onslaught was always the worst. After he had closed his doors no aid from any one would be forthcoming, and the politicians would have against him the additional grievance that he had concealed the fact of the defalcation. They might claim that if he had told them they would have aided him gladly in order to avoid exposure. It now seemed to Cowperwood the part of wisdom to go to Butler, who was really his friend, and urge upon him the necessity of doing as much as possible to support the market and prevent his, Cowperwood's, failure in order to avoid a political scandal. To just what extent the politicians would feel the force of this necessity Cowperwood could not be sure. Still, in Stener's absence, it was the only thing he had to rely upon. He re-entered his runabout and drove swiftly to old Butler's home.

When he arrived there the famous contractor was at dinner. He had not heard the calling of the extras, and, of course, did not understand as yet the significance of the fire. The servant's announcement of Cowperwood brought him smiling to the door.

"Won't you come in and join us? We're just havin' a light supper. Have a cup of coffee or tea, now—do."

"I can't," replied Cowperwood, good-naturedly, viewing the stout Irishman with a literary and half-humorous eye. He could never quite resist the impulse to see the old gentleman as something different from the thing he really was—a successful man of affairs. He seemed just the least bit of a caricature of the normal—like Hosea Whitney and Andrew Pohlhemus used to be on 'change. To-night, however, he was in no mood for light reflection. "Not to-night," he thanked Mr. Butler; "I'm in too much of a hurry. I want to see you for just a few moments, and then I'll be off again. I won't keep you very long."

"Why, if that's the case, I'll come right out." And Butler returned to the dining-room to put down his napkin. Aileen, who was also dining, had heard Cowperwood's voice, and was on the *qui vive* to see him. She wondered what it was that could have brought him at this time of night to see her father. She could not leave the table at once, but hoped to before he went. Cowperwood was thinking of her, even in the face of this impending storm, as he was of his wife, and many other things. If his affairs came down in a heap it would go hard with those attached to him. In this first clouding of disaster, he could not tell how things would eventuate. He meditated on this desperately, but he was not panic-stricken. His naturally even-molded face was set in fine, classic lines; his eye was as hard as chilled steel.

"Well, now," exclaimed Butler, returning, his countenance manifesting a decidedly comfortable relationship with the world as at present constituted. "What's up with you to-night? Nawthin' wrong, I hope. It's been too fine a day."

"Nothing very serious, I hope myself," replied Cowperwood; "but I want to talk with you for a few minutes, anyhow. Don't you think we had better go up to your room?"

"I was just going to say that," replied Butler—"the cigars are up there."

They started from the reception-room to the stairs, Butler preceding; and, as the contractor mounted, Aileen came out from the dining-room. She was dressed in a silk evening gown of rich garnet, and as she came her skirts frou-froued. Her splendid hair was drawn up from the base of the neck and the line of the forehead into some quaint convolutions which constituted a reddish-golden crown. Her complexion was glowing, and she had all the gay force of white arms and bare shoulders which so attracted Cowperwood. He thought her neck and shoulders were exquisite, and he told her so often. To-night he was not so conscious of her charms as he was of his own troubles. She was not conscious of the trouble which was besetting him; but the moment she saw his face she realized that there was something wrong. Her nature was so akin to his, so much in accord with it at present, that she felt instantly that he was laboring under some burden.

"Oh, Mr. Cowperwood, how do you do?" she exclaimed, coming forward and holding out her hand as her father went on up-stairs. She was delaying him deliberately in order to have a word with him, and this bold acting was for the benefit of others. It struck them both as silly at times, however necessary it might be. To-night the thought of the falsity of their position was nothing. He was troubled, and she was immediately anxious.

"What's the trouble, honey?" she whispered, when her father was out of hearing. "You look worried."

"Nothing much, I hope, sweet," he said. "Chicago is burning up, and there's going to be trouble to-morrow. I have to talk to your father."

She had time only for a sympathetic, distressed "Oh, my honey!" before he withdrew his hand and strolled onward. She squeezed his arm, and went through the reception-room to the parlor, where the piano was. She sat down, thinking, for never before had she seen Cowperwood's face wearing such an expression of stern, disturbed calculation. It was placid, like fine, white wax, but quite as cold; and those deep, vague, inscrutable eyes! So Chicago was burning. What would happen to him? Was he very much involved? He had never told her in detail of his affairs. He could not, if he had tried. They were too complicated. She would not have understood fully any more than would have Mrs. Cowperwood. But she was worried, nevertheless, because it was her Frank, and because she was bound to him by what to her seemed insoluble ties.

Shall we pause to speculate for a moment on this sympathetic ebullition of temperament? Literature, outside of the masters, has given us but one idea of the mistress, the subtle, calculating siren who delights to prey on the souls of men. The journalism and the moral pamphleteering of the time seem to foster it with almost partisan zeal. You would imagine that a censorship of life had been established by divinity, and the care of its execution given into the hands of the utterly conservative. Yet there is that other form of liaison which has nothing to do with conscious calculation. In the vast majority of cases it is without design or guile. The average woman, controlled by her affections and deeply in love, is no more capable of anything save sacrificial thought than a child—the desire to give; and so long as this state endures, she can only do this. She may change. Hell hath no fury, etc. But the sacrificial, yielding, solicitous attitude is the chief characteristic of the mistress; and it is this very attitude in contradistinction to the grasping legality of established matrimony that has caused so many wounds in the defenses of the latter. The temperament of man, either male or female, cannot help falling down before and worshiping this non-seeking, sacrificial note. It approaches vast distinction in life. It appears to be related to that last word in art, that largeness of spirit which is the first characteristic of the great picture, the great building, the great sculpture, the great decoration—namely, a giving, freely and without stint of itself, of beauty. Hence the significance of this particular mood in Aileen.

Cowperwood went up-stairs thinking of her for the moment, and then of his wife. All the subleties of the present combination troubled him.

"Sit down, sit down. You won't take a little somethin'? You never do. I remember now. Well, have a cigar, anyhow. Now, what's this that's troublin' you to-night?"

"Extra! Extra! All about the big Chicago fire! Chicago burning down!"

You could hear the voices calling faintly in the distance, far off toward the thicker residential sections.

"Just that," replied Cowperwood. "Have you heard the news?"

"No. What's that they're calling?"

"It's a big fire out in Chicago."

"Oh," replied Butler, still not gaining the significance of it.

"It's burning down the business section there, and I fancy it's going to disturb financial conditions here to-morrow. That is what I have come to see you about. How are your investments? Pretty well drawn in?"

Butler suddenly gained the idea from Cowperwood's expression, which was stern, though normal enough to all appearances, and from the distant calling voices that there was something serious in the wind. He put up his large hand as he leaned back in his big leather chair, and covered his mouth and chin with it. Over those big knuckles, and bigger nose, thick and cartilaginous, his large, shaggy-eyebrowed eyes gleamed. His gray, bristly hair stood up stiffly in a short, even growth all over his head.

"So that's it," he said. "You're expectin' trouble to-morrow. How are your own affairs?"

"I'm in pretty good shape, I think, all told, if the money element of this town doesn't lose its head and go wild. There has to be a lot of common sense exercised. You know we are facing a real panic. It may not last long, but while it does it will be bad. Stocks are going to drop to-morrow ten or fifteen points on the opening. The banks are going to call their loans unless some arrangement can be made to prevent them. No one man can do that. It will have to be a combination of men. You and Mr. Simpson and Mr. Mollenhauer might do it—that is, you could if you would persuade the big banking people to combine to back the market. There is going to be a raid on local street-railways. Unless they are sustained the bottom is going to drop out. I have always known that you were long on those. I thought you and Mr. Mollenhauer and some of the others might want to act. If you don't I might as well confess that it is going to go rather hard with me. I am not strong enough to face this thing alone."

Cowperwood looked at Butler, meditating on how he should tell the whole truth in regard to Stener.

"Well, now, that's pretty bad," said Butler, calmly and meditatively. He was thinking of how his own affairs stood exactly. A panic was not good for him either—meant considerable trouble for him, but he was not in a desperate state. He could not fail. He might lose some money, but not a vast amount—before he could adjust things. Still he did not care to lose any money.

"How is it you're so bad off?" he asked, curiously. He was wondering how the fact that the bottom was going to drop out of local street-railways would affect Cowperwood so seriously. "You're not carryin' any of them things, are you?" he added.

It was now a question of lying or telling the truth, and Cowperwood was literally afraid to risk lying in this dilemma. If he did not gain Butler's comprehending support he might fail, and if he failed the truth would come out, anyhow.

"I might as well make a clean breast of this, Mr. Butler," he said, throwing himself on the old man's sympathies and looking at him with that brisk assurance which Butler so greatly admired in him. He felt as proud of Cowperwood at times as he did of his own sons. He felt that he had helped to put him where he was.

"The fact is that I have been buying street-railway stocks, but not for myself exactly. I am going to do something now which I think I ought not to do, but I cannot help myself. If I don't do it, it will be to injure you and a lot of people whom I do not wish to injure. I know you are naturally interested in the outcome of the fall election. The truth is I have been carrying a lot of stocks for Mr. Stener and some of his friends. I do not know that all the money has come from the city treasury, but I think that most of it has. I know what that means to Mr. Stener and the Republican party and your interests in case I fail. I don't think Mr. Stener started this of his own accord in the first place—I think I am as much to blame as anybody—but it grew out of other things. As you know, I handled that matter of city loan for him and then some of his friends wanted me to invest in street-railways for them. I have been doing that ever since. Personally I have borrowed considerable money from Mr. Stener at two per cent. In fact, originally the transactions were covered in that way. Now I don't want to shoulder the blame on any one. It comes back to me and I am willing to let it stay there, except that if I fail Mr. Stener will be blamed and that will reflect on the administration. Naturally, I don't want to fail. There is no excuse for my doing so. Aside from this panic I have never been in a better position in my life. But I cannot weather this storm without assistance, and I want to know if you won't help me. If I pull through I will give you my word that I will see that the money which has been taken from the treasury is put back there. Mr. Stener is out of town or I would have brought him here with me."

Cowperwood was lying out of the whole cloth in regard to bringing Stener with him, and he had no intention of putting the money back in the city treasury except by degrees and in such manner as suited his convenience; but what he had said sounded well and created a great seeming of fairness.

"How much money is it Stener has invested with you?" asked Butler. He was a little confused by this curious development. It put Cowperwood and Stener in an odd light.

"About five hundred thousand dollars," replied Cowperwood.

The old man straightened up. "Is it as much as that?" he said.

"Just about—a little more or a little less; I'm not sure which."

The old contractor listened solemnly to all that Cowperwood had to say on this score, thinking of the effect on the Republican party and his own contracting interests. He liked Cowperwood, but this was a rough thing the latter was telling him—rough, and a great deal to ask. He was a slow-thinking and a slow-moving man, but he did well enough when he did think. He had considerable money invested in Philadelphia street-railway stocks— perhaps as much as eight hundred thousand dollars. Mr. Mollenhauer had perhaps as much more. He did not know that, but he had heard rumors to that effect. Whether the interesting Senator Simpson had much or

THE FINANCIER

little he could not tell. Cowperwood had told him in the past that he thought the Senator had a good deal. Most of their holdings, as in the case of Cowperwood's, were hypothecated at the various banks for loans and these loans invested in other ways. It was not advisable or comfortable to have these loans called, though the condition of no one of the triumvirate was anything like as bad as that of Cowperwood. They could see themselves through without much trouble, though not without probable loss unless they took hurried action to protect themselves.

The thing that interested Butler most at this time was this matter of Stener. He had not heard much about Stener's doings since the time when the city loan issue was turned over to Cowperwood, but he fancied he was getting along well enough. These small-fry politicians, quite like the large ones, were always getting up some little scheme in one way and another, to make some money. They had to be watched right along to see that their schemes did not become too ambitious, or their plottings infringe on the perquisites of the big politicians or injure the party, but beyond that nothing was thought about it. He would not have thought so much of it if Cowperwood had told him that Stener was involved, say, to the extent of seventy-five or a hundred thousand dollars. That might be adjusted. But five hundred thousand dollars!

"That's a lot of money," said Butler, thinking of the amazing audacity of Stener, but failing at the moment to identify it with the astute machinations of Cowperwood. Cowperwood had always seemed so conservative in his plannings. It must be others behind Stener.

"Well, now, that's something to think about," he said. "There's no time to lose if there's going to be a panic in the morning. How much good will it do ye if we did support the market?"

"A great deal," returned Cowperwood, "although of

course I have to raise money in other ways. I have that one hundred thousand dollars of yours on deposit. Is it likely that you'll want that right away?"

"It may be," said Butler.

"It's just as likely that I'll need it so badly that I can't give it up without seriously injuring myself," added Cowperwood. "That's just one of a lot of things. If you and Senator Simpson and Mr. Mollenhauer were to get together—you're the largest holders of street-railway stocks—and were to see Mr. Drexel and Mr. Cooke, you could fix things so that matters would be considerably easier. I will be all right if my loans are not called, and my loans will not be called if the market does not slump too heavily. If it does, all my securities are depreciated, and I can't hold out."

Old Butler got up. "This is serious business," he said. "I wish you'd never gone in with Stener in that way. It's bad business. Still, I'll do what I can. I can't promise much. I'm not the only one that has a hand in things in this town." He was thinking it was right decent of Cowperwood to forewarn him this way in regard to his own affairs and the city election, even though he was saving his own neck by so doing. He meant to do what he could.

"I don't suppose you could keep this matter of Stener and the city treasury quiet for a day or two until I see how I come out?" suggested Cowperwood, warily.

"I can't promise that," replied Butler. "I'll have to do the best I can. I won't lave it go any further than I can help—you can depend on that." He was thinking how the effect of Stener's crime could be overcome if Cowperwood failed.

"Owen!"

He stepped to the door, and, opening it, called down over the banister.

"Yes, father."

"Have Dan hitch up the light buggy and bring it

around to the door. And you get your hat and coat. I want you to go along with me."

"Yes, father."

He came back.

"Sure that's a nice little storm in a teapot, now, isn't it? Chicago begins to burn, and I have to worry here in Philadelphia. Well, well—" Cowperwood was up now and moving to the door. "And where are you going?"

"Back to the house. I have several people coming there to see me."

"Well, good night. I'll see you later, then, I suppose. I'll tell you what I find out."

He went back in his room for something, and Cowperwood descended the stair alone. From the hangings of the reception-room entryway Aileen signaled him silently to draw near.

"I hope it's nothing serious, honey?" she questioned, looking into his solemn eyes.

It was not time for love, and he felt it.

"No," he said, almost coldly, "I think not."

"Frank, don't let this thing make you forget me for long, please. I love you so."

"I won't! I can't! Don't you know I won't?" He had started to kiss her, but a noise disturbed him. "'Sh!"

He walked to the door, and she followed him with eager, sympathetic eyes.

What if anything should happen to her Frank? What if anything could? What would she do? That was what was troubling her. What would, what could she do to help him?

CHAPTER XXVIII

THE condition of the Republican party at this time in
Philadelphia, its relationship to George W. Stener,
Edward Malia Butler, Henry A. Mollenhauer, Senator
Mark Simpson, and others, will have to be briefly indicated here, in order to foreshadow Cowperwood's actual
situation. Butler, as we have seen, was normally interested in and friendly to Cowperwood. George
W. Stener was Cowperwood's tool. Henry A. Mollenhauer and Senator Simpson were strong rivals of Butler
in the control of city affairs. Mr. Simpson represented
the Republican control of the State legislature, which
could dictate to the city if necessary, making new election laws, revising the city charter, starting political investigations, and the like. He had many influential
newspapers, corporations, banks, and the like at his beck
and call. Mr. Mollenhauer represented the Germans,
some Americans, and some large stable corporations—a
very solid and respectable man. All three were strong,
able, and dangerous politically. The two latter counted
on Butler's influence, particularly with the Irish, and a
certain number of ward leaders and Catholic politicians
and laymen, who were as loyal to him as though he were
a part of the church itself. Butler's return to these fol-
lowers was protection, influence, aid, and good-will generally. The city's return to him, *via* Mollenhauer and
Simpson, was contracts—fat ones—street-paving, bridges,
viaducts, sewers. And in order for him to get these
contracts the affairs of the Republican party, of which
he was a beneficiary as well as a leader, must be kept
reasonably straight. At the same time it was no more

a part of his need to keep the affairs of the party straight than it was of either Mollenhauer's or Simpson's, and Stener was not his appointee. The latter was more directly responsible to Mollenhauer than to any one else.

As Butler stepped into the vehicle with Owen he was thinking about this, and it was puzzling him greatly.

"Cowperwood's just been here," he said to his son Owen, who had been rapidly coming into a sound financial understanding of late, and was already a shrewder man politically and socially than his father, though he had not the latter's political and social magnetism. "He's been tellin' me that he's in a rather tight place," confided Butler, solemnly. "You hear that?" he indicated, as some voice in the distance was calling "Extra! Extra!" "That's Chicago burnin', and there's goin' to be trouble on the stock exchange to-morrow. We have a lot of our street-railway stocks around at the different banks. If we don't look sharp they'll be callin' our loans. We have to 'tend to that the first thing in the mornin'. Cowperwood has a hundred thousand of mine with him that he wants me to let stay there, and he has some money that belongs to Stener, he tells me."

Butler did not care to tell Owen at once what he knew about the condition of the city treasurer. He was wondering whether he should tell him.

"Stener?" asked Owen, curiously. "Has he been dabbling in stocks?" Owen had heard some rumors concerning Stener and others only very recently, which he had not credited nor yet communicated to his father. He wondered whether there was any truth in them, or trouble in that direction. "How much money of his has Cowperwood?" he asked. He thought of warning his father in case he did not know.

Butler meditated. Owen was his son and a very capable one. He could be trusted. Why shouldn't he tell him? It would be best to talk the whole thing over with him. "Quite a bit, I'm afraid," he finally said. "As a matter of fact, it's a great deal—about five hundred thousand dollars. If that should become known, it would be makin' a good deal of noise, I'm thinkin'."

"Whew!" exclaimed Owen in astonishment. "Five hundred thousand dollars! Good Lord, father! Do you mean to say Stener has got away with five hundred thousand dollars? He's been robbing the place wholesale. Why, I wouldn't say he was clever enough to do that. Five hundred thousand dollars! It will make a nice row if that comes out."

"Aisy, now! Aisy, now!" replied Butler, doing his best to keep all phases of the situation in mind. "We can't tell exactly what the circumstances were yet. He mayn't have meant to take so much. It may all come out all right yet. The money's invested. Cowperwood hasn't failed yet. It may be put back. The thing to be settled on now is whether anything can be done to save him. If he's tellin' me the truth—and I never knew him to lie— he can get out of this if street-railway stocks don't break too heavy in the mornin'. I'm going over to see Henry Mollenhauer and Mark Simpson. They're in on this. Cowperwood wanted to see if I couldn't get them to get the bankers together and to help stand by the market. He thought we might protect our loans by comin' on and buyin' and holdin' up the price."

Owen was running swiftly in his mind over Cowperwood's affairs—as much as he knew of them. He felt keenly that the banker ought to be shaken out. This dilemma was his fault, not Stener's—he felt. It was strange to him that his father did not see it and resent it.

"You see what it is, father," he said, dramatically, after a time. He had been thinking of what he had heard recently of Cowperwood's growing street-railway investments. "Cowperwood's been using this money of Stener's to pick up stocks, and he's in a hole. If it hadn't been for this fire he'd have got away with it; but now he wants you and Simpson and Mollenhauer and the others to pull him out. He's a nice fellow, and I like him fairly well; but you're a fool if you do. He has more than belongs to him already. I heard the other day that he has the Front Street line, and almost all of Green and Coates; and that he and Stener own the Seventeenth and Nineteenth; but I didn't believe it. I've been intending to ask you about it. I think Cowperwood has a majority for himself stowed away somewhere in every instance. Stener is a pawn. He moves him around where he pleases. I know it. It must be so."

Owen's eyes gleamed avariciously, opposingly. Why should his father help Cowperwood to become rich, when he might just as well let him sink now and buy up as much of his street-railway holdings as he could? Cowperwood was a crook. He had led Stener on. This condition of the treasury might hurt the party some, but certainly not enough to warrant his father's allowing himself to be used as a catspaw. Cowperwood ought to be punished, sold out, driven out of the street-railway business in which Owen was anxious to rise.

"Now you know," observed Butler, thickly and solemnly, "I always thought that young felly was clever, but I hardly thought he was as clever as all that. So that's his game. You're pretty shrewd yourself, aren't you? Well, we can fix that, if we think well of it. The thing that's troublin' me is this matter of Stener and the city treasury. If somethin' isn't done about that it may go hard with the party this fall, and with some of our contracts. You don't want to forget that an election is comin' along in November. If Cowperwood should fail and that money couldn't be put back—" He broke off abstractedly. "I'm wonderin' if I ought to call in that one hundred thousand dollars. It's goin' to take considerable money to meet my loans in the mornin'."

It is a curious matter of psychology, but it was only now that the real difficulties of the situation were beginning to dawn on Butler. In the presence of Cowperwood he was so influenced by that young man's personality and his magnetic presentation of his need and his own liking for him that he had not stopped to consider all the phases of his own relationship to the situation. Out here in the cool night air, talking to Owen, who was ambitious on his own account and anything but sentimentally considerate of Cowperwood, he was beginning to sober down and see things in their true light. He had to admit that Cowperwood had seriously compromised the city treasury and the Republican party, and incidentally Butler's own private interests. Nevertheless, he liked Cowperwood. He was in no way prepared to desert him. He was now going to see Mollenhauer and Simpson as much to save the party and his own affairs and a scandal as anything, but also with the kindly feeling that he ought to do something to help the young man, if anything could help him. He might even leave his hundred-thousand-dollar loan with him until the last hour, as Cowperwood had requested, if the others were friendly.

"Well, father," said Owen, after a time, "I don't see why you need to worry any more than Mollenhauer or Simpson. If you three want to help him out, you can; but for the life of me I don't see why you should. I know this thing will have a bad effect on the election, if it comes out before then; but I can't see that it needs to, exactly. It could be hushed up until then. Anyhow, your street-railway holdings are more important than this election, and if you can see your way clear to getting the street-railway lines in your hands you won't need to worry about any elections. My advice to you is to call that one-hundred-thousand-dollar loan of yours in the morning, and meet the drop in your street-railway stocks that way. It may make Cowperwood fail, but that won't hurt you any. You can go into the market and buy his stocks. I wouldn't be surprised if he would run to you and ask you to take them. You ought to get Mollenhauer and Simpson to scare Stener so that he won't loan

Cowperwood any more money. If you don't, Cowperwood will run there and get more. Stener's in too far now. If Cowperwood won't sell out, well and good; the chances are he will bust, anyhow, and then you can pick up as much on the market as any one else. I think he'll sell. You can't afford to worry about Stener's five hundred thousand dollars. No one told him to loan it. Let him look out for himself. It may hurt the party, but you can look after that later. You and Mollenhauer can fix the newspapers so they won't talk about it till after election."

Butler's canny son paused and stared out into the dark. He was thinking how long Cowperwood had been a favorite of his father, and that it was high time that the latter's sons took his place. Owen was ambitious to become a factor in the street-railway world himself, and this was an easy way to do it. Butler was thinking whether he wanted to be so hard on his former lieutenant or not.

"Aisy! Aisy!" was all the old contractor would say. He was thinking hard.

The residence of Mr. Henry A. Mollenhauer was located, at that time, in a section of the city which was not quite though almost as new as that in which Mr. Butler was living. It was in South Broad Street, near a handsome library building which had been recently erected. It was a spacious house of the type ordinarily affected by men of new wealth in those days—a structure four stories in height of yellow brick and white stone, built after no school which one could readily identify, but not unattractive in its architectural composition. A broad flight of steps leading to a wide veranda gave into a decidedly ornate door, which was set on either side by narrow windows and ornamented to the right and left with pale-blue jardinières of considerable charm of outline. The interior, divided into twenty rooms, was paneled and parqueted in the most expensive manner for homes of that time. There was a great reception-hall, a large parlor or drawing-room, a dining-room at least thirty feet square paneled in oak; and on the second floor were a music-room devoted to the talents of Mollenhauer's three ambitious daughters, a library and private office for himself, a boudoir and distinguished bath for his wife, and a conservatory.

Mr. Mollenhauer was, and felt himself to be, a very important man. His financial and political judgment was exceedingly keen. Although he was a German, or rather an American by German parentage, he was a man of rather notable American presence. He was tall and heavy and shrewd and cold. His large chest and wide shoulders supported a head of distinguished proportions, both round and long when seen from different angles. The frontal bone descended in a protruding curve over the nose, and projected solemnly over the eyes. The latter burned with a shrewd, inquiring gaze. And the nose and mouth and chin below, as well as his smooth, hard cheeks, confirmed the impression that he knew very well what he wished in this world, and was very able without regard to let or hindrance to get it. It was a big face, impressive, well modeled. He was an excellent friend of Edward Malia Butler's, as such friendships go, and his regard for Mark Simpson was as sincere as that of one tiger for another. He respected ability; he was willing to play fair when fair was the game. When it was not, the reach of his cunning was not easily measured.

When Edward Butler and his son arrived on this Sunday evening, this distinguished representative of one-third of the city's interests was not expecting them. He was in his library reading and listening to one of his daughters playing. His wife and the other two girls, which constituted his complete ménage, had gone to church. He was of a domestic turn of mind. Still, Sunday evening being an excellent one for conference purposes generally in the world of politics, he was not without the thought that some one or other of his distinguished confrères might call. His was not the sort of mind that anticipates calamitous developments of any kind; and when they did occur he was not disposed to be very much disturbed by them. A few minutes before Butler was announced he was thinking that he would like to look in on him some day soon, as the local political slate for the coming election, which had been agreed on between them and chosen some time before, needed further discussion. Simpson had been to his office a few days before on this same business, and had said then that he might call round this Sunday evening. In all ways Mr. Mollenhauer was in a pleasant and amicable frame of mind this evening; and when the combination footman and butler, who answered the bell regularly, announced the presence of Edward Malia Butler and his son, he was well pleased.

"So there you are," he remarked to Butler, genially, when the later was shown up, and extending his hand. "I'm certainly glad to see you. And Owen! How are you, Owen? What will you gentlemen have to drink, and what will you smoke? I know you'll have something. John"—to the servitor—"see if you can find something for these gentlemen. I have just been listening to my daughter Caroline play; but I think you've frightened her off for the time being."

He moved a chair which was near by into position for Butler, and indicated to Owen another on the other side of the table. In a moment his servant had returned with a silver tray of elaborate design, carrying whiskies and wines of various dates and cigars in profusion. Owen was the new type of young financier who neither smoked nor drank. His father in a mild way did both.

"It's a comfortable place you have here," said Butler, without any indication of the important mission that had brought him. "I don't wonder you stay at home Sunday evenings. What's new in the city?"

"Nothing much, so far as I can see," replied Mollenhauer, pacifically. "Things seem to be running smooth enough. You don't know anything that we ought to worry about, do you?"

"Well, yes," said Butler, draining off the remainder of a brandy and soda that had been prepared for him. "One thing. You haven't seen an avenin' paper, have you?"

"Not at all," said Mollenhauer, straightening up. "Is there one out? What's the trouble, anyhow?"

"Nothing—except Chicago's burning, and it looks as though we'd have a little money-storm here in the morning."

"You don't say! I didn't hear that. There's a paper out, is there? Well, well—is it much of a fire?"

"The city is burning down, so they say," put in Owen, who was watching the face of the distinguished politician with considerable interest.

"Well, that *is* news. I must send out and get a paper. John!" he called. His man-servant appeared. "See if you can get me a paper somewhere." The servant disappeared. "What makes you think that would have anything to do with us?" observed Mollenhauer, returning to Butler.

"Well, there's one thing that goes with it that I didn't know till a little while ago. Our man Stener is apt to be short in his accounts, I hear, unless things come out better than some people seem to think," suggested Butler, calmly. "That might not look so well before election, would you say?"

Mollenhauer eyed him searchingly.

"Where did you get that?" he said. "He hasn't deliberately taken much money, has he? How much has he taken—do you know?"

"Quite a bit," replied Butler, quietly. "Nearly five

hundred thousand, so I understand. Only I wouldn't say that it has been taken as yet. It's in danger of being lost."

"Five hundred thousand!" exclaimed Mollenhauer in amazement, and yet preserving his usual calm. "You don't tell me! How long has this been going on? What has he been doing with the money?"

"He's loaned a good deal—about five hundred thousand dollars to this young Cowperwood in Third Street, that's been handlin' city loan. They've been investin' it for themselves in one thing and another—mostly in buyin' up street-railways." (At the mention of street-railways Mollenhauer's impassive countenance underwent a barely perceptible change.) "This fire, accordin' to Cowperwood, is certain to produce a panic in the mornin', and unless he gets considerable help he doesn't see how he's to hold out. If he doesn't hold out, there'll be five hundred thousand dollars missin' from the city treasury which can't be put back. Stener's out of town and Cowperwood's come to me to see what can be done about it. As a matter of fact, he's done a little business for me in times past, and he thought maybe I could help him now—that is, that I might get you and the Senator to see the big bankers with me and help support the market in the mornin'. If we don't he's goin' to fail, and he thought the scandal would hurt us in the election. He doesn't appear to me to be workin' any game—just anxious to save himself and do the square thing by me—by us, if he can." Butler paused.

Mr. Mollenhauer was quite astonished at this unexpected development. He had never thought of Stener as having any particular executive or financial ability. Cowperwood he knew of indirectly. He had profited by his manipulation of city loan. Evidently the banker had made a fool of Stener, and had used the money for street-railway shares! He and Stener must have quite some private holdings. That interested Mollenhauer greatly.

"Five hundred thousand dollars!" he repeated, when Butler had finished. "That is quite a little money. If merely supporting the market would save Cowperwood we might do that, although if it's a severe panic I do not see how anything we can do will be of very much assistance to him. If he's in a very tight place and a severe slump is coming, it will take a great deal more than our merely supporting the market to save him. I've been through that before. You don't know what his liabilities are?"

"I do not," said Butler.

"He didn't ask for money, you say?"

"He wants me to l'ave a hundred thousand he has of mine until he sees whether he can get through or not."

"Mr. Stener is really out of town, I suppose?" Mollenhauer was innately suspicious.

"So Cowperwood says. We can send and find out."

Mollenhauer was thinking of the various aspects of the case. Supporting the market would be all very well if that would save Cowperwood. Stener would then be compelled to restore the five hundred thousand dollars to the city treasury. He consulted with Butler and learned that Cowperwood had agreed to do this. But what assurance had any one that Cowperwood could be so saved? And if he were saved would he give the money back to Stener? If he required actual money, who would loan it to him in a time like this—in case a sharp panic was imminent? What security could he give? On the other hand, under pressure from the right parties he might be made to surrender all his street-railway holdings for a song—his and Stener's. If he (Mollenhauer) could get them he would not particularly care whether the election was lost this fall or not, although he felt satisfied, as had Owen, that it would not be lost. It could be bought, as usual. The defalcation—if Cowperwood's failure made Stener's loan into one—could be concealed long enough, Mollenhauer thought, to win. Personally he would like to have time to frighten Stener into refusing Cowperwood additional aid, and then to raid the latter's street-railway stock in combination with everybody else's, for that matter—Simpson's and Butler's included. One of the big sources of future wealth in Philadelphia lay in these lines. For the present, however, he had to pretend an interest in saving the party at the polls.

"I can't speak for the Senator, that's sure," pursued Mr. Mollenhauer, reflectively. "I don't know what he may think. As for myself, I will be perfectly willing to do what I can to keep up the price of stocks, if that will do any good. I would do so naturally in order to protect my loans. The thing that we ought to be thinking about, in my judgment, is how to prevent exposure, in case Mr. Cowperwood does fail, until after election. We have no assurance, of course, that however much we support the market we will be able to sustain it."

"We have not," replied Butler, solemnly.

Owen thought he could see Cowperwood's approaching doom quite plainly. At that moment the door-bell rang again. A maid, in the absence of the footman, brought in the name of Senator Simpson.

"Just the man," said Mollenhauer. "Show him up. You can see what he thinks."

"Perhaps I had better leave you alone now," suggested Owen to his father. "Perhaps I can find Miss Caroline, and she will sing for me. I'll wait for you, father," he added.

Mollenhauer cast him an ingratiating smile, and as he stepped out Senator Simpson walked in.

A more interesting type of his kind than Senator Mark Simpson never flourished in the State of Pennsylvania, which has been productive of interesting types. Contrasted with either of the two men who now greeted him warmly and shook his hand, he was not so impressive, physically speaking. His body was not so large as Mollenhauer's, nor so rotund as Butler's. He did not possess the chest expansion of either, nor did he convey the sense of ruddy blood which was obvious in the others. By comparison he was rather a small man—five feet nine inches, to Mollenhauer's six feet and Butler's five feet eleven inches and a half. His face was smooth, with a receding jaw, which was not as impressive as this pugnacious feature in the other two. His eyes were not as frank as those of Mr. Butler, nor as defiant as those of Mr. Mollenhauer; but for subtlety they were unmatched by either—deep, strange, receding, cavernous eyes which contemplated you as might those of a cat looking out of a dark hole, and suggestive of all the artfulness that ever distinguished the feline family. He had a strange mop of black hair sweeping down over a fine, low, white forehead, and a skin as pale and bluish as poor health might make it; but there was, nevertheless, resident here a strange, resistant, capable force that ruled men by the force of political ideas —the subtlety with which he knew how to feed cupidity with hope and gain and the ruthlessness with which he repaid those who said him nay. He was a still man, as such a man might well have been—feeble and fish-like in his hand-shake, wan and slightly lackadaisical in his smile, but speaking always with eyes that answered for every defect. Mr. Mollenhauer had the profoundest respect for him; and he was a strong man, from whom only strong men could win acknowledgment. Butler scarcely understood him, but realized that he was powerful, and in a close political game could be thoroughly relied upon. Butler knew that his own sincerity was appreciated by Simpson, and Simpson believed that Butler was well worth while in a city which was honored by the presence of Mr. Mollenhauer.

"Av'nin', Mark, I'm glad to see you," was Butler's greeting.

"How are you, Edward?" came the quiet reply.

"Well, Senator, you're not looking any the worse for wear. Can I pour you something?"

"Nothing to-night, Henry," replied Simpson. "I haven't long to stay. I just stopped by on my way home. My wife's over here at the Cavanagh's, and I have to stop by to fetch her." He was referring to the family of a steam-railway manipulator of great distinction.

"Well, it's a good thing you dropped in, Senator, just when you did," began Mollenhauer, seating himself after his guest. "Butler here has been telling me of a little political problem that has arisen since I last saw you. I suppose you've heard that Chicago is burning?"

"Yes; Cavanagh was just telling me. It looks to be quite serious. I think the market will drop heavily in the morning."

"I wouldn't be surprised myself," put in Mollenhauer, laconically.

"Here's the paper now," said Butler, as John, the servant, came in from the street bearing the paper in his hand. Mollenhauer took it and spread it out before them. It was among the earliest of the extras that were ever issued in this country, and contained a rather impressive spread of type announcing that the conflagration in the lake city was growing hourly worse since its inception the day before.

"Well, that is certainly dreadful," said Simpson. "I'm very sorry for Chicago. I have many friends there. I shall hope to hear that it is not so bad as it seems."

The man had a rather grandiloquent manner which he never in his later years abandoned under any circumstances.

"The matter that Butler was telling me about," continued Mollenhauer, after Simpson had ceased to scan the head-lines and had read the rather disjointed intelligence beneath them, "has something to do with this in a way. You know the habit our city treasurers have of loaning out their money at two per cent.?"

"Yes?" said Simpson, inquiringly.

"Well, Mr. Stener, it seems, has been loaning out a

good deal of the city's money to this young Cowperwood, in Third Street, who has been handling city loan."

"You don't say!" said Simpson, putting on an air of surprise. "Not much, I hope?" The Senator, like Butler and Mollenhauer, was profiting greatly by cheap loans from the various designated city depositories.

"Well, it seems that Stener has loaned him as much as five hundred thousand dollars, and this fire threatens to cause a panic in the morning. If by any chance Cowperwood shouldn't be able to weather this storm, Stener is apt to be short that amount, and that wouldn't look so good as a voting proposition to the people in November. Mr. Cowperwood owes Mr. Butler here one hundred thousand dollars, and because of that he came to see him to-night. He wanted Butler to see if something couldn't be done through us to tide him over. If not"—he waved one hand suggestively—"well, he might fail."

Mr. Simpson fingered his strange, wide mouth with his delicate hand. "What have they been doing with the five hundred thousand dollars?" he asked.

"Oh, the boys must make a little somethin' on the side," said Butler, cheerfully. "I think they've been buyin' up street-railways, for one thing." He stuck his thumbs in the armholes of his vest. Both Mollenhauer and Simpson smiled wan smiles.

"Quite so," said Mr. Mollenhauer. Senator Simpson merely looked the deep things that he thought.

He, too, was thinking how useless it was for any one to approach a group of politicians with a proposition like this, particularly in a crisis such as bid fair to occur. He reflected that if he and Butler and Mollenhauer could get together and promise Cowperwood protection in return for the surrender of his street-railway holdings it would be a very different matter. It would be very easy in this case to carry the city treasury loan along in silence and even issue more money to support it; but it was not sure, in the first place, that Cowperwood could be made to surrender his stocks, and in the second place that either Butler or Mollenhauer would enter into any such deal with him, Simpson. Essentially Butler was a fair man. He had come here to say a good word for Cowperwood. Mollenhauer and Simpson himself were silent rivals. Although they worked together politically it was toward essentially different financial ends. They were allied in no one particular financial proposition, any more than Simpson and Butler were. And besides, in all probability Cowperwood was no fool. He was not guilty with Stener; the latter had loaned him money. The Senator reflected on whether he should broach some such subtle solution of the situation as had occurred to him to his colleagues, but he decided not. Really Mollenhauer was too treacherous a man to work with on a thing of this kind. It was a splendid chance but dangerous. He had better go it alone. For the present they should demand of Stener that he get Cowperwood to return the five hundred thousand dollars if he could. If not, Stener should be made a sacrifice of for the benefit of the party, if need be. Cowperwood's stocks, with this tip as to his condition, would, Simpson reflected, offer a good opportunity for a little stock-exchange work on the part of his own brokers. They could spread rumors as to Cowperwood's condition and then offer to take his shares off his hands—for a song, of course. It was an evil moment that led Cowperwood to Butler.

"Well, now," said the Senator, after a prolonged silence, "I might sympathize with Mr. Cowperwood in his situation, and I certainly don't blame him for buying up street-railways if he can; but I really don't see what can be done for him very well in this crisis. I don't know about you, gentlemen, but I am rather certain that I am not in a position to pick other people's chestnuts out of the fire if I wanted to, just now. It all depends on whether we feel that the danger to the party is sufficient to warrant our going down into our pockets and assisting him."

At the mention of real money to be loaned Mr. Mollenhauer pulled a long face. "I can't see that I will be able to do very much for Mr. Cowperwood," he sighed.

"Begad," said Mr. Butler, with a keen sense of humor, "it looks to me as if I'd better be gettin' in my one hundred thousand dollars. That's the first business of the early mornin'."

Neither Mr. Simpson nor Mr. Mollenhauer condescended on this occasion to smile even the wan smile they had smiled before. They merely looked wise and solemn.

"But this matter of the city treasury now," said Senator Simpson, after the atmosphere had been allowed to settle a little, "is something to which we shall have to devote a little thought. If Mr. Cowperwood should fail, and the treasury lose that much money, it would embarrass us no little. What lines are they," he added, as an afterthought, "that this man has been particularly interested in?"

"I really don't know," replied Butler, who did not care to say what Owen had told him on the drive over. The Senator could find out for himself. Mollenhauer did not even condescend to reply.

"I don't see," said Mollenhauer, "unless we can make Mr. Stener get the money back before this man Cowperwood fails, how we can save ourselves from considerable annoyance later; but if we did anything which would look as though we were going to compel restitution, he would probably shut up shop anyhow. So there's no remedy in that direction. And it wouldn't be very kind to our friend Edward here to do it until we hear how he comes out on his affair."

He was referring to Butler's loan.

"Certainly not," said Senator Simpson, with true political sagacity and feeling.

"I'll have that one hundred thousand dollars in the

mornin'," said Butler, "and never fear." He saw, as far as that was concerned, that if he really wished to be sure of his money he had better call his loan in the morning. Whether he would really do it was, even at this late hour, an open question. Butler was not unsympathetic in his attitude toward Cowperwood. He remembered with pleasure the favors he had done the young financier in earlier days.

"I think," said Simpson, "if anything comes of this matter that we will have to do our best to hush it up until after the election. The newspapers can just as well keep silent on that score as not. There's one thing I would suggest"—and he was now thinking of the street-railway properties which Mr. Cowperwood had so judiciously collected—"and that is that the city treasurer be cautioned against advancing any more money in a situation of this kind. He might readily be compromised into advancing much more. I suppose a word from you, Henry, would prevent that."

"Yes; I can do that," said Mollenhauer, solemnly.

"My judgment would be," said Butler, in a rather obscure manner, thinking of Cowperwood's mistake in appealing to these noble protectors of the public, "that it's best to let sleepin' dogs run be thimselves."

Thus ended Frank Cowperwood's dreams of what Butler and his political associates might do for him in this hour of his distress.

CHAPTER XXIX

THE energies of Cowperwood, after leaving Butler—after having made the one arrangement which held, as he thought, any considerable hope for the morrow—were devoted to the task of seeing others who might be of some assistance to him. He had left word with Mrs. Stener that if any message came from her husband he was to be notified at once. He hunted up Walter Leigh, of Drexel & Co., Avery Stone, of Jay Cooke & Co., President Davison of the Girard National Bank, and others in order to consult about his loans. He wanted to see what they thought of the situation, what they had heard, if anything. If he offered them such and such sets of securities in the morning, what could he get on them? He wanted to negotiate a loan with President Davison covering all his real and personal property.

"I can't tell you, Frank," Walter Leigh insisted, when Cowperwood, after many conferences, had called at his house. "I don't know how things will be running by to-morrow noon. I'm glad to know how you stand. I'm glad you're doing what you're doing—getting all your affairs in shape. It will help a lot. I'll favor you all I possibly can. But if the chief decides on a certain group of loans to be called, they'll have to be called, that's all. I'll do my best to make things look better. If the whole of Chicago is wiped out the insurance companies—some of them, anyhow—are sure to go, and then look out. I suppose you'll call in all your loans?"

"Not any more than I have to."

"Well, that's just the way it is here—or will be."

The two men shook hands. They liked each other.

Leigh was of the city's fashionable coterie, a society man to the manner born, but with a wealth of common sense and a great deal of worldly experience. Cowperwood was fitted by brains and tact to adorn any station; but he was of a lower stratum, not of the élite by birth. Still, Leigh liked him very much.

"I'll tell you, Frank," he observed, at parting, "I've always thought you were carrying too much street-railway. It's great stuff if you can get away with it, but it's just in a pinch like this that you're apt to get hurt. You've been making money pretty fast out of that and city loan."

He looked directly into his long-time friend's eyes, and they smiled. Cowperwood liked Leigh, and Leigh liked Cowperwood. But business is business.

It was the same with Avery Stone, President Davison, and others. They had all already heard rumors of disaster when he arrived. They were not sure what the morrow would bring forth. It looked very unpromising. President Davison was doubtful about Cowperwood's house and real estate. He would do what he could. If anybody could do it for him he would. Cowperwood returned to his own home late—not so much depressed as energetically nervous and questioning; but before doing so he stopped in to see Edward Butler, whose interview with Mollenhauer and Simpson was now over. Butler, who had been meditating what he should say to Cowperwood, was not unfriendly in his manner. "So you're back," he said, when Cowperwood appeared.

"Yes, Mr. Butler," Cowperwood replied.

"Well, I'm not sure that I've been able to do anything for you. I'm afraid not," Butler said, cautiously. "It's a hard job you set me. Mr. Mollenhauer seems to think that he'll support the market, on his own account. I think he will. Mr. Simpson has interests which he has to protect. I'm goin' to buy for myself, of course."

He paused to reflect.

"I couldn't get them to call a conference with any of the big moneyed men as yet," he added, warily. "They'd rather wait and see what happens in the mornin'. Still, I wouldn't be down-hearted if I were you. If things turn out very bad they may change their minds. I had to tell them about Mr. Stener. It's pretty bad, but they're hopin' you'll come through and straighten that out. I hope so. About my own loan—well, I'll see how things are in the mornin'. If I raisonably can I'll lave it with you. You'd better see me again about it. I wouldn't try to get any more money out of Stener if I were you. It's pretty bad as it is."

Butler was friendly, but non-committal, and Cowperwood could see that he was not to get much aid from the politicians. The one thing that disturbed him was this reference to Stener. Had they already communicated with him—warned him? If so, his own coming to Butler had been a bad move; and yet from the point of view of his possible failure on the morrow it had been advisable. At least now the politicians knew where he stood. If he got in a very tight corner he would come to Butler again—the politicians could assist him or not, as they chose. If they did not help him and he failed, and the election were lost, it was their own fault. Anyhow, if he could see Stener first the latter would not be such a fool as to stand in his own light in a crisis like this.

"Things look rather dark to-night, Mr. Butler," said Cowperwood, smartly, "but I still think I'll come through. I hope so, anyhow. I'm sorry to have put you to so much trouble. I wish, of course, that you gentlemen could see your way clear to assist me, but if you can't, you can't. I have a number of things that I can do. I hope that you will leave your loan as long as you can."

He went briskly out, and Butler meditated. "A clever young chap that," he said. "It's too bad. He may come out all right at that." He was thinking of that peculiar thing about Cowperwood, his personal magnetism, which did not permit him (Butler) to get angry, although Cowperwood had put the interests of the Republican party in such jeopardy·that it might eventually affect him. "A clever felly," he said, as he went off to his room, "but he's goin' a little too fast, I'm thinkin'. He'd be doin' better if he took his time."

Cowperwood hurried to his own home only to find his father awake and brooding. To him he talked with that strong vein of sympathy and understanding which is usually characteristic of those drawn by ties of flesh and blood. He liked his father. He sympathized with his painstaking effort to get up in the world covering years and years of effort. He could not forget that as a boy he had had the loving sympathy and interest of his father. The loan which he had from the Third National, on somewhat weak Union Street Railway shares, he could probably replace if stocks did not drop too tremendously. He must replace this at all costs. But his father's investments in street-railways, which had risen with his own ventures, and which now involved an additional two hundred thousand—how could he protect these? These shares were hypothecated and the money was used for other things. Additional collateral would have to be furnished the several banks carrying them. It was nothing except loans, loans, loans, and the need of protecting them. If he could only get an additional deposit of two or three hundred thousand dollars from Stener. But that, in the face of possible financial difficulties, was rank criminality. All depended on the morrow. All depended on how much the market broke. If Simpson, Mollenhauer, and Butler did anything at all, and the several big banking concerns could be induced to stand together, it might help a little; but how, in the last analysis, was that going to save him? Were the banks going to be generous to him? How could they be? They would have to ask him for additional guarantees up to the limit of the various shrinkages, and he would have to meet them. Would they loan him money? On what? More city loan which he might get from Stener? Would the latter get back in time? He would have to pretend to Stener to have sold the additional city loan in order to get it. But, also, if he got it, he would have to account for it later, and that might not be so easy. That was the arrangement he had always had—to call for as much city loan as he had sold on 'change. He could mortgage his house, his real estate; but it all depended on how much this shrinkage would be. He would have to go on 'change himself along with Arthur Rivers (who was now out of Tighe & Co. and acting for himself), and see at what rate he could protect or close out his holdings. Simpson, Mollenhauer, Butler, and the big banking houses, because of his shrewd suggestion of the night before, were probably going to support the market to a certain extent anyhow, in order to protect their own interests. Under cover of this, if he could sell enough, even at ten points off, to realize five hundred thousand dollars he would come out all right. Could he? He went to bed finally very late, but he did not stay there long.

Monday, the 9th, opened gray and cheerless. He was up early with the dawn, shaved and dressed, and went over, under the gray-green pergola, to his father's house. The latter was up, also, and stirring about, for he had not been able to sleep. His gray eyebrows and gray hair looked rather shaggy and disheveled to Cowperwood, and his side-whiskers rather pointless and anything but decorative. The old gentleman's eyes were tired, and his face was gray. Cowperwood could see that he was worrying. He looked up from a small, ornate escritoire of buhl, which Ellsworth had found somewhere, and which was full of his private papers, and smiled wanly. He was quietly tabulating a list of his resources and liabilities, and Cowperwood winced. He hated to see his father worried, but he could not help it. He had hoped sincerely, when they built their houses together, that the days of worry for his father had gone forever.

"Counting up?" he asked, familiarly, with a smile. He wanted to hearten the old gentleman as much as possible.

"I was just running over my affairs again to see where I stood in case—" He looked quizzically at his son, and Frank smiled again.

"I wouldn't worry, father. I told you how I fixed it so that Butler and that crowd will support the market. I have Rivers and Targool and Harry Eltinge on 'change helping me sell out, and they are the best men there. They'll handle the situation carefully. I couldn't trust Ed or Joe in the case, for the moment they began to sell everybody would know what was going on with me. This way my men will seem like bears hammering the market, but not hammering too hard. I ought to be able to unload enough at ten points off to raise five hundred thousand. The market may not go lower than that. You can't tell. It isn't going to sink indefinitely. If I just knew what the big insurance companies were going to do! The morning paper hasn't come yet, has it?"

He was going to pull a bell, but remembered that the servants would scarcely be up as yet. He went to the front door himself. There were the *Press* and the *Public Ledger* lying damp from the presses. He picked them up and glanced at the front pages. His countenance fell. On one, the *Press*, was spread a great black map of Chicago, a most funereal-looking thing, the black portion indicating the burned section. He had never seen a map of Chicago before in just this clear, definite way. He had seen maps; but because of a lack of financial interest in the matter, he had never paid any attention to them. Now the city stood out ominously clear to his eye. He could not have explained to himself why it impressed him so. There was the lake rolling wide before it as a white portion, and there was the Chicago River dividing the city into three almost equal portions —the north side, the west side, the south side. He saw at once that the city was curiously arranged, somewhat like Philadelphia, and that the business section was probably an area of two or three miles square, set at the juncture of the three sides, and lying south of the main stem of the river, where it flowed into the lake after the southwest and northwest branches had united to form it. This was a significant central area; but, according to this map, it was all burned out. "Chicago in Ashes" ran a great side-heading set in heavily leaded black type. "The business section already a mass of smoldering ruins, and the fire still raging in outlying portions; banks, wholesale and retail houses, office buildings, and the magnificent trading section entirely destroyed." It went on to detail the sufferings of the homeless, the number of the dead, the number of those whose fortunes had been destroyed. Then it descanted upon the probable effect in the East.

Cowperwood set his teeth. If only the newspapers had been called upon to minimize this disaster! He had forgotten that. Butler, Mollenhauer, Simpson, and the banks could have done it. It might have been discussed more gradually. This blast of woe would frighten investors. It would cause a rush to sell. Now, unless the great money organizations stood firm, there would be a terrific slaughter, and he might not be able to realize the sum he needed. Still, there was no use to despair! He would fight this thing out as he had planned. He would go on 'change himself, a thing he rarely did. His personal influence might help some. He was considered very strong.

"I wish I were out of this d—d stock-jobbing business," he said to himself. "I wish I had never gotten into it."

He went back into the room and laid the papers down.

"Well, it looks as though Chicago were really done for.

We'll have to see how the street feels." And he excused himself, saying he wanted to go back to his room for a few minutes. He had planned the night before with his father all the moves that they could possibly make together. His father was going to see to many things personally. He came back after a time and talked to his brothers, giving them careful and detailed instructions. Then, though it was still early, he asked his father if he were going down-town, for he knew the telegraphic messages might be beginning to arrive even at this early hour—orders to sell, cancellations of orders to buy, orders to sell short. They drove down in their own light buggy; and when Cowperwood reached his own office, quite the first to arrive, it was as he expected. There were already messages, a dozen or more, to cancel or sell. While he was standing there a messenger-boy brought him three more. One was from Stener and said that he would be back by twelve o'clock, the very earliest he could make it. Cowperwood was relieved and yet distressed. He would need large sums of money to meet various loans before three. Every hour was precious. He must arrange to meet Stener at the station and talk to him before any one else should see him. Cowperwood saw clearly that this was going to be a hard, dreary, strenuous day. He would not be able to forget it very soon. That was certain. At ten minutes of eight in the morning this was very clear.

CHAPTER XXX

THIRD STREET, by the time Cowperwood reached there, was stirring with other bankers and brokers who had been called forth by the exigencies of the occasion. The shutters were open in many places where these were still maintained, and the doors wide. There was a suspicious hurrying of feet—that intensity which makes all the difference in the world between a hundred people placid and a hundred people disturbed. At Third and Dock, where the exchange stood, and as the time drew near for it to open, the atmosphere was feverish. The crowd intending to do business for the day was larger than usual, for the company of regular floor-men who represented the different firms and interests of the city was already augmented by those who had a right to operate on 'change but seldom came—men like Cowperwood and head dealers generally. The big financiers had sent their best men, seen from time to time in strenuous days past, and their very presence only seemed to intensify the general feeling of fear and unrest. The bears were eager, defiant, jubilant. The bulls were apprehensive, determined to cover (sell) in the subtlest ways if possible, shy of indicating by look or glance what they really thought. It was nothing strange to see big men here at this occasion, for older operators recalled and explained to their confidential assistants that it was always so in times like this. What would you expect?

"There's going to be h—l to pay here, Charlie, in a few minutes," one floor-man observed to his second. "You keep a close eye on me. I'll give you the quotations as near as I can get them, and you sell fast until I call a halt."

337

THE FINANCIER

He was going to go short of Northern Pacific, which was the great road building by Jay Cooke & Co., and he hoped to sell enough on a sliding scale down to sixty to assure him a fortune if he succeeded, and then to buy enough below that figure for his deliveries. It was one of those notable occasions which the shrewd are always looking for, and which only iron nerve can execute. It required so much strength to fight one's way to the center of operations and snap the bargains. So much shrewdness of mind to see the drift of things. So much courage to stay. At every pole on the floor—Northern Pacific, city street-railways, sugar, coal, mines, State securities—small crowds were gathered listening to rumors, discussing possibilities, pretending indifference, trying to figure out from the smooth surface of able faces whether there was to be a determined facing down of panic or a rush to sell. Arthur Rivers came in after a time with Simpson Talbot, an operator; and a little later Newton Targool appeared, an older man by thirteen years than when Cowperwood had first observed him. He had not changed so much—there is little change between forty and sixty. The same shrewd, inscrutable face,—the same keen sensing of the cunning nature of wealth. He was too shrewd a man to preach disaster even to his most intimate associates. It was his policy never to admit its possibility, whatever he might think, even to himself. But this morning he was satisfied that it was going to go hard with all current values the moment the bell struck. He had orders to buy certain street railway stocks up to a certain point, and to sell more of the same under cover of any stability down to seventy. After that he was to get instructions direct from Cowperwood, who was to be on the floor. Rivers had the same orders—each to unload one hundred thousand worth above seventy, if possible—to seek advice later. Both Targool and Rivers were going short on other lines in the face of the splendid opportunity to make something as bears. They said nothing at all of this to

338

Cowperwood, though he suspected it. It could not be helped. It was one of the points of the situation.

When the opening hour came the floor of 'change had become a seething mass, for the room was not notably large and the facilities for handling a crowd were insufficient. In one corner of the room the telegraph-machines—with their operators before them, a dozen or more in number, in shirt-sleeves or light-gray seersucker office-coats—were clicking rapidly and even irritatingly, the operators scribbling or ticking as the messenger brought or took information away. There were messenger-boys and 'change boys calling names—"Mr. Appleby! Mr. Hale! Mr. Thompson!"—singsonging them out in a musical but indifferent tone. About the poles the groups of men were gathering closer and closer, their coats buttoned tight, their bodies pulled erect, their faces set, their one thought being, when the gong struck, to hurl themselves like madmen at each other in order to be first to fill a bid or grab an offer. So many of them had urgent orders to sell, sell, sell; others to buy below certain figures. There were so many like Rivers and Targool and Tighe, who was also present, who were secretly determined to depress the market and buy later.

At the sound of the gong the shrill, staccato uproar began. Its metallic vibrations were still in the air when the two hundred men, who composed this local organization at its utmost stress of calculation, threw themselves upon each other in a gibbering struggle to dispose of or seize the bargains of the hour. The interests were so varied that it was impossible to say at which pole it was best to sell or buy. Those who knew most about a given stock, or a given line of stocks, had crowded around the pole which represented the center of their interests. Others, who had no specific interest but were inclined to bear the market generally, were anxious to pick the center of greatest activity and be represented at the minor poles by agents. The pole covering railroad securities, particularly the Northern Pacific, was a great center, and that of the local street-car securities was another, for of these many knew much. They were considered weak under the present circumstances, and a great killing was expected.

At this pole Cowperwood did not take his stand immediately, for he could not leave his office at once. Targool and Rivers had been delegated to stay at the center of things, Joseph and Edward to hover around on the outside and to pick up such opportunities of selling as might offer a reasonable return on the stock. The bears were determined to jam things down, and it all depended on how well the agents of Mollenhauer, Simpson, Butler, and others supported things in the street-railway world whether those stocks retained any strength or not. The last thing Butler had said the night before was that they would do the best they could. They would buy up to a certain point. Whether they would support the market indefinitely he would not say. He could not vouch for Mollenhauer and Simpson. Nor did he know the condition of their affairs. Cowperwood remained at his office, or rather in the street, visiting the various banks and trust companies where he had loans, and seeing how much he could raise on his house, his real estate, and some government bonds which he had.

At the pole where his lieutenants were stationed, things were raging. Walnut and Chestnut, one of the Simpson lines, opened at ninety, but dropped immediately to eight-four, for there were scores of offers from wild-eyed bears who were anxious to profit here—"Eighty-nine! Eighty-eight! Eighty-seven! Eighty-six! Eighty-five! Eighty-four!" "Any part of three thousand at eighty-four," some one was calling, and it meant that there was terrific unloading here on the part of some frightened speculator. Martin Schreyer, an operator, was buying for Simpson's broker, and he called, defiantly, "Take the lot"; but he no sooner did so than he was confronted by a second offer, "Any part of two thousand Walnut and Chestnut at eighty-four."

One could see the market going glimmering.

With Fifth and Sixth Street it was worse, for that was a Mollenhauer organization, and not so strong. The profits were not so great, and there had been a notable attempt at inflation here. The stocks had been unloaded freely right and left, and were now coming out.

"Any part of five thousand Fifth and Sixth at eighty-five! Eighty-four! Eighty-three! Eighty-two! Eighty-one! Eighty! Seventy-nine! Seventy-eight! Seventy-seven! Seventy-six!" It was staggering to listen to it. The expected support was not there. Mollenhauer held a control in this line already and did not need to buy. Apparently he was not even buying to protect his loans. Finally, at seventy-five, a second agent called "Sold," and there was a rush to offer him more of the same. Fifteenth and Sixteenth, Seventeenth and Nineteenth, Green and Coates, opened in the same way, only lower, for these were Butler and Cowperwood holdings, and dropped in the face of Rivers's and Targool's purchases to seventy-one, sixty-nine, sixty-three, and sixty, respectively. It was grim business, and offered small chance of unloading any quantity of anything above sixty.

While the excitement was at its highest, coats being tugged at, shoulders shaken by frantic hands, men being borne almost to the floor in the onrush to take a bid or complete a trade, Cowperwood came in. He had had a number of non-committal interviews. No one knew how the New York market was going to behave. It was uncertain how the insurance companies would weather the storm. None had failed as yet; but there was no knowing at what moment the telegraph would click out some ominous information which would have to be posted on the board. As he stood in the door looking to catch the eye of Rivers, who, at his station near the local railway post, was buying small lots to maintain a semblance of strength, the 'change gong sounded, and trading stopped. All the brokers and traders faced about to the little balcony, where the secretary of the 'change made his announcements; and there he stood, the door open behind him, a small, dark, clerkly man of thirty-eight or forty, whose spare figure and pale face bespoke the methodic mind that knows no venturous thought. In his right hand he held a slip of white paper.

"The American Fire Insurance Company of Boston announces its inability to meet its obligations." The gong sounded again.

Immediately the storm broke anew, more voluble than before, because, if after one hour of investigation on this Monday morning one insurance company had gone down, what would four or five hours or a day or two bring forth? It meant that men who had been burned out in Chicago would not be able to resume business. It meant that all loans connected with this concern had been, or would be called now. And the cries of frightened bulls offering thousand and five thousand lot holdings in Northern Pacific, Illinois Central, Reading, Lake Shore, Wabash; in all the local street-car lines; and in Cowperwood's city loans at constantly falling prices was sufficient to take the heart out of all concerned. By dint of buying for the sinking-fund, Cowperwood had maintained city loan at par; but this morning it was selling—such few sales as were made —at eighty-eight, and was constantly falling. The margin he would have to supply the banks to continue their interest in this security, if they did not call his loans instantly, was large. He had hurried to Arthur Rivers's side in the lull; but there was little he could say to him.

"It looks as though the Mollenhauer and Simpson crowds aren't doing much for the market," he observed, gravely.

"They've had advices from New York. It can't be supported very well. There are three insurance companies over there on the verge of going down, I understand. I've expected to see them posted every moment."

They stepped aside, as pandemonium began again, to discuss ways and means. Under his agreement with Stener, Cowperwood could buy up to one hundred thousand dollars of city loan, above the customary wash sales, or market manipulation, by which they were making money. This was in case the market had to be genuinely supported. He decided to buy sixty thousand worth now, and use this to sustain his loans elsewhere. Stener would pay him for this instantly, giving him more ready cash. It might help him in one way and another; and, anyhow, it might tend to strengthen the other securities long enough at least to allow him to realize a little something now at better than ruinous rates. If only he had the means "to go short" on this market! If only doing so did not really mean ruin to his present position. It was characteristic of the man that even in this storm and stress of a crisis he should be seeing how the very thing that of necessity, because of his present obligations, might ruin him, might also, under slightly different conditions, yield him a great harvest. He could not take advantage of it, however. He could not be on both sides of this market. It was either bear or bull, and of necessity he was bull. It was strange but true. His subtlety could not avail him here. He was about to turn and hurry to see a certain banker who might loan him something on his house, when the gong struck again. Once more trading ceased. Arthur Rivers, from his position at the State securities post, where city loan was sold, and where he had started to buy for Cowperwood, looked significantly at him. Newton Targool hurried to Cowperwood's side.

"You're up against it," he exclaimed. "I wouldn't try to sell against this market. It's no use. They're cutting the ground from under you. The bottom's out. Things are bound to turn in a few days. Can't you hold out? Here's more trouble."

He raised his eyes to the announcer's balcony.

"The Eastern and Western Fire Insurance Company of New York announces that it cannot meet its obligations."

A low sound something like "Haw!" broke forth.

The announcer's gavel struck for order.

"The Erie Fire Insurance Company of Rochester announces that it cannot meet its obligations."

Again that "H-a-a-a-w!"

Once more the gavel.

"The American Trust Company of New York has suspended payment."

"H-a-a-a-w!"

The storm was on.

"What do you think?" asked Targool. "You can't brave this storm. Can't you quit selling and hold out for a few days? Why not sell short?"

"They ought to close this thing up," Cowperwood said, shortly, thinking of what years later was actually done in a crisis in New York. "It would be a splendid way out. Then nothing could be done." He hurried to consult with those who, finding themselves in a similar predicament with himself, might use their influence to bring it about. It was a mean trick to play on those who, now finding the market favorable to their designs in its falling condition, were harvesting a fortune. But that was nothing to him. Business was business. There was no use selling at ruinous figures, and he gave his lieutenants orders to stop. Unless the bankers favored him heavily, or the stock exchange was closed, or Stener could be induced to deposit an additional three hundred thousand with him at once, he was ruined. He knew his assets and his liabilities as he knew his ten fingers. He hurried down the street to various bankers and brokers suggesting that they do this—close the exchange. At a few minutes before twelve o'clock he drove rapidly to the station to meet Stener; but to his great disappointment the latter was not there. It looked as though he had missed his train. Cowperwood sensed something, some trick; and in driving back to his office to see if any message had arrived, decided also to go to the city hall and to Stener's house. Perhaps he had arrived and was trying to avoid him. After what Butler had said and the evidence of non-support on the market, Cowperwood was inclined to think that Stener was being reached and influenced against him—frightened into getting out of the market entirely. It gave him a feeling of cold untoward treachery.

On the strength of this feeling Cowperwood drove swiftly to Stener's office, and, not finding him there, direct to his house. Here he was not surprised to meet Stener just coming out, looking very pale and distraught. At the sight of Cowperwood he actually blanched.

"Why, hello, Frank," he exclaimed, sheepishly, "where do you come from?"

"What's up, George?" asked Cowperwood, realizing something untoward in Stener's action, but seeking not to embarrass him. "I thought you were coming into Broad Street."

"So I was," returned Stener, foolishly, "but I thought I would get off and change my clothes. I've a lot of things to 'tend to yet this afternoon. I was coming in to see you." After Cowperwood's urgent telegram this was silly, but the young banker let it pass.

"Jump in, George," he said. "I have something very important to talk to you about. I told you in my telegram about the likelihood of a panic. It's on. There isn't a moment to lose. Stocks are 'way down, and most of my loans are being called. I want to know if you won't let me have three hundred and fifty thousand dollars for a few days at four or five per cent. I'll pay it all back to you. I need it very badly. If I don't get it I'm likely to fail. You know what that means, George. It will tie up every dollar I have. Those street-car holdings of yours will be tied up with me. I won't be able to let you realize on them, and that will put those loans of mine from the treasury in bad shape. You won't be able to put the money back, and you know what that means. We're in this thing together. I want to see you through safely, but I can't do it without your help. I had to go to Butler last night to see about a loan of his, and I'm doing my best to get money from other sources. But I can't see my way through on this, I'm afraid, unless you're willing to help me." Cowperwood paused. He did not know what Stener had heard. He wanted to put the whole case clearly and succinctly to him before he had a chance to refuse—to make him realize it as his own predicament.

As a matter of fact, what Cowperwood had keenly suspected was literally true. Stener had been reached. The moment Butler and Simpson had left him the night before, Mr. Mollenhauer had sent for his very able secretary, Mr. Abner Sengstack, and despatched him to learn the truth about Stener's whereabouts. Mr. Sengstack, still following instructions, had then sent a long wire to Mr. Strobik, who was with Stener, urging him to caution the latter against Cowperwood. The state of the treasury was known. Stener and Strobik were to be met by Sengstack whenever they arrived at Wilmington (this to forefend against the possibility of Cowperwood's reaching Stener first)—and the whole state of affairs was to be made perfectly plain. No more money was to be issued under penalty of prosecution. If Mr. Stener wanted to see any one he must see Mollenhauer. Mr. Sengstack, having received a telegram from Strobik informing him of their proposed arrival at noon the next day, had proceeded to Wilmington to meet them. The result was that Stener did not come direct into the business heart of the city, but instead got off at West Philadelphia, proposing to go first to his house to change his clothes and then to see Mr. Mollenhauer before seeing

Cowperwood. He was very badly frightened and wanted time to think.

Now at the mention of three hundred and fifty thousand dollars he stirred nervously, and at the mention of Butler he moved. Strobik had told him that Cowperwood had practically confessed to Butler and the others that he was bankrupt.

"I can't do it, Frank," Stener pleaded, piteously. "I'm in pretty bad in this matter, it looks to me just now. Mr. Mollenhauer's secretary met the train out at Wilmington just now to warn me against this situation, and Strobik is against it. They know how much money I've got outstanding. You or somebody has told them. I can't go against Mollenhauer. I owe everything I've got to him, in a way. He got me this place."

Cowperwood's eyes clouded ominously. He pretended to be properly astonished at this development, as he might well have been; and yet he was not astonished, either. Stener was such a tool. He was more surprised at what Stener told him of Mollenhauer. That explained in a way why Mollenhauer and Simpson had refused to act the night before. Either Mollenhauer, Simpson, and Butler had combined against him, instead of assisting him as he had expected, or Mollenhauer and Simpson had refused Butler's proposition, or Mollenhauer was driving at him alone—he could not tell which. It looked to his shrewd mind, for the time being, as if all three had suddenly combined to strike him, and were using Stener and the panic in combination to undo him. He was angered and chagrined, but he did not see just what was to be done about it at the moment. Perhaps a few clear words from him to Stener would bring the latter to his senses.

"George," he said, "there's no use being angry with me for going to Butler. I had to do it to save the day. If I hadn't been able to reach you before a day or two, and the politicians hadn't helped me—as it turns out they haven't—I would have failed, and you and the party would have been in a bad hole and we wouldn't even have got the credit of telling the truth about it. I did it as much for your sake as my own. Butler couldn't or didn't do what I wanted him to do—get Mollenhauer and Simpson to support the market. Instead of that they are hammering it. They've got a game of their own. It is up to you and me, George, to save ourselves, and that's what I'm here for now. If you don't let me have three hundred and fifty thousand dollars—three hundred thousand, anyhow—you and I are ruined. It will be worse for you, George, than for me, for I'm not involved in this thing in any way—not legally, anyhow. But that's not what I'm thinking of. I want to save my business and you want to save your name and money."

"But what can I do, Frank?" pleaded Stener, weakly. "I can't go against Mollenhauer. They can prosecute me if I do that. They can do it, anyhow. I can't do that. I'm not strong enough. If they didn't know, if you hadn't told them, it might be different, but this way—" He shook his head sadly, his gray eyes filled with a pale distress.

"George," replied Cowperwood, who realized now that only the sternest arguments would have any effect here, "don't talk about what I did. What I did I had to do. You're in danger of losing your head and your nerve and making a serious mistake here, and I don't want to see you make it. I have five hundred thousand of the city's money invested for you—partly for me, and partly for you, but more for you than for me"—which, by the way, was not true—"and here you are hesitating in an hour like this as to whether you will protect your interest or not. I can't understand it. This is a crisis, George. Stocks are tumbling on every side—everybody's stocks. You're not alone in this—neither am I. This is a panic, brought on by a fire, and you can't expect to come out of a panic alive unless you do something to protect yourself. You say you owe your place to Mollenhauer and that you're afraid of what he'll do. If you look at your own situation and mine, you'll see that it doesn't make much difference what he does, so long as I don't fail. If I fail, where are you? Who's going to save you from prosecution? Will Mollenhauer or any one else come forward and put five hundred thousand dollars in the treasury for you? He will not. If Mollenhauer and the others have your interests at heart, why aren't they helping me on 'change to-day? I'll tell you why. They want your street-railway holdings and mine, and they don't care whether you go to jail afterward or not. Now if you're wise you will listen to me. I've been loyal to you, haven't I? You've made money through me—lots of it. If you're wise, George, you'll go to your office and write me your check for three hundred thousand dollars, anyhow, before you do a single other thing. Don't see anybody and don't do anything till you've done that. You can't be hung any more for a sheep than you can for a lamb. No one can prevent you from giving me that check. You're the city treasurer. Once I have that I can see my way out of this, and I'll pay it all back to you next week or the week after—this panic is sure to end in that time. With that put back in the treasury we can see them about the five hundred thousand a little later. In three months, or less, I can fix it so that you can put that back. As a matter of fact, I can do it in fifteen days once I am on my feet again. Time is all I want. You won't have lost your holdings and nobody will cause you any trouble if you put the money back. They don't care to risk a scandal any more than you do. Now what 'll you do, George? Mollenhauer can't stop you from doing this any more than I can make you. Your life is in your own hands. What will you do?"

Cowperwood was cool, determined, patient, and impatient. He had taken a firm stand here, clearly outlined the issue, given Stener a definite choice. He wanted to do it—wanted to make him see very clearly exactly what it was he was in danger of doing. If he, Cowperwood, failed, Stener was certainly in a bad way. The man would be charged with embezzlement. As for himself, things were not so bad. He would not, technically, be charged with embezzlement, though he might be accused of compounding a felony. Nevertheless, he would be broken financially, and that was the one thing he dreaded most of all—the loss of his wealth. He could not stand that. Fortune was too nearly within his reach. It would be too much to lose it. Still he fronted the possibility with a steady eye.

Stener sat there ridiculously meditating when, as a matter of fact, his very financial blood, to use a simile, was oozing away. His wound was a fatal one, and he realized it. Yet he was afraid to act. He was afraid of Mollenhauer, afraid of Cowperwood, afraid of life and of himself. The thought of panic, loss, was not so much a definite thing connected with his own property, his money, as it was with his social and political standing in the community. Few people have the sense of financial individuality strongly developed. They do not know what it means to be a controller of wealth, to have that which releases the sources of social action—its medium of exchange. In most people thoughts of financial supremacy are not high and strong. They want money, but not for money's sake. They want it for what it will buy in the way of simple comforts, whereas the financier wants it for what it will control—for what it will represent in the way of dignity, force, power. Cowperwood wanted money in that way; Stener not. That was why he had been so ready to let Cowperwood act for him; and now, when he should have seen more clearly than ever the significance of what Cowperwood was proposing, he was frightened and his reason obscured by such things as Mollenhauer's probable opposition and rage, Cowperwood's possible failure, his own inability to face a real crisis, and things of that sort. Cowperwood's real innate financial ability did not reassure Stener in this hour. The banker was too young, too new. Mollenhauer was older, richer. So was Simpson; so was Butler. These men, with their wealth, represented the big forces, the big standards in his world as yet. Mollenhauer's word, as long as he, Stener, had been dealing with Cowperwood, and as much as he had prospered, was still a law to him. And besides, Cowperwood confessed that he was in great danger—that he was in a corner. That was the worst possible confession to make to Stener—although under the circumstances it was the only one that could be made—for he had no courage to face danger.

So he sat beside Cowperwood meditating—pale, flaccid, unable to see the main line of his interests quickly, unable to follow them definitely, surely, vigorously—while they drove to his office. Cowperwood entered it with him for the sake of continuing his plea.

"Well, George," he said, earnestly, "I wish you'd tell me. Time's short. We haven't a moment to lose. Give me the money, won't you, and I'll get out of this quick. We haven't a moment, I tell you. Don't let those people frighten you off. They're playing their own little game; you play yours."

"I can't, Frank," said Stener, finally, very weakly, his sense of his own financial future, successful and wonderful, overcome for the time being by the thought of Mollenhauer's hard, controlling face. The latter was his political God. He (Stener) was but one among many servitors. "I'll have to think. I can't do it right now. Strobik was just in here, and—"

"Good God, George," exclaimed Cowperwood, scornfully, "don't talk about Strobik! What's he got to do with it? Think of yourself. Think of where you will be. It's your future—not Strobik's—that you have to think of."

"I know, Frank," persisted Stener, weakly; "but, really, I don't see how I can. Honestly I don't. You say yourself you're not sure whether you can come out of things all right, and three hundred thousand more is three hundred thousand more. I can't, Frank. I really can't. It wouldn't be right. Besides, I want to talk to Mollenhauer first, anyhow."

"Good God, how you talk!" exploded Cowperwood, angrily, looking at him with ill-concealed contempt. "See Mollenhauer—that's the thing to do. Let him tell you how to cut your own throat for his benefit. It wouldn't be right to loan me three hundred thousand dollars more, but it would be right to let the five hundred thousand dollars you have loaned stand unprotected and lose it. That's right, isn't it? That's just what you propose to do—lose it, and everything else besides. I want to tell you what it is, George—you've lost your mind. You've let a single message from Mollenhauer frighten you to death, and because of that you're going to risk your fortune, your reputation, your standing—everything. Do you really realize what this means if I fail? You will be a convict, I tell you, George. You will go to prison. This fellow Mollenhauer, who is so quick to tell you what not to do now, will be the last man to turn a hand for you once you're down. Why, look at me—I've helped you, haven't I? Haven't I handled your affairs satisfactorily for you up to now? What in Heaven's name has got into you? What have you to be afraid of?"

Stener was just about to make another weak rejoinder when the door from the outer office opened, and Mr. Albert Stires, Mr. Stener's chief clerk, entered. Stener was too flustered to really pay any attention to Stires for the moment; but Cowperwood, being so well known to the latter, took matters in his own hands.

"What is it, Albert?" he asked, familiarly.

"Mr. Sengstack from Mr. Mollenhauer to see Mr. Stener."

At the sound of this dreaded name Stener wilted like a leaf. Cowperwood saw it. He realized that his last hope of getting the three hundred thousand dollars was now probably gone. Still he did not propose to give up as yet.

"Well, George," he said, after Albert had gone out leaving word that Mr. Stener would see Mr. Sengstack in a moment, "I see how it is. This man has got you mesmerized. You can't act for yourself now—you're too frightened. I'll let it rest for the present; I'll come back. But for Heaven's sake pull yourself together. Think what it means. I'm telling you exactly what's going to happen if you don't. You'll be independently rich if you do. You'll be a convict if you don't. There's the long and the short of it, and there's no third way out."

CHAPTER XXXI

AFTER leaving Stener in his office Cowperwood decided to make one more effort in the street before seeing Butler again, and after him Stener for a final appeal. He jumped into his light spring runabout, which he so often used in fair weather—a handsome little yellow-glazed vehicle, with a yellow-leather cushion-seat, drawn by a young, high-stepping bay mare, and sent her scudding from door to door, throwing down the lines indifferently and bounding up the steps of banks and into office doors, the while she looked around curiously as though wondering what it was all about. It never occurred to him that she would run away. No horse of his ever had.

In these offices, after seeing Stener, he was literally pleading for his life. And, curiously, it never occurred to him that he was pleading. It was all business. If he could induce these people to close the exchange, to give him more on his house and property than under the circumstances they would ordinarily give; if they could be induced to give him twenty-four or thirty-six or forty-eight hours of grace, why, so much the better. It wasn't their charity—it was his magnetism that was doing it. He didn't think they would do it unless he made them. He had no more regard for them actually than he had for any other human being—no less so. They were all hawks—he and they. They were all tigers facing each other in a financial jungle. If they were surfeited, if they were happy, if the mood were on them—any one or many of them—they might let him go, otherwise not. And if they did, thanks; but what of it? And if they didn't, no thanks; but what of that? They were none

354

the less the same as they always were—wolves at one moment, smiling, friendly human beings at another. Such was life. He had no illusions.

So to-day he said to Walter Leigh, now one of the big men in Drexel & Co.:

"Walter, they haven't supported the market as I thought they would. You know the bottom's out. What about my loans? Are you people going to call them?"

Leigh had previously explained that he couldn't get any support for the closing-the-exchange idea. Too many bears or "shorts" were anxious for their winnings.

"I tell you, Frank," he said, at one point, "I think Mollenhauer and Simspon are trying to shake you out."

"I thought so myself," replied Cowperwood, "when I saw how things were going on 'change this morning. Somebody is hammering my lines. But what about my loans?"

"Well, you know, Frank, how it is," replied Leigh, directly. "They are already twenty points under what we took them at"—he was referring to Cowperwood's hypothecated securities on which the loans had been advanced—"and we have one rule. I don't see what I can do."

"I'm expecting to raise about three hundred thousand by to-morrow noon," replied Cowperwood, with a great air of calm and courage, as though he were not in reality already too pressed for means. "I can't throw my holdings on the market. It's no use. I'd rather take them to private individuals and put them up. I can get more. But I can't do it in an hour. I have to have a little time. Can't you give me until to-morrow noon, or say Wednesday noon?"

Leigh liked Cowperwood very much. He really rejoiced in his clear-minded, unterrified determination and ability to fight in extremes. There was something dramatic about the man as he stood here, his naturally smooth, hard-fleshed face a little pale, but so handsome.

His eyes, usually glazed with a subtle haze, were now clear and brilliant. There was nothing of the nervous coward in him. He was almost jaunty in his appearance, a light-brownish-gray wool suit covering his body neatly, and a new fall brown derby hat setting squarely above his eyes. His formerly short mustache had become longer and silky. It was turned up in quite a distinguished manner about his cheeks.

"I'd like to, Frank," replied Leigh. "I'll see what I can do. It depends on how the old man feels. He's in a fighting mood to-day. He smells blood." And he looked at Cowperwood grimly—quite as one fighting brave looks at another.

Leigh, for all his friendship, was helping to hammer Cowperwood's stock, for from what he (Cowperwood) had said the night before and early this morning, he knew that his fellow-financier was hard pressed. He would probably go down, or be sheared of most of his holdings. Why should he refuse to help in this noble and profitable labor? Business was business. Still, in the face of this, if he could help him get a few days' grace on his loans, it would be all right. He did not object to doing that—rather wanted to for old sake's sake.

"I can't get at the old man right now. He's in there talking to Ticknor. When he's through I'll talk to him. I'll send you word before two."

Cowperwood went out not crestfallen, but brisk and determined. You would have thought by his shoulders that he had loaned somebody money at good interest, rather than that he had been begging for an extension of time. But he hadn't been begging it. He had been attempting to compel it.

"Wonderful fellow that," said Leigh. "They'll never down him. He'll squirm out somehow."

He waited thoughtfully for Ticknor to come out, and then stated Cowperwood's case to Francis Drexel, the head of the firm. The latter was a solidly built man of about fifty years of age—grave, reserved, and of a financial cast of countenance. He was a big man, a big thinker.

"I'll give him until to-morrow noon only," replied the white-mustached financier, indifferently. "He's in a bad hole. He's been spreading himself out too thin. He's a bright young fellow, but he's too ambitious."

He turned to his papers.

Leigh went out.

"Here, boy," he called, writing a note, "take that to Cowperwood and Company."

It contained Francis Drexel's ultimatum.

It was the same with Cooke & Co., Clark & Co., the First National Bank, the Girard National Bank. All were interested, considerate; but things were very uncertain. The Girard National Bank refused an hour's grace, and he had to send a large bundle of his most valuable securities to cover his stock shrinkage there. Word came from his father at two that as president of the Third National he would have to call for his one hundred and fifty thousand dollars due there. The directors were suspicious of his stocks. He at once wrote a check against fifty thousand dollars of his deposits in that bank, took twenty-five thousand of his available office funds, called a loan of fifty thousand against Tighe & Co., and sold sixty thousand Green & Coates, a line he had been tentatively dabbling in, for one-third their value—and, combining the general results, sent them all to the Third National. His father was immensely relieved from one point of view, but sadly depressed from another. He knew what it meant to Frank. He, Cowperwood, Sr., hurried out at the noon-hour to see what his own holdings would bring. He was compromising himself in a way by doing it, but his parental heart, as well as his own financial interests, were involved. By mortgaging his house, furniture, carriages, lots, and stocks, he managed to raise one hundred thousand in cash, and deposited it in his own bank to Frank's credit; but it was a very light anchor to windward in this swirling storm, at that. Frank had been counting on getting all of his loans extended three or four days at least. When he saw his situation at two o'clock of this Monday afternoon, he said, thoughtfully but grimly: "Well, Stener *has* to loan me three hundred thousand—that's all there is to it. And I'll have to see Butler now, or he'll be calling his loan before three."

He hurried out, jumped into his runabout, and was off again to Butler's house, driving like mad.

Things had changed greatly overnight, since last Mr. Cowperwood talked with Mr. Butler. Although friendly at the time when the proposition was made that he should combine with others to sustain the market, and which had resulted as we have seen, yet on this Monday morning at nine o'clock, as Butler was leaving his house for Owen's office, an additional complication had been added to this already tangled situation which had changed his attitude completely. As he was coming down his house steps to enter the runabout—Owen had preceded him by three-quarters of an hour—the postman, coming up, handed him four letters for himself, all of which he paused for a moment to glance at. One was from a sub-contractor by the name of O'Higgins, complaining of his inability to complete a certain piece of work because of unnecessary delay in the delivery of material due him from a stone-crushing company; the second was from Father Michael, his confessor, of St. Timothy's rectory, thanking him for a contribution to the parish poor-fund; a third was from Drexel & Co., relating to a deposit; and the fourth was an anonymous communication, written on cheap trade stationery, from some one who was apparently not very literate, a woman, most likely, in a scrawling hand, which read:

DEAR SIR,—This is to warn you that your daughter Aileen is running around with a man that she shouldn't—Frank A. Cowperwood, the banker. If you don't believe it, watch the house at 931 North Tenth Street. Then you can see for yourself.

There was neither signature nor mark of any kind to indicate from whence it might have come. Butler got the impression strongly that it might have been written by some one living in the vicinity of the number indicated, so keen are our intuitions. As a matter of fact, it was written by a girl, a member of St. Timothy's Church, who did live in the vicinity of the house indicated, and who knew Aileen by sight and was jealous of her airs and her position, as well as the wealth of her family. She was a thin, anemic, dissatisfied creature who had the type of brain which can reconcile the gratification of personal spite with a comforting sense of having fulfilled a moral duty. There are many such. Her home was some five doors north of the unregistered Cowperwood domicile on the opposite side of the street, and by degrees, in the course of time, she made out, or imagined that she had, the significance of this institution, piecing fact to fancy and fusing all with that keen intuition which is so closely related to fact. She really never did know exactly, but she believed with a belief worthy of a better cause. The result was eventually this letter which now spread clear and grim before Mr. Butler's eyes.

The Irish are a practical and philosophic race. Their first and strongest instinct is to make the best of a bad situation—to put a better face on evil than it will normally wear. On first reading these lines the intelligence they conveyed sent a peculiar chill and thrill over Mr. Butler's sturdy frame. His jaw instinctively closed, and his gray, hair-shaded eyes narrowed. A keener sense of the subtlety of the character of Frank Algernon Cowperwood than he had ever had before came to him. Could this be true? If it were not, would the author of the letter say so practically, "If you don't believe it, watch the house at 931 North Tenth Street"? Wasn't that in itself proof positive—the hard, matter-of-fact realism of it? And this was the man who had come to him the night before seeking aid—whom he had done so much to assist. There forced itself into his naturally slow-moving but rather accurate mind a sense of the distinction and charm of his daughter—a considerably sharper picture than he had ever had before, and at the same time a keener understanding of the personality of Frank Algernon Cowperwood. How was it he had failed to detect any of the real subtlety of this man? How was it he had never seen any sign of it, if there had been anything between Cowperwood and Aileen? Parents are frequently inclined, because of a time-flattered sense of security, to take their children for granted. Nothing ever has happened, so nothing ever will happen. They see their children every day, and through the eyes of affection; and despite their natural charm and their own strong parental love, the children are apt to become not only commonplaces, but ineffably secure against evil. Mary is naturally a good girl—a little wild, but what harm can befall her? John is a straightforward, steady-going boy—how could he get into trouble? They are home almost every evening. The astonishment of most parents at the sudden accidental revelation of evil in connection with any of their children is almost invariably pathetic. "My John! My Mary! Impossible!" But it is possible. Very possible. Decidedly likely. Some, through lack of experience or understanding, or both, grow hard and bitter on the instant. They feel themselves astonishingly abased in the face of notable tenderness and sacrifice. Others collapse and go to pieces before the grave manifestation of the insecurity and uncertainty of life and mortal chemistry. Others, taught roughly by life, or furnished broadly by understanding or intuition, or both, see in this the latest manifestation of that incomprehensible chemistry which we call *life* and personality, and, knowing that it is quite vain to hope to gainsay it, save by greater subtlety, put the best face they can upon the matter and call a truce until they can think. We all know that life is unsolvable—we who think. The remainder imagine a vain thing, and are full of sound and fury signifying nothing.

So Edward Butler, being a man of much wit and hard, grim experience, stood there on his doorstep holding in his big, rough hand this thin slip of cheap paper which contained this terrific indictment of his daughter. There came to him now a picture of her as she was when she was a very little girl—she was his first baby girl—and how keenly he had felt about her all these years. She was a beautiful child—her red-gold hair had been pillowed on his breast many a time, and his hard, rough hand and fingers had stroked her soft cheeks, lo, these thousands of times. Aileen, his lovely, dashing daughter of twenty-three! What a forceful girl she was—how aggressive, how sensible, how practical! He had been drawn to her this long time, much more so than he was to his wife or Norah, his younger daughter, by the practical character of the mind concealed in her pretty head. She was forthright and self-sufficient and posy at times; but she had good sense, too, and a will of her own. That was what always pleased him most these late years—this will of her own. It defied him sometimes—him and his wife and Owen and Callum—to say "no," that she wouldn't, or "yes," that she would, in spite of anything they might say.

"I don't care," she would declare, firmly. "I know what I want. I won't do it."

"Well, why won't you?"

"Well, because I won't,—that's why."

There was no moving her once her mind was set, and she was coming to be very much the master in this household. Callum frequently asked her what she thought of the clothing he was about to order or purchase. Norah pleaded with her to intercede with her mother or father for her for things that she wanted and feared she could not obtain. Mrs. Butler, the mother, constantly leaned on her for advice in social matters. As a matter of fact, Aileen provided all the social information this household obtained or considered. Owen traded ideas with her gingerly, for he did not quite understand her—never had. Butler loved her as a big, strong man always loves a strong, self-sufficient, thoroughly human woman. He was drawn to her, to her exhibition of a natural understanding of things, and yet he attempted to deceive himself with the thought that she could have large understanding and be a veritable simpleton of a girl into the bargain. This tragic hour undeceived him, and yet he was not sure that the letter was not an ugly, malicious lie. His daughter Aileen! Could it really be? It couldn't be! And yet, that note! "If you don't believe it, watch the house at 931 North Tenth Street."

He turned back and entered his door again, thinking to go to his room and call Aileen, but he stayed himself on the threshold. Why should he do this? It might not be true. His daughter might expect that he would have more faith in her. Supposing it wasn't true— couldn't be proved; what would she think? They were more like dear old friends than father and daughter. She seemed to understand him, his idiosyncrasies, more of late than ever before. Was this due to sorrow for her concealed evil—the injustice being done him and his wife, her mother? Why hadn't she married? He had urged, suggested so often. Wasn't that a point against her? It was, surely.

He stood there in his door debating these things uncertainly, his broad, coarse face a study in strongly modeled, grim, sad lines, and then he went out again. Never in his life had he been thrown into so deep a pit of doubt so quickly. He was lost in dark, strange, unhappy speculations, and he was without any present ability to think or say or do the right thing. He did not know what the right thing was at present, he finally confessed to himself. Aileen! Aileen! His Aileen! If her mother knew this it would break her heart. She mustn't! She mustn't! And yet mustn't she?

The heart of a father! The world wanders into many strange by-paths of affection. The love of a mother for her children is dominant, leonine, selfish, and unselfish. It is concentric. The love of a husband for his wife, or of a lover for his sweetheart, is a sweet bond of agreement and exchange—fair trade in a lovely contest. The love of a father for his son or daughter, where it is love at all, is a broad, generous, sad, contemplative giving without thought of return, a hail and farewell to a troubled traveler whom he would do much to guard, a balanced judgment of weakness and strength, with pity for failure and pride in achievement. It is a lovely, generous, philosophic blossom which rarely asks too much, and seeks only to give wisely and plentifully. "That my boy may succeed! That my daughter may be happy!" Who has not heard and dwelt upon these twin fervors of fatherly wisdom and tenderness?

As Butler drove down-town his huge, slow-moving, in some respects chaotic mind turned over as rapidly as he could all of the possibilities in connection with this unexpected, sad, and disturbing revelation. Why had Cowperwood not been satisfied with his wife? Why should he neglect or endanger the reputation of his children in this way? Why should he enter into his (Butler's) home, of all places, to establish a clandestine relationship of this character? Was Aileen in any way to blame? She was an able, sufficient, attractive, self-willed girl, and was not without mental resources of her own. She must have known what she was doing. She was a good Catholic, or, at least, had been raised so. All the years she had been going regularly to confession and communion. True, of late Butler had noticed that she did not care so much about going to church, would sometimes make excuses and stay at home on Sundays; but she had gone, as a rule. And now, now—his thoughts would come to the end of a blind alley, and then he would start back, as it were, mentally to the center of things, and begin all over again.

There was another puzzle. Why had no signs of affection ever been shown between Cowperwood and Aileen? Aileen had never been out evenings much, except with Norah, Callum, Owen, her mother, or the family, and they always knew where she was. She drove some. Yes, there was one chance for Cowperwood. And she rode. There was another. She took music-lessons, and she went to the library—a private circulating library—occasionally afternoons. Yes, here were the loopholes through which she might have escaped. But there had never been a sign, not a single glance, so far as he knew. Cowperwood had rarely asked after her. He had never looked at her significantly. She had never spoken of him in a curious or enthusiastic way. He would have said that Cowperwood was probably the one man she was not interested in. She went to the Cowperwood home occasionally, not so much of late; and she went down-town now and then. Had she stopped in his office to see him? It was a queer tangle, another blind alley. And so he strolled back to the central fact again—the letter. Could it be true? Was Aileen guilty? Should he ask her? Should he accuse Cowperwood? What good would that do? It would merely give them warning. They would deny everything, and he would have no chance of finding out. Should he watch her? What good would that do? If discovered, she might be enraged and defy him. The strange force of the girl's character was lurking oddly in his mind. He could not, try as he would, think of dealing with her as he would with an ordinary girl. He must get his evidence or talk to her and persuade her to confess. If she broke down and confessed he might attempt to punish Cowperwood; but wasn't he going to be punished enough as it was? He was probably going to fail. He would be punished that much, anyhow, and right away, very likely. Was he anxious to kill him or punish him physically? He was too old a man, too reverent a Catholic, too wise in the ways of the world to think of any such thing. He knew too much about life. But he was angry, hurt, shamed, and disappointed. Aileen! His Aileen! How could she?

He went up the stairs to his own office slowly. He went in and sat down, and thought and thought. Ten o'clock came, and eleven. His son bothered him with an occasional matter of interest, but, finding him moody, finally abandoned him to his own speculations. It was twelve, and then one, and he was still sitting there thinking, when the presence of Frank A. Cowperwood was announced.

Cowperwood, after his herculean labors of the morning, had, as has been said, driven rapidly to Butler's house; but, finding him out, and not encountering Aileen, he had driven back to Fourth Street, and had hurried up to the office of the Edward Butler Contracting Company, which was also the center of some of Butler's street-railway interests. The floor space controlled by the company was divided into the usual official compartments, with sections for the bookkeepers, the road-managers, the treasurer, and so on. Owen Butler and his father had small but attractively furnished offices in the rear, where they transacted all the important business of the company.

During this drive, curiously, by reason of one of those strange psychologic intuitions which so often precede a human difficulty of one sort or another, Cowperwood had been thinking of Aileen. He was thinking of the peculiarity of his relationship to her, and of the fact that now, in spite of what Butler would consider a great evil done him in respect to his daughter, he was running to him for assistance. He was going to ask of the man whose daughter the world would say he had seduced that this loan of one hundred thousand dollars should not be called, and in addition that Butler loan him one hundred thousand dollars more, if possible. Butler had of late been less generous in his investments through Cowperwood; but he had not entirely ceased the relationship, by any means, and this additional loan, if he were not too frightened by current developments, would not disturb him greatly. The old gentleman was rich enough to loan him several hundred thousand dollars if he were so minded.

In regard to Aileen, Cowperwood was satisfied that no suspicion of his relationship to her had ever even flickered into light; and because of her practical wisdom and his own there was small danger of it, he thought. Still, he was thinking of her this afternoon, for some reason, and of how resentful her family would be if they knew. He had often wondered what the results would be if that should happen, though the thought hadn't troubled him any. Death? Scarcely. They would not risk a public scandal. Could Aileen be removed from his influence and restrained? He questioned it. She was too individual—too much of a fighter herself. More than once they had discussed what she would do in case charges based on suspicions or something less than actual evidence were made against her and himself.

"I'd deny it," declared Aileen, heartily. "I'd deny everything until I knew what they knew."

"But, supposing they said that I had said, for instance—" He outlined a supposititious case, trying to fathom the extent of her tact and caution.

"I'd deny it," she repeated. "I'd deny everything until I had positive proof that they knew. I'd never admit anything more than a foolish friendship, under any circumstances, even then. Never!"

Her clear eyes glowed with self-protective defiance, and he knew from that time on that they would have great difficulty in extracting anything of the truth from her. Her version of the Japanese aphorism would have been, "It is better to lie much than to suffer at all."

This afternoon, therefore, whenever he thought of her at odd moments, it was with the feeling that all was well in that quarter; but he could not help wondering why it was that he should be thinking at all of her so much. He did not believe so thoroughly in pyschic intuitions, although there were times when he thought he had them. As he mounted the stairs to Butler's office he had a peculiar sense of the untoward; but he could not, in his view of life, give it countenance. He sent in his name, and was received in a few moments by Mr. Butler in person; but one glance showed him that something had gone amiss. Butler was not so friendly; his glance was dark, and there was a certain sternness to his countenance which had never previously been manifested there in Cowperwood's memory. He perceived at once that it was something different from a mere intention to refuse him aid and call his loan. That could not be a very bad thing to Butler personally. He might pull a long face, but it would not be a hard, grim, sad one, set in such lines as his features now showed; and Butler was not in the habit of doing this sort of thing, anyhow. What was it? Aileen? The thought occurred to him, and he stuck to it. It must be that. Somebody had suggested something. They had been seen together. Well, even so, nothing could be proved. Butler would obtain no sign from him. But his loan—that was to be called, surely. And as for an additional loan, he could see now, before a word had been said, that that thought was useless. He would get no money here—nor any consideration. Something had happened. Was Butler going to tell him?

"I came to see you about that loan of yours, Mr. Butler," he observed, briskly, with an old-time, jaunty air. You could not have told from his presence or his face that he had heard, seen, or observed anything out of the ordinary anywhere. Butler was to him, apparently, his old-time recourse, and he expected, unquestionably, all the consideration and aid which one might look for in a friend under such circumstances.

Butler, who was alone in the room—Owen having

gone into an adjoining room—merely stared at him from under his shaggy brows.

"I'll have to have that money," he said, darkly, brusquely.

An old-time Irish rage suddenly welled up in his bosom as he contemplated this jaunty, sophisticated undoer of his daughter's virtue. He fairly glared at him as he thought of him and her.

"I judged from the way things were going this morning that you might want it," Cowperwood replied, quietly, without sign of tremor. "The bottom's out, I see."

"The bottom's out, and it 'll not be put back soon, I'm thinkin'. I'll have to have what's belongin' to me today. I haven't any time to spare."

"Very well," replied Cowperwood, who saw clearly how treacherous the situation was. The old man was in a dour mood. His (Cowperwood's) presence was an irritation to him, for some reason—a deadly provocation. Cowperwood felt clearly that it must be Aileen, that Butler must know or suspect something. He had best close this conversation at once and get out—not argue. Why exchange words or make foolish inquiries? The least phrase might set the fires blazing. He must pretend business hurry and end this. "I'm sorry. I thought I might get an extension; but that's all right. I can get the money, though. I'll send it right over."

He turned and walked quickly to the door.

Butler got up. He had thought to manage this differently. He had thought to denounce or even assault this man. He was about to make some insinuating remark which would compel an answer, some direct charge; but Cowperwood was out and away as jaunty as ever.

The old man was flustered, enraged, disappointed. He opened the small office door which led into the adjoining room, and called, "Owen!"

"Yes, father."

"Send over to Cowperwood's office and get that money."

"You decided to call it, eh?"

"I have."

Owen was puzzled by the old man's angry mood. He wondered what it all meant, but thought he and Cowperwood might have had a few words. He went out to his desk to write a note and call a clerk. Butler went to the window and stared out. He was angry, bitter, brutal in his vein.

"The dirty dog!" he suddenly exclaimed to himself, in a low voice. "I'll take every dollar he's got before I'm through with him. I'll send him to jail, I will. I'll break him, I will. Wait!"

He clinched his big fists and his teeth.

"I'll fix him. I'll show him. The dog! The damned scoundrel!"

Never in his life before had he been so bitter, so cruel, so relentless in his mood.

He walked his office thinking what he could do; but there was nothing that he really could do, apparently. He wanted to go back to Aileen and see what she had to say. If her face, or her lips, told him that his suspicion was true, he would deal with Cowperwood later. This city treasury business, now. It was not a crime in so far as Cowperwood was concerned; but it might be made to be. He would see. Anyhow, he was not through with Cowperwood. No, not by these many, many days.

CHAPTER XXXII

BUTLER finally decided that before his sons returned for the evening he would go out to the house and see if he could find Aileen. So nonplussed was he that he took his hat in a very secretive way and slipped away, telling the clerk to say to Owen that he had gone down the street for a few moments. He took a car and rode out to his house, where he found his elder daughter just getting ready to leave on an errand of some sort. She wore a purple-velvet street dress edged with narrow, flat gilt braid, and a striking gold-and-purple turban. She had on dainty new boots of bronze kid and long gloves of lavender suede. In her ears were one of her latest affectations, a pair of long jet earrings. The old Irishman realized, on this occasion, when he saw her, perhaps as clearly as he ever had in his life, that he had grown a bird of rare plumage, and that it would be difficult to compel her to accept the simple details of a commonplace existence such as his home offered and had offered for some years. She was too high-strung in her fancies, perfervid in her tastes. To-day her color was high, and she had an air of great force, as though she were experiencing to the utmost her exceptional health and vigor.

"Where are you going, daughter?" he asked, with a rather unsuccessful attempt to conceal his fear, distress, and smoldering anger.

"To the library," she said, easily, and yet with a sudden realization that all was not right with her father. His face was too heavy and gray. He looked tired and gloomy.

"Come up to my office," he said, "a minute. I want to see you before you go."

THE FINANCIER

Aileen heard this with a strange feeling of curiosity and wonder. It was not customary for Butler to want to see his daughter in his office just when she was going out; and his manner indicated, in this instance, that the exceptional procedure portended a strange revelation of some kind. Aileen, like every other person who offends against a rigid convention of the time, was conscious of and sensitive to the possible disastrous results which would follow exposure. She had often thought what her family would think if they knew what she was doing; she had never been able to satisfy herself in her mind as to what they would do. Her father was a very vigorous man. She had never known him to be cruel or cold in his attitude toward her or any other member of the family, but especially not toward her. Always he seemed too fond of her to be completely alienated by anything that might happen; yet she could not be sure. This thing that she was doing was completely beyond any experience which had ever confronted him in his life, and she really could not imagine what he would think or do, once he knew. As in Cowperwood's case, his attitude to-day caused her to feel that, by some untoward fling of chance, he might have become aware of what she was doing. "The wicked flee when no man pursueth."

Butler led the way, planting his big feet solemnly on the steps as he went up. Aileen followed with a single glance at herself in the tall pier-mirror which stood in the hall, realizing at once how charming she looked and how uncertain she was feeling about what was to follow. What could her father want? It made the color leave her cheeks for the moment, as she thought what he might want.

Butler strolled into his stuffy room and sat down in the big leather chair, disproportioned to everything else in the chamber, but which, nevertheless, accompanied his desk. Before him, against the light, was the visitor's chair, in which he liked to have those sit whose faces he was anxious to study. When Aileen entered he motioned her to it, which was also ominous to her, and said, "Sit down there."

She took the seat, not knowing what to make of his procedure. On the instant her promise to Cowperwood to deny everything, whatever happened, came back to her. If her father was about to attack her on that score, he would get no satisfaction, she thought. He would not get any! She owed it to Frank. Her pretty, nonplussed face strengthened and hardened on the instant. Her fine, white teeth set in two even rows; and her father saw quite plainly that she was consciously bracing herself for an attack of some kind. He feared by this that she was guilty, and he was all the more distressed, ashamed, outraged, made wholly unhappy. He fumbled in the left-hand pocket of his coat, which never fitted him very well, and drew forth from among the various papers the fatal communication so cheap in its physical texture. His big fingers fumbled almost tremulously as he fished the letter-sheet out of the small envelope and unfolded it without saying a word. Aileen watched his face and his hands, wondering what it could be that he had here, uncertain whether to expect the worst or some foolish, friendly communication. She was steeling herself to meet his glance, while he was fixing himself to put into practice his usual tactic of watching her face as she read what he was going to show her. He handed the paper over, small in his big fist, and said, "Read that."

Aileen took it, and for a second was relieved to be able to lower her eyes to the paper. Her relief vanished in a second, when she realized how in a moment she would have to raise them again and look him in the face.

DEAR SIR,—This is to warn you that your daughter Aileen is running around with a man that she shouldn't—Frank A. Cowperwood, the banker. If you don't believe it, watch the house at 931 North Tenth Street. Then you can see for yourself.

In spite of herself Aileen's hands shook for the least fraction of a second as she steeled herself to withstand this blow. The color fled from her cheeks instantly, only to come back in a hot, defiant wave.

"Why, what a lie!" she said, lifting her eyes to her father's. "To think that any one should write such a thing of me! How dare they! I think it's a shame!"

Old Butler looked at her narrowly, solemnly. He was not deceived to any extent by her bravado. If she were really innocent, he knew she would have jumped to her feet in her defiant way. Protest would have been written all over her. As it was, she only stared haughtily. He read through her eager defiance to the guilty truth.

"How do ye know, daughter, that I haven't had the house watched?" he said, quizzically. "How do ye know that ye haven't been seen goin' in there?"

Only Aileen's solemn promise to her lover could have saved her from this subtle thrust. As it was, she paled nervously; but she saw Frank Cowperwood, solemn and distinguished, asking her what she would say if she were caught.

"It's a lie!" she said, catching her breath. "I wasn't at any house at that number, and no one saw me going in there. How can you ask me that, father?"

In spite of his mixed feelings of uncertainty and yet unshakable belief that his daughter was guilty, he could not help admiring her courage—she was so defiant, as she sat there, so set in her determination to lie and thus defend herself. Her beauty helped her in his mood, raised her in his esteem. After all, what could you do with a woman of this kind? She was not a ten-year-old girl any more, as in a way he sometimes continued to fancy her.

"Ye oughtn't to say that if it isn't true, Aileen," he said. "Ye oughtn't to lie. It's against your faith. Why would anybody write a letter like that if it wasn't so?"

"But it's not so," insisted Aileen, pretending anger and outraged feeling, "and I don't think you have any right to sit there and say that to me. I haven't been there, and I'm not running around with Mr. Cowperwood. Why, I hardly know the man except in a social way."

Butler shook his head solemnly.

"It's a great blow to me, daughter. It's a great blow to me," he said. "I'm willing to take your word if ye say so; but I can't help thinkin' what a sad thing it would be if ye were lyin' to me. I haven't had the house watched, because I love ye too much for that. And what's written here may not be so. But we'll not say any more about that now. If there is anythin' in it, and ye haven't gone too far yet to save yourself, I want ye to think of your mother and your sister and your brothers, and be a good girl. Think of the church ye was raised in, and the name we've got to stand up for in the world. Why, if ye were doin' anythin' wrong, and the people of Philadelphy got a hold of it, the city, big as it is, wouldn't be big enough to hold us. Your brothers have got a reputation to make, their work to do here. Ye and your sister want to get married sometime. How could ye expect to look the world in the face and do anythin' at all, if ye are doin' what this letter says ye are, and it was told about ye?"

The old man's voice was thick with a strange, sad, alien emotion. He did not want to believe that his daughter was guilty, even though he knew she was. He did not want to face what he considered in his vigorous, religious way to be his duty, that of reproaching her sternly. There were some fathers who would have turned her out, he fancied. There were others who might possibly kill Cowperwood after a subtle investigation. This course was not for him. If vengeance he was to have, it must be through politics and finance—he must drive him out. But as for doing anything desperate in connection with Aileen, he could not think of it.

"Oh, father," returned Aileen, with considerable histrionic ability in her assumption of pettishness, "how
can you talk like this when you know I'm not guilty?
When I tell you so?"

The old Irishman saw through her make-believe with
profound sadness—the feeling that one of his dearest
hopes had been shattered. He had believed so stead-
fastly in her social virtue as he understood that quality.
To see her coloring and pretending here was too terrible.
He had expected so much of her socially and matri-
monially. Why, any one of a dozen remarkable young
men might have married her, and she would have had
lovely children to comfort him in his old age. Was that
gone, as many another important thing had gone in this
world (as they go for all of us), leaving his hope unsatisfied?

"Well, we'll not talk any more about it now, daughter,"
he said, wearily. "Ye've been so much to me during
all these years that I can scarcely belave anythin' wrong
of ye. I don't want to, God knows. Ye're a grown
woman, though, now; and if ye are doin' anythin'
wrong I don't suppose I could do so much to stop ye.
I might turn ye out, of course, as many a father would;
but I wouldn't like to do anythin' like that. But if ye
are doin' anythin' wrong"—and he put up his hand to
stop a proposed protest on the part of Aileen—"remember, I'm certain to find it out in the long run, and
Philadelphy won't be big enough to hold me and the man
that's done this thing to me. I'll get him," he said,
getting up dramatically. "I'll get him, and when I do—"
He turned a livid face to the wall, and Aileen saw clearly
that Cowperwood, in addition to any other troubles which
might beset him, had her father to deal with. Was this
why Frank had looked so sternly at her the night before?
Was this why his face was so set? He had not told her.

"Why, your mother would die of a broken heart if
she thought there was anybody could say the least word

against ye," pursued Butler, in a shaken voice. "This man has a family—a wife and children. Ye oughtn't to want to do anythin' to hurt them. They'll have trouble enough, if I'm not mistaken — facin' what's comin' to them in the future," and Butler's jaw hardened just a little. "Ye're a beautiful girl. Ye're young. Ye have money. There're dozens of young men'd be proud to make ye their wife. Whatever ye may be thinkin' or doin', don't throw away your life. Don't destroy your immortal soul. Don't break my heart entirely."

Aileen, not ungenerous—fool of mingled affection and passion—could now have cried. She pitied her father from her heart; but her allegiance was to Cowperwood, her loyalty unshaken. She wanted to say something, to protest much more; but she knew that it was useless. Her father knew that she was lying.

"Well, there's no use of my saying anything more, father," she said, getting up. The light of day was fading in the windows. The down-stairs door closed with a light slam, showing that one of the boys had come in. Her proposed trip to the library was now without interest to her. "You won't believe me, anyhow. I tell you, though, that I'm innocent just the same."

Butler lifted his big, brown hand to command silence, to indicate that he did not care to hear any more. She saw that this shameful relationship, so far as her father was concerned, had been made quite clear, and that this trying conference was now at an end. She turned and walked shamefacedly out. He waited until he heard her steps fading into faint nothings down the hall toward her room.

Then he arose. Once more he clinched his big fists.

"The scoundrel!" he said. "The scoundrel! I'll drive him out of Philadelphy, if it takes the last dollar I have in the world." His parental love was back of his anger.

CHAPTER XXXIII

THAT five minutes that Cowperwood had spent in Butler's presence was one of the most illuminating that had occurred to him recently. For the first time in his life he was in the presence of that interesting social phenomenon, the outraged sentiment of a parent. He himself was a father, the possessor of two rather interesting children. The boy, Frank, Jr., was to him not so remarkable. But Lillian, second, with her dainty little slip of a body and bright, hair-aureoled head, had always appealed to him. She was going to be a charming woman some day, he thought, and he was going to do much to establish her safely. He used to tell her that she had "eyes like blue buttons," "feet like a pussy cat," and "hands that were just five cents' worth," they were so little. The child admired her father, and would often stand by his chair in the library or the sitting-room, or his desk in his private office, when he worked at peculiar columns of figures, at times, or by his seat at the table, asking him questions.

"Papa, do they, now, in fractions—do they, now, multiply the numerators together first?"

"Yes, now, little girlie, now—they do, now," he used to mock her, chucking her under the chin or squeezing her waist.

"Now, papa, now, I don't think that's any way to talk, now. Is it, mama?"

"You'd better not bother your father any longer," Mrs. Cowperwood would conservatively reply. "Come round here and sit down. Your soup is getting cold."

"Now, I don't either, now," was Cowperwood's reply,

rather gaily if not attentively put, answering her original protests.

This attitude toward his own daughter made him see clearly how Butler might feel toward Aileen. The old Irishman had probably had just such sympathetic experiences with his children as Cowperwood was having with his. He wondered how he would feel if it were his own little Lillian, and still he did not believe he would make much fuss over the matter, either with himself or with her, if she were as old as Aileen. Children and their lives were more or less above the willing of parents, anyhow, and it would be a difficult thing for any parent to control any child, unless the child were naturally docile-minded and willing to be controlled. As he drove away from Butler's office he had no absolute knowledge as to why the latter had been so enraged, but he felt certain that Aileen was the reason. At any rate, he must take considerable thought of this added complication. Instead of a friend in Butler, he now had an enemy to fight, and Butler was very powerful. It almost made him smile, in a grim way, to see how fate was raining difficulties on him. He was distressed, too, about Aileen—what she would say and do if she were confronted by her father. If he could only get to see her! But if he met Butler's call for his loan, and the others which would come yet to-day or on the morrow, there was not a moment to lose. If he did not pay he must assign at once. Many personalities had occurred to him even as he stood before Butler, to whom he might or must appeal. You would suppose that all of his thoughts would have been concerned with Butler's rage, Aileen, his own danger. Not so. He was thinking of these things quickly, incidentally; but his mind never wavered from the main point, which was to save himself financially. With wealth one can do almost anything to protect oneself. Without it—well, that is another story. Wealth, the position, and force which means give, was to him as his right arm. He must have it or be crippled until, to vary the simile, he could, like the lobster, grow another claw. He hurried to visit George Waterman; David Wiggin, his wife's brother, who was now fairly well to do; Joseph Zimmerman, the wealthy dry-goods dealer who had dealt with him in the past; Judge Kitchen, a private manipulator of considerable wealth; Frederick Van Nostrand, the State treasurer, who was interested in local street-railway stocks, and others. He was determined that he would not dispose of his street-railway holdings at any price. He would suspend first, though it was a disastrous thing to do, and the chances were that they would be sold out at a sacrifice. But before that he would go to Stener again, to see if he could not frighten him into coming to his rescue. He went by turns to all the people he had in mind, laying the situation in which he found himself rapidly before them. Of all those to whom he appealed one was actually not in a position to do anything for him; another was afraid; a third was calculating eagerly to drive a hard bargain; a fourth was too deliberate, anxious to have much time. All scented the true value of his situation, all wanted time to consider, and he had no time to consider.

Judge Kitchen did agree to lend him thirty thousand dollars—a paltry sum. Joseph Zimmerman would only risk twenty-five thousand dollars, when he should have loaned him two hundred thousand dollars. It was quite the same in the other cases. He could see where, all told, he might raise seventy-five thousand dollars by hypothecating double the amount in shares; but this was ridiculously insufficient. He had figured again, to a dollar, and he must have at least two hundred and fifty thousand dollars above all his present holdings, or he must close his doors. To-morrow at two o'clock he would know. If he didn't he would be written down as "failed" on a score of ledgers in Philadelphia. What a pretty pass for one to come to whose hopes had so recently run so high!

There was a loan of one hundred thousand dollars from the Girard National Bank which he was particularly anxious to clear off. This bank was the most distinguished in the city, and if he retained its friendship by meeting this loan promptly he might hope for very many valuable favors in the future, whatever happened. Mr. Davison, the president of the bank, had been most agreeable to him in the past. He had suggested ways and means of raising money when Cowperwood had not always been able to think of them at the moment. He had recommended him to other banks, had called at his house socially, and in other ways, by his friendship, had tended to make his various deals possible and secure. The loss of the friendship of Mr. Davison would be most serious. Supposing he did fail. Mr. Davison, by his good-will, might help him to get on his feet again. It was most necessary to meet this loan, because it meant much to him in future patronage; and yet, at the moment, Cowperwood did not see how he could do it. He decided, however, after some reflection that he would deliver the stocks which Judge Kitchen, Zimmerman, and others had agreed to take and get their checks or cash yet this night. Then he would persuade Stener to let him have a check for the sixty thousand dollars' worth of city loan he had purchased this morning on 'change. Out of it he could take twenty-five thousand dollars to make up the balance due President Davison, and so retain the friendship of the latter at least, and still have thirty-five thousand for himself, free and clear, which he needed badly.

The one unfortunate thing about such an arrangement was that by it he was building up a rather complicated situation in regard to these same certificates. Since their purchase in the morning, he had not deposited them in the sinking-fund, where they belonged (they had been delivered to his office by half past one in the afternoon), but, on the contrary, had immediately hypothecated them to cover another loan. It was a risky thing to have done, considering that he was in danger of failing and that he was not absolutely sure of being able to take them up in time—he could not tell how this storm would eventuate.

But, he reasoned, he had a working agreement with the city treasurer, illegal of course, which would make such a transaction rather plausible, and almost all right, even if he failed, and that was that none of his accounts were supposed necessarily to be put straight until the end of the month. If he did it by then, all was customarily all right. In this case, if he failed and the certificates were not in the sinking-fund, he could say, as was the truth, that he was in the habit of taking his time, and had forgotten. This collecting of a check, therefore, for these as yet undeposited certificates would be technically, if not legally and morally, plausible. The city would only be out an additional sixty thousand dollars—making five hundred and sixty thousand dollars all told, which in view of its probable loss of five hundred thousand did not make so much difference. But his caution clashed with his need on this occasion, and he decided that he would not call for the check unless Stener finally refused to aid him with three hundred thousand more, in which case he would claim it as his right. In all likelihood Stener would not think to ask whether the certificates were in the sinking-fund or not. If he did, he would have to lie—that was all.

He drove rapidly back to his office, and, finding Butler's note, as he expected, wrote a check on his father's bank for the one hundred thousand dollars which had been placed there to his credit by his loving parent, and sent it around to Butler's office. There was another note, from Mr. Stener's secretary, Mr. Albert Stires, advising him not to buy or sell any more city loan—that until further notice such transactions would not be honored. Cowperwood immediately sensed the source of this warning. Stener had been in conference with Butler or Mollenhauer, and had been warned and frightened. Nevertheless, he proposed to go to him again. It was his last recourse. He got in his buggy again and drove directly to the city treasurer's office.

Since Cowperwood's visit in the morning Stener had talked still more with Mr. Sengstack, Mr. Strobik, and others, all sent to see that a proper fear of things financial had been put in his heart. The result was decidedly one which spelled opposition to Cowperwood.

Strobik was considerably disturbed himself. He and Wycroft and Harmon had also been using money out of the treasury—much smaller sums, of course, for they had not Cowperwood's financial imagination—and they were disturbed as to how they would return what they owed before the storm broke. If Cowperwood failed, and Stener was short in his accounts, the whole budget might be investigated, and then their loans would be brought to light. The thing to do was to return what they owed, and then, at least, no charge of malfeasance would lie against them. They were very much concerned, and did raise considerable of what they owed by noon the next day, which was credited on the treasurer's books, but at this date these unseemly transactions were not entirely closed. The matter of Cowperwood was still exceedingly significant to Strobik, and he thought hard.

"Go to Mollenhauer," he said to Stener, shortly after Cowperwood had left the latter's office, "and tell him the whole story. He put you here. He was strong for your nomination. Tell him just where you stand and ask him what to do. He'll probably be able to tell you. Offer him your holdings to help you out. You have to. You can't help yourself. Don't loan Cowperwood another damned dollar, whatever you do. He's got you in so deep now you can hardly hope to get out. Ask Mollenhauer if he won't help you to get Cowperwood to put that money back. He may be able to influence him." This last was advice Sengstack had advised Strobik to give Stener.

There was more in this conversation to the same effect, and then Stener hurried as fast as his legs could carry him to the office of Henry A. Mollenhauer, in Market Street. He was so frightened that he could scarcely breathe, and he was quite ready to throw himself on his knees before the big German-American financier and leader. Oh, if Mr. Mollenhauer would only help him! he thought. If he could just get out of this without going to jail! His house, his real estate, his holdings in Cowperwood's and Strobik's and Harmon's affairs—Mollenhauer could have them all if only he, Stener, were not sent to jail. The thought of the grim, gray walls of the Eastern Penitentiary, which he frequently passed coming downtown from his outlying home, looming hard and cold against their commonplace background, frightened him. He had read in the papers of the nature of the solitary confinement endured there by convicts who had been sentenced for offenses in no way worse than his. He was not guilty actually—other treasurers had done as he had done; but the Chicago fire and Cowperwood's impending failure made it look so bad. The money was not in the treasury, that was one thing sure. He had loaned it out without legal authority from the city or the State. It was gone unless Cowperwood brought it back, and he was a criminal. Great heavens, think of that! It was a warm October day, the sun shining brightly, but the perspiration on his brow and hands and neck was ice-cold.

"Oh, Lord! Oh, Lord! Oh, Lord!" he repeated, over and over to himself, as he walked. "What shall I do?"

The attitude of Henry A. Mollenhauer, grim, political boss that he was—trained in a hard school—was precisely the attitude of every such man in all such trying but somewhat self-advantaging circumstances. In a way Stener was his appointee. Stener had carried out Mollenhauer's political orders at the time the big political leader wanted to realize on his large holdings of city warrants—the time he had sent Stener to Cowperwood; but he had not imagined that Stener's efforts to create and sell city loan, in order to take up his holdings of city warrants at a good price, would result in any such relationship as existed at present between Stener and Cowperwood. What Butler and, later, Strobik had told him concerning the condition of affairs in the city treasurer's office had surprised him greatly. He did not give Stener credit for so much shrewdness and daring, and could see at once that it must be Cowperwood.

When Stener was shown in on this very catastrophic Monday afternoon, Mollenhauer was cool, meditative, smiling—except in Stener's presence. He was wondering, in view of what Butler had told him, in just how much he could advantage himself in this situation by acquiring additional street-railway stock. If he could, he wanted to get control of what Stener now had (through Cowperwood's skill) without in any way compromising himself. Stener's shares could easily be transferred on 'change through his (Mollenhauer's) brokers to a dummy, who would eventually transfer them to himself (Mollenhauer). Stener must be squeezed thoroughly, though, this afternoon, and as for his five hundred thousand dollars' indebtedness to the treasury, Mr. Mollenhauer did not see what could be done about that. If Cowperwood could not pay it, the city would have to lose it; but the scandal must be hushed up until after election. Stener, unless the various party leaders had more generosity than Mollenhauer imagined, would have to suffer exposure, arrest, trial, confiscation of his property, and possibly sentence to the penitentiary, though this might easily be commuted by the governor, once public excitement died down. He did not trouble to think whether Cowperwood was criminally involved or not. A hundred to one he was not. Trust a shrewd man like that to take care of himself. But if there were any way to shoulder the blame onto Cowperwood, and so clear the treasurer and the skirts of the party, he would not object to that. He wanted to hear the full

story of Stener's relations with the broker first. He did
not believe it could be done; but he would see. More
talks were eventually coming between himself, Butler,
and Simpson. Meanwhile, the thing to do was to seize
what Stener had to yield.

The troubled city treasurer, on being shown into Mr.
Mollenhauer's presence, at once sank feebly in a chair
and collapsed. He was entirely done for mentally. His
nerve was gone, his courage exhausted like a breath.

"Well, Mr. Stener?" queried Mr. Mollenhauer, impressively, pretending, even though he had sent Sengstack,
not to know what brought him.

"I came about this matter of my loans to Mr. Cowperwood."

Mr. Mollenhauer had kept Mr. Stener waiting a full
half-hour, in order to melt him, and he was properly
melted.

"Well, what about them?"

"Well, he owes me, or the city treasury rather, five
hundred thousand dollars, and I understand that he is
going to fail and that he can't pay it back."

"Who told you that?"

"Mr. Sengstack, and since then Mr. Cowperwood has
been to see me. He tells me that I will have to loan him
some more money to help him out. He wants to borrow
three hundred thousand dollars more. He says he must
have it."

"So!" said Mr. Mollenhauer, impressively, and with an
air of astonishment which he did not feel. "You would not
think of doing that, of course. You're badly involved as it
is. If he wants to know why, refer him to me. Don't
advance him another dollar. If you do, and this case
comes to trial, no court would have any mercy on you.
It's going to be difficult enough to do anything for you
as it is."

At this suggestion of mercy, possible aid, George Stener,
hopeless infant that he was financially, slipped from his

chair, which was facing Mollenhauer's, and to which the latter had waved him on entering, to his knees and folded his hands in the uplifted attitude of a devotee before a sacred image.

"Oh, Mr. Mollenhauer," he choked, beginning to cry, "I didn't mean to do anything wrong. Strobik and Wycroft told me it was all right. You sent me to Mr. Cowperwood in the first place. I only did what I thought the others had been doing. Mr. Bode did it, just like I have been doing. He dealt with Tighe and Company. I have a wife and four children, Mr. Mollenhauer. My youngest boy is only seven years old. Think of them, Mr. Mollenhauer! Think of what my arrest will mean to them! I don't want to go to jail. I didn't think I was doing anything very wrong—honestly I didn't. I'll give up all I've got. You can have my stocks and houses and lots—anything—if you'll only get me out of this. You won't let 'em send me to jail, will you?"

His fat, white lips were trembling—wabbling nervously—and big, hot tears were coursing down his previously pale but now, from exciting prayer, flushed cheeks. He presented one of those almost unbelievable pictures which are yet so intensely human and so true. If only the great financial and political giants would for once accurately reveal the details of their lives!

Mollenhauer looked at him calmly, meditatively. How often had he seen weaklings no more dishonest than himself, but without his courage and subtlety, pleading to him in this fashion, not on their knees exactly, but intellectually so! Life to him, as to every other man of large practical knowledge and insight, was an inexplicable tangle. What were you going to do about the so-called morals and precepts of the world? This man Stener fancied that he was dishonest, and that he, Mollenhauer, was honest. He was here, self-convicted of sin, pleading to him, Mollenhauer, as he would to a righteous, unstained saint. As a matter of fact, Mollenhauer knew that he was simply shrewder, more far-seeing, more calculating, not less dishonest. Stener was lacking in force and brains—not morals. This lack was his principal crime. There were people who believed in some esoteric standard of right—some ideal of conduct absolutely and very far removed from practical life; but he had never seen them practise it save to their own financial (not moral—he would not say that) destruction. They were never significant, practical men who clung to these fatuous ideals. They were always poor, nondescript, negligible dreamers. He could not have made Stener understand all this if he had wanted to, and he certainly did not want to. Stener, like thousands and millions of others, was one of those men who are born to be ruled by men like himself, for instance. The shrewd, calculating, thinking man—other things being equal—nearly always rules. These significant thoughts passed vaguely through Mollenhauer's mind as he saw Stener kneeling before him; but in spite of them he felt a little sorry for the man, just a little. It was too bad about Mrs. Stener and the little Steners. No doubt she had worked hard, as had Stener, to get up in the world and be something— just a little more than miserably poor; and now this unfortunate complication had to arise to undo them—this Chicago fire. What a curious thing that was! If any one thing more than another made him doubt the existence of a kindly, overruling Providence, it was the unheralded storms out of clear skies which so often brought ruin and disaster to so many.

"Get up, Mr. Stener," he said, calmly, after a few moments. "You mustn't give way to your feelings like this. You must not cry. These troubles are never unraveled by tears. You must do a little thinking for yourself. Perhaps your situation isn't so bad."

As he was saying this Stener was putting himself back in his chair, getting out his handkerchief, and sobbing hopelessly in it.

"There, Mr. Stener, there. I'll do what I can. I won't promise anything. I can't tell you what the result will be. There are many peculiar political forces in this city. I may not be able to save you, but I am perfectly willing to try. You must put yourself absolutely under my direction. You must not say or do anything without first consulting with me. I will send my secretary, Mr. Sengstack, to you from time to time. He will tell you what to do. You must not come to me unless I send for you. Do you understand that thoroughly?"

"Yes, Mr. Mollenhauer."

"Well, now, dry your eyes. I don't want you to go out of this office crying. Go back to your office and I will send Mr. Sengstack to see you. He will tell you what to do. Follow him exactly. And whenever I send for you come at once."

He got up, large, self-confident, reserved. Stener, buoyed by the subtle reassurance of his remarks, recovered to a degree his equanimity. Mr. Mollenhauer, the great, powerful Mr. Mollenhauer, was going to help him out of his scrape. He might not have to go to jail after all. He left after a few moments, his face a little red from weeping, but otherwise recovered from telltale marks, and returned to his office.

In three-quarters of an hour Mr. Sengstack called for the second time this day—Mr. Abner Sengstack, small, dark-faced, club-footed, a great sole of leather three inches thick under his short, withered right leg, his slightly Slavic, highly intelligent countenance burning with a pair of keen, piercing, inscrutable black eyes. Mr. Sengstack was a fit secretary for Mr. Mollenhauer. You could see at one glance that he would make Mr. Stener do exactly what Mr. Mollenhauer suggested. His business was to induce Mr. Stener to part with his street-railway holdings at once through Tighe & Co., Butler's brokers, to the political subagent who would eventually transfer them to Mollenhauer. What little Stener received for them might well go into the treasury. Tighe & Co. would manage the "'change" subtleties of this without giving any one else a chance to bid, while at the same time making it appear an open-market transaction. At the same time Sengstack went carefully into the state of the treasurer's office for his master's benefit—finding out what it was that Strobik, Wycroft, and Harmon had been doing with their loans. *Via* another source they were ordered to disgorge at once or face prosecution. They were a part of Mr. Mollenhauer's political machine. Then, having cautioned Mr. Stener not to set over the remainder of his property to any one, and not to listen to any one, most of all to the Machiavellian counsel of Mr. Cowperwood, Mr. Sengstack left. Needless to say, Mr. Mollenhauer was greatly gratified by this turn of affairs. Cowperwood was now most likely in a position where he would have to come and see him, or if not, a good share of the properties he controlled, Mr. Stener's end of them, were already in his, Mollenhauer's, possession. If by some hook or crook he could secure the remainder, Mr. Simpson and Mr. Butler might well talk to him about this street-railway business. His holdings were now as large as any, if not quite the largest.

CHAPTER XXXIV

IT was in the face of this very altered situation that Cowperwood arrived late this Monday afternoon—it was almost five o'clock—to see Mr. Stener.

Stener was quite alone, worried and distraught. He was anxious to see Cowperwood, and at the same time afraid to meet him. His running to Mollenhauer this afternoon, at Strobik's suggestion, and telling him of Cowperwood's request, was in its way a form of treachery. He should not have done it, seeing that he had hitherto so thoroughly shared in all the schemes and profits of Cowperwood; but he had not dared do otherwise. The man was frightened and senseless.

"George," said Frank, briskly, on seeing him, "I haven't much time to spare now, but I've come, finally, to tell you that you'll have to let me have three hundred thousand more if you don't want me to fail. Things are looking very bad to-day. They've caught me in a corner on my loans; but this storm isn't going to last. You can see by the very character of it that it can't." He was looking at Stener's face, and seeing fear and a painful necessity for opposition written there. "Chicago is burning, but it will be built up again. Business will be all the better for it later on. Now, I want you to be reasonable and help me. Don't get frightened." Stener stirred uneasily. "Don't let these politicians scare you. It will all blow over in a few days, and then we'll be better off than ever. Did you see Mollenhauer?"

"Yes."

"Well, what did he have to say?"

"He said just what I thought he'd say. He won't let

me do this. I can't, Frank, I tell you!" exclaimed Stener, jumping up. He was so nervous that he had had a hard time keeping his seat during this short, direct conversation. Cowperwood's searching glance was troubling him as might a hundred needle-points pricking his spine. "I can't! They've got me in a corner! They're after me! They all know what we've been doing. Oh, say, Frank" —he threw up his arms wildly—"you've got to get me out of this. You've got to let me have that five hundred thousand back and get me out of this. If you don't, and you should fail, they'll send me to the penitentiary. I've got a wife and four children, Frank. I can't go on in this. It's too big for me. I never should have gone in on it in the first place. I never would have if you hadn't persuaded me, in a way. I never thought when I began that I would ever get in as bad as all this. I can't go on, Frank. I can't! I'm willing you should have all my stock. Only give me back that five hundred thousand, and we'll call it even." His voice rose nervously as he talked, and he wiped his wet forehead with his hand and stared at Cowperwood pleadingly, foolishly.

Cowperwood stared at him in return for a few moments with a cold, fishy eye. He knew a great deal about human nature, and he was ready for and expectant of any queer shift in an individual's attitude, particularly in time of panic; but this shift of Stener's was quite too much. If it had not been for his own dire predicament he would not have thought anything of it, would have walked out and let the man go; but now, *in extremis*, to hear him emitting a sinking wail like this, when he expected at least understanding and appreciation of his own situation, was too much. It did not vitally disturb his own clear thinking machinery, however. He merely stared at Stener for a few minutes, in order to convey to him something of his own surprise and chagrin—to hearten him with a sense of the contempt he had for any such weakness if long persisted in—and then he asked: "Who else have you been talking to, George, since I saw you? Who have you seen? What did Sengstack have to say?"

"He says just what Mollenhauer does, that I mustn't loan any more money under any circumstances, and he says I ought to get that five hundred thousand back as quickly as possible."

"And you think Mollenhauer wants to help you, do you?" inquired Cowperwood, finding it hard to efface the contempt which kept forcing itself into his voice. Still, he said to himself, if you wish to manipulate fools you must bear with their follies—their idiosyncrasies. He had to placate this man.

"I think he does, yes. I don't know who else will, Frank, if he don't. He's one of the big political forces in this town."

"Listen to me," began Cowperwood, eying him fixedly. Then he paused. "What did he say you should do about your holdings?"

"Sell them through Tighe and Company and put the money back in the treasury, if you won't take them."

"Sell them to whom?" asked Cowperwood, thinking of Stener's last words.

"To any one on 'change who'll take them, I suppose. I don't know."

"I thought so," said Cowperwood, comprehendingly. "I might have known as much. They're working you, George. They're simply trying to get your stocks away from you. You must know it if you know anything at all. Mollenhauer is leading you on. Tighe and Company are his agents. He knows I can't do what you want—give you back the five hundred thousand dollars. He wants you to throw your stocks on the market so that he can pick them up. Depend on it, that's all arranged for already. When you do, he's got me in his clutches, or he thinks he has—he and Butler and Simpson. They want to get together on this local street-railway situation, and I know it, I feel it. I've felt it coming all along. They want to shake us out—shake me out—and they are using you right now to hit me. Mollenhauer hasn't any more intention of helping you than he has of flying. Once you've sold your stocks he's through with you—mark my word. Do you think he'll turn a hand to keep you out of the penitentiary once you're out of this street-railway situation? He will not. And if you think so, you're a bigger fool than I take you to be, George. Don't go crazy. Don't lose your head. You've gone wild overnight. Somebody's frightened the life out of you. Be sensible. Look the situation in the face. Let me explain it to you. You can see for yourself just how things are, if you will only stop for a moment and try to see what it is you are going to do. If you don't help me now—if you don't let me have three hundred thousand dollars by to-morrow noon, at the very latest, I'm through, and so are you. There is not a thing the matter with our situation. Those stocks of ours are as good to-day as they ever were. Why, great heavens, man, the railways are there behind them. They're paying. The Seventeenth and Nineteenth Street line is earning one thousand dollars a day right now. What better evidence do you want than that? Green and Coates is earning five hundred dollars. You're frightened, George. These damned political schemers have scared you. Why, you've as good a right to loan that money as Bode and Murtagh had before you. They did it. You've been doing it for Mollenhauer and the others, only so long as you do it for them it's all right. What's a designated city depository but a loan?" Cowperwood was referring to the system under which certain portions of city money, like the sinking-fund, were permitted to be kept in certain banks at a low rate of interest or no rate—banks in which Mollenhauer and Butler and Simpson were interested. This was their safe graft. "Don't throw your chances away, George. Don't quit now. You're a rich man if you

THE FINANCIER

don't. You'll be worth millions in a few years, and you won't have to turn a hand. All you will have to do will be to keep what you have. If you don't help me, mark my word, they'll throw you over the moment I'm out of this, and they'll let you go to the penitentiary. There's not a single one of these fellows will turn a hand the moment I'm through. Who's going to put up five hundred thousand dollars for you, George? Where is Mollenhauer going to get it, or Butler, or anybody, in these times? They can't. They don't intend to. When I'm through, you're through, and you'll be exposed quicker than any one else. They can't hurt me, George. I'm an agent. I didn't ask you to come to me. You came to me in the first place of your own accord. If you don't help me, you're through, I tell you, and you're going to be sent to the penitentiary as sure as there are jails. Why don't you take a stand, George? Why don't you hold your ground? You have your wife and children to look after. You can't be any worse off loaning me three hundred thousand more than you are right now. What difference does it make—five hundred thousand or eight hundred thousand? It's all one and the same thing, if you're going to be tried for it. You might as well be tried for a sheep as a lamb. Besides, if you loan me this, there isn't going to be any trial. I'm not going to fail. This storm will blow over in a week or ten days, and we'll be rich again. For Heaven's sake, George, don't go to pieces this way! Be sensible! Be reasonable!"

He paused, for Stener's face had become a jelly-like mass of woe. The man was beside himself with these thoughts of his own folly and of the penitentiary possibly yawning for him, of Mollenhauer's using him as a tool and playing him false, of Cowperwood's doing, as Mollenhauer and his secretary, Sengstack, had suggested, the same thing. He had no courage for great occasions, no vitality, no physical stamina. This idea of a large burden of responsibility being suddenly thrust upon him was too

394

much for him. His physical and intellectual knees
knocked together.

"I can't, Frank," he wailed. "I tell you I can't.
They'll punish me worse than ever if I do that. They'll
never let up on me. You don't know these people."

The political underling, the tool, the man trained to
obey, spoke here. So long had he helped to carry the
trains of the strutting political potentates that their
slightest nod was as an unbreakable command to him.
In his very crumpling, jelly-like weakness Cowperwood
read his own fate. What could you do with a man like
that? How brace him up? You couldn't! And with
a gesture of infinite understanding, disgust, noble indifference, he threw up his hands and started to walk
out. At the door he turned.

"George," he said, "I'm sorry. I'm sorry for you,
not me. I'll come out of things all right, eventually. I'll
be rich. But, George, you're making the one great mistake of your life. You'll be poor; you'll be a convict, and
the blame will be all to yourself. There isn't a thing the
matter with this money situation except the fire. There
isn't a thing wrong with my affairs except this slump in
stocks—this panic. You sit there, a fortune in your hands,
and you allow a lot of schemers, highbinders, who don't
know any more of your affairs or mine than a rabbit,
who have no power over you except your own fear, and
no interest in you except to plan what they can get out
of you, to frighten you and prevent you from doing the
one thing that will save your life. Three hundred thousand paltry dollars that in three or four weeks from
now I can pay back to you four and five times over, and
for that you will see me go broke and yourself to the
penitentiary. I can't understand it, George. It isn't
reason. It's obsession. You're out of your mind. You're
going to rue this the longest day that you live, and if
you ever meet me you'll tell me so."

Cowperwood waited a few moments to see if this, by

any twist of chance, would have any effect; then, noting that Stener still remained a wilted, helpless mass of nothing, he shook his head gloomily and walked out. It was the first time in his life that Cowperwood had ever shown the least sign of weakening or despair. He had felt all along as though there were nothing to the Greek theory of being pursued by the furies. Now, however, there seemed an untoward fate which was pursuing him. It looked that way. Still, fate or no fate, he was put on this earth to achieve somewhat, and he did not propose to be daunted. Even in this very beginning of a tendency to feel despondent he threw back his head, protruded his chest, and walked as briskly as ever.

In the large room outside Mr. Stener's private office he encountered Albert Stires, Stener's chief clerk and secretary. He and Albert had exchanged many friendly greetings in times past, and all the little minor transactions in regard to city loan, the entering of transfers on given dates, the mailing or sending of checks, etc., had been discussed between them, for Albert knew more of the intricacies of finance and financial bookkeeping than Stener would ever know.

At the sight of Stires the thought in regard to the sixty thousand dollars' worth of city loan certificates previously referred to flashed suddenly through Cowperwood's mind. He had not deposited them in the sinking-fund, and did not intend to for the present—could not, unless considerable free money were to reach him shortly—for he had used them to satisfy other pressing demands, and had no free money to buy them back—or, in other words, release them. And he did not want to just at this moment. Under the law governing transactions of this kind with the city treasurer, he was supposed to deposit them at once to the credit of the city, and not to draw his pay therefor from the city treasurer until he had. To be very exact, the city treasurer, under the law, was not supposed to pay him for any transaction of this kind until he or his agents presented a voucher from the bank or other organization carrying the sinking-fund for the city showing that the certificates so purchased had actually been deposited there. As a matter of fact, under the custom which had grown up between him and Stener, the law had long been ignored in this respect. He could buy certificates of city loan for the sinking-fund up to any reasonable amount, hypothecate them where he pleased, and draw his pay from the city without presenting a voucher. At the end of the month sufficient certificates of city loan could usually be gathered from one source and another to make up the deficiency, or the deficiency could actually be ignored, as had been done on more than one occasion, for long periods of time, while he used money secured by hypothecating the shares for speculative purposes. This was morally wrong and actually illegal; but neither Cowperwood nor Stener saw it in that light or cared. It might be wrong, but it was profitable; and, anyhow, there was no immediate danger of exposure. Stener was affable and willing; the city treasury was usually more than plentifully supplied with cash. What would you?

The trouble with this particular transaction was the note that he had received from Stener ordering him to stop both buying and selling, which put Cowperwood's relations with the city treasury on a very formal basis. He had bought these certificates before receiving this note, but had not deposited them. He was going now to collect his check; but since Stener was evidently "at outs" with him, and might sever relations entirely, or be compelled to, the old, easy system of balancing matters at the end of the month might not be said to obtain any longer. Anyhow, Stires might ask him to present a voucher of deposit. If so, he could not now get this check for sixty thousand dollars, for he did not have the certificates to deposit. If not, he might get the money; but, also, it might constitute the basis of some subsequent legal action. If he did not eventually deposit the certificates before failure, some charge such as that of larceny might be brought against him. Still, he said to himself, he might not really fail even yet. If any of his banking associates should, for any reason, modify their decision in regard to calling his loans, he would not. But, barring this, he would fail; and then Stener could say, when it was discovered that these certificates were not in the sinking-fund, that he, Cowperwood, had said they were, or obtained the check under false pretense. That was larceny. Beyond question it was grand larceny, and yet he could plead custom, lack of time to adjust his financial affairs, intention to deposit, and the like. Would Stener make a row about this if he so secured this check? Would the city officials pay any attention to him if he did? Could you get any district attorney to take cognizance of such a transaction, if Stener did complain? No, not in all likelihood; and, anyhow, nothing would come of it. No jury would punish him in the face of the understanding existing between him and Stener as agent or broker and principal. And, anyhow, once he had the money, it was a hundred to one Stener would think no more about it. It would go in among the various unsatisfied liabilities, and nothing more would be thought about it. It did not occur to him at this moment that his relations with Edward Malia Butler and his daughter might possibly create a special situation in which any flaw in his legal status would be eagerly utilized to cause him trouble. Like lightning the entire situation flashed through his mind. He would risk it. He stopped before the chief clerk's desk.

"Albert," he said, in a low voice, "I bought sixty thousand dollars' worth of city loan for the sinking-fund this morning. Will you give my boy a check for it in the morning, or, better yet, will you give it to me now? I got your note about no more purchases. I'm going back to the office. You can just credit the sinking-fund with eight hundred certificates at from seventy-five to eighty. I'll send you the itemized list later."

"Certainly, Mr. Cowperwood, certainly," replied Albert, with alacrity. "Stocks are getting an awful knock, aren't they? I hope you're not very much troubled by it?"

"Not very, Albert," replied Cowperwood, smiling, the while the chief clerk was making out his check. He was wondering if by any chance Stener would appear and attempt to interfere with this. It was a legal transaction. He had right to the check provided he deposited the certificates, as was his custom, with the trustee of the fund. Still, in his nervous frenzy Stener might object and take counsel with Mollenhauer. Then, no doubt, he, Cowperwood, would have to bring the certificates to the treasurer's office, or a receipt from the trustee of the sinking-fund, the Drovers' and Traders' Bank, before he could get his check. Since he himself had used the certificates to fill a crying need for additional securities, he could not do this. It would be fatal to his plan. If he could not get the check, he could not pay the Girard National Bank its call-loan; and if he did not pay this call-loan promptly, he lost the friendship of W. C. Davison, his present good ally. He waited tensely while Albert wrote, and as he tore the check from the stub-book and handed it to Cowperwood the latter breathed a sigh of relief. Here, at least, was sixty thousand dollars, and to-night's work would enable him to cash the seventy-five thousand that had been promised him. To-morrow, once more he must see Leigh, Kitchen, Jay Cooke & Co., Edward Clark & Co.—all the long list of people to whom he owed loans—and see what could be done. If he could only get time! If he could get just a week!

CHAPTER XXXV

TIME was not a thing to be had in this emergency. With the seventy-five thousand dollars his friends had extended to him, and sixty thousand dollars secured from Stires, Cowperwood met, the next morning, the Girard call, and placed the balance, thirty-five thousand dollars, in a private storage-box in his own home. He visited all the bankers and financiers again. It was not within reason that they should assist him under the circumstances, and by twelve o'clock he had exhausted his resources. There was nothing for it but that he must default on his payments. He saw clearly in this hour all the work of years disappearing. They would sell out his holdings against a depressed market, unless, by a credit conference and legal proceedings started solely to delay matters, he could prevent it; and then, even then, he would be "done" out of most of the holdings he had worked so industriously to acquire. He did not commiserate himself in this hour. He looked out of his office window into the little court upon the grass and the red-brick wall, and sighed. What more could he do? He sent a note to his father, asking him to call for lunch. He sent a note to his own lawyer, Harper Steger, a man of his own age, whom he liked very much, and asked him to call also. He evolved in his own mind various plans of delay, addresses to creditors, and the like; but, alas! he was going to fail. And the worst of it was that this matter of the city treasurer's loans was bound to become a public, and more than a public, a political scandal. The matter of the sixty thousand dollars' worth of city loan certificates, unless he could pay his father's bank, where he had hypothecated them, and deposit them in the Drovers' and Traders' for the sinking-fund, where they belonged, might be contorted into a charge of larceny as bailee, although heretofore, during the times he had dealt with the city treasurer, he had drawn his cash promptly from the treasury and taken his time about depositing the certificates. He could fail with them in his possession, having the excellent excuse that he intended to do so but had forgotten it. It might look better so. There ought to be plenty of assets for his creditors to quarrel about. Alas! the charge of conniving, if not illegally, at least morally, at the misuse of the city's money was the one thing that would hurt him most. And how industriously his rivals would advertise this fact! He might get on his feet again if he failed; but it would be uphill work. And his father! His father would be pulled down with him. The old gentleman could not stand this collapse financially and socially. He might weather it if no odium attached to his financial relationship with his son; but if this were discussed, it was probable that he would be forced out of the presidency of his bank. It would be so easy, Cowperwood saw, to make it appear that his father was identified with all that he did. It would not be so bad if it were not for the city treasurer's defalcation; but that—that would throw a cloud of shame over the whole thing. Stener! The fool! The ingrate! The coward! To risk a penitentiary sentence rather than fight his way to success and victory! Such was the stuff of which some men were made. With these thoughts Cowperwood sat there waiting, for counsel with his father and Steger was most important. As he did so Aileen Butler was announced by his office-boy, and at the same time Albert Stires.

"Show in Miss Butler," he said, getting up. "Tell Mr. Stires to wait." And he turned to look into the little court, where the grass was still green and the sky blue overhead between the red-brick walls. Aileen came briskly, vigorously in, her beautiful body clothed as decoratively as ever. The street suit that she wore was of a light golden-brown broadcloth, faceted with small, dark-red buttons. Her head was decorated with a brownish-red shako of a type she had learned was becoming to her, brimless and with a trailing plume, and on which Cowperwood had complimented her more than once; and her throat was graced by a three-strand necklace of gold beads. Her hands were smoothly gloved as usual, and her little feet dainty to behold. There was a look of girlish distress in her eyes, which, however, she was doing her best to conceal.

"Honey," she exclaimed, on seeing him, her arms extended—the room was incased in solid hardwood panels, giving no opportunity for observation from without— "what is the trouble? I wanted so much to ask you the other night. You're not going to fail, are you? I heard father and Owen talking about you last night."

"What did they say?" he inquired, putting his arm about her and looking quietly into her nervous eyes.

"Oh, you know, I think papa is very angry with you. He suspects. Some one sent him an anonymous letter. He tried to get it out of me last night, but he didn't. I denied everything. I was in here twice this morning to see you, but you were out. I was so afraid that he might see you first, and that you might say something."

"Me, Aileen?"

"Well, no, not exactly. I didn't think that. I don't know what I thought. Oh, honey, I've been so worried. You know, I didn't sleep at all. I thought I was stronger than that; but I was so worried about you. You know, he put me in a strong light by his desk, where he could see my face, and then he showed me the letter. I was so astonished for a moment I hardly know what I said or how I looked."

"What did you say?"

"Why, I said: 'What a shame! It isn't so!' But I

didn't say it right away. My heart was going like a trip-hammer. I'm afraid he must have been able to tell something from my face. I could hardly get my breath."

"He's a shrewd man, your father," he commented. "He knows something about life. Now you see how difficult these situations are. It's a blessing he decided to show you the letter instead of watching the house. I suppose he felt too bad to do that. He can't prove anything now. But he knows. You can't deceive him."

"How do you know he knows?"

"I saw him yesterday."

"Did he talk to you about it?"

"No; I saw his face. He simply looked at me."

"Honey! I'm so sorry for him!"

"I know you are. So am I. But it can't be helped now. We should have thought of that in the first place."

"But I love you so. Oh, honey, he will never forgive me. He loves me so. He mustn't know. I won't admit anything. But, oh dear!"

She put her hands tightly together on his bosom, and he looked consolingly into her eyes. This was a grim occasion for him—a sad hour. There were so many things converging to make a dramatic dénouement.

"Never mind," he replied; "it can't be helped now. Where is my strong, determined Aileen? I thought you were going to be so brave? Aren't you going to be? I need to have you that way now."

"Do you?"

"Yes."

"Are you in trouble?"

"I think I am going to fail, dear."

"Oh no!"

"Yes, honey. I think I'm at the end of my rope. I don't see any way out just at present. I've sent for my father and my lawyer. You mustn't stay here, sweet. Your father may come in here at any time. We must

meet somewhere—to-morrow, say—to-morrow afternoon.
You remember Indian Rock, out on the Wissahickon?"

"Yes."

"Could you be there at four?"

"Yes."

"Look out for who's following. If I'm not there by
four-thirty, don't wait. You know why. It will be because
I think some one is watching. There won't be, though,
if we work it right. And now you must run, sweet. We
can't use Nine-thirty-one any more. I'll have to rent
another place somewhere else."

"Oh, honey, I'm so sorry."

"Aren't you going to be strong and brave? You see,
I need you to be."

He was almost, for the first time, a little sad in his
mood.

"Yes, honey, yes," she declared, slipping her arms
under his and pulling him tight. "Oh yes! You can
depend on me. Oh, sweet, I love you so! I'm so sorry.
Oh, I do hope you don't fail! But it doesn't make any
difference, dear, between you and me, whatever happens,
does it? We will love each other just the same. You
will love me, and I will love you. Oh, honey, I'll do anything for you! I'll do anything you say. You can trust
me. They sha'n't know anything from me."

She looked at his chill face, and a fearful determination to fight for him welled up in her heart. Her love was
unjust, illegal, outlawed; but it was love, just the same,
and had much of the fiery daring of the outcast from
justice.

"I love you! I love you! I love you!" she declared.
He unloosed her hands.

"Run, sweet. To-morrow at four. Don't fail. And
don't talk. And don't admit anything, whatever you do."

"I won't."

"And don't worry about me. I'll be all right."

And then Mr. Albert Stires was admitted.

Cowperwood barely had time to straighten his tie, to assume a nonchalant attitude by his window, when in hurried Mr. Stener's chief clerk—pale, disturbed, obviously out of key with himself.

"Mr. Cowperwood! You know that check I gave you last night? Mr. Stener says it's illegal, that I shouldn't have given it to you, that he will hold me responsible. He says I can be arrested for compounding a felony, and that he will discharge me and have me sent to prison if I don't get it back. Oh, Mr. Cowperwood, I am only a young man! I'm just really starting out in life. I've got my wife and little boy to look after. You won't let him do that to me? You'll give me that check back, won't you? I can't go back to the office without it. He says you're going to fail, and that you knew it, and that you haven't any right to it."

His face was a study in clerkly distress. He was one of your typical clerical assistants, young, methodical, unschooled in the larger tricks of the world, fearsome and careful of his future. This matter of the check, these possible charges, were as life and death to him. He knew that the practical, inconsiderate machinery of politics would only make short work of him. His future! His wife and child! His salary! This threat of jail and of forfeiting his sureties had frightened the soul out of him.

Cowperwood looked at him curiously. He was surprised at the variety and character of these emissaries of disaster. Surely, when troubles chose to multiply they had great skill in presenting themselves in rapid order. Stener had no right to make any such statement. The transaction was not illegal. The man had gone wild. True, he, Cowperwood, had received an order after these securities were bought not to buy or sell any more city loan, but that did not invalidate previous purchases. Stener was browbeating and frightening this poor underling, a better man than himself, in order to get back this sixty-thousand-dollar check. What a petty creature he was! How true it was, as somebody had remarked, that you could not possibly measure the petty meannesses to which a fool could stoop!

"You go back to Mr. Stener, Mr. Stires, and tell him that it can't be done. The certificates of loan were purchased before his order arrived, and the records of the exchange will prove it. There is no illegality here. I am entitled to that check and could have collected it in any qualified court of law. The man has gone out of his head. I haven't failed yet. You are not in any danger of any legal proceedings; and if you are, I'll help defend you. I can't give you the check back because I haven't it to give; and if I did, I wouldn't. That would be allowing a fool to make a fool of me. I'm sorry, very, but I can't do anything for you."

"Oh, Mr. Cowperwood!" Tears were in Mr. Stires's eyes. "He'll discharge me! He'll forfeit my sureties. I'll be turned out into the street. I have only a little property of my own—outside of my salary!"

He wrung his hands, and Cowperwood shook his head sadly.

"This isn't as bad as you think, Albert. He won't do what he says. He can't. It's unfair and illegal. You can bring suit and recover your salary. I'll help you in that as much as I'm able. But I can't give this sixty-thousand-dollar check, because I haven't it to give. I couldn't if I wanted to. It isn't here any more. I've paid for the securities I bought with it. The securities are not here. They're in the sinking-fund, or will be."

He paused, wishing he had not mentioned that fact. It was a slip of the tongue, one of the few he ever made, due to the peculiar pressure of the situation. Stires pleaded longer. It was no use, Cowperwood told him. Finally he went away, crestfallen, fearsome, broken. There were tears of suffering in his eyes. Cowperwood was very sorry.

And then his father was announced.

CHAPTER XXXVI

THE elder Cowperwood brought a haggard face. He and Frank had had a long conversation the evening before, lasting until early this Tuesday morning; but it had not been productive of much save uncertainty. Cowperwood, the father, had reported that his enemies in the bank, particularly Adam Davi, the vice-president, were secretly gratified at the turn affairs had taken, and that they were watching his manœuvers closely. If by any chance Frank failed and the city were defrauded of so large a sum as five hundred thousand dollars, there would surely be an uproar. The unostentatious conservative public, which knows so little of what is going on politically, and appears as a rule not to care, though it really does, being merely helpless, would begin to make inquiries. Where had the money gone? Who got it? What part did Frank Algernon Cowperwood play in this transaction? How much did Henry Worthington Cowperwood, his father, get? If that question were raised there would be perturbation in his own bank. Adam Davi would find his excuse for speaking. The secondary element that is present everywhere and is always seeking a change, hoping to profit thereby, would find in this its strong, legitimate excuse. Henry Worthington Cowperwood would have to resign; and after that where would he go? Who would have him? What bank? Bank presidencies are not lying around loose for the asking. Men with flaws in their record are not necessary to their control. The pressure to achieve these distinguished positions is so great that only the flawless—speaking from a public point of view—are eligible. A man must be im-

peccable, his honor not open to suspicion, as far as the
general public is concerned—certainly not open to provable
dishonor. Besides, he was old—a little over sixty years.

Cowperwood, Jr., had been thinking of this all along.
Cowperwood, Sr., had been worrying about it almost
fatally. This last night he had spent in his garden of
Gethsemane. "And he prayed that this cup might pass
from him." He thought of his wife, a little, quiet, helpless woman, who believed in him so thoroughly. She believed in Frank. His two boys, Edward and Joseph—they
were not yet placed in the world, except as assistants to
Frank. Now they never would be. Anna Adelaide, because of her looks and temperament, had not been able
to make a worth-while marriage. Joseph was just now
thinking of getting married, and this would affect that.
He, the father, would lose his house, its fine furniture, his
connections, his friends; Frank and he would be practically without a dollar in the world. He thought once of
impounding some money—concealing some securities; but
his conscience would not let him. His conscience was part
of his methodical mental machinery. He could not lie. He
had never been able to. Frank had always been so able,
plain-spoken, practical, that he had been hypnotized into
believing that everything he did was right. When Frank
had explained Stener's desire to have him bring city
loan to par, in the first place, it was nothing but a nice,
fortunate, desirable, delightful bit of luck. Since then
all other subtleties had followed one by one, as a spider
spins a web, and they were apparently so harmless.
"Other city treasurers." How that phrase, carrying its
palliative and yet hopeless thought, jangled in his brain!
"Other city treasurers." Yes, by their wrong conduct,
their wretched precedent, they had digged the pit into
which his son Frank had now fallen. By their unrebuked
custom of using the city's funds without interest, they
had set and baited the trap by which Frank was now
caught fast. And then this Chicago fire. What a

strange, catastrophic, fatalistic thing it was! Chicago burns, stocks tumble, Frank's securities are depreciated, his loans called, the city treasurer cannot get his money, and exposure follows! It was unfair, unkind on the part of fate; and yet so it was. Stener would go to the penitentiary, surely; but how about Frank and himself? Frank! His talented son! His millionaire boy! The man whom so many men respected, feared, looked up to. Why, these last few years he had heard scarcely anything save wonderful things about his son until it was a distinguished thing to be his father. His strength—half of it, at least—with the Third National was due to the success and prominence of his boy. And now—now!

When he was alone he rose from his chair in his room, or from his desk at the bank, and walked the floor. He pressed his bony hands together. He laid his pale hand over his mouth and stared at the floor. His eyes, rather deep-set and hollow at all times, were now sad caverns filled with a pale woe. He could not eat; he could not sleep. He could only think and calculate and hurry here and there in an aimless way. He was losing flesh, and he was as weak as though he were ill. Philadelphia, the eyes of the public, the minds of his friends, were as so many burning, blistering rays concentrated by a sun-glass and cast upon one spot, his brain. His sense of pride and position! His Frank! His personal honor! His bank presidency! His sons and daughter! His wife! And he was old now.

Let no one underestimate the need of pity. We live in a stony universe whose hard, brilliant forces rage fiercely. From the prowling hunger of the Hyrcan tiger to the concentric grip of Arcturus and Canopus there is this same ruthless, sightless disregard of the individual and the minor thing. Life moves in an ordered hierarchy of forces of which the lesser is as nothing to the greater. Ho, slave! And in the midst of the rip of desperate things —in odd crannies and chance flaws between forces—there spring and bloom these small flowers of sentiment. Tenderness! Mercy! Affection! Sorrow! The Hindus worship an image of pain. And well they may. It is a classic amid the painless, the indifferent—Nirvana. Blessed are the merciful, for they shall receive mercy! No, no. Blessed are the merciful, for they create mercy. Of such is the kingdom of the ideal.

"Hello, father," Cowperwood exclaimed, cheerfully, noting the former's gloom as he walked in. He was satisfied that there was scarcely a coal of thought to be raked out of these ashes of despair; but there was no use admitting the possibility of it. Discussion was worth something, seeing that everything they had was at stake. There was this final transaction in regard to the Girard National Bank and the sixty thousand dollars' worth of city loan, for instance. He owed the sinking-fund that much, and the certificates were not in his possession. They could be traced. How would he explain that? He could not believe that his luck had deserted him— that there was not some way out.

"Well," said his father, lifting his sad eyes in a peculiar way. He had a habit of raising his eyelids and eyebrows in a simulated expression of surprise, which was purely mechanical—a habit acquired through years and years of what seemed to him essential commercial practice, as some people look up over and along their noses; and now, in this hour of distress, he did it with a peculiar touch of vacuity to the action. It was mechanical and pathetic. Frank was so used to him he scarcely noticed it.

"Well, it looks like stormy weather, doesn't it? I've decided to call a meeting of my creditors, father, and ask for time. There isn't anything else to do. I can't realize enough on anything to make it worth while talking about. I thought Stener might change his mind, but he's worse rather than better. His head bookkeeper just went out of here."

"What did he want?" asked Henry Cowperwood.

"He wanted me to give him back a check for sixty thousand that he paid me for some city loan I bought yesterday morning." Frank did not explain to his father, however, that he had hypothecated the certificates this check had paid for, and used the check itself to raise money enough to pay the Girard National Bank and to give himself thirty-five thousand in cash besides.

"Well, I declare!" replied the old man. "You'd think he'd have better sense than that. That's a perfectly legitimate transaction. When did you say he notified you not to buy city loan?"

"Yesterday noon."

"He's out of his mind," Cowperwood, Sr., commented, laconically.

"It's Mollenhauer and Simpson and Butler, I know. They want my street-railway lines. Well, they won't get them. They'll get them through a receivership, and after the panic's all over. Our creditors will have first chance at these. If they buy, they'll buy from them. If it weren't for that five-hundred-thousand-dollar loan I wouldn't think a thing of this. My creditors would sustain me nicely. But the moment that gets noised around! . . . and this election!"

He foresaw what the creditors would think. He foresaw what his father's directors would think—for the time being, anyhow. Nothing is so senseless, so pointless, so indiscriminate as popular clamor. While that was on anything foolish and evil might be done. And this sixty thousand? What would Stener—or, rather, his advisers, now—do about that?

"I hypothecated those city loan certificates because I didn't want to get on the wrong side of Davison. I expected to take in enough by now to take them up. They ought to be in the sinking-fund, really," Cowperwood finally added.

The old gentleman saw the point at once, and winced.

"They might cause you trouble there, Frank."

"It's a technical question," replied his son. "I might have been intending to take them up. As a matter of fact, I will if I can before three. I've been taking eight and ten days to deposit them in the past. In a storm like this I'm entitled to move my pawns as best I can."

Cowperwood, the father, put his hand over his mouth again. He felt very disturbed about this. He saw no way out, however. He was at the end of his own resources. He felt the side-whiskers on his left cheek. He looked out of the window into the little green court. It was a technical question. Precedent probably governed. Still, it was dangerous—not straight. If Frank could get them out and deposit them it would be so much better.

"I'd take them up if I were you and I could."

"I will if I can."

"How much money have you?"

"Oh, twenty thousand, all told. If I suspend, though, I'll have to have a little ready cash."

"I have eight or ten thousand, or will have by night, I hope."

He was thinking of some one who would give him a second mortgage on his house.

Cowperwood looked quietly at him. There was nothing more to be said to his father. "I'm going to make one more appeal to Stener after you leave here," he said. "I'm going over there with Harper Steger when he comes. If he won't change I'll send out notice to my creditors, and notify the secretary of the exchange. I want you to keep a stiff upper lip, whatever happens. I know you will, though. I'm going into the thing head down. If Stener had any sense—" He paused. "But what's the use talking about a damn fool?"

He turned to the window, thinking of how easy it would have been if Aileen and he had not been exposed by this anonymous note to have arranged all with Butler. Rather than injure the party, Butler, *in extremis*, would have assisted him, so he thought, gone into partnership, possibly. Now. . .!

He turned back, for his father had got up. The latter was as stiff with despair as though he were suffering from cold. Once more he put his hand to his mouth.

"Well," he said, wearily.

Cowperwood suffered intensely for him. What a shame! His father! He felt a great surge of feeling and sorrow sweep to his brain, and then he settled down to his brilliant, defiant thinking. His father went out. Harper Steger was brought in. They shook hands, and at once started for Stener's office. He saw Stener; but Mr. Sengstack, with his small body and club foot, was there in the background of an outer room, and this visit was useless. Stener had sunk in on himself like an empty gas-bag, and no efforts were sufficient to inflate him. They went out, finally, defeated.

"I tell you, Frank," said Steger, "I wouldn't worry. We can tie this thing up legally until election and after, and that will give all this row a chance to die down. Then you can get your people together and talk sense to them. They're not going to give up good properties like this, even if Stener does go to jail."

Steger did not know of the sixty thousand dollars' worth of hypothecated securities as yet. Neither did he know of Aileen Butler and her father's boundless rage.

CHAPTER XXXVII

WE must turn a moment from the affairs of Mr. Frank Algernon Cowperwood to those of his wife.

During the years that had elapsed since the time when Frank Cowperwood and his wife were married many and notable changes had taken place. Cowperwood had filled out from the daring, aggressive frame of youth to the broader, more impassive solidity of manhood. He knew so much more of life now—of the actual practical workings of life—than he had thirteen years before, when he suspected everything. Experience had given him a larger tolerance, a kindlier understanding of weakness, without in the least modifying that practical control of affairs—that ability to say *no* and do *no* when it served his interests so to do—which was his chiefest and most imposing characteristic. Those who have come closest to men of large understanding and great executive judgment have always marveled at the seeming cruelty which stops short of nothing to achieve a given desired point. Failure is their *bête noir*. Weakness the real crime in an individual. They take into account only the significant things of life, and those only in their finest flower—health, strength, wisdom, courage, magnetism, and, above all, that subtlest of all qualities, *the luck to succeed*, which they put above every virtue. "I am no spiritualist nor theosophist," wrote one not long since, "but this gift, or occasional visitation of Providence, or whatever else people may choose to call it, to which I am subject at intervals, has saved me from being financially shattered at least two or three times every year. I do not indulge in any table-tapping or dark séances, as did the elder Vanderbilt;

but this strange, peculiar, and admonitory influence has always clung to me in times of approaching squalls more tenaciously than at any other. It has enabled me to take points on the market in at one ear and dispose of them through the other without suffering any evil consequences therefrom. I have known others who have had these mysterious forebodings, but who recklessly disregarded them; and this has been the rock on which they have split in speculative emergencies."

Cowperwood had this sixth sense, or gift, or psychic control, or whatever else you may choose to call it; he expected it in others—in those he worked with closely. He insisted on dealing with them solely in so far as this was practicable. In his own home he introduced an element of this demand for perfection more and more as he grew older. But his wife. It was just a little over thirteen years since he married her, and she was nearing forty—well within her thirty-ninth year, which was five years older than he was now. That original glamour which five years of quiet married life had not removed at the time he first saw her, was practically gone. She was not so plump for her size as she originally had been —more noticeably angular. If you could have looked under her chin you would have noticed now that a little network of wrinkles had come, which is to the life-loving woman such a discouraging forerunner of approaching age. Her eyes at the edges, her lips at the corners, her nose at its clear juncture with her face, had those faint, suspicious depressions which women dread so much. She was graceful yet, and charming; practical, too, in a narrow way, not grieving over life and death. But that, perhaps, was just what he missed most of all, if one would have believed it—that keen sense of the pathos of things that makes the exceptional woman. Aileen had something of it—a hearty understanding of the vast difference between success and failure. She seemed quite aware that she was at the zenith of her beauty. She was quite capable in a slightly crude way of telling what it meant to him and to her.

"There's one thing," she said to him, one day, "I'm ten years younger than you are. I'll still be all right when you're fifty."

He smiled at this keen understanding of life. It was these psychological touches, this occasional brilliant flash of raw, almost brutal understanding that fascinated him. He knew how she was figuring — on a physical basis purely. He felt that Edward Butler and his wife— their brute strength—were not entirely unrepresented in her. And what she said was probably true. He was not sure of that, but he loved her beauty just the same, and her mind—her awareness.

"Yes, sweet, I think you will. I hope so, anyhow. You deserve to be."

She felt sure that she was to have him all to herself some day — how, she could not say; but she would.

"Do you think you'll ever get a divorce?" she occasionally asked.

"You'll have to wait, honey. I'll do the best I can. When I do, we get married at once."

Her eyes sparkled.

Oh, to be Mrs. Frank Algernon Cowperwood!

Explain me this riddle if you can.

And now he was worried, at times, as to how he would ever rid himself of his wife easily and without publicity, and he thought and thought. There was no feasible way. There was no reasonable excuse for being brutal. He did not know that he wanted to be. That would be quite too unfair. But his life was so much larger and broader now. If he only had Aileen now, how much more suitably arranged he would be! Then came this storm; and the same day that brought Edward Butler the anonymous communication in regard to his daughter brought almost a duplicate of it in the same hand to Mrs.

Frank Algernon Cowperwood, only in this case the name
of Aileen Butler had curiously been omitted.

Perhaps you don't know that your husband is running with another woman. If you don't believe it, watch the house at 931
North Tenth Street.

Mrs. Cowperwood was in the conservatory of her own
home watering some plants when this letter was brought
by her maid on this fatal Monday morning. She was
most placid in her thoughts, for she did not know what
all the conferring of the night before meant. Frank was
occasionally troubled by financial storms, but they did
not seem to harm him.

"Lay it on the table in the library, Annie. I'll get it."
She thought it was some social note.

In a little while, such was her deliberate way, she put
down her sprinkling-pot and went into the library. There
it was lying on the green leather sheepskin which constituted a part of the ornamentation of the large library
table. She picked it up, glanced at it curiously because it
was on cheap paper, and then opened it. Her face, always placid, paled slightly as she read it; and then her
hand trembled—not much. Hers was not a soul that
ever loved passionately, hence she could not suffer passionately. She was hurt, disgusted, enraged some for the
moment, and frightened; but she was not broken in spirit
entirely. Thirteen years of life with Frank Cowperwood
had taught her a number of things. He was selfish, she
knew now, self-centered, and not as much charmed by
her now as he had been. The fear she had originally
felt as to the effect of her preponderance of years had
been to some extent justified by the lapse of time. Frank
did not love her as he had—he had not for some time;
she had felt it. What was it? she had asked herself at
times—almost, who was it? Business was so engrossing
to him. Finance was such a master. Did this mean the
end of her régime? she queried. Would he cast her off?

Where would she go? What would she do? She was not helpless, of course, for she had money of her own which he was manipulating for her. Who was this other woman? Curiously, the other woman did not seem so vastly important—that is, who she was. Was she young, beautiful, of any social position? Was it—? Suddenly she stopped. Was it? Could it be, by any chance—her mouth opened—Aileen Butler?

She stood still staring at this letter, for she could scarcely countenance her own thought. She had observed often, in spite of all their caution, how nice Aileen had been to him and he to her. He liked her; he never lost a chance to defend her. Lillian had thought of them at times as being curiously suited to each other temperamentally. He liked young people. But, of course, he was married, and Aileen was infinitely beneath him socially, and he had two children and herself. And his social and financial position was so fixed and stable that he did not dare trifle with it. Still she paused; for forty years and two children, and some slight wrinkles, and the suspicion that we may be no longer loved as we once were, is apt to make any one pause, even in the face of the most significant financial position. Where would she go if she left him? What would people think? What about the children? Could she prove this liaison? Could she entrap him in a compromising situation? Did she want to?

Greater knowledge of Frank Cowperwood had given her a form of awe of him which was not unmixed with sincere admiration. She was in the least way a little afraid of him. Those keen, searching eyes of his so often ran her over, and she felt that he was estimating her materially, even when she could not tell what he was thinking. She felt that she knew him, and yet she didn't. He was never given to tantrums. He did not burst out into revealing fits of rage. If he were disappointed in anything, he was apt to say so shortly but not meanly.

There was always present a sense of latent force—great strength and judgment that need not be used at all. Too, he was not inclined to talk about his affairs any more. Once, in the beginning, he had talked quite confidentially—how fully, she could not have said. She had never had the feeling that he was telling her everything. Now, however, of late—say the last three or four years—he had scarcely talked at all. Their conversation had become more and more perfunctory. He had talked, to be sure, easily, pleasantly, of all the little household concerns and cares, but not about the things in which he was vastly interested. Occasionally he would say something —that he expected to make a good thing out of a certain line of stocks. She heard more, if anything, through chance snatches of conversation which came borne by sound-waves when he and his father were talking. The two men occasionally sat in one or the other of the two family libraries or sitting-rooms or private offices, and talked sometimes so softly you could not hear; at other times so clearly that you got some faint inkling of what it was all about—rarely anything more than that. Frank and his father were doing very well; she knew that. They were in street-railways. Her own money was invested in some way in them. The city treasurer and the State treasurer and the city councilmen, a few of them, and Butler and Mr. Leigh, of Drexel's, and others, were somehow all involved—how, she did not know. It seemed to her that Frank had a vast network of connections; that he knew a very large number of people financially. He must be a very remarkable man, indeed. And yet it was all summed up in one strange, enigmatic, non-understandable word—business. Frank was a great business man, a financier. He was scarcely human enough to be a good lover any more. And yet he was so fascinating when he wanted to be.

This letter, though—how it tormented her! She saw now, by the very state of mind she was in, that she did not love him as some women loved their husbands. She was not wild about him. In a way she had been taking him for granted all these years, had thought that he loved her enough not to be unfaithful to her; at least fancied that he was so engrossed with the more serious things of life that no petty liaison such as this letter indicated would trouble him or interrupt his great career. Now, though, this was evidently not true. This apparently very solid and distinguished home was, after all, built on shifting sands. What should she do? What say? How act?

She dropped the letter after a time and stood there, then picked it up and went into her private boudoir. She hid it in her bosom, and wondered how she would go about it to watch this house, if she did at all. Could she? What about the children, her friends, her social station? She wrung her hands after a time, for it was only after an hour of thinking that she began, as she fancied, to catch the significance of it all. Frank Cowperwood was lost to her. Could she regain him? Could she hold him? There had been in times past some little silly feeling between them over Aileen in regard to the question of entertaining her, liking her; but this was so different, so much more important. Her none too brilliant mind was not of much service in this crisis. She did not know very well how either to plan or to fight.

The conventional mind is at best a petty piece of machinery. It is oyster-like in its functioning, or, perhaps better, clam-like. It has its little siphon of thought-processes forced up or down into the mighty ocean of fact and circumstance; but it uses so little, pumps so faintly, that the immediate contiguity of the vast is not disturbed. Nothing of the subtlety of life is perceived. No least inkling of its storms or terrors is ever discovered except through accident. When some crude, suggestive fact, such as this letter proved to be, suddenly manifests itself in the placid flow of events, there is great agony or

disturbance and clogging of the so-called normal processes. The siphon does not work right. It sucks in fear
and distress. There is great grinding of mal-adjusted
parts—not unlike sand in a machine—and life, as is so
often the case, ceases or goes lamely ever after.

Mrs. Cowperwood was possessed of a conventional
mind. She was charming, but she really knew nothing
about life. And life could not teach her. Reaction in
her from salty thought-processes was not possible. She
was not alive in the sense that Aileen Butler was, and yet
she thought that she was very much alive. All illusion.
She wasn't. She was charming if you loved placidity.
If you did not, she was not. She was not engaging,
brilliant, or forceful. Frank Cowperwood might well
have asked himself in the beginning why he married her.
He did not do so now because he did not believe it was
wise to question the past as to our failures and errors.
It was, according to him, most unwise to regret. He kept
his face and thoughts to the future.

But Mrs. Cowperwood was truly distressed in her way,
and she went about the house thinking, feeling wretchedly. She decided, since the letter asked her to see for herself, to wait. She must think how she would watch this
house, if at all. Frank must not know. If it were
Aileen Butler by any chance—but surely not—she thought
she would expose her to her parents. Still, that meant
exposing herself. She determined to conceal her mood as
best she could at dinner-time—but Cowperwood was not
able to be there. He was so rushed, so closeted with individuals, so closely in conference with his father and
others, that she scarcely saw him this Monday night, nor
the next day, Tuesday, nor for many days.

For on Tuesday afternoon at two-thirty Frank Cowperwood had issued a call for a meeting of his creditors,
and at five-thirty he decided to go into the hands of a
receiver. Old Cowperwood was beside himself with grief.
He foresaw the end of all his dignities, comforts, honors.

In his own home, after the meeting, in his private room, he walked the floor and wrung his hands, struck them together again and again. He got out his private account-books and went over his affairs, only to shake his head ruefully. He was ruined. Frank's connection with the city treasurer's office would be exposed. He himself would be ousted from his presidency. He and his wife and his sons and daughter and Frank's wife and his grandchildren would have to move. There was an air about his house and Frank's now, he thought, as though some one had died in them. You could feel a sense of dissolution. And yet Frank Cowperwood, as he stood before his principal creditors — a group of thirty men—in his office, did not feel that his life was ruined. He was temporarily embarrassed. Certainly things looked very black. The city-treasurership deal would make a great fuss. Those hypothecated city loan certificates, to the extent of sixty thousand, would make another, if Stener chose. Still, he did not feel that he was utterly destroyed.

"Gentlemen," he said, in closing his address of explanation at the meeting, quite as erect, secure, defiant, convincing as he had ever been, "you see how things are. These securities are worth just as much as they ever were. There is nothing the matter with the properties behind them. If you will give me fifteen days or twenty, I am satisfied that I can straighten the whole matter out. I am almost the only one who can, for I know all about it. The market is bound to recover. Business is going to be better than ever. It's time I want. Time is the only significant factor in this situation. I want to know if you won't give me fifteen or twenty days—a month, if you can. That is all I want."

He stepped aside and out of the general room, where the blinds were drawn into his private office, in order to give his creditors an opportunity to confer privately in regard to his situation. He had friends in the meeting who were for him. He waited one, two, nearly three hours while they talked. Finally Walter Leigh, Judge Kitchen, Avery Stone, of Jay Cooke & Co., and several others came in. They were a committee appointed to gather further information.

"Nothing more can be done to-day, Frank," Walter Leigh informed him, quietly. "The majority want the privilege of examining the books. There is some uncertainty about this entanglement with the city treasurer which you say exists. They feel that you'd better announce a temporary suspension, anyhow; and if they want to let you resume later they can do so."

"I'm sorry for that, gentlemen," replied Cowperwood, the least bit depressed. "I would rather do anything than suspend for one hour, if I could help it, for I know just what it means. You will find assets here far exceeding the liabilities if you will take the stocks at their normal market value; but that won't help any if I close my doors. The public won't believe in me. I ought to keep open. It's not fair to charge this Chicago fire up to me, although I know that's legitimate enough under the circumstances."

"Sorry, Frank, old boy," observed Leigh, pressing his hand affectionately. "If it were left to me personally, you could have all the time you want. There's a crowd of old fogies out there that won't listen to reason. They're panic-struck. I guess they're pretty hard hit themselves. You can scarcely blame them. You'll come out all right, though I wish you didn't have to shut up shop. We can't do anything with them, however. Why, damn it man, I don't see how you can fail, really. In ten days these stocks will be all right."

Judge Kitchen commiserated with him also; but what good did that do? He was being compelled to suspend. An expert accountant would have to come in and go over his books. Butler might spread the news of this city-treasury connection. Stener might complain of this last city-loan transaction. It was a serious matter if he could not open his doors in the morning; and he couldn't. He was never left alone by a half-dozen of his helpful friends from then on until morning; but he had to suspend just the same. And when he did that he knew he was practically defeated in this first brilliant race for wealth and fame.

Once, and once only, when he was really and finally quite alone in his private bedroom at four in the morning —he and his wife had always occupied separate rooms in the new house—he stared at himself in the mirror. His face was pale and tired, he thought, but strong and effective. "Pshaw!" he said to himself, "I'm not whipped. I'll get out of this. Certainly I will. I'll find some way."

And he began to undress, cogitating heavily, wearily. Finally he sank upon his bed, and in a little while, strange as it may seem, with all the tangle of trouble around him, slept. He could do that — sleep and gurgle most peacefully, the while his old father paced the floor in his room, refusing to be comforted. All was dark before the older man—the future hopeless. He turned wearily to and fro in his short space and sighed. Frank only turned once in his slumber, and he did not dream. He was intensely weary.

Mrs. Frank Cowperwood in her room turned and tossed in the face of a new calamity. It had suddenly appeared from news from her father and Frank and Anna and her mother-in-law that Frank was about to fail, or would, or had—it was almost impossible to say just how it was. Frank was too busy to explain. The Chicago fire was to blame. There was no mention as yet of the city treasurership. Frank was caught in a trap, and was fighting for his life.

In this crisis, for the moment, she forgot about the note as to his infidelity, or rather ignored it. She was astonished, frightened, dumfounded, confused. Her little, placid, beautiful world was going around in a dizzy ring.

THE FINANCIER

It was as though the tables and chairs of her own home had begun to move of their own volition and without any exterior aid. It was somewhat like an earthquake, in which things tumble and fall about, or like a storm at sea. The charming ornate ship of their fortune was being blown most ruthlessly here and there. She felt it a sort of duty to stay in bed and try to sleep; but her eyes were quite wide, and her brain hurt her. Hours before Frank had insisted that she should not bother about him, but rest, that she could do nothing; and she had gone, wondering more than ever what and where was the line of her duty. To stick by her husband, convention told her; and so she decided. Yes, religion dictated that, also custom. There were the children. They must not be injured. Frank must be reclaimed, if possible. He would get over this. But what a blow! She also turned from side to side wearily, and by dawn had not had a single wink of sleep.

CHAPTER XXXVIII

THE suspension of the banking house of Frank A. Cowperwood & Co. created a great stir on 'change and in Philadelphia generally. It was so unexpected, and the amount involved was comparatively so large. Actually he failed for one million two hundred and fifty thousand dollars; and his assets, under the depressed condition of stock values, barely totaled seven hundred and fifty thousand dollars. There had been considerable work done on the matter of his balance-sheet by him, and also by his father and Harper Steger, his lawyer, before it was finally given to the public; but when it was, stocks dropped an additional three points generally, and the papers the next day devoted notable head-lines to it. Cowperwood had no idea of failing permanently; he merely wished to suspend temporarily, and later, if possible, to persuade his creditors to allow him to resume. There were only two things which stood in the way of this: the matter of the five hundred thousand dollars borrowed from the city treasury at a ridiculously low rate of interest, which showed plainer than words what had been going on, and the other, the matter of the sixty-thousand-dollar check. Cowperwood had the fear of disaster ensuing from these causes, if any such thought in him could be called fear; and he had done his very best up to the final hour to make his chances of resuming —barring these two difficulties—as secure as possible. His financial wit told him there were ways to assign his holdings in favor of his largest creditors, who would help him later to resume; and he was swift to do this. Harper

Steger, his lawyer, drew up documents which named Jay Cooke & Co., Edward Clark & Co., Drexel & Co., and others as preferred. He knew that even though dissatisfied holders of smaller shares in his company brought suit and compelled readjustment or bankruptcy later, the intention shown to prefer some of his most influential aids was important. They would like it, and might help him later when all this was over. Besides, suits in plenty are an excellent way of tiding over a crisis of this kind until stocks and common sense are restored, and he was for many suits. Harper Steger smiled once rather grimly, even in the whirl of the financial chaos where smiles were few, as they were figuring it out.

"Frank," he said, "you're a wonder. You'll have a network of suits spread here shortly, which no one can break through. They'll all be suing each other."

Cowperwood smiled.

"I only want a little time, that's all," he replied. Nevertheless, for the first time in his life he was a little depressed; for now this business, to which he had devoted years of active work and thought, was ended. He, Frank A. Cowperwood, was insolvent. His house and many interesting private belongings were in danger of being immediately swept away. His father, because of him, was a bankrupt also, and might immediately be removed unless something were done to restore the credit of his son. The worst thing, of course, was the matter of the treasury loan, and what it represented. This notable defection of Stener worried Cowperwood. He sensed the cunning and animosity of bigger men behind it—possibly Butler now, for he knew the latter's estranged attitude to be a certainty; and he did not see clearly how the matter was to be arranged without some talk, and possibly action, which would be injurious. He did think of going to Mollenhauer, whom he knew of indirectly, and laying the whole matter before him, but he was so busy with other matters for the first day or two that he had no time to attend to it. He was more than satisfied that he would before long.

The thing that was troubling Cowperwood most in all of this was not the five hundred thousand dollars which was owing the city treasury, and which he knew would stir political and social life to the center once it was generally known—that was a legal or semi-legal trans-action, at least—but rather the minor, though to him, in reality, so far as legal retribution was concerned, the major matter of the sixty thousand dollars' worth of un-restored city loan certificates which he had not been able to replace in the sinking-fund. Actually, it was a crime not to have done that, under the circumstances, though heretofore, in fair weather, he had taken his time about it. Technically, he would say that he had always been in the habit of taking his time. His accounting with the treasury was never made until the first of the month. But could he say, honestly, that he had intended at the time that he asked Albert Stires for the sixty-thousand-dollar check to replace the absent city loan certificates in the sinking-fund? He had already owed the city five hundred thou-sand dollars in illegally borrowed money at that time. He had been told by Stener that he could not have any more. He had not asked Stener's permission to call for this check, and the latter would probably tell his superiors that this additional sum had literally been stolen without his knowl-edge or consent, and after he, Stener, had broken with him. Cowperwood pondered over the situation a good deal. The thing to do, he thought, if he went to Mollen-hauer or Simpson, or both (he had never met either of them, but in view of Butler's desertion they were his only recourse), was to say that, although he could not at present return the five hundred thousand dollars, if no injurious action were taken against him now, such as would prevent his resuming his business on a normal scale a little later, he would pledge his word that every dollar of the involved five hundred thousand dollars would eventually be returned to the treasury. If they refused, and injury was done him, he proposed to let them wait until he was "good and ready," to use an American phrase, which in all probability would be never, before he returned a dollar. But, really, it was not quite clear how action against him was to be prevented—even by them. The money was down on his books as owing the city treasury, and it was down on the city treasury's books as owing from him. Besides, there was a local organization known as the Citizens' Municipal Reform Association which occasionally conducted investigations in connection with public affairs. His defalcation would be sure to come to the ears of this body. A public investigation, which must surely follow, would reveal it. Various private individuals knew of it already. His creditors, for instance, who were now examining his books.

To ask for time—to ask the politicians, for the sake of avoiding a scandal, to hush up—was all very good if they *could* hush up. But could they? The situation had become already so dangerous.

This matter of seeing Mollenhauer or Simpson, or both, was important, anyhow, he thought; but before doing so he decided to talk all this over with Harper Steger, his lawyer, and get the legal end of it, so far as the sixty-thousand-dollar check was concerned, straight in his mind. So several days after he had closed his doors, he sent for Steger and told him all about the transaction, except that he did not make it clear that he had not intended to put the certificates in the sinking-fund unless he survived quite comfortably. Steger was a little dubious; though he thought that, seeing how loosely city funds had always been handled, how close the relations of Cowperwood and Stener were, nothing would come of it before a jury.

"Let them proceed against you," he said, his brilliant legal mind taking in all the phases of the situation at once. "I don't see that there is anything more here than a technical charge. If it ever came to anything like that, which I don't think it will, the charge would be embezzlement or perhaps larceny as bailee. In this instance, you were the bailee. And the only way out of that would be to swear that you had received the check with Stener's knowledge and consent. Then it would only be a technical charge of irresponsibility on your part, as I see it, and I don't believe any jury would convict you on the evidence of how this relationship was conducted. Still, it might; you never can tell what a jury is going to do."

"What would that mean, Harper, legally, if I were tried on a charge of larceny as bailee, as you put it, and convicted? How many years in the penitentiary at the outside?"

Steger thought a minute, rubbing his chin with his elegant hand. "Let me see," he said, "that is a serious question, isn't it? The law says one to five years at the outside; but the sentences usually average from one to three years in embezzlement cases. Of course, in this case—"

"Would I have to go to jail at any time during the proceedings—before a final adjustment of the case by the higher courts?" interrupted Cowperwood. He was thinking of the long legal fights that usually surround trials of this kind where money is concerned, and where it is available for attorneys' fees; most defendants, he thought, usually managed to avoid jail sentence if they had the price.

Steger began a careful explanation of just what the motions and delays were in a case like this, while Cowperwood meditated solemnly, his mind running quickly and surely forward through all the ramifications of his case. What would he do if he were sentenced? he thought. Steger was wondering if Cowperwood really thought he was to be tried by any chance of fate or ill-luck in this way, and whether he considered himself guilty. So far Cowperwood had indicated that he had bought the cer-

THE FINANCIER

tificates well enough, but that he had not been able to deposit them, and had been compelled to use the check and the certificates for another purpose. True enough, he had not thought he was going to fail, though he had not seen any way out at the time. It was more a matter of hope than anything else. Would a jury take any stock in that? Steger asked himself.

The young banker sat there staring out of the window, and Steger observed, "It is a bit complicated, isn't it?"

"Well, I should say so," returned Frank; and he added to himself: "Jail! Five days in prison!" That would be a terrific slap, all things considered. Five days in jail pending the obtaining of a certificate of reasonable doubt, if one could be obtained! He must avoid this! He got up and went out to a creditors' meeting with Steger; but the thought was with him all the time. Jail! The penitentiary! His commercial reputation would never survive that.

CHAPTER XXXIX

FRANK ALGERNON COWPERWOOD was not a weakling given to wild ideas of financial prosperity; he was not of the kind who in prosperity cut throats indiscriminately and in disaster sit down and weep over their own woes. Whatever he was, he was neither a hypocrite nor a fool. He did not delude himself concerning himself or others. He did not capitalize the future. He thought, thought, thought all the time, in prosperity and in times when he was not so prosperous. He based everything on thought, after he made due allowance for chance and opportunity, which he could not control. He would have agreed with Machiavelli that, other things being equal, fortune is always with him who plans. He was no fatalist; or if he was, he would not give fate the opportunity to say that he had not put up a good fight—had not taken advantage of every single opportunity. He was no coward; and, above all, he was no moralist suffering from an uneducated time conscience. He saw no morals anywhere—nothing but moods, emotions, needs, greeds. People talked and talked, but they acted according to their necessities and desires, just as he did, only as a rule they were not quick and clever as he was. For this, sometimes, he was sorry for them. At other times he was not. He knew he had a splendid mind. He knew he had a marvelous physique. He knew he had a magnetic and dominating will. Few people, in extremes, could face him out. By his steady eye, his set jaw, and his urgent will to achieve a victory, he could almost, in the face of defeat, snatch success from the hands of fate. He had done it time and again. He had seen himself ten years before as a boy on 'change leap in when hope seemed hopeless, and wrest something from an apparently uncompromising situation. Ever since then he had been doing this to a greater or lesser degree. He had done things one week before which no other financier had dreamed of doing. He had organized, or attempted to do so, at least, opposition to impending overwhelming disaster. If these bankers and brokers had only taken his advice and closed the exchange he would have been safe. But they hadn't! The trick had been all in his favor. Once he had dreamed of laying by a reserve of government bonds for just such a crisis as this; but he had never done it. He had been too busy making money —seizing his growing opportunities. Now he was facing the first severe crisis of his life, and it was an astonishing one. The wonder of it was its suddenness—its thunder-clap nature—and the fact that he had not the least thing to do with it, neither previous warning nor present opportunity. His every dollar was entangled, involved, and he was fighting for his financial life. Was he really going to lose entirely? He meditated this gravely, wondering what he should do the while he worked with creditor after creditor, but he saw no light.

The question as to whether Edward Malia Butler could do anything to injure the financial and social prosperity of Cowperwood, once he had become so incensed against him, was one which occupied the thoughts of both Butler and Cowperwood after their final interview, and after Butler had talked so directly to his daughter.

The latter had met Cowperwood as he had planned, the day after he closed his doors, at four o'clock in the afternoon, at Indian Rock on the Wissahickon, stealing an expensive hour from him to do it, but eager to know as to his affairs. It cost him a severe struggle to arrange it. At that time he was thirty-four and Aileen was twenty-four years of age; and the beauty which she had always counted on to hold him, when he should be fifty and she forty, was still in perfect bloom. It was the thing which interested and fascinated him most, though her mind meant much. We say beauty loosely in this way, when in reality we mean so often charm of soul or temperament in addition to exquisite facial and physical outlines; and it was so in this case. Charm of temperament, as much as physical beauty, was holding Cowperwood in Aileen's case. Although long since he had rifled her of every physical delight, she was still dear to him. He had found that it was not that alone. She was like him in many respects—courageous, resourceful, debonair. He thought of her as some one of much more physical force than his wife, far better able to bear a social struggle for place. She had never lost for one moment the inspiriting sense of her own charm, which had been heightened by his continuous affection for her; and his affection had never been sufficiently fed by her continued presence to weaken his interest. She had been able to be with him so little, guarded as she was by her family; and this sudden possibility of losing her among so many other important things, owing to the wrath of her father, was sufficient to make him see her in a more enchanting form—the form that beauty wears when it is most elusive. Besides, in this storm, she, of all people, was now bringing him the most unstinted and unqualified fondness—the love that asks only affectionate recognition in return—if we may call that unqualified. At least she was asking no material reward and forcing no claim. Her large eyes were filled with a warm, sympathetic appreciation of his woes, and in this hour he craved it.

It was bright weather, fortunately, when he drove swiftly out—he did not trouble to go on horseback this day—and his mind relaxed a little of its intense working when he saw her standing beside a gray stone up the road awaiting his coming. Her eyes were so solicitous. She looked so youthful, blooming, and efficient as a woman, which is what affection requires. Her riding-habit was of the smoothest, closest-fitting character. Her high silk riding-hat, such as was worn in those days, sat jauntily above her red-gold hair. She carried a bright-yellow whip in her hand, and looked very much as she had that day, several years before, when he had persuaded her to consider how complete, finally, their union must be. He marveled a little at himself—taking the time on this day of all days to come and see her—but he said to himself that one need never regret the bright moments of love and yearning affection as lost. They were not numerous enough. Aileen looked to see if there were any one else in sight in either direction; but there was not. When he jumped down from his light little runabout, letting the reins fall between the whip and the dash-board, she threw her arms around his neck and held him close, her lips crushed to his. His young bay mare pawed and snorted vigorously, throwing her ears forward and back and swishing her neatly trimmed tail.

"Oh, honey, honey, honey!" was all Aileen could murmur. "Oh, my darling boy!" She was so distressed by recent developments that she could scarcely speak.

She stroked his hair and neck sympathetically, and he pulled her tight to him, feeling her cheek over her shoulder with his free hand. Curiously enough, he noted the undying coquetry of her, which had led her to cut and paste below her left eye a small speck of black court-plaster, in order to emphasize and make more beautiful the color of her cheeks and hair. Sorrow for him somehow did not affect or modify her interest in herself. She figured that she must always be very beautiful and attractive to make him happy, for she had learned that he loved beauty. Repeated hours with him in North Tenth Street had taught this, and she wanted to keep it for him as long as she could.

"I have only a few minutes to stay, sweet," were his first words after he had shared their long embrace. "I am terribly rushed. You don't know. Has anything new developed with your father?"

"No. I only saw him for a few minutes this morning. He's very busy. I know he is thinking of me, though. I saw it by his looks. Oh, poor daddy! But never mind that. What about you? You haven't really failed, have you? I heard them say you had."

"Heard who say?"

"Callum and Owen."

"Not failed, no. I've assigned temporarily for the benefit of my creditors. My lawyer is drawing up the papers. But don't let that worry you, pet," he added, as he saw a widening look of distress in her eyes. "I'll come out all right. Stocks are going to recover shortly. I'm going to assign all my holdings in favor of my largest creditors. You don't understand that, Aileen; but you needn't worry about it. I'll be quite all right again in a few months. Things are going to be better than ever. I'll go right on. There are a lot of things in connection with it all that I ought to be attending to right now. So there is nothing new at your house?"

He seemed a little preoccupied to Aileen, as he might well; but she did not quite see why he should neglect her in his thoughts. Still, his troubles were now obviously so great that she could forgive him temporarily. They had little altercations at times, as all lovers do; but she did not crave one now.

"Oh, sweet, I'm disturbed about you," she replied, earnestly. "Isn't there a single thing I can do to help you?" He smiled genially but sardonically at this. "I know— Oh, women are so helpless." She threw back her head and looked away wearily.

"Baby, it's sweet of you to think of this, but it can't be done. You don't understand finance. I have to go it alone. There isn't a thing you can do but love me, and that is all I want from you. It is a good deal."

He tightened his arms around her, and she took his head in her hands.

"Oh, I do that; but Frank—honey, it is so little! If I could only be with you! If I could only share in some way! I know you are in trouble. I can feel it."

He shut her mouth with his.

"There, there, pet, don't worry. I'll come out all right. I really will," he said, for almost the first time in his life emotionally moved by her keen sympathy and tenderness. It was a new sensation. "It's a little rough just now, but I will be all right later."

He could not talk finance to her. She was too incapable of understanding.

"For the present it is all over with Nine-thirty-one, I suppose," he said, referring to the North Tenth Street domicile, and thinking of the resources which its contents offered. His day of any such liberal provision for profane love was temporarily over. Besides, the house was, no doubt, watched. "I'll have to close that up and get a new address shortly. Meanwhile we'd better say here again on Saturday, unless it rains; and if it does, make it Monday. You can't come over to the house very well, either, just at present." He was thinking of her father.

Aileen realized the danger of it all.

"No," she replied, "I can't; that's so. I hadn't thought of that. And just when you need me most. What shall we do?"

He did feel a special craving for affection just now, when everything was going so badly, but he did not let it master him.

"You mustn't fret. Things are coming out. Just be patient now. I'll find some place where we can meet."

They looked at the long, stream-skirted road, where was no one, and listened to the ripple of the water over the stones. There were birds singing in the autumn-tinted foliage overhead, and a general air of restfulness and peace here centered in great beauty. The thought came to him how little his tangle of affairs seemed to matter in the general scheme of things; but he shut it out. He was too practical, too efficient to think of anything save of untangling a tangle and making much of the material of which life is woven. He squeezed her hands; but he was restless, and she could see it.

"We might as well go, then," she observed; and he agreed with alacrity.

"You'd better let me go first," he said; and giving her a farewell kiss, he jumped into his run-about. For the first time it came home sharply to Aileen how much his affairs meant to him. They were really first, and love was a thing apart—a diversion. It hurt her.

"Still, he wouldn't be what he is if it weren't so," she thought; "and if he weren't what he is I might not love him."

She watched him speeding down the ochre-hued road, wistfully and admiringly, then jumped to her own saddle and was off. In all the world there was no one to her like Frank Cowperwood. She went to her room and wrote him, pouring out her heart in a long, comforting letter; but that did not avail, either. She wanted to be with him.

In spite of his lenient attitude toward his daughter, Butler felt an increasing tide of revengeful anger toward Cowperwood. The old man was of that peculiarly human turn which loves to assist when its sympathies and interests are involved, but which also loves to humiliate when its sympathies have been lacerated or its generosities betrayed. Butler considered that he had been exceedingly generous to Cowperwood during the eight or nine years in which he had known him. As will be remembered, he had assisted Cowperwood to get a section of one of the civil-war loans, which had netted him twenty thousand dollars in his early banking days; and since then he had been kind to him in other directions, speculating from time to time in stocks through the young banker, and buying blocks of street-railway stock in certain struggling or slowly developing lines which he hoped to acquire. The hundred-thousand-dollar loan which he had with Cowperwood had been carried at six per cent., when, as a matter of fact, it would have brought a much higher rate of interest in other places. Butler, after having called his loan and seeing Cowperwood fail the next day, was puzzled as to what else he could do to injure his one-time friend and protégé. Ordinarily he was not vindictive; but he considered that Cowperwood had surely repaid him very badly for all he had done, and that his further continuance in political and financial affairs in Philadelphia was a menace. Whether he, Butler, could do anything to prevent or delay him in his future progress, whether he could hinder his resumption of business or destroy his possibly profitable political affiliations, was another matter. The one thing that occurred to Butler at this time as having great significance was the matter of the five hundred thousand dollars which Cowperwood had received from the city treasury, and which was involved with the success of the Republican party at the November election. His talk with Mollenhauer and Simpson had not cleared up definitely what was to be done about this, and further conferences were yet to come. Obviously something should be done. He wondered whether Cowperwood would really be able to get on his feet after having put the Republican party in such a desperate position, and whether he ought to let him. He did not hesitate to take thought as to some personal means of reprisal, though he did not know at the moment just what those would be. One thing that occurred to him, after a few days, was that he might buy into Cowperwood's affairs (secretly, of course) in order to become a creditor, in which case he could cause him a great deal of trouble. He was not so poor a financier but what he could see, as both Mollenhauer and Simpson had seen, that, if Cowperwood could not get money to pay his debts and could not get his creditors to agree to let him go on until such time as the values of his stocks had recovered, he would have to part with all his holdings. Butler had sat in enough creditors' meetings in his time to know how easy it is for one creditor, by standing out for a hundred cents on the dollar, or "payment in full," as it is called, to prevent a resumption even when all the other creditors are willing. It would be easy to buy into Cowperwood's affairs now through some disgruntled creditor who needed cash, and so become a factor in his financial difficulties—one of the judges who might say whether he was to resume or not. At the same time it might be advisable—in fact, it was very tempting—to unite with Mollenhauer and Simpson by pooling their properties so as to jointly control all the street-railway interests of the city. That was what Owen had suggested to him; and it had stuck in his mind. Some such union of street-railway properties had been vaguely in his own mind all these years, only he had been thinking of controlling these interests alone. He did not know that this had been Cowperwood's ambitious thought also. The idea of combination was just beginning to manifest itself in those days—in so far as American affairs were concerned—and it was in the air. It was occurring to other people in many other walks of life.

It is interesting to see how readily our ambitions and desires for advancement combine frequently with our outraged sense of justice and our craving for revenge. This is a very human failing, or, let us say, capability. It was decidedly true in the case of Butler. The old man, brooding over the injury done him through his affection for his daughter, was actually comforted by what he thought he could do to Cowperwood in return. As this avenue of reprisal opened to him his eyes fairly gleamed in their dark, fulgurous way, and he decided to make use of it. He also thought persistently of how Cowperwood could be identified with the punishment that would, in all

probability, eventually have to be meted out to Stener.
Butler did not wish to injure the party; but if it were
necessarily to be injured in the long run, Cowperwood
might as well be made to suffer for his share in the transaction. What could he do about that? Butler asked himself. How could he connect Cowperwood with it? A
few days after Cowperwood's failure he decided to go
around to the city hall and see for himself what the
situation was. He did not care to talk to Stener personally—Mollenhauer was handling him—but there were
others. Mr. David Pettie, for instance—the outgoing
district attorney—was one of his protégés—a man whom
he had started years before with a few small legal cases.
Pettie would know; it would be his duty to find out all
about it. Butler strolled down there the very afternoon
the idea occurred to him, and was closeted with Pettie
for three-quarters of an hour. At the end of that time
he had learned all of the details in regard to the five-
hundred-thousand-dollar defalcation, and also the peculiar
circumstances attending the transfer of the final check
for sixty thousand dollars, of which he had not previously
known.

Mr. David Pettie was a little man physically, so far
as height was concerned, rather stocky of body and broad
of shoulders, whose full, fat face was set with a pair of
goggle eyes, over which were placed again a pair of large,
gold-rimmed glasses. He was a contentious person of
considerable force, and was fairly suited to his peculiar
duties as prosecutor, though not very good as an organizer
—a faculty which his office required. Beholden to Butler for favors in the past, he was expectant of additional
ones in the future, and anxious to serve him in any way
that he might. So Butler had no difficulty in finding out
anything he wished to know.

"What is this, Mr. Pettie," he asked, after he inquired
about some little legal matter in connection with a city
contract, which he pretended had brought him there,

"that I hear about Stener and his broker? Is it true that he's lost a lot of money in Third Street, as they say he has?"

Butler, as was his custom, pretended an ignorance as to what was going on, when, as a matter of fact, he knew nearly all about it.

"Oh, that is a bad mess, Mr. Butler," replied Pettie, respectfully, and with every desire to be properly communicative. "Mr. Mollenhauer's secretary, Mr. Sengstack, was in here yesterday to see me about it. It looks as though Mr. Stener was short all of five or six hundred thousand dollars, if not more. You understand how it happened, of course? Since then I have heard there is a row on between Mr. Stener and Mr. Cowperwood about a part of it—some check for sixty thousand dollars, which Stener says he never intended to give him. Stener says he ought to be arrested for embezzlement, though I don't suppose there's much in that. They've been using city money together on this plan for six or seven years."

At this remark concerning a quarrel over a sixty-thousand-dollar check, and a charge of embezzlement, Butler pricked up his ears.

"You don't tell me," he said, easily. "Is it as bad as that? Six hundred thousand! They must have been havin' a great deal of fun with their money. Just what was this check, do you know?"

Pettie proceeded to explain the incident of Cowperwood's having taken the sixty-thousand-dollar check from Stires, allegedly without Stener's consent, and his failure to deposit in the sinking-fund the certificates which this money was supposed to represent. An ordinary man as much interested as Butler was in this intelligence would have straightened up and manifested in a measure what he felt. Butler only looked as placid as he had before.

"Is it as bad as that?" he repeated. "You don't tell me! I suppose young Cowperwood could be punished for that under the law. What is the penalty for a crime like that, anyhow?"

"Five years is the maximum," replied Pettie, briskly. "A man in his position takes an awful chance doing a thing like that. This will make it pretty bad for the party if it comes out before the election, I suppose."

"We'll have to see that it doesn't come out, if we can help it, before election, anyhow," replied Butler. "After that it wouldn't matter so much; but I don't see that anything very much can be done for this fellow Stener. He's certainly got himself in a bad scrape."

He returned to the subject of the city contract, which he had made it appear had brought him there, and then left. He was thinking what he could do to further this embezzlement charge against Cowperwood, in case it proved to be as Pettie said. He proposed to have Owen go to the Drovers' and Traders' Bank to see if the certificates were really absent from the sinking-fund, and when the time came, as it would in a very few hours, no doubt, when he and Mollenhauer and Simpson would again confer, he would recommend what he thought ought to be done. It might be—certainly was—advisable to hush this whole matter up until after election; but beyond that there would be no necessity. Stener might be convicted—it would really be essential to convict him if the matter came to the ears of the public, for looks' sake, even if the leaders had to get him pardoned afterward; and if he were convicted there was no reason why Cowperwood should not be also, so long as the coming election was not affected by it one way or the other.

CHAPTER XL

T HE necessity of a final conference between Butler, Mollenhauer, and Simpson was speedily reached, for this situation was hourly growing more serious. Rumors were floating about in Third Street that in addition to having failed for so large an amount as to have further unsettled the already panicky financial situation induced by the Chicago fire, Cowperwood had involved the city treasury to the extent of five hundred thousand dollars. The question was how was the matter to be kept quiet until after election, which was still three weeks away. Bankers and brokers were communicating odd rumors to each other on the street-corners and in their private offices, and there was danger that it would come to the ears of that very uncomfortable political organization known as the Citizens' Municipal Reform Association, of which a well-known iron-manufacturer of great probity and moral rectitude, one Skelton C. Wheat, no less, who for years had been following on the trail of the dominant Republican administration in a vain attempt to bring it to a sense of some of its political iniquities, was president.

On the day following Butler's discovery of Cowperwood's very suspicious action in extracting an additional sixty thousand dollars from the city treasury when it was understood that he was to have no more, a messenger coming from Mr. Simpson to Mr. Butler and Mr. Mollenhauer advised that they come together for a final conference on the city-treasurership at once. Senator Simpson had learned that the rumors in Third Street were becoming very thick and threatening, and the newspaper editors were already looking for information on this very dangerous topic. As a consequence the two invited leaders journeyed to Senator Simpson's house at four in the afternoon, and were closeted with him there for several hours. The conference this time was in the Senator's library, and he received his colleagues with the genial air of one who has much to gain and little to lose. There were whiskies, wines, and cigars on the table; and while Mollenhauer and Simpson exchanged the commonplaces of the day awaiting the arrival of Butler, they lighted cigars and kept their inmost thoughts to themselves.

It so happened that upon the previous afternoon, at the very hour when Mr. Butler had been learning from Mr. Pettie of the sixty-thousand-dollar-check transaction, this same matter had been brought to Mollenhauer's attention by Stener himself. The former worthy, on Stener's frightened arrival, explaining that, in spite of his positive instructions, Cowperwood, by a subtle trick in connection with Albert Stires, had managed to get sixty thousand dollars more, had instantly seen how he could use this piece of information, which he assumed to be private, to his own enrichment alone, and, by taking advantage of Cowperwood's difficult situation, fleece him out of his street-railway shares without letting Butler or Simpson know anything about it. Mollenhauer's thought at this time was that if Cowperwood had committed embezzlement, as it looked, he himself would, providing he could hush up all conversation about the matter, have the former in his power. He could send for him, once the matter of the absence of the certificates was established, and say to him in so many words: "Now you clear out of the street-railway business or you go to the penitentiary. I do not want to be unduly harsh, but you will have to part with your holdings to me for a merely nominal consideration, or this matter will be brought to the attention of the courts. Do as I say, and I will do all I can to assist you."

Mollenhauer really did not know the stuff of which Frank A. Cowperwood was made; and, anyhow, his game was blocked, as he was soon to learn, by the asinine conversational powers of Stener. When questioned as to whom he had told, he had to admit, to Mollenhauer's intense disgust and dissatisfaction, that he had already conferred with Strobik and Harmon, who had been in his office, and that he could not say whom else they had told. Mollenhauer had a profound contempt for the city treasurer and his situation—never greater than at this moment. Although he suspected that the plan he had in mind was already frustrated beforehand, he nevertheless preferred, being the cautious man that he was, to find out just what chance he had of putting his idea into force. Strobik and Harmon might not have told any one else before he could reach them and seal their lips also. He did not know that both these gentlemen had talked to Pettie, who was their very good friend, and who had been helping them in the matter of their suretyship trouble with Stener, and that even at this hour Pettie was telling Butler. So Abner Sengstack, Mr. Mollenhauer's faithful secretary, was now sent for and told to go first to the Drovers' and Traders' Bank and learn if the certificates were really in the sinking-fund, as Cowperwood had said—the fact that the latter had by now closed his doors would give great significance to their absence—and then, such being the case, with all possible speed to find and caution Strobik and Harmon. He returned to say that the sixty thousand dollars' worth of certificates was not in the sinking-fund, and that, although he had given Strobik and Harmon the desired warning, he feared that some damage had already been done, as they admitted having informed Mr. Pettie. Mr. Mollenhauer decided to confer with that official also, and sent for him, only to find that it was too late. He had talked with Mr. Butler, and the latter knew. Mollenhauer thereupon decided that if need be he would make a virtue of this necessity, and share with Butler the pleasure of plucking the Cowperwood goose. It was essentially a delicate political situation.

Butler was not long in arriving, and apologized for the delay.

"It's a lively life I'm leadin', what with every bank in the city wantin' to know how their loans are goin' to be taken care of," he said, taking up a cigar and striking a match.

"It does look a little threatening," said Senator Simpson, smiling. "Sit down. I have just been talking with Avery Stone, of Jay Cooke and Company, and he tells me that the talk in Third Street about Mr. Stener's connection with this Cowperwood failure is growing very strong, and that the newspapers are bound to take up the matter shortly, unless something is done about it. He says that the financial reporters of the *Press* and the *Ledger* have been around to him asking him for information; and I am sure that the news is certain to reach Mr. Wheat, of the Citizens' Reform Association, very shortly. We ought to decide now, gentlemen, what we propose to do. One thing, I am sure, is to eliminate Mr. Stener from the ticket as quietly as possible. This really looks to me as if it might become a very serious issue, and we ought to be doing what we can now to offset its effect later."

"There is one thing sure," continued Senator Simpson, after a time, seeing that no one else spoke, "and that is, if we do not begin a prosecution on our own account within a reasonable time, some one else is apt to; and that would put rather a bad face on the matter. My own opinion would be that we wait until it is very plain that prosecution is going to be undertaken by some one else— possibly the Municipal Reform Association—but that we be ready to step in and act in such a way as to make it look as though we had been planning to do it all the time. The thing to do is to gain time; and so I would suggest that it be made as difficult as possible to get at the treas-

urer's books. An investigation there, if it begins at all
—as I think is very likely—should be very slow in producing the facts."

The Senator was not at all for mincing words with his
important confrères, when it came to vital issues. He
preferred, in his grandiloquent way, to call a spade a
spade.

"Now that sounds like very good sense to me," said
Butler, sinking a little lower in his chair for comfort's
sake. "The boys could easily make that investigation
last three weeks, I should think. They're slow enough
to do everything else, if me memory doesn't fail me."

"Yes; that isn't a bad idea," said Mollenhauer, solemnly, blowing a ring of smoke.

"We ought to have our programme worked out very
carefully," continued Senator Simpson, "so that if we
are compelled to act we can do so very quickly. I believe myself that this thing is certain to come to an issue
within a week, if not sooner, and we have no time to lose.
If my advice were followed now, I should have the mayor
write the treasurer a letter asking for information, and
the treasurer write the mayor his answer, and also have
the mayor, with the authority of the common council,
suspend the treasurer for the time being—I think we have
the authority to do that—or, at least, take over his principal duties. We ought to have these letters ready to
show to the newspapers at once, in case this action is
forced upon us."

"I could have those letters prepared, if you gentlemen
have no objection, and have my secretary show them to
you," put in Mollenhauer, quietly, but quickly.

"Well, that strikes me as sinsible," said Butler, easily.
"It's about the only thing we can do under the circumstances, unless we could find some one else to blame it
on, and I have a suggestion to make in that direction.
Maybe we're not as helpless as we might be, all things
considered."

There was a slight gleam of triumph in his eye as he said this.

The idea of a scapegoat had not occurred to Senator Simpson up to this time, knowing nothing, as he did, of the sixty-thousand-dollar-check transaction. He had not followed the local-treasury dealings very closely, nor had he talked to either of his confrères since the original conference between them. Nor had he imagined up to now that Cowperwood was acting as anything more than a broker for Stener, carrying money on deposit at two per cent. or more, which left him quite free and beyond prosecution.

"Just what do you mean?" asked the Senator, looking at Butler interestedly. "There haven't been any outside parties mixed up with this, have there?"

"No-o. I wouldn't call him an outside party, exactly. It's Cowperwood himself I'm thinkin' of. There's somethin' that has come up since I saw you gentlemen last that makes me think that perhaps that young man isn't as innocent as he might be. It looks to me as though he was the ringleader in this business, as though he had been leadin' Stener on against his will. I've been lookin' into the matter on me own account, and as far as I can make out this man Stener isn't as much to blame as I thought. From all I can learn, Cowperwood's been threatenin' Stener with one thing and another if he didn't give him more money, and only the other day he got a big sum on false pretinses, which might make him aqually guilty with Stener. There's sixty thousand dollars of city loan certificates that has been paid for that aren't in the sinkin'-fund. I don't see that we need to have any particular consideration for him."

The old man had shot his first arrow, and he felt considerably relieved. He looked before him with a steady gleam in his eye, and both the Senator and Mollenhauer were surprised at his change of front. At their last meeting he had appeared rather friendly to the young banker,

and this recent discovery was no occasion for any vicious
attitude on his part. Mollenhauer in particular was surprised, for he had been counting on Butler's friendship for
Cowperwood as a means of interesting the contractor
to take over Cowperwood's holdings by some hocus-pocus
which would save the banker from prosecution, leave
the city nothing, and themselves everything.

"Um-m, you don't tell me!" observed Senator Simpson, thoughtfully, stroking his mouth with his pale hand.

"Yes, I can confirm that," said Mollenhauer, quietly,
seeing his own little private plan of browbeating Cowperwood out of his street-railway shares going glimmering.
"I had a talk with Mr. Stener the other day about this
very matter, and he told me that Mr. Cowperwood had
been trying to force him to give him three hundred
thousand dollars more, and that when he refused Cowperwood managed to get sixty thousand dollars further
without his knowledge or consent."

"How could he do that?" asked Senator Simpson, in-
credulously. Mollenhauer explained the transaction.

"Oh," said the Senator, when Mollenhauer had finished,
"that indicates a rather sharp person, doesn't it? And
the certificates are not in the sinking-fund, eh?"

"They're not," chimed in Butler, with considerable
enthusiasm.

"Well, I *must* say," said Simpson, rather relieved in
his manner, "this looks like a rather good thing to me.
We need something like this. I see no reason under the
circumstances for trying to protect Mr. Cowperwood.
We might as well try to make a point of that, if we have
to. The newspapers might just as well talk loud about
that as anything else. They are bound to talk; and if we
give them the right angle, I think that the election might
well come and go before the matter could be reasonably
cleared up, even though Mr. Wheat does interfere. I
will be glad to undertake to see what can be done with the
papers."

"Well, that bein' the case," said Butler, "I don't see that there's so much more we can do now; but I do think it will be a mistake if Cowperwood isn't punished with the other one. He's aqually guilty with Stener, if not more so, and I for one want to see him get what he deserves. He belongs in the penitentiary, and that's where he'll go if I have my say."

Both Mollenhauer and Simpson turned a reserved and inquiring eye on their usually genial associate. What could be the reason for his sudden determination to have Cowperwood punished? Cowperwood, as Mollenhauer and Simpson saw it, and as Butler would ordinarily have seen it, was well within his human, if not his strictly legal rights. They did not blame him half as much for trying to do what he had done as they blamed Stener for letting him do it. But, since Butler felt as he did, and there was an actual technical crime here, they were perfectly willing that the party should have the advantage of it, even if Cowperwood went to the penitentiary. It was not such a nice thing for powerful political gentlemen to be doing—jumping on a man who was already financially down and in no position to help himself—but party and personal self-interest were much stronger here than the ethical and social privileges of any individual. Cowperwood was a scapegoat, self-made to their hand, and it would be folly to ignore him in case they needed him in that capacity.

"You may be right," said Senator Simpson, cautiously. "You might have those letters prepared, Henry; and if we have to bring any action at all against anybody before election, it would, perhaps, be advisable to bring it against Mr. Cowperwood. Include Mr. Stener if you have to. I leave it to you two, as I am compelled to start for Pittsburg next Friday; but I know you will not overlook any point."

The Senator arose. His time was always valuable. Mollenhauer, having been obliged to abandon his private designs upon Cowperwood's holdings, had been intending to bring up the matter of the joint control of all the local street-railway properties, but decided to let it rest. The continued panicky state of the market was bringing out various holdings which he was doing his best to acquire, and the more he had in his possession at some crucial time when they should talk over any plan of uniting, the better would be his personal position. The matter could well rest. Butler was highly gratified by what he had accomplished. He had succeeded in putting the trium-virate on record against Cowperwood as the first victim, in case of any public disturbance or demonstration against the party. All that was now necessary was for that disturbance to manifest itself; and, from what he could see of local conditions, it was not far off. There was now the matter of Cowperwood's disgruntled creditors to look into; and if by buying in these he should succeed in preventing the financier from resuming business, he would have him in a very precarious condition indeed. It was a sad day for Cowperwood, Butler thought—the day he had first tried to lead Aileen astray—and the time was not far off when he could prove it to him.

CHAPTER XLI

IN the meanwhile the affairs of Frank Algernon Cowperwood had not been improving. Since the day when he had first talked over the matter of his city-loan dilemma with Harper Steger, his lawyer, several things had transpired which made him reasonably certain that the politicians would try to make a scapegoat of him, and that shortly. For one thing, Albert Stires had called only a few days after Cowperwood had closed his doors and imparted a significant piece of information. Albert was still connected with the city treasury, as was Stener, and engaged with Secretary Sengstack and another personal appointee of Mollenhauer's in going over the treasurer's books and explaining their financial significance. Albert had come to Cowperwood primarily to get additional advice in regard to the sixty-thousand-dollar check and his personal connection with it; for Stener, after Albert had failed to bring back the check from Cowperwood, had threatened, as Stires had already reported to Cowperwood on the day of the latter's failure, to have his chief clerk prosecuted, saying that he was responsible for the loss of the money, and that his bondsmen could be held responsible. If Albert's bondsmen were held, that would simply mean that they in turn would attach his property to satisfy their loss, and probably have him punished in the bargain. On this second call from Stires, Cowperwood had merely laughed good-naturedly at their threat, and assured Albert that there was nothing in it.

"Albert," he had said, smilingly, "I tell you positively there's nothing in it. You're not responsible for delivering that check to me, and they wouldn't think of attaching your property, or making any move whatsoever, if you openly defied them. I'll tell you what you do, now. Go and consult my lawyer, Mr. Steger. It won't cost you a cent, and he'll tell you exactly what to do. If anybody makes a move he will simply write them a letter of some kind, and that will be the end of it. Now go on back, and don't worry any more about it. I am sorry this move of mine has caused you so much trouble; but it's a hundred to one you couldn't have kept your place with a new city treasurer, anyhow, seeing how things are; and if I see any place where you can possibly fit in I'll let you know."

Albert had been properly grateful, and as a consequence he had told Cowperwood of a little scene which had transpired, not in his presence, but in the presence of a fellow-employee, Robert Wotherspoon, a henchman of Strobik's; which scene, repeated by Wotherspoon, was a mere shadow of something else much more important. Wotherspoon, it appears, had been in the mayor's office the day before, when there had been a conference between Strobik, Harmon, and the mayor in regard to Stener; and these three underlings were commenting on what "the big three," as Mollenhauer, Butler, and Simpson were known, were likely to do. According to Wotherspoon, Harmon had said to Strobik and Borchardt that Mollenhauer had said to Butler, in some conference which had been reported to Harmon: "The party's got to have somebody else besides Stener to prosecute." And Butler had replied: "What's the matter with this man Cowperwood? Can't we fix this on him in some way? He's as guilty as the other fellow." "And," said Wotherspoon to Stires, "Strobik said, 'They've got that sixty-thousand-dollar check on him, and they're going to send him up.'"

This alleged conversation between Butler, Mollenhauer, and Simpson had no relation to the actual one which had occurred at Senator Simpson's house. It was a freak product of the imagination of those who instinctively felt what ought to, or at least might, happen. Harmon did not know that Butler and Mollenhauer and Simpson had conferred about anything; he had merely seen Butler coming out of District-Attorney Pettie's office and Sengstack entering Stener's. That was enough. The rest might be looked upon as a tribute to his constructive imagination. Nevertheless, it was important enough to Cowperwood.

"I thought you'd like to know about this, Mr. Cowperwood," had said Stires, who, in spite of the former's treatment of him, bore him no ill-will. Outside of that particular incident Cowperwood had always been uniformly courteous to him and considerate. "If they're going to do anything, it's better you should know about it beforehand. I thought you might want to do something yourself. You've been very nice to me all along, Mr. Cowperwood, and I appreciate it."

"Oh, don't mention it, Albert," Cowperwood had replied, cheerfully, concealing the real impression this intelligence made on him. "I certainly am much obliged to you, and it will be useful to me. I thought they might be doing something of that sort. But you go and see Mr. Steger now, and don't worry about me. I'll be all right."

Albert departed, and then Cowperwood's brow clouded. So this was the first evidence of Butler's or Mollenhauer's or Simpson's ill-will—very likely Butler's.

Another thing, brought to Cowperwood's attention shortly after the call from Stires, by a letter from Aileen, was a conversation which had taken place at the Butler dinner-table one evening when Butler, the elder, was not at home. It was one of those commonplace little talks which so constantly take place in connection with public events in every family—based, in this instance, on the public event of Cowperwood's failure. (The picturesque details Aileen did not relate.) Callum had come in fresh from Third Street, in the neighborhood of which his father's offices were, and where he continually labored gathering the news of the day from one person and another. On this day he had been talking with some one who knew something of the treasury defalcation, and also of Cowperwood's final mistake in extracting the sixty-thousand-dollar check, which since the recent conference of the great triumvirate was being rumored.

"Well," said Callum, apropos of a guarded hint in the morning *Press* concerning the need of a sounder public morality, to which Owen laughingly referred, "there's no doubt that fellow's one shifty person, all right. He's got this finance business going around like a pinwheel. Bob Sibert, over in the county clerk's office, was telling me that he got a last check out of Stener for sixty thousand dollars by some trick or other, and that they're going to send him up for it. I didn't think he'd do that. You didn't hear anything about that, did you, Owen?"

Aileen, at the mention of Cowperwood's name, and the opening attack by Callum, had pricked up her ears and flared up dangerously, seeing that her father was not present; but when Callum added the data about the sixty-thousand-dollar check she calmed down again and paled a little. She was terribly afraid they would do something to Cowperwood. It was on her tongue to ask since when Cowperwood had become so shifty in Callum's eyes, seeing that he had gone to Cowperwood's house gaily enough in times past.

"Yes, I heard a little something about it," replied Owen, guardedly. He knew all about it, for his father had confided the matter to him as quickly as he had heard it; but, since Butler had asked him to say nothing of it for the time being, he had not done so. Since it was obviously getting around now, though, he did not mind. Butler had told him nothing of Aileen, of course. "I'm sorry that fellow's turned out so badly. He's made a mistake if he's done that. They'll get him yet, sure."

"What do you mean by 'get him yet,' Owen?" put in

Norah, who was quite a young lady now, with a very definite leaning toward a certain eligible young gentleman, and who was certain to be married within the next year. "You don't mean they'll send him to the penitentiary, do you?"

"Something like that, I'm afraid, Sis," he replied. "He's got himself in a very bad hole through this Stener business."

Aileen's heart twitched involuntarily, and hurt her. She could not think of her Frank having got himself in such a desperate situation. The penitentiary! Good heavens! Her appetite deserted her, and she shortly arose and left the table, giving as an excuse the lie that she had had too much lunch. Her dear lover, she thought, once she was in her room—her beloved Frank! Could anything like this really happen to him? She ran cold. She wrote him a letter at once, and told him all she had heard, which made him set his even teeth in two gleaming rows. He would have to do something about this, he thought—see Mollenhauer or Simpson, or both, and make some offer to the city. He could not promise them money for the present—only notes; but they might take that. Surely they could not be intending to make a scapegoat out of him over such a trivial and uncertain matter as this check transaction. It was too uncertain, too vague, from a legal point of view. It was too complicated with the history of his transactions with Stener. Still, they might. He must see Mollenhauer. A public storm might break loose at any hour now, even though all the politicians, Butler included, might wish to have the matter hushed up until after election, as he knew they did.

This matter of seeing Mollenhauer and Simpson, once Cowperwood had the idea, was gone about with his customary energy; but it resulted in nothing. Simpson was out of the city for a period of ten days; and Mollenhauer, having in mind the suggestion made by Butler, and confirmed by Simpson, in regard to utilizing Cowperwood's misdeed for the benefit of the party, and knowing what wide circulation had been given in the last few days to the report of Cowperwood's criminal involvement with Stener, had very little hope to offer. (Since the conference between Butler, Mollenhauer, and Simpson, the smaller politicians, taking their cue from the overlords, had been industriously spreading the story of the sixty-thousand-dollar check, and insisting that the burden of guilt for the treasury defalcation lay on the banker.) The moment Mollenhauer laid eyes on Cowperwood he realized, however, that he had a young but powerful personality to deal with, and that he could not use the terrors of his political power on him any more than he could on any other man as powerful as himself. Cowperwood gave no evidence of fright. He merely stated, in his bland way, that he had been in the habit of borrowing money from the city treasury at a low rate of interest, and that this panic had involved him so that he could not possibly return it at present.

"I have heard rumors, Mr. Mollenhauer," he said, "to the effect that some charge was to be brought against me as a partner with Mr. Stener in this matter; but I am hoping that the city will not do that, and I thought I might enlist your influence to prevent it. My affairs are not in a bad way at all, if I had a little time to arrange matters. I am making all of my creditors an offer of fifty cents on the dollar now, and giving notes at one, two, and three years; but in this matter of the city treasury loans, if I could come to terms, I would be glad to make it a hundred cents—only I would want a little more time. Stocks are bound to recover, as you know, and, barring my losses at this time, I will be all right. I realize that the matter has gone pretty far already. The newspapers are apt to start talking at any time. But if I could be kept out of the general proceedings as much as possible, my standing would not be injured, and I would have a better chance of getting on my feet. It would be better for the city, for then I could certainly pay what I owe it."

Mollenhauer looked at this young financial David with an interested eye. If he could have seen a way to accept this proposition of Cowperwood's, so that the money offered would have been eventually payable to him, and if Cowperwood had had any reasonable prospect of getting on his feet soon, he would have considered carefully what he had to say. For then Cowperwood could have assigned his recovered property to him. As it was, there was small likelihood of this situation ever being straightened out. The Citizens' Municipal Reform Association, once it came to their ears, as it was certain to do, would unquestionably follow it closely to the end—particularly the eventual disposition of this five hundred thousand.

"The trouble with this situation, Mr. Cowperwood," he said, very blandly, "is that it has gone so far that it is practically out of my hands. I really have very little to do with it. I don't suppose, though, really, it is this matter of the five-hundred-thousand-dollar loan that is worrying you so much, as it is this other matter of the sixty-thousand-dollar check you received the other day. Mr. Stener insists that you secured that illegally, and he is very much wrought up about it. The mayor and the other city officials know of it now, and they may force some action of some kind. I don't know."

Mollenhauer was obviously not frank in his attitude— a little bit evasive in his sly reference to his official tool, the mayor; and Cowperwood saw it. It irritated him greatly. It portended subtle opposition; but he was tactful enough to be quite suave and respectful.

"I did get a check for sixty thousand dollars, that's true," he replied, with apparent frankness, "the day before I assigned. It was for certificates I had purchased, however, on Mr. Stener's order, and was due me. I needed the money, and asked for it. I don't see that there is anything illegal in that."

"Not if the transaction was completed in all its details," replied Mr. Mollenhauer, blandly. "As I understand it, the certificates were bought for the sinking-fund, and they are not there. How do you explain that?"

"An oversight, merely," replied Cowperwood, innocently, and quite as blandly as Mollenhauer. "They would have been there if I had not been compelled to assign so unexpectedly. It was not possible for me to attend to everything in person. It has not been our custom to deposit them at once. Mr. Stener will tell you that, if you ask him."

"You don't say," replied Mollenhauer. "He did not give me that impression. However, they are not there, and I believe that that makes some difference legally. But I'm merely commenting on it. I have no interest in the matter one way or the other, more than that of any other good Republican, I fancy. I don't see exactly what I can do for you. What did you think I could do?"

"I don't believe you can do anything for me, Mr. Mollenhauer," replied Cowperwood, a little tartly, "unless you are willing to deal quite frankly with me. I am not a beginner in politics in Philadelphia. I know something about the powers in command. I thought (if you want to hear me) that you could stop any plan to prosecute me in this matter, and give me time to get on my feet again. I am not any more criminally responsible for that sixty thousand dollars than I am for the five hundred thousand dollars that I had as loan before it—not as much so. I did not create this panic. I did not set Chicago on fire. Mr. Stener and his friends have been reaping some profit out of dealing with me. I certainly was entitled to make some effort to save myself after all these years of service, and I can't understand why I should not receive some courtesy at the hands of the present city administration, after I have been so useful to it. I certainly have kept city loan at par; and as for Mr. Stener's

money, he has never wanted for his interest on that, and
more than his interest."

"Quite so," replied Mollenhauer, looking Cowperwood
in the eye steadily and estimating the force and accuracy
of the man at their real value. "I understand exactly
how it has all come about, Mr. Cowperwood. No doubt
Mr. Stener owes you a debt of gratitude, as does the remainder of the city administration. I'm not saying what
the city administration ought or ought not do. All I
know is that you have put yourself in a dangerous situation, and that public sentiment in some quarters is already very strong against you. The Republican party
is in a very bad position, so far as this election is concerned. In a way, however innocently, you have helped
to put it there, Mr. Cowperwood. I sympathize with you
greatly; but I do not know exactly what I can do. I
am only one of those who have a slight say in the affairs
of Philadelphia—not all. You had better see some of
the others—Mr. Butler and Mr. Simpson, for instance."

Mollenhauer expected that Cowperwood would make
some offer of his own holdings, but he did not. Instead,
at the mention of the name Butler, and that too in
connection with this very aloof and equivocal attitude on
the part of Mollenhauer, Cowperwood saw how futile
his appeal was. He realized that, with Butler opposing
strongly, Mollenhauer would do nothing, even if he could
—would not try it.

"I'm very much obliged to you, Mr. Mollenhauer,"
he said, in the end, "for the courtesy of this interview.
I believe you would help me if you could. I shall just
have to fight it out the best way I can. Good day."

Cowperwood bowed himself out. He saw clearly how
hopeless his quest was. Butler and the party interests
and the public were, or shortly would be, allied against
him. What could he do? Fighting bankruptcy suits
was about all that was left for him to do, and that gave
no evidence of a fortunate outcome in the long run.

CHAPTER XLII

IN the meanwhile public rumor had been growing, and the matter of defalcation had finally reached the ear of that very estimable citizen, Mr. Skelton C. Wheat, the president of the Citizens' Municipal Reform Association, who had long been wondering whether just such a situation as this would not come about in connection with the city treasury.

His mind, thereupon, offered that singular paradox so frequently characteristic of the human thought organ —namely, the open question whether he was more disgusted with this evidence of public misconduct in office than he was pleased at finding that it was ready to his hand to reprimand. The occasion was such an excellent one, too—the eve of an important municipal and State election. Nevertheless, it was a serious charge to make against any one, the sum in question was so imposingly large; and the rumors involved Cowperwood, who was a private citizen of unstained record. Mr. Wheat was not so anxious to proceed but what he wished also to exercise due caution. And so he delayed for a few days before doing anything, collecting data. On the evening of October 20, 1871, ten days after the failure of Cowperwood, finding that the rumors were growing in volume, and that no one appeared to be willing to take steps to straighten the matter out, Mr. Wheat called together the committee of ten estimable Philadelphians of which he was chairman.

It was decided to appoint a subcommittee "to investigate," to quote the statement eventually given to the public, "the peculiar rumors now affecting one of the most important and distinguished officers of our municipal government," and to report at the next meeting, which was set for the following evening at nine o'clock. The meeting adjourned, and the following night at nine reassembled, four individuals of very shrewd financial judgment having meantime been about the task assigned them. They drew up a very elaborate statement, not wholly in accordance with the facts, but as nearly so as could be ascertained in so short a space of time.

"It appears [read the report, after a preamble which explained why the committee had been appointed] that it has been the custom of city treasurers for years, when loans have been authorized by councils, to place them in the hands of some favorite broker for sale, the broker accounting to the treasurer for the moneys received by such sales at short periods, generally the first of each month. In the present case Frank A. Cowperwood has been acting as such broker for the city treasurer. But even this vicious and unbusiness-like system appears not to have been adhered to in the case of Mr. Cowperwood. The accident of the Chicago fire, the consequent depression of stock values, and the subsequent failure of Mr. Frank A. Cowperwood have so involved matters temporarily that the committee has not been able to ascertain with accuracy that regular accounts have been rendered; but from the manner in which Mr. Cowperwood has had possession of bonds (city loans) for hypothecation, etc., it appears that the transfers for bonds thus pledged have been repudiated. It would appear that he has been held to no responsibility in these matters, and that there have always been under his control several hundred thousand dollars of cash or securities belonging to the city, which he has manipulated for various purposes; but the details of the results of these transactions are not easily available.

"Some of the operations consisted of hypothecation of large amounts of these loans before the certificates were issued, the lender seeing that the order for the hypothecated securities was duly made to him on the books of the treasurer. Such methods appear to have been occurring for a long time, and it being incredible that the city treasurer could be unaware of the nature of the business, there is indication of a complicity between him and Mr. Cowperwood to benefit by the use of the city credit, in violation of the law.

"At the very time these hypothecations were being made, and the city paying interest upon such loans, the money representing them was in the hands of the treasurer's broker and bearing no interest to the city. The payment of municipal warrants was postponed, and they were being purchased at a discount in large amounts by Mr. Cowperwood with the very money that should have been in the city treasury. The *bona fide* holders of the orders for certificates of loans are now unable to obtain them, and thus the city's credit is injured to a greater extent than the present defalcation, which amounts to over five hundred thousand dollars. An accountant is now engaged at the treasurer's books, and a few days will make clear the whole *modus operandi*. It is hoped that the publicity thus obtained will break up such vicious practices."

There was appended along with this report a quotation from the law governing the abuse of a public trust; and the committee went on to say that, unless some taxpayer chose to initiate proceedings for the prosecution of those concerned, the committee itself would be called upon to do so, although such action hardly came within the object for which it was formed.

This report was immediately given to the papers. Such a public announcement had been anticipated in one form or other by Cowperwood and the politicians; but this was, nevertheless, a severe blow—a real thunder-clap to the public at large, and it created the storm of ill feeling and social opposition that might have been expected. Cowperwood was not surprised. It was merely one additional ill among many. But Stener, who was now being used wholly as a tool in this situation, was beside himself with fear. These days he lay in his bed at his new home in Spring Garden Street, and scanned all the daily papers, the while his wife looked after the ordering of the breakfast. He broke into a cold sweat when he saw the announcement which was conservatively headed by all of the papers, "Meeting of the Municipal Reform Association." All of the papers were so closely identified with the political and financial powers of the city that they did not dare to come out openly and say what they thought. The chief facts had already been in the hands of the various editors and publishers for a week and more, but the word had also gone around from Mollenhauer, Simpson, and Butler to press down on the soft pedal for the present. No great fuss must be made. It was not good for Philadelphia, for local commerce, etc., to make a row. The fair name of the city would be injured. It was the old story.

That desperate scheme to cast the blame on Cowperwood temporarily, which had been concocted by Mollenhauer, Butler, and Simpson, to get the odium of the crime outside the party lines for the time being, was now lugged forth and put in operation. It was interesting and strange to note how quickly the newspapers, and even the Citizens' Municipal Reform Association, got the notion that Cowperwood was largely, if not solely, to blame. Stener had loaned him the money, it is true—put bond issues in his hands for sale—but somehow every one seemed to gain the impression that Cowperwood had desperately misused the treasurer. The fact that he had taken a sixty-thousand-dollar check for certificates which were not in the sinking-fund was hinted at, though until they could actually confirm this for themselves both the newspapers and the committee were too fearful of the State libel laws to say so. Nevertheless, the general impression was that Cowperwood was the scoundrel. All the little politicians like Strobik, Harmon, Wycroft, District-Attorney Pettie, and others were wagging their heads solemnly and saying only those things which they were told to say. In due time were brought forth those noble municipal letters, purporting to be a stern call on the part of the mayor, Mr. Jacob Borchardt, on Mr. George W. Stener for an immediate explanation of his conduct, and the latter's reply, which were at once given to the newspapers and the Citizens' Municipal Reform Association. These letters were enough to show, so the politicians figured, that the Republican party was anxious to purge itself of any miscreant within its ranks, and they also helped to pass the time until after election. The thing to do was to get past the election safely, when Stener and Cowperwood might well be dealt with as occasion warranted. Mr. Mollenhauer, Mr. Butler, and Mr. Simpson watched with interest to see what effect these letters would have, though Butler was not anxious to have anything interfere with the ultimate punishment which he felt was due Cowperwood. Mollenhauer had not told him as yet of Cowperwood's call. Here are the letters:

OFFICE OF THE MAYOR OF THE CITY OF PHILADELPHIA

GEORGE W. STENER, Esq.,   *October 18, 1871.*
      City Treasurer.

DEAR SIR,—Information has been given me that certificates of city loan to a large amount, issued by you for sale on account of the city, and, I presume, after the usual requisition from the mayor of the city, have passed out of your custody, and that the proceeds of the sale of said certificates have not been paid into the city treasury.

I have also been informed that a large amount of the city's money has been permitted to pass into the hands of some one or more brokers or bankers doing business on Third Street, and that said brokers or bankers have since met with financial difficulties, whereby, and by reason of the above generally, the interests of the city are likely to be very seriously affected.

I have therefore to request that you will promptly advise me of the truth or falsity of these statements, so that such duties as devolve upon me as the chief magistrate of the city, in view of such facts, if they exist, may be intelligently discharged.

                  Yours respectfully,   JACOB BORCHARDT.

OFFICE OF THE TREASURER OF THE CITY OF PHILADELPHIA

HON. JACOB BORCHARDT.   *October 19, 1871.*

DEAR SIR,—I have to acknowledge the receipt of your communication of the 21st instant, and to express my regret that I cannot at this time give you the information you ask. There is undoubtedly an embarrassment in the city treasury, owing to the delinquency of the broker who for several years past has negotiated the city loans, and I have been, since the discovery of this fact, and still am occupied in endeavoring to avert or lessen the loss with which the city is threatened.   I am, very respectfully,

                           GEORGE W. STENER.

THE FINANCIER

October 21, 1871.

GEORGE W. STENER, Esq.,
      City Treasurer.

DEAR SIR,—Under the existing circumstances you will consider this as a notice of withdrawal and revocation of any requisition or authority by me for the sale of loan, so far as the same has not been fulfilled. Applications for loans, authorized and not issued, may for the present be made at this office.

Very respectfully,

JACOB BORCHARDT,
Mayor of Philadelphia.

And do you think, dear reader, that Mr. Jacob Borchardt wrote the letters to which his name was attached? He did not. Mr. Abner Sengstack wrote them in Mr. Mollenhauer's office, and Mr. Mollenhauer's comment when he saw them was that he thought they would do— that they were very good, in fact. And do you think Mr. George W. Stener, city treasurer of Philadelphia, wrote his very politic reply? You know he did not. Mr. Stener was in a state of complete collapse, even crying at one time at home in his bath-tub. Mr. Abner Sengstack wrote that, and had Mr. Stener sign it. And Mr. Mollenhauer's comment on that, before it was sent, was that he thought it was "all right." It was a time when all the little rats and mice were scurrying to cover because of the presence of a great, fiery-eyed public cat somewhere in the dark, and only the older and wiser rats were able to act. Mr. Mollenhauer, Mr. Butler, and Mr. Simpson, who had now returned, were conferring frequently. They were sending orders to Mr. Borchardt, the mayor of the city, Mr. Strobik, president of council, and Mr. Stener, semi-defunct city treasurer, as you would send orders to a hall-boy.

They were considering with Mr. Pettie, the district attorney, just what could be done about Cowperwood, if anything, and just what defense, if any, could be made

467

for Mr. Stener. Butler was strong for Cowperwood's prosecution, of course. The latter was very much in the public eye just now. Butler argued the public seemed to want to blame him. He was rich. A fine opportunity. Mr. Pettie did not see that any defense could be made for Stener; but Cowperwood—"Let me see," he said. They were figuring that, first of all, whatever the justice of the facts, it would be good policy to arrest Cowperwood, and if necessary try him. Stener's story of how Cowperwood secured sixty thousand dollars *via* Albert Stires and a false claim seemed to constitute a good basis for action. His disposal of the sixty-thousand-dollar check without making any return to the city, up to now, constituted larceny or larceny as bailee, or embezzlement or embezzlement on a check. He could be readily arrested on any one or two, or all four, of these charges, for that matter, and locked up and tried. It was Mr. Pettie who offered these various suggestions. Cowperwood's mere arrest, Butler and the others reasoned, would seem like a great evidence of virtuous indignation on the part of the other officers of the administration; and in a way this would divert attention from the evil nature of the dear, darling party until after election—which was what was wanted.

So finally, on October 23d, two days after Mr. Skelton C. Wheat had issued the first thunderous blast—when there was not a moment longer to lose—the several letters so carefully and forcefully prepared were properly sent and received, and finally given to the papers, which were clamoring for information; and then Mr. Mollenhauer and Mr. Simpson and Mr. Butler conferred some more. Finally, on the afternoon of October 26, 1871, Mr. Edward Strobik, president of the common council of Philadelphia, and acting in that capacity solely for the city, appeared before the mayor, as finally ordered by Mr. Mollenhauer, after a conference, and charged by affidavit that Mr. Frank A. Cowperwood, as broker, employed by the treasurer to sell the bonds of the city, had committed embezzlement and larceny as bailee. It did not matter that he charged Mr. George W. Stener with embezzlement at the same time. Cowperwood was the scapegoat they were after.

In that minor world of the small politicians—those below Simpson, Mollenhauer, and Butler—which concerned Mr. Borchardt, Mr. Strobik, Mr. Wycroft, Mr. Harmon, Mr. Stener, and others, things were equally subtle, treacherous, uncertain, and anything but pleasant to contemplate. These gentlemen, aside from their connection with Mr. Mollenhauer, which was dark, safe, and never to be spoken of, had all been making a little money out of the pliability and financial immorality of Mr. Stener, to say nothing of the cleverness of Mr. Cowperwood. As has been said, Mr. Strobik, Mr. Wycroft, and Mr. Harmon were on Mr. Stener's bond as treasurer, which was against the law in the first place. They had no business to be; but it was profitable.

Then they had all shared Mr. Stener's earlier earnings. Now, however, Mr. Stener's bond was in danger of being forfeited. His affairs were being investigated. Did friendship last? It did not. They, all of them, were now watching each other like a lot of cats and rats, each figuring how he could protect himself as to his bond and his holdings by getting Stener to make over his property to him, individually, instead of to all three of them collectively, and before it could or should (owing, perhaps, to public clamor) be perforce seized by some one for the city.

There was much running to and fro here. There was much conferring with Mr. Stener and whispering with each other. It was, of course, against the law for Mr. Stener to assign his property—such little of it as there was left after his transactions with Mr. Mollenhauer—to any one, seeing that he was indebted to the city to the extent of five hundred thousand dollars; but under the advice of Mr. Strobik—and with promise of the latter's aid as president of council—he did so do, giving Mr. Strobik secretly the lion's share. These men, Strobik, Wycroft, Harmon, and others, had always been slapping each other on the back in great good-humor during their days of prosperity. They had dined at Stener's house time and again. They had gone off with him, or rather taken him along on week-end junkets, some of which were anything but admirable; and he had been properly repentant afterward, for he was not a man with any courage outside of the conventions.

Now his one-time friends all turned on him with subtle eyes, contemptuous of his weakness, anxious to save themselves, and caring absolutely nothing of what became of him. He was a sinking ship. Only the fear of the public and the political bosses ruled with these men. They did not dare to be too eager in their scurrying to shelter, for fear Mr. Mollenhauer, or some one else, might become politically disgusted with them. Depend on it, however, Mr. George W. Stener's political carcass was being as rapidly and as effectively picked clean and bare to the bone as this particular flock of political buzzards knew how to pick him.

Such is life.

CHAPTER XLIII

THIS charging of Cowperwood by the politicians with "larceny, larceny as bailee, embezzlement, and embezzlement on a check," as Mr. Pettie had framed this matter for them, was a severe and dangerous blow to him. He was in so bad a state financially, asking for credits and extensions here and there, and doing his best to have his creditors agree to let him go on, that to have this high-sounding and complicated charge laid at his door was very destructive. His wife saw it the following morning after it was made, blazoned in the head-lines of the papers; and she and his mother and father were all compelled to witness it—with what feelings, one can imagine. Old Cowperwood read his own personal doom in it so far as the presidency of the Third National Bank was concerned; and Mrs. Cowperwood, Frank's wife, saw her own and his fortune, as she thought, going straightway to nothing. How could he recover from a slap like this? Who would believe him in the future, seeing that in addition he had failed for so large a sum? Butler, Sr., was delighted (concerned though he was about party success at the polls); for, now he had this villain in the toils, he would see that the matter was properly followed up. Cowperwood would have a fine time getting out of this. The incoming district attorney to succeed David Pettie, in case the Republican party was again successful at the polls, was an appointee of Butler's—a young Irishman who had done considerable legal work for him—one Dennis Shannon. Shannon was a smart, athletic, good-looking young Irishman, all of five feet ten inches in height, sandy-haired, pink-cheeked, blue-

eyed, considerable of an orator, and a fine legal fighter.
Through him Butler had of late won quite a few damage
suits instituted against himself. Shannon was very proud
to be in the old man's favor, to have been put on the ticket
by him, and would, if elected, do his bidding to the best
of his knowledge and ability. Besides, even if it was
technically owing to Stener that the treasury was now
short five hundred thousand dollars, it was, in the public
mind, primarily due to Cowperwood and his wretched
machinations. The papers made it look that way. For
a little while the Citizens' Municipal Reform Association,
too, was deceived. Cowperwood had gone personally
to Skelton C. Wheat and tried to explain his side of the
situation, alleging that what he had done was no different
from what many others had done before him, and were
still doing, but Wheat was dubious. He did not see how
it was that the sixty thousand dollars' worth of certificates
were not in the sinking-fund. Cowperwood's explanation
of *custom* did not avail. Nevertheless, Mr. Wheat saw
that others in politics had been profiting quite as much as
Cowperwood in other ways; but he could not do anything
about that now. He advised Cowperwood to turn State's
evidence, if they would let him, which the latter promptly
refused to do. He was no "squealer," and indicated as
much to Mr. Wheat. The latter smiled wryly.

Butler on his part kept himself busy indicating to all
with whom he came in contact how evil Cowperwood really
was. He did not want the financier to escape by any
chance. Aileen was beside herself with distress; but she
could do nothing. She scarcely realized what was going on.
Butler argued with himself that she was still young and
must have another chance. If he did something radical
now to break off this liaison she could still be established
in merit and decency. So far as the world knew—he
could not tell how far the gossip which had produced the
letter had gone, but he hoped it had not gone far—she was
still unsoiled and unspoiled. With her position and her

money she could still make a fine match. It would take a drastic move like this, though, to open her eyes. She would have to see Cowperwood charged with a crime in this manner, convicted, and sent to the penitentiary, if necessary, before she would let go, and before he would let go. Convict stripes would do it. They would cure her and properly smoke out and ostracize Cowperwood. Butler had no whit of sympathy for the young financier, once he realized how thoroughly he himself had been put upon.

"The man's no good," he said, one day, to District-Attorney Pettie, in talking over the case with him and indicating what he thought ought to be done. "He's a sharper—you can see that. Look how he worked that check business. Only a sharper could do that. We needn't be worryin' about him, I'm thinkin'. He'll look after himself." He said the same thing to young Dennis Shannon; and, of course, that young, ambitious political aspirant immediately took sides against Cowperwood. He became his subtle enemy, waiting only until he should get into office in order to prosecute him properly.

There was only one fly in this ointment, so far as some of the politicians were concerned; and that was due to the fact that if Cowperwood were convicted, Stener must needs be also. There was no escape for the city treasurer. If Cowperwood was guilty of securing by trickery sixty thousand dollars' worth of the city money, Stener was guilty of securing five hundred thousand dollars. The prison term for this was five years. There was no escape. He might plead not guilty, and, by submitting as evidence that what he did was due to custom, save himself from the odious condition of pleading guilty; but he would be convicted, nevertheless. No jury could get by the fact in regard to him. In spite of public opinion, when it came to a trial there might be considerable doubt in Cowperwood's case. There was none in Stener's.

The practical manner in which the situation was furthered, after Cowperwood and Stener were formally charged, may be quickly noted. Steger, Cowperwood's lawyer, who, as an active participant, was in close touch with Mr. David Pettie, the district attorney, learned privately beforehand that Cowperwood was to be prosecuted. He arranged at once to have his client appear before any warrant could be served, and so forestall the newspaper palaver which would follow if he had to be searched for.

The mayor, following Strobik's charge, issued a warrant for Cowperwood's arrest; and, in accordance with Steger's plan, Cowperwood immediately appeared before Borchardt in company with his lawyer and gave bail in twenty thousand dollars (W. C. Davison, president of the Girard National Bank, was his surety) for his appearance at the central police station on the following Saturday for a hearing. Marcus Oldslaw, a lawyer, had been employed by Strobik, as president of the common council, to represent him in prosecuting for the city the dastardly crime of Cowperwood. Mr. Stener did not appear at the same time. The mayor, when Cowperwood came in, looked at him curiously, for he, being comparatively new to the political world of Philadelphia, was not so familiar with him as others were; and Cowperwood returned the look pleasantly enough.

"This is a great dumb show, Mr. Mayor," he observed once to Borchardt, quietly; and the latter replied, with a smile and a kindly eye, that in as far as he was concerned it was a form of procedure which was absolutely unavoidable at this time.

"You know how it is, Mr. Cowperwood," he observed.

The latter smiled. "I do, indeed," he said.

He and Steger went out quickly after a few moments' conversation with Borchardt; but the newspapers were soon out with all the details, and the aggregation of anxious souls in Girard Avenue were compelled to witness this latest development in his affairs.

Later there followed several more or less perfunctory

appearances in a local police court, known as the Central Court, where Cowperwood when arraigned pleaded not guilty, and finally his appearance before the November grand jury, where, owing to the complicated nature of the charge drawn up against him by David Pettie, he thought it wise to appear. He was properly indicted by the latter body (Mr. Shannon, the newly elected district attorney, making a demonstration in force), and his trial ordered for December 5th before a certain Judge Payderson in Part I of Quarter Sessions, which was the local branch of the State courts dealing with crimes of this character. Cowperwood's indictment did not occur, however, before the coming and going of the much-mooted fall election.

This election, thanks to the fine political suggestions and manipulations of Mr. Mollenhauer and Mr. Simpson (ballot-box stuffing and personal violence at the polls not barred), resulted, in spite of the black record of the dominant party, in another victory, by, however, a greatly reduced majority. This injected the personality of Mr. Dennis Shannon into the treasury case—as district attorney to succeed Mr. Pettie, retired—who immediately took hold in a brisk and effective way, doing all he could to further the interests of his superior, Butler, who seemed set on Cowperwood's conviction. The Citizens' Municipal Reform Association, in spite of a resounding defeat at the polls which could not have happened except for fraud, continued to fire courageously away at those whom it considered to be the chief malefactors.

The contrasting pictures presented by George W. Stener and Frank Algernon Cowperwood at this time is well worth a moment's consideration. Cowperwood, despite his solemn thoughts concerning a possible period of incarceration which this hue and cry now suggested, was as calm and collected as one might suppose his great mental resources would permit him to be. He was in no way apparently disturbed. During all this whirl of disaster he had never once lost his head or his courage. That thing *conscience*, which obsesses and rides some people to destruction, did not trouble him at all. He had no consciousness of what is currently known as sin. He never gave a thought to the vast palaver concerning evil which is constantly going on. There were just two faces to the shield of life from the point of view of his peculiar mind—strength and weakness. Right and wrong? He did not know about those. They were bound up in metaphysical abstrusities about which he did not care to bother. Good and evil? Those were toys of clerics, by which they made money. Morality and immorality? He never considered them. But strength and weakness —oh yes! If you had strength you could protect yourself always and be something. If you were weak—pass quickly to the rear and get out of the range of the guns. He was strong, and he knew it; and somehow he always believed in his star. Something—he could not say what, it was the only metaphysics he bothered about—was doing something for him. It had always helped him. It made things come out right at times. It put excellent opportunities in his way. Why had he been given so fine a mind? Why always favored financially, personally? He had not deserved it, earned it. Accident, perhaps; but somehow the thought that he would always be protected —these intuitions, the "hunches" to act which he frequently had—could not be so easily explained. Life was a dark, insoluble mystery; but, whatever it was, strength and weakness were its two constituents. Strength would win; weakness lose. He must rely on swiftness of thought, accuracy, his judgment, and on nothing else.

At each addition to the shadowy flock of disasters which of late had arrived and were circling about him, he merely contemplated them more accurately as a juggler might contemplate additional spheres cast into the air and spinning about his head, and which he must maintain in motion without dropping any of them. These disasters must not light. He must shoo them away. New woes might arrive hourly; but Cowperwood would not cease to estimate them at their true value—to weigh and place them as they came. How much damage could this new one do? How would it affect all the old ones? Where would he place it so it would do the least damage? How would he forfend against its possible evil effect? How many disasters could he keep up in the air at once without letting them fall? His lightning brain followed with photographic accuracy all the probable ramifications of each new woe in all its subtle reaches, and ran to do battle. He had no sense of fear—only a defensive and constructive awareness. He was really a brilliant picture of courage and energy—moving about briskly in a jaunty, dapper way, his mustaches curled, his clothes pressed, his nails manicured, his face clean-shaven and tinted with health. He was not pale or distraught. What was behind that steady, inscrutable eye you might not say. It gave you not the slightest indication of what was going on in the brain behind.

On the other hand, consider Stener. On the morning, for instance, when Cowperwood was looking at the first notice of his own complicity in the defalcation of the city treasurer as announced by the Citizens' Municipal Reform Association, never turning a hair, wondering how long it would take this destructive publicity to die down and what he could do to make his own skirts seem sweet and clean —Stener, as we have seen, was lying in his bed absolutely collapsed. The cold sweat of the first few moments gave way to complete nervous inertia a few moments later, and there he lay. He might readily have died of heart failure. His face was grayish white, his lips blue. He had been warned well enough beforehand by the fact of Cowperwood's failure that this publicity was to come; but for all this he was not prepared. He had been running all week in an agonized way to Mollenhauer, Strobik,

Jacob Borchardt, and others, listening helplessly to every suggestion as to how best he should evade the consequences of his deeds; but he had no resource within himself. His own mind did not tell him what to do. His so-called conscience—which was what others thought, or what they pretended they were thinking—seared him like a white flame. Like Cowperwood's father, only much faster, he was rapidly getting thin. A new suit of brown clothes that ten days before fitted him perfectly now hung on him loosely. His big stomach was steadily lessening in girth.

"Oh!" he groaned. "Oh!" and the force of the sigh affected his whole frame. It was like the crinkling effect of a rapidly deflating gas-bag.

"Why, George," asked his wife, coming in—she was a small, homely, hard-worked woman, whose pinching labor of former years had removed nearly all traces of feminine charm—"what's the matter? What's happened?"

"Nothing," he sighed, wearily, when he could get his breath; but she knew better. She knew well enough why he was scanning the papers every day so closely. The Chicago fire, Cowperwood's failure, their united investments had been no secret to her. She had heard Stener expatiate too fulsomely in times past concerning his prospects, Cowperwood's, those of Strobik, Wycroft, and Harmon. Cowperwood's skill, their joint investments, their future prospects—all had been discussed; and now she knew well enough that disaster was near. She did not know that her inefficient husband could actually be sent to the penitentiary; only that his prosperity was all over. In the agonized expression of his face she read all the horrors of debasement and difficulty with which he invested the future. Their property was to be swept away; their children reduced to penury. Like every dependent woman of this class, usually far more resourceful than her lord and master, she tried to help him think. She was not versed in finance, however. She knew nothing of politics or stock-jobbing. All she could reason from was data which Stener gave her, and he did not know. Worst of all, she now realized in a rather clear way that he did not know—that he was an implement—a tool in the hands of other people.

If life presents a more painful spectacle than this, one would like to know it. The damnable scheme of things which we call existence brings about conditions whereby whole masses suffer who have no cause to suffer, and, on the other hand, whole masses joy who have no cause to joy. It rains on the just and the unjust impartially. We suffer for our temperaments, which we did not make, and for our weaknesses and lacks, which are no part of our willing or doing. Who by taking thought can add one cubit to his stature? Who can make his brain better? His thoughts swifter? His courage greater? Who is it that can do anything it was not given him to do? All good things are gifts. There are no *creations* of the mind alone. Creations, achievements, distinguished results always sink back into so many other things. They have their roots in inherited ability, in environment, in fortune, in a lucky star. There is no possible contradiction of this. It is so. So was it ever. So will it be from everlasting to everlasting.

The little woman, watching her husband this morning, experienced a sinking of heart at the evidence of his weakness.

"Is there something in the paper?" she asked, coming over—suspecting—really knowing full well that there was.

"No," he said. "Yes, there is, too—a little mention." She picked it up and read the long, solemn rigmarole concerning the state of her husband's office, which had been issued by the Citizens' Municipal Reform Association. An expert was going over his books. There was as much as five hundred thousand dollars missing. She had not known that.

"Is it as much as five hundred thousand dollars?" she paused to ask.

"I think so," he admitted, weakly. "I'm not quite sure yet. It may be less."

"And can't you get any of it back from him? He must have money." She was referring to Cowperwood.

"I don't think so," replied Stener, weakly. "I don't know. He led me into this." There followed then that weighing of resources by her which women in these circumstances almost always undertake. She made a dozen earnest suggestions in regard to Mollenhauer, Simpson, Cowperwood, and Strobik; but, alas! it was merely conversation. Stener had tried all these. There was no loophole for him. He was not considered. Because of his temperament, his inability to reason, he had been marked for a victim, and no one proposed to assist him to evade that rôle. He was the one who was going to be punished, unless the powers above him willed that it was not necessary. It all depended on that. His wife went out of the room after a time; but it was only to go into another bedroom and stare out of a window onto the faded grass of the fall. What was to become of her and her husband? She always thought of him and herself and children as a collective unit. There were four children, all told, fortunately well grown now. They would be very poor again, and, worst of all, disgraced. That was what hurt her. She stared and twisted her bony little hands. Her eyes did not moisten, but an ineffable sadness filled them. Sometimes the mediocre and the inefficient attain to a classic stature when dignified by pain.

CHAPTER XLIV

THE peculiarity and wonder of this situation, which has been indicated rather swiftly on its technical, financial, and legal sides, was its related human or rather affectional and social ramifications—in the two Cowperwood households, in the Butler household, in the city administration—through Stener, in the financial and social sections—anywhere and everywhere in Philadelphia, in short, where the personality or the fame or the business relations of Frank A. Cowperwood personally, or Frank A. Cowperwood & Co., had had time to penetrate.

During all this time Aileen Butler was following the trend of his outward vicissitudes as heralded by the newspapers and the local gossip with as much interest and bias and enthusiasm for him, and all that related to him, as her powerful physical and affectional nature would permit. She was no great reasoner where affection entered in, but shrewd enough without it; and, although she saw him often and he told her much—as much as his natural caution would permit—she yet gathered from the newspapers and private conversation, at her own family's table and elsewhere, that, as bad as they said he was, he was not as bad as he might be. One item only, clipped from the Philadelphia *Public Ledger* of about this time, a little while after Cowperwood had been publicly accused of embezzlement, comforted and consoled her. She cut it out and carried it in her bosom; for, somehow, it seemed to show that her adored Frank was far more sinned against than sinning. It was a part of one of those very numerous pronunciamientos or reports issued

by the Citizens' Municipal Reform Association, which
was persistently probing into this affair, and it ran:

The aspects of the case are graver than have yet been allowed to
reach the public. Five hundred thousand dollars of the deficiency
arises not from city bonds sold and not accounted for, but from loans
made by the treasurer to his broker. The committee are also informed, on what they believe to be good authority, that the loans
sold by the broker were accounted for in the monthly settlements
at the lowest prices current during the month, and that the difference between this rate and that actually realized was divided
between the treasurer and the broker, thus making it the interest
of both parties to "bear" the market at some time during the month,
so as to obtain a low quotation for settlement. Nevertheless, the
committee can only regard the prosecution instituted against the
broker, Mr. Cowperwood, as an effort to divert public attention
from more guilty parties while those concerned may be able to
"fix" matters to suit themselves.

"There," thought Aileen, when she read it, "there
you have it." These politicians were trying to put the
blame of their own evil deeds on her Frank. He was not
nearly as bad as he was painted. The report said so.
She went over the lines where it said, "The committee can
only regard the prosecution instituted against the broker,
Mr. Cowperwood, as an effort to divert public attention
from more guilty parties while those concerned may be
able to 'fix' matters to suit themselves," with the most
loving care. She gloated over the words "an effort
to divert public attention from more guilty parties."
That was just what her Frank had been telling her in
those happy, private hours when they had been together
recently in one place and another, particularly the
new rendezvous in South Sixth Street which he had
established, since the old one had to be abandoned. He
had stroked her rich hair, caressed her body, and told her
it was all a prearranged political scheme to cast the
blame as much as possible on him and make it as light as
possible for Stener and the party generally. He would
come out of it all right, he said, but he cautioned her

carefully not to talk. He did not deny his long and profitable relations with Stener. He told her exactly how it was. She understood, or thought she did. Anyhow, her Frank was telling her, and that was enough.

In the Cowperwood household—the two Cowperwood households—things had been simmering to a deadly cold. The life was going out of them. Frank Algernon Cowperwood was that life. He was the courage and force of his father, the spirit and opportunity of his brothers, the hope of his children, the estate of his wife, the dignity and significance of the Cowperwood name. All that meant opportunity, force, emolument, dignity, and happiness to those connected with him, he was. And his marvelous sun was waning apparently to a black eclipse.

To begin with, there was the problem of Cowperwood's wife and his two children. Since the fatal morning when she had received that utterly destructive note, like a cannon-ball ripping through her domestic affairs, Lillian had been walking like one in a trance. Each day now for weeks she had been going about her duties placidly enough to all outward seeming, but inwardly she was running with a troubled tide of thought. She was so utterly unhappy. Her fortieth year had come for her, and here she was just passing into the time when a woman ceases to be interesting to men, devoted to her children, feeling innately that life ought naturally to remain grounded on a fixed and solid base, and yet torn bodily from the domestic soil in which she was growing and blooming, and thrown out indifferently in the blistering noonday sun of circumstance to wither. You have seen fish caught ruthlessly in a net and cast indifferently on a sandy shore to die. They have no value save to those sea-feeding buzzards which sit on the shores of some coasts and wait for such food. It is a pitiable spectacle—a gruesome one; but it is life. That is exactly

the way life works. She saw in this turmoil of hurry and
work and conference and talk that her husband's affairs
were in a deadly state of collapse. The newspapers were
full of the news of the panic and the fire. After a few days
they were full of the failure or suspension of Frank Algernon Cowperwood, and of his connection with the city
treasury. Yet a few days more and the reports of the
Citizens' Municipal Reform Association began to appear
in the papers. These openly and lucidly indicated Frank
Algernon Cowperwood and the city treasurer as con-
spiring to defraud the city, though later this very committee raised the question whether Cowperwood was not
more sinned against than sinning. She had seen the same
item that Aileen was carrying about with her. It was a
many-sided problem. Few people saw but more than an
angle or a facet of it all. Harper Steger, Cowperwood's
lawyer, was actually convinced that Cowperwood had
a human, if not a moral right to attempt to save himself as he had; and he proposed, if Mollenhauer and the
others attempted to shoulder the blame onto Cowperwood, and make a legal scapegoat of him, to burn them
up argumentatively before a jury. (He could do it, too,
for he had a bitter, incisive, argumentative capacity.)
But to Cowperwood's wife the situation was like a ghastly
maze in which she wandered as one walking in her sleep.

Cowperwood senior's situation at his bank and elsewhere was rapidly nearing a climax. As has been said,
he had tremendous faith in his son and loyalty to him; but
he could not help seeing that an error had been committed,
as he thought, and that Frank was suffering greatly for it
now. He considered, of course, that Frank had been entitled to try to save himself as he had; but he so regretted
that his son should have put his foot into the trap of any
situation which could stir up discussion of the sort that was
now being aroused. Frank was wonderfully brilliant. He
need never have taken up with the city treasurer or the
politicians to have succeeded marvelously. Local street-

railways and speculative politicians were his undoing. Nevertheless, it was all over now—the possibility of rectifying it. The milk was spilled. The old man walked the floor all of the days, realizing that his sun was setting, that with Frank's failure he failed, and that this disgrace— these public charges—meant his own undoing. His hair was very gray, his step slow, his face pallid, his eyes sunken. His rather showy side-whiskers looked tremendously out of place now. They seemed like flags or ornaments of a better day that was gone. His only consolation in it all was that Frank had actually got out of his relationship with the Third National Bank without owing it a single dollar. Still the directors of that institution realized that Frank had merely cleared up everything here in order to save his father. He would not have done so if his father had not been there. Anyhow, the bank could not possibly tolerate the presence of a man whose son had helped loot the city treasury, and whose name was now in the public prints in this connection. Besides, Cowperwood, Sr., was too old. He ought to retire.

The crisis came for him when Frank was arrested on the embezzlement charge. The directors wanted Cowperwood, Sr., to have sense enough and courtesy enough to take the initiative and resign at once. There was absolutely no hope of his remaining. Adam Davi, the first vice-president, realized it. There was a semi-concealed light of triumph in his eyes on the day the arrest happened. Cowperwood, Sr., realized that his hour had struck. He saw it all suggested in their faces. He hardly had the courage to go to the bank. It was like struggling under the weight of a heavy stone to do it. Still he went; but he wrote his resignation the next morning, after a sleepless night, to Frewen Kasson, the chairman of the board of directors. Nothing had been said to him. He wrote Mr. Kasson to come in, if it were possible, on this morning, and then he told him in a vague, nervous way that he realized that this failure of his son had done the bank—owing to his connection with it—great injury.

"I know," he said, strumming with his thin, white, bony fingers on his handsome mahogany desk, which would soon be his no longer, "that my connection with the bank now is a serious handicap to it."

Frewen Kasson, a short, stocky, well-built, magnetic, attractive man of fifty, breathed an inward sigh of relief. It was so urgent that Cowperwood, Sr., should do this. "I have been with it now nearly thirty-eight years," Henry Cowperwood continued; but at the thought of the long, long years, which had really been his life, spent with this one institution, his voice failed him, and he got up and went to the widow. A suspicious stiffening of the shoulders told Mr. Kasson that he was undergoing a great inward struggle, and the latter felt sorry for him. He came back after a time, however, and sat down.

"It's hard; it's hard," he said, suddenly rubbing his hands weakly; and he got up again, unable to speak.

Mr. Kasson choked slightly.

"I know it is, Mr. Cowperwood," he said, sympathetically. "I wish you wouldn't try to talk now. I know exactly what you would wish to say. We—and I can speak for the other members of the board, for although we haven't talked about it as yet, I know how they feel—we feel keenly the unfortunate nature of your position. We know exactly how it is that your son has become involved in this matter. He is not the only banker who has been involved in the city's affairs. It is an old system. We appreciate, all of us, keenly, the services you have rendered this institution. They have been notable and unbroken. If there were any possible way in which we could help to tide you over your difficulties at this time, we would be glad to do so; but as a banker yourself you realize just how difficult this is just now. Everything is in a turmoil. If things were settled—if we knew how soon this would blow over—" He paused, for he felt that he could not go on and say that he or the bank was sorry to be forced to lose Mr. Cowperwood in this way at present. Mr. Cowperwood himself would have to speak.

Cowperwood, Sr., had been doing his best to pull himself together. He had gotten out a large white linen handkerchief and blown his nose, and he had straightened himself in his chair, and laid his hands rather peacefully on his desk. Still he was intensely wrought up. He didn't attempt to speak any more. Instead, he fished in his right coat pocket for his very hardly concocted letter of resignation, which was nicely enveloped and addressed, and handed it over to Mr. Kasson.

"I can't stand this!" he suddenly exclaimed. "I wish you would leave me alone now."

Mr. Kasson, very carefully dressed and manicured, arose and walked out of the room for a few moments. The moment the door was closed Cowperwood put his head in his hands and shook and shook convulsively. "I never thought I'd come to this," he said. "I never thought it." Then he wiped away his salty hot tears, and went to the window once more to recover. It was a terrible day and a terrible siege for him.

CHAPTER XLV

IT was with this general atmosphere prevailing that the
time was drifting toward that uncertain December
5, 1871, the day set apart on the court docket for Cowperwood's trial. Aileen had been periodically bringing
him news concerning the attitude of her father, which
made it perfectly clear that Butler was not through with
him, and would not be, in all likelihood, unless he chose
to leave Philadelphia permanently, or unless Butler
should die. The election being over and Stener and
Cowperwood properly indicted, and Butler's young protégé, Dennis Shannon, elected to the office of district attorney (in which direction it was plain to Cowperwood
that great injury might be done him), the old man was determined to find some additional thing which would further
his campaign against the young banker and result in
eliminating him from the city and the life of Aileen entirely. One thing that occurred to him was the fact that
the particular Judge Payderson to whose court Cowperwood's case had been assigned was one of those judges
who owed his position to the influence of the politicians.
Payderson should be given an opportunity to learn that
Cowperwood was deserving of punishment. Beyond
Payderson lay the State Supreme Court and the governor, where Butler's word, or the fact that he had been
injured by Cowperwood, would be of great weight. He
need not speak directly—but there were plenty who
would talk for him.

The plan of buying out some of Cowperwood's creditors—particularly those who held street-railway stocks—
had remained in Butler's mind and finally been acted

upon. Cowperwood had been offering only fifty cents on the dollar in notes at one, two, and three years (and that by the courtesy of some of his financial friends who proposed to assist him to take them up at maturity), but the creditors would not accept it. Butler was ready to offer them cash, and more than fifty cents, when necessary, which would give him a voice in the matter of Cowperwood's resumption; for, as every business man knows, no business can be resumed without the full consent of all creditors. In order that Cowperwood might not know at the time that these holdings were transferred, Butler had them taken over by a small bank in which he was secretly interested and carried on its books as belonging to it. Butler then had the feeling that, if Cowperwood wished to resume, he would have to pay dollar for dollar for the stock—which was considerable—or remain a bankrupt.

In addition Butler was planning some move in his own home which, without causing him to tell his wife what the trouble was, would bring about the elimination of Aileen from the situation, locally speaking. As time went on he grew more and more puzzled and restive as to his duty in regard to her. He was sure by her furtive manner, her lack of frankness, and apparent desire to avoid him, that she was still in touch with Cowperwood in some way, and that this would bring about a social disaster of some kind. He thought once of going to Mrs. Cowperwood and having her bring pressure to bear on her husband; but he decided that would not do. He was not really positive as yet that Aileen was secretly having to do with Cowperwood; and, besides, Mrs. Cowperwood might not know of her husband's duplicity. He thought also of going to Cowperwood personally and threatening him; but that would be a severe measure, and again, as in the other case, he lacked proof. He hesitated to appeal to a public detective agency on account of Aileen, and he did not care to take the other members of the family into his confidence. He did go out and scan the neighborhood of 931 North Tenth Street once, looking at the house; but that helped him little. Cowperwood had already abandoned his connection with that, and the place was for rent. Butler finally hit upon the plan of having Aileen invited to go somewhere some distance off —Boston or New Orleans, where a sister of his wife lived. It was a delicate matter to engineer, and in such matters he was not exactly the soul of tact; but he undertook it. He wrote once personally to his wife's sister at New Orleans, and asked her if she would not, without indicating in any way that she had heard from him, write his wife and ask if she would not permit Aileen to come and visit her, writing Aileen an invitation at the same time; but he tore the letter up. A little later he learned accidentally that Mrs. Mollenhauer and her three daughters, Caroline, Felicia, and Alta, were going to Europe early in December to visit Paris, the Riviera, and Rome; and he decided to ask Mollenhauer if he would persuade his wife to invite Norah and Aileen, or Aileen only, to go along, giving as an excuse that his own wife would not leave him, and that the girls ought to go. It would be a fine way of disposing of Aileen for the present. The party was to be gone six months. Mollenhauer was glad to do so, of course. The two families were fairly intimate. Mrs. Mollenhauer was willing—delighted from a politic point of view—and the invitation was extended. Norah was overjoyed. She wanted to see something of Europe, and had always been hoping for some such opportunity. She was not particularly interested in any one place abroad, but everything over-sea must be fine. Aileen was pleased from one point of view that Mrs. Mollenhauer should invite her; years before she would have accepted in a flash. But now she felt that it only came as a puzzling interruption, one more of the minor difficulties that were tending to interrupt her relations with Cowperwood. She immediately threw cold water on the proposition, which was made one evening at dinner by Mrs. Butler, who did not know of her husband's share in the matter, but had received a call that afternoon from Mrs. Mollenhauer, when the invitation had been extended.

"She's very anxious to have you two come along, if your father don't mind," volunteered the mother, "and I should think ye'd have a fine time. They're going to Paris and the Riveera." (This was Mrs. Butler's pronunciation of the Riviera.)

"Oh, fine!" exclaimed Norah. "I've always wanted to go to Paris. Haven't you, Ai? Oh, wouldn't that be fine?"

"I don't know that I want to go," replied Aileen, subtly, who saw in this merely another untoward slap of fate, a trick. She did not care to compromise herself by showing any interest at the start. "It's coming on winter, and I haven't any clothes. I'd rather wait and go some other time."

"Oh, Aileen Butler!" exclaimed Norah. "How you talk! I've heard you say a dozen times you'd like to go abroad some winter. Now when the chance comes—besides you can get your clothes made over there."

"Couldn't you get somethin' over there?" inquired Mrs. Butler. "Besides, you've got two or three weeks here yet."

"They wouldn't want a man around as a sort of a guide and advisor, would they, mother?" put in Callum, attempting to pick a chicken wing with his knife and fork. He was interested in Alta Mollenhauer. He smiled a quizzical smile.

"I might offer my services in that capacity myself," observed Owen, reservedly.

"I'm sure I don't know," returned Mrs. Butler, smilingly, chewing a lusty mouthful. "You'll have to ast them, my sons."

Aileen still persisted. She did not want to go. It

was too sudden. It was this. It was that. Just then old Butler came in and took his seat at the head of the table. Knowing all about it, he was most anxious to appear not to.

"You wouldn't object, Edward, would you?" queried his wife, explaining the proposition in general.

"Object!" he echoed, with a well simulated but rough attempt at gaiety. "A fine thing I'd be doing for me-self—objectin'. I'd be glad if I could get shut of the whole pack of ye for the time."

"What talk ye have!" said his wife. "A fine mess you'd make of it, livin' alone."

"I'd not be alone, belave me," replied Butler, stolidly. "There's many a place I'd be welcome in this town—no thanks to ye."

"And there's many a place ye wouldn't have been if it hadn't been for me. I'm tellin' ye that," retorted Mrs. Butler, genially.

"And that's not stretchin' the troot much, aither," he answered, fondly.

Aileen was not interested in this by-play. She wanted to escape any discussion of a European trip now, and the subsequent observations and arguments on this matter, both on the part of Norah and her mother, had no effect whatever. She was adamant. Butler witnessed the failure of his plan with considerable dissatisfaction; but he was not through. He wanted Aileen to go, and he was determined to make her—go somewhere, anyhow. He thought once of speaking to her about the matter—using strong words—but he realized that he had not sufficient evidence to go on. The mere receipt of the letter with which he had confronted her was not enough. She had denied that. The possibility of watching the house at 931 North Tenth Street was gone—had been the moment he had shown her the letter. He should have watched that first, he thought, and confirmed the letter. He decided after a while to employ a detective; but this was not until all hope of persuading Aileen to accept the Mollenhauer proposition had been abandoned. When that was gone and Aileen was still going to and fro in Philadelphia as careless and nonchalant as before, he became determined. She pretended to be visiting her friends, many of whom she did visit—social personages whom she had met through Cowperwood, and girls who had gone to school with her; but Butler was suspicious. She rode, drove, and visited the libraries and the shops alone or with her mother; but he was haunted with the idea that she might be with Cowperwood. Neither he nor his sons, if he had been inclined to take them into the secret, which he was not, could watch her very well, he thought. Her movements were too complicated. It had to be some outside agency; and he wondered which or what it would be.

At that time, owing to his career in connection with the Civil War and Abraham Lincoln, the reputation of William A. Pinkerton, of detective fame, and of his agency was great. The man had come up from poverty through a series of vicissitudes to a high standing in his peculiar and, to many, distasteful profession; but to any one in need of such in themselves calamitous services, his very famous and decidedly patriotic connection with the Civil War and Abraham Lincoln was a recommendation. He, or rather his service, had guarded the latter all during his stormy incumbency at the executive mansion. There were offices for the management of the company's business in Philadelphia, Washington, and New York, to say nothing of other places. Butler was familiar with the Philadelphia sign, but did not care to go to the office there. It was too local, too conspicuous. He decided, once his mind was made up on this score, that he would go over to New York, where he was told the principal offices were located.

He made the simple excuse one day of business, which was common enough in his case, and journeyed to New

York—nearly five hours away as the trains ran then—
arriving at two o'clock. With much caution of manner
and clearness of mind he found the principal offices, which
were in lower Broadway, and asked to see the manager.
The latter he found to be a large, gross-featured, heavy-
bodied man of fifty, gray-eyed, gray-haired, puffily outlined as to countenance, but keen and shrewd, and with
short, fat-fingered hands, which drummed idly on his
desk as he talked. He was dressed in a suit of dark-
brown wool cloth, which struck Butler as peculiarly showy,
and wore a large horseshoe diamond pin. The old man
himself invariably wore conservative gray.

"How do you do?" said Butler, when a boy ushered
him into the presence of this worthy, whose name was
Martinson—Gilbert Martinson, of American and Irish extraction. The latter nodded and looked at Butler shrewdly,
recognizing him at once as a man of force and probably
of position. He therefore rose and offered him a chair.

"Sit down," he said to Butler, studying the old Irishman from under thick, bushy eyebrows. "What can I
do for you?"

"You're the manager, are you?" asked Butler, solemnly, eying the man with a shrewd, inquiring eye.

"Yes, sir," replied Martinson, simply. "That's my
position here."

"This Mr. Pinkerton that runs this agency—he wouldn't
be about this place, now, would he?" asked Butler, carefully. "I'd like to talk to him personally, if I might,
meaning no offense to you."

"Mr. Pinkerton is in Chicago at present," replied Mr.
Martinson. "I don't expect him back for a week or ten
days. You can talk to me, though, with the same confidence that you could to him. I'm the responsible head
here. However, you're the best judge of that."

Butler debated with himself in silence for a few moments, estimating the man before him. "Are you a
family man yourself?" he finally asked, oddly.

"Yes, sir, I'm married," replied Mr. Martinson, solemnly. "I have a wife and two children."

Butler blinked his eyes; and Martinson, from long experience, conceived by this that it must be some matter of family misconduct—a son, daughter, wife—which had brought Butler here. Such cases as that were not infrequent.

"I thought I would like to talk to Mr. Pinkerton himself, but if you're the responsible head—" Butler paused and looked at Mr. Martinson again.

"I am," replied the latter. "You can talk to me with the same freedom that you could to Mr. Pinkerton. Won't you come into my private office? We can talk more at ease in there."

He led the way into an adjoining room which had two windows looking down into Broadway; an oblong table, heavy, brown, smoothly polished; four leather-backed chairs; and some pictures of the Civil War battles, in which the North had been victorious. Butler followed doubtfully. He hated very much to take any one into his confidence in regard to Aileen. He was not sure that he would, even at present. He wanted to "look these fellys over," as he said in his mind. He would decide then what he wanted to do. He went to one of the windows and looked down into the street, where there was a perfect swirl of omnibuses and vehicles of all sorts. Mr. Martinson quietly closed the door.

"Now then, if there's anything I can do for you, Mr.—" Martinson paused. He thought by this little trick to elicit Butler's real name—it often "worked"—but in this instance the name was not forthcoming. Butler was too shrewd.

"I'm not so sure that I want to go into this," said the old man, solemnly. "Certainly not if there's any risk of the thing not being handled in the right way. There's somethin' I want to find out about—somethin' that I ought to know; but it's a very private matter with me, and—" He paused to think and conjecture, looking at Mr. Martinson the while. The latter understood his peculiar state of mind. He had seen many such cases.

"Let me say right here, to begin with, Mr.—"

"Scanlon," interpolated Butler, easily; "that's as good a name as any if you want to use one. I'm keepin' me own to meself for the present."

"Scanlon," continued Martinson, easily. "I really don't care whether this is your right name or not. I was just going to say that it might not be necessary to have your right name under any circumstance—it all depends upon what you want to know. But, so far as your private affairs are concerned, they are as safe with us, this agency, as if you had never told them to any one. Our business is built upon confidence, and we never betray it. We wouldn't dare. We have men and women who have been in our employ for over thirty years, and we never retire any one except for cause, and we don't pick people who are likely to need to be retired for cause. Mr. Pinkerton is a good judge of men. There are others here who consider that they are. We handle over ten thousand separate cases in all parts of the United States every year. We work on a case only so long as we are wanted. We seek to find out only such things as our customers want. We do not pry unnecessarily into any-body's affairs. When we think we have found out what you want, or decide that we cannot find out for you, we are the first to say so. Many cases are rejected right here in this office before we ever begin. Yours might be such a one. We don't want cases merely for the sake of having them, and we are frank to say so. Some matters that involve public policy, or some form of small per-secution, we don't touch at all—we won't be a party to them. You can see how that is. You look to me to be a man of the world. I hope I am one. Does it strike you that an organization that has attained to the stand-ing that we have would be in the business of betraying any one's confidence?" He paused and looked at Butler for confirmation of what he had just said.

"It wouldn't seem likely," said the latter; "that's the truth. It's not aisy to bring your private affairs into the light of day, though," added the old man, sadly.

They both rested.

"Well," said Butler, finally, "you look to me to be all right, and I'd like some advice. Mind ye, I'm willing to pay for it well enough; and it isn't anything that 'll be very hard to find out. I want to know whether a certain man where I live is goin' with a certain woman, and where. You could find that out aisy enough, I be-lave—couldn't you?"

"Nothing easier," replied Mr. Martinson. "We are doing it all the time. We simply appoint some man or woman, or some men or women, whom we trust to watch the houses, stores, offices, and places of amusement of those whom we wish to find out about. It doesn't take long, as a rule. You might do it yourself, if you had people whom you could trust."

"That's just the point," said Butler. "It's the matter of trusting them. I have the people—plenty of them— and they'd be glad enough to do my word; but I don't trust them in this case. I'd rather trust outsiders if I could. I've heard of your people before."

Mr. Martinson nodded his head sagely. "Let me see if I can help you just a moment, Mr. Scanlon, in order to make it easier for you. It is very plain to me that you don't care to tell any more than you can help, and we don't care to have you tell any more than we absolutely need to assist us to do what you want. We will have to have the name of the city, of course, and the name of either the man or the woman; but not necessarily both of them, unless you want to help us in that way. Some-times if you give us the name of one party—say the man, for illustration—and the description of the woman— an accurate one—or a photograph, we can tell you after a little while exactly what you want to know. Of course, it's always better if we have full information. You suit yourself about that. Tell me as much or as little as you please, and I'll guarantee that we will do our best to serve you, and that you will be satisfied afterward. You tell me now or not, just as you choose. It's all the same to us."

He smiled genially.

Butler felt, all things considered, that he was in the hands of a rather fair man. Like most men of affairs, Cowperwood included, he was mistrustful of people in general, looking on them as aimless forces rather than as self-regulating bodies, though he was nevertheless religious-minded. Nothing save the will of God could save anybody in the long run, Butler thought; but you were in duty bound to help God by helping yourself. Such was his philosophy. The devil represented all untoward forces within and without ourselves which made people— weak elements—do the strange things they did. He could not have explained life any better than that; but in a rough way he felt that he was serving God when he did his best to punish Cowperwood and save Aileen.

"Well, that bein' the case," said Butler, finally taking the leap, with many mental reservations, however, "I'll be plain with you. My name's not Scanlon. It's Butler. I live in Philadelphy. There's a man there, a banker by the name of Cowperwood—Frank A. Cowperwood—"

"Wait a moment," said Martinson, drawing an ample pad out of his pocket and producing a lead-pencil; "I want to get that. How do you spell it?"

Butler told him.

"Yes; now go on."

"He has a place in Third Street—Frank A. Cowperwood—any one can show you where it is. He's just failed there recently."

"Oh, that's the man," interpolated Martinson. "I've

heard of him. He's mixed up in some city embezzlement
case over there. I suppose the reason you didn't go to
our Philadelphia office is because you didn't want our
local men over there to know anything about it. Isn't
that it?"

"That's the man, and that's the reason," said Butler,
answering both questions at once. "I don't care to have
anything of this known in Philadelphy. That's why I'm
here. This man has a house on Girard Avenue—Nineteen-
thirty-seven. You can find that out, too, when you get
over there."

"Yes," agreed Mr. Martinson.

"Well, it's him that I want to know about—him—and
a certain woman, or girl, rather." The old man paused
and winced at this necessity of introducing Aileen into
the case. He could scarcely think of it—he was so fond
of her. He had been so proud of Aileen. A dark, smoldering rage burned in his heart against Cowperwood.
To think he should have given him so much trouble and
so much shame!

"A relative of yours—possibly, I suppose," remarked
Martinson, tactfully. "You needn't tell me any more—
just give me a description if you wish. We may be able
to work from that." He saw quite clearly what a fine
old citizen in his way he was dealing with here, and also
that the man was greatly troubled. Butler's heavy,
meditative face showed it. "You can be quite frank with
me, Mr. Butler," he added; "I think I understand. We
only want such information as we must have to help you,
nothing more."

"Yes," said the old man, dourly. "She is a relative.
She's my daughter, in fact. You look to me like a sinsible,
honest man. I'm her father, and I wouldn't do anything
for the world to harm her. It's tryin' to save her I am.
It's him I want." He suddenly closed one big fist forcefully.

Mr. Martinson, who had two daughters of his own,

observed the suggestive movement. It told more plainly than anything Butler could say how keenly the old man was feeling, and he sympathized with him. Butler's emotion came across to him like a breath of cold air. He must love this daughter very much. But it looked bad for Cowperwood, Martinson thought, if it should turn out that he was running with this man's daughter. It was a bad move on Cowperwood's part. He was rather sorry for him. Still, business was business.

"I understand how you feel, Mr. Butler," he observed. "I am a father myself. We'll do all we can for you. If you can give me an accurate description of her, or let one of my men see her at your house or office, accidentally, of course, I think we can tell you in no time at all if they are meeting with any regularity. That's all you want to know, is it—just that?"

"That's all," said Butler, solemnly.

"Well, that oughtn't to take any time at all, Mr. Butler —three or four days possibly, if we have any luck—a week, ten days, two weeks. It depends on how long you want us to shadow him in case there is no evidence the first few days."

"I want to know, however long it takes," replied Butler, bitterly. "I want to know, if it takes a month or two months or three to find out. I want to know." The old man got up as he said this, very positive, very rugged. Mr. Martinson was quite astonished at the force and vigor of him. "And don't send me men that haven't sinse—lots of it, plase. I want men that are fathers, if you've got 'em—and that have sinse enough to hold their tongues—not b'ys." He fairly glared at Martinson, making the latter feel the significance of all this to him.

Martinson nodded.

"I understand, Mr. Butler," he replied. "Depend on it, you'll have the best we have, and you can trust them. They'll be discreet. You can depend on that. The way I'll do will be to assign just one man to the case at first, some one whom you can see for yourself whether you like or not. I'll not tell him anything. You can talk to him. If you like him, tell him, and he'll do the rest. Then, if he needs any more help, he can get it. What is your address?"

Butler gave it to him.

"And there'll be no talk about this?"

"None whatever—I assure you."

"And when 'll he be comin' along?"

"To-morrow, if you wish. I have a man whom I could send to-night. He isn't here now or I'd have him talk with you. I'll talk to him, though, and make everything clear. You needn't worry about anything. Your daughter's reputation will be safe in his hands."

"Thank you kindly," commented Butler, softening the least bit in a gingerly way. "I'm much obliged to you. I'll take it as a great favor, and pay you well."

"Never mind about that, Mr. Butler," replied Martinson. "You're welcome to anything this concern can do for you at its ordinary rates."

He showed Butler to the door, and the old man went out. He was feeling very depressed over this—very shabby. To think he should have to put detectives on the track of his Aileen, his daughter! Still, he thought, he would know positively if what she said were untrue or not; and that would help him to adjust matters with her finally. He could not think of reforming her really unless he knew, and now he would know.

He returned to Philadelphia at once.

CHAPTER XLVI

THE business of establishing Aileen's relationship to Cowperwood was quickly undertaken and completed. The very next day there called at Butler's office from New York a long, lean, preternaturally solemn man of noticeable height and angularity, dark-haired, dark-eyed, sallow, with a face that was long and leathery, and particularly hawk-like, who talked with Butler for over an hour and then departed. That evening he came to the Butler house around dinner-time, and, being shown into Butler's room, was given a look at Aileen by a ruse. Butler sent for her while he was in there. Aileen came quickly. As it was planned between the detective and Butler, the latter stood in the door just far enough to one side to prevent Aileen from coming in, but, nevertheless, to yield a good view of her. The detective stood behind one of the heavy curtains which had already been put up for the winter, pretending to look out into the street. As a matter of fact, he was watching the door between the folds which almost concealed him.

"Did any one drive Sissy this mornin'?" asked Butler of Aileen, inquiring after a favorite family horse. Butler's plan, in case the detective was seen, was to give the impression that he was a horseman who had come either to buy or to sell. His name was Jonas Alderson, and he looked sufficiently like a horse-trader to be one.

"I don't think so, father," replied Aileen. "I didn't. I'll find out."

"Never mind. What I want to know is did you intend using her to-morrow?"

"No, not if you want her. Jerry suits me just as well."
She was referring to another horse.

"Very well, then. Leave her in the stable." Butler
quietly closed the door. Aileen concluded at once that
it was a horse conference. She knew he would not dispose of any horse in which she was interested without
first consulting her, and so she thought no more about it.

After she was gone Alderson stepped out and declared
that he was satisfied. "That's all I need to know," he
said. "I'll let you know in a few days if I find out anything."

He departed, and within thirty-six hours the house and
office of Cowperwood, the house of Butler, the office of
Harper Steger, Cowperwood's lawyer, and Cowperwood
and Aileen separately and personally were under complete surveillance. It took six men to do it at first, and
eventually a seventh, when the second meeting-place,
which was located in South Sixth Street, was discovered.
All the detectives were from New York. The personalities of Aileen and Cowperwood were pointed out
to each detective as Alderson introduced him to the case,
and then the watch was taken up. In a week all was
known to Alderson. It had been agreed between him
and Butler that if Aileen and Cowperwood were discovered to have any particular rendezvous Butler was
to be notified some time when she was there, so that he
could go immediately and confront her in person, if he
wished. He did not intend to kill Cowperwood—and
Alderson would have seen to it that this should not be
allowed; but he would give him a good tongue-lashing,
fell him to the floor, in all likelihood, and march Aileen
away. There would be no more lying on her part as
to whether she was or was not going with Cowperwood.
She would not be able to say after that what she would
or would not do. Her father would lay down the law to
her. She would reform, or he would send her to a reformatory. Think of her effect on her sister, or on any

good girl—knowing what she knew, or doing what she was doing! She would go to Europe after this, or any place he chose to send her.

In working out this plan of action the detective in charge made plain his determination to safeguard Cowperwood's person. It was one of the rules of the agency that no violence must be permitted in any case of this kind with which they were connected. Evidence, yes; but no violence.

"We couldn't allow you to strike any blows or do any violence," Alderson told Butler, when they first talked about it. "It's against the rules. You can go in there on a search-warrant, if we have to have one. I can get that for you without anybody's knowing anything about your connection with the case. We can say it's for a girl from New York. But you'll have to go in in the presence of my men. They won't permit any trouble. You can get your daughter all right—we'll bring her away, and him, too, if you say so; but you'll have to make some charge against him, if we do. Then there's the danger of the neighbors seeing. You can't always guarantee you won't collect a crowd that way." Butler had many misgivings about the matter. It was fraught with great danger of publicity. Still he wanted to know. He wanted to terrify Aileen if he could—to reform her drastically.

Within a week Alderson learned that Aileen and Cowperwood were visiting an apparently private residence, which was anything but that. The house in South Sixth Street was one of assignation purely; but in its way it was superior to the average institution of this kind. It was of a high order of refinement, if the latter word may be permitted in this connection—of red brick, white-stone trimmings, four stories high, and all the rooms, some eighteen in number, furnished in a showy but cleanly way. It was not an institution of general but rather of a highly exclusive patronage, only those being admitted who were known to the mistress, having been introduced by others. This guaranteed that privacy which the illicit affairs of this world so greatly require. The mere phrase, "I have an appointment," was sufficient, where either of the parties was known, to cause them to be shown to an exclusive suite of rooms, where they could await the completion of their rendezvous at leisure. Cowperwood had known of the place from previous experiences, and when it became necessary to close the place on North Tenth Street he had directed Aileen to meet him here.

The matter of entering a place of this kind and trying to find any one was, as Alderson informed Butler on hearing of its character, a treacherous matter. It involved the right of search, which was difficult to get. To enter by sheer force was easy enough in most instances where the business conducted was in contradistinction to the moral sentiment of the community; but sometimes one encountered violent opposition from the tenants themselves. It might be so in this case. The only sure way of avoiding such opposition would be to take the woman who ran the place into one's confidence, and by paying her sufficiently insure silence. "But I do not advise that in this instance," Alderson had told Butler, "for I believe this woman is particularly friendly to your man. It might be better, in spite of the risk, to take it by surprise." To do that, he explained, it would be necessary to have at least three men in addition to the leader—perhaps four, who, once one man had been able to make his entrance into the hallway, on the door being opened in response to a ring, would appear quickly and enter with and sustain him. Quickness of search was the next thing—the prompt opening of all doors. The help would have to be overpowered and silenced in some way. Money sometimes did this; force accomplished it at other times. Then one of the detectives simulating a servant could tap gently at the different doors— Butler and the others standing by—and in case a face

17   505

appeared identify it or not, as the case might be. If
the door was not opened and the room was not empty,
it would eventually be forced. The house was one of a
solid block, so that there was no chance of escape save
by the front and rear doors, which were to be safeguarded.
It was a daringly conceived scheme. In spite of all this,
secrecy in the matter of removing Aileen was to be attained.

When Butler heard of this he was nervous about the
whole terrible procedure. He thought once that without going to the house he would merely talk to his daughter, declaring that he knew and that she could not possibly deny it. He would then give her her choice between
going to Europe or going to a reformatory. A sense of
the raw brutality of Aileen's disposition, and something
essentially coarse in himself, made him adopt the other
method eventually. He told Mr. Alderson to perfect his
plan, and once he found Aileen or Cowperwood entering
the house to inform him quickly. He would then drive
there, and with the assistance of these men confront her.

It was a foolish scheme, a brutalizing thing to do,
both from the point of view of affection and any corrective theory he might have had. No good ever springs
from violence—none. But Butler did not see that. He
wanted to frighten Aileen, to bring her by shock to a
realization of the enormity of the thing she was doing.
He waited fully a week after his word had been given;
and then, one afternoon, when his nerves were worn
almost thin from fretting, the climax came. He sensed
a deadly contest with his daughter in case he tried to
carry through this scheme to its ultimate conclusion—
reformatory and all; but still he did not desist. He
really wanted to know definitely for himself.

It was one afternoon, about November 20th, when
Cowperwood was most busy with the many lawsuits and
other things that were troubling him, that Butler finally
took the contemplated action. Cowperwood had already

been indicted, and was now awaiting trial. Aileen had been bringing him news, from time to time, of just how she thought her father was feeling toward him. She did not get this evidence direct from Butler, of course—he was too secretive, in so far as she was concerned, to let her know how relentlessly he was engineering Cowperwood's final downfall—but from odd bits confided to Owen, who had confided them to Callum, who in turn, innocently enough, confided them to Aileen. She could see that her father was doing something—just what or how much she could not make out. It was irritating her greatly. For one thing, she had learned in this way of the new district attorney elect—his probable attitude—for he was a constant caller at the Butler house or office, and Owen had told Callum that he thought Shannon was going to do his best to send Cowperwood "up"—that the old man thought he deserved it. Aileen was already bitter against her father for this. She felt it was because of her relation with Cowperwood, and nothing more.

In the next place she learned that her father did not want Cowperwood to resume in business—did not feel he deserved to be allowed to. "It would be a God's blessing if the community were shut of him," he had said to Owen one morning, apropos of some notice in the papers of Cowperwood's legal struggles; and Owen had asked Callum why he thought the old man was so bitter. The two sons could not understand it. Callum had passed the query on to Aileen. She saw the point, of course. Cowperwood heard all this from her, and more—bits about Judge Payderson, the judge who was to try him, who was a friend of Butler's—also about the fact that Stener might be sent up for the full term of his crime, but that he would be pardoned out. Aileen could not learn that anything was to be done for Cowperwood, which enraged her, for she saw from what Cowperwood told her that there was a conspiracy on to "railroad" him, as a new term had it, or to make it just as hard for him as possible. Apparently Cowperwood was not very much frightened, for he told her that he had powerful financial friends who would appeal to the governor to pardon him in case he was convicted; and, anyhow, that he did not think that he could be convicted. The evidence was not strong enough. He was merely a political scapegoat through public clamor and her father's influence; since the latter's receipt of the letter about them he had been the victim of Butler's enmity, and nothing more. "If it weren't for your father, honey," he declared, "I could have this indictment quashed in no time. Neither Mollenhauer nor Simpson has anything against me personally, I am sure. They want me to get out of the street-railway business here in Philadelphia, and, of course, they wanted to make things look better for Stener at first; but depend upon it, if your father hadn't been against me they wouldn't have gone to any such length in making me the victim. Your father has this fellow Shannon and these minor politicians just where he wants them, too. That's where the trouble lies. They have to go on."

"Oh, I know," replied Aileen. "It's me, just me, that's all. If it weren't for me and what he suspects he'd help you in a minute. He wouldn't now any more, but he would have. Sometimes, you know, I think I've been very bad for you. I don't know what I ought to do. If I thought it would help you any I'd not see you any more for a while, though I don't see what good that would do now. Oh, I love you, love you, Frank! I would do anything for you. I don't care what people think or say. I love you."

"Oh, you just think you do, petty," he replied, jestingly. "You'll get over it. There are others. But there's no use crying over spilled milk. I don't see what's to be done about this right now."

"Others!" echoed Aileen, resentfully and contemptuously—she was foolish about this financial genius. "After you there aren't any others. They're all insipid. They won't do. I just want one man, my Frank. If you ever desert me, I'll go to hell. You'll see. You'll be the cause."

"Don't talk like that, Aileen," he replied, almost irritated. "I don't like to hear you. You wouldn't do anything of the sort. I love you. You know I'm not going to desert you. It would pay you to desert me just now."

"Oh, how you talk!" she exclaimed. "Desert you! It's likely, isn't it? But if ever you desert me, I'll do just what I say. I swear it."

"Don't talk like that. Don't talk nonsense."

"I swear it. I swear by my love. I swear by your success—my own happiness. I'll do just what I say. I'll go to hell."

Cowperwood got up. He was a little afraid now of this deep-seated passion he had aroused. It was dangerous. He could not tell where it would lead.

Following this conversation came the discovery of Aileen in the South Sixth Street house, which the employment of the detective agency foreshadowed. Butler was in his office on the afternoon named when Alderson, who had been informed of the presence of Aileen and Cowperwood by the detective on guard, drove rapidly up and invited Butler to come with him. The latter hurried down in a most perturbed state of mind. In spite of the letter and Aileen's guilty eyes, and her peculiarly antagonistic attitude toward the European trip, he could not believe that he was actually to find her. What would he say to her if he did? How reproach her? What would he do to Cowperwood? They drove rapidly to within a few doors of the place, and a second detective on guard across the street approached. Butler and Alderson descended from the vehicle, and together they approached the door. It was now almost four-thirty in the afternoon. In a room within the house, Cowperwood was listening to Aileen's account of her troubles. Certainly the situation was a pressing one, and it must be met.

"You know I get desperately frightened, sometimes," said Aileen, at one place in the conversation that was going on, referring to her father. "He might be watching us, you know. I've often wondered what I'd do if he did. I couldn't lie out of this, could I?"

"You certainly couldn't," said Cowperwood, who never failed to respond to the incitement of her charms. She had such lovely smooth arms, a full, luxuriously tapering throat and neck; her golden-red hair floated like an aureole about her head, and her large eyes sparkled. The wondrous vigor of a full womanhood was hers— errant, ill-balanced, romantic, but exquisite.

"You might as well not cross that bridge until you come to it," Cowperwood continued. "I myself have been thinking that we had better not go on with this for the present. That letter ought to have been enough to stop us for the time."

He came over to where she stood by the dressing-table, adjusting her hair.

"You're a pretty minx," he said. "Don't worry. There isn't anything going to happen here. He slipped his arm about her and kissed her pretty mouth. "Nothing sweeter than you this side of Paradise," he whispered in her ear.

While this was enacting, Butler and the extra detective had stepped out of sight, to one side of the front door of the house, while Alderson, taking the lead, rang. A negro servant appeared.

"Is Mrs. Davis in?" he asked, genially, using the name of the woman in control. "I'd like to see her."

"Just come in," said the maid, unsuspectingly, and indicated a reception-room on the right. Alderson took off his soft, wide-brimmed hat and entered it. When the maid went up-stairs he immediately returned to the door and let in Butler and the second detective, who was now accompanied by a third. The four stepped into the reception-room unseen. In a few moments the "madam."

as the current word characterized this type of woman, appeared.

Those who are at all familiar with the underworld may at once anticipate a type which will not be far wrong: of good height, buxom, usually over forty, blonde—more often from choice than from nature—and with a specialized wisdom concerning life gathered by a form of contact which cannot by any stretch of the imagination be considered pleasant. This particular woman, Mrs. Davis, was tall, fair, rugged, and not at all unpleasant to look upon. She had light-blue eyes and a genial smile. Long contact with the police and the brutalities of sex in her early life had made her wary, a little afraid of how the world would use her. This particular method of making a living being illicit, and she having no other practical knowledge at her command, she was as anxious to get along peacefully with the police and the public generally as any struggling tradesman in any walk of life might have been. She had on a loose, blue-flowered *peignoir* or dressing-gown open at the front, tied with blue ribbons and showing a little of her expensive underwear beneath. A large opal ring graced her left middle finger, and turquoises of vivid blue were pendent from her ears. She wore yellow-leather slippers with bronze buckles; and altogether her appearance was not out of keeping with the character of the reception-room itself, which was a composite of gold-flowered wall-paper, blue and cream-colored Brussels carpet, heavily gold-framed engravings of reclining nudes, and a gilt-framed pier-mirror which rose from the floor to the ceiling. Needless to say that Butler was shocked to the soul of him by this suggestive atmosphere which was supposed to include his daughter in its destructive reaches.

Mr. Alderson motioned one of his detectives to get behind the woman—between her and the door—which he did.

"Sorry to trouble you, Mrs. Davis," he said, using her

current name, "but we are looking for a couple who are in your house here. We're after a runaway girl. We don't want to make any disturbance—merely to get her and take her away." Mrs. Davis paled and opened her mouth. "Now don't make any noise or try to scream, or we'll have to stop you. My men are all around the house. Nobody can get out. Do you know anybody by the name of Cowperwood?"

Mrs. Davis, fortunately from one point of view, was not of a particularly nervous nor yet contentious type. She was more or less philosophic. She was not in touch with the police here in Philadelphia, hence subject to exposure. What good would it do to cry out? she thought. The place was surrounded. There was no one in the house at the time save Cowperwood and Aileen. She did not know Cowperwood by his name, nor Aileen by hers. They were a Mr. and Mrs. Montague to her.

"I don't know anybody by that name," she replied, nervously, fearing that she was to be made to pay severely for her unwitting part in a private tragedy.

"Isn't there a girl here with red hair?" asked one of Alderson's assistants who had been on guard, and who now pushed forward. "And a man with a gray suit and a light-brown mustache? They came in here half an hour ago. You remember them, don't you?"

"There's just one couple in the house, but I'm not sure whether they're the ones you want. I'll ask them to come down, if you wish. Oh, I wish you wouldn't make any disturbance. This is terrible."

"We'll not make any disturbance," replied Alderson, "if you don't. Just you be quiet. We merely want to see the girl and take her away. Now, you stay where you are. What room are they in?"

"In the second one in the rear up-stairs. Won't you let me go, though? It will be so much better. I'll just tap and ask them to come out."

"No. We'll tend to that. You stay where you are.

You're not going to get into any trouble. You just stay where you are," insisted Alderson.

He motioned to Butler, who, however, now that he had embarked on his grim task, was thinking that he had made a mistake. Aileen was a grown woman with a will of her own. What could he do? What good would it do him to tap personally on the door or force his way in and make her come out, unless he intended to kill Cowperwood? If she were made to come down here, that would be enough. She would then know that he knew all. He did not care to quarrel with Cowperwood, he now decided, in any public way. He was afraid to. He was afraid of himself.

"Let her go," he said, grimly, doggedly. "You watch her. Tell the girl to come down-stairs to me."

Mrs. Davis, realizing on the moment that this was some family tragedy, and hoping in an agonized way that she could slip out of it peacefully, started at once with Alderson and his assistants at his heels. They ascended the stairs, and, reaching the door of the room occupied by Cowperwood and Aileen, she tapped lightly. At the first knock Aileen blanched and leaped to her feet. She was usually not so nervous; but to-day, for some reason, she anticipated trouble. Cowperwood's eyes instantly hardened, losing that color of mirth which had filled them before.

"Don't be nervous," he said, "it's nothing, I fancy. The servant wants to give you something. I'll go."

He started, but Aileen interfered. "Wait," she said. Meanwhile the tap came again. Then she went to the door and opened it the least bit.

"Mrs. Montague," exclaimed Mrs. Davis, in an obviously nervous, forced voice, "there's a gentleman down-stairs who wishes to see you!"

"A gentleman to see me!" exclaimed Aileen, astonished and paling. "Are you sure?"

"Yes; he says he wants to see you. There are several

other men with him. I think it's some one who belongs
to you, maybe."

Aileen realized on the instant, as did Cowperwood,
what had in all likelihood happened. Butler or Mrs.
Cowperwood had trailed them—in all probability her
father. He wondered what he should do to protect her.
It was not at all improbable that Butler might want to
kill him; but that did not disturb him. He really did
not pay any attention to that thought, and he was not
armed.

"I'll go down," he said, when he saw her pale face.
"You stay here. I'll get you out of this—now, don't you
worry. This is my affair. Let me go first."

Aileen's mind was working like a rapidly moving machine. She was wondering whether this really could be
her father. Perhaps it was not. Might there be some
other Mrs. Montague—a real one? Supposing it was her
father—he had been so nice to her in not telling the family,
in keeping her secret thus far. He loved her—she knew
that. It makes all the difference in the world in a child's
attitude on an occasion like this whether she has been
loved and petted and spoiled, or the reverse. Aileen had
been loved and petted and spoiled. She could not think
of her father doing anything terrible physically to her or
to any one else. But it was so hard to confront him—to
look into his eyes. When she had attained a proper
memory of him, her fluttering wits told her what to do.

"No, Frank," she whispered, excitedly; "if it's father,
you'd better let me go. I know how to talk to him. He
won't say anything to me. If it is he, and you go down,
it might make him very angry. You stay here. I'm
not afraid—really, I'm not. If I want you, I'll call you."

He had come over and taken her pretty chin in his
hands, and was looking solemnly into her eyes.

"You mustn't be afraid," he said. "I'll go down.
If it's your father, you can go away with him. I don't
think he'll do anything either to you or to me. If it is

he, write me something at the office. I'll be there. If I can help you in any way, I will. We can fix up something. There's no use trying to explain this. Say nothing at all."

He had on his coat and overcoat, and was standing with his hat in his hand. When she was ready—hat, gloves, and all—he said:

"Now let me go first. I want to see."

"No; please, Frank," she begged, courageously. "Let me. I know it's father. Who else would it be? You can come if I call. Nothing's going to happen. I understand him. He won't do anything to me. If you go it will only make him angry. Let me go. You stand in the door here. If I don't call, it's all right. Will you?"

She put her two pretty hands on his shoulders, and he weighed the matter very carefully. "Very well," he said, "only I'll go to the foot of the stairs with you."

They went to the door, and he opened it. Outside were Mr. Alderson, Mr. Slattery, a detective, Mr. Woywod, a detective, and Mrs. Davis, standing perhaps five feet away.

"Well," said Cowperwood, commandingly, looking at Mr. Alderson.

"There's a gentleman down-stairs wishes to see the lady," said Alderson. "It's her father, I think," he added, quietly.

Cowperwood made way for Aileen, who swept by, furious at the presence of men and this exposure. Her courage had entirely returned. She was angry to think her father would make a public spectacle of her. Cowperwood started to follow.

"I'd advise you not to go down there right away," cautioned Alderson, sagely. "That's her father. Butler's her name, isn't it? He don't want you so much as he wants her. You may save trouble."

Cowperwood nevertheless walked slowly toward the head of the stairs, listening.

"What made you come here, father?" he heard Aileen ask.

Butler's reply he could not hear.

In the room, confronted by Butler, Aileen was now attempting to stare defiantly, to look reproachful. Butler's deep, shaggy gray eyes beneath their brows revealed a weight of weariness and despair which she had never seen there before. To think he should find his daughter here! To think she should put him to this shame! He shook his head solemnly. And the worst of it was that Aileen obviously did not realize her wretched state. She was still too young, too foolish, too erratic, too emotionally strange. Nevertheless, she was his daughter.

"I never expected to find you in a place like this, daughter," he said, when she appeared. "I should have thought you would have thought better of yourself."

It was then Aileen asked: "What made you come here, father?" which Cowperwood heard. She carried herself with quite an air, due to her pumped-up courage, and her anger, which she felt she had to have to see her through. The old man, in spite of all her airs, could not be angry, save against Cowperwood. He was too sad.

"I know who you're with," he said, shaking his head sadly. "The dog! I'll get him yet. I've had men watchin' you all the time. Oh, the shame of this day! The shame of this day! You'll be comin' home with me now."

"That's just it, father," began Aileen. "You've had men watching me. I should have thought—" She stopped, because he put up his hand in a strange, agonized, and yet frightening way.

"None of that! none of that!" he said, glowering under his strange, sad gray brows. "I can't stand it! Don't tempt me! We're not out of this place yet. He's not! You'll come home with me now."

Aileen understood. It was Cowperwood he was referring to. That frightened her. She hushed at once.

"I'm ready," she replied, nervously.

The old man led the way broken-heartedly. He felt he would never live to forget the agony of this hour.

CHAPTER XLVII

IN spite of Butler's rage and his determination to do many things to the financier, if he could, he was, nevertheless, so wrought up and shocked by the attitude of Aileen that he could scarcely believe he was the same man he had been twenty-four hours before. Aileen was so nonchalant, so defiant. He had expected to see her wilt completely when confronted with her guilt. Instead, he found, to his despair, after they were once safely out of the house, that he had aroused a fighting quality in the girl which was not incomparable to his own. She had some of his own and Owen's grit. She sat beside him in the little runabout—not his own—in which he was driving her home, her face coloring and blanching by turns, as different waves of thought swept over her, determined to stand her ground now that her father had so plainly trapped her, to declare for Cowperwood and her love and her position in general. What did she care, she asked herself, what her father thought now? What good would what he thought do her? She was in this thing. She loved Cowperwood; she was permanently disgraced in her father's eyes. He had fallen so low in his parental feeling as to spy on her and expose her before other men —strangers, detectives, Cowperwood. What real affection could she have for him after this? He had made a mistake, according to her. He had done a foolish and a contemptible thing, which was not warranted however bad her actions might have been. What could he hope to accomplish by rushing in on her in this way and ripping the veil from her very soul before these other men—

these crude detectives? Oh, the agony of that walk from the bedroom to the reception-room! She would never forgive her father for this—never, never, never! He had now killed her love for him—that was what she felt. It was to be a battle royal between them from now on; he would be trying to make her do one thing, and she would be wanting to do, and would be doing, another—depend on that. As they rode—in complete silence for a while— her hands clasped and unclasped defiantly, her nails cutting her palms, and her mouth hardened. Never had there been such an intense and bitter look of opposition on Aileen's face. It was really hard and sad, but intensely defiant—a look that was to be seen much more frequently in later years.

It is an open question whether raw opposition ever accomplishes anything of value in this world. It seems so inherent in this mortal scheme of things that it appears to have a vast validity. It is more than likely that we owe this spectacle called *life* to it, and that this can be demonstrated scientifically; but when that is said and done, what is the value? What is the value of the spectacle? And what the value of a scene such as this enacted between Aileen and her father?

The old man saw nothing for it, as they rode on, save a grim contest between them which could end in what? What could he do with her? They were riding away fresh from this awful catastrophe, and she was not saying a word! She had even asked him why he had come there! How was he to subdue her, when the very act of trapping her had failed to do so? His ruse, while so successful materially, had failed so utterly spiritually. They reached the house, and Aileen got out. The old man, too nonplussed to wish to go further at this time, drove back to his office with the strange horse, and left it to be called for. He then went out and walked by himself—a peculiar thing for him to do; he had done nothing like that in years and years—walking to think. Coming to an open Catholic church, he went in and prayed for enlightenment, the growing dusk of the interior, the single everlasting lamp before the repository of the chalice, and the high, white altar set with candles soothing his troubled feelings. What should he do about Aileen? he asked his God. What about this man Cowperwood? Was Aileen to blame entirely, or Cowperwood, or both? They had both acted vilely. But Aileen!

He came out of the church after a time and returned home. Aileen did not appear at dinner, and he could not eat. He went back into his private room after a while and shut the door—thinking, thinking, thinking. The dreadful spectacle of Aileen in a house of ill repute burned in his brain. To think that Cowperwood should have taken her there of all places—his Aileen, convent-bred, so well educated, so refined, as he thought. In spite of his prayers, his uncertainty, her opposition, the puzzling nature of the situation, she must be got out of this, must be made to cease. He had asked her before, and she had lied. Well, she could not lie now. She could not explain—there was nothing to explain. She must go away for a while, give the man up, and the law would run its course with him. In all likelihood Cowperwood would go to the penitentiary—if ever a man richly deserved to go, it was he. Butler would see that no stone was left unturned. He would make it a personal issue, if necessary. All he had to do was to let it be known in judicial circles that he wanted it so—was convinced of Cowperwood's black character—and this would have great weight. He could not suborn a jury, that would be criminal; but he could see that the case was properly and force-fully presented; and if Cowperwood were convicted, Heaven help him. The appeal of his financial friends would not save him. The judges of the lower and superior courts knew on which side their bread was buttered. They would strain a point in favor of the highest political opinion of the day, and he certainly could influence that.

He had never been so grimly determined on that score as he was now.

Aileen meanwhile was contemplating the peculiar nature of her situation. In spite of their silence on the way home, she knew that a conversation was coming with her father. It had to be. He would want her to go somewhere. Most likely he would revive the European trip in some form—she now suspected the invitation of Mrs. Mollenhauer as a trick; and she had to decide whether she would go. Would she leave Cowperwood just when he was about to be tried? She could not. She was determined she would not. She wanted to see what was going to happen to him. She would leave home first —run to some relative, some friend, some stranger, if necessary, and ask to be taken in. She had some money— a little. Her father had always been very liberal with her. She could take a few clothes and disappear. They would be glad enough to send for her after she had been gone awhile. Her mother would be frantic; Norah and Callum and Owen would be beside themselves with wonder and worry; her father—she could see him. Maybe that would bring him to his senses. In spite of all her emotional vagaries, she was the pride and interest of this home, and she knew it.

Notwithstanding her various social connections and acquaintances, the people to whom Aileen could run in an emergency of the present kind were not numerous. She could scarcely think of any one who would be likely to take her in for any lengthy period, without question. There were a number of young women of her own age, married and unmarried, who were very friendly to her, but there were few with whom she was really intimate. The only person who stood out in her mind as having any real possibility of refuge for a period was a certain Mary Calligan, better known as "Mamie" among her friends, who had attended school with Aileen in former years and was now a teacher in one of the local schools.

The Calligan family was limited, consisting of Mrs. Katharine Calligan, the mother, a dressmaker by profession and a widow—her husband, a house-mover by trade, having been killed by a falling wall some ten years before—and Mamie, her twenty-three-year-old daughter, who lived in a small two-story brick house in Cherry Street, near Fifteenth. Mrs. Calligan was not a very good dressmaker, not good enough, at least, for the Butler family to patronize in their present exalted state. Aileen went there occasionally for gingham house-dresses, underwear, pretty dressing-gowns, and alterations on some of her more important clothing which was made by a very superior modiste in Chestnut Street. Aileen visited the house largely because she had gone to school with Mamie at St. Agatha's, when the outlook of the Calligan family was much more promising. Since then, owing to the father's death, and the superior change in Aileen's social position, she had not seen so much of her, and the mother and daughter had not done so well. Mamie was earning forty dollars a month as the teacher of a sixth-grade room in one of the near-by public schools, and Mrs. Calligan averaged on the whole about two dollars a day—sometimes not so much. The house they occupied was their own, free and clear, and the furniture which it contained suggested the size of their joint income, which was somewhere near eighty dollars a month. Mamie Calligan had a piano, which she could play only fairly well; and Mrs. Calligan had a comfortable work-room fitted with the implements of her trade.

In this crisis it was to the home of the Calligans that Aileen turned in thought. If her father really was not nice to her, and she had to leave home for a time, she could go to the Calligans. They would receive her and say nothing. They would not ask her too many questions. They were not sufficiently well known to the other members of the Butler family to have the latter suspect that she had gone there. She might readily dis-

THE FINANCIER

appear into the privacy of Cherry Street and not be seen
or heard of for weeks. The Calligans would be delighted
to have her until she could make up her mind what to
do. It is an interesting fact to contemplate that the
Calligans, like the various members of the Butler family,
never suspected Aileen of the least tendency toward a
wayward existence. Hence her flight from her own
family, if it ever came, would be laid more to the door of
a lovely temperamental pettishness than anything else.

CHAPTER XLVIII

THE decision of Butler to compel Aileen to accept
some form of change which would take her out of
Philadelphia for the time being—out of the bosom of
the family where he so much loved to have her—was,
once he had thought it all over and made up his mind,
unalterable. He did not forget that Cowperwood had
been properly indicted and would in all probability be
convicted—he certainly hoped so; but even that did not
assure him that Aileen would cease her relations with the
banker. Besides, it was not absolutely certain that Cowperwood would not be acquitted; and in that case he,
Butler, would have the spectacle of his erring daughter
continuing relations with a man whom respectable people
would hereafter not care to know. Aileen must be got
out of this atmosphere, got out soon, whatever happened;
and since Mrs. Mollenhauer's proposition had been so
incontinently rejected, something else would have to be
arranged for. Butler was ready to consider any proposition which would save her; but it must be a sound one—
one not open to her whimsical moods or the guidings or
leadings of romance. Again he thought of his wife's sister
in New Orleans, and again of getting her to Europe in
some way. If he could just think of something that would
interest her to do—something that would not seem, in
spite of the fact that it was, like idle incarceration or
alienation. New Orleans would scarcely be lively enough.
It would be difficult to keep her there except under surveillance, and he did not care to attempt that unless it
was absolutely necessary. Something must be done. He

must take her in hand and save her. She was absolutely a menace to the family as things stood. Heaven only knew how much harm she had done already. He must act. He cudgeled his weary brain, thinking of a reformatory known as the Good Shepherd, near Philadelphia, which was in charge of an order of sisters, where Aileen might be enticed and restrained; but that must be a last resort. He thought of intelligent sisters who could be employed as chaperons —one to accompany Aileen and Norah on a trip, or Aileen alone. That was a fine idea, he thought. Why had not that occurred to him before? Suddenly he recalled the sister who had taught Aileen music at St. Agatha's, Sister Constantia, who still came occasionally to see them, a woman of fifty, and charming from his point of view. Why not her? Aileen had liked her—did yet. Sister Constantia! Certainly! Then, suggested by her, another thought came to him—that was music. Why should not Aileen go abroad to wherever they went for that purpose, with Sister Constantia as a chaperon, and study music? A capital idea. It was not too late. Aileen was not too old. She must accept this; she must go at once. He got up, the third day, from where he was sitting in his private office meditating this dread situation, having meanwhile not had one word with Aileen, and decided to act. She must go. He must compel her. He must talk to her at once, tell her what he thought, reproach her with her sins and her state of mind, and then by sheer force of will-power compel her to go. It was a strenuous hour for him—a deadly one.

He came home from his office very early in the afternoon, hoping to find Aileen there, in order that he might have a private interview with her, and by good luck found her in. She was sitting in her room reading. She had had no taste to go out into the world these last few days—she was too expectant of trouble to come. She had been reading aimlessly anything that came to her hand, or pretending to do so, and thinking. She had written Cowperwood

how things stood, and had asked for a rendezvous out
on the Wissahickon, in spite of the detectives. She must
see him. Her father, she said, had done nothing; but
she was sure he would attempt to do something. He was
merely recovering from this shock of surprise. If he
attempted to coerce her in any way, she was thinking of
running away. She wanted to talk to Cowperwood about
that. She was merely waiting patiently until the next
afternoon, when she would go out to meet him. Old
Butler spoke to her gently when he came in.

"Come into my room a little while, Aileen," he said.

Aileen arose and followed.

When they were closeted together, safe from the hearing of the other members of the family, he began without
any preliminaries of any kind.

"I've been thinkin' about ye, Aileen, and what ought
to be done in this case. You're on the road to ruin if
ever there was one. I tremble when I think of your
immortal soul. I want to do somethin' for ye, my child,
before it's too late. I've been reproachin' myself for the
last month and more, thinkin', perhaps, it was somethin'
I had done, or maybe had failed to do, aither me or your
mother, that has brought ye to the place where ye are
to-day. Needless to say, it's on my conscience, me child.
It's a heartbroken man you're lookin' at this day. I'll
never be able to hold me head up again. Oh, the shame
—the shame! That I should have lived to see it!"

"But father," protested Aileen, who was a little distraught at the thought of having to listen to a long preach-
ment which would relate to her duty to God and the
Church and her family and her mother and him. She
realized that all these were important in their way; but
Cowperwood and his point of view had given her another
outlook on life. They had discussed this matter of
families—parents, children, husbands, wives, brothers,
sisters—from almost every point of view. Cowperwood's
laissez-faire attitude had permeated and colored her mind

completely. She saw things through his cold, direct "I satisfy myself" attitude. He was sorry for all the little differences of personality that sprang up between people, causing quarrels, bickerings, opposition, and separation; but they could not be helped. People outgrew each other. Their points of view altered at varying ratios— hence changes. Religion—he smiled. It was for the weak, the fearsome. Morals—those who had them had them; those who didn't, didn't. There was no explaining. As for him, he saw nothing wrong in the sex relationship. Between those who were mutually compatible it was innocent and delicious. Aileen in his arms, unmarried, but loved by him, and he by her, was as good and pure as any living woman—a great deal purer than most. Without propinquity—nearness of blood, mood, mind, sentiment, such a relationship was impossible. It would not occur. With these things, marriage or no marriage, it was perfect, delightful. One found oneself in a given social order, theory, or scheme of things. For purposes of social success, in order not to offend, to smooth one's path, make things easy, avoid useless criticism, and the like, it was necessary to create an outward seeming—ostensibly conform. Beyond that it was not necessary to do anything. Never fail, never get caught. If you did, fight your way out silently and say nothing. That was what he was doing in connection with his present financial troubles; that was what he had been ready to do the other day when they were caught. It was something of all this that was coloring Aileen's mood as she listened at present.

"But father," she protested, "I love Mr. Cowperwood. It's almost the same as if I were married to him. He will marry me some day when he gets a divorce from Mrs. Cowperwood. You don't understand how it is. He's very fond of me, and I love him. He needs me."

Butler looked at her with strange, non-understanding eyes. He scarcely comprehended what she was talking about, so remote was all this from his understanding and theory of life.

"Needs you, does he?" he asked, sarcastically. "You're in love with him, and him a married man? What about his wife and children? I don't suppose they need him, do they? What talk have ye?"

Aileen flung her head back defiantly. She thought she saw how useless argument was with her father. He did not understand her point of view. Could not, of course. "It's true, nevertheless," she reiterated. "You just don't understand."

Butler could scarcely believe his ears. He had never heard such talk before in his life from any one, let alone his own daughter. It amazed and shocked him. He was quite aware of all the subtleties of politics and business, but these of romance were too much for him. He knew nothing about them. To think a daughter of his should be talking like this! and he and she Catholics—or she ought to be. He could not understand where she got such notions unless it was from the Machiavellian, corrupting brain of Cowperwood.

"How long have ye had these notions, my child?" he suddenly asked, calmly and soberly. "Where did you get them? Ye certainly never heard anything like that in this house, I warrant. Ye talk as though ye had gone out of yer mind."

"Oh, don't talk nonsense, father," flared Aileen, angrily. "I'm not a child any more. I'm twenty-four years of age. You just don't understand. Mr. Cowperwood doesn't like his wife. He's going to get a divorce when he can, and will marry me. I love him, and he loves me, and that's all there is to it."

"Is it, though?" asked Butler, grimly determined, by hook or by crook, to bring this girl to her senses. He could see that Cowperwood had had an easy victim here, whatever he (Butler) might have originally thought. She was a strange, wayward, determined girl. "Ye'll be takin' no thought of his wife and children then? The fact that he's goin' to jail, besides, is nawthin'. Ye'd love him just as much in convict stripes, I suppose—more, maybe." (The old man was at his best, humanly speaking, when he was a little sarcastic.) "Ye'll have him that way, likely, if at all."

Aileen blazed at once to a furious heat. "Yes, I know," she sneered. "That's what you would like. I know what you've been doing. Frank does, too. You won't hurt him. You can't! You want to punish him on my account; but he doesn't care. I'll marry him anyhow. I love him, and I'll wait for him and marry him; and you can do what you please. So there!"

"Ye'll marry him, will you?" asked Butler, nonplussed and further astounded. "So ye'll wait for him and marry him? Ye'll take him away from his wife and children, where, if he were half a man, he'd be stayin' this minute instead of gallivantin' around with you, and marry him? Ye'd disgrace your father and yer mother and yer family. Ye'll stand here and say this to me, I that have raised ye, cared for ye, and made somethin' of you? Where would you be if it weren't for me and your poor, hard-workin' mother, schemin' and plannin' for you year in and year out? Ye're smarter than I am, I suppose. Ye know more about the world than I do, or any one else that might want to say anythin' to ye. I've raised ye to be a fine lady, and this is what I get. Talk about me not bein' able to understand, and ye lovin' a convict-to-be, a robber, an embezzler, a bankrupt, a lyin', thavin'—"

"Father!" exclaimed Aileen, determinedly. "I'll not listen to you talking that way. He's not any of the things that you say. I'll not stay here." She moved toward the door; but Butler stepped in between her and it. His face for the moment was flushed and swollen with anger.

"But I'm not through with him yet," he went on, ignoring her. "I'll get him as sure as I have a name. There's law in this land, and I'll have it on him. I'll show him whether he'll come sneakin' into dacent homes and robbin' parents of their children."

He paused after a time, for Aileen's face was hard and tense by now, resigned but indifferent.

"It's too bad, daughter," he said, quietly, after a moment. "I'm lettin' my anger get the best of me. It wasn't that I intended talkin' to ye about when I ast ye to come in. It's somethin' else I have on me mind. I was thinkin', perhaps, ye'd like to go to Europe for the time bein' to study music." Butler was really a tactless person in a situation of this kind. He really knew very little about women and romance. He scarcely knew how to introduce his proposition. He had made one mistake by allowing his anger to get the better of him, and now he was making another, following up this attack with a plea for a trip to Europe. "Ye're not quite yourself just at present. Ye're needin' a rest. It would be good for ye to go away for a while. Ye could have a nice time over there. Norah could go along with ye, if you would, and Sister Constantia that taught you. Ye wouldn't object to havin' her, I suppose?"

At the mention of this idea of a trip to Europe again, with Sister Constantia and music thrown in to give it a slightly new form, Aileen bridled. She was not such a fool but what she could see that her father was trying to be nice to her—that he was taking the situation in which he had discovered her in the best possible way from his own point of view, but she did not want to be made to be grateful. It meant taking her away from Cowperwood. She did not propose to leave Philadelphia —never, never, never!—so long as Frank was in so much trouble. And she was opposed to conversation on this score. How could she? Her sole idea of happiness was to be near him.

"I wish you wouldn't talk about that, father," she

began, having softened under his explanation. "I don't want to go to Europe now. I don't want to leave Philadelphia. I know you want me to go; but I don't want to think of going now. I can't."

Butler's brow darkened again. "But it would be so fine for ye. Ye surely can't expect to stay here after—" He paused, for he was going to say "what has happened." He knew she was very sensitive on that point. His own conduct in hunting her down had been such a breach of fatherly courtesy that he knew she felt resentful, and in a way properly so. Still, what could be greater than her own crime? "After," he concluded, "ye have made such a mistake ye surely wouldn't want to stay here. Ye won't be wantin' to keep up that—committin' a mortal sin. It's against the laws of God and man."

He did so hope the thought of sin would come to Aileen —the enormity of her crime from a spiritual point of view—but Aileen did not see it at all.

"You don't understand me, father," she exclaimed, hopelessly, toward the end. "You can't. I have one idea, and you have another. I don't believe in any religion any more."

The moment Aileen had said this she wished she had not. It was a slip of the tongue. Butler's face took on an inexpressibly sad, despairing look.

"You don't believe?" he asked.

"No, not exactly—not like you do."

He shook his head.

"The harm that has come to yer soul!" he replied. "It's plain to me, daughter, that somethin' terrible has happened to ye. This man has ruined ye, body and soul. Somethin' must be done. I don't want to be hard on ye, but ye must leave Philadelphy. Ye can't stay here. I can't permit ye. Ye can go to Europe, or ye can go to yer aunt's in New Orleans; but ye must go somewhere. I can't have ye stayin' here—it's too dangerous. It's sure to be comin' out. The papers 'll be havin' it next. Ye're young yet. Yer life is before you. I tremble for yer soul; but so long as ye're young and alive ye may come to yer senses. It's me duty to be hard. It's me obligation to you and the Church. Ye must quit this life. Ye must lave this man. Ye must never see him any more. I can't permit ye. He's no good. He has no intintion of marrying ye, and it would be a crime against God and man if he did. No, no! Never that! The man's a bankrupt, a scoundrel, a thafe. If ye had him, ye'd soon be the unhappiest woman in the world. He wouldn't be faithful to ye. No." He paused. "Ye must go away. I say it once and for all. I mane it kindly. I have yer best interests at heart. I love ye; but ye must. I'm sorry to see ye go—I'd rather have ye here. No one will be sorrier; but ye must. Ye must make it all seem natcheral and ordinary to yer mother; but ye must go —d'ye hear? Ye must."

He paused, looking sadly but firmly at Aileen under his shaggy gray eyebrows. She knew he meant this. It was his most solemn, his most religious expression.

"Now get all the clothes ye want," he said. "Fix yourself up in any way you plase. Say where ye want to go, but get ready."

"But I won't, father," replied Aileen, equally solemnly, equally determinedly. "I won't go! I won't leave Philadelphia."

"Ye don't mane to say ye will deliberately disobey me when I'm asking ye to do somethin' that's intended for yer own good, will ye, daughter?"

"Yes, I will," replied Aileen, determinedly. "I won't go! I'm sorry, but I won't!"

"Ye really mane that, do ye?" asked Butler, sadly, but grimly.

"Yes, I do," replied Aileen, grimly, in return.

"Then I'll have to see what I can do, daughter," replied the old man. "Ye're still my daughter, whatever ye are, and I'll not see ye come to wreck and ruin for

want of doin' what I know to be my solemn duty. I'll
give ye a few more days to think this over. I'll not stint
ye in money or the likes of that. Ye can go to Europe,
or anywhere ye plase, in charge of Sister Constantia. Ye
can study singin' or anythin' ye choose; but go ye must.
There's an end of that. There are laws in this land
still. There are things that can be done to those who
won't obey the law. I found ye this time—much as it
hurt me to do it. I'll find ye again if ye try to disobey
me. Ye must change yer ways. I can't have ye goin'
on as ye are. Ye understand now. It's the last word.
Give this man up, and ye can have anything ye choose.
Ye're my girl—I'll do everything I can in this world to
make ye happy. Why, why shouldn't I? What else
have I to live for but me children? It's ye and the rest
of them that I've been workin' and plannin' for all these
years. Come now, be a good girl. Ye love your old
father, don't ye? Why, I rocked ye in my arms as a
baby, Aileen. I've watched over ye when ye were not
bigger than what would rest in me two fists here. I've
been a good father to ye—ye can't deny that. Look at
the other girls you've seen. Have any of them had more
nor what ye have had? Ye won't go against me in this.
I'm sure ye won't. Ye can't. Ye love me too much—
surely ye do—don't ye?"

He paused and put a big, brown, horny hand on Aileen's
arm. She had listened to his plea not unmoved—really
more or less softened—because of the hopelessness of it.
She could not give up Cowperwood. Her father just did
not understand. He did not know what love was. Unquestionably he had never loved as she had. Her Frank
—to think of deserting him!

She stood quite silent while Butler appealed to her.

"I'd like to, father," she said. "Really I would. I
do love you. I want to please you; but I can't in this—
I can't! I love Mr. Cowperwood. You don't understand—really you don't!"

At the repetition of Cowperwood's name Butler's mouth hardened. He could see that she was infatuated—that his carefully calculated plea had failed. It was all true, all that he had said; but she would not—could not. So he must think of some other way.

"Very well, then," he said, as Aileen turned away. "Have it yer own way, if ye will. Ye must go, though, willy-nilly. It can't be any other way. I wish to God it could."

Aileen went out, very solemn, and Butler went over to his desk and sat down. "Such a situation!" he said to himself. "Such a complication!"

But she must go. She must be got out of the clutches of Cowperwood. He would spend almost any sum of money to make her happy; but she must no longer trifle with this villainous man in this shameful way. It was inconceivable, impossible. He would spend any sum of money now to see that Cowperwood did not escape the clutches of the law on the charge laid against him. He must act at once.

At the same time, Aileen sat in her room and thought and thought as to what she was to do next.

CHAPTER XLIX

THE situation which confronted Aileen was really a trying one. A girl of less innate courage and determination would have weakened and yielded. In spite of the fact, however, that she had been in and of her family, living by its Butler-provided resources, she was not so dependent on it mentally and emotionally as it was on her. She needed, or thought she did, the money which her father provided her to live on; but the Butler family literally needed the light of her countenance to keep them appropriately cheerful, and if she went away there would be a distinct gulf or blank that would not soon be overcome.

Aileen understood this clearly enough in a way. She knew her father and mother were more or less dependent on her. She had never said anything about it, but it was evident. She took it as a matter of course. Now, when it came to thinking of leaving and shifting for herself, in order to avoid a trip which she did not care to be forced into, her courage was based largely on this keen sense of her own significance to the family. They could not do without her very well. She thought over what Butler had said, and decided she must act at once. She dressed for the street the next morning, after her father had gone, and decided to step in at the Calligans's about noon, when Mamie would be at home for luncheon. Then she would take up the matter casually. If they had no objection, she would go there. She sometimes wondered why Cowperwood did not suggest, in his great stress, that they leave for some part unknown; but she also felt that he must know best what he could do. His increasing troubles depressed her.

The Calligans, as might have been expected, were delighted when she arrived. Aileen, for once, was a little depressed. Her home state had always appeared so delightful to the Calligans that she knew they would be greatly surprised. Nevertheless they would say nothing in opposition to her mood. After exchanging the gossip of the day with Mrs. Calligan, who was alone—Mamie not having come in yet—she went to the piano and played a melancholy air. Mrs. Calligan asked after her father and mother and Norah, though she rarely saw them, or any of Aileen's other relatives or friends.

"Sure it's lovely the way you play," said Mrs. Calligan. "I like to hear you, Aileen. I wish you'd come oftener to see us. You're so rarely here nowadays."

"Oh, I've been so busy, Mrs. Calligan," replied Aileen. "I've had so much to do this fall. I just couldn't. They wanted me to go to Europe; but I didn't feel that I ought to go. Oh dear!" she sighed, and in her playing swept off with a movement of sad, romantic significance. As she was doing this the door opened and Mamie came in. Her commonplace face brightened at the sight of Aileen.

"Well, Aileen Butler!" she exclaimed. "Where did you come from? Where have you been keeping yourself so long?"

Aileen rose to exchange kisses. "Oh, I've been very busy, Mamie. I've just been telling your mother. How are you, anyway? How are you getting along in your work?"

Mamie recounted at once some school difficulties which were puzzling her—the growing size of classes and the amount of work expected. While Mrs. Calligan was setting the table Mamie went to her room to tidy herself up, and Aileen followed her. As she stood before her mirror Aileen stopped and looked at her meditatively—an act which was not customary with Aileen—and Mamie noticed it.

"There is something the matter with you to-day, Aileen Butler," observed Mamie, coming over to her and looking in her face. The young school-teacher was very fond of the contractor's daughter. "You're not like yourself at all."

"I've got something on my mind," replied Aileen— "something that's worrying me. I don't know just what to do—that's what's the matter."

"Well, whatever can it be?" commented Mamie. "I never saw you act this way before. Can't you tell me? What is it?"

"No, I don't think I can—not now, anyhow." Aileen paused. "Do you suppose your mother would object," she asked, suddenly, "if I came here and stayed a little while? I want to get away from home for a time for a certain reason."

"Why, Aileen Butler, how you talk!" exclaimed her friend. "Object! You know she'd be delighted, and so would I. Oh, dear—*can* you come? But what makes you want to leave home?"

"That's just what I can't tell you—not now, anyhow," replied Aileen. "You mustn't ask me. But I want to come if you'll let me. Will you speak to your mother, or shall I?"

"Why, I will," said Mamie, struck with wonder at this remarkable development; "but it's silly to do it. I know what she'll say before I tell her, and so do you. You can just bring your things and come. That's all."

Aileen looked at her solemnly. "But neither of you must tell anybody that I'm here. I don't want any-body to know—particularly no one of my family."

"You're not going to run away for good, are you, Aileen?" asked Mamie, curiously and gravely.

"Oh, I don't know; I don't know what I'll do. I know that I want to come away for a while, anyhow."

18   537

"Well, of all things," replied her friend. "Wonders never cease, do they, Aileen? But it will be so lovely to have you here. Mama will be so pleased. Of course, we won't tell anybody if you don't want us to. Hardly any one ever comes here; and if they do, you needn't see them. You can have this big room next to me. Oh, that will be *so* nice! I'm perfectly delighted." The young school-teacher's spirits rose to a decided height, illustrating the old saw that it's an ill wind that blows nobody any good. "Come on. We'll tell mama right now."

They went down the stairs together, Aileen lingering behind a little as they neared the bottom. Mamie burst in upon her mother with: "Oh, mama, isn't it lovely? Aileen's coming to stay with us for a while. She doesn't want any one to know, and she's coming right away." Aileen entered the room just as this was being said. Mrs. Calligan, who was holding a sugar-bowl in her hand, turned to survey her with a surprised but smiling face. She was immediately curious as to why Aileen should want to come—why leave home. To her, however, Butler's daughter was a woman grown, capable of regulating her own affairs, and welcome, of course, as the honored member of so important a family. It was very flattering to the Calligans to think that she would want to come under any cirumstances, whatever they might think.

"I don't see how your parents can let you go, Aileen; but you're certainly welcome here as long as you want to stay." The hearty, comprehending manner in which she said this, and Mamie's normal enthusiasm, caused Aileen to breathe a sigh of relief. The matter of the expense of her presence to the Calligans came into her mind.

"I want to pay you, of course," she said to Mrs. Calligan, "if I come."

"The very idea, Aileen Butler!" exclaimed Mamie.

"You'll do nothing of the sort. You'll come here and live with me as my guest."

"No, I won't! If I can't pay I won't come," replied Aileen. "You'll have to let me do that." She knew that the Calligans could not afford to keep her.

"Well, we'll not talk about that now, anyhow," replied Mrs. Calligan. "You can come when you like and stay as long as you like. Reach me some clean napkins, Mamie."

Aileen remained for luncheon, and afterward went away satisfied that her chiefest problem had been solved. Now her way was clear. She could come here if she wanted to. It was all a matter of collecting a few necessary things, or coming without bringing anything away. She must now go to meet Cowperwood in the hope that he had been able to keep his appointment and would have something to suggest.

CHAPTER L

BEGINNING with that dramatic moment when he
saw Aileen going down the stairs to meet her angry
father Cowperwood had realized that he had in Butler
a mortal enemy. It had astonished him greatly that the
thing had ended so peacefully even for the present—he
had expected to encounter Butler or Owen or Callum, or
all three, and possibly be shot. His reason told him that
Butler had no particular claim on Aileen's action—she
was old enough to know what to do; but he also realized
that the old man was inordinately fond of her, and, from
what she had told him from time to time, that her father
did not realize quite that she was grown up. He was
really astonished to think that Butler was so foolish as to
come there and get her, for, in his judgment, if anything
could finally snap the tie of affection which so closely
bound Aileen to her family, this would do it. She would
count herself from now on more or less of an outcast,
whether her father wanted her to or not. Practically
speaking, Cowperwood considered it quite all right that
she should have left with her father, promising to write,
and also that he himself should not have appeared before
Butler—that could only have been fraught with danger,
and would not have served any good purpose. Aileen
had not wanted him to defend her against her father
under the circumstances, and he knew from his past
connection with the family that it was not necessary
to do so.

Aside from being sorry for Aileen, Cowperwood was decidedly irritated that three or four detectives should have
been employed by Butler to spy out his movements, and

that now these people knew that he was guilty of this liaison. While it was not such a fatal thing for a man of his position to be caught in a resort of this kind, it might readily be used in future situations against him. It might come out—one never could tell—these detectives whom he did not know might spread it; though he fancied that Butler, for Aileen's sake, had taken good care that they should not. He was surprised that the detectives had allowed him to walk off so nonchalantly, as he did after Butler and Aileen went away, saying no further word whatever. He was wondering what Butler would do next. If the old contractor had been angry before, what would he be now; and if he had done so much before, what would he not now do? Cowperwood returned to his office curious to hear the final outcome of the argument between Aileen and her father, and speculating, of course, as to what his various court proceedings held in store for him.

He made no effort to communicate with Aileen, but awaited her letter, which came promptly. It was, as usual, long, optimistic, affectionate, and defiant. Her father had not been able to do anything with her, she said, up to that time. (When she wrote this letter the final conversation with Butler had not been held.) She did not intend that he should. He might want her to go to Europe or somewhere, but she would not. If necessary, she would leave home first. This thought puzzled Cowperwood very much. He had never imagined that Aileen would be compelled to leave home before he was prepared to take her; and if she did now, it might stir up complications which would be anything but pleasant to contemplate. Aileen in the bosom of her family, smart and well cared for, was one thing. Aileen out in the world dependent on him was another. Still he was fond of her, very, and would do anything to make her happy. He could support her in a very respectable way even yet, if he did not eventually go to prison, and even there he might manage to make some shift for her. It would be so much better, though, if he could persuade her to remain at home until he knew exactly what his fate was to be. He never imagined but that some day, whatever happened, within a reasonable length of time, he would be rid of all these complications and well-to-do again, in which case, if he could get a divorce, he would be glad to take Aileen as his wife. If not, he would like to take her with him, anyhow, and from this point of view it might be just as well if she broke away from her family now. But from the point of view of present complications—the search Butler would make, the espionage he might cast over his (Cowperwood's) affairs—it might be dangerous. *In extremis* Butler might publicly charge him with abduction—but no, he concluded, Butler would not do that. It would create too large a scandal. Aileen had told him that her father had not told her mother or any one else, and his own experience in the house of assignation with Aileen's father had indicated as much. If Butler had wanted to countenance publicity something deadly would have happened to him (Cowperwood) then. He decided, if he could, to persuade Aileen to stay at home, drop meetings and communications for the time being if necessary, and even go abroad. He would be all right until she came back, and so would she—common sense ought to rule in this case. But Aileen was headstrong and very much in love. She might not want to do it.

When he received her letter suggesting an appointment, he decided to keep it, though he felt it was a little dangerous. He drove out at the appointed hour, which was three, and heard Aileen's story of her argument with her father, and her intention of leaving. Cowperwood saw that if she carried out this intention Butler would think she had run to him, which was what he did not want. He did not want Aileen to complicate the situation so much that he would have no opportunity whatever of adjusting his affairs locally. He loved her in his shrewd, intelligent way: but he did not propose that she should injure him, for in so doing, of course, she would injure herself also in the long run.

"Are you sure," he asked, after he had listened to her description of the Calligan homestead, "that you will like that place? That sounds rather poor to me."

"Yes, but I like them so much," replied Aileen.

"And you're sure they won't tell on you?"

"Oh no; never, never!"

"Very good," he concluded. "You know what you're doing. I don't want to advise you against your will. If I were you, though, I'd take your father's advice and go away for a while. He'll get over this then, and I'll still be here. I can write you occasionally, and you can write me."

The moment Cowperwood said this Aileen's brow clouded. "Why, how you talk!" she exclaimed. "You know I won't leave Philadelphia now. You certainly don't expect me to leave you." Did he really love her? she asked herself. Was he going to desert her just when she was going to do the thing which would bring them nearer together? In her judgment it was important to defy her father. Butler had outraged her sense of justice and fair play in putting detectives on her trail and in his present attempt to force her to leave Philadelphia. To think that Frank, after all his protestations of affection, should suggest conforming now was too much. It hurt her. Anyhow, she would not stay at home, whatever Frank did. She had a right to combat her father, and she would. Her love for Frank— Her eyes clouded, for she was terribly hurt.

Cowperwood saw it all very clearly. He was too shrewd not to. He was immensely fond of her. Good heaven, he thought, he would not hurt her feelings for the world!

"Honey," he said, quickly, when he saw her eyes, "you don't understand. I want you to do what you want to do. You've planned this out in order to be with me; so now you do it. Don't think any more about me or anything I've said. I was merely thinking that it might make matters worse for both of us; but I don't believe it will. You think your father loves you so much that after you're gone he'll change his mind. Very good; go. I think you're right. But we must be very careful, sweet —you and I—really we must. This thing is getting serious. You'd better not try and see me often for the present—not any oftener than we can possibly help. If we had used common sense and stopped when your father got that letter, this wouldn't have happened. Write me, and I'll write you. You haven't any money, have you?"

He went down in his pocket for the first time since he had known Aileen and produced a layer of bills. "Here's two hundred dollars, sweet," he said, "until I see or hear from you. I'll see that you have whatever you need; and now don't think that I don't love you. You know I do. I'm crazy about you."

Aileen protested that she did not need so much—that she did not really need any—she had some at home; but he put that aside. He knew that she must have money.

"Don't talk, honey," he said; "I know what you need." She had been so used to receiving money from her father and mother in comfortable amounts from time to time that she thought nothing of it. Frank loved her so much that it made everything right between them. She softened in her mood and they discussed the matter of letters, reaching the conclusion that a private messenger would be safest for him—to be sent to Cherry Street. When finally they parted, Aileen, from being sunk in the depths by his uncertain attitude, was now once more on the heights. She decided that he did love her, and went away smiling. She had her Frank to fall back on— she would teach her father. Cowperwood shook his head, following her with his eyes. She represented an additional burden in his way, and Butler would be furious; but, "What can I do?" he asked himself. Give her up? Certainly not. Tear the veil from this illusion of affection and make her feel so wretchedly when he cared for her so much? No. There was really nothing for him to do but what he had done. He did not want to lose her. No least cloud must come over this perfect scene of affection. It would be a shame to spoil it. His artistic nature revolted at the thought. Better chance whatever might happen. After all, he reflected, it might not work out so badly. It might be made pretty clear that she had not run to him, and any detective work that Butler might choose to do would prove that. If at any moment it became necessary to bring common sense into play to save the situation from a deadly climax, he could have the Butlers secretly informed as to Aileen's whereabouts. That would show he had little to do with it, and they could try to persuade Aileen to come home again. Good might result—one could not tell. He would deal with the evils as they arose. He drove quickly back to his office, and Aileen returned to her home determined to put her plan into action. Her father had given her some little time in which to decide—possibly he would give her longer—but she would not wait. Having always had her wish granted in everything, she could not understand why she was not to have her way this time. It was about five o'clock now. She would wait until all the members of the family were comfortably seated at the dinner-table, which would be about seven o'clock, and then slip out.

CHAPTER LI

ON arriving home, however, Aileen was greeted by an unexpected reason for suspending action. This was the presence of a certain Mr. and Mrs. Steinmetz—the former a well-known engineer who drew the plans for many of the works which Butler undertook. It was the day before Thanksgiving, and they were eager to have Aileen and Norah accompany them for a fortnight's stay at their new home in West Chester—a structure concerning the charm of which Aileen had heard much. Mr. and Mrs. Steinmetz were exceedingly agreeable people—comparatively young and surrounded by a coterie of interesting friends. Aileen, in view of the protest Cowperwood had originally made and the fact that her father and mother, particularly her father, for some reason, seemed most friendly to the project, decided to delay her flight and go. She could not very well escape the presence of the Steinmetzes, who were staying for dinner, and besides she judged from her father's attitude that he had not made up his mind to anything radical as yet. He was most cordial. She did not realize that he had not solved for himself yet how he would compel her to go anywhere without the rest of the family becoming fully aware of the situation, and that the presence and invitation of the Steinmetzes was as much of a relief to him as it was to her. He had hoped that his solemn threat would be sufficient to compel Aileen to acquiescence, but if it were not he was glad of a little further time in which to arrange a plan of action. West Chester being forty miles from Philadelphia, it was unlikely that Aileen would attempt to meet Cowperwood while there—her actions would be too closely remarked by her friends; so, on hearing the proposal of the Steinmetzes he had shown approval at once. Aileen wrote Cowperwood of the changed condition and departed; and the latter breathed a sigh of relief, fancying at the time that this storm had probably permanently blown over.

In the meanwhile the day of Cowperwood's trial had been drawing near. Owing to the various facts which had been communicated to him by Aileen and others, Cowperwood himself was under the impression that an attempt was going to be made to convict him whether the facts warranted it or not. He did not see any way out of his dilemma, however, unless it was to abandon everything and leave Philadelphia for good, which was impossible. The only way to guard his future and retain his financial friends was to stand trial as quickly as possible, and trust them to assist him to his feet in the future in case he failed. He discussed the possibilities of an unfair trial with Steger, who did not seem to think that there was so much to that. In the first place, a jury could not easily be suborned by any one. In the next place, most judges were honest, in spite of their political cleavage, and would go no further than party bias would lead them in their rulings and opinions, which was, in the main, not so far.

The Court of Quarter Sessions, Part I, where this trial was to take place, was held in the famous Independence Hall, at Sixth and Chestnut Streets, which was at this time, as it had been for all of a century before, the center of local executive and judicial life. It was a low two-story building of red brick, with a white wooden central tower of old Dutch and English derivation, compounded of the square, the circle, and the octagon. The total structure consisted of a central portion and two T-shaped wings lying to the right and left, whose small, oval-topped old-fashioned windows and doors were set with those many-paned sashes so much admired by those who love what is now known as Colonial. Here and in an addition known as State House Row (since torn down), which extended from the rear of the building toward Walnut Street, were located the offices of the mayor, the chief of police, the city treasurer, the chambers of council, and all the other important and executive offices of the city, together with the four branches of Quarter Sessions, which sat to hear the growing docket of criminal cases. The mammoth city hall which was subsequently completed at Broad and Market Streets was then building.

An attempt had been made to make the reasonably large court-rooms presentable by putting in them raised platforms of dark walnut surmounted by large, dark-walnut desks, behind which the judges sat; but the attempt was not very successful. The desks, jury-boxes, and railings generally were made too large, and so the rooms looked squat. A cream-colored wall was considered the appropirate thing to go with black-walnut furniture, so that was added; but time and dust had made the combination dreary. There were no pictures or ornaments of any kind, save the stalky, over-elaborated gas-brackets which stood on his honor's desk, and the single swinging chandelier suspended from the center of the ceiling. Fat bailiffs and court officers, concerned only in holding their workless jobs, did not add anything to the spirit of the scene. Two of them in the particular court in which this trial was held (Judge Payderson's— Part I) contended hourly as to which should hand his honor a glass of water. One preceded his honor like a fat, stuffy, dusty majordomo to and from his honor's dressing-room. His business was to call loudly, when the latter entered, "His honor the Court, hats off. Everybody please rise," while a second bailiff, standing at the left of his honor when he was seated, and between the jury-box and the witness-chair, recited in an absolutely unintelligible way that beautiful and dignified old court-call, which begins, "Hear ye! hear ye! hear ye!" and ends, "All those of you having just cause for complaint draw near and ye shall be heard." You would have thought it was of no importance in the world, this beautiful and noble statement based on the majesty of the law in so far as it is based on the will of the people; but, nevertheless, it was. Only custom and indifference had allowed it to fall so badly from grace. A third bailiff guarded the door of the jury-room; and in addition to these there was present a court clerk—small, pale, candle-waxy, with colorless milk-and-water eyes, and thin, pork-fat-colored hair and beard, who looked for all the world like an Americanized and decidedly decrepit Chinese mandarin —and a court stenographer.

Part One, or Room One, where this, to Cowperwood, very significant trial was to take place, was presided over at this time by Judge Wilbur Payderson, a lean herring of a man, who had sat in this case originally as the examining judge when Cowperwood had been indicted by the grand jury, and who had bound him over for trial at this term. Payderson was a peculiarly interesting type of judge, as judges go. He was so meager and thin-blooded that it was interesting to contemplate him. Technically, he was learned in the law; actually, so far as life was concerned, absolutely unconscious of that subtle chemistry of things that transcends all written law and makes for the spirit and, beyond that, for the absolute inutility of all law, as all wise judges know. You could have looked at this lean, pedantic body, his frizzled gray hair, his fishy, blue-gray eyes, without any depth of speculation in them, and his nicely modeled but unimportant face, and told him that he was without imagination; but he would not have believed you—would have fined you for contempt of court. By the careful garnering of all his little opportunities, the furbishing up of every meager advantage; by listening slavishly to the voice of party, and following as nearly as he could the behests of intrenched property, he was where he was. It was not very far along, at that. His salary was only six thousand dollars a year. His little fame did not extend beyond the meager realm of local lawyers and judges. But the sight of his name quoted daily as being about his duties, or rendering such and such a decision, was a great satisfaction to him. He thought it made him a significant figure in the world. "Behold I am not as other men," he often thought, and this comforted him. He was very much flattered when a prominent case came to his calendar; and as he sat enthroned before the various litigants and lawyers he felt, as a rule, very significant indeed. Now and then some subtlety of life would confuse his really limited intellect; but in all such cases there was the letter of the law. He could hunt in the reports to find out what really thinking men had decided.

Payderson could scarcely be pointed to as an unjust judge; but he was a party judge—Republican in principle, or rather belief, beholden to the dominant party councils for his personal continuance in office, and as such willing and anxious to do whatever he considered that he reasonably could do to further the party welfare and the private interests of his masters. Most people never trouble to look into the mechanics of the thing they call their conscience too closely. They have no great subtlety at getting the matter of ethics and morals straight for themselves. Whatever the opinion of the time is, whatever the weight of great interests dictates, that they conscientiously believe. Some one has since invented the phrase "a corporation-minded judge." There are many such.

Payderson was one. He fairly revered property and power. To him Butler and Mollenhauer and Simpson were great men—reasonably sure to be right always because they were so powerful. How did they come to be so powerful if they were not fair? This matter of

THE FINANCIER

Cowperwood's and Stener's defalcation he had long heard
of. He knew by associating with one political light and
another just what the situation was. The party, as the
leaders saw it, had been put in a very bad position by
Cowperwood's subtlety. He had led Stener astray—more
than an ordinary city treasurer should have been led
astray—and, although Stener was primarily guilty as the
original mover in the criminality, Cowperwood was more
so for having led him on so magnificently. Besides, the
party needed a scapegoat—that was enough for Payderson, in the first place. Later, when the election was won,
and it appeared that the party had not suffered so much,
he did not understand quite why it was that Cowperwood
was still so carefully included in the proceedings; but he
had faith to believe that the leaders had some just grounds
for not letting him off. From one source and another he
learned that Butler had some private grudge against
Cowperwood. What it was no one seemed to know
exactly. The general impression was that Cowperwood
had led Butler into some unwholesome financial transactions. Anyhow, it was generally understood that for the
good of the party, and in order to teach a wholesome
lesson to dangerous subordinates—men like Cowperwood
—it had been decided to allow these several indictments to
take their course. Cowperwood was to be punished quite
as severely as Stener for the moral effect on the community.
The broker was to be sent up, if possible, for being unfair
to the bosses. Stener was to be sentenced the maximum
sentence for his crime in order that the party and the
courts should appear properly righteous. Beyond that
he was to be left to the mercy of the governor, who could
ease things up for him if he chose, and if the leaders wished.
In the silly mind of the general public the various judges
of Quarter Sessions, like girls incarcerated in boarding-
schools, were supposed in their serene aloofness from life
not to know what was going on in the subterranean realm
of politics; but they knew well enough, and, knowing

551

particularly well from whence came their continued position and authority, they were duly grateful. What the leaders wanted, within reason, and what the judges could give without too great self-sacrifice they had—Judge Wilbur Payderson included.

CHAPTER LII

THE court-room on the morning the trial began was no different from that of any other where cases of this kind are tried, though because of the notoriety of the fact and the importance of the personages involved the room was crowded. Judge Payderson was not in the room when Cowperwood and his lawyer and his father and President Davison arrived—the latter separately, but at the same hour, seeing that he had been summoned as a witness. But the scene was hardly less vivid than if Payderson had arrived, for there was an expectant hush over the place and an air of intense curiosity. The largeness of the amount involved in Stener's defalcation, Cowperwood's share in it, the lurid background of fire and panic, the subsequent newspaper comment—all had combined to whet that native human curiosity which has so little to feed itself on in the ordinary drift of humdrum affairs. Besides, the moment you introduce the elements of chance, accident, or fate into any human situation such as this you immediately arouse human curiosity to the fullest. Fate, chance, accident in the guise of the Chicago fire had made Cowperwood and Stener alleged felons. The newspapers had already freely commented on how strange it was, and yet how true to life that a fire in Chicago, nearly a thousand miles away, should have made a criminal of a man here in Philadelphia. Now the public wanted to see the man who had made a fortune out of the cupidity of Stener, and who had thus inauspiciously lost it.

When Cowperwood entered with Harper Steger and his father, quite fresh and jaunty (looking the part of the shrewd financier, the resourceful manipulator, the man

553

of affairs), they all stared. It was really too much to expect, most of them thought, that a man like this would be convicted. He was, no doubt, guilty; but, also, no doubt, he had ways and means of evading the law. His lawyer, Harper Steger, looked very shrewd and canny to them. It was very cold, and both men wore long, dark, bluish-gray overcoats, cut in the latest mode. Cowperwood was given to small *boutonnières* in fair weather, but to-day he wore none. His tie, however, was of heavy, impressive silk, of lavender hue, set with a large, clear, green emerald, which was cut narrow and long, and set bias to the line of his waistcoat buttons. He wore only the thinnest of watch-chains, and no other ornaments of any kind. He always looked reserved, impressive, jaunty, good-natured, and yet capably self-sufficient; and he never looked more so than he did to-day.

Judge Payderson came in after a time, accompanied by his undersized but stout court attendant, who looked more like a pouter pigeon than a human being; and as they came, Bailiff Sparkheaver rapped on the judge's desk, beside which he had been slumbering, and mumbled, "Please rise!" The audience arose, as is the rule of all courts.

When the judge finally cleared away the various minor motions pending, he ordered his clerk, Mr. Able Protus, to call the case of the City of Philadelphia *versus* Frank A. Cowperwood, which was done in a clear voice. Both Mr. Dennis Shannon, the district attorney, and Mr. Steger, Cowperwood's counsel, were on their feet at once. Steger and Cowperwood, together with Shannon and Strobik, who had now come in and was standing as the representative of the State of Pennsylvania—the complainant—had seated themselves at the long table inside the railing which inclosed the space before the judge's desk. Steger proposed to Judge Payderson, for effect's sake more than anything else, that this indictment be quashed, but was overruled. A jury to try the case was now quickly impaneled—twelve men out of the usual list called to serve for the month—and was then ready to be challenged by the opposing counsel. The business of impaneling a jury was a rather simple thing so far as this court was concerned. It consisted in the mandarin-like clerk taking the names of all the jurors called to serve in this court for the month—some fifty in all—and putting them, each written on a separate slip of paper, in a whirling drum, spinning it around a few times, and then lifting out the first slip which his hand encountered, thus glorifying *chance* and settling on who should be juror No. 1. His hand reaching in twelve times drew out the names of the twelve jurymen, who were, as their names were called, ordered to take their places in the jury-box in the order called.

Cowperwood observed this proceeding with a great deal of interest. What could be more important than the men who were going to try him? The process was too swift for accurate judgment, but he received a faint impression of middle-class men. One man in particular, however, an old man of sixty-five, with iron-gray hair and beard, shaggy eyebrows, sallow complexion, and stooped shoulders, struck him as having that kindness of temperament and breadth of experience which he could command for his own benefit in this case. Another, a small, sharp-nosed, sharp-chinned commercial man of some kind, he took an immediate dislike to.

"I hope I don't have to have that man on my jury," he said to Steger, quietly.

"You don't," replied Steger. "I'll challenge him. We have the right to fifteen peremptory challenges on a case like this, and so has the prosecution."

Cowperwood settled back in his chair with a sense of relief. He proposed to decide for himself whether some of these men were fit or not. When the jury-box was finally full, the two lawyers waited for the clerk to bring them the small board upon which slips of paper bearing the names of the twelve jurors were fastened in rows in order of their selection—jurors one, two, and three being in the first row; four, five, and six in the second, and so on. It being the prerogative of the attorney for the prosecution to examine and challenge the jurors first, Mr. Shannon arose, and, taking the board, began to question them as to their trades or professions, their knowledge of the case before the court, and their possible prejudice for or against the prisoner.

The collection of men which now faced Cowperwood and his lawyer, as well as the district attorney, who hoped for a conviction, was fairly representative of that assorted social fry which the drag-nets of the courts, cast into the ocean of the city, bring to the surface for purposes of this sort. It was made up in the main of managers, agents, tradesmen, editors, engineers, architects, furriers, grocers, traveling salesmen, authors, and every other kind of working citizen whose experience had fitted him for service in proceedings of this character. Rarely would you have found a man of great distinction; but very frequently a group of men who were possessed of no small modicum of that interesting quality known as hard common sense.

Each lawyer asked each juror whether he knew the present defendant, whether he was known to Stener, or had lost money in the panic, or was a hide-bound Republican, etc. Both lawyers looked them over now rather curiously (those twelve plain men they had never seen before), and Steger decided quite at once that when his turn came he would prefer to dispose of a certain long-faced, serene-eyed mechanical draftsman, with an undue rigidity of jaw and an air of self-controlling conviction, whom he saw before him.

"I will ask you to step out of the box, Mr. Simonton," he said, smilingly, and without any further explanation; and Mr. Shannon, who was a good judge of men, smiled also. He knew why. The old man, with kindly gray eyes, slanting shoulders, a full gray beard, and not too nicely trimmed hair, Steger decided to keep, because he looked wise, and as though he had suffered much. Such a man would not be too irritably eager to enforce the letter or the spirit of the law. Unfortunately, Mr. Shannon had decided in his own mind that he did not want him. Cowperwood, on his own behalf, was quietly examining the men, and he was an accurate judge of their qualities. A young florist, who was possessed of a pale skin, a wide, speculative forehead, and anemic hands, struck him as being sufficiently impressionable to his personal charm to be worth while. He whispered as much to Steger, who was standing beside him. There was a shrewd Jew, a furrier, who was challenged because he had read all the news of the panic and had lost two thousand dollars in street-railway stocks. There was a stout wholesale butcher with red cheeks, blue eyes, and flaxen hair, whom Cowperwood said he thought was easily prejudiced and stubborn. He was eliminated. There was a thin, dapper manager of a small retail clothing store, very anxious to be excused, who declared, falsely, that he did not believe in swearing at all by the Bible. Judge Payderson, eying him severely, let him go. There were some ten more in all—men who knew of Cowperwood, men who admitted they were prejudiced, men who were hide-bound Republicans and resentful of this crime, men who knew Stener—who were pleasantly eliminated. One man was dropped because he was a contractor, and most likely friendly to the administration, though he said not. He was an Irishman. Another because he was a Southerner with a peculiar streak of prejudice and narrowness showing in his eyes. So it went. Oh, for a modern Frans Hals or Rembrandt to paint a jury!

By twelve o'clock, however, a jury reasonably satisfactory to both sides had been chosen. Cowperwood looked them over finally; he thought they seemed like fairly sensible, considerate men—young and old—and so he said that as far as he was concerned they might be sworn. Shannon accepted them also without further criticism.

CHAPTER LIII

AT two o'clock sharp Dennis Shannon, as district
attorney, charged to present the case to the jury,
began his opening address. In all such cases it is the
district attorney who states to the jury the nature of the
case that the people, through the agency of the court,
are about to present to it. He stated in a very simple,
kindly way—for he had a most engaging manner—that the
indictment as here presented charged Mr. Frank A. Cowperwood, who was sitting at the table inside the jury-rail,
first with larceny, second with embezzlement, third with
larceny as bailee, and fourth with embezzlement of a certain sum of money—a specific sum, to wit, sixty thousand
dollars—on a check given him (drawn to his order)
October 9, 1871, which was intended to reimburse him
for a certain number of certificates of city loan, which he
as agent or bailee of the check was supposed to have purchased for the city sinking-fund on the order of the city
treasurer (under some form of agreement which had been
in existence between them, and which had been in force
for some time)—said fund being intended to take up
such certificates as they might mature in the hands of
holders and be presented for payment—for which purpose,
however, the check in question had never been used.

"Now, gentlemen," said Mr. Shannon, very quietly and
innocently, "before we go into this very simple question
of whether Mr. Cowperwood did or did not on the date
in question get from the city treasurer sixty thousand
dollars, for which he made no honest return, let me explain to you just what the people mean when they charge
him first with larceny, second with embezzlement, third

with larceny as bailee, and fourth with embezzlement on a check—that is, the check for sixty thousand dollars which he secured on the date in question without making any adequate return, or, indeed, any return whatsoever. Now, as you see, there are four counts here, as we lawyers term them, and the reason there are four counts is as follows: A man may be guilty of larceny and embezzlement at the same time, or of larceny or embezzlement separately, and without being guilty of the other, and the district attorney representing the people might be uncertain, not that he was not guilty of both, but that it might not be possible to present the evidence under one count, so as to insure his adequate punishment for a crime which in a way involved both. In such cases, gentlemen, it it customary to indict a man under separate counts, as has been done in this case. Now, the four counts in this case, in a way, overlap and confirm each other, and it will be your duty, after we have explained their nature and character and presented the evidence in regard to the fact, to say whether the defendant is guilty on one count or the other, or on two or three of the counts, or on all four, just as you see fit and proper—or, to put it in a better way, as the evidence warrants. Larceny, as you may or may not know, is the act of taking away the goods or chattels of another without his knowledge or consent, and embezzlement is the fraudulent appropriation to one's own use of what is intrusted to one's care and management, especially money. Larceny as bailee, on the other hand, is simply a more definite form of larceny wherein one fixes the act of carrying away the goods of another without his knowledge or consent on the person to whom the goods were delivered in trust—that is, the agent or bailee. Embezzlement on a check, which constitutes the fourth charge, is simply a more definite form of fixing charge number two in an exact way and signifies appropriating the money on a check given for a certain definite purpose. All of these charges, as you can see, gentlemen, are in a way synonymous. They overlap and overlay each other. The people, through their representative, the district attorney, contend that Mr. Cowperwood, the defendant here, is guilty of all four charges. So now, gentlemen, we will proceed to the history of this crime, which proves to me as an individual that this defendant has one of the most subtle and dangerous minds of the criminal financial type, and we hope by witnesses to prove that to you, also."

Mr. Shannon, because the rules of evidence and court procedure admit of no interruption of the prosecution in presenting a case, went on to describe from his own point of view how Cowperwood had first met Stener; how he had wormed himself into his confidence; how little financial knowledge Stener had, and so forth; coming down finally to the day the check for sixty thousand dollars was given Cowperwood; how Stener, as treasurer, claimed that he knew nothing of its delivery, which constituted the base of the charge of larceny; how Cowperwood, having it, misappropriated the certificates supposed to have been purchased for the sinking-fund, if they were purchased at all—all of which Shannon said constituted the crimes with which the defendant was charged, and of which he was unquestionably guilty.

"We have direct and positive evidence of all that we have thus far contended, gentlemen," Mr. Shannon concluded violently. "This is not a matter of hearsay or theory, but of fact. You will be shown by direct testimony which cannot be shaken just how it was done. If, after you have heard all this, you still think this man is innocent—that he did not commit the crimes with which he is charged—it is your business to acquit him. On the other hand, if you think the witnesses whom we shall put on the stand are telling the truth, then it is your business to convict him, to find a verdict for the people as against the defendant. I thank you for your attention."

The jurors stirred comfortably and took positions of ease, in which they thought they were to rest for the time; but their idle comfort was of short duration for Mr. Shannon, now called out the name of Mr. George W. Stener, who came hurrying forward very pale, very flaccid, very tired-looking. His eyes, as he took his seat in the witness-chair, laying his hand on the Bible and swearing to tell the truth, roved in a restless, nervous manner. Cowperwood studied him a moment carefully as he sat down and their eyes met. Stener had no courage, apparently, any more—no viewpoint. He could not endure Cowperwood's steady, examining eye, though he knew now, for the first time, that Cowperwood was bent on discrediting his truthful testimony with a hard, barefaced lie. He twisted nervously in his chair; his hands kept opening and closing and moving forward and backward on the high side-arms.

"He certainly has got into a bad state physically," observed Cowperwood to Steger, calmly; and the latter agreed quite pleasantly. They watched him as Mr. Shannon began, and all through his testimony; but he never again looked at Cowperwood—he could not for some reason, though he really had the more truthful end of the argument.

Was he George W. Stener? Yes. Where did he live? At present at 1112 Spring Garden Street. What was his business or occupation on October 9th last? He was treasurer of the city of Philadelphia. And did he know the defendant, Frank A. Cowperwood, who was sitting at this table here behind the speaker? He did. Would he tell the gentlemen of the jury where, how, and under what circumstances he had first met the defendant, and would he please try to speak very loud and clear, so that all the members of the jury might hear—the furthest member over here, even?

Mr. Stener cleared his voice, which was a little weak. He had first met Mr. Cowperwood in the early months of 1866—he could not remember the exact day; it was during his first term as city treasurer—he had been elected to the office in the fall of 1864. He had been troubled about the condition of city loan, which was below par, and which could not be sold by the city legally at anything but par. Mr. Cowperwood had been recommended to him by some one—Mr. Strobik, he believed, though he couldn't be sure. It was the custom of city treasurers to employ brokers, or a broker, in a crisis of this kind, and he was merely following what had been the custom. He went on to describe, under steady promptings and questions from the incisive mind of Mr. Shannon, just what the nature of this first conversation was—he remembered it fairly well; how Mr. Cowperwood had said he thought he could do what was wanted; how Cowperwood had gone away and drawn up a plan or thought one out; and how he had returned and laid it before Stener. Under Mr. Shannon's skilful guidance Stener elucidated just what this scheme was—which wasn't exactly so flattering to the honesty of men in general as it was a testimonial to their subtlety and skill. After much discussion of Stener's and Cowperwood's relations the story finally got down to the preceding October, when by dint of companionship, long business understanding, mutually prosperous relationship, etc., the place had been reached where it was explained Cowperwood was not only handling several millions of city loan annually, buying and selling for the city and trading in it generally, but in the bargain had secured some five hundred thousand dollars' worth of city money at an exceedingly low rate of interest, which was being invested for himself and Stener in profitable street-car ventures of one kind and another. Stener was not anxious to be altogether clear on this point; but Shannon, seeing that he was later to prosecute Stener himself for this very crime of embezzlement, and that Steger would soon follow in cross-examination, was not willing to let him be hazy. Shannon wanted to fix Cowperwood in the minds of the jury as a clever, tricky financial person, and he certainly managed to indicate a very subtle-minded man. The jurors occasionally, as one sharp point of his skill after another was brought out and made moderately clear, turned to look at Cowperwood. He merely gazed Stenerward with a steady air of intelligence and comprehension.

The examination now came down to the matter of the particular check for sixty thousand dollars which Albert Stires had handed Cowperwood on the afternoon—late— of October 9, 1871. Mr. Shannon showed Mr. Stener the check itself. Had he ever seen it? Yes. Where? In the office of District-Attorney Pettie on October 20th, or thereabouts, last. Was that the first time he had seen it? Yes. Had he ever heard about it before then? Yes. When? On October 10th last. Would he kindly tell the jury in his own way just how and under what circumstances he first heard of it then? Mr. Stener twisted uncomfortably in his chair. It was a hard thing to do. It was not a pleasant commentary on his own character and degree of moral stamina, to say the least. However, he cleared his throat again and began a description of that small but bitter section of his life's drama in which Cowperwood, finding himself in a tight place and about to fail, had come to him at his office and demanded that he loan him three hundred thousand dollars more in one lump sum.

There was considerable bickering just at this point between Mr. Steger and Mr. Shannon, for the former was very anxious to make it appear that Mr. Stener was lying out of the whole cloth about this—that his client had never said that he was about to fail, and that the sum had not been as much as three hundred thousand dollars. Steger got in his objection at this point, and created a considerable diversion from the main theme, because Stener kept saying he "thought" or he "believed."

"Object!" shouted Steger, repeatedly. "I move that that be stricken from the record as incompetent, irrelevant, and immaterial. The witness is not allowed to say what he thinks, and the prosecution knows it very well."

"Your honor," insisted Shannon, "I am doing the best I can to have the witness tell a plain, straightforward story, and I think that it is obvious that he is doing so."

"Object!" reiterated Steger, vociferously. "Your honor, I insist that the district attorney has no right to prejudice the minds of the jury by flattering estimates of the sincerity of the witness. What he thinks of the witness and his sincerity is of no importance in this case. I must ask that your honor caution him plainly in this matter."

"Objection overruled," declared Judge Payderson; and Shannon went on with his case.

During this testimony Cowperwood stared at Stener in a curious way. You would have thought he was trying to influence him mentally in some fashion. He was pleased to see that Stener had no intention or opportunity to shift or lie on any particular points. The preceding district attorney had framed this case so as to try it solely on the merits of the question whether or not Cowperwood, knowing that he was a bankrupt at the time, had feloniously appropriated to his own use sixty thousand dollars' worth of the city's money. All the evidence admitted to the records of the case must tend either to affirm or deny this fact. Stener's testimony, in one respect, was most important, for it made plain what Mr. Cowperwood did not want brought out—namely, that Cowperwood and Stener had had a dispute before this; that Stener had distinctly told Cowperwood that he would not loan him any more money; that Cowperwood had told Stener, on the day before he secured this check, and again on that very day, that he was in a very desperate situation financially, and that if he were not assisted to the extent of three hundred thousand dollars he would fail, and that then both he and Stener would be ruined.

On the morning of this day, according to Stener, he had sent Cowperwood a letter ordering him to cease purchasing city loan certificates for the sinking-fund. It was after their conversation on the same afternoon that Cowperwood surreptitiously secured the check for sixty thousand dollars from Albert Stires without his (Stener's) knowledge; and it was subsequent to this latter again that Stener, sending Albert to demand the return of the check, was refused, though the next day at five o'clock in the afternoon Cowperwood made an assignment. This was dark testimony for Cowperwood.

If any one imagines that all this was done without many vehement *objections* and *exceptions* made and taken by Mr. Steger, and subsequently when he was cross-examining Mr. Stener, by Mr. Shannon, they will err greatly. The chamber was coruscating at times with these two gentlemen's bitter wrangles, and his honor was compelled to hammer his desk with his gavel, and to threaten both with contempt of court, in order to bring them to a sense of order. Mr. Steger was most bitter in his characterization of Mr. Shannon's motives, and finally they nearly came to blows over the question as to whether Mr. Shannon was a shyster, as charged by Mr. Steger. The jury was amused and interested. Judge Payderson was highly incensed.

"You gentlemen will have to stop this, or I tell you now that you will both be heavily fined. This is a court of law, not a bar-room. Mr. Steger, I expect you to apologize to me and your colleague at once. Mr. Shannon, I must ask that you use less aggressive methods. Your manner is offensive to me. It is not becoming to a court of law. I will not caution either of you again."

Both lawyers apologized as lawyers do on such occasions, but it really made but little difference. Their individual attitudes and moods continued about as before.

"What did he say to you," asked Mr. Shannon of Mr. Stener, after one of these troublesome interruptions, "on that occasion, October 9th last, when he came to you and demanded the loan of an additional three hundred thousand dollars? Give his words as near as you can remember—exactly, if possible."

"Object!" interposed Mr. Steger, vigorously. "His exact words are not recorded anywhere except in Mr. Stener's memory, and his memory of them cannot be admitted in this case. The witness has testified to the general facts."

Judge Payderson smiled grimly. "Objection over-ruled," he returned, chewing his pencil-point to pass the time.

"Exception!" shouted Mr. Steger.

"He said, as near as I can remember," replied Stener, drumming on the arms of the witness-chair in a nervous way, "that if I didn't give him three hundred thousand dollars he was going to fail, and I would be poor and go to the penitentiary."

"Object!" shouted Mr. Steger, leaping to his feet. "Your honor, I object to the whole manner in which this examination is being conducted by the prosecution. The evidence which the district attorney is here trying to extract from the uncertain memory of the witness is in defiance of all law and precedent, and has no definite bearing on the facts of the case, and could not disprove or substantiate whether Mr. Cowperwood thought or did not think that he was going to fail. Mr. Stener might give one version of this conversation or any conversation that took place at this time, and Mr. Cowperwood an-other. As a matter of fact, their versions are different. I see no point in Mr. Shannon's line of inquiry, unless it is to prejudice the jury's minds toward accepting certain allegations which the prosecution is pleased to make and which it cannot possibly substantiate. I think you ought to caution the witness to testify only in regard to things that he recalls exactly, not to what he thinks he remem-bers; and for my part I think that all that has been testified to in the last five minutes might be well stricken out."

"Objection overruled," replied Judge Payderson, rather indifferently; and Steger, who had been talking merely to overcome the weight of Stener's testimony in the minds of the jury, sat down.

Mr. Shannon once more approached Mr. Stener.

"Now, as near as you can remember, Mr. Stener, I wish you would tell the jury what else it was that Mr. Cowperwood said on that occasion. He certainly didn't stop with the remark that you would be ruined and go to the penitentiary. Wasn't there other language that was employed on that occasion?"

"He said, as far as I can remember," replied Stener, "that there were a lot of political schemers who were trying to frighten me, that if I didn't give him three hundred thousand dollars we would both be ruined, and that I might as well be tried for stealing a sheep as a lamb."

"Ha!" yelled Shannon. "He said that, did he?"

"Yes, sir; he did," said Stener.

"How did he say it, exactly? What were his exact words?" Shannon demanded, emphatically, pointing a forceful forefinger at Stener in order to key him up to a clear memory of what had transpired.

"Well, as near as I can remember, he said just that," replied Stener, vaguely. "You might as well be tried for stealing a sheep as a lamb."

"Exactly!" exclaimed Mr. Shannon, whirling around past the jury to look at Cowperwood. "I thought so."

"Pure pyrotechnics, your honor," said Steger, rising to his feet on the instant. "All intended to prejudice the minds of the jury. Acting. I wish you would caution the counsel for the prosecution to confine himself to the evidence in hand, and not act for the benefit of his case."

The spectators smiled; and Judge Payderson, noting

it, frowned severely. "Do you make that as an objection, Mr. Steger?" he asked.

"I certainly do, your honor," insisted Steger, resourcefully.

"Objection overruled. Neither counsel for the prosecution nor for the defense is limited to a peculiar routine of expression."

Steger himself was ready to smile, but he did not dare to.

When Mr. Shannon was through bringing out this unsatisfactory data, Mr. Steger took Mr. Stener in hand; but he could not make as much out of him as he hoped. In so far as this particular situation was concerned, Stener was telling the exact truth; and it is hard to weaken the effect of the exact truth by any subtlety of interpretation, though it can, sometimes, be done. With painstaking care Steger went over all the ground of Stener's long relationship with Cowperwood, and tried to make it appear that Cowperwood was invariably the disinterested agent— not the ringleader in a subtle, really criminal adventure. It was hard to do, but he made a fine impression. Still the jury listened with skeptical minds. It might not be fair to punish Cowperwood for seizing with avidity upon a splendid chance to get rich quick, they thought; but it certainly was not worth while to throw a veil of innocence over such palpable human cupidity. Finally, both lawyers were through with Stener for the time being, anyhow, and then Mr. Albert Stires was called to the stand.

He was the same thin, pleasant, alert, rather agreeable soul that he had been in the heyday of his clerkly prosperity—a little paler now, but not otherwise changed. His small property had been saved for him by Cowperwood, who had advised Steger to inform the Municipal Reform Association that Stires's bondsmen were attempting to sequestrate it for their own benefit, when actually it should go to the city if there were any real claim against him—which there was not. That watchful organization had issued one of its numerous reports covering this point, and Albert had had the pleasure of seeing Strobik and the others withdraw in haste. Naturally he was grateful to Cowperwood, even though once he had been compelled to cry in vain in his presence. He was anxious now to do anything he could to help the banker, but his naturally truthful disposition prevented him from telling anything except the plain facts, which were partly beneficial and partly not.

Stires testified that he recalled Cowperwood's saying that he had purchased the certificates, that he was entitled to the money, that Stener was unduly frightened, and that no harm would come to him, Albert. He identified certain memoranda in the city treasurer's books, which were produced, as being accurate, and others in Cowperwood's books, which were also produced, as being corroborative. His testimony as to Stener's astonishment on discovering that his chief clerk had given Cowperwood a check was against the latter; but Cowperwood hoped to overcome the effect of this by his own testimony later.

During all the examination and cross-examination by his lawyer and Shannon, Cowperwood sat solemnly gazing at the witness. For once he was fairly interested in this dizzy process of law. He could not control this straightforward flow of evidence by Albert. He did not know that he wanted to. In the main, it was not unfavorable. Altogether it was a very complicated case, and the jury showed it in their faces. Up to now both Steger and Cowperwood felt that they were doing fairly well, however, and that they need not be surprised if they won their case.

The subtlety of law!

CHAPTER LIV

THE trial moved on. The witnesses for the prosecution followed one another until the State had built up an arraignment that satisfied Mr. Dennis Shannon, when he announced that he rested. Steger at once arose and began a long argument for the dismissal of the case, but Judge Payderson would have none of it. He knew how important the matter was in the local political world.

"I don't think you had better go into all that now, Mr. Steger," he said, wearily, after allowing him to proceed a reasonable distance. "I am familiar with the custom of the city, and the indictment as here made does not concern the custom of the city. I would like to hear your argument, but I don't believe it will do any good. As I understand this case, it is specifically a question of fact—one fact—namely, whether Mr. Cowperwood, your client, did or did not on a certain date obtain a certain sum of money under false pretenses, did or did not fail to perform certain duties under a given agreement—which in this case, as I understand, constitutes the charge of larceny as bailee. Now I can't enter into a discussion of that before a jury has had a chance to pass on the facts alleged. Your argument is with the jury, not with me. I couldn't enter into that now. You may renew your motion at the close of the defendants' case. Motion denied."

District-Attorney Shannon, who had been listening attentively, sat down. Steger, seeing there was no chance to soften the judge's mind by any subtlety of argument, returned to Cowperwood, who smiled at the result.

"We'll just have to take our chances with the jury," said Steger.

"I was sure of it," replied his employer.

Steger then approached them, and, having outlined the case briefly from his angle of observation, continued by telling them what he was sure the evidence would show from his point of view.

"As a matter of fact, gentlemen, there is no essential difference in the evidence which the prosecution can present and that which we, the defense, can present. The difference is not so much in testimony, as you will soon see, for we are not going to dispute that Mr. Cowperwood received a check from Mr. Stener for sixty thousand dollars, or that he failed to put the certificate of city loan which that sum of money represented, and to which he was entitled in payment as agent, in the sinking-fund, which the prosecution now claims he should have done; we are going to claim that he had a right, as the agent of the city, doing, and having done, business with the city through its treasury department for four years, to withhold, under an agreement which he had with the city treasurer, all payments of money and all deposits of certificates in the sinking-fund until the first day of each succeeding month—the first month following any given transaction. The prosecution is going to ask you to believe that Mr. Cowperwood knew at the time he received this check that he was going to fail; that he did not buy the certificates, as he claimed, with the view of placing them in the sinking-fund; and that, knowing he was going to fail, and that he could not subsequently deposit them, he deliberately went to Mr. Albert Stires, Mr. Stener's secretary, told him that he had purchased such certificates, and on the strength of a falsehood, implied if not actually spoken, secured the check, and walked away.

"Now, gentlemen, I am not going to enter into a long-winded discussion of these points at this time, since the testimony is going to show very rapidly what the facts are. We have a number of witnesses here, and we are all anxious to have them heard. What I am going to ask you to remember is that there is not one scintilla of testimony outside of that which may possibly be given by Mr. George W. Stener, which will show either that Mr. Cowperwood knew, at the time he called on the city treasurer, that he was going to fail, or that he had not purchased the certificates in question, or that he had not the right to withhold them from the sinking-fund as long as he pleased up to the first of the month, the time he invariably struck a balance with the city. Mr. Stener, the ex-city treasurer, may possibly testify one way. Mr. Cowperwood, on his own behalf, will testify another. It will then be for you gentlemen to decide between them, to decide which one you prefer to believe—Mr. George W. Stener, the ex-city treasurer, the former commercial associate of Mr. Cowperwood, who, after years and years of profit, solely because of conditions of financial stress, fire, and panic, preferred to turn on his one-time associate from whose labors he had reaped so much profit, or Mr. Frank A. Cowperwood, the well-known banker and financier, who did his best to weather the storm alone, who fulfilled to the letter every agreement he ever had with the city, who has even until this hour been busy, unremunerated in his efforts, to remedy, in so far as within him lies, the unfair financial difficulties forced upon him by fire and panic, and who only yesterday made an offer to the city that, if he were allowed to continue in uninterrupted control of his affairs, and so bring order out of chaos, he would gladly repay as quickly as possible every dollar of his indebtedness (which is really not all his), including the five hundred thousand dollars under discussion between him and Mr. Stener and the city, and so prove by his works, not talk, that there was no basis, in fact, for this unfair suspicion of his motives. As you perhaps surmise, the city has not chosen to accept his offer, and I shall try and tell you why later, gentlemen. For the present we will proceed with the testimony, and for the defense all I ask is that you give very close attention to all that is testified to here to-day. Listen very carefully to Mr. W. C. Davison when he is put on the stand — study him. Listen equally carefully to Mr. Frank A. Cowperwood when we call him to testify. Follow the other testimony closely, and then you will be able to judge for yourselves. See if you can distinguish a just motive for this prosecution. I can't. I am very much obliged to you for listening to me, gentlemen, so carefully."

He then, on behalf of Cowperwood, put on Arthur Rivers, who had acted for Cowperwood on 'change as special agent during the panic, to testify to the large quantities of city loan he had purchased to stay the market; and then after him, Cowperwood's brothers, Edward and Joseph, who had come to court later in the day, and who testified to instructions received from Rivers as to buying and selling city loan on that occasion—principally buying.

The next witness after these was President W. C. Davison of the Girard National Bank. He was a large man physically, not so round of body as full and broad. His shoulders and chest were ample. He had a big blond head, with an ample breadth of forehead, which was high and sane-looking. He had a thick, squat nose, which, however, was forceful, and thin, firm, even lips. There was the faintest touch of cynical humor in his hard blue eyes at times; but mostly he was friendly, alert, placid-looking, without seeming in the least sentimental or even kindly. His business, as one could see plainly, was to insist on hard financial facts, and one could see also how he would naturally be drawn to Frank Algernon Cowperwood without being mentally dominated or upset by him. Cowperwood had the type of financial mind which he admired. As he took the chair very quietly, and yet one might say significantly, it was obvious that he felt that this sort of legal-financial palaver was above the average man and beneath the dignity of a true financier—in other words, a bother. The drowsy Sparkheaver holding up a Bible beside him for him to swear by might as well have been a block of wood. His oath was a personal matter with him. It was good business to tell the truth at times. He looked over to where Cowperwood sat, but did not attempt to take his eye. He knew that Cowperwood knew that he liked him and would do anything within the lines of financial safety and his personal comfort to assist him. His testimony was very direct and very simple.

He had known Mr. Frank Algernon Cowperwood for nearly ten years. He had done business with or through him nearly all of that time. He knew nothing of his personal relations with Mr. Stener, and did not know Mr. Stener personally. As for the particular check of sixty thousand dollars—yes, he had seen it before. It had come into the bank on October 10th along with other collateral to offset an overdraft on the part of Cowperwood & Co. It was placed to the credit of Cowperwood & Co. on the books of the bank, and the bank secured the cash through the clearing-house. No money was drawn out of the bank by Cowperwood & Co. after that to create an overdraft. The bank's account with Cowperwood was squared.

Nevertheless, Mr. Cowperwood might have drawn heavily, and nothing would have been thought of it. Mr. Davison did not know that Mr. Cowperwood was going to fail—did not suppose that he could, so quickly. He had frequently overdrawn his account with the bank; as a matter of fact, it was the regular course of his business to overdraw it. It kept his assets actively in use, which was the height of good business. His overdrafts were protected by collateral, however, and it was his custom to send bundles of collateral or checks, or both, which were variously distributed to keep things straight. Mr. Cowperwood's account was the largest and most active in the bank, Mr. Davison kindly volunteered. When Mr. Cowperwood had failed there had been over ninety thousand dollars' worth of certificates of city loan in the bank's possession which Mr. Cowperwood had sent there as collateral. Mr. Shannon, on cross-examination, tried to find out for the sake of the effect on the jury whether Mr. Davison was not for some ulterior motive especially favorable to Mr. Cowperwood. It was not possible for him to do that. Mr. Steger followed, and did his best to render the favorable points made by Mr. Davison in Mr. Cowperwood's behalf perfectly clear to the jury by having him repeat them. Mr. Shannon objected, of course, but it was of no use. Mr. Steger managed to get in his point.

Steger now decided to have Cowperwood take the stand, and at the mention of the latter's name in this connection the whole court-room bristled up.

Cowperwood came forward briskly and quickly, and one could scarcely expect a witness to present a surer, more effective, more reasonable appearance on the witness-stand. He was so calm, so jaunty, so defiant of life, and yet so courteous to it. These lawyers, this jury, this straw-and-water judge, these machinations of fate, did not basically disturb or humble or weaken him. He saw through the mental equipment of the jury at once. He estimated Mr. Shannon and Mr. Steger at their true and respective worths. He wanted to assist Mr. Steger to disturb and confuse Mr. Shannon, but his reason told him that only an indestructible fabric of fact or seeming would do it. He believed in the financial *rightness* of the thing he had done. He was entitled to do it. Life was war—particularly financial life; and strategy was its keynote, its duty, its necessity. Why should he bother about petty, picayune minds which could not understand this? He did not propose to bother. His business was to deceive or to elude them, to feed their voracious non-understanding with a fat *seeming* of some kind. Let them be fed with emotional, sentimental, or academic straw, if possible, and be persuaded to believe that it was solid food. As for him, he would go his way, get strong and powerful, because he could not so be fed. He went over his history for Mr. Steger and the jury, and put the sanest, most comfortable light on it that he could. He had not gone to Mr. Stener in the first place, he said—he had been called. He had not urged Mr. Stener to anything. He had merely shown him and his friends financial possibilities which they were only too eager to seize upon. And they had seized upon them. (It was not possible for Mr. Shannon to discover at this period how subtly he had organized his street-car companies so that he could have "shaken out" Mr. Stener and his friends without their being able to voice a single protest, so he talked of these things as opportunities which he had made for Stener and others. Mr. Shannon was not a financier, neither was Mr. Steger. They had to believe in a way, though they doubted it, partly—particularly Shannon.) Cowperwood was not responsible for the custom prevailing in the office of the city treasurer, he said. He was a banker and broker. The jury looked at him, and believed all except this matter of the sixty-thousand-dollar check. When it came to that he explained it all plausibly enough. When he had gone to see Stener those several last days, he had not fancied that he was really going to fail. He had asked Stener for some money, it is true—not so very much, all things considered—one hundred and fifty thousand dollars; but, as Stener should have testified, he (Cowperwood) was not disturbed in his manner. Stener had merely been one resource of his. He was satisfied at that time that he had many others. He had not used the forceful language or made the urgent appeal which Stener said he had, although he had pointed out to Stener that it was a mistake to become panic-stricken in any way or to withhold further credit. Stener was his easiest, his quickest resource, but not his only one. He thought, as a matter of fact, that his credit would be greatly extended by his principal money friends if necessary, and that he would have ample time to patch up his affairs and keep things going until the storm should blow over. He had told Stener of his extended purchase of city loan to stay the market on the first day of the panic, and of the fact that sixty thousand dollars was due him. Stener had made no objection. It was just possible that he was too mentally disturbed at the time to pay close attention. After that, to his, Cowperwood's, surprise, unexpected pressure on great financial houses from unexpected directions had caused them to be not willingly but unfortunately severe with him. This pressure, coming collectively the next day, had compelled him to close his doors, though he had not really expected to up to the last moment. His call for the sixty-thousand-dollar check at the time he had called for it was purely fortuitous. He needed the money, of course, but it was due him, and his clerks were all very busy. He merely asked for and took it personally to save time. Stener knew if it had been refused him he would have brought suit. The matter of depositing city loan certificates in the sinking-fund, when purchased for the city, was something to which he never gave any personal attention whatsoever. His bookkeeper, Mr. Stapley, attended to all that. He did not know, as a matter of fact, that they had not been deposited. (This was a barefaced lie. He did know.) As for the check being turned over to the Girard National Bank, that was fortuitous. It might just as well have been turned over to some other bank if the conditions had been different.

He was through finally, and the effect on the jury of his testimony and his personality was peculiar. The young florist, Mr. Richard Marsh, with his waxen face and weak eyes, believed that all that he said was quite true. He had not intended to rob the city of sixty thousand dollars. On the other hand, a juror by the name of Moultrie, the owner and manager of a small wholesale chicken and egg business—Philip Moultrie, juror No. 1— studied Cowperwood's face with a great deal of interest, and decided that he was lying. He could not see how it was possible that Cowperwood could not know the day before that he was going to fail. He must have known, he thought. Anyhow, the whole series of transactions between him and Stener seemed deserving of some punishment, and all during this testimony he was thinking how, when he got in the jury-room, he would vote guilty. He even thought of some of the arguments he would use to convince the others that Cowperwood was guilty. Juror No. 2, on the contrary, Simon Glassberg, a clothier, thought he understood how it all came about, and decided to vote for acquittal. He did not think Cowperwood was innocent, but he did not think he deserved to be punished. Juror No. 3, Fletcher Norton, an architect, thought Cowperwood was guilty, but at the same time that he was too talented to be sent to prison. Juror No. 4, Charles Hillegan, an Irishman, a contractor, and a somewhat religious-minded person, thought Cowperwood was guilty and ought to be punished. Juror No. 5, Philip Lukash, a coal merchant, thought he was guilty, and at present he thought little more about it. Juror No. 6, Benjamin Fraser, a mining expert, thought he was probably guilty, but he could not be sure. Uncertain what he would do, juror No. 7, J. J. Bridges, a broker in Third Street, small, practical, narrow, thought Cowperwood was shrewd and guilty and deserved to be punished. He would vote for his punishment. Juror No. 8, Guy E. Tripp, general manager of a small steamboat company, was uncertain. Cowperwood might or might not be guilty. He did not know. Juror No. 9, Joseph Tisdale, a retired glue manufacturer, thought Cowperwood was probably guilty as charged, but to Tisdale it was no crime. Cowperwood was entitled to do as he had done under the circumstances. Tisdale would vote for his acquittal. Juror No. 10, Richard Marsh, the young florist, was, as we have seen, for Cowperwood in a sentimental way. He had, as a matter of fact, no real convictions. Juror No. 11, Richard Webber, a grocer, small financially, but heavy physically, was for Cowperwood's conviction. He thought him guilty. "He is guilty," he said to himself, stoutly. Juror No. 12, Washington B. Thomas, a wholesale flour merchant, thought Cowperwood was guilty, but believed in a recommendation to mercy after pronouncing him so. Men ought to be reformed, was his slogan.

So they stood, and so Cowperwood left them, wondering whether anything he had said had had a favorable effect or not.

CHAPTER LV

THE legal arguments for the defendant and for the State had drawn to their weary close; both Steger and Shannon had done their best with the evidence at their command, and the case was ready to go to the jury. It had grown quite dark, and by the flare of the street lamps outside one could see that it was snowing. The judge stirred among his papers, turned solemnly to the jurors, and began the customary explanation of the law known as his instructions. This formality occupied some twenty minutes, during which time Cowperwood looked at the jury curiously, wondering what they had actually thought—were thinking. What would they decide? He sat and meditated on this while Judge Payderson finished his instructions and asked the jury to retire, which they did, passing down a side aisle toward which Cowperwood was facing. Judge Payderson left the bench for the time being. Cowperwood then turned to his father, who now came over across the fast-emptying court, and said:

"Well, we'll know now in a little while all about this."

"Yes," replied Cowperwood, Sr., a little wearily. "I hope it comes out right. I saw Butler back there a little while ago."

"Did you?" queried Cowperwood, to whom this had a peculiar interest.

"Yes," replied his father. "He's just gone."

So, Cowperwood thought, Butler was curious enough as to his fate to want to come here and watch him tried. He had slipped in, not expecting to be seen, possibly. Shannon was his tool. Judge Payderson was his emissary, in a way. He, Cowperwood, might defeat him in the matter of his daughter, but it was not so easy to defeat him here unless the jury should happen to take a sympathetic attitude. They might convict him, and then Butler's Judge Payderson would have the privilege of sentencing him—giving him the maximum of sentence. That would not be so nice—five years! He cooled a little as he thought of it, but there was no use worrying about what had not yet happened. Steger came forward and told him that his bail was now ended—had been the moment the jury left the room—and that he was at this moment actually in the care of the sheriff, whom he knew—Sheriff Adlai Jaspers. Unless he were acquitted by the jury, Steger added, he would have to remain in the sheriff's care until an application for a certificate of reasonable doubt could be made and acted upon.

He and Cowperwood and the latter's father now stalked off with the sheriff's subordinate—a small man by the name of "Eddie" Zanders, who had approached to take charge. They entered a small room called the pen at the back of the court, where all those on trial whose liberty had been forfeited by the jury's leaving the room had to wait pending its return. It was a dreary, high-ceiled, four-square place, with a window looking out into Chestnut Street, and a second door leading off into somewhere—one had no idea where. It was dingy, with a worn wooden floor, some heavy, plain, wooden benches lining the four sides, no pictures or ornaments of any kind. A single two-arm gas-pipe descended from the center of the ceiling. It was permeated by a peculiarly stale and pungent odor, obviously redolent of all the flotsam and jetsam of life—criminal and innocent—that had stood or sat in here from time to time, waiting patiently to learn what a deliberating fate held in store.

Cowperwood was, of course, disgusted; but he was too self-reliant and capable to show it. All his life he had been immaculate, almost fastidious in his care of himself.

Here he was coming, perforce, in contact with a form of life to which he objected very much, and it jarred upon him greatly. Jails, penitentiaries—they were compounded of atmospheres like this. Horrible! And this was only a brief foretaste of what, in the uncomfortable providence of chance, might become in a few moments a more enduring reality. Five days—in a little while longer, years. Ghastly! His jaw stiffened, and he pulled himself together in order not to make some remark which would show that he was thinking of this. Steger, who was beside him, very cheerful and optimistic, made some comforting, explanatory, apologetic remarks.

"Not as nice as it might be," he said; "but you won't mind waiting a little while. The jury won't be long, I fancy."

"That may not help me," he replied, walking to the window. Afterward he added: "What must be, must be."

His father winced. Suppose Frank was on the verge of a long prison term, which meant an atmosphere like this. Good heavens! For a moment he trembled; then, for the first time in years, he made a silent prayer—an appeal, which prayer is.

Meanwhile the great argument had been begun in the jury-room, and all the points that had been meditatively speculated upon in the jury-box were now being openly discussed here. The man who is supposed to take charge of the jury in the jury-room, and in a way to organize it —a purely perfunctory labor—is juror No. 1—in this instance Philip Moultrie, the wholesale chicken and egg dealer; but because he was a little backward Mr. Simon Glassberg, who had served on many juries, spoke up and said he thought that the best way to begin would be to take a ballot.

"Dot's de way we usually work on juries," he volunteered with a slightly German accent, and genially offered around some cigars. All but Webber, the grocer, and

Washington Thomas had cigars of their own, and produced them; but these two accepted. Richard Marsh, the young florist, who had been persuaded in a way by Cowperwood's looks, at first had been shaken a little in his faith by Shannon's sneering attack. Marsh was not much of a personality, all told—not much of an individuality. Mr. Moultrie, having had his duty, or rather the custom of his position, indicated to him by Mr. Glassberg, took his seat in the central chair, and said he would ask all those in favor of acquittal to hold up their hands. The first ballot stood: Guilty, 7; Not Guilty, 5—a curious result of the general cogitations of the jury up to this time, which needs to be explained.

Although the law provides that it must never be known who voted how on any jury, whatever the result, it is permissible to explain in this instance. Philip Moultrie; Charles Hillegan, the Irish-American contractor; Philip Lukash, the coal merchant; Benjamin Fraser, the young mining expert; J. J. Bridges, the little broker; Richard Webber, the grocer, and Washington B. Thomas, the flour merchant, all voted guilty for various and sundry reasons —some positively, some uncertainly, some tentatively. On the other hand, Simon Glassberg, the Jew clothier; Fletcher Norton, the architect; Guy E. Tripp, the steamboat manager; Joseph Tisdale, the rather old, retired glue manufacturer; and Richard Marsh, the uncertain young florist, all voted not guilty. Young Marsh's vote was very uncertain. Fletcher Norton's was rather positive. On the other side, Benjamin Fraser was not at all certain, and Washington B. Thomas was thinking hard. The others were fairly well fixed. Guy E. Tripp was not certain. He was trying to think that Cowperwood deserved a show; but he really did not believe it. His conscience was troubling him. On argument he would change his vote, and he felt it.

It is amazingly interesting to see how a jury will waver and speculate in a case like this—how curious and uncertain is the process by which it makes up its so-called mind. So-called truth is such a nebulous thing at best; facts are capable of such curious inversion and interpretation, honest and otherwise. This jury had a strongly complicated problem before it, and it went over it and over it, one juror after another venturing a thought, one juror after another asking a question.

"Isn't it a fact," asked J. J. Bridges, in one place, his little red-rimmed eyes taking in his fellow-jurors smartly—quite like an impertinent crow—"that we have to decide this question solely on the evidence as to whether Cowperwood did or did not take that sixty-thousand-dollar check after he knew he was going to fail, and whether he had or had not put the certificates he said he had purchased in the sinking-fund? There isn't any other question, is there? His early dealings with Stener haven't anything to do with this trial, as I understand it. Wasn't that what Judge Payderson pointed out?"

"It was," echoed Charles Hillegan, the contractor, with a faint Irish tinge in his voice. You could have read conviction in that voice if you had heard it—Cowperwood's fate.

"It's quite true," observed Simon Glassberg, generously, "dot technically speaking we can only consider dose facts what you mention, but hactually we gotta look at de t'ing as a whole. Dose two fellows were doing business togedder. Dey weren't observing de law, ever. But dey didn't start dis business in de first place. Udder city treasurers and brokers done dot before dey did. I doan'd see but what, under de circumstances, Cowperwood had a right to expect dot de udder feller would stand by him. If he had I guess he wouldn't be in no position like vot he is to-day. Anyhow, dot's de way I feel about it. He may be guilty—all right. I t'ink he is. But do we want to punish him—dot's de question. It ain'd de same as if he broke into a house and took t'ree hundred dollars or knocked a man down on de street and robbed him. You gotta look at de way de whole t'ing come about. He wouldn't 'a' took de sixty t'ousand dollars if he hadn't been doin' business with de city treasury in dot way, dot's one t'ing sure."

Mr. Glassberg went on to speculate more in this vein, but he was interrupted by Mr. Washington B. Thomas, the flour merchant, whose ordinary commercial manner had long since been glossed over by a rather philosophic air. He was inclined to look very wisely and quizzically over his spectacles.

"Gentlemen," he said, pleasantly, "I think we will have to look at this question from many points of view before we can reach a decision. There is no doubt in my mind that there is much to be said for the first gentleman's argument—I don't know your name," he paused, catching Mr. Bridges's eye.

"Bridges is my name—J. J. Bridges."

"There is much to be said for Mr. Bridges's point, and equally as much I think for Mister"—he turned to Glassberg, who supplied his own name promptly—"for Mr. Glassberg's. There is something in both these points of view. No doubt legally we must adhere strictly to the evidence concerning the actual transfer of this check, and no doubt morally we ought to think of what Mr. Glassberg suggests. In addition, I believe we ought to consider Mr. Cowperwood himself, his moral reformation, and the justice we owe to the city of Philadelphia. As I look on it now, it strikes me that Mr. Cowperwood and Mr. Stener are men without any moral conscience whatsoever. They don't seem to know or to have known what respect for law is. There is no question in anybody's mind, I presume, that these two men and all the other men that were associated with them knew what they were doing. That is, they knew they were breaking the law. But you see, so far as the evidence shows, it didn't make any difference to either of them. I don't suppose Mr. Cowperwood or Mr. Stener ever thought of the people of Philadelphia or the fact that the money they were risking didn't belong to them."

"They did not," suggested Mr. Hillegan, the Irishman, emphatically. Mr. Hillegan's manner amused Mr. Fletcher Norton, who smiled to himself delightedly. None of the others seemed to notice it.

"And I don't suppose," continued Mr. Thomas, "that they would have cared if they had thought. The rights of the people who make up the city of Philadelphia would not have meant anything to either of them. It was their own advancement they were seeking at the expense of everybody, and they thought that was just right. Now the question is, to my mind, What are you going to do with a man when you catch him red-handed in a thing of that sort? I know there are plenty of people nowadays who believe that he is justified in such conduct—looking after himself regardless of everybody else; but where is the limit? What laws, if any, do you or don't you have to obey? Isn't there a duty that comes in here somewhere to other people—to the city of Philadelphia, for instance? And if a man hasn't that sense of duty to his fellow-men, how are you going to give it to him? When you catch somebody like Cowperwood or Stener, what are you going to do with him—turn him loose again? Will he do any better if you don't punish him? Will he have any sense of duty, any conscience, in the future?"

He paused and looked around, and found that he had interested the whole company of men. They were looking at him as a thinker, or at least that *rara avis*, a man with convictions. Mr. Thomas was a rather well-set-up man of fifty-five, with a full but not over-heavy body of perhaps five feet nine inches tall and a nicely proportioned Socrates-like head. He wore a full beard and mustache — cut rather close, though — and a pair of black-steel-rimmed spectacles. His hair and beard were blackish gray, and his whole make-up breathed a certain well-preserved vitality of body and solidarity of thought. He was quite a personage, intellectually, even if he was a flour merchant.

"Gentlemen, I suggest dot we take anodder vote," observed Mr. Glassberg; and at this Mr. Moultrie, seeing how the previous vote had gone, asked all those in favor of conviction to raise their hands. All but Mr. Glassberg and Mr. Tisdale did so.

The jurors heaved a kind of sigh. They were glad (the majority) that the general consensus of opinion was shaping up.

"Well, that makes ten to two for conviction, gentlemen," observed Mr. Moultrie, in a rather naïve though sufficiently business-like manner. It is amazing how a manner sometimes persists under the most *outré* circumstances. "Can't we get together on this, gentlemen, and agree to make it unanimous? None of us wants to stay here any longer than we can help."

Fletcher Norton got up, strolled to the window, and announced that it was snowing hard. He extracted a cigarette from his case and lit it. Charles Hillegan and Philip Lukash, who sat beside him, joined in a private conversation, agreeing that there was no question as to Cowperwood's guilt, and wondering how any of the jurors could stand out. Simon Glassberg and J. J. Bridges joined in an issue as to facts, and Guy E. Tripp sought out Washington B. Thomas for further confirmation of his wavering mind. Mr. Webber sat alone smoking solemnly, and when Benjamin Fraser tried to strike up a conversation with him it was without much success. He wasn't very bright, and his ideas about life in general were few and fixed. Mr. Richard Marsh, the florist, went over to listen to the discussion between J. J. Bridges and Simon Glassberg.

It is curious what it is that causes juries to reach not so much definite conclusions as verdicts. Very often a jury will have concluded little so far as its individual members are concerned, when yet it will have reached a verdict. The matter of time, as all lawyers know, plays a part in this. Juries, speaking of the members collectively and frequently individually, object to the amount of time it sometimes takes to decide a case. They do not enjoy sitting and deliberating over a problem unless it is tremendously fascinating. The ramifications of the mystery or the syllogism become a weariness and a bore. The jury-room itself becomes a dull agony. They become sick of every detail. On the other hand, no jury contemplates a disagreement with any degree of satisfaction. There is something so inherently constructive in the human mind that to leave a problem unsolved is plain misery. It haunts the average individual like any other important task left unfinished. Men in a jury-room, like those scientifically demonstrated atoms of a crystal which scientists and philosophers love to speculate upon, love finally to arrange themselves into an orderly and artistic whole, to present a compact, intellectual front, to be whatever they have set out to be, properly and right—a compact, sensible jury. One sees this same instinct magnificently displayed in every other phase of nature—in the drifting of sea-wood to the Sargasso Sea, in the geometric interrelation of air-bubbles on the surface of still water, in the marvelous unreasoned architecture of so many insects and atomic forms which make up the substance and the texture of this world. It would seem as though the physical substance of life—this apparition of form which the eye detects and calls real—were shot through with some vast subtlety that loves order, that is order. The atoms of our so-called *being*, in spite of our so-called *reason*—the dreams of a mood—know where to go and what to do. They represent an order, a wisdom, a willing that is not of us. They build orderly in spite of us. So the subconscious spirit of a jury. At the same time, one does not forget the strange hypnotic effect of one personality on another, the varying effects of varying types on each other, until a solution—to use the work in its purely chemical sense—is reached. In a jury-room the thought or determination of one or two or three men, if it be definite enough, is likely to pervade the whole room and conquer the reason or the opposition of the majority. One man "standing out" for the definite thought that is in him is apt to become either the triumphant leader of a pliant mass or the brutally battered target of a flaming, concentrated intellectual fire. Men despise dull opposition that is without reason. In a jury-room, of all places, a man is expected to give a reason for the faith that is in him—if one is demanded. It will not do to say, "I cannot agree." Jurors have been known to fight. The bitterest antagonisms have been generated in these close quarters which have lasted for years. Recalcitrant jurors have been hounded commercially in their local spheres for their unreasoned oppositions or conclusions. Men in jury-rooms want thought, explanation, agreement; and if they cannot have it they become sullen, darkling, bitter, like stagnant water.

CHAPTER LVI

THIS general discussion ended in nothing special. All the phases of the trial were gone over in detail by one group and another. Richard Marsh, by listening to Simon Glassberg and J. J. Bridges arguing, was left mentally about where he was before. He had voted both guilty and not guilty, and still he was not quite certain. Guy E. Tripp, the spare general manager of the Delaware Navigation Company, after his extended conversation with Washington B. Thomas, was considerably comforted. These men were somewhat alike in their speculative mental attitude, only Thomas was more of the clear reasoner, speaking from an idealistic standpoint. Simon Glassberg, for all his vulgarity of address, had more of the realist's clearness of vision. The trouble with Glassberg was that if he found himself in a hopeless minority for long he was apt to compromise—to give the game to the majority merely because it was the majority and because he did not care to clog up the processes of life, whatever they might be—good, bad, or indifferent.

Joseph Tisdale, who had voted not guilty, Philip Moultrie, and Fletcher Norton had joined in an interesting argument finally as to whether the court had insisted, as Mr. Bridges had explained at the opening of these deliberations, that only the proof as to whether Cowperwood had or had not received the check as testified, and whether he had or had not deposited the city loan certificates as required by law, was to rule in reaching a verdict. Were none of his previous relations with Stener to weigh in the matter? Tisdale insisted they must.

Philip Moultrie declared *no*. Simon Glassberg and J. J. Bridges came up finally, and the second very interesting question was raised as to whether this should not be referred back to Judge Payderson for further instructions. Charles Hillegan and Philip Lukash, who had agreed absolutely as to Cowperwood's guilt, were not certain now as to whether one could reasonably find him guilty on all four counts. Although they had heard quite clearly what the court had said, they decided that the judge might have meant something else. There was a solemn filing out in the lonely, poorly lighted court-room; then after a time the rather morose and disgruntled return of Judge Payderson, who went over the situation again at length, trying to clear up their minds, and finally sent them back. Cowperwood was not in the room at the time, and he was a little disturbed when he learned that the jury had been in. It looked ominous, but Steger assured him that juries frequently came back for further instructions, and then disagreed. It was not a bad sign at all. So they continued to wait in the bare, dreary pen, lighted by a thin two-jet gas-arm, while the jury went on with its deliberations.

The argument in the jury-room again waxed strong and importunate. Simon Glassberg contended solemnly that, in spite of the instructions of the court, the jury should think of how Cowperwood had assisted Stener and vote not guilty—give him another chance. Joseph Tisdale said he thought it was a shame to punish a man for doing exactly what any other man would do under the circumstances. During the drag of moments and half-hours those who had made up their minds conclusively came to feel sick of the waste of time. Why sit here and cogitate when ten men, all equally good in brain and understanding of life, were agreed that the defendant was guilty? Why keep ten good men, tried and true, waiting? Philip Moultrie was anxious to get home to his wife and his comfortable bed. Fletcher Norton had originally planned an evening at his club, and was now restless and irritated. Simon Glassberg felt this, and began to waver. If ten men felt so strongly about this, why shouldn't he give in? Why argue? Cowperwood was not innocent, by any means. A recommendation to the court for mercy would do as well, or nearly so. Still Joseph Tisdale's determination to stick strengthened him for a time. After a third, a fourth, a fifth, and a sixth ballot, in which the vote stood ten to two, and much argument was indulged in—even some hard feeling— Glassberg finally shifted, saying: "Vell, I doaned want to stand out if all you fellers feel dis way. I t'ink we ought to ask de court to be lenient, dough."

Joseph Tisdale was all alone now, and an interesting but sorry fight he made of it. He was not a strong man physically. He was no longer young, and he did not believe that Cowperwood was innocent. He merely felt that he was able and deserving. It seemed such a shame to him, though, to punish a man for doing exactly what any other man would do under the same circumstances. He saw Cowperwood's position as a whole. Still, he did not know the man from any other man. He had never seen him before. He had merely read about him. It was now ten-thirty. Tisdale faced the united gaze of Philip Moultrie, Philip Lukash, Charles Hillegan, Richard Webber, and J. J. Bridges, and these men were determined. The others were not so significant for some reason, and yet the attitudes of Washington B. Thomas and Guy E. Tripp appealed to him more. They talked about the mercy of the court and the duty of the jury to Philadelphia, etc. About midnight he yielded, and then only because he wondered why he was fighting so hard for Cowperwood, who was nothing to him, and why he should thus inconvenience himself when he was so very tired. Perhaps, after all, Cowperwood deserved some punishment. There was more wrangling now as to whether the verdict should be guilty on all four counts, as charged in the indictment. Since the jury did not understand how to differentiate between the various charges very well, they decided it should be on all four, and a recommendation to mercy added. Afterward this last was eliminated, however; either he was guilty or he was not. The judge could see as well as they could all the extenuating circumstances—perhaps better. Why tie his hands? As a rule no attention was paid to such recommendations, anyhow, and it only made the jury look wabbly. So, finally, at ten minutes after twelve, they were ready to return a verdict; and Judge Payderson, who, because of his interest in the case and the fact that he lived not so far away, had decided to wait up this long, was recalled. Steger and Cowperwood were sent for. The court-room was fully lighted. The bailiff, the clerk, and the stenographer were there. The jury filed in, and Cowperwood, with Steger at his right, took his position at the gate which gave into the railed space, where prisoners always stand to hear the verdict and listen to any commentary of the judge. He was accompanied by his father, who was very nervous.

He stood here now, looking at this jury, the members of which did not look at him, waiting for Judge Payderson and wondering what they had really decided. For the first time in his life he felt as though he were walking in his sleep. Was this the real Frank Cowperwood of two months before—so wealthy, so progressive, so sure? Was this only December 5th or 6th now (it was after midnight)? And on October 5th last he was unconscious that the Chicago fire was about to break out. Why was it the jury had deliberated so long? What did it mean? Here it was midnight and they had just agreed—this midnight jury. Here they were now, standing and gazing solemnly before them; and here now was Judge Payderson, mounting the steps of his rostrum, his frizzled hair standing out in a strange, attractive way, his familiar bailiff rapping for order. He did not look at Cowperwood—it would not be courteous—but at the jury, who gazed at him in return. At the words of the clerk, "Gentlemen of the jury, have you agreed upon a verdict?" Mr. Moultrie spoke up, "We have."

"Do you find the defendant guilty or not guilty?"

"We find the defendant guilty as charged in the indictment."

Cowperwood felt an odd, unusual thrill pass over him. What a strange position for him to be in—he, Frank Cowperwood! All these years he had been plunging so briskly, so energetically ahead toward wealth and, he would have added, fame; but he could not be sure that he cared so much for fame. Anyhow, fame went with great wealth greatly achieved—and now suddenly he was stopped. It was truly as though all of a sudden a strong wall had come between him and his future, and—unpleasant thought!—it was a prison-wall! Here it was right here before him now, and there were the twelve men who were making it possible for it to be there—who were putting it there as a matter of fact. How had they come to do this? Because he had taken a check for sixty thousand dollars which did not belong to him? But in reality it did. Good Lord, what was sixty thousand dollars in the sum total of all the money that had passed back and forth between him and George W. Stener? Nothing, nothing! A mere bagatelle in its way; and yet here it had risen up, this miserable, insignificant check, and become a mountain of opposition, a stone wall, a prison-wall barring his further progress. It was astonishing. He looked around him at the court-room. How large and bare and cold it was! Still he was Frank A. Cowperwood. Why should he let such queer thoughts disturb him? His fight for freedom and privilege and restitution was not over yet. Good heavens! It had only begun. In five days he would be out again on bail. Steger would take an appeal. He would be out, and he would have two long months in which to make an additional fight. He was not down yet. He would win his liberty. This jury was all wrong. A higher court would say so. It would reverse their verdict, and he knew it. He turned to Steger, where the latter was having the clerk poll the jury, in the hope that some one juror had been over-persuaded, made to vote against his will.

"Is that your verdict?" he heard the clerk ask of Philip Moultrie, juror No. 1.

"It is," replied that worthy, solemnly.

"Is that your verdict?" The clerk was pointing to Simon Glassberg.

"Yes, sir."

"Is that your verdict?" He pointed to Fletcher Norton.

"Yes."

So it went through the whole jury. All the men answered firmly and clearly, though Steger thought it might barely be possible that one would have changed his mind. The judge thanked them and told them that in view of their long services this night, they were dismissed for the term. The only thing remaining to be done now was for Steger to persuade Judge Payderson to grant a stay of sentence pending the hearing of a motion by the State Supreme Court for a new trial.

Judge Payderson looked at Cowperwood very curiously as Steger asked that the pending sentence be stayed until a motion for a new trial could be entertained by the Supreme Court, and owing to the importance of the case and the feeling he had that the Supreme Court might very readily grant a certificate of reasonable doubt in this case, he agreed. There was nothing left, therefore, but for Cowperwood to return at this late hour with the deputy sheriff to the county jail, where he must now remain for five days at the least—possibly longer.

The jail in question, which was known locally as

Moyamensing Prison, was located at Tenth and Reed Streets, and from an architectural and artistic point of view was not so displeasing to the eye. It consisted of a central portion—prison, residence for the sheriff or what you will—three stories high, with a battlemented cornice and a round battlemented tower about one-third as high as the central portion itself, and two wings, each two stories high, with battlemented turrets at either end, giving it a highly castellated and consequently, from the American point of view, a very prison-like appearance. The façade of the prison, which was not more than thirty-five feet high for the central portion, nor more than twenty-five feet for the wings, was set back at least a hundred feet from the street, and was continued at either end, from the wings to the end of the street block, by a stone wall all of twenty feet high. The structure was not severely prison-like, for the central portion was pierced by rather large, unbarred apertures hung on the two upper stories with curtains, and giving the whole front a rather pleasant and residential air. The wing to the right, as one stood looking in from the street, was the section known as the county jail proper, and was devoted to the care of prisoners serving out short-term sentences on some judicial order. The wing to the left was devoted exclusively to the care and control of untried prisoners. The whole building was built of a smooth, light-colored stone, which on a snowy night like this, with the few lamps that were used in it glowing feebly in the dark, gave it an eery, fantastic, almost supernatural appearance. Artistically, it was not displeasing in the least.

It was a rough and blowy night when Cowperwood started for this institution under duress. The wind had sprung up, driving the snow before it in curious, interesting whirls. Eddie Zanders, the sheriff's deputy on guard at the court of Quarter Sessions, who accompanied Cowperwood and his father and Steger to the jail, was a little man, dark, with a short, stubby mustache, and a shrewd though not highly intelligent eye, who was anxious first to uphold his dignity as a deputy sheriff, which was a very important position in his estimation, and next to turn an honest penny if he could. He knew little save the details of his small world, which consisted of accompanying prisoners to and from the courts and the jails, and seeing that they did not get away. He was not unfriendly to a particular type of prisoner—the well-to-do or moderately prosperous—for he had long since learned that it paid to be so. To-night he offered a few sociable suggestions—*viz.*, that it was rather rough, that the jail was not so far but that they could walk, and that Sheriff Jaspers would, in all likelihood, be around or could be aroused. Cowperwood scarcely heard. He was thinking of his mother and his wife and of Aileen.

When the jail was reached Cowperwood was led to the door of the central portion, as it was here that the sheriff, Adlai Jaspers, had his private office. Jaspers had recently been elected to office, and was inclined to conform to all the outer appearances, in so far as the proper conduct of his office was concerned, without in reality inwardly conforming. Thus it was generally known among the politicians that one way he had of fattening his rather lean salary was to rent private rooms and grant special privileges to prisoners who had the money to pay for the same. Other sheriffs had done it before him. In fact, when Jaspers was inducted into office several prisoners were already enjoying these privileges, and it was not a part of his scheme of things to disturb them. The rooms that he let to the "right parties," as he invariably put it, were in the central portion of the jail, where were his own private living quarters. They were unbarred, and not at all cell-like. There was no particular danger of escape, for a guard stood always at his private door instructed "to keep an eye" on the general movements of all the inmates. A prisoner so accommodated was in many respects quite a free person. His meals were served to him in his room, if he wished. He could read or play cards, or receive guests; and if he had any favorite musical instrument, that was not denied him. There was just one rule that had to be complied with. If he were a public character, and any newspaper men called, he had to be brought down-stairs into the private interviewing room in order that they might not know that he was not confined in a cell like any other prisoner. Nearly all of these facts had been noted and brought to Cowperwood's attention beforehand by Steger; but for all that, when the jail was reached and the central door opened, Cowperwood crossed the threshold with a peculiar sensation of strangeness—in a way, of defeat. They knocked, and were opened to by a sleepy turnkey, and then Cowperwood went into a little office to the left of the entrance, where were only a desk and a chair, dimly lighted by a low-burning gas-jet. Sheriff Jaspers, rotund and ruddy, came down, not at all cantankerous for being disturbed in this manner, greeting them in quite a friendly way. Zanders was dismissed, and went briskly about his affairs.

"A bad night, isn't it?" observed Jaspers, turning up the gas and preparing to go through the routine of registering his prisoner. Steger came over and held a short, private conversation with him in his corner, over his desk. The sheriff's face shortly lit up.

"Oh, certainly, certainly! That's all right, Mr. Steger, to be sure! Why, certainly!"

Cowperwood, eying the fat sheriff from his position on the stone floor, understood what it was all about. He had regained completely his not cynical—he really never had been that—but critical attitude, his cool, intellectual poise. So this was the jail, and this was the fat mediocrity of a sheriff who was to take care of him. Very good. He would make the best of it. He wondered whether he was to be searched—prisoners usually were—but he soon found out not.

"That's all right, Mr. Cowperwood," said Mr. Jaspers, getting up. "I guess I can make you comfortable, after a fashion. We're not running a hotel here, as you know"—he chuckled to himself—"but I guess I can make you comfortable. John," he called to a sleepy factotum, who appeared from another room, rubbing his eyes, "is the key to Number Six down here?"

"Yes, sir."

"Let me have it."

John disappeared and returned, while Steger explained to Cowperwood that anything he wanted in the way of clothing, etc., could be brought. Steger himself would stop round next morning and confer with him, as would any of the members of Cowperwood's family whom he wished to see. Cowperwood immediately explained to his father the less of this the better. His father could stop by that night and tell his wife the result of the trial. Joseph or Edward might come in the morning and bring a grip full of underwear, etc.; but as for the others, let them wait until he got out or had to remain permanently. Then would be time enough. He did think of writing Aileen, cautioning her to do nothing; but the sheriff now beckoned, and he quietly followed. Accompanied by his father and Steger, he ascended to his new room.

It was a simple, white-walled chamber fifteen by twenty feet in size, rather high-ceiled, supplied with a high-backed, yellow wooden bed, a yellow bureau, a small imitation-cherry table, three very ordinary cane-seated chairs with carved hickory-rod backs, cherry-stained also, and a wash-stand of yellow-stained wood to match the bed, containing a wash-basin, a pitcher, a soap-dish, uncovered, and a small, cheap, pink-flowered tooth and shaving brush mug, which did not match the other ware and which probably cost ten cents. The value of this room to Sheriff Jaspers was what he could get for it in cases like this—twenty-five to thirty-five dollars a week. Cowperwood would pay thirty-five.

On entering his room Cowperwood walked briskly to the window, which gave out on the lawn in front, now embedded in snow, and said he thought this was all right. Both his father and Steger were willing and anxious to confer with him for hours, if he wished; but there was nothing to say. He did not wish to talk.

"Let Ed bring in some fresh linen in the morning and a couple of suits of clothes, and I will be all right. George can get my things together." He was referring to the family servant who acted as valet and in other capacities. "Tell Lillian not to worry. I'm all right. I'd rather that she would not come here so long as I'm going to be out in five days. If I'm not, it will be time enough then. Kiss the kids for me." And he smiled good-naturedly.

Steger was glad to see him so cheerful. The decent character of the room had evidently had a good effect on him. After his unfulfilled predictions in regard to the result of this preliminary trial Steger was almost afraid to suggest confidently what the State Supreme Court would or would not do; but he had to say something.

"I don't think you need worry about what the outcome of my appeal will be. I'll get a certificate of reasonable doubt, and that's as good as a stay of two months, perhaps longer. I don't suppose the bail will be more than thirty thousand dollars at the outside. You'll be out again in five or six days, whatever happens."

Cowperwood said that he hoped so, and suggested that they drop matters for the night. After a few fruitless parleys Steger and Cowperwood senior finally said good night, and then Cowperwood turned to his own private reflections. He was tired, however, and in his customary way made short work of that, throwing off his clothes, tucking himself in his mediocre bed, and going fast asleep.

CHAPTER LVII

SAY what one will about prison life in general, modify it never so much by special chambers, obsequious turnkeys, a general tendency to make one as comfortable as possible, a jail is a jail; and there is no getting away from that. Cowperwood in his new private room, which was not in any way inferior to that of the ordinary boarding-house, was nevertheless conscious of the character of that section of this real prison which he was not in. He knew that there were cells there, probably greasy and smelly and vermin-infested from contact with a long line of human victims who had either sat or lain in them, and that they were inclosed by heavy iron bars, which would have as readily clanked on him as on those who were now therein incarcerated if it had not been that he had the price to pay for something better. As a matter of fact, when he had come in down-stairs the first night he had caught a whiff of that peculiarly stale chemical odor which accompanies most prisons, a faint combination of unwashed offal pots, soap-suds, and lime. So much for the alleged equality of man, he thought, which gives to one man, even within the grim confines of the machinery of justice, such personal liberty as he himself was now enjoying, and denies to another, because he lacks wit or presence or friends or wealth, these more comfortable things which money will buy. Could any one blame him, Cowperwood thought, for putting the emphasis in this world on money? Did the lack of cash bring any one anything save compulsory subservience and a lack of consideration? No, money was very important, as this present situation had proved; and

20

it was his business to get it and keep it. Only he must never be so foolish another time as to permit himself to be caught within the toils of the law. This present difficulty was due merely to a lack of forethought. If he had kept his lines drawn tighter, had held a reserve n government bonds in case of a possible panic, he would not be in his present doubtful state. However, here he was, and it was necessary to make the best of it.

The morning after the trial, on waking, he stirred curiously, and then it suddenly came to him that he was no longer in the free and comfortable atmosphere of his own bedroom, but in a jail-cell, or rather its very comfortable substitute, a sheriff's rented bedroom. He got up and looked out the window. The ground outside and Passayunk Avenue were white with snow. Some wagons were lumbering by silently. A few Philadelphians were visible here and there, going to and fro on morning errands. He began to think at once what he must do, how he must act to carry on his business, his efforts to rehabilitate himself; and as he did so he dressed and pulled the bell-cord, which had been indicated to him, and which would bring him an attendant who would build him a fire and later bring him something to eat. His problems were large and significant, and he meditated on them while a shabby prison attendant in a blue uniform, conscious of Cowperwood's superiority because of the room he occupied, laid wood and coal in the grate and started a fire, and later brought him his breakfast, which was anything but prison fare, though poor enough at that. He had to take what the sheriff served him—ham and eggs, coffee, bread and butter, and a little jelly, which Cowperwood ate solemnly by himself, speculating on how readily it might have been worse.

He was compelled to wait in patience several hours, in spite of the sheriff's assumption of solicitous interest, before his brother Edward was admitted with his clothes. An attendant, for a consideration, brought him the morning papers, and these he read wearily. Late in the afternoon Steger arrived, saying he had been busy having certain proceedings postponed, but that he had arranged with the sheriff for Cowperwood to be permitted to see such of those as had important business with him.

Between the visits of his father, brothers, several of his commercial assistants and his creditors, the five days finally passed, at which time Steger's appeal for a certificate of reasonable doubt was granted, and Cowperwood was permitted to leave the jail.

He returned to his home a rather grim and sobered person. The thought of how to overcome a possible prison sentence—the effects of which would be to destroy his commercial interests entirely—was with him night and day.

It was while Cowperwood was in his room in Moyamensing, meditating on the vagaries of fortune and wondering how he would overcome the effect of this setback, that the crisis in Aileen's relations with her father occurred. Cowperwood had been in his rented room four days, and was destined to come out on the morrow (for although he did not then know it, his appeal for a certificate of reasonable doubt was to be granted), when Aileen concluded that it was best for her to leave home. Cowperwood had written her under no circumstances to try to see him, as he would be out by the tenth, and if not then, there would be plenty of time after that. He did not want to compromise her any more than he had already done, and he was afraid on this account to have her appear at the jail. She wanted greatly to see him; but she fancied, because of her emotional tension at this time, that she was under surveillance by the detectives employed by her father. This was no better grounded in reason than in the fact that one morning when she was coming out of the post-office, where Cowperwood had taken a lock-box, she thought she saw one of the men who had assisted in discovering her in South Sixth Street.

This was not true, but it preyed on her fancy, and, combined with some derogatory remarks dropped by Owen and Callum at the dinner table, proved almost too much for her fiery, nervous disposition. The imaginary sight of the detective brought back all the shame of the clumsy method Butler had employed to track her down; and the curt observation of Owen—who was entirely unconscious of her relationship to Cowperwood—that so far as he could see the financier was getting about what he deserved, made her feel that her father had secretly confided in her brother, and that what the latter said was intended as a back-handed slap at her. This at once humiliated and infuriated her; but she made no move until she read on the morning of the tenth that Cowperwood's plea for a certificate of reasonable doubt had been granted, and that he would once more, for the time being at least, be a free man. This gave her courage to do what she had long wanted to do, and that was to teach her father that she could get along without him and that he could not make her do anything that she did not want to do. She still had the two hundred dollars Cowperwood had given her at the time she thought she would leave before, and some additional cash of her own—perhaps three hundred and fifty dollars all told. This she thought would be sufficient to see her to the end of her adventure, or at least until such time as she could make some other arrangement for her personal well-being. From what she knew of the feeling of her family for her, she felt that the agony would all be on their side, not hers. Perhaps when her father saw how determined she was he would decide to let her alone and make peace with her. She was determined to try it, anyhow; and on the night when she knew that Cowperwood was free she stopped in at the Calligans' to say that she would be coming in a day or two, and to caution them to tell no one. To Mrs. Calligan she confided that because of the opposition of her parents to something she wanted to do she was very unhappy.

Mrs. Calligan looked upon it as a bit of family temper which would soon blow over, and welcomed Aileen, because she liked her and because a favor extended to her now might tend to benefit herself in the future.

Aileen also stopped to send word to Cowperwood where she was going, to make an appointment, and to welcome him to freedom. In a way he was rather gratified by the message, for he felt that his present plight, bitter as it was, was largely due to Butler's opposition, and he had no compunction now in striking him through his daughter. His former feeling as to the wisdom of not enraging Butler further had proved rather futile, he thought, and since the old man could not be placated it might be just as well to have Aileen demonstrate to him that she was not without resources of her own and could live without him. She might force him to change his attitude toward her, and possibly even to modify some of his political machinations against him, Cowperwood. Any port in a storm—and besides he had now really nothing to lose, or if he had, Butler's attitude was more likely to be favorably affected than not, particularly if it was demonstrated by Aileen's flight that her affection and attitude were largely of her own free will and volition. It was a knotty question—but instinct told him that her move was likely to prove more favorable than otherwise, so he did nothing to prevent it.

CHAPTER LVIII

THE night following her letter to Cowperwood Aileen decided to act. She took her jewels, some underwear, a couple of dresses which she thought would be serviceable, and a few other things; packed them in the most capacious portmanteau she had; and prepared to leave. Shoes and stockings came into consideration, and, despite her efforts, she found that she could not get in all that she wished. Her nicest hat, which she was determined to take, had to be carried outside. She made a separate bundle of it, which was not pleasant to contemplate. Still she decided to take it. It was dark. She rummaged in a little drawer where she kept her money and jewels, and found the three hundred and fifty dollars all told which was hers, and put it in her purse. It wasn't much, as Aileen could herself see, but Cowperwood would help her. If he did not arrange to take care of her, and her father would not relent, she would have to get something to do. Little she knew of the steely face the world presents to those who have not been practically trained and are not economically efficient. She did not understand the bitter reaches of life at all. She waited, humming for effect, until she heard her father go down-stairs to dinner, then leaned over the upper balustrade to make sure that Owen, Callum, Norah, and her mother were at the table, and that Katy, the housemaid, was not anywhere in sight. Then she slipped into her father's den, and, taking a note from her bosom, laid it on his desk, and went out. It was addressed to "Father," and read:

DEAR FATHER,—I just cannot do what you want me to. I have made up my mind that I love Mr. Cowperwood too much, so I am going away. Don't look for me with him. You won't find me where you think. I am not going to him; I will not be there. I am going to try to get along by myself for a while, until he wants me and can marry me. I'm terribly sorry; but I just can't do what you want. I can't ever forgive you for the way you acted to me. Tell mama and Norah and the boys good-by for me.

AILEEN.

She laid it under the light of the green table-lamp, which was turned low, and, to insure its discovery, picked up Butler's heavy-rimmed spectacles which he employed always when reading, and laid them on it. During the last two hours, for the first time in all this situation, separate waves of feeling had swept over her. As she was gathering up her clothing, as she wrote the note, and later when she was leaning over the balustrade listening to detect the several voices of the family, she felt very strange, somewhat like a thief—a new sensation for her; and as she laid the letter on her father's desk she felt a momentary sense of ingratitude coupled with pain. Perhaps she was doing wrong. Her father had been very good to her. Her mother would feel so very bad. Norah would be sorry, and Callum and Owen. Still, they did not understand her any more. She had outgrown their world. Cowperwood's was so much bigger. Her loyalty was due to him in his present troubles. She was resentful of her father's attitude toward Cowperwood and toward her love for him. He might have seen what the point was; but no, he was too old, too hide-bound in religion and conventional ideas—he never would. He might never let her come back. Very well, she would stay—she would get along somehow. She would teach him. She might get a place as a school-teacher, and live with the Calligans a long while, if necessary, or teach music. She stole down-stairs and out into the vestibule, opening the outer door and looking out into the street. The lamps were already flaring in the dark, and a cool wind was blowing. Her portmanteau was quite heavy, but she was very strong. She walked briskly to the corner, which was some fifty feet away, and turned south, walking rather nervously and irritably, for this was a very new experience for her. It was all so undignified—so anything but what she was used to doing. She was not so vastly distressed about her family now that she was out. She was thinking about finding a boy, and of getting to Mamie's as quickly as possible. She put her bag down on a street-corner finally to rest herself, and waited. A boy whistling in the distance attracted her attention. As the lad drew nearer—an idle-mannered urchin coming home from work of some form or other—she called to him: "Boy! Boy! Oh, boy!"

He came over, looking at her curiously.

"Do you want to earn some money?"

"Yes, ma'm," he replied, politely, adjusting a frowsy cap over one ear.

"Carry this bag for me," Aileen said; and he picked it up and marched off, finally getting it up on one of his shoulders for comfort's sake. In due time Aileen arrived at the Calligans', and amid much astonishment and excitement was installed in the bosom of her new home. She took her situation with much nonchalance, once she was properly located, distributing her toilet articles and those of personal wear with quiet care. The fact that she was not any longer to have the services of Kathleen, the maid who had served her, her mother, and Norah jointly, was odd, though not trying. She scarcely felt that she had parted from these luxuries permanently, and so made herself comfortable. She talked to Mamie and her mother, who were delighted with her fine looks, her artistic clothing, her self-conscious manner, and natural hauteur. They were adoring slaveys to her, and so she was not entirely out of the atmosphere which she craved and to which she was used.

Meanwhile in the Butler home a peculiar scene was

being enacted. Butler, meditating constantly on how soon he should speak to Aileen again, if at all, and wondering just what particular move he could make in case her attitude should not have been changed by the result of Cowperwood's trial in the way that he had hoped, had been going about in a mute world of his own. Never in his life had he been confronted by such a problem as this.

If Cowperwood's certificate of reasonable doubt were ultimately denied by the Supreme Court and he were sent to the penitentiary, which might easily happen within two months, Aileen would perforce be permanently cured. She must see then that she could not stay in love with a convict. But supposing in the mean time she and Cowperwood should run away together? He did not really believe that Cowperwood would do this; but still the thought, once it occurred, was a horror to him. Scarcely any action on his part to prevent such a thing could be too drastic.

It was in this mood that he had come to the table tonight. He was actually feeling badly physically, to say nothing of how he felt mentally. His appetite was gone. His eyes had sunken rings under them. He had suffered politically and financially at times when reverses had come upon him; but what had they been to this?

He noticed that Aileen was not at table. He thought nothing of it. She did not always precede him. Mrs. Butler was sitting in rotund complacency at the foot of the table, her gray hair combed straight back from her round, shiny forehead. She had on a medium-dark-gray silk dress finished with white-and-gray-striped trimmings, which also had a touch of red and green in them—dots. It suited her florid temperament admirably. Aileen had dictated her mother's choice, and had seen that it had been made properly. Norah was refreshingly youthful in a pale-green house-dress, with red-velvet cuffs and collar. She looked young, slender, gay. Her eyes, complexion, and hair were fresh and healthy. She was trifling with a string of coral beads which her mother had just given her.

Butler walked heavily in and took his seat.

"It's gettin' colder, I'm thinkin'," said Butler, by way of conversation, and eying Aileen's empty chair. She would come soon now—his heavy problem. He had been very tactful these last two months—avoiding any reference in so far as he could help to Cowperwood in Aileen's presence, but he had not always been successful. Aileen was called, and the maid said she answered.

"It's colder," remarked Owen, "much colder. We'll soon see real winter now."

Old John began to offer the various dishes in order; but when all had been served Aileen had not yet come.

"See where Aileen is, John," observed Mrs. Butler, interestedly. "The meal will be gettin' cold."

Old John sent the maid again. This time Aileen was not in her room.

"She's not in her room," he said, returning after a time. "Annie says she can't find her."

"Sure she must be somewhere," commented Mrs. Butler, only slightly perplexed. "She'll be comin', though, never mind, if she wants to. She knows it's meal-time."

Old Butler decided that Aileen's mind was telling against her appetite. It was not strange. The conversation drifted from a new water-works that was being planned to the new city hall, then nearing completion; Cowperwood's financial and social troubles, and the state of the stock market generally; a new gold-mine in Arizona; the departure of Mrs. Mollenhauer the following Tuesday for Europe, with appropriate comments by Norah and Callum; and a Christmas ball that was going to be given for charity.

"Aileen 'll be wantin' to go to that," commented Mrs. Butler.

"I'm going, you bet," put in Norah.

"Who's going to take you?" asked Callum.

"That's my affair, mister," she replied, smartly.

The meal was over, and Mrs. Butler strolled up to Aileen's room to see what had become of her. Butler entered his den, wishing so much that he could take his wife into his confidence concerning all that was worrying him. On his desk, as he sat down and turned up the light, he saw the note. He recognized Aileen's handwriting at once. What could she mean by writing him? A sense of the untoward came to him, and he tore it open slowly, and, putting on his glasses, contemplated it solemnly.

The old man stared at each word as if it had been written in fire. So Aileen was gone. She said she had not gone with Cowperwood. It was possible, just the same, that he had run away from Philadelphia and taken Aileen with him. This was the last straw. This ended it. Aileen lured away from home—to where—to what? Butler could scarcely believe, though, that Cowperwood had tempted her to do this. He had too much at stake; it would involve his own and Butler's families. The papers would be certain to get it quickly. But as to Aileen, the girl was crazy. She was out of her mind. Still, she was gone. He got up, crumpling the paper in his hand, and turned about at a noise. His wife was coming in. He pulled himself together and shoved the letter in his pocket.

"Aileen's not in her room," she said, curiously. "She didn't say anything to you about going out, did she?"

"No," he replied, truthfully, wondering how soon he should have to tell his wife.

"That's odd," observed Mrs. Butler, doubtfully. "She must have gone out after somethin'. It's a wonder she wouldn't tell somebody."

Butler gave no sign. He dared not. "She'll be back," he said, more in order to gain time than anything else. "She's thought of some one she wanted to see and gone." He was sorry to have to pretend. Mrs. Butler went out, and he closed the door. Then he took out the letter and read it again. The girl was crazy. She was doing an absolutely wild, inhuman, senseless thing. Where could she go, except to Cowperwood? She was on the verge of a public scandal, and this would produce it. There was just one thing to do as far as he could see. Cowperwood, if he were still in Philadelphia, would know. He had her in complete control. He would go to him—threaten, cajole, actually destroy him, if necessary. Aileen must come back. She need not go to Europe, perhaps, but she must come back and behave herself at least until Cowperwood could legitimately marry her. That was all he could expect now. She would have to wait, and some day perhaps he could bring himself to accept her wretched proposition. Horrible thought! It would kill her mother, disgrace her sister. He got up, took down his hat, put on his overcoat, and started out.

CHAPTER LIX

AT nine o'clock Butler, having decided that Cowperwood must know and must be made, if he were still in Philadelphia, to help straighten out this terrific tangle in regard to Aileen, rang at his door, and was shown into the reception-room. Cowperwood at the time was in his private den looking over some papers. During the time that he had been in jail the two Cowperwood households had been in a state of utter collapse. With Henry, the father, out of his position, and the two brothers in a way publicly discredited by Cowperwood's fall, there was nothing to do for any of them save to wait and see what happened in connection with him. His wife had now not the courage to think of anything save the possibility of his restoration to his former financial state. His attitude toward Aileen was now a secondary consideration. The real animus of Butler had never been revealed to any of them, and they still thought that his seeming indifference to Cowperwood in this crisis was due to his political affiliations. In order to save the good name of the party he had had to join with the other leaders in ignoring him—so Cowperwood's relatives thought.

When the name of Butler was announced to him Frank immediately arose and went down-stairs. It was characteristic of the man that the announcement of Butler's presence created no stir in him whatever. He knew what it was all about. So Butler had come. That meant, of course, that Aileen had gone. Now for a battle, not of words, but of weights of personalities.

"Good evening, Mr. Butler," said Cowperwood, cheerfully, when he saw him, extending his hand. He deemed it best to assume an air of friendly civility, even though Butler would not want it to prevail. "What can I do for you?"

"Ye can take that away from in front of me, for one thing," said Butler, grimly referring to his hand. "I have no need of it. It's my daughter I've come to talk to ye about, and I want plain answers. Where is she?"

"You mean Aileen?" said Cowperwood, looking at him with steady, curious, unrevealing eyes, and merely interpolating this to obtain a moment for reflection. "What can I tell you about her?"

"Ye can tell me where she is, that I know. And ye can make her come back to her home, where she belongs. It was bad fortune that ever brought ye across my doorstep; but I'll not bandy words with ye here. Ye'll tell me where my daughter is, and ye'll leave her alone from now, or I'll—" The old man's fists closed like a vise, and his chest heaved with suppressed rage. "Ye'll not be drivin' me too far, man, if ye're wise," he added, after a time, recovering his equanimity in part. "I want no thruck with ye. I want my daughter."

"Listen, Mr. Butler," said Cowperwood, quite calmly, relishing the situation for the sheer sense of superiority it gave him. Butler was strong, old, tempestuous. He had done much to injure him, Cowperwood, but if he had triumphed in every other matter, he had not done so in connection with this one thing—the most important to him, his daughter. Cowperwood reflected by contrast that he was young and calm, really the victor in this. Much to his astonishment, there was more in Aileen's move than he had realized, and he might use it to improve his own position somewhat. Obviously, Butler was determined not to expose him or her if he could help it. It was a great advantage. "I want to be perfectly frank with you, if you will let me. I may know where your daughter is, and I may not. I may wish to tell you, and I may not. She may not wish me to. But unless you wish to talk with me in a civil way there is no need of our going on any further. You are privileged to do what you like. Won't you come up-stairs to my room? We can talk more comfortably there."

Butler looked at his former protégé in utter astonishment. He had never before in all his experience come up against a more ruthless type—suave, bland, forceful, unterrified. This man had certainly come to him as a sheep, and had turned out to be a ravening wolf. His incarceration had not put him in the least awe.

"I'll not come up to your room," Butler said, "and ye'll not get out of Philadelphia with her if that's what ye're plannin'. I can see to that. Ye think ye have the upper hand of me, I see, and ye're anxious to take it. Well, ye've not. It wasn't enough that ye come to me as a beggar, cravin' the help of me, and that I took ye in and helped ye all I could—ye had to steal my daughter from me in the bargain. If it wasn't for the girl's mother and her sister and her brothers—dacenter men than ever ye'll know how to be—I'd brain ye where ye stand. Takin' a young, innocent girl and makin' an evil woman out of her, and ye a married man! It's a God's blessin' for ye that it's me, and not one of me sons, that's here talkin' to ye, or ye wouldn't be alive to say what ye'd do."

The old man was grim but impotent in his rage.

"I'm sorry, Mr. Butler," replied Cowperwood, quietly. "I'm willing to explain, but you won't let me. I'm not planning to run away with your daughter, nor to leave Philadelphia. You ought to know me well enough to know that I'm not contemplating anything of that kind; my interests are too large. You and I are practical men. We ought to be able to talk this matter over together and reach an understanding. I thought once of coming to you and explaining this; but I was quite sure you wouldn't listen to me. Now that you are here I would like to talk to you. If you will come up to my room I will be glad to—otherwise not. Won't you come up?"

Butler saw that Cowperwood had the upper hand of him. In spite of his rage, slowly but surely this man's tentacles were fastening themselves upon him. He might as well go up. Otherwise it was plain he would get no information. He hated Cowperwood; but he had to do it.

"Very well," he said.

Cowperwood led the way quite amicably, and, having entered his private office, closed the door behind him. He saw as plainly as anything that Butler was a victim of his feeling for Aileen. He prepared to talk to him very sensibly and explain the whole situation. Perhaps he could soothe Butler so that he would cease his political attacks on him.

"We ought to be able to talk this matter over and reach an understanding," he said again, when they were in the room and he had closed the door. "I am not as bad as you think, though I know I appear very bad." Butler stared at him in contempt. "I love your daughter, and she loves me. I know you are asking yourself how I can do this while I am still married; but I assure you I can, and that I do. I am not happily married. I had expected, if this panic hadn't come along, to arrange with my wife for a divorce and marry Aileen. My intentions are perfectly good. The situation which you can complain of, of course, is the one you encountered a few weeks ago. It was indiscreet, but it was entirely human. Your daughter does not complain—she understands."

At the mention of his daughter in this connection Butler flushed with rage, but he controlled himself.

"And ye think because she doesn't complain that it's all right, do ye?" he asked, sarcastically.

"From my point of view, yes; from yours, no. You have one view of life, Mr. Butler, and I have another."

"Ye're right there," put in Butler, "for once, anyhow."

"I want to marry Aileen," Cowperwood repeated, for emphasis' sake. "She wants to marry me. Under the circumstances, however you may feel, you can have no real objection to my doing that, I am sure; yet you go on fighting me—making it hard for me to do what you really know ought to be done."

Cowperwood smiled inwardly at this subtle presentation of his case. He knew now, by Butler's very attitude, that he had him in a vulnerable position and could do something to improve his own.

"Ye're a clever man," said Butler, seeing through his motives quite clearly. "Ye're a sharper, to my way of thinkin', and it's no child of mine I want connected with ye. I'm not sayin', seein' that things are as they are, that if ye were a free man it wouldn't be better that she should marry ye. It's the one dacent thing ye could do —if ye would, which I doubt. But that's nayther here nor there now. What can ye want with her hid away somewhere? Ye can't marry her. Ye can't get a divorce. Ye've got your hands full fightin' your lawsuits and kap- in' yourself out of jail. She'll only be an added expense to ye, and ye'll be wantin' all the money ye have for other things, I'm thinkin'. Why should ye want to be takin' her away from a dacent home and makin' some- thing out of her that ye'd be ashamed to marry if you could? The laist ye could do, if ye were any kind of a man at all, and had any of that thing that ye're plazed to call love, would be to lave her at home and keep her as respectable as possible. Mind ye, I'm not thinkin' she isn't ten thousand times too good for ye, whatever ye've made of her. But if ye had any sinse of dacency left, ye wouldn't let her shame her family and break her old mother's heart, and that for no purpose except to make her worse than she is already. What good can ye get out of it, now? What good can ye expect to come of it? Be hivins, if ye had any sinse at all I should think ye could see that for yourself. Ye're only addin' to your troubles, not takin' away from them—and she'll not thank ye for that later on."

He stopped, rather astonished that he should have been drawn into an argument with Cowperwood at all. His contempt for the man was so great that he could scarcely look at him, but his duty and his need was to get Aileen back. Cowperwood looked at him as one who gives serious attention to another. He seemed to be thinking deeply over what Butler had said.

"To tell you the truth, Mr. Butler," he said, "I did not want Aileen to leave your home at all; and she will tell you so, if you ever talk to her about it. I did my best to persuade her not to, and when she insisted on going the only thing I could do was to be sure she would be comfortable wherever she went. She was greatly outraged to think you should have put detectives on her trail. That, and the fact that you wanted to send her away somewhere against her will, was the principal reason for her leaving. I assure you I did not want her to go. I think you forget sometimes, Mr. Butler, that Aileen is a grown woman, and that she has a will of her own. You think I control her to her great disadvantage. As a matter of fact, I am very much in love with her, and have been for three or four years; and if you know anything about love you know that it doesn't always mean control. I'm not doing Aileen any injustice when I say that she has had as much influence on me as I have had on her. I love her, and that's the cause of all the trouble. You come and insist that I shall return your daughter to you. As a matter of fact, I don't know whether I can or not. I don't know that she would go if I wanted her to. She might turn on me and say that I didn't care for her any more. That is not true, and I would not want her to feel that way. She is greatly hurt, as I told you, by what you did to her, and the fact that you want her to leave Philadelphia. You can do as much to remedy that as I can. I could tell you where she is, but I do not know that I want to. Certainly not until I know what your attitude toward her and this whole proposition is to be."

He paused and looked calmly at the old contractor, who eyed him grimly in return. It was a wonderful situation.

"What proposition are ye talkin' about?" asked Butler.

"Well, it's simple enough," replied Cowperwood. "I should like to have you withdraw your opposition to Aileen's remaining in Philadelphia, for one thing; and for another, I should like you to stop your attacks on me." Cowperwood smiled in an ingratiating way. He hoped really to placate Butler in part by his generous attitude throughout this procedure. "I can't make you do that, of course, unless you want to. I really did not think I could when I said it. I merely bring it up, Mr. Butler, because I am sure that if it hadn't been for Aileen you would have taken a very different attitude toward me. I understood you received an anonymous letter, and that afternoon you called your loan with me. Since then I have heard from one source and another that you were strongly against me, and I merely wish to say that I wish you wouldn't be. I am not guilty of embezzling any sixty thousand dollars, and you know it. My intentions were of the best. I did not think I was going to fail at the time I used those certificates, and if it hadn't been for several other loans that were called I would have gone on to the end of the month and put them back in time, as I always have. I have always valued your friendship very highly, and I am very sorry to lose it. Now I have said all I am going to say."

Butler looked at Cowperwood with shrewd, calculating eyes. He knew as well as any one how fine this rôle was that Cowperwood had enacted. The man had some merit, but much unconscionable evil in him. Butler knew very well how he had taken the check, and a good many other things in connection with it. The manner in which he had played his cards to-night was on a par with the way he had run to him on the night of the fire. He was just shrewd and calculating and heartless. Butler was not without guile himself, particularly in situations of this kind. He wanted nothing to do with him, but he wanted his daughter back at once for his wife's sake.

"I'll make ye no promise," he said. "Tell me where my daughter is, and I'll think the matter over. Ye have no claim on me now, and I owe ye no good turn. But I'll think it over, anyhow."

"That's quite all right," replied Cowperwood. "That's all I can expect. But what about Aileen? Do you expect her to leave Philadelphia?"

"Not if she settles down and behaves herself; but there must be an end of this between you and her. She's disgracin' her family and ruinin' her soul in the bargain. And that's what you are doin' with yours. It 'll be time enough to talk about anything else when you're a free man. More than that I'll not promise."

Cowperwood, satisfied that this move on Aileen's part had done her a real service if it had not aided him especially, was convinced that it would be a fine thing for her to return to her home at once. He could not tell how his appeal to the State Supreme Court would eventuate. His motion for a new trial which was now to be made under the privilege of the certificate of reasonable doubt might not be granted, in which case he would have to serve a term in the penitentiary. Butler might not aid him—in all likelihood would not—but he might not be so vigorous in his prosecution of him. Anyhow, it was good policy to have Aileen return. She would be safe in the bosom of her family, and, if he were compelled to go to the penitentiary, that was where she ought to be. His own hands were going to be exceedingly full for the next two months until he knew how his appeal was coming out. And after that—well, after that he would fight on, whatever happened.

"The best thing that I can do under the circumstances," he said, after a time, "would be to see Aileen in two or three days, and ask her what she wishes to do. I can explain the matter to her, and if she wishes to go back, she can. I will promise to tell her anything that you say."

"Two or three days!" exclaimed Butler, irritably. "Two or three fiddlesticks! She must come home to-night. Her mother doesn't know she's left the place yet. To-night is the time! I'll go and fetch her meself to-night."

Cowperwood had to smile at the old man's impetuous burst of feeling, though it was not a facial smile. "No, that won't do," he said. "I shall have to go myself. If you wish to wait here I will see what can be done, and let you know."

"Very well," grunted Butler, who was now walking up and down with his hands behind his back. "But for Heaven's sake be quick about it. There's no time to lose." He was thinking of Mrs. Butler. Cowperwood called the servant, ordered his runabout, and told George to see that his private office was not disturbed. Then, as Butler strolled to and fro in this, to him, objectionable room, Cowperwood sped rapidly away.

CHAPTER LX

ALTHOUGH it was nearly eleven o'clock when he arrived at the Calligans', Aileen had not yet gone to bed. In her bedroom upstairs she was confiding to Mamie and Mrs. Calligan some of her social experiences when a ring came at the door, and Mrs. Calligan went down and opened it to Cowperwood.

"Miss Butler is here, I believe," he said. "Will you tell her that there is some one here from her father?"

Although Aileen had instructed that her presence here was not to be divulged even to the members of her family, the force of Cowperwood's presence and the mention of Butler's name cost Mrs. Calligan her presence of mind.

"Wait a moment," she said; "I'll see."

She stepped back, and Cowperwood promptly stepped in, taking off his hat with the air of one who was satisfied. Aileen was there. "Say to her that I only want to speak to her for a few moments," he called, as Mrs. Calligan went up-stairs, raising his voice in the hope that Aileen might hear. She did, and came down promptly. She was very much astonished to think that Cowperwood should come so soon, and fancied, in her vanity, that there must be great excitement in her home. She would have greatly grieved if there had not been.

The Calligans would have been pleased to hear, but Cowperwood was cautious. As she came down the stairs he put his finger to his lips in sign for silence, and said, "This is Miss Butler, I believe."

"Yes," replied Aileen, with a secret smile. Her one desire was to kiss him. "What's the trouble?" she asked, softly.

"You'll have to go back, dear, I'm afraid," whispered Cowperwood. "You'll have everything in a turmoil if you don't. It may be a good deal of help to me if you do. Your father is over at my place now, waiting for you. Let me tell you—" He went off into a complete description of his conversation with Butler and his own views in the matter. Aileen's expression changed from time to time as the various phases of the matter were put before her; but, persuaded by the clearness with which Cowperwood put the matter, and by his assurance that they could continue their relations as before uninterrupted, once this was settled, she decided to return. In a way, her father's surrender was a great triumph. She made her farewells to the Calligans, saying, with a smile, that they could not do without her at home, and that she would send for her belongings later, and returned with Cowperwood to his own door. He asked her to wait in the runabout while he sent her father down.

"Well?" said Butler, turning on him when he opened the door, and not seeing Aileen.

"You'll find her down-stairs in my runabout," observed Cowperwood. "You may use that if you choose. I will send my man for it."

"No, thank you; we'll walk," said Butler.

Cowperwood called his servant to take charge of the vehicle, and Butler stalked solemnly out.

He had to admit to himself that the influence of Cowperwood over his daughter was deadly, and probably permanent. The best he could do would be to keep her within the precincts of the home, where she might still, possibly, be brought to her senses. He did not know what to think. He held a very guarded conversation with her on his way home, for fear that she would take additional offense. Argument was out of the question.

"Ye might have talked with me once more, Aileen," he said, thinking of what the house would have been without her, "before ye left. Yer mother would be in a terrible state if she knew ye were gone. She doesn't know yet. Ye'll have to say ye stayed somewhere to dinner."

"I was at the Calligans," replied Aileen. "That's easy enough. Mama won't think anything about it."

"It's a sore heart I have, Aileen. I hope ye'll think over your ways and do better. I'll not say anythin' more now."

Aileen returned to her room, decidedly triumphant in her mood for the moment, and things went on apparently in the Butler household as before. But those who imagine that this defeat permanently altered the attitude of Butler toward Cowperwood are mistaken.

In the mean while Cowperwood was going on doing his best to repair his shattered forces. He took up his work where he left off; but the possibility of reorganizing his business was distinctly modified since his conviction. Because of his action in trying to protect his largest creditors at the time of his failure, he fancied that once he was free again, if ever he got free, his credit, other things being equal, would be good with those who could help him most—say, Cooke & Co., Clark & Co., Drexel & Co., and the Girard National Bank, providing his personal reputation was not so badly injured by his sentence that all his friends were alienated. Would they be? That was a knotty question. Some of them, like Davison and Leigh, would certainly not be, he hoped. Fortunately for his own hopefulness of mind, he failed fully to realize what a depressing effect a legal decision of this character, sound or otherwise, has on the minds of even the most enthusiastic supporters.

"You know," observed President Davison of the Girard National to one of his friends, the morning after Cowperwood was convicted, "I don't believe that it will be possible to put young Cowperwood on his feet after this. It looks pretty bad to me. There have been a good many men who were friendly to him, but this will alienate them.

I confidently expected that he would be acquitted, but since he hasn't—" He shook his head significantly.

"Quite right," replied the other, who was also a financier. "Give a dog a bad name."

They drifted to other subjects; but it was quite plain from this which way the wind was blowing. Cowperwood's best friends in the financial world, whom he had done considerable to protect at the time of his assignment, were convinced that his was a sinking ship. It was some student of finance that once observed that nothing is so sensitive as money, and the financial mind partakes largely of the quality of the thing in which it deals. There was no use trying to do much for a man who might be going to prison for a term of years. It couldn't be done. Something might be done for him possibly in connection with the governor, providing he lost his case before the Supreme Court and was actually sentenced to prison; but that was two months off, or more, and they could not tell what the outcome of these would be. So Cowperwood's repeated appeals for assistance, extension of credit, or the acceptance of some plan he had for his general rehabilitation, were met with the kindly evasions of those who were doubtful. They would think it over. They would see about it. Certain things were standing in the way. And so on, and so forth, through all the endless excuses of those who do not care to act. Cowperwood went about the money world in his customary jaunty way, greeting all those whom he had known there many years and pretending, when asked, to be very hopeful, to be doing very well; but they did not believe him, and he really did not care whether they did or not. His business was to persuade or over-persuade any one who could really be of assistance to him, and at this task he worked untiringly, ignoring all others.

"Why, hello, Frank," his friends would call, on seeing him. "How are you getting on?"

"Fine! Fine!" he would reply, cheerfully. "Never

better," and he would explain in a general way how his
affairs were being handled. He conveyed much of his
own optimism to all those who knew him and were interested in his welfare, but of course there were many who
were not.

He and Steger were constantly appearing in courts of
law; he was constantly being re-examined in some petition in bankruptcy or waiting on some banker who
might tell him something favorable a little later. It was
a heartbreaking task, but he did not flinch. He wanted
to stay in Philadelphia and fight the thing to a finish—
putting himself where he had been before, rehabilitating
himself in the eyes of the public. He felt that he could
do it, too, if he were not actually sent to prison for a
long term; and even then he might when he got out
again; but he did not want to go to prison, and he did
not want his quondam friends to be so pessimistic about
his condition now. But he was in a very deep slough of
despair, and only he could have seen any possibility of getting out of it so far as Philadelphia was concerned.

His worst anxiety was that if he were sent to the penitentiary, or adjudged a bankrupt, or both, he would
probably lose the privilege of a seat on 'change, and that
would close to him the most distinguished avenue of his
prosperity here in Philadelphia for some time, if not
forever. At present, because of his complications, his
seat had been attached as an asset, and he could not
act. Edward and Joseph, almost the only employees he
could afford, were still acting for him in a small way; but
the other members of 'change naturally suspected his
brothers as his agents, and any talk that they might
raise of going into business for themselves merely indicated to other brokers and bankers that Cowperwood was
contemplating some concealed move which would not
necessarily be advantageous to his creditors, and against
the law anyhow. Yet he must remain on 'change, whatever happened, potentially if not actively; and so in his

quick mental searchings he hit upon the idea that in order to forfend against the event of his being put into prison or thrown into bankruptcy, or both, he ought to form a subsidiary silent partnership with some man who was or would be well liked on 'change, and whom he could use as a cat's-paw and a dummy.

He began to think on whom his silent partner would be, convicted or no, and finally he hit upon a man whom he thought would do. He did not amount to much—had a small business; but he was honest, and he liked Cowperwood. His name was Wingate—Stephen Wingate—and he was eking out a not too robust existence in South Third Street as a broker. He was forty-five years of age, of medium height, fairly thick-set, not at all unprepossessing, and rather intelligent and active, but not too forceful and pushing in spirit. He really needed a man like Cowperwood to make him into something, if ever he was to be made. He had a seat on 'change, and was well thought of; respected, but not so very prosperous. In times past he had asked small favors of Cowperwood—the use of small loans at a moderate rate of interest, tips, and so forth; and Cowperwood, because he liked him, felt a little sorry for him, had granted them. Now Wingate was slowly drifting down toward a none too successful old age, and was as tractable as such a man would naturally be. No one for the time being would suspect him of being a hireling of Cowperwood's, and the latter could depend on him to execute his orders to the letter. He sent for him three weeks after he was convicted for embezzlement and was out on bail again, and had a long conversation with him. He told him just what the situation was, what he thought he could do for him (Wingate) if the latter were his partner, how much of his business he would want for himself, and so on, and found him agreeable. Wingate knew Cowperwood, of course, as a brilliant operator, and thought that in spite of his present and future handicap he would be successful. He was not doing at all well himself just at this stage, and this was a chance to connect himself with a very able man. The panic had almost sunk his frail little craft. So he consented cheerfully.

"I'll be glad to do anything you say, Mr. Cowper-wood," he assured the latter, when he heard his story. "I know whatever happens that you'll protect me, and there's nobody in the world I would rather work with or have greater respect for. This storm will all blow over, and you'll be all right. We can try it, anyhow. If it don't work out you can see what you want to do about it later."

Cowperwood looked at his latest acquisition in a critical manner. Would he do? Very likely. Edward and Joseph could be introduced into the business later, if it war-ranted. Wingate promised to come daily to the prison, if such a thing were ever necessary or possible; and so this relationship was tentatively entered into now. Cowperwood began to act in a small way through him already. But he had little time. Suits and counter-suits against him were either being tried or filed almost daily. He was being examined at odd times in various bank-ruptcy proceedings. He had so many people to see and things to do that he could not devote himself much to the main task of making money, which was so essential.

CHAPTER LXI

MEANWHILE four weeks had passed since Cowperwood had been released upon a certificate of reasonable doubt, and at the end of that time both Harper Steger and Dennis Shannon appeared before the judges of the State Supreme Court, and argued pro and con as to the reasonableness of granting him a new trial. Through his lawyer, Steger, Cowperwood made a learned appeal to the Supreme Court judges, showing how he had been unfairly indicted in the first place, how there was no real substantial evidence on which to base a charge of larceny or anything else. The jury, an ordinary body of men not trained in finance, were not capable mentally, he urged, of dealing with such a subtle problem. They could not possibly be made to understand the ramifications of finance. All they saw was the particular check of sixty thousand dollars and its technically illegal disappearance. They could not be made to understand how this was all accidentally involved with a condition of which he was not aware at the time—his insolvency—and of a system and precedent which he did not create. Such a case, he maintained, should not be tried by a jury at all. It ought to be submitted to a committee of financial experts, men in Third Street, who knew. It took Harper Steger two hours and ten minutes to make his argument, and District-Attorney Shannon longer to make his reply, during which the five judges on the bench, men of considerable legal experience but no great financial understanding, listened with great attention. Three of them, Judges Smithson, Rainey, and Beckwith, men most amen-

able to the political feeling of the time and the wishes of
the bosses, were little interested in this story of Cowperwood's transaction, particularly since his relations with
Butler's daughter and Butler's consequent opposition
to him had come to them. They fancied that in a way
they were considering the whole matter fairly and impartially; but the manner in which Cowperwood had
treated Butler was never out of their minds. Two of
them, Judges Marvin and Rafalsky, who were men of
larger sympathies and understanding than the other
three, but of no greater political freedom, did feel that
Cowperwood had been badly used thus far, but they did
not see what they could do about it. He had put himself in a most unsatisfactory position, politically and
socially. They understood and took into consideration
his great financial and social losses which Steger described
accurately; and one of them, Judge Rafalsky, because
of a similar event in his own life in so far as a girl was
concerned, was inclined to argue strongly against the
conviction of Cowperwood; but, owing to his political
connections and obligations, he realized that it would
not be wise politically to stand out against what was
wanted. Still, when he and Marvin learned that Judges
Smithson, Rainey, and Beckwith were inclined to convict Cowperwood without much argument, they decided
to hand down a dissenting opinion. The point involved
was a very knotty one. Cowperwood might carry it to
the Supreme Court of the United States on some funda-
mental principle of liberty of action. Anyhow, other
judges in other courts in Pennsylvania and elsewhere
would be inclined to examine the decision in this case,
it was so important. The minority decided that it would
not do them any harm to hand down a dissenting opinion.
The politicians would not mind as long as Cowperwood
was convicted—would like it better, in fact. It looked
better, fairer. Besides, Marvin and Rafalsky did not
care to be included, if they could help it, with Smithson

Rainey, and Beckwith in a sweeping condemnation of Cowperwood. There was much to be said for his point of view. His treatment of Butler, through the latter's daughter—well, that was a very human matter. The flesh is weak. So all five judges fancied they were considering the whole matter rather fairly and impartially, as men will under such circumstances. Cowperwood was not innocent by any means. His whole career indicated that. If he must be denied a new trial, it was a good thing that he was really guilty of many things and deserving of punishment. At least, Smithson, Rainey, and Beckwith thought so. The former, speaking for himself and Judges Rainey and Beckwith (the opinion was written by Judge Smithson, and handed down on the eleventh of February, 1872), wrote as follows:

The defendant, Frank A. Cowperwood, asks that the finding of the jury in the lower court (the State of Pennsylvania *vs.* Frank A. Cowperwood) be reversed and a new trial granted. This court cannot see that any substantial injustice has been done the defendant. [Here followed a rather lengthy résumé of the history of the case, in which it was pointed out that the custom and precedent of the treasurer's office, to say nothing of Cowperwood's easy method of doing business with the city treasury, could have nothing to do with his responsibility for failure to observe both the spirit and the letter of the law.] The obtaining of goods under color of legal process [went on Judge Smithson, speaking for the majority] may amount to larceny. In the present case it was the province of the jury to ascertain the felonious intent. They have settled that against the defendant as a question of fact, and the court cannot say that there was not sufficient evidence to sustain the verdict. For what purpose did the defendant get the check? He was upon the eve of failure. He had already hypothecated for his own debts the loan of the city placed in his hands for sale—he had unlawfully obtained five hundred thousand dollars in cash as loans; and it is reasonable to suppose that he could obtain nothing more from the city treasury by any ordinary means. Then it is that he goes there, and, by means of a falsehood implied if not actual, obtains sixty thousand dollars more. The jury has found the intent with which this was done.

It was in these words that Cowperwood's appeal for a new trial was denied by the majority.

For himself and Judge Rafalsky, Judge Marvin, dissenting, wrote:

It is plain from the evidence in the case that Mr. Cowperwood did not receive the check without authority as agent to do so, and it has not been clearly demonstrated that within his capacity as agent he did not perform or intend to perform the full measure of the obligation which the receipt of this check implied. It was shown in the trial that as a matter of policy it was understood that purchases for the sinking-fund should not be known or understood in the market or by the public in that light, and that Mr. Cowperwood as agent was to have an absolutely free hand in the disposal of his assets and liabilities so long as the ultimate result was satisfactory. There was no particular time when the loan was to be bought, nor was there any particular amount mentioned at any time to be purchased. Unless the defendant intended at the time he received the check fraudulently to appropriate it he could not be convicted even on the first count. The verdict of the jury does not establish this fact; the evidence does not show conclusively that it could be established; and the same jury, upon three other counts, found the defendant guilty without the semblance of shadow of evidence. How can we say that their conclusions upon the first count are unerring when they so palpably erred on the other counts? It is the opinion of the minority that the verdict of the jury in charging larceny on the first count is not valid, and that that verdict should be set aside and a new trial granted.

Judge Rafalsky, a meditative and yet practical man of Jewish extraction but peculiarly American appearance, felt called upon to write a third opinion which should especially reflect his own cogitation and be a criticism on the majority as well as a slight variation from and addition to the points on which he agreed with Judge Marvin. It was a knotty question, this of Cowperwood's guilt, and, aside from the political necessity of convicting him, nowhere was it more clearly shown than in these varying opinions of the superior court. Judge Rafalsky held, for instance, that if a crime had been committed at all, it was not that known as larceny, and he went on to add:

It is impossible, from the evidence, to come to the conclusion either that Cowperwood did not intend shortly to deliver the loan or that Albert Stires, the chief clerk, or the city treasurer did not intend to part not only with the possession, but also and absolutely with the property in the check and the money represented by it. It was testified by Mr. Stires that Mr. Cowperwood said he had bought certificates of city loan to this amount, and it has not been clearly demonstrated that he had not. His non-placement of the same in the sinking-fund must in all fairness, the letter of the law to the contrary notwithstanding, be looked upon and judged in the light of custom. Was it his custom so to do? In my judgment the doctrine now announced by the majority of the court extends the crime of constructive larceny to such limits that any business man who engages in extensive and perfectly legitimate stock transactions may, before he knows it, by a sudden panic in the market or a fire, as in this instance, become a felon. When a principle is asserted which establishes such a precedent, and may lead to such results, it is, to say the least, startling.

These opinions were handed down on February 11th, six weeks after Steger had made his appeal and two months and more after Cowperwood had been tried and convicted. While he was notably comforted by the dissenting opinions of the judges in minority, which he could use to his advantage in his future commercial relations, and while he had been schooling himself to expect the worst in this connection and had been arranging his affairs as well as he could in anticipation of it, he was still bitterly disappointed. It would be untrue to say that, strong and self-reliant as he normally was, he did not suffer. He was not without sensibilities of the highest order, only they were governed and controlled in him by that cold iron thing, his reason, which never forsook him. There was no appeal from this appeal save to the United States Supreme Court, as Steger pointed out, and there only on the constitutionality of some phase of the decision and his rights as a citizen, of which the Supreme Court of the United States must take cognizance. This was a tedious and expensive thing to do. It was not exactly obvious at the moment on what point he could make an appeal. It would involve a long delay—perhaps a year and a half, perhaps longer—at the end of which period he might have to serve his prison term anyhow, and pending which he would certainly have to undergo incarceration for a time.

On hearing the news of Cowperwood's conviction (it was three o'clock of a Wednesday afternoon), Steger had sent for Cowperwood to come over to his office, and on receiving the note the latter had instinctively known what it was about. He was still in his old banking office in Third Street, where, because he could be of most use to himself and others, he had constantly retained a room; and on this afternoon he was engrossed in a plan to disentangle the old Seventeenth and Nineteenth Street railway lines from his other assets, and have it bought in for his benefit by the Drexel company, or Davison and an allied group of friends, who would let him manage it and possibly, eventually, buy it. On the receipt of Steger's note he took down his hat from the little private locker and went over to see him.

Steger was waiting, serious, concerned, hardly knowing how to face out this last blow, and yet gratified that he had been so obviously coincided with by two of the judges.

"Well, Harper," said Cowperwood, on arriving, a peculiar twinkle in his eye, which was not wholly gay, "I suppose I've lost. I don't know what else you could want just now."

"Yes, Frank," replied Steger; "that's just it. We've lost. I thought you might think it was that. Still, I didn't want to say so. Three to two against us. I've sent for a transcript of the opinions."

He paused and looked at Cowperwood, who in turn looked speculatively at the floor for a moment.

"Well, I don't see that there is anything more to be done in this matter one way or the other," he replied, at last, looking up. "I don't see what can be done. You say the matter can be carried to the Supreme Court on a technicality, but that won't stop me from going to jail just now. I have to go or I have to leave the country, and I've made up my mind to go. I can fight this out right here in Philadelphia in the long run and win. I can get that decision reversed in the Supreme Court, or I can get the governor to pardon me after a time, I think. I'm not going to run away, and everybody knows I'm not. These people that think they have got me down haven't got one corner of me whipped. I'll get out of this thing after a while, and when I do I'll show some of these petty little politicians what it means to put up a real fight. They'll never get a damned dollar out of me now—not a dollar. I did intend to pay that five hundred thousand dollars some time if they had let me go. Now they can whistle."

He set his teeth for the moment with an ugly Cowperwoodish set, and his gray eyes fairly snapped their determination; but his face modified a moment after to its usual bland, pleasant expression.

"Well, I've done all I can, Frank," pleaded Steger, sympathetically. "You'll do me the justice to say that I put up the best fight I knew how. I may not know how—you'll have to answer for that—but within my limits I've done the best I can. I can do a few things more to carry this thing on, if you want me to, but I'm going to leave it to you now. Whatever you say goes."

"Don't talk nonsense at this stage," replied Cowperwood, testily. "I know whether I'm satisfied or not, and I'd soon tell you if I wasn't. I think you might as well go on and see if you can find some definite grounds for carrying it to the Supreme Court, but meanwhile I'll begin my sentence. I suppose Payderson will be naming a day to have me brought before him now shortly."

"It depends on how you'd like to have it, Frank. I could get a stay of sentence for a week, maybe, or ten days, if it will do you any good. Shannon won't make any objection to that, I'm sure. There's only one hitch.

Jaspers will be around here to-morrow looking for you. It's his duty to take you into custody again, once he's notified that your appeal has been denied. He'll be wanting to lock you up unless you pay him, but we can fix that. If you do want to wait, and want any time off, I suppose he'll arrange to let you out with a deputy; but I'm afraid you'll have to stay there nights. They're pretty strict about that since that Albertson case of a few years ago."

Steger referred to the case of a noted bank cashier who, being let out of the county jail at night in the alleged custody of a deputy, was permitted to escape. There had been emphatic and severe condemnation of the sheriff's office at the time, and since then, repute or no repute, money or no money, convicted criminals were supposed to stay in the county jail at night at least.

Cowperwood meditated this calmly, looking out of the lawyer's window into Second Street. He did not much fear anything that might happen to him in Jaspers's charge since his first taste of that popular gentleman's hospitality, although he did object to spending nights in the county jail when his general term of imprisonment was being reduced no whit thereby. All that he could do now in connection with his affairs, unless he could have months of freedom, could be as well adjusted from a prison cell as from his Third Street office—not quite, but nearly so. Anyhow, why parley? He was facing a prison term, and he might as well accept it without further ado. He might take a day or two finally to look after his affairs; but beyond that, why bother?

"When, in the ordinary course of events, if you did nothing at all, would I come up for sentence?"

"Oh, Friday or Monday, I fancy," replied Steger. "I don't know what move Shannon is planning to make in this matter. I thought I'd walk around and see him in a little while."

"I think you'd better do that," replied Cowperwood

"Friday or Monday will suit me, either way. I'm really not particular. Better make it Monday if you can. You don't suppose there is any way you can induce Jaspers to keep his hands off until then? He knows I'm perfectly responsible."

"I don't know, Frank, I'm sure; I'll see. I'll go round and talk to him to-night. Perhaps a hundred dollars will make him relax the rigor of his rules that much."

Cowperwood smiled grimly.

"I fancy a hundred dollars would make Jaspers relax a whole lot of rules," he replied, and he got up to go.

Steger arose also. "I'll see both these people, and then I'll call round at your house. You'll be in, will you, after dinner?"

"Yes."

They slipped on their overcoats and went out into the cold February day, Cowperwood back to his Third Street office, Steger to see Shannon and Jaspers.

CHAPTER LXII

THE business of arranging Cowperwood's sentence for Monday was soon disposed of through Shannon, who had no personal objection to any reasonable delay.

"That's all right, Mr. Steger," he observed, most cordially, after the proposition had been put to him. "No opposition on my part, not in the least. I want to congratulate you on the way you conducted your case. I thought you'd win, to tell you the truth. If public sentiment weren't as strong as it is against Cowperwood and Stener, I think you would have. Anyhow, you divided the Supreme Court. That's something. I have no hard feelings if you haven't."

Steger smiled cordially. "Certainly not," he said. He shook hands and then went away, not bearing any resentment in the least.

He next visited the county jail, close on to five o'clock, when it was already dark. Sheriff Jaspers was pleased to see him. He came lolling out from his private library, where he had been engaged upon the noble work of cleaning his pipe.

"How are you, Mr. Steger?" he observed, smiling blandly. "How are you? Glad to see you. Won't you sit down? I suppose you're round here again on that Cowperwood matter. I just received word from the district attorney that he had lost his case."

"That's it, Sheriff," replied Steger, ingratiatingly. "He just asked me to step around and see what you wanted him to do in the matter. Judge Payderson has just fixed the sentence time for Monday morning at ten o'clock. I don't suppose you'll be much put out if he doesn't show up here before Monday at eight o'clock, will you, or Sunday night, anyhow? He's perfectly reliable, as you know." Steger was sounding Jaspers out, politely trying to make the time of Cowperwood's arrival a trivial matter in order to avoid paying the hundred dollars, if possible. But Jaspers was not to be so easily disposed of. His fat face lengthened considerably. How could Steger ask him such a favor and not even suggest the slightest form of remuneration?

"It's ag'in' the law, Mr. Steger, as you know," he began, cautiously and complainingly. "I'd like to accommodate him, everything else being equal, but since that Albertson case three years ago we've had to run this office much more careful, and—"

"Oh, I know, Sheriff," interrupted Steger, blandly, "but this isn't an ordinary case in any way, as you can see for yourself. Mr. Cowperwood is a very important man, and he has a great many things to attend to. Now if it were only a mere matter of seventy-five or a hundred dollars to satisfy some court clerk with, or to pay a fine, it would be easy enough, but—" He paused and looked wisely away, and Mr. Jaspers's face began to relax at once. The law against which it was ordinarily so hard to offend was not now so important. Steger saw that it was needless to introduce any additional arguments.

"It's a very ticklish business, this, Mr. Steger," put in the sheriff, complainingly, but yieldingly. "If anything were to happen, it would cost me my place practically. I don't like to do it under any circumstances, and I wouldn't, only I happen to know both Mr. Cowperwood and Mr. Stener, and I like 'em both. I don't think they got their rights in this matter, either. I don't mind making an exception in this case if Mr. Cowperwood don't go about too publicly. I wouldn't want any of the men in the district attorney's office to know this. I don't suppose he'll mind if I keep a deputy somewhere near all the time for looks' sake. I have to, you know, really, under the law. He won't bother him any. Just keep on guard like. Then if anything should happen I can say, 'Well, I was just lettin' him out for a half-hour or so on somethin' very special.'" Mr. Jaspers looked at Mr. Steger very flatly and wisely—almost placatingly under the circumstances—and Mr. Steger nodded.

"Quite right, Sheriff, quite right. You're quite right," and he drew out his purse while the sheriff led the way very cautiously back into his library.

"I'd like to show you the line of law-books I'm fixing up for myself in here, Mr. Steger," he observed, genially, but meanwhile closing his fingers gently on the small roll of ten-dollar bills Mr. Steger was handing him. "We have occasional use for books of that kind here, as you see. I thought it a good sort of thing to have them around." He waved one arm comprehensively at the line of State reports, revised statutes, prison regulations, etc., and Steger pretended to look.

"Quite so, Sheriff, quite so. A good idea, I think. Very good, indeed. So you think if Mr. Cowperwood gets around here very early Monday morning, say eight or eight-thirty, that it will be all right?"

"I think so," replied the sheriff, curiously nervous, but agreeable, anxious to please. "I don't think that anything will come up that will make me want him earlier. If it does I'll let you know, and you can produce him. I don't think so, though, Mr. Steger; I think everything will be all right." They were once more in the main hall now. "Glad to have seen you again, Mr. Steger— very glad," he added. "Call again some day."

Steger went to the outer door, where a turnkey stood on guard, and waved the sheriff a pleasant, albeit solemn, farewell. Then he hurried on his way to Cowperwood's house.

When Cowperwood came home from his office in the evening, after having been notified by Steger of the loss of his appeal, he decided to make the announcement in an offhand way in order to forfend against any show of feeling on anybody's part later in case he might have to go quickly. He did not know how soon he might have to leave—Steger's errand might not be successful, and, anyhow, he might have to be sentenced the first thing Friday morning. This might be his last night here. The sheriff might not be willing for him to remain out of his custody even one night. You would not have thought, seeing Cowperwood mount the front steps of his handsome residence in his neat gray suit and well-cut overcoat, that he was thinking that this might be his last night here and that henceforth he might not even come to this charming spot any more. His air and walk indicated no weakening of spirit. He entered the hall, where an early lamp was aglow, and encountered "Wash" Sims, an old negro factotum, who was just coming up from the basement, carrying a bucket of coal for one of the fire-places.

"Mahty cold out, dis evenin', Mistah Coppahwood," said Wash, to whom anything less than sixty degrees was very cold. His one regret was that Philadelphia was not located in North Carolina, where he came from.

" 'Tis sharp, Wash," replied Cowperwood, absent-mindedly. He was thinking for the moment of the house and how it had looked, as he came toward it west along Girard Avenue. What the neighbors were thinking of him, too, these days, was also in his mind. He fancied they were observing him from time to time out of their windows. It was clear and cold. The lamps in the reception-hall and sitting-room had been lit, for he had permitted no air of funereal gloom to settle down over this place since his troubles had begun. In the far west of the street a last tingeing gleam of lavender and violet was showing over the cold white snow of the roadway. The house of gray-green stone, with its lighted windows, and cream-colored lace curtains, had looked especially attractive. He had thought for the moment of the pride he had taken in putting all this here, decorating and ornamenting it, and whether, ever, he could secure it for himself again. "Where is your mistress?" he added to Wash, when he bethought himself.

"In the sitting-room, Mr. Coppahwood, ah think."

Cowperwood ascended the stair, thinking curiously that Wash would soon be out of a job now, unless Mrs. Cowperwood, out of all the wreck of other things, chose to retain him, which was not likely. He entered the sitting-room, and there sat his wife by the oblong center-table, sewing a hook and eye into one of Lillian, second's, petticoats. She looked up, at his step, with the peculiarly uncertain smile she used these days—indication of her pain, fear, suspicions, and so on—and inquired, "Well, what is new with you, Frank?" Her smile was something like a hat or belt or ornament of one kind or another which one puts on or off at will.

"Nothing in particular," he replied, in his offhand way, "except that I understand I have lost that appeal of mine. Steger is coming here in a little while to let me know. I had a note from him, and I fancy it's about that."

He did not care to say squarely that he had lost. He knew that she was sufficiently distressed as it was, and he did not care to be too rough just now. He was thinking of the penitentiary and what it would be like—whether Steger could get him any special privileges there. He had heard that the rules of the Eastern Penitentiary, where he was destined to go, were ordinarily very strict, though Steger had assured him, and he knew himself, that the terrors of most prisons were worse in the minds of inexperienced sentimentalists than they were in fact. Still, no doubt whatever, they were bad enough.

"You don't say!" replied Lillian, with surprise and fright in her voice, and getting up.

She had been so used to a world where prisons were scarcely thought of, where things went on smoothly from day to day without any noticeable intrusion of such distressing things as courts, jails, and the like, that these last few months had driven her nearly mad. Cowperwood had so definitely insisted on her keeping in the background—he had told her so very little that she was all at sea anyhow in regard to the whole procedure. Nearly all that she had had in the way of intelligence had been from his father and mother and Anna, and from a close and almost secret scrutiny of the newspapers.

At the time he had gone to the county jail she did not even know anything about it until his father had come back from the court-room and the jail and had broken the news to her. It had been a terrific blow to her. Now to have this thing suddenly broken to her in this offhand way, even though she had been expecting and dreading it hourly, was too much.

She was a decidedly charming-looking woman as she stood holding her daughter's garment in her hand, even if she was forty years old to Cowperwood's thirty-five. She was robed in one of the creations of their late prosperity, a cream-colored gown of rich silk, with dark-brown trimmings—a fetching combination for her. Her eyes were a little hollow, and reddish about the rims, but otherwise she gave no evidence of her keen mental distress. There was considerable evidence of the former tranquil sweetness that had so fascinated him ten years before, but not enough, and he felt sorry.

"Isn't that terrible?" she said, weakly, her hands trembling in a nervous way. "Isn't it dreadful? Isn't there anything you can do, anything more? You won't really have to go to prison, will you?" He objected to her distress and her nervous fears. He preferred a stronger, more self-reliant type of woman, but still she was his wife, and in his day he had loved her much.

"It looks that way, Lillian," he said, with the first note of real sympathy he had used in a long while. He was afraid to go any further along that line, however, for fear it might give her a false sense as to his present attitude, which was more of sorrow for her than anything else. She was not so dull but what she could see that the consideration in his voice had been brought about in just this way. The other factor of his manner—his face and eyes—indicated as much. Still it appealed to her as a touch of the old time. She wished sincerely that there was more of it.

"I don't want you to feel distressed about me, though," he went on, before she could say anything to him. "I'm not through with my fighting. I'll get out of this. I have to go to prison, it seems, in order to get things straightened out properly. What I would like you to do is to keep up a cheerful appearance in front of the rest of the family—father and mother particularly. They need to be cheered up." He thought once of taking her hand, then decided not. She noted mentally his hesitation, the great difference between his attitude now and that of ten or twelve years before. It did not hurt her now as much as she once would have thought. Then he was so enthusiastic, so constantly trespassing on her time. Now, when he was going to prison—a blow sufficient to have broken her heart a few years before—he was telling her of it at long range, as it were. She looked at him, scarcely knowing what to say. There was really not so much to say.

"Will you have to go soon, if you do have to go?" she ventured, wearily.

"I can't tell yet. Possibly to-night. Possibly Friday. Possibly not until Monday. I'm waiting to hear from Steger. I expect him here any minute."

He turned to go to his little private office, where a number of papers, some certificates of stock, and other things, which he would have to seal up and turn over to Steger for safe keeping, were kept.

Mrs. Cowperwood stood there as he turned. She wondered in a way what she could do. "Is there anything I can get for you?" she asked, starting forward as if out of a dream. "Do you want me to do anything? Don't you think perhaps you had better leave Philadelphia, Frank? You needn't go to prison unless you want to."

She was a little beside herself, for the first time in her life shocked out of a deadly calm; and she was not making the sanest suggestions for him, not saying the things that would appeal to him now.

He paused and looked at her for a moment in his direct, examining way, his hard commercial business judgment restored on the instant.

"That would be a confession of guilt, Lillian, and I'm not guilty," he replied, almost coldly. "I haven't done anything that warrants my running away or going to prison, either. I'm merely going there to save time at present. I can't be litigating this thing forever. I'll get out—be pardoned out or sued out in a reasonable length of time. Just now it's better to go, I think. I wouldn't think of running away from Philadelphia. Two of five judges found for me in the decision. That's pretty fair evidence that the State has no case against me."

His wife saw she had made a mistake. It clarified her judgment on the instant. "I didn't mean it that way, Frank," she replied, apologetically. "You know I didn't. Of course I know you're not guilty. Why should I think you were, of all people?"

She paused, expecting some retort, some further argument. He had quietly turned to his desk and was thinking of other things.

Suddenly the anomaly of her own state came over her again. Why trespass on his time? she asked herself. Why bother? He really did not care for her any more—that was it. Nothing could make him, nothing could bring them together, not even this tragedy. Why explain? He was interested in another woman—Aileen; and so her foolish thoughts and explanations, her fear, sorrow, distress, were not important to him. He could take her agonized wish for his freedom as a comment on his probable guilt, a doubt of his innocence, a criticism of him! She turned away for a minute, and he came out and went into another room. Then he came out of that and crossed to the hall again on his way to the other house to see his father.

"I'll be back again in a few moments," he volunteered. "Are the children here?"

"Yes, they're up in the play-room," she answered, sadly, utterly nonplussed and distraught. What was she to do in a situation of this kind? What say?

"Oh, Frank!" she had it on her lips to cry, but before she could utter it he had bustled down the steps and was gone. She turned back to the table, her left hand to her mouth, her eyes in a queer, hazy, melancholy mist. Could it be, she thought, that life could really come to this—that love could so utterly, so thoroughly die? Ten years before—but, oh, why go back to that? Obviously it could, and thoughts concerning that would not help now. Twice now in her life her affairs had seemed to go to pieces—once when her first husband had died, and now when her second had failed her, had fallen in love with another and was going to be sent off to prison. What was she going to do? Where go? She had no idea, of course, for how long a term of years he would be sent away. It might be one year or it might be five years, as the papers had said. Good heavens! The children could almost forget him in five years. She put her other hand to her mouth also, and then to her forehead, where there was a dull ache. She tried to think further than this, but somehow, just now, there was no further thought. Suddenly quite outside of her own volition, with no thought that she was going to do such a thing, her bosom began to heave, her throat contracted in four or five short, sharp, aching spasms, her eyes burned, and she shook in a vigorous, anguished, desperate, almost one might have said dry-eyed cry, so hot and few were the tears. She could not stop for the moment, just stood there and shook, and then after a while a dull ache succeeded, and she was quite as she had been before.

"Why cry?" she suddenly asked herself, fiercely—for her. "Why break down in this stormy, useless way? Would it help?"

But, in spite of her speculative, philosophic observations to herself, she still felt the echo, the distant rumble, as it were, of the storm in her own soul. "Why cry? Why not cry?" She might say she wouldn't, but, in spite of herself and all her logic, she knew that this tempest which had so recently raged over her was now merely circling round her soul's horizon and would return to break again.

CHAPTER LXIII

THE arrival of Steger with the information that no move of any kind would be made by the sheriff until Monday morning, when Cowperwood could present himself, eased matters. The forceful banker had time to think—to adjust home details at his leisure. He broke the news to his father and mother in a consoling way and talked with his brothers and father about getting matters immediately adjusted in connection with the smaller houses to which they were now shortly to be compelled to move. There was much conferring among the different members of this collapsing organization in regard to the minor details; and what with his conferences with Steger, his seeing personally Davison, Leigh, Avery Stone, of Jay Cooke & Co., George Waterman (his old-time employer Henry was dead), ex-State Treasurer Van Nostrand, who had gone out with the last State administration, and others, he was very busy, and the time passed. Cowperwood, now that he was really going into prison, wanted his financial friends to get together and see if they could get him out by appealing to the governor.

The division of opinion among the judges of the State Supreme Court was his excuse and strong point. He wanted Steger to follow this up after he should be gone, and he spared no pains in trying to see all and sundry who might be of use to him—Edward Tighe, of Tighe & Co., who was still in business in Third Street; Newton Targool; Arthur Rivers; Joseph Zimmerman, the dry-goods prince, now a millionaire; Judge Kitchen; Terrence Relihan, the former representative of the money element at Harrisburg; and many others.

Cowperwood wanted Relihan to approach the newspapers and see if he could not readjust their attitude so as to work to get him out, and he wanted Walter Leigh to head the movement of getting up a signed petition which should contain all the important names of money people and others, asking the governor to release him. Leigh agreed to this heartily, as did Relihan speaking for his work in connection with the newspapers.

"I'll do everything I can, Frank," Leigh assured him, heartily; and as for Relihan, he simply said, "You may depend on me, Mr. Cowperwood," and he meant it. Relihan informed Cowperwood now, as had others before, that he knew that the local political poohbahs, Mollenhauer, Simpson, and Butler, were against him—that they had been anxious all along to see him convicted, and for what reason he, Relihan, could not quite make out, unless it was to break up his local street-railway activity. Relihan had heard of Cowperwood's relation to Aileen Butler, but he did not care to speak about it.

"And I can't see why, either," was his comment, "unless it's because you were getting too deep in the street-car game here."

Cowperwood lifted his eyes. "That's one good reason, anyhow, isn't it?" he replied.

Aileen had one last opportunity of seeing her lover outside the prison walls. They met on Saturday before the Monday of his sentence, and there was enacted one of those peculiar scenes—peculiar to the privileged classes—which money and mental resourcefulness guarantee as both possible and socially safe. Cowperwood had not come in contact with her since the decision of the Supreme Court had been rendered, but he had had a letter at a private mail-box, and had made an appointment for Saturday at a small hotel in Camden, which, being across the river, was safer, in his judgment, than anything in Philadelphia. He was a little uncertain as to how Aileen would take the possibility of not seeing him soon again after Monday, and how she would act generally once he was where she could not confer with him as often as she chose. He was very anxious to talk to her on many counts, not the least of which was that of his love, and his sorrow at being compelled to part with her in this way.

Aileen, who through all this long period of disaster had been repeating her assurances of faith and affection, was no less emphatic in her protestations than she had ever been; in fact, was much more so. She went at her beloved in that direct, forceful way which only she could attempt with him, a sort of mannish impetuosity which he both enjoyed and admired, and slipping her arms around his neck, said: "Honey, you needn't tell me. I saw it in the papers the other morning. Don't you mind, honey. I love you. I'll wait for you. I'll be with you yet, if it takes a dozen years of waiting. It doesn't make any difference to me if it takes a hundred, only I'm so sorry for you, sweetheart. I'll be with you every day through this, darling, loving you with all my might. Oh, my lovely Frank, my boy!"

She caressed his solid head while he looked at her in that quiet way which betokened at once his self-poise and yet his interest and satisfaction in her. He couldn't help loving Aileen, he thought. He couldn't help admiring her tremendously, now more than ever, because literally, in spite of all his intellectual strength, he really could not rule her. She went at him, even when he stood off in a calm, critical way, as if he were her special property, her toy. She would talk to him always, and particularly when she was excited, as if he were just a baby, her pet; and sometimes he felt as though she would really overcome him mentally, make him subservient to her, she was so individual, so sure of her importance as a woman.

Now on this occasion she went babbling on as if he were broken-hearted, in need of her greatest care and tenderness, although he really wasn't at all; and for the moment she actually made him feel as though he was.

"It isn't as bad as that, Aileen," he ventured to say, eventually; but she went on forcefully, paying no heed to him.

"Oh yes, it is, too, honey. I know. Oh, my poor Frank! But I'll see you. I know how to manage, whatever happens. How often do they let visitors come out to see the prisoners there?"

She had seen in the papers the name of the institution to which he would probably have to go.

"Only once in three months, pet, so they say, but I think we can fix that after I get there; only do you think you had better try to come? Aren't you in danger of stirring up your father? He might cause a lot of trouble out there if he were so minded."

"Only once in three months!" she exclaimed, with rising emphasis, as he began this explanation. "Oh, Frank, no! Surely not! Once in three months! Oh, I won't do it! Oh, I can't stand that! I won't! I'll go and see the warden myself. He'll let me see you. I'm sure he will, if I talk to him."

"Stop a minute, Aileen," said Cowperwood, firmly, while he drew her to a chair and pulled her down on his lap. He was thinking, in spite of all his other calculations, how charming she was looking to-day. How young she kept, and how forceful! While he was nearing his full maturity she was a comparatively young girl, and as beautiful as ever. She was wearing a black-and-white-striped silk in the curious bustle style of the times, and a set of sealskin furs, including a little sealskin cap on top of her jaunty red-gold head.

"You're not thinking what you're saying, Aileen," he continued. "You're not thinking. Remember your father! Remember your family! Your father may know the warden out there. You don't want it to get all over town that you're running out there to see me. Your father will cause you trouble. You don't know the small party politicians as I do. They gossip like a lot of old women. You'll have to be very careful what you do and how you do it. I don't want to lose you. I want to see you. But you'll have to mind what you're doing. Don't try to see me at once. I want you to, but I want to find out how the land lies, and I want you to find out too. You won't lose me. I'll be there, well enough."

He paused as he thought of the long tier of iron cells which must be there, one of which would be his—for how long?—and of Aileen seeing him through the door of it or in it.

"I know, I know," replied Aileen, firmly. "But think of three months! Honey, I can't! I won't! It's non-sense. Three months! I know that my father wouldn't have to wait any three months if he wanted to see any-body out there, nor anybody else that he wanted to ask favors for. And I won't, either. I'll find some way."

Cowperwood had to smile. You could not defeat Aileen so easily.

"But you're not your father, honey; and you don't want him to know."

"I know I don't, but they don't need to know who I am. I can go heavily veiled. I don't think that the warden knows my father. He may. Anyhow, he doesn't know me; and he wouldn't tell on me if he did—if I talked to him. He'd help me, not hurt me."

Her confidence in her charms, her personality, her earthly privileges was quite anarchistic. Cowperwood shook his head.

"Honey, you're about the best and the worst there is when it comes to a woman," he observed, affectionately, pulling her lips down to his, "but you'll have to listen to me just the same. I have a lawyer, Steger—you know him. He's going to take up this matter with the warden out there—is doing it to-day. He may be able to fix things, and he may not. I'll know to-morrow or Sun-day, and I'll write you. But don't go and do anything rash until you hear. I'm sure I can cut that visiting limit in half, and perhaps down to once a month or once in two weeks even. I'm not sure. They only allow me to write one letter in three months"—Aileen exploded again —"and I'm sure I can have that made different—some; but don't write me until you hear, or at least don't sign any name or put any address in. They open all mail and read it. If you see me or write me you'll have to be cautious, and you're not the most cautious person in the world. Now be good, will you?"

They talked much more—of his family, his court appearance Monday, whether he would get out soon to attend any of the suits still pending, or be pardoned. Aileen was enraged at her father for his part in the local political attitude toward Cowperwood and anxious to see the latter come out and triumph again. She believed in his future still. She had read the opinions of the dissenting judges in his favor, and that of the three agreed judges against him. She was sure his day was not over in Philadelphia, and that he would some time re-establish himself and then take her with him somewhere else. She was sorry for Mrs. Cowperwood, but she was convinced that she was not suited to him—that Frank needed some one more like herself, some one with youth and beauty and force—her, no less. She clung to him now in ecstatic embraces until it was time to go. So far as a plan of procedure could have been adjusted in a situation so incapable of accurate adjustment, it had been done. She was desperately downcast at the last moment, as was he, over their parting; but she pulled herself together with her usual force and faced the dark future with a steady eye.

CHAPTER LXIV

THE matter of sentencing Cowperwood was carried out with that due regard for the forms of so-called justice which make the final disposition of any individual case always interesting as a spectacle. In spite of Stener's decision not to stand trial at the time that Cowperwood was being tried, when it came to the actual matter of pleading guilty he had changed his mind, as has been said, and on the advice of friends pleaded not guilty, standing trial rather than bear the odium of acknowledged guilt. Judge Payderson, for a romantic legal reason of his own, and because Stener's change of heart had thrown his trial over into the January term of court, had decided to sentence both Cowperwood and him at the same time. He had readily granted a stay of sentence in Stener's case because he wanted to see how Cowperwood's appeal eventuated. When that failed, he ordered both men brought before him at the same time, proposing to make a fine moral example of their conviction. He had even framed up the language in which he would set forth their error to them separately, and he had both speeches committed to memory at the time they were finally brought before him.

The process of bringing them there was interesting enough, as things legal go. Once the decision of the Supreme Court was reached, it was entered on the court records at the court itself and a notice mailed to the district attorney of the district in which the appellant had been tried. He in turn notified the court before whom the case had been tried, and the latter then fixed a day for sentence and ordered the prisoner to be brought before him. It was the business of the sheriff, once he was notified of the defeat of an appeal, to see that the individual whom it concerned was promptly brought into his care. Cowperwood, through Steger and Jaspers, as we have seen, was illegally freed from being asked to come to the county jail and surrender himself. Payderson having fixed Monday, the sixteenth, at ten o'clock in the morning, for both Cowperwood's and Stener's sentence, the former was asked by Sheriff Jaspers to present himself at the jail at eight o'clock, in order that there might be ample time for all possible contingencies. There were papers to be filled out and signed and other formalities to be complied with. In ordinary cases there was a wagon which went around to the different courts from the jail carrying prisoners then on trial or subject to sentence, and taking them away again; and this would have carried Cowperwood, except that for the price he had paid he was able to make a different arrangement—that is, walk with a deputy. There was a little antechamber connected with every court where prisoners were detained under surveillance and produced or returned to jail or discharged as ordered by the court, and it was to the most available entrances to these that the jail-wagon ran or the prisoner was taken. In connection with the Criminal Court, Part I, where Cowperwood had been tried and where he was to be sentenced, there was such an anteroom, as we have seen, and it was here that he was to be conducted this Monday morning. In the court-room there was a large aisle, the same which led to the jury-room in which he was first convicted, where, the first thing in the morning, after the court had got through listening to pleas for dismissals, motions for new trials, pleas for delays, etc.—the general business of arranging the day's docket—the prisoners who were to hear their fate on this day were brought forth. They were lined up by bailiffs in a long row, if there were many, against the wall in this aisle; and as each prisoner's name was called he stepped forward to his proper position in front of the court-rail gate where the judge could see and hear him. Then the final pleas of the lawyers for clemency, the letters of friends and relatives, the prisoner's own statement, and anything else that might be either for or against him were considered, and the sentence administered accordingly. It might have been supposed that in a case of such importance as Stener's and Cowperwood's, the two men being fairly prominent, they would have been brought in in some unobtrusive way and sentenced; but such was not the case here. Judge Payderson was a stickler for form and order in his court, never giving way except to notable political influence, which was conspicuously lacking in Cowperwood's case. So he and Stener had to accept the rather disagreeable arrangement of being brought in with decidedly ordinary criminals and lined up on the side wall in the aisle, which was a thing neither of them ever forgot afterward.

When they reached the court the same little pen in which Cowperwood had awaited the verdict of his jury several months before was waiting to receive them, or him. Owing to a lively sense of possible favors to come, Eddie Zanders was not insistent on Cowperwood's entering at once, knowing well how offensive the pen was to him.

"We can sit outside here," he observed, "or walk around. We got a half-hour yet before we need to go in there."

Because it was cold—still snow on the ground—it then occurred to him that they might visit a near-by saloon which was visible from where they stood. It was a thought quite inappropriate to Cowperwood's father, and to Cowperwood himself in a way, though he did not so much mind, but Zanders could not be expected to see this. His standards were of the jail and the average court hanger-on. "It's warm over there," he volunteered, genially, "and you can get something to drink if you want." Then, bethinking him that he was in the presence of perhaps a rather conservative company so far as liquor was concerned, he added: "I don't know whether you gentlemen ever take anything. Maybe you don't."

Cowperwood, senior, was very much opposed to saloons in general. To him they were the curse of God, the visible evidence of a personal devil, operating on this earth. He himself never took anything stronger than water; though these many years, for custom's sake and owing to the degenerate habits of that superior world into which, by degrees, he had been rising, he had allowed wine to be served on his table. A noted brand of French wine in a dusty bottle over which other bankers and men of importance smacked their lips and pretended or evinced a real interest was one thing; a saloon filled with commonplace sots and brawlers, as he fancied them to be —he had never been inside one in his life—was another matter. On this occasion, therefore, this suggestion hurt him no little, because he was not sure that his several sons might not want to go. Cowperwood had to smile, for he knew his father's attitude. He had no objection to saloons good, bad, or indifferent, if there were any object in his going into them. He drank nothing stronger than water, except good wine on occasion, though he was perfectly willing that others should, and bought liberally for those who did. Joseph and Edward had been drinking at bars occasionally, for company, these many years, without their father's knowing it, however.

"No," said Cowperwood, considerately, "father's opposed to that sort of thing. We'd better go to a restaurant."

Cowperwood, senior, in spite of his other troubles, felt relieved. It was something not to have to go to a saloon even if your son was being—sent to the penitentiary. They finally compromised on a near-by restaurant, where coffee was ordered; and then, when the time was up, they entered the "pen," awaiting momentarily the order of the court to have all prisoners up for sentence brought before him. Cowperwood, senior, and his two free sons were compelled to leave after a moment, as it was against the rules for them to remain here. They sought places in the court - room proper. Eddie Zanders remained with his charge. Stener and a deputy by the name of Wilkerson were in the room; and because of their original quarrel Cowperwood and Stener pretended now not to see each other. Cowperwood had no objection to talking to his former associate, but he could see that he was diffident and ashamed. So he let the situation pass without look or word of any kind. After some three-quarters of an hour of dreary waiting the door leading into the court-room proper opened and a bailiff in blue stepped in.

"All prisoners up for sentence," he called.

There were some six, all told, including Cowperwood and Stener. Two of them were house-breakers who had worked as confederates and had been caught red-handed at their midnight task. Both of them had taken off their shoes, as the trial had proved, and put them under the basement steps of the house in which they were operating, where a prowling officer had discovered them. They had fled on hearing the approach of the police, and had only been captured after a hard chase; but despite the absence of their shoes they had denied that they were the persons wanted, and had stood trial, alleging that they were not without shoes, and that the police were "railroading" them. This was their second offense.

Another prisoner was no more and no less than a plain horse-thief, a young man of twenty-six, who had been convicted by a jury of stealing a rather commonplace grocer's horse and selling it. He had not previously been guilty of any crime in so far as the court records showed, and it was thought that he would get off with a light sentence, though there was not so much of the mercy-for-first-offenders theory operative in that day. The last man was a negro, a tall, shambling, illiterate, nebulous-minded black, who had walked off with an apparently discarded section of lead pipe which he had found in a lumber-yard. His idea was to sell or trade it for a drink. He really did not belong in this court at all; but, having been caught by an undersized American watchman charged with the care of the property, and having at first refused to plead guilty, not quite understanding what was to be done with him, he had been perforce bound over to this court for trial. Afterward he had changed his mind and admitted his guilt, so he now had to come before Judge Payderson for sentence or dismissal. The lower court before which he had originally been brought had lost jurisdiction by binding him over to the higher court for trial. Eddie Zanders, in his self-appointed position as guide and mentor to Cowperwood, had confided nearly all of this data to him as he stood waiting.

The court-room was crowded. It was very humiliating to Cowperwood to have to file in this way along the side aisle, preceded by the negro, the confederated house-breakers, and the horse-thief, and followed by Stener, well dressed but sickly-looking and disconsolate. Cowperwood, by reason of his physical health, his face, his keen, intellectual eyes, his good clothes, cut and worn with the greatest care, stood out in marked contrast to the shambling, grinning, half-witted negro; to the queer, fox-like, lantern-jawed faces of the house-breakers, who looked rugged enough, yet anemic, as if the fluids of their bodies were but ill compounded, and as though they had been reared in slums and cellars, slinking all their days through an unintelligible world. The young horse-thief, who fortunately stood directly in front of him instead of the negro, who he feared by some irony of fate might be there, looked as though he might have been very hard pressed at the time he stole the horse. He was obviously of German extraction but born in America, of a stocky build, all of five feet ten inches, with light, straight yellow hair and a skin that would have been ruddy if he had been well fed. His face was not remarkably intelligent; neither was it utterly dull. His shoes, as Cowperwood noted, were run down at the heels, his trousers frayed at the bottom, his coat and trousers not so much dirty as baggy, having lost all kinship with new, tidy garments. No doubt he had been lying in one of those miserable cells in the county jail, Cowperwood thought, which he, for a price, had escaped. Cowperwood looked at his thin but not badly shaped ears, noticing that they were dirty. Why shouldn't they be, though? he asked himself, knowing a little more now of jails than he ever had before. The man had but small chance to wash, no doubt. In his hands he held a faded cap of some cross-barred cheviot, which he kept rolling and unrolling nervously. Cowperwood understood quite well now. He forgave him all his sins because of the stress of life that had no doubt staggered and overcome his feeble intellect. He felt sorry now for this entire shabby row of convicts like himself, sorry for all who were in jails, men who were here now or would be or had been. It is a grim, bitter world we were all born into, he reflected. Who was to straighten out the matter of the unjust equipment with which most people began? Who was to give them strong minds in place of feeble ones, able bodies instead of wretched ones? Where were they to get pure tendencies instead of impure ones, as the world looked on these things? The world was full of jails and laws and maxims and theories, and some men were strong and some weak. Some were sent into the world filled with a great lust and a great ability for wealth like himself, a mind swift to see, a body strong to endure; and some were sent half equipped, almost shapeless and formless—like this negro at the head of the line, or this poor weakling of a boy, or these burglars—"ditch delivered of a drab," as Shakespeare had put it. How were they going to win in life, how do anything important, how save their pointless lives from being ground between the upper and the nether millstones of strength? Strength and weakness—there lay the key, the answer. Between upper and lower wheels of strength lay weakness. Were you strong, or were you weak? If you were not strong enough to win, heaven help you! In the center of life were its great prizes, where intolerant men were always battling as he had battled, as he was battling still. The weaklings had to die. And here was this pale, thin, dusty Payderson, high on his bench, with his weak, milky-blue eyes, and his thin-frizzled, yellowish-white hair, looking down on them now. His whole soul was convinced that he was executing some very important function of life—acting in accordance with some inherent fact of our being for the benefit of the people. Good heavens! Payderson! And the shifty, tricky lawyers! And the wabbling law! Why had not the wabbling law seen to it that he had not had one kind of treatment at the county jail and the poor scrubs now before him another? Why had not the wabbling law prevented him from being indicted not so much as a real offender as a scapegoat? Why had not the wabbling law prevented the politicians from influencing this court and the one above it? Law—fiddlesticks! Justice—nonsense! He had no quarrel with things in particular. He was just a little weary of the endless misunderstandings and topsy-turvy nature of life. You could not put your fingers on any definite facts save those of strength and weakness, subtlety or the lack of it; and he had his fingers there, safely enough. But this poor silly negro! Would Payderson have the hardihood really to punish him for his crime? And this horse-thief!

CHAPTER LXV

IT was not very long after Cowperwood thought this that he found out what Payderson would do. Payderson had been listening to the usual arguments between the assistants of the district attorney's office and the lawyers for the defense in criminal cases as to why certain cases were or were not ready. The arrangement of the day's trial docket was always the first business of the morning. Having finished with this, he was now ready to hear from the court clerk, Abel Protus, the names and the crimes of all those who were to be sentenced this morning, in their order. Protus, as was customary in all such cases, had handed him, by the courtesy of the district attorney's office, the papers in the case of Charles Ackerman, the negro, who was the first on the list.

"How is it this man comes before me?" asked Payderson, peevishly, when he saw the amount in cash, the value of the property Ackerman was supposed to have stolen.

"Your honor," the assistant district attorney explained, promptly, "this negro was before a lower court and refused, because he was drunk, or something, to plead guilty. The lower court, because the complainant would not forego the charge, was compelled to bind him over to this court for trial. Since then he has changed his mind and has admitted his guilt to the district attorney. He would not be brought before you except we have no alternative. He has to be brought here now in order to clear the calendar."

Judge Payderson stared quizzically at the negro, who was leaning comfortably on the gate or bar before which

662

the average criminal stood erect and terrified. The latter was obviously not very much disturbed by this examination, for he had been before police-court magistrates before on one charge and another—drunkenness, disorderly conduct, and the like. His whole attitude was rather innocent, shambling, lackadaisical, amusing, like that of a large Newfoundland dog.

"Well, Ackerman," inquired his honor, severely, "did you or did you not steal this piece of lead pipe as charged here—four dollars and eighty cents' worth?"

"Yassah, I did," began the negro. "I tell you how it was. I was a-comin' along past dat lumber-yard one Saturday afternoon, and I hadn't been wuckin', an' I saw dat piece o' pipe thoo de fence, lyin' inside, and I jes' reached thoo with a piece o' boad I found dere and pulled it over to me an' tuck it. An' aftahwahd dis Mistah Watchman man"—he waved his hand oratorically toward the witness-chair, where, in case the judge might wish to ask him some questions, the complainant had taken his stand—"come around tuh where I live an' accused me of done takin' it."

"But you did take it, didn't you?"

"Yassah, I done tuck it."

"Well, don't you know it's wrong to do anything like that? Didn't you know when you reached through that fence and pulled that pipe over to you that you were stealing? Didn't you?"

"Yassah, I knowed it was wrong," replied Ackerman, sheepishly. "I didn't think 'twus stealin' like zackly, but I done knowed it was wrong. I done knowed I oughtn' take it, I guess."

"Of course you did. Of course you did. That's just it. You knew you were stealing, and still you took it."

His honor was very emphatic, but, troubled by a new thought, he turned to the assistant district attorney, who was standing near him.

"Has the man to whom this negro sold the lead pipe

been apprehended yet?" he inquired, sharply. "He should be, for he's more guilty than this negro, a receiver of stolen goods."

"Yes, sir," replied the assistant. "His case is before Judge Yawger."

"Quite right. It should be," replied Payderson, severely. "This matter of receiving stolen property is one of the worst offenses, in my judgment."

He then turned his attention to Ackerman again. "Now, look here, Ackerman," he exclaimed, irritated at having to bother with such a petty case, "I want to say something to you, and I want you to pay strict attention to me. Straighten up, there! Don't lean on that gate! You are in the presence of the law now." Ackerman had sprawled himself comfortably down on his elbows as he would have if he had·been leaning over a back-fence gate talking to some one, but he immediately drew himself straight, still grinning foolishly and apologetically, when he heard this. "You are not so dull but that you can understand what I am going to say to you. The offense you have committed—stealing a piece of lead pipe—is a crime. Do you hear me? A criminal offense—one that I could punish you very severely for. I could send you to the penitentiary for one year if I chose—the law says I may—one year at hard labor for stealing a piece of lead pipe. Now, if you have any sense you will pay strict attention to what I am going to tell you. I am not going to send you to the penitentiary right now. I'm going to wait a little while. I am going to sentence you to one year in the penitentiary—one year. Do you understand?" Ackerman blanched a little and licked his lips nervously. "And then I am going to suspend that sentence—hold it over your head, so that if you are ever caught taking anything else you will be punished for this offense and the next one also at one and the same time. Do you understand that? Do you know what I mean? Tell me. Do you?"

"Yassah! I does, sir," replied the negro. "You'se gwine to let me go now—tha's it."

The audience grinned, and his honor made a wry face to prevent his own grim grin.

"I'm going to let you go only so long as you don't steal anything else," he thundered. "The moment you steal anything else, back you come to this court, and then you go to the penitentiary for a year and whatever more time you deserve. Do you understand that? Now, I want you to walk straight out of this court and behave yourself. Don't ever steal anything. Get something to do! Don't steal, do you hear? Don't touch anything that doesn't belong to you! Don't come back here! If you do, I'll send you to the penitentiary, sure."

"Yassah! No, sah, I won't," replied Ackerman, nervously. "I won't take nothin' more that don't belong tuh me."

He shuffled away, after a moment, urged along by the guiding hand of a bailiff, and was put safely outside the court, amid a mixture of smiles over his simplicity and Payderson's undue severity of manner. But the next case was called and soon engrossed the interest of the audience.

It was that of the two house-breakers, Albert Hursted and William Eugster, whom Cowperwood had been and was still studying with much curiosity. In all his life before he had never witnessed a sentencing scene of any kind. He had never been in police or criminal courts of any kind—rarely in any of the civil ones. He had on several occasions been summoned, but had always managed to evade jury duty. He was curious about his own case—somewhat uncertain and disturbed—but not so much so but that he could take an interest in these other examples. They seemed to parallel, and in a way foreshadow, his own doom. He was glad to see the negro go, and gave Payderson credit for having some sense and sympathy—more than he had expected. He won-

THE FINANCIER

dered whether by any chance Aileen was here. He had objected to her coming, but she might have. She was, as a matter of fact, in the extreme rear, pocketed in a crowd near the door, heavily veiled, but present. She had not been able to resist the desire to know quickly and surely her beloved's fate—to be near him in his hour of real suffering, as she thought. She was greatly angered at seeing him brought in with a line of ordinary criminals and made to wait in this, to her, shameful public manner, but she could not help admiring all the more the dignity and superiority of his presence even here. He was not even pale, she thought, just the same firm, forceful man she had always known him to be. My, how badly life had used him in these last several months—how cruel it had been to him!

When the name of William Eugster was called—the two house-breakers, although their offenses were identical, were nevertheless sentenced separately—he followed with his peculiarly suggestive walk to the rail. Eugster did not walk directly forward on the soles of his feet, but rather pivoted circularly on his heels. He was a slathery type of man, in the sense in which the Irish use the word —meaning loose-jointed, pugnacious, dour, and other things. He was not capable of looking anything under the present circumstances save uncertain. Naturally, he was apprehensive of a severe sentence, as was his companion, and perhaps with a view to concealing the significance of his eyes, kept them to the floor. His hands, as Cowperwood noted, were not long and shapely like those of a craftsman of any kind, but short and stubby, with round, homely nails. No doubt, he thought, the police had the right man in this instance, as in the case of his partner, who was of a somewhat different type; but how could one tell? How could one figure out the devious course by which they had come here?

"William Eugster," said his honor, after the second bailiff had asked his name, address, age, profession or

666

calling, and whether he had ever been convicted before, and the court stenographer had taken it down, "you have been convicted of the crime of burglary in the first degree by a jury of your own selection, and under circumstances which it seems to me should have made you hesitate to put the State to the unnecessary expense of prosecuting you, seeing that the evidence was sufficiently definite to insure your conviction at any time. At the time you were first brought before me I gave you the opportunity of pleading guilty and saving the State this expense, and I told you then that, seeing this was your second offense, it would go hard with you, but that I would not let a plea of guilty go without some consideration on my part. You chose not to accept that offer, but to insist instead on a jury trial, which has resulted as you have seen. I have, therefore, no sympathy with you in your position at this time. You have been guilty of house-breaking before under circumstances no less reprehensible than those which bring you before me to-day. The crime of which you have been convicted was undertaken in the most calculating and deadly spirit, as the shoes under the steps, the burglar's tools and knife and revolver found on your person amply demonstrate. Society deserves to be protected against such criminals as you, and I would be lacking in my duty as a servant of the law and a representative of the will of the people if I did not to the fullest extent of the authority granted me protect society against you and your kind. Finding absolutely nothing to modify or extenuate your guilt, I sentence you to fifteen years' imprisonment in the State Penitentiary for the Eastern District, at labor."

He turned calmly from his victim, while the latter stared, and then hurried away, being marched rapidly along past Cowperwood, who followed him with his eyes, only to turn back when the latter's companion in crime, Albert Hursted, was placed at the rail. The latter looked grimly around while his honor sentenced him in almost the same terms. It was the same crime, the same weapons; the same opportunity to plead guilty had been offered and refused. Cowperwood looked at this man as interestedly as he had at Eugster, realizing that he should have both of them for companions at the penitentiary for the Eastern District. Think, he might even encounter them there—have to work with them!

As Albert Hursted passed by him back to the little "pen" room, shunted along by a controlling bailiff, August Nunnekamp, the young man charged with horse-stealing, was called forward, and stood at the rail, rolling his cap, quite pale, evidently underfed, having endured, no doubt, a great mental strain for some time past. As usual his record was taken by the court stenographer and a bailiff, and then Judge Payderson, staring at the indictment and the subsequent history of his case, asked:

"Where did you come from, when you first came to Philadelphia, Nunnekamp?"

"Trenton, sir."

"What did you do there?"

"I worked in a pottery."

"How did it come that you didn't stay there?"

"They shut down, most of them, sir, last spring."

"And then you came to Philadelphia?"

"Yes, sir."

"Why didn't you admit you stole this horse in the first place, Nunnekamp, instead of putting the State to all this expense of trying you? You did steal it, didn't you?"

"I—I—"

The victim swallowed and licked his lips. He had stolen the horse truly enough, but he had been badly advised, or not properly influenced to tell the truth in the first place. A spindling fourth-rate lawyer had been appointed by the court to defend him (seeing that he had no money), and Nunnekamp had no confidence in the latter. He had been afraid to admit that he had stolen the horse, because he fancied an effort was being made to trap him. Consequently, he had lied to him. The silly lawyer, an undersized American, was standing beside him now.

"You'd better say yes," he whispered to Nunnekamp. "It 'll make it easier for you."

"You did, didn't you?" shouted Payderson, very much irritated by Nunnekamp's uncertainty as to whether he would tell the truth or not even yet. The evidence at the trial had indicated very plainly that he had stolen the horse.

"Yes, sir," he finally said.

"Of course! That's it! You had to put the State to all the expense of trying you, although you knew all the time that you had stolen the horse and that you ought to be punished."

Payderson could not know that Nunnekamp had been brought up through a rather hard boyhood and, being not too strong mentally, had often sought to dodge suffering by lies.

"Well, Nunnekamp, I don't know what to think of you. I guess you don't amount to much, really. You know you stole the horse. The evidence shows that you worked for this grocer a little while, and then when he couldn't keep you any more"—Nunnekamp had been discharged because he was really not quick enough to be a grocer's clerk—"you went back and stole his horse. That shows a very bad trait in you, Nunnekamp. You're dull, and you're lacking in gratitude and honesty. I did think some of letting you go, seeing this is your first offense, so far as this court knows, but, all things considered, I think a year in the penitentiary will do you good. It will rouse you to a sense of the significance of the law, and make you understand that the property of others is sacred and not to be trifled with. My judgment is that you be confined in the penitentiary for the Eastern District of Pennsylvania for one year, and that you repay to this grocer the value of this horse, as estimated here—

one hundred and thirty-five dollars—out of your future earnings."

Nunnekamp had sold the horse to a passing peddler for forty dollars.

He was led away, rolling his cap, uncertain, inefficient, not knowing what to think of his crime or his future.

When it came to Cowperwood's turn to be called, his honor himself stiffened and straightened up, for this was a different type of man, and he could not be handled in the same way. Payderson became much more self-conscious.

"Frank Algernon Cowperwood," called the clerk.

Cowperwood stepped briskly forward as his name was called, sorry for himself, ashamed of his position, in a way, but showing it neither in look nor manner. He stood very straight in front of the gate, very simple-mannered, unassuming, and yet courageous. Payderson eyed him as he had the others.

"Name?" asked the bailiff, for the benefit of the court stenographer.

"Frank Algernon Cowperwood."

"Residence?"

"Nineteen hundred thirty-seven Girard Avenue."

"Occupation?"

"Banker and broker."

Cowperwood had been joined by Steger the moment he stepped forward, and the latter stood close beside him, very dignified, very forceful, ready to make a final statement for the benefit of the court and the public, when the time should come. Aileen from her position in the crowd near the door was for the first time in her life biting her fingers nervously, and there were great beads of perspiration on her brow. Cowperwood's father was tense with excitement, and his two brothers looked quickly away, doing their best to hide their fear and sorrow.

"Ever convicted before?"

"Never," replied Steger for Cowperwood, quietly.

"Frank Algernon Cowperwood," called the clerk, in

his nasal singsong way, coming forward, "have you anything to say why judgment should not now be pronounced upon you? If so, speak."

Cowperwood started to say no, but Steger put up his hand.

"If the court please, my client, Mr. Cowperwood, the prisoner at the bar, is neither guilty in his own estimation, nor in that of two-fifths of the Pennsylvania State Supreme Court—the court of last resort in this State," he exclaimed, loudly and clearly, so that all might hear. One of the interested listeners and spectators at this point was Edward Malia Butler, who had just stepped in from another court-room where he had been talking to a judge. An obsequious court attendant had warned him that Cowperwood was about to be sentenced. He had really come here this morning in order not to miss this sentence, but he cloaked his motive under the guise of another errand. He did not know that Aileen was there, nor did he see her. The crowd was quite large. The Cowperwoods, father and sons, were so intent on Frank that they did not see him. Butler had a peculiar look of interest on his face—not malicious, but strangely grim and determined.

"As he himself testified at the time of his trial," went on Steger, "and as the evidence clearly showed, he was never more than an agent for the gentleman whose offense was subsequently adjudicated by this court; and as an agent he still maintains, and two-fifths of the State Supreme Court agree with him, that he was strictly within his rights and privileges in not having deposited the sixty thousand dollars' worth of city loan certificates at the time, and in the manner which the people, acting through the district attorney, complained that he should have. My client is a man of rare financial ability. By the various letters which have been submitted to your honor in his behalf, you will see that he commands the respect and the sympathy of a large majority of the most forceful and eminent men in his particular world. He is a man of distinguished social standing and of notable achievements. Only the most unheralded and the unkindest thrust of fortune has brought him here before you to-day —a fire and its consequent panic which involved a financial property of the most thorough and stable character. In spite of the verdict of the jury and the decision of three-fifths of the State Supreme Court, I maintain that my client is not an embezzler, that he has not committed larceny, that he should never have been convicted, and that he should not now be punished for something of which he is not guilty.

"I trust that your honor will not misunderstand me or my motives when I point out in this situation that what I have said is true. I do not wish to cast any reflection on the integrity of this court, nor of any court, nor of any of the processes of law. I appreciate the peculiar and distinguished position which your honor holds in this matter. But I do condemn and deplore the untoward chain of events which has built up a seeming situation, not easily understood by the lay mind, and which has brought my distinguished client within the purview of the law. I think it is but fair that this should be finally publicly stated here and now. I ask that your honor be lenient, and that if you cannot conscientiously dismiss this charge you will at least see that the facts, as I have indicated them, are given due weight in the measure of the punishment inflicted."

Steger stepped back; and Judge Payderson nodded, as much as to say he had heard all the distinguished lawyer had to say, and would give it such consideration as it deserved—no more. Then he turned to Cowperwood, who was standing as erect as before, and, summoning all his judicial dignity to his aid, he began:

"Frank Algernon Cowperwood, you have been convicted by a jury of your own selection of the offense of larceny. The motion for a new trial, made in your behalf by your learned counsel, has been carefully considered and overruled, the majority of the court being entirely satisfied with the propriety of the conviction, both upon the law and the evidence. Your offense was one of more than usual gravity, the more so that the large amount of money which you obtained belonged to the city. And it was aggravated by the fact, of which we have judicial knowledge, that you had in addition thereto unlawfully used and converted to your own use several hundred thousand dollars of the loan and money of the city. For such an offense the maximum punishment affixed by the law is singularly merciful. Nevertheless, the facts in connection with your hitherto distinguished position, the circumstances under which your failure was brought about, and the courteous appeal of your numerous friends and financial associates, will be given due consideration by this court. It is not unmindful of any important fact in your career." Payderson paused as if in doubt what further to say, though he knew very well how he was about to proceed. It was all written out and in his mind. He knew what his superiors expected of him.

"If your case points no other moral," he went on, after a moment, toying with the briefs, "it will at least teach the lesson, long needed at the present time, that the treasury of the city is not to be invaded and plundered with impunity under the thin disguise of a business transaction, and that there is still a power in the law to vindicate itself and to protect the public.

"The sentence of the court," he added, solemnly, the while Cowperwood gazed on unmoved, "is, therefore, that you pay a fine of five thousand dollars to the commonwealth for the use of the county, that you pay the costs of prosecution, and that you undergo imprisonment in the State Penitentiary for the Eastern District by separate or solitary confinement at labor for a period of four years and six months, and that you stand committed until this sentence is complied with."

The judge dropped the papers and moved to pick up those in connection with Stener, who was to follow, satisfied that he had given the financiers no chance to say he had not given due heed to their plea in Cowperwood's behalf, and yet certain that the politicians would be pleased that he had so nearly given Cowperwood the maximum, while appearing to have given due heed to the pleas for mercy in his case. Cowperwood saw through the trick at once; but it did not disturb him. It struck him as rather weak and contemptible. A bailiff came forward and started to hurry him away.

"Allow the prisoner to remain a moment," called Judge Payderson.

The name of George W. Stener had been called by the clerk, and the ex-city treasurer was now quite near. Cowperwood did not quite understand why it was that he was detained, but he soon learned. It was that he might hear the opinion of the court in connection with his co-partner in crime. The latter's record was taken, as had been Cowperwood's. Roger O'Mara, the Irish political lawyer who had been his counsel all through his troubles, stood near him, but had nothing to say beyond asking the judge to consider Stener's previously honorable career. Cowperwood's father, who had borne up rather courageously until the actual sentence was pronounced, was concealing his wet eyes behind the back of his son Edward, who was leaning over with his elbows on the seat before him, his head in his hands. Aileen was biting her lower lip and clinching her hands to keep down rage and disappointment and tears. "Four years and six months," she thought. That would make a terrible gap in his life —in hers. Still, she could wait. It was better than eight or ten years, as she had feared it might be. Perhaps now, once this was really over and Cowperwood in prison, the governor would pardon him, as he thought. Oh, if he only would!

While she was thinking Judge Payderson was beginning to address Stener, who made no such figure as Cowperwood had, standing before the rail or gate. He was too pale, too limp, too sagged in on himself. He looked very tired and very sickly.

"George W. Stener," said his honor, while the audience, including Cowperwood, listened attentively, "the rule for a new trial in your case having been refused and the motion in arrest of judgment overruled, it remains for the court to impose such sentence as the nature of your offense requires. I do not desire to add to the pain of your position by any extended remarks of my own; but I cannot let the occasion pass without expressing my emphatic condemnation of your offense. The misapplication of public money has become the great crime of the age. If not promptly and firmly checked, it will ultimately destroy our institutions. When a republic becomes honeycombed by corruption its vitality is gone. It must crumble upon the first pressure.

"In my opinion, the public are much to blame for your offense and others of a similar character. Heretofore, official fraud has been regarded with too much indifference. What we need is a higher and purer political morality—a state of public opinion which would make the improper use of public money a thing to be execrated. It was the lack of this which made your offense possible. Beyond that I see nothing of extenuation in your case." Judge Payderson paused for emphasis. He was coming to his finest flight, and he wanted it to sink in.

"The people had confided to you the care of their money," he went on, solemnly. "It was a high, a sacred trust. You should have guarded the door of the treasury even as the cherubim protected the Garden of Eden, and should have turned the flaming sword of impeccable honesty against every one who approached it improperly. Your position as the representative of a great community warranted that. You have sinned against the light.

"In view of all the facts in your case the court can do no less than impose a major penalty. The seventy-fourth section of the Criminal Procedure Act provides that no convict shall be sentenced by the court of this commonwealth to either of the penitentiaries thereof, for any term which shall expire between the fifteenth of November and the fifteenth day of February of any year, and this provision requires me to abate three months from the maximum of time which I would affix in your case—namely, five years. The sentence of the court is, therefore, that you pay a fine of five thousand dollars to the commonwealth for the use of the county"—Payderson knew well enough that Stener could never pay that sum—"and that you undergo imprisonment in the State Penitentiary for the Eastern District, by separate and solitary confinement at labor, for the period of four years and nine months, and that you stand committed until this sentence is complied with."

He laid down the briefs and rubbed his chin reflectively, thinking how nearly he had complied with the wish of his political superiors, that Cowperwood and Stener be given the same sentence, and both the latter were hurried out. Butler was the first to leave after the sentence—quite satisfied. Seeing that all was over so far as she was concerned, Aileen stole quickly out; and after her, in a few moments, came Cowperwood's father and brother. They were to await him outside, or he was to await them, and they were to go with him to the penitentiary. The remaining members of the family in Girard Avenue were eagerly awaiting intelligence of the morning's work, and Joseph Cowperwood was at once despatched to tell them. Cowperwood did not think it necessary to go back home at present. Steger told him that he was sure he would be wanted in the bankruptcy court the following Thursday, and if he chose he could visit his home then. Seeing that he had actually been sentenced, the sheriff was anxious to get Cowperwood off his hands—out of his jurisdiction, as it were. He had given Zanders orders to take him straight away after obtaining the final commitment paper of the court, which was now ready.

The day had now become cloudy, lowery, and it looked as if it might snow a little. Eddie Zanders, who had been given all the papers in the case, announced that there was no need to return to the county jail. In consequence the five of them—Zanders, Steger, Cowperwood, his father, and Edward—got into a street-car which ran to within a few blocks of the prison. Within half an hour they were at the gates of the Eastern Penitentiary.

CHAPTER LXVI

THE Eastern District Penitentiary of Pennsylvania, located at Fairmount Avenue and Twenty-first Street in Philadelphia, where Cowperwood was now to serve his sentence of four years and six months, was a large, gray-stone structure—or wall and inclosed prison ten acres in extent—solemn and momentous in its mien, not at all unlike the palace of the Sforzas at Milan, although not so distinguished. It stretched its gray length for several blocks along four different streets, and looked as lonely and forbidding as a prison should. The wall which inclosed its great acreage and gave it so much of its solemn dignity was thirty-five feet high and some seven feet thick. The prison proper, which was not visible from the outside, consisted of seven arms or corridors, ranged octopus-like around a central room or court, and occupying in their sprawling length about two-thirds of the ten-acre yard inclosed within the walls, so that there was but little space for the charm of lawn or sward. The corridors, forty-two feet wide from outer wall to outer wall, were one hundred and eighty feet in length, and in four instances two stories high, and extended in their long reach in every direction. There were no windows in the corridors, only narrow slits of skylights, three and one-half feet long by perhaps eight inches wide, let in the roof; and the ground-floor cells were accompanied in some instances by a small yard ten by sixteen—the same size as the cells proper—which was surrounded by a high brick wall in every instance. The cells and floors and roofs were made of stone, and the corridors, which were only ten feet wide between the cells, and in the case of the single-story portion only fifteen feet high, were paved with stone. If you stood in the central room, or rotunda, and looked down the long stretches which departed from you in every direction, you had a sense of narrowness and confinement not compatible with their length. The iron doors, with their outer accompaniment of wooden ones, which were used at times to shut the prisoner from all sight and sound, were grim and unsatisfactory to behold. The halls were light enough, being whitewashed frequently and set with the narrow skylights, which were closed with frosted glass in winter; but they were, as are all such matter-of-fact arrangements for incarceration, bare—wearisome to look upon. Life enough there was in all conscience, seeing that there were four hundred prisoners here at the time, and that nearly every cell was occupied; but it was a life of which no one individual was aware of as a spectacle. He was of it; but he was not. Some of the prisoners, after long service, were used as "trusties" or "runners," as they were locally called; but not many. There was a bakery, a machine-shop, a carpenter-shop, a store-room, a flour-mill, and a series of gardens, or truck patches; but the manipulation of these did not require the services of a large number.

The prison proper dated from 1822, and it had grown, wing by wing, until its present considerable size had been reached. Its population consisted of individuals of all degrees of intelligence and crime, from murderers to minor practitioners of larceny. It had what was known as the "Pennsylvania System" of regulation for its inmates, which was nothing more nor less than solitary confinement for all concerned—a life of absolute silence and separate labor in separate cells.

When Cowperwood and his party, walking along Fairmount Avenue, were confronted by the great gray Gothic gate of the penitentiary, with its iron-riveted doors and its sentinel towers and the dreary expanse of high wall disappearing to either side, it was beginning to blow a few fat, feathery flakes of snow, which gave the whole place a somewhat melodramatic and stagy appearance, which was not lost on him. Barring his comparatively recent experience in the county jail, which after all was not an accurate one, he had never been in a prison in his life. Once, when a boy, in one of his perambulations with "Spat" McGlathery and others through several of the surrounding towns, he had passed a village "lock-up," as the town prisons were then called—a small, square, gray building with long iron-barred windows, and he had seen, at one of these rather depressing apertures on the second floor, a none too prepossessing drunkard or town ne'er-do-well who looked down on him with bleary eyes, unkempt hair, and a sodden, waxy, pallid face, and called—for it was summer and the jail window was open:

"Hey, sonny, get me a plug of tobacco, will you?"

Cowperwood, who had looked up, shocked and disturbed by the man's disheveled appearance, had called, quite without stopping to think:

"Naw, I can't."

"Look out you don't get locked up yourself sometime, you little runt," the man had replied, savagely, only half recovered from his debauch of the day before.

Cowperwood had been a little sickened and frightened by the spectacle, and he remembered having a keen desire to get away. He had not thought of this particular scene in years, but now suddenly it came back to him. Here he was on his way to be locked up in this dull, somber prison, and it was snowing, and he was being cut out of human affairs as much as it was possible for him to be cut out.

When Cowperwood arrived with his father, brother, Steger, and Zanders, he was informed that his relatives could only go with him to the outer gate. No friends were permitted to accompany him beyond that—not even Steger for the time being, though he might visit him later in the day. This was an inviolable rule. Zanders being known to the gate-keeper, and bearing his commitment paper, was admitted at once. The others turned solemnly away. They bade an affectionate farewell to Cowperwood, who, however, attempted to make it as matter-of-fact as possible.

"Well, good-by for the present," he said, shaking hands. "I'll be all right. Tell Lillian not to worry."

He stepped inside, and the gate clanked solemnly behind him. Zanders led the way through a dark, somber hall, wide and high-ceiled, to a farther gate, where a second gateman, trifling with a large key, unlocked a barred door at his bidding. Once inside the prison yard, Zanders turned to the left into a small office, presenting his prisoner before a small, chest-high desk, where stood a prison officer in uniform of blue. The latter, the receiving overseer of the prison—a thin, practical, executive-looking person with narrow gray eyes and light hair, took the paper which the sheriff's deputy handed him and read it. This was his authority for receiving Cowperwood. In his turn he handed Zanders a slip, showing that he had so received the prisoner; and the latter left, receiving gratefully the tip which Cowperwood pressed in his hand.

"Well, good-by, Mr. Cowperwood," he said, with a peculiar twist of his detective-like head. "I'm sorry. I hope you won't find it so bad here."

He wanted to impress the receiving overseer with his familiarity with this distinguished prisoner, and Cowperwood, true to his policy of make-believe, shook hands with him cordially.

"I'm much obliged to you for your courtesy, Mr. Zanders," he said.

Zanders went out. Cowperwood turned to his new master with the air of a man who is determined to make a good impression. He was now in the hands of petty officials, he knew, who could modify or increase his comfort at will. He wanted to impress this man with his utter willingness to comply and obey—his sense of respect for his authority—without in any way demeaning himself. He had no particular use for the individual before him, intellectually speaking; but the latter could be of use to him, and so he prepared to be nice to him. He was depressed but efficient, even here in the clutch of that eventual machine of the law, the State penitentiary, which he had been struggling so hard to evade.

The receiving overseer, Mr. Roger Kendall, though thin and clerical, was a rather capable man, as prison officials go—shrewd, not particularly well educated, not over-intelligent naturally, not over-industrious, but sufficiently energetic to hold his position. He knew something about convicts—considerable—for he had been dealing with them for nearly twenty-six years. His attitude toward them was cold, cynical, critical; for he had had to do for nearly half of his life with individuals whom he considered to be innately liars, cutthroats, thieves, robbers, with a modest sprinkling of comparatively decent men. Most of them were dirty, afraid of a real bath, and physically defective in some way or other. They were as ignorant as natural deficiency and lack of opportunity could make them.

He did not permit any of them to come into personal contact with him, but he saw to it that underlings in his presence carried out the requirements of the law.

When Cowperwood entered, dressed in his very good clothing—a dark gray-blue twill suit of pure wool, his light, well-made gray overcoat, a black derby hat of the latest shape, his shoes new and of good leather, his tie of the best silk, heavy and conservatively colored, his hair and mustache showing the attention of an intelligent barber, and his hands well manicured—the receiving overseer saw at once that he was in the presence of some one of superior intelligence and force, such a man as the fortune of his trade rarely brought into his net. Mr.

Kendall could tell at once by Cowperwood's simple manner, his direct, unaffected glance that he was sane and wise and that he was looking, in a forceful way, to be unobtrusive and not to give offense.

Cowperwood stood in the middle of the room without apparently looking at any one or anything, though he saw all. "Convict number 3633," Kendall called to a clerk, handing him at the same time a yellow slip of paper on which was written Cowperwood's full name and his record number, counting from the beginning of the penitentiary itself.

The underling, a convict, whose name was Magerson, took it and entered it in a book, reserving the slip at the same time for the penitentiary "runner" or "trusty," who would eventually take Cowperwood to the "manners" gallery.

"You will have to take off your clothes and take a bath," said Mr. Kendall to Cowperwood, solemnly, eying him curiously. "I don't suppose you need one, but it's the rule."

"Thank you," replied Cowperwood, pleased that his personality was counting for something even here. "Whatever the rules are, I want to obey."

Mr. Kendall made no comment, seeing that Cowperwood was a prisoner. He realized that he was dealing with his superior, mentally and socially, but Cowperwood was beneath him here, and that was enough. When Cowperwood started to take off his coat, however, he put up his hand delayingly and tapped a bell. There now issued from an adjoining room an assistant, a prison servitor, a weird-looking specimen of the genus "trusty." He was a small, dark, lop-sided individual, one leg being slightly shorter, and therefore one shoulder lower, than the other. He was hollow-chested, squint-eyed, and rather shambling, but spry enough withal. He was dressed in a.thin, poorly made, baggy suit of striped jeans, the prison stripes of the place, showing a soft roll-collar shirt underneath,

and wearing a large, wide-striped cap, peculiarly offensive
in its size and shape to Cowperwood. He could not help
thinking how uncanny the man's squint eyes looked under
its straight out-standing visor. The trusty had a silly,
sycophantic manner of raising one hand in salute. He was
a professional "second-story man," "up" for ten years,
but by dint of good behavior he had attained to the honor
of working about this office without the degrading hood
customary for prisoners to wear over the cap. For this
he was properly grateful. He now considered his superior
with nervous dog-like eyes, and looked at Cowperwood
with a certain cunning appreciation of his lot and a show
of initial mistrust.

One prisoner is as good as another to the average convict; as a matter of fact, it is their only consolation in
their degradation that all who come here are no better
than they. The world may have misused them; but they
misuse their confrères in their thoughts. The "holier
than thou" attitude, intentional or otherwise, is quite the
last and most deadly offense within prison walls. This
particular "trusty" could no more understand Cowperwood than could a fly the motions of a fly-wheel; but with
the cocky superiority of the underling of the world he
did not hesitate to think that he could. A crook was a
crook to him—Cowperwood no less than the shabbiest
pickpocket. His one feeling was that he would like to
demean him, to pull him down to his own level. Alas,
he was to have no great opportunity.

"You will have to take everything you have out of
your pockets," Kendall said to Cowperwood. Ordinarily
he would have said, "Search the prisoner."

Cowperwood stepped forward and laid out a purse
with twenty-five dollars in it, a pen-knife, a lead-pencil, a
small note-book, and a little ivory elephant which Aileen
had given him once, "for luck," and which he treasured
solely because she gave it to him. Kendall looked at the
latter curiously. "Now you can go on," he said to the

"trusty," referring to the undressing and bathing process which was to follow.

"This way," said the latter, addressing Cowperwood, and preceding him into an adjoining room, where three closets held three old-fashioned, iron-bodied, wooden-top bath-tubs, with their attendant shelves for rough crash towels, yellow soap, and the like, and hooks for clothes.

"Get in there," said the trusty, whose name was Thomas Kuby, pointing to one of the tubs.

Cowperwood realized that this was the beginning of petty official supervision; but he deemed it wise to appear friendly even here.

"I see," he said. "I will."

"That's right," replied the attendant, somewhat placated. "What did you bring?"

Cowperwood looked at him quizzically. He did not understand. The prison attendant realized that he had said something here which was superior to Cowperwood. The latter did not know the lingo of the place. "What did you bring?" Kuby repeated, in a weird, superior way. "How many years did you get?"

"Oh!" exclaimed Cowperwood, comprehendingly. "I understand. Four and a half."

He decided to humor the man. It would probably be better so.

"What for?" inquired Kuby, familiarly.

For the first time Cowperwood winced as if he had been stuck with a knife. His blood chilled slightly. "Larceny," he said.

"Yuh got off easy," commented Kuby. "I'm up for ten. A rube judge did that to me."

Kuby had never heard of Cowperwood's crime. He would not have understood its subtleties if he had. To him a criminal was a criminal like himself. Cowperwood did not want to talk to this man; he did not know how. He wished he would go away; but that was not likely. He wanted to be put in his cell and let alone.

"That's too bad," he answered; and the convict realized clearly that Cowperwood was really not one of them, or he would not have said anything like that. Kuby went to the two hydrants opening into the bath-tub and turned them on. Cowperwood had been undressing the while, and now stood naked, but not ashamed, in front of this eighth-rate intelligence.

"Don't forget to wash your head, too," said Kuby, and went away.

Cowperwood stood there while the water ran, meditating on his fate. It was strange how life had dealt with him of late—so severely. Unlike most men in his position, he was not suffering from a consciousness of evil. He did not think he was evil. As he saw it, he was merely unfortunate. To think that he should be actually in this great, silent penitentiary, a convict, waiting here beside this cheap iron bath-tub, not too sweet or hygienic to contemplate, with this crack-brained criminal to watch over him! How different from his home, his old life! What were his friends and acquaintances thinking? His father had left him with such a queer, disconsolate look in his eyes.

He got in the tub and washed himself briskly with the biting yellow soap, getting out finally and drying himself on one of the rough, only partially bleached towels. He looked for his underwear, but there was none.

At this point the attendant looked in again.

"Out here," he said, inconsiderately.

Cowperwood followed, naked. He was led through the receiving overseer's room into a third or record and measurement room, where were scales, implements of measurement, a record-book, etc. The attendant who stood guard at the door now came over, and the clerk who sat in the corner automatically took down a record-blank. Kendall surveyed Cowperwood's rather forceful figure, inclining already, however, to a slight stomach.

His skin was peculiarly white in contrast to his ruddy face and brown hands.

"Step on the scale," said the attendant, brusquely.

Cowperwood did so. The former adjusted the weights and scanned the record carefully.

"Weight, one hundred and seventy-five," he called. "Now step over here."

He indicated a spot in the side wall where was fastened in a thin slat—which ran from the floor to about seven and one half feet above, perpendicularly—a small movable wooden indicator, which, when a man was standing under it, could be pressed down on a level with his head. At the side of the slat were the total inches of height, laid off in halves, quarters, eighths, and so on, and to the right a length measurement for the arm. Cowperwood understood what was wanted, and stepped under the indicator, standing quite straight.

"Feet level, back to the wall," urged the attendant. "So. Height, five feet nine and ten-sixteenths," he called. The clerk in the corner noted it. He now produced a tape-measure and began measuring Cowperwood's arms, legs, chest, waist, hips, etc. He called out the color of his eyes, his hair, his mustaches, and, looking into his mouth, exclaimed, "Teeth, all sound."

After Cowperwood had once more given his address, age, profession, whether he knew any trade, etc.—which he did not—he was allowed to return to the bath-room, and put on the clothing which the prison provided for him. He put them on in order—first the rough, prickly underwear, then the cheap soft roll-collar, white-cotton shirt, then the thick bluish-gray cotton socks of a quality such as he had never worn in his life, and over these a pair of indescribable rough-leather clogs, which felt to his feet as though they were made of wood or iron —oily and heavy. He then drew on the shapeless, baggy trousers with their telltale stripes, and over his arms and chest the loose-cut shapeless coat and waistcoat. He felt and looked very strange, and as he stepped out into the overseer's room again he experienced a peculiar sense of depression, a gone feeling which he did his best to conceal. This, then, was what society did to the criminal, he thought to himself. It took him and tore away from his body and his life the habiliments of his state and left him these. He felt sad and grim, and, try as he would, he could not help showing it for a moment. It was always his business and his intention to conceal his real feelings, but now it was not quite possible. He felt degraded, impossible, in these clothes, and he knew that he looked it. Nevertheless, he did his best to pull himself together and look unconcerned, willing, obedient, considerate of those above him. After all, he said to himself, it was all like a play to him, a dream—nothing more. It could not last. He was acting some strange, unfamiliar part on the stage, this stage of life that he knew so well. Surely it could not last. It was too insignificant, too unimportant, all this. Nevertheless, he was depressed.

Kendall did not waste any time looking at him, however. He merely said to his assistant, "See if you can find a cap for him"; and the latter, going to a closet containing numbered shelves, took down a cap—a high-crowned, straight-visored, shabby, striped affair which Cowperwood was asked to try on. It fitted well enough, slipping down close over his ears, and he thought now his indignities must be about over. There could be no more of these discomforting accoutrements. But he was mistaken.

"Now, Kuby, you can take him to Mr. Chapin," said Kendall.

Kuby understood. He went back into the wash-room and produced what Cowperwood had heard of but never before seen—a blue-and-white-striped cotton bag about half the length of an ordinary pillow-case and half again as wide, which Kuby unfolded and shook out as he came toward him. The use of this hood was a custom, dating from the earliest days of the prison, intended to humiliate and drive home to the incoming prisoner the fact that all sense of social connection was hereby ended. The hood was intended to destroy all sense of association with fellow-prisoners, and by preventing a sense of location and direction obviate any attempt to escape. Thereafter during all his stay he was not supposed to walk with or talk to or see another prisoner—or even, to any extent, converse with his superiors, except as the latter were compelled to instruct him. It was a grim theory, and was really worked out to a very notable extent, although when it came to actual practice there were modifications, as there are in every theory.

"You'll have to put this on," Kuby said, and opened it in such a way that it could be put over Cowperwood's head.

The latter understood. He had heard of it in some way, in times past—not through Steger, but in some general gossip. Little had he ever thought that this would come to him. All his wealth, all his shrewdness had not been able to prevent it, apparently. He was a little shocked—looked at it first with a touch of real surprise, but a moment after lifted his hands and helped pull it down.

"Never mind," cautioned the guard, "put your hands down. I'll get it over."

Cowperwood dropped his arms. When it was fully on, it came to about his chest, giving him little means of seeing anything. He felt very strange, very humiliated, very downcast. This simple thing of a blue-and-white-striped bag over his head almost cost him his sense of self-possession. Why could not they have spared him this indignity? he thought.

"This way," said his attendant, and, without seeing anything more of Kendall or his assistants or the room or the path he was following, he was led out—to where he could not say.

"If you hold it out in front you can see to walk," said

his guide; and Cowperwood pulled it out, thus being able to discern his feet and a portion of the floor below. He was thus conducted—seeing nothing in his transit—down a short walk, then through a long corridor, then through a room of uniformed guards, and finally up a narrow flight of iron steps, leading to the overseer's office on the second floor of one of the two-tier blocks. When he was there, he heard the voice of Kuby saying, "Mr. Chapin, here's another prisoner for you from Mr. Kendall."

"I'll be there in a minute," came a peculiarly pleasant voice from the distance, an older, more friendly one. Cowperwood could feel it. Presently a big, heavy hand closed about his arm, and he was conducted still further.

"You hain't got far to go now," the voice said, "and then I'll take that bag off," and Cowperwood felt for some reason—a sense of sympathy, perhaps—as though he would choke.

CHAPTER LXVII

THE further steps were not many.

A cell door was reached and unlocked by the inserting of a great iron key. It was swung open, and the same big hand guided him through. A moment later the bag was pulled easily from his head, and he saw that he was in a narrow, whitewashed cell, not very light and not very dark, windowless, but lighted from the top by a small skylight of frosted glass three and one half feet long by four inches wide. For a night light there was a tin-bodied lamp swinging from a hook near the middle of one of the side walls. A rough iron cot, furnished with a straw mattress and two pairs of dark blue, possibly unwashed blankets, stood in one corner. There was a hydrant and small sink in another. A shelf for books or razor cup and strop, or what you will, occupied the wall opposite the bed. A plain wooden chair with a homely round back stood at the foot of the bed, and a fairly serviceable broom was standing in one corner. There was an iron stool or pot for excreta giving, as he could see, into a large drain-pipe which ran along the inside wall, and which was obviously flushed by buckets of water being poured into it. Rats and other vermin infested this, and it gave off an unpleasant odor which filled the cell. The floor was of stone. Cowperwood's clear-seeing eyes, somewhat touched with regret at his predicament, took it all in at a glance. He also took in Mr. Chapin, the homely, good-natured cell overseer whom he now saw for the first time—a large, heavy, lumbering man, rather dusty and misshapen-looking, whose uniform did not fit him well, and whose manner of standing made him look as though he would much prefer to sit down. He was obviously bulky, but not strong, having somewhat of a paunch, and a kindly face covered with a short growth, of grayish-brown whiskers. His hair was cut badly and stuck out in odd strings or wisps from underneath his big cap. Nevertheless, Cowperwood was not at all unfavorably impressed—quite the contrary—and he felt at once that this man might be more considerate of him than the others had been. He hoped so, anyhow. He did not know that he was in the presence of the overseer of the "manners squad," who would have him in charge for two weeks only, instructing him in the rules of the prison, and that he was only one of twenty-six, all told, who were in Chapin's care.

Cowperwood looked around Chapin's broad, stooping shoulders, which were those of a man of fifty-eight, to the hard cell door, which was barred and cross-barred with great round rods of steel, and fastened with a thick, highly polished lock. He saw also that beyond this was a heavy wooden door, which could shut him in even more completely than the iron one. There was no chance for any clear, purifying sunlight here. Cleanliness depended entirely on whitewash, soap and water and sweeping, which in turn depended on the prisoners themselves. The thought came to him as to who had occupied this cell before him, and where he had gone. And also that this would be a most unsatisfactory place to live for any length of time.

Mr. Chapin, by way of easy introduction, went over to Mr. Cowperwood's future bed and seated himself on it. He pointed to the hard wooden chair, which Cowperwood drew out and sat on.

"Well, now you're here, hain't yuh?" asked Mr. Chapin, familiarly, for he was an unlettered man, generously disposed, of long experience with criminals, and inclined, as Cowperwood had judged by his voice and his big hand, to deal kindly with them. It was so plain to Cowperwood that in the sphere to which he himself belonged Chapin was a man whom he might employ as a gardener or workman of some kind, never anything more, but that down here he was a genial, good-natured lord. Age and a naturally kindly temperament and a form of religious belief—Quakerism—had inclined him to be merciful, and yet his official duties, as Cowperwood later found out, seemed to have led him to the conclusion that most criminals were innately bad. Like Mr. Kendall, he regarded them as weaklings and ne'er-do-wells with evil streaks in them, and in the main he was not mistaken. Yet he could not help being what he was, a fatherly, kindly old man, having faith in those shibboleths of the weak and inexperienced mentally—human justice and human decency.

"Yes, I'm here, Mr. Chapin," Cowperwood replied, simply, remembering his name from the attendant, and flattering the keeper by the use of it.

To old Chapin the situation was more or less puzzling. This was the famous Frank A. Cowperwood whom he had read about, the noted banker and treasury-looter. He and his co-partner in crime, Stener, were destined to serve, as he had read, comparatively long terms here. Five hundred thousand dollars was a large sum of money in those days, much more to Mr. Chapin than five million would have been forty years later. He was awed by the thought of what had become of it—how Cowperwood managed to do all the things the papers had said he had done. He had a little formula of questions which he usually went through with each new prisoner — asking him if he was sorry now for the crime he had committed, if he meant to do better with a new chance, if his father and mother were alive, etc.; and by the manner in which they answered these questions—simply, regretfully, defiantly, or otherwise—he judged whether they were being adequately punished or not. To him all prisoners who came here were guilty; there was no doubt of that. He had great faith in the machinery of justice. If men were punished, it was a thousand to one that they deserved to be. But in the case of men like Cowperwood he could not understand how they had come to do the things with which they were charged. He could not talk to Cowperwood as he would to the average second-story burglar, store-looter, pickpocket, and plain cheap thief and swindler, of whom there were so many. Yet he scarcely knew how else to talk.

"Well, now," he went on, looking at Cowperwood in a quizzical, uncertain way, while the latter eyed him in an attempt to appear interested and docile without at the same time appearing amused or superior, "I don't suppose you ever thought you'd get to a place like this, did you, Mr. Cowperwood?"

"I never did," replied Frank, simply. "I wouldn't have believed that I could have arrived here a few months ago, Mr. Chapin. I don't think I deserve to be here now, though of course there is no use of my telling you that."

He saw that old Chapin wanted to moralize a little, and he was only too glad to fall in with his mood. He would soon be alone with no one to talk to perhaps, and if a sympathetic understanding could be reached with this man now, so much the better. Any port in a storm; any straw to a drowning man.

"Well, no doubt all of us makes mistakes," continued Mr. Chapin, superiorly, with an amusing faith in his own value as a moral guide and reformer. "We can't just always tell how the plans we think so fine are coming out. You're here now, an' I suppose you're sorry certain things didn't come out just as you thought; but if you had a chance I don't suppose you'd try to do just as you did before, would yuh?"

"No, Mr. Chapin, I wouldn't, exactly," said Cowperwood, truly enough, "though I believed I was right in everything I did. I don't think legal justice has really been done me." In spite of his depressed state he could not suppress a whimsical smile over the old man's attitude.

"Well, that's the way," continued Chapin, meditatively, not bothering to pay any attention to Cowperwood's thoughts, but following his own very carefully, and scratching his grizzled head and looking genially about. "Sometimes, as I allers says to some of these here young fellers that comes in here, we don't know as much as we thinks we does. We forget that others are just as smart as we are, and that there are allers people that are watchin' us all the time. These here courts and jails and detectives—they are here all the time, and they get us. I gad"—Mr. Chapin's moral version of "by God"—"they do, if we don't behave."

"Yes," Cowperwood replied, "that's true enough."

"Well," said the old man after a time, after he had made a few more solemn, owl-like, and yet well-intentioned remarks, "now here's your bed, and there's your chair, and there's your wash-stand, and there's your water-closet. Now keep 'em all clean and use 'em right." (You would have thought he was making Cowperwood a present of a fortune.) "You're the one's got to make up your bed every mornin' and keep your floor swept and your toilet flushed and your cell clean. There hain't anybody here'll do that for yuh. You want to do all them things the first thing in the mornin' when you get up, and afterward you'll get sumpin' to eat, about six-thirty. You're supposed to get up at five-thirty."

"Yes, Mr. Chapin," Cowperwood said, politely. "You can depend on me to do all those things promptly. I don't want to cause you any annoyance. I'll do whatever you tell me."

"There hain't so much more," added Chapin. "You're supposed to wash yourself all over once a week, an' I'll give you a clean towel for that. You gotta wash this floor up every Friday mornin'." Cowperwood winced without showing it. "You kin have hot water for that if you want it. I'll have one of the runners bring it to you. An' as for your friends and relations"—he got up and shook himself like a big Newfoundland dog. "You gotta wife, hain't yuh?"

"Yes," replied Cowperwood.

"Well, the rules here are that your wife or your friends kin come to see you once in three months, and your lawyer—you gotta lawyer, hain't yuh?"

"Yes, sir," replied Cowperwood, amused.

"Well, he kin come every week or so if he likes—every day, I guess—there hain't no rules about lawyers. You kin only write one letter once in three months yourself, an' if you want anything like tobaccer or the like o' that, from the store-room, you gotta sign an order for it, if you got any money with the warden, an' then I can git it for you."

The old man was really above taking small tips in the shape of money. He was a hold-over from a much more severe and honest régime, but subsequent presents or constant flattery were not amiss in making him kindly and generous. Cowperwood read him accurately.

"Very well, Mr. Chapin; I understand," he said, getting up as the old man did. "I'll do exactly as you say."

"Then when you have been here two weeks," added Chapin, rather accidentally (he had forgot to state this to Cowperwood before), "the warden 'll come and git yuh and give yuh yer regular cell summers down-stairs. Yuh kin make up yer mind by that time what y'u'd like tuh do, what y'u'd like to work at. If you behave yourself proper, more'n like they'll give yuh a cell with a yard. Yuh never can tell."

He went out, locking the door with a solemn click; and Cowperwood stood there, a little more depressed than he had been, because of this latest intelligence. Only two weeks, and then he would be transferred from this kindly old man's care to another's, whom he did not know and with whom he might not fare so well. He had forgotten for the moment—in his pleasant talk with Chapin—his shabby prison suit, his rough underwear, his hard shoes, the sickening checker-board cap he had on his head, the bad odor of the cell, and its narrowness. Now they all came back to him with a rush. Here he was in this narrow cell, locked in.

"If ever you want me for anything—if ye're sick er sumpin' like that," called Chapin, after he had walked a few paces away, but returning, "we have a signal here of our own. Just hang your towel out through these here bars. I'll see it, and I'll stop and find out what yuh want, when I'm passin'."

Cowperwood, whose spirits had sunk, revived for the moment.

"Yes, sir," he replied; "thank you, Mr. Chapin."

The old man walked away, and Cowperwood heard his steps dying down the cement-paved hall. He stood and listened, his ears being greeted occasionally by a distant cough, a faint scraping of some one's feet, the hum or whir of some machine, or the iron scratch of a key in a lock. None of the noises was loud. Rather they were all faint and far away. He went over and looked at the bed, which was not very clean, and without linen, and anything but wide or soft, and felt it curiously. He was sickened by the thought of possible vermin. How could he tell? The one chair was abominable. The skylight was weak. He tried to think of himself as becoming accustomed to the situation, but he rediscovered the offal pot in one corner, and that discouraged him. It was possible that rats might come up here—it looked that way. No pictures, no books, no scene, no person, no space to walk—just the four bare walls and silence, which would probably be shut in tight at night by the thick door. What a horrible fate!

He sat down and contemplated his situation. So here he was at last in the Eastern Penitentiary, and doomed, according to the judgment of the politicians (Butler among others), to remain here four long years and longer. Stener, it suddenly occurred to him, was probably being put through the same process he had just gone through. Poor old Stener! What a fool he had made of himself, all told! Nevertheless, he deserved all he was getting. Only they would let Stener out. Perhaps already they were easing his punishment in some way that he, Cowperwood, did not know. He put his hand to his chin, thinking—his business, his house, his friends, his family, Aileen. He felt for his watch, but remembered that they had taken that. There was no way of telling the time. Neither had he any note-book, pen, or pencil with which to amuse or interest himself. He had had nothing to eat since morning. Still, that mattered little. What did matter was that he was shut up here tight from the world, quite alone, quite lonely, without knowing what time it was, and that he could not attend to any of the things he ought to do. Steger would probably come to see him after a while. That would help a little. It was a strange thing to be a solitary prisoner. His own steps and movements sounded so loud. He walked to the cell door and looked out through the thick bars, but there was nothing to see—nothing save a portion of two cell doors opposite, something like his own. He came back and sat in his single chair, meditating, but, getting weary of that finally, stretched himself on the dirty prison bed to try it. It was not uncomfortable entirely. He got up after a while, however, and sat, then walked, then sat. What a narrow place to walk, he thought. This was terrible, horrible—something like a living tomb. And to think he should be here now, day after day and day after day, until—

Until what?

Until the governor pardoned him or his time was up, or his fortune eaten away—or—

So he cogitated while the hours slipped by. It was

nearly five o'clock before Steger was able to return, and then only for a little while. He had been arranging for Cowperwood's appearance on the following Thursday, Friday, and Monday in his several court proceedings. When he was gone, however, and the night fell and Cowperwood had to trim his little, shabby oil-lamp and to drink the strong tea and eat the rough, poor bread made of bran and white flour, which was shoved to him through the small aperture in the door by the trencher trusty who was accompanied by the overseer to see that it was done properly (trenchermen shoving great carts of these delectable supplies about to the cells), he really felt very bad. The center wooden door of his cell was presently closed and locked by a trusty who slammed it rudely and said no word. Nine o'clock would be sounded somewhere by a great bell, he understood, when his smoky oil-lamp would have to be put out promptly and he would have to undress and go to bed. There were punishments, no doubt, for infractions of these rules—reduced rations, the straight-jacket, stripes, perhaps—he scarcely knew what. He felt grim, disconsolate, weary. He had put up such a long, unsatisfactory fight. After washing the heavy stone cup and tin plate for holding his tea and bread at his hydrant, he took off the sickening uniform and shoes and even the drawers of the scratching underwear, and, going to his bed, stretched himself wearily. He tried to make himself comfortable between the blankets—for it was chill here—but it was of little use.

"This will never do," he said to himself. "This will never do. I'm not sure whether I can stand much of this or not."

Still he turned his face to the wall, and after several hours sleep eventually came.

CHAPTER LXVIII

THOSE who by any pleasing courtesy of fortune, accident of birth, inheritance, or the wisdom of parents or friends, have succeeded in avoiding making that anathema of the prosperous and comfortable, "a mess of their lives," will scarcely understand the mood of Cowperwood, sitting rather gloomily in his cell these first days, wondering, in spite of his great ingenuity, what was to become of him. The strongest have their hours of depression. There are times when life to the greatest brains—perhaps mostly to the greatest—takes on a somber hue. They see so many phases of its dreary subtleties. It is only when the soul of man has been built up into some strange self-confidence, some curious faith in its own powers, based, no doubt, on the actual presence of these same powers subtly involved in the body, that it fronts life unflinchingly. It would be too much to say that Cowperwood's mind was of the first order. It was subtle enough in all conscience—and involved, as is common with the executively great, with a strong sense of personal advancement. It was a big mind, turning, like a vast searchlight, a glittering ray into many a dark corner; but it was not sufficiently disinterested to search the ultimate dark. He realized, in a way, what the great astronomers, sociologists, philosophers, chemists, physicists, and physiologists were meditating; but he could not be sure in his own mind that, whatever it was, it was important for him. No doubt life held strange secrets. Perhaps it was essential that somebody should investigate them. However that might be, the call of his own soul was in another direction. His business was to make money—to organize something which would make him much money, or, better yet, save the organization he had begun. But this, as he now looked upon it, was almost impossible. It had been too disarranged and complicated by evil circumstances. He might, as Steger pointed out to him, string out these bankruptcy proceedings for years, tiring out one creditor and another, but in the meanwhile the properties involved were being seriously damaged. Interest charges on his unsatisfied loans were making heavy inroads; court costs were mounting up; and, to cap it all, he had discovered with Steger that there were a number of creditors who would never accept anything except the full value of their claims. These were the ones who had sold out to Butler, and incidentally to Mollenhauer. His one hope now was to save what he could by compromise a little later, and to build up some sort of profitable business through Stephen Wingate. The latter was coming in a day or two, as soon as Steger had made some working arrangement for him with Warden Michael Desmas— a man whom Cowperwood had not seen as yet, but who came the second day to have a look at him.

Desmas was a big man physically—Irish by birth, a politician by training—who had been one thing and another in Philadelphia from a policeman in his early days and a corporal in the Civil War to a ward captain under Mollenhauer. He was a canny man, tall, raw-boned, singularly muscular-looking, who for all his fifty-seven years looked as though he could give a splendid account of himself in a physical contest. His hands were big and bony, his face more square than either round or long, and his forehead high. He had a vigorous growth of short-clipped, iron-gray hair and a bristly iron-gray mustache, very short; keen, intelligent blue-gray eyes; a florid complexion; and even-edged, savage-looking teeth, which showed the least bit in a slightly wolfish way

when he smiled. He was really not as hard a person
as he looked to be; nevertheless, he was to a certain
extent hard, and on occasions savage. He was quite
ready to recognize that there was a mental and social
difference between prisoners, and that now and then one
was apt to appear here who, with or without political
influences, was eminently worthy of special consideration. Seeing that the prison was a public institution apt to be visited at any time by lawyers, detectives, doctors, preachers, propagandists, and the public
generally, and that certain rules and regulations had to
be enforced, if for no other reason than to keep a moral
and administrative control over his own help, it was
necessary to see that much discipline, system, and order
were maintained, and it was not possible to be too
liberal with any one. There were, however, exceptional
cases—men of wealth and refinement, victims of those
occasional uprisings which so shocked the political leaders
generally—who had to be looked after in a friendly way.

Desmas, not unlike all the other politicians, was quite
aware of the history of Cowperwood and Stener. He knew
how money had always been illegitimately loaned, and
that the Chicago fire was the thing which had really
brought about Cowperwood's downfall. The politicians,
Strobik and others, had already given him warning that
Stener, because of his past services to the community,
was to be treated with special consideration. Not so much
was said about Cowperwood, although they did admit in
conversation with Desmas that his lot was rather hard.

"Butler is down on him," Strobik said to Desmas,
on one occasion. "It's that girl of his that's at the bottom
of it all. If you listened to Butler you'd feed him on
bread and water, but he isn't a bad fellow. As a matter
of fact, if George had had any sense Cowperwood wouldn't
be where he is to-day. But the big fellows wouldn't
let Stener alone. They wouldn't let him give Cowperwood any money."

Although Strobik had been one of those who under pressure from Mollenhauer had advised Stener not to let Cowperwood have any more money, yet here he was pointing out the folly of the victim's course. The thought of the inconsistency involved did not trouble him in the least.

Desmas, who had been speculating on how he would have to treat Cowperwood and Stener, decided that he might have to make a difference between them. If Cowperwood were *persona non grata* to the "Big Three," it might be necessary to be indifferent to him, or at least slow in extending him any special favors. For Stener a good chair, clean linen, special cutlery and dishes, the daily papers, privileges in the matter of mail, the visits of friends, and the like. For Cowperwood—well, he would have to look at Cowperwood and see what he thought. The politicians might not want him to be nice. At the same time, Steger's intercessions—which, though tentative, had been forcible—were not without their effect on Desmas. He had not been there to see Cowperwood when he came into the prison, and had decided to wait some hours until the rigors of the place had had time to soak in. But the morning after Cowperwood's entrance the warden received a letter from Terrence Relihan, the Harrisburg potentate, indicating that any kindness shown to Mr. Cowperwood would be duly appreciated by him. Upon the receipt of this letter Desmas went up into Overseer Chapin's block and looked through Cowperwood's iron door. On the way he had a brief talk with Chapin, who told him what a nice man he thought Cowperwood was.

Desmas had never seen Cowperwood in his life before, but in spite of the shabby uniform, the clog shoes, the cheap shirt, and the wretched cell, he was impressed. Instead of the weak, anemic body and the shifty eyes of the average prisoner, he saw a man whose form was vigorously erect and whose well-shaped head, rising

THE FINANCIER

above his wretched clothes, betokened the spirit which no conditions can demean. He lifted his head when Desmas appeared, glad that any form should have appeared at his door, and looked at him with large, clear, examining eyes—those eyes that in the past had inspired so much confidence and surety in all those who had known him. Desmas was interested on the moment. Compared with Stener, whom he knew in the past and whom he had met on his entry, this man was a force, a power. Say what you will, one forceful man inherently respects another. They are like wolves and tigers that run best in packs. They may eat one another ultimately, but never so long as there is anything else to eat.

Cowperwood, never having seen Desmas, did not know who was looking at him, but on the instant he suspected it must be the warden. "This isn't Mr. Desmas, is it?" he asked, courteously and pleasantly. The glitter of his past estate still radiated in his manner.

"Yes, sir, I'm the man. These rooms are not as comfortable as they might be, are they?" The warden's even teeth showed in a friendly yet wolfish way.

"They certainly are not, Mr. Desmas," replied Cowperwood, standing very erect and soldier-like. "I didn't imagine I was coming to a hotel, however." He smiled.

"There isn't anything special I can do for you, is there?" asked Desmas, curiously. "I've been talking to your lawyer."

"I don't want to be asking anything, Warden, which you cannot reasonably give," returned Cowperwood, politely. "There are a few things I would change if I could. I wish I might have sheets for my bed, and I could afford better underwear if you would let me wear it. This that I have on annoys me a great deal."

"They're not the best wool, that's true enough," replied Desmas, solemnly. "They're made for the State out here in Pennsylvania somewhere. I suppose there's no objection to your wearing your own underwear if you

704

want to. I'll see about that. And the sheets, too. We might let you use them if you have them. We'll have to go a little slow about this. There are a lot of people that take a special interest in showing the warden how to tend to his business." His even teeth showed in the slightest way again, grimly, and his eyes wrinkled at the outer edges. You have seen a wolf or collie dog grin, perhaps. Mr. Desmas looked not unlike that.

"I'm certainly very much obliged to you, Mr. Desmas," said Cowperwood, feelingly.

"That's all right," said Desmas, now that he had gone so far as to be friendly to Cowperwood. "I can't promise to do much. Prison rules are prison rules. There are some things that can be done, because it's the rule to do them for other men when they behave themselves. You can have a better chair than that, possibly, and something to read. If you're in business yet, I wouldn't want to do anything to stop that. We can't have people running in and out of here every fifteen minutes, and you can't turn a cell into a business office—that's not possible. It would break up the order of the place. Still, there's no reason why you shouldn't see some of your friends now and then. As for your mail—well, that will have to be opened in the ordinary way for the time being, anyhow. I'll have to see about that. I can't promise too much. You'll have to wait until you come out of this block and down-stairs. Some of the cells have a yard there; if there are any empty—" The warden cocked his eye wisely, and Cowperwood saw that his lot was not to be as bad as he had anticipated—though bad enough. The warden spoke to him about the different trades he might follow, and asked him to think about the one he would prefer. "You want to have something to keep your hands busy, whatever else you want. You'll find you'll need that. They all want to work."

Cowperwood thanked Desmas profusely. The horror of idleness in silence and in a cell scarcely large enough to turn around in comfortably had already begun to creep over him, and the thought of being able to see Wingate and Steger frequently, and to have his mail reach him, after a time, untampered with, was a great relief. He was to have his own underwear, silk and wool—thank God!—and perhaps they would let him take off these shoes after a while. With these modifications and a trade, and perhaps the little yard which Desmas had referred to, his life would be, if not ideal, at least tolerable. The prison was a prison still, but it looked as though it might not be so much of a terror to him as to some other people.

During the two weeks in which Cowperwood was in the "manners squad," in care of Mr. Chapin, he learned nearly as much as he ever learned of the general nature of prison life; for this was not an ordinary penitentiary in the sense that the prison yard, the prison squad, the prison lock-step, the prison dining-room, and prison associated labor make the ordinary penitentiary. There was, for him and for the very large majority of those confined there, no general prison life whatsoever. The large majority were supposed to work silently in their cells at the particular tasks assigned them, and not to know anything of the remainder of the life which went on around them, the rule of this prison being solitary confinement, and few being permitted to work at the limited number of outside menial tasks provided. Old Chapin, with whom Cowperwood became quite friendly within a few days, because of his subtle courtesy to the old man, informed him that not more than seventy-five of the four hundred prisoners confined here were so employed, and not all of these regularly—cooking, gardening in season, milling, and general cleaning being the only avenues of escape from solitude. Even they were strictly forbidden to talk, and although they did not have to wear the objectionable hood when actually employed, they were supposed to wear it in going to and from their work. Cowperwood saw them occasionally tramping by his cell door, and it struck him as strange, grim, uncanny. He wished sincerely that he were to be under old Chapin permanently; but it was not to be. His two weeks soon passed—drearily enough in all conscience, but they passed, interlaced with his few commonplace tasks of bed-making, floor-sweeping, dressing, eating, undressing, rising at five-thirty, and retiring at nine, washing his several dishes after each meal, etc. The food, he found, was such a fall from that to which he had been accustomed that he thought he would never get used to it. Breakfast, as has been said, was at six-thirty, and consisted of coarse black bread made of bran and some white flour, and served with black coffee. Dinner was at eleven-thirty, and consisted of bean or vegetable soup, with some coarse meat in it, and the same bread. Supper was at six, of tea and bread, very strong tea and the same bread—no butter, no milk, no sugar. Cowperwood did not smoke, so the small allowance of tobacco which was permitted was without value to him. Steger called in every day for two or three weeks, until Cowperwood had become used to his condition; and after the second day, when Warden Desmas called on him, Stephen Wingate, as his new business associate, was permitted to see him also—once every day, if he wished, Desmas stated, though the latter felt he was stretching a point in permitting this so soon. Both of these visits rarely occupied more than an hour, or an hour and a half, and after that the day was long. Cowperwood was taken out on several days on a court order, between nine and five, to testify in the bankruptcy proceedings against him, which caused the time in the beginning to pass quickly.

CHAPTER LXIX

THE day of Cowperwood's sentence, in so far as the
newspapers and the public in Philadelphia were concerned, was one of great moment. Civic virtue evidently had triumphed; the malefactors who had preyed
on the city's innocence were properly punished. It
mattered little that the new city treasurer, recently inducted into office, was already about the work of loaning
money as Stener had loaned it—the interest to go to him
personally, or to those who were close to him. Butler,
Mollenhauer, and Simpson knew that this would be done;
they were quite as ready to borrow money from the city
treasurer at this rate of interest—two and one-half per
cent.—as any one else, when they needed it. Cowperwood's crime, as he often said afterward, was the Chicago
fire. However, ostensible justice had been done, and such
varied personalities as Butler, Skelton C. Wheat, various
minor newspaper editors, and a number of Cowperwood's
rivals in business were glad that he was gone—out of the
way. It was curious, once he was in prison, safely shut
from the world for a period of years apparently, how
quickly all thought of assisting him, in so far as his finances
were concerned, departed from the minds of those who
had been most friendly. He was done, through—so most
of the financiers thought—the best of them. The only
thing they could do now would be to use their influence
to get him out and possibly loan him sufficient money
to get a start in a small way again some time; how soon,
they could not guess. Beyond that there was nothing.
He would never really be of any great importance to any

one any more. It was very sad, very tragic, if you will, but he was gone—his place knew him not.

"A bright young man, that," observed President Davison of the Girard National, on reading of Cowperwood's sentence and incarceration. "Too bad! Too bad! He made a great mistake."

It did not occur to Davison that there was anything so radically wrong in Cowperwood being made a political scapegoat. He, too, had heard of Aileen. Perhaps, after all, Cowperwood was merely being properly punished for a general tendency to play fast and loose. Anyhow, he was found out, caught; and that, after all, was the principal evil. Walter Leigh reflected, as did Arthur Rivers and others, that after this, really, they would scarcely be permitted to know Cowperwood socially. They could speak to him, appear friendly, do a little business, perhaps—but really, you know, an ex-convict! It couldn't be expected. Cowperwood, in so far as his old social life was concerned, was a pariah, and he himself knew it.

Only his parents, Aileen, and his wife—the latter with mingled feelings of resentment and sorrow—really missed him. Aileen, because of her great passion for him, was really suffering most of all. She returned direct to her room after the sentence, and, locking the door, sat down and cried bitterly. Four years and six months! she thought. If he did not get out before then she would be nearing twenty-nine and he would be nearing forty. Would he want her then? Would she be so nice? And would nearly five years change his point of view? He would have to wear a convict suit all that time, and be known as a convict forever after. It was hard to think about, but she had to face it all; and petted as she had always been by her family, there was no one to whom she could run with this sorrow. Her mother would have sympathized with her greatly if she had known, and Butler also if he had not been opposed to Cowperwood, but they could not know. So she looked out of the window at the hard street, where the snow had begun to fall afresh, and wiped her red eyes and her quivering lips. Then she turned to her mirror to compose her face, determined to cling to Frank whatever happened and to help him all she could.

The day after Cowperwood's incarceration Aileen had driven out and looked at the grim gray walls of the penitentiary, which impressed her greatly. Knowing nothing absolutely of the vast and complicated process of law and penal servitude, it seemed especially terrible to her. What might not they be doing to her Frank? She drove home, determined to see him; but as he had originally told her that visiting days were only once in three months, and that he would have to write her when the next one was, or when she could come, or when he could see her on the outside, she scarcely knew what to do. Secrecy was the thing.

The day after his entrance to the prison Cowperwood had had a letter from her, describing the drive she had taken past the prison on the stormy afternoon before—the terror of the thought that he was behind those grim gray walls—and declaring her determination to see him soon. The next day he wrote her a letter in reply, which he gave to Wingate to mail. It ran:

DEAR PETTY,—I fancy you are a little downhearted to think I cannot be with you any more soon, but you mustn't be. I suppose you read all about the sentence in the paper. I came out here yesterday morning—nearly noon. If I had time, dearest, I'd write you a long letter describing the situation so as to ease your mind; but I haven't. It's against the rules, and I am really doing this secretly. I'm here, though, safe enough, and wish I were out, of course. Sweetest, you must be careful how you try to see me. You can't do me much service outside of cheering me up, and you may do yourself great harm. Sometimes, now, I think I have done you much more harm than I can ever make up to you for. I am to be in the Court of Special Pleas, Sixth and Chestnut, on Friday at two o'clock; but you cannot see me there. I'll be out in charge of my counsel. You must be careful. Perhaps you'll think better, and not come here.

This last touch was one of pure gloom, the first Cowper-wood had ever introduced into their relationship, for he had never been in a position where a gloomy thought could intrude itself in regard to her. Hitherto he had been in the position of the superior being, the one who was being sought—although Aileen was and had been well worth seeking—and he had thought that he might escape unscathed, and so grow in dignity and power until she might not possibly be worthy of him any longer. He had had that thought. But here, in stripes, it was a different matter. Aileen's position, reduced in value as it was by her long, ardent relationship with him, was now, nevertheless, superior to his—apparently so. She ought not to become a convict's bride. She ought not to want to, and she might not want to, for all he knew; she might change her mind. She ought not to wait for him. Her life was not yet ruined. The public did not know, so he thought—not generally, anyhow—that she had been his mistress. She might marry. Did he not owe it to her, to a sense of fair play in himself, to ask her to give him up, or at least think over the wisdom of doing so?

He did her the justice to believe that she would not want to give him up; and in his position, however harm-ful it might be to her, it was an advantage, a connecting link with the finest period of his past life, to have her continue to love him. He could not, however, scribbling this note in his cell in Wingate's presence, and giving it to him to mail (Overseer Chapin was kindly keeping a respectful distance, though he was supposed to be pres-ent), refrain from adding, at the last moment, this little touch of doubt which, when she read it, struck Aileen to the heart. She read it as gloom on his part—great depression. The penitentiary was really breaking his spirit then, and he had held up so courageously so long. She was madly eager to get to him, to console him, even though it was difficult, perilous. Her father's possible future discoveries in connection with her did not interest

her. He had done his worst. Since the day she had seen
Frank convicted she had turned on her father once for
all. She could not love him any more—she knew that.
Frank Cowperwood was superior. The life he had offered
her was better than her home life, and he need not have
gone to the penitentiary, she reasoned, if it had not been
for old Butler. That might be good wrath; but it certainly was not kindness, humanity, religion. Her father
could go to the devil now. She did not love him any
more. There was an end of it. In spite of Cowperwood's
incarceration and her feeling that she might be exposed
publicly by the reckless desire which still drew her to
him, she realized in the back of her feverish brain that
nothing but marriage with him would save her now. Her
future position, whatever it was to be, depended on him.
She was too old, too enlightened by him to care for any
one but him. He must save her.

In regard to visits from the various members of his
family—his mother and father, his brother, his wife, and
his sister—Cowperwood made it plain to them on one of the
days on which he was out attending a bankruptcy hearing
that even providing it could be arranged he did not think
they should come oftener than once in three months,
unless he wrote them or sent word by Steger. He expected
to be coming out from time to time yet on court orders.
He really did not care to see much of any of them at
present. He was sick of the whole social scheme of
things. He wanted to be rid of the turmoil he had been
in, seeing it had proved so useless. He had used nearly
fifteen thousand dollars thus far in defending himself—
court costs, family maintenance, Steger, etc.; but he did
not mind that. He expected to make some little money
working through Wingate. His family were not utterly
without funds, sufficient to live in a small way. He had
advised them to take very commonplace houses, which
they did—his mother and father and brothers and sister
moving to a three-story brick of about the caliber of the

old Buttonwood Street house, and his wife to a smaller, less expensive two-story one on North Twenty-first Street, near the penitentiary, not unlike that of the Calligans' on Cherry Street, a portion of the money saved out of the thirty-five thousand dollars extracted from Stener under false pretenses aiding to sustain it. It was a terrible descent from the Girard Avenue mansion for the elder Cowperwood; for here was none of the furniture which characterized the other somewhat gorgeous domicile— merely store-bought, ready-made furniture, and neat but cheap hangings and fixtures generally. The assignees, to whom all Cowperwood's personal property belonged, and to whom Cowperwood, the elder, had surrendered all his holdings, would not permit anything of importance to be retained. It all had to be sold for the benefit of creditors. A few very small things, but only a few, had been kept, as everything had been inventoried some time before. One of the things which old Cowperwood wanted was the private desk which Frank had had designed for him; but as it was valued at one hundred and fifteen dollars and could not be relinquished by the sheriff except on payment of that sum, or by auction, and as Henry Cowperwood had no such sum to spare, he had to let the desk go. There were many things they all wanted, and Anna Adelaide had literally purloined a few; but it was dangerous, and she did not admit the matter to her parents until long afterward.

There came a day when the two houses in Girard Avenue were the scene of a sheriff's sale, during which the general public, without let or hindrance, were permitted to tramp through the rooms which Cowperwood and his relatives had occupied, and examine all the things which had constituted his private world. The pictures, statuary, and objects of art generally, which he had spent years in collecting, were now scrutinized in detail and knocked down to the highest bidder. Considerable fame had attached to Cowperwood's activities in this field, owing in the first place to the real merit of what he had brought together, and in the next place to the enthusiastic comment of such men as Wilton Ellsworth, Fletcher Gray, Gordon Strake— architects and art dealers whose judgment and taste were considered important in Philadelphia. In their social meanderings these men had described Cowperwood as an enthusiastic collector and a man of real taste. Now in this hour of disintegration, many who had known him socially as well as commercially and who appreciated his innate force, were here to see what the sheriff, acting for his creditors, had to offer. All of these lovely things by which he had set great store—small bronzes, representative of the best period of the Italian Renaissance; bits of Venetian glass which he had collected with great care— a full curio case; statues by Powers, Hosmer, and Thorwaldsen—things which would have been smiled at thirty years later, but which were of high value then; all of his pictures by representative American painters from Gilbert to Eastman Johnson, together with a few specimens of the current French and English schools, went for a song. Art judgment in Philadelphia at this time was not exceedingly high; and some of the pictures, for lack of appreciative understanding, were disposed of at much too low a figure. Gordon Strake, Fletcher Gray, and Wilton Ellsworth were all present and bought liberally. Senator Simpson, Mr. Mollenhauer, and our good friend Strobik entered to see what they could see. The smallfry politicians were there, *en masse*. But Senator Simpson, calm judge of good art, secured practically the best of all that was offered; for he had the money and was perfectly willing to pay a good price. To him went the curio case of Venetian glass; one pair of tall blue-and-white Mohammedan cylindrical vases; fourteen examples of Chinese jade, including several artists' water-dishes and a pierced window-screen of the faintest tinge of green. To Mr. Mollenhauer went the furniture and decorations of the entry-hall and reception-room of Henry Cowperwood's house, and to Edward Strobik two of Cowperwood's bird's-eye-maple bedroom sets for the most modest of prices. Adam Davi was present and secured the secrétaire of buhl which the elder Cowperwood prized so highly. To Fletcher Gray went the four Greek vases —a kylix, a water-jar, and two amphoræ—which he had sold to Cowperwood and which he valued highly. Various objects of art, including a Sevres dinner set, a Gobelin tapestry, Barye bronzes, and pictures by Detaille, Fortuny, and George Inness, went to Walter Leigh, Arthur Rivers, Joseph Zimmerman, Judge Kitchen, Harper Steger, Terrence Relihan, Trenor Drake, Mr. and Mrs. Simeon Jones, W. C. Davison, Frewen Kasson, Fletcher Norton, and Judge Rafalsky. Judge Wilbur Payderson stopped in on the second day of this sale, but purchased nothing. Within four days after the sale began the two houses were bare of their contents. Even the objects which Cowperwood had had in the house at 931 North Tenth Street had been withdrawn from storage, where they had been placed at the time it was deemed advisable to close this institution, and placed on sale with the other objects in the two homes. It was at this time that the senior Cowperwoods first learned of something which seemed to indicate a mystery which had existed in connection with their son and his wife. No one of all the Cowperwoods was ever present during all this gloomy distribution; and Aileen, reading of the disposition of all the wares, and knowing their value to Cowperwood, to say nothing of their charm to her, was greatly depressed; yet she was not long despondent, for she was convinced that Cowperwood would some day regain his liberty and be more distinguished than ever.

Walking up and down in his cell, meditating on the various phases of his fortune during the weeks immediately following his incarceration, Cowperwood meditated constantly on these things. If he could only strike it again in some way financially—if he could only get rich once more. His poor father, hunting for work! His distressed mother! His hopeless wife! If he wanted really to be fair to his wife in leaving her, he ought to have money to give her. That he could not now do unless he made it again; and would he? And then there was Aileen—four or five months away from her would be a long time, let alone four or five years! What was she thinking? He had not seen her these first few weeks—had only had letters, and had written her in return. When would she come? When would it be advisable? He did not know that by now she was fairly desperate with desire to see him, and determined to reach him, whatever happened.

CHAPTER LXX

IN the meanwhile Cowperwood had been transferred to a new cell and a new overseer. At the end of two weeks, as Chapin had told him, he was removed from the "manners squad" to a cell in Block 3 on the ground floor, which was like all the others in size, ten by sixteen, but to which was attached the small yard, of the same size, that had been mentioned as possibly coming to him. Warden Desmas came up two days before he was transferred, and had another short conversation with him through his cell door.

"You'll be transferred on Monday," he said, in his reserved, slow way. "They'll give you a yard, though it won't be much good to you—we only allow a half-hour a day in it. I've told the overseer about your business arrangements. He'll treat you right in that matter. Just be careful not to take up too much time that way, and things will work out. I've decided to let you learn caning chairs. That 'll be the best for you. It's easy, and it 'll occupy your mind."

The warden and some allied politicians made a good thing out of this prison industry, which was enforced. It was really not hard labor—the tasks set were simple and not oppressive, but all that were made were promptly sold and the profits pocketed. It was good, therefore, to see all prisoners working, and it did them good. Cowperwood was glad of the chance to do something, for he really did not care for books, and his connection with Wingate and his old affairs were not sufficient now to employ his mind in a satisfactory way. His hands moving would be better. He thought, if he seemed strange now how much stranger he would seem then, behind these narrow bars working at so commonplace a task as caning chairs. He thanked Warden Desmas for the sheets which had been permitted to be brought in, and the toilet articles.

"That's all right," replied the latter, pleasantly and softly. "It's no more than your due. We know that there are men and men here, the same as anywhere. If a man knows how to use these things and wants to be clean, I wouldn't be one to put anything in his way."

He went away, and Cowperwood awaited his transfer with interest. It would be better, even though he liked old man Chapin so much, to have a yard and a trade. Both would help him to pass the time and to think of better days to come. The new overseer had been instructed to be considerate of him. That would make a difference, too, he thought. He was quite cheerful over the prospect. He began to gather up his things on the day of his transfer, for, being an ordinary convict, he had to transfer all his personal belongings by hand to his new quarters; and old man Chapin, seeing him, observed: "Well, you're goin' to go now, hain't yuh? Well, I've done all I could for yuh. I've taught yuh the rules as best I know. I'll see you down there, maybe, now and then. Yuh hain't goin' so far but what I kin find yuh. Maybe, if everything goes right, you'll get out a little earlier than you expect. I see one and another here go that way from time to time."

Cowperwood grasped the old man's hand. "You've been very nice to me, Mr. Chapin," he said, warmly. "I certainly appreciate your kindness. And if I ever get out of here, I shall not forget it."

Chapin was too old a man to expect anything much from life in any form. He was, nevertheless, flattered by the interest and good-will of Cowperwood, for the average character of his charges was not high.

"That's all right, Mr. Cowperwood. I never expect anythin' fur doin' what I consider right. I hope you git out, though, fer I think very likely you deserve to. You look that way to me. You've had a taste o' this place now, and ye see what it is. If I can ever do anythin' for you, I'll be glad to."

Cowperwood, who was actually moving at the time, gathered up an armful of linen, underwear, books, and the like, and went his way. In his ill-fitting, semi-cotton, striped, cheap suit, and with his arms full of movables, he looked anything but the financier who had been such a striking personage in Third Street.

The new overseer with whom Cowperwood had to deal was a very different person from Elias Chapin. His name was Walter Bonhag, and he was not more than thirty-seven years of age—a big, flabby sort of person with a crafty mind, whose principal object in life was to see whether this prison situation as he found it would not furnish him a better income than his normal salary provided. A close study of Bonhag would have seemed to indicate that he was a stool-pigeon of Desmas, but this was really not true except in a limited way. Because Bonhag was shrewd and sycophantic, quick to see a point in his or anybody else's favor, Desmas instinctively realized that he was the kind of man who could be trusted to be lenient on order or suggestion. That is, if Desmas had the least interest in a prisoner he need not say as much to Bonhag; he might merely suggest that this man was used to a different kind of life, or that, because of some past experience, it might go hard with him if he were handled roughly; and Bonhag would strain himself to be pleasant. The trouble was that to a shrewd man of any refinement his attentions were objectionable, being obviously offered for a purpose, and to a poor or ignorant man they were brutal and contemptuous. He had a score of methods of making money out of the prisoners by selling them extra allowances of things which he secretly brought into the prison. It was strictly against the rules, in theory at least, to bring in anything which was not sold in the store-room—tobacco, writing-paper, pens, ink, whisky, cigars, or delicacies of any kind. It is true that tobacco of inferior grade was provided, and wretched pens, ink, and paper; but no self-respecting man, if he could help it, would endure them. Whisky was not allowed at all, and delicacies were abhorred as indicating rank favoritism; nevertheless, they were brought in. If a prisoner had the price and was willing to see that Bonhag secured something for his trouble, almost anything would be forthcoming. The privilege of being sent into the general yard as a "trusty," or of being allowed to stay in the little private yard which some cells possessed, longer than the half-hour ordinarily permitted, was to be had for a consideration. Bonhag had a peculiar face, which was anything but weak, yet not straightforward. It was rather well modeled, but often either leering or lowering. Sometimes it was gay, but in the coarse, vulgar, animal fashion. The man had no wit, in the best sense of the word. He was without a real sense of humor. His mind was really too centered on his material improvement to be of the least value to anybody else, and only fools would really trust him. One look on Cowperwood's part, on his arrival, satisfied him that all the things which have here been said of Bonhag were true. He saw that he could use him by making it worth his while, and of course he proposed to do so.

One of the things which worked in Cowperwood's favor was the fact that Bonhag was friendly with the overseer who had Stener in charge. Stener, because of his political friends, was, as has been said, being liberally treated, and Bonhag knew of this. He was not a careful reader of newspapers, nor had he any intellectual grasp of important events; but he knew by now that both Stener and Cowperwood were individuals of great importance in the community, that Cowperwood was the more important of the two, and that, as Bonhag suspected, he still had money. And so, entirely aside from Warden Desmas's recommendation, which was given in a very quiet, non-committal way, Bonhag was interested to see what he could do for Cowperwood for a price. He was actually afraid that if he did not do something, Steger, who looked very important to him, and Wingate, who had a very considerable air as a business man, although he was not a remarkable one, might say something to Desmas, whom he fancied they knew. Cowperwood might complain, and the latter not being like those friendless creatures in the other cells who had no one to speak their woes to, Bonhag would be in danger of criticism on some score. Trust the sycophant promptly to see on which side his bread is buttered.

The day Cowperwood was installed here, having been brought over by Chapin, Bonhag lolled up to the door, which was open, and said, in a semi-patronizing way, "Got all your things over yet?" It was his business to lock the door once Cowperwood was inside it.

"Yes, sir," replied Cowperwood, who had been shrewd enough to get the new overseer's name from Chapin; "this is Mr. Bonhag, I presume?"

"That's me," replied Bonhag, easily and curiously. He was anxious to study Cowperwood, to see what type of man he was. The latter was more than a match for the situation. His manner betrayed just that amount of deference and confidence, without sycophancy, which would be grateful to the thick-witted overseer. He wanted to patronize Cowperwood, and yet to be considered by him. Exactly what he expected he received. Cowperwood was alert, courteous, industrious. He fell into an easy conversation with this master of the hall which was confiding and yet not familiar. In a reserved way he described Mr. Chapin and his pleasure in being with him.

"You'll find it a little different down here from up

there," observed Bonhag. "It ain't so stuffy. These doors out in the yards make a difference." He looked toward the tightly sealed door which gave into the narrow space outside as though it were some tremendous privilege for which Cowperwood should be vastly grateful.

"Oh yes," said Cowperwood. "That is the yard Mr. Desmas spoke about."

If Bonhag had been a horse his ears would have been seen to lift at the mention of this magic name. If Cowperwood was so friendly with Desmas that the latter had described to him the type of cell he was to have beforehand, it behooved Bonhag to be especially careful.

"Yes, that's it, but it ain't much," he observed. "They only allow a half-hour a day in it. Still it would be all right if a person could stay there longer."

This was the first hint at graft, favoritism; and Cowperwood distinctly caught the sound of it in Bonhag's voice. He could see that some time, if he wished, Bonhag would stretch a point in this matter.

"That is too bad," said Cowperwood. "I don't suppose good conduct helps a person to get more." He smiled in a friendly, impressive way.

"I'd better teach you your trade," said Bonhag, genially. "You've got to learn to cane chairs, so the warden says. If you want, we can begin right now."

Cowperwood expressed himself as delighted, and Bonhag went off, locking the door as he went, returning after a time with three unvarnished frames of chairs and a bundle of cane strips or withes, which he deposited on the floor. "Now I'll show you if you'll watch me," he said; and he began showing Cowperwood how the strips were to be laced through the apertures on either side, cut, and fastened with little hickory pegs. He had brought a forcing awl, a small hammer, a box of pegs, and a pair of clippers. After several brief demonstrations with different strips, as to how the geometric forms were designed, he allowed

722

Cowperwood to take the matter in hand, watching over his shoulder. The latter, quick at anything, manual or mental, went at it in his customary energetic fashion, and in five minutes demonstrated that, barring the skill and speed, which would only come with practice, he could do it as well as another. "You'll make out all right," said Bonhag. "You're supposed to do ten of those a day. We won't count the next few days, though, until you get your hand in. I'll come around now and then and see how you're getting along. You understand about the towel on the door, don't you?" he inquired. He was referring to the prisoners' method of calling attention to their needs.

"Yes, Mr. Chapin explained that to me," replied Cowperwood. "I think I know what most of the rules are now. I'll try not to break any of them."

Bonhag went away, and Cowperwood was left to himself, contemplating the years that were before him here. He must get Steger and Wingate and his father and others to work hard in order to get him out. It was intolerable to him to think that he should be compelled to stay here even so much as a single year.

The days which followed brought a number of modifications of his prison lot, but not sufficient by any means to make it acceptable to him. In spite of his supposed influence with Desmas, the helpful connections he maintained with Steger, Wingate, and others, and the financial understanding he managed to effect with Bonhag, he was very uncomfortable and unhappy, though he bore it all like a stoic. Bonhag, during the first few days in which he trained Cowperwood in the art of caning chairs, managed to make it perfectly clear that there were a number of things he would be willing to do for him. "I see you have your lawyer and your partner here every day," he said to him, one morning. "There isn't anybody else you'd like to have visit you, is there? It's against the rules to have your wife or sister or anybody like that, except on visiting-days, but all the rules ain't kept around here, by a long shot."

Bonhag had been impressed by the fact that Stener's friends were coming to see him in larger numbers than Cowperwood's, sending him an occasional basket of fruit, which he gave to the overseers, and that his wife and children had been already permitted to visit him outside the regular visiting-day. This was a cause for jealousy on Bonhag's part. His fellow-overseer was lording it over him—telling him, as it were, of the high jinks in Block 4. Bonhag really wanted Cowperwood to spruce up and show what he could do, socially or otherwise.

Cowperwood was not the man to lose a chance of this kind. "I'll tell you how it is, Mr. Bonhag," he said, very politely, but with that engaging frankness which caused even Bonhag to feel as if he were one of his oldest friends. "I believe you understand my position better than most men would, and that I can talk to you. There are people who would like to come here, but I have been afraid to let them come. I did not know that outside of Mr. Wingate and Mr. Steger it could be arranged. If it could be, I would be very grateful. You and I are practical men—I know that if any favors are extended some of those who help to bring them about must be looked after. I wish I could make you my agent in this matter, and if you would be willing I would make it well worth your while. I am in prison, and I do not want to make any more trouble than I have to. I am not used to this life, and it's going rather hard with me. If you can do anything to make it a little more comfortable for me I will show you that I appreciate it. I haven't any money on my person, but can always get it, and I will see that you are properly looked after."

Bonhag's short, thick ears tingled. This was the kind of talk he liked to hear. "I can fix anything like that, Mr. Cowperwood," he replied, servilely. "You leave it to me. If there's any one you want to see at any time, just let me know. Of course I have to be very careful, but that's all right, too. If you want to stay out in that yard a little longer in the mornings or get out there afternoons or evenings, I can fix that. I'll just leave the door open. If the warden or anybody else should be around, I'll just scratch on your door with my key, and you come in and shut it. If there's anything you want from the outside I can get it for you—jelly or eggs or butter or any little thing like that. You might like to fix up your meals a little that way."

Cowperwood wanted to smile. Bonhag's proposition tended to make this penitentiary a very comfortable caravansary. He kept a straight face, however.

"In regard to that other matter," went on Bonhag, referring to the matter of extra visitors, "I can fix that any time you want to. I know the men out at the gate. If you want anybody to come here, just write 'em a note and tell 'em to ask for me. They'll let 'em in all right. When they get here you can talk to 'em in your cell. Only when I tap they have to come out. So just you let me know."

Cowperwood was exceedingly grateful. He said so in direct, choice language. It occurred to him at once that this was Aileen's opportunity, and that he could now notify her to come. If she veiled herself sufficiently she would probably be safe enough. He decided to write her, and when Wingate came he gave him a letter to mail. Two days later, at three o'clock in the afternoon—the time appointed by him—Aileen came to see him for the first time in the prison. She was dressed in gray broadcloth with white-velvet trimmings and cut-steel buttons which glistened like silver, and wore, as additional ornaments, as well as a protection against the cold, a cap, stole, and muff of snow-white ermine. Over this rather striking costume she had slipped a long dark circular cloak, which she meant to lay off immediately upon her arrival. She had made a very careful toilet as to her shoes, gloves, hair, and the gold ornaments which she wore. Her face was concealed by a thick green veil, as Cowperwood had suggested; and she arrived at an hour when, as near as he had been able to prearrange, he would be alone. Wingate usually came at four, after business, and Steger in the morning, when he came at all. She was very nervous over this strange adventure, leaving the street-car some distance away and walking up a side street. The cold weather and the gray walls under a gray sky gave her a sense of defeat, but she had worked very hard to look nice in order to cheer her lover up. She knew how readily he responded to the influence of her beauty when properly displayed.

Cowperwood, in view of her coming, had made his cell as acceptable as possible. It was clean, because he had swept it and made his own bed; and he had shaved and combed his hair, and otherwise put himself to rights. The caned chairs on which he was working had been put in the corner at the end of the bed. His few dishes were washed and hung up, and his clogs brushed with a brush which he now kept for the purpose. Never before, he thought to himself, with a peculiar feeling of artistic degradation, had Aileen seen him like this. She had always admired his good taste in clothes, and the way he carried himself in them; and now she was to see him in garments which no dignity of body could make presentable. A stoic sense of his own soul-dignity came over him, however. He was Frank A. Cowperwood, and that was enough, whatever he wore. He would be free and rich some day again, and, anyhow, his looks under these circumstances would make no difference to Aileen. She would only love him the more. It was her ardent sympathy that he was afraid of. He was so glad that Bonhag had suggested that she might enter the cell, for it would be a grim procedure talking to her through a barred door. Steger and Wingate had been allowed to confer with him in his cell from the beginning.

THE FINANCIER

When Aileen arrived she asked for Mr. Bonhag, and was permitted to go to the central rotunda, where he was sent for. When he came she murmured: "I wish to see Mr. Cowperwood, if you please"; and he exclaimed, "Oh yes, just come with me." As he came across the rotunda floor from his corridor he was struck by the evident youth of Aileen, even though he could not see her face. This now was something in accordance with what he had expected of Cowperwood. A man who could steal five hundred thousand dollars and set a whole city by the ears must have wonderful adventures of all kinds, and Aileen looked like a true adventure. He led her to a little room where he kept his desk and detained visitors, and bustled down to Cowperwood's cell, scratching on the door with his key. "There's a young lady here to see you. Do you want to let her come inside the cell?" he said to Cowperwood, who was working at one of his chairs.

"Thank you, yes," replied Cowperwood; and Bonhag hurried away, unintentionally forgetting, in his boorish incivility, to unlock the cell door, so that he had to open it in Aileen's presence. The long corridor, with the mathematically spaced gratings and gray-stone pavement, caused Aileen to feel faint at heart. It chilled her usually courageous spirit and shriveled it up. She followed Bonhag nervously, for all her smart air; for these hard, steel bars seemed very menacing to her. What a terrible place for her Frank to be! What a horrible thing to have put him here! Judges, juries, courts, laws, jails seemed like so many foaming ogres ranged about the world, glaring down upon her and her love-affair. The clank of the key in the lock, and the heavy outward swinging of the door, completed her sense of the untoward. And then she saw Cowperwood.

Because of the price he was to receive, Bonhag, after admitting her, strolled discreetly away.

Aileen looked at Cowperwood from behind her veil, afraid to speak until she was sure Bonhag had gone.

THE FINANCIER

Cowperwood, who was retaining his self-possession by an effort, signaled her after a moment or two. "It's all right," he said. "He's gone away." She lifted her veil, removed her cloak, and took in, without seeming to, the stuffy, narrow thickness of the room, his wretched shoes, the cheap, misshapen suit, the iron door behind him leading out into the little yard attached to his cell. Against such a background, with his partially caned chairs visible at the end of the bed, he seemed strange, unnatural. It was useless for her to try to speak for the moment, and then she suddenly said, putting her arms around him and stroking his head:

"My poor Frank, my brave boy. Is this what they have done to you?"

Cowperwood did his best to retain his sense of composure in the face of this sudden onslaught; but for the first time in his life, and the only time in all his life, he lost it. He lost it by some inexplicable trick of chemistry—that chemistry of the body, of blind forces which so readily supersede reason at times. The depth of Aileen's feeling, the cooing sound of her voice, the velvety tenderness of her hands, that beauty that had drawn him all the time—more radiant here perhaps within these hard walls, and in the face of his physical misery, than it had ever been before—completely unmanned him. He did not understand how it could; he tried to defy the mood, but he could not. When she held his head close and caressed it, of a sudden, in spite of himself, his breast felt thick and stuffy, and his throat hurt him. He felt, for him, an astonishingly strange feeling, a desire to cry, which he did his best to overcome; it shocked him so. There then combined and conspired to defeat him a strange, rich picture of the great world he had so recently lost, of the lovely, magnificent world which he hoped some day to regain. He felt more poignantly at this moment than ever he had before the degradation of the clog shoes, the cotton shirt, the striped suit, the reputation of a convict permanent and not to be laid aside. He felt now the real injustice of the great Chicago fire, the panic, the tricky political situation which had entrapped him and sent him here. Now he was quite alone—still fighting to win, but alone. His friends had almost deserted him; his family and home life were practically disintegrated. Outside of the business he was trying to build up with Wingate day by day, he had nothing. Really Aileen was with him no longer—belonging to an outside world which abhorred stripes. It came to him, all, in a rich, colorful way—more romance really than he had ever experienced; and because she had pulled his head down to her shoulder under her soft chin and was stroking it, he began to cry. He drew himself quickly away from her, turned his back, clinched his hands, drew his muscles taut; but it was too late. He was crying, and he could not stop.

"Oh, damn it!" he exclaimed, half angrily, half self-commiseratingly, in combined rage and shame. "Why should I cry? What the devil's the matter with me, anyhow?"

Aileen saw it. She fairly flung herself in front of him, seized his head with one hand, his shabby waist with the other, and held him tight in a grip that he could not have readily released.

"Oh, honey, honey, honey!" she exclaimed, pityingly, feverishly. "I love you, I adore you. They could cut my body into bits if it would do you any good. To think that they should make you cry! Oh, my sweet, my sweet, my darling boy!"

She pulled his still shaking body tighter (now completely unmanned by her emotion), and with her free hand caressed his head. She kissed it, his eyes, his hair, his cheeks. He pulled himself loose again after a moment, exclaiming, "What the devil's got into me?" but she drew him back.

"Never mind, honey, don't you be ashamed to cry. Cry here on my shoulder. My honey, my baby!"

She kissed his hair and eyes and cheeks and ears, the while Bonhag paced the hall in the distance. She loved him desperately, agonizingly, with a strong effusion of vital, animal temperament. She was really his, body and soul. He quieted down after a few moments, cautioning her against Bonhag, and regaining his former composure.

"You're a great girl, pet," he said. "You're all right, just what I need; but don't worry any longer about me, though. I'm all right. How are you?"

Aileen on her part was not to be soothed so easily. His many woes, including his wretched position here, outraged her sense of justice and decency. To think her fine, wonderful Frank should be compelled to come to this—to cry. She stroked his head, tenderly, while wild, deadly, unreasoning opposition to life and chance and untoward opposition surged in her brain. Her father—damn him! Her family—pooh! What did she care? Her Frank—her Frank—was all she thought about. She clung to him in silence while she fought in her brain an awful battle with life and law and fate and circumstance. Law—nonsense! People—they were brutes, devils, enemies, hounds! She was delighted, eager, crazy to make a sacrifice of herself. She would go anywhere for or with her Frank now. She would do anything for him. Her family was nothing—life nothing, nothing, nothing. She would do anything he wished, nothing more, nothing less; anything she could do to save him, to make his life happier, but nothing for any one else. How was it she had come to stay away so long?

CHAPTER LXXI

THE days passed. Once the understanding with Bonhag was reached, Cowperwood's wife, mother, and sister were allowed to appear on occasions. It established a visiting relation between him and Aileen. He was very careful to arrange that they did not appear on the same day as Aileen; that was easy enough, for no one of them came sufficiently often to make a clash possible. Cowperwood, in his solemn brooding over his chair-caning, decided to speak frankly to his wife, now that he was so thoroughly removed from her, and one day did so. He had such an excellent excuse now, he reasoned. She was in the little home for which he was paying, and his financial obligations to her were satisfied by Wingate, who paid her one hundred and twenty-five dollars a month for him. He realized that he owed her more, if he could pay more, but he was sailing rather close to the wind financially, these days, for him. The final collapse of his old interests had come in March, when he had been legally declared a bankrupt, and all his properties forfeited to satisfy the claims against him. The city's claim of five hundred thousand dollars would have eaten up more than could have been realized at the time, had not a pro rata payment of thirty cents on the dollar been declared. Even then the city never received its due, for by some hocus-pocus it was declared to have forfeited its rights. Its claims had not been made at the proper time in the proper way. This left larger portions of real money for the others.

Cowperwood had now begun to see by a little experimenting that his business relations with Wingate were certain to be moderately profitable. The latter broker had made it clear that he intended to be perfectly straight with him. He had employed Cowperwood's two brothers, at very moderate salaries—one to take care of the books and look after the office, and the other to act on 'change with him, for their seats in that organization had never been sold. He gathered all the information he possibly could daily, and told it all to Cowperwood, whose keen mind and wide experience permitted him to make suggestions which almost invariably turned out well. They were handicapped, of course, by a lack of means; and Cowperwood did not care to have it known at present that he was operating through Wingate. He was afraid it would not do the house any good. He did make suggestions as to how money could be secured and where, how certificates could be hypothecated and capital pyramided, which Wingate's average mind would never have dreamed of. He used to look at Cowperwood at times with dog-like eyes, while that worthy solved some complicated problem for him in a rather offhand manner, and then sent him cheerfully on his way. Cowperwood showed Wingate how to use Edward and Joseph to the best advantage, and by considerable effort finally got Cowperwood, senior, a place as a clerk, Wingate having notified the old gentleman of a vacancy in a bank.

To see old Cowperwood bustling off from his new but very much reduced home at half after seven in the morning in order to reach the small bank, which was some distance away and not accessible by street-car line, was one of those pathetic sights which the fortunes of trade so frequently offer. He carried his lunch in a small box because it was inconvenient to return home in the time allotted for this purpose, and because his new salary did not permit the extravagance of a purchased one. It was his one ambition now to eke out a respectable but unseen existence until he should die, which he hoped would not be long. Day in and day out he went shuttlewise back and forth in this manner, pointed out occasionally by those who had known him in his better days as the ex-president of the Third National who had come to grief through his son. He was a pathetic figure with his thin legs and body, his gray hair, and his snow-white side-whiskers. He was very lean and angular, and, when confronted by a difficult problem, a little uncertain or vague in his mind. The habit of putting his hand to his mouth and of opening his eyes in an assumption of surprise, which had no basis in fact, grew upon him. He really degenerated into a mere automaton. Life strews its shores with such interesting and pathetic wrecks.

Cowperwood speculated for some time as to how he would bring up the matter of his indifference to his wife, and his desire to end their relationship, but he did not see anything for it save the brutality of plain truth. She was persisting in her pretense of devotion, uncolored, apparently, by suspicion of any kind, when as a matter of fact she had never ceased to brood over what had happened. Since his trial and conviction she had been hearing from one source and another that he was still intimate with Aileen, and it was only her thought of his concurrent woes, and the fact that he might possibly be spared to a successful financial life, that had deterred her from speaking. Now that he was shut up in a cell, she really felt very sorry for him, but she did not love him as she once had. She felt that he was deserving of re-proach for his general unseemly conduct, and that this was probably intended by the Governing Power of the world, which makes for morality, to cause him to see the error of his way.

One can imagine how much this attitude would appeal to Cowperwood once he detected it. He could see by a dozen little signs, in spite of the fact that she brought him delicacies, and commiserated him on his fate, that she felt a little reproachful, a little depressed and sad.

If there was one thing that Cowperwood objected to at all times it was the funereal air. As contrasted with the cheerful combative hopefulness and enthusiasm of Aileen, the wearied uncertainty of Mrs. Cowperwood was, to say the least, a little tame. Aileen, after her first burst of rage over his fate, which really did not develop any tears on her part, was apparently convinced that he would get out and be very successful again. She naturally talked success and his future all the time because she believed in it. She seemed instinctively to realize that he must be great, and that prison walls could not make a prison for him. On the first day she left she handed Bonhag ten dollars and thanked him in her attractive voice—without showing her face, however—which sealed that ambitious materialist's fate completely. There was nothing the overseer would not do for the young lady in the dark cloak. She might have stayed in Cowperwood's cell for a week if the visiting-hours of the penitentiary had not made it impossible.

The day that Cowperwood brought up the weariness of his present married state and his desire to be free of it was some four months after he had entered the prison. He had become inured to his convict life by that time. The silence of his cell and the menial tasks he was compelled to perform, which had at first been so distressing, banal, maddening, in their pointless iteration, had now become merely commonplace—dull, but not painful. He had learned many of the little resources of the solitary convict, such as that of using his lamp to warm up some delicacy which he had saved from a previous meal or from some basket which had been sent him by his wife or Aileen. He had got rid of the sickening odor of his room in part by persuading Bonhag to bring him small packages of lime, which he used with great freedom. He defeated some of the venturesome rats with traps; and with Bonhag's permission, after his cell door had been properly locked at night and sealed with the outer wooden

THE FINANCIER

door, he would take his chair, if it were not too cold, out into the little yard back of his cell and look at the sky, where, when the nights were clear, the stars were to be seen. He was satisfied at times that he heard the footsteps of other convicts in these yards, but he could not be sure, the high walls not permitting him to see. He had never taken any interest in astronomy as a scientific study, but now the Pleiades, the belt of Orion, the Big Dipper and the North Star, to which one of its lines pointed, caught his attention, almost his fancy. He wondered why the stars of the belt of Orion came to assume the peculiar mathematical relation to each other which they held, as far as distance and arrangement were concerned, and whether that could possibly have any intellectual significance. The nebulous conglomeration of the suns in Pleiades suggested a soundless depth of space, and he thought of the earth floating like a little ball in immeasurable reaches of ether. His own life became very trivial in view of these things, and he found himself asking whether it was all really of any significance or importance. He shook these moods off with ease, however, for the man was possessed of a sense of grandeur, largely in relation to himself and his affairs, and his temperament was essentially material and vital. Something kept telling him that he must grow to be a significant personage, one whose fame would be heralded the world over—who must try, try, try. It was not given all men to see far or to do brilliantly; but to him it was given, and he must be what he was cut out to be. There was no more escaping the greatness that was inherent in him than there was for so many others the littleness that was in them.

Mrs. Cowperwood came in one afternoon quite solemnly, he thought, bearing several changes of linen, a pair of sheets, some potted meat and a pie which she wished him to have. She was not exactly doleful, but Cowperwood thought that she was tending toward it, largely because of her brooding over his relationship to Aileen, which he knew that she knew. Something in her manner decided him to speak before she left; and after asking her how the children were, and listening to her inquiries in regard to the things that he needed, and so forth, he said to her, sitting on his single chair while she sat on his bed:

"Lillian, there's something I've been wanting to talk with you about for some time. I should have done it before, but it's better late than never. I know that you know that there is something between Aileen Butler and me, and we might as well have it open and above board. I am very fond of her, and if ever I get out of here I want to arrange it so that I can marry her. That means that you will have to give me a divorce, if you will; and I want to talk to you about that now. This can't be so very much of a surprise to you, because you must have seen this long while that our relationship hasn't been all that it might have been."

Mrs. Cowperwood's thought, when he first broached this proposition, was that she ought to make some demonstration of astonishment or wrath; but when she looked into his steady, examining eye, so free from the illusion of or interest in demonstrations of any kind, she realized how useless it would be. He was so utterly matter-of-fact in what seemed to her quite private and secret affairs —very shameless. She had never been able to understand quite how he could take the subtleties of life as he did, anyhow. Certain things which she always fancied should be hushed up he spoke of with the greatest nonchalance. Somebody's daughter was a prostitute; some other individual, high in moral affairs, was much more than a squire of dames—he said so frankly. Her ears tingled sometimes at the way he would dispose of a social situation; but she thought in view of his large affairs that somehow this must be characteristic of notable men, and so there was nothing to be said about it. Certain men did as they pleased; society did not seem to be able to deal with them in any way. Perhaps God would, later

—she was not sure. Anyhow, bad as he was, direct as he was, forceful as he was, he was far more interesting than some of the more conservative type in whom the social virtues of polite speech and modest thoughts were seemingly more predominate.

"I know, Frank," she said, rather peacefully, although with a touch of anger and resentment in her voice. "I've known all about it all this time. I expected you would say something like this to me some day. It's a nice reward for all my devotion to you; but it's just like you, Frank. When you are set on something, nothing can stop you. It wasn't enough that you were getting along so nicely and had two children whom you ought to love, but you had to take up with this Butler creature until her name and yours are a by-word throughout the city. I know that she comes to this prison. I saw her out here one day as I was coming in, and I suppose every one else knows it by now. I should think you would be ashamed, Frank, to go on the way that you have, when you are certain to have such a hard fight to get yourself on your feet, as it is. If she had any sense of decency she would not have anything to do with you—the shameless thing."

Cowperwood looked at his wife with unflinching eyes. He expected some such outburst, of course; it was natural that she should feel grieved and angry. He did not mind that she called Aileen a "thing" and a "creature." Of course Aileen was a strumpet in her eyes; but what of it? He read in her remarks just what his observation had long since confirmed—that she was sympathetically out of touch with him. He was a very different man from the one he had been thirteen years before when he married her. She was no longer so attractive physically, and intellectually she was not Aileen's equal. Socially she was not so much; he had learned that long since. Many of the society women who had deigned to grace his home in his greatest hour of prosperity had proved that to him conclusively. Aileen was not so vastly better, but she was young and could be improved. Opportunity would make Aileen. It had not been able to make Mrs. Cowperwood. The thing to do was to make it perfectly clear to her now that the day of their comfortable marital relationship was over, and that it would be much better and simpler, from all points of view, to have her forsake him, set him free. He would provide for her and the children properly, as he saw that his means would permit—very liberally, no doubt, later on—but just now she must let him go, set him free, so that when he came out of prison he would be at liberty to do as he chose. This was the very important business in hand.

"I'll tell you how it is, Lillian," he said; "I'm not sure that you are going to get what I mean exactly, but you and I are not at all well suited to each other any more."

"You didn't seem to think that three or four years ago," interrupted his wife, bitterly.

"I married you when I was twenty-one," went on Cowperwood, quite brutally, not paying any attention to her interruption, "and I was really too young to know what I was doing. I was a mere boy. It doesn't make so much difference about that. I am not using that as an excuse. The point that I am trying to make is this— that right or wrong, important or not important, I have changed my mind since. I don't love you any more, and I don't feel that I want to keep up a relationship, however it may look to the public, that is not satisfactory to me. You have one point of view about life, and I have another. You think your point of view is the right one, and there are thousands of people who will agree with you; but I don't think so. We have never quarreled about these things, because I didn't think it was important to quarrel about them. I don't see under the circumstances that I am doing you any great injustice when I ask you to let me go. I don't intend to desert you or the children—you will get a good living-income from me as long as I have the money to give it to you—but I want my personal freedom when I come out of here, if ever I do, and I want you to let me have it. The money that you had and a great deal more you will get back when I am on my feet again." He smoothed the leg of his prison trousers in a thoughtful way, and plucked at the sleeve of his coat. Just now he looked very much like a highly intelligent workman as he sat here, rather than like the important personage that he was.

Mrs. Cowperwood was very resentful. Her feeling that Cowperwood needed her, in spite of his misconduct, and that, if given a chance, the crash that the error of his way had brought about would cause him to reform, was hereby set at naught. His assurance that he would take care of her, however, and return her her money, however material and objectionable it might seem on that score, had real value, for it set at rest her fears as to her own fate financially, and that of the children. In so far as money matters were concerned, his word was as good as his bond. He would do what he said if he had it to do with. Nevertheless she resented his looking upon money as the sole consideration.

"That's a nice way to treat me!" she exclaimed, dramatically, rising and walking the short space—some two steps —that lay between the wall and the bed. "I might have known that you were too young to know your own mind when you married me. Money, of course, that's all you think of and your own gratification. You haven't any sense of justice in you, I do believe. I never saw such a man as you are. You have treated me like a dog all through this affair; and all the while you have been running with that little snip of an Irish thing, and telling her all about your affairs, I suppose. You let me go on believing that you care for me up to the last moment, and then you suddenly step up and tell me that you want a divorce. I'll not do it. I'll not be put upon in this way. I'll not give you a divorce, and you needn't think it."

Mrs. Cowperwood went on to complain of his indifference to his children and to her, long before Aileen Butler appeared as a direct influence in his affairs.

Cowperwood listened in silence. His position, in so far as this marital tangle was concerned, was very advantageous. He was a convict, to be out of personal contact with his wife for a long period of time to come, which would gradually school her to do without him. When he came out it would be very easy for her to get a divorce from a convict, particularly if she could allege misconduct with another woman, which he would not deny. He hoped to keep the name of Aileen out of it. She could give any false name if he made no contest. Mrs. Cowperwood was not a very strong person, intellectually and temperamentally speaking. He could bend her to his will. There was no need of saying much more now; the ice had been broken, the situation had been put before her, and time would do the rest. Mrs. Cowperwood, who was dressed in a dark, inconspicuous brown, stood in the short space between the bed and the wall, wringing her hands, thinking over her multiplied woes.

"Don't be dramatic, Lillian," commented Cowperwood, indifferently. "I'm not such a loss to you if you have enough to live on. I don't think I want to live in Philadelphia if ever I come out of here. My idea is to go West, and I think I want to go alone. I sha'n't get married right away again even if you do give me a divorce. I don't care to take anybody along. It would be better for the children if you would stay here and divorce me. The public would think better of them and you."

Cowperwood was very specious. He did not think half so badly of his future as he said.

"I'll not do it," declared Mrs. Cowperwood. "I'll never do it, never; so there! You can say what you choose. You owe it to me to stick by me and the children after all I've done for you, and I'll not do it. You needn't ask me any more; I'll not do it."

THE FINANCIER

"Very well," replied Cowperwood, quietly, getting up. "We needn't talk about it any more now. Your time is nearly up, anyhow." (Twenty minutes was supposed to be the regular allotment for visitors.) "Perhaps you'll change your mind sometime."

Mrs. Cowperwood, whose life now, for some reason (although her husband was in the penitentiary and destined apparently to remain there for years more), seemed clouded over, gathered up her muff and the shawl-strap in which she had carried her gifts, and turned to go. It had been her custom to kiss Cowperwood in a make-believe way, but it was not worth while doing so any more, so angry was she. And yet she was sorry, too—sorry for herself and, she thought, for him.

"Frank," she declared, dramatically, at the last moment, "I never saw such a man as you. I don't believe you have any heart. You're not worthy of a good wife. You're worthy of just such a woman as you're getting. The idea!" Suddenly tears came in her eyes, and she flounced scornfully and yet sorrowfully out.

Cowperwood stood there. At least there would be no more useless kissing between them, he congratulated himself. It was hard in a way, but purely from an emotional point of view. He was not doing her any essential injustice, he reasoned—not an economic one—which was the important thing. The children would not be injured, any more than they had been. He would look after them properly in the future. She was angry to-day, but she would get over it, and in time come to see his point of view. He reminded one of nothing so much, as he stood there, as of a young chicken picking its way out of the shell of an old estate. Although he was in a cell of a penitentiary, with nearly four years more to serve, he felt, within himself, that the whole world was still before him. He could go West if he could not re-establish himself in Philadelphia; but he must stay here long enough to win the approval of those who had known him formerly—to obtain, as it were, a letter of credit which he could carry to other parts.

"Hard words break no bones," he said to himself, referring to what Mrs. Cowperwood had said of him and Aileen, and then thinking of his future and what he might do. "A man's never done till he's done. I'll show some of these people yet." Of Bonhag, who came to close the cell door, he asked whether it was going to rain, it looked so dark in the hall.

"It's sure to before night," replied Bonhag, who was wondering over Cowperwood's tangled affairs as he heard them retailed here and there.

The ex-financier fell to working at his allotment of chairs, measuring the withes and driving in the pegs, wondering what else he could do to further his future, which was sure to come—and soon, he thought.

CHAPTER LXXII

THE time that Cowperwood spent in the Eastern Penitentiary of Pennsylvania was exactly thirteen months from the day of his entry to his discharge. The influences which brought about this result were partly of his willing, and partly not. For one thing, some six months after he had been incarcerated, Edward Malia Butler died, expired sitting in his chair in his private office at his home. The conduct of Aileen had been a great strain on him, and his contest with Cowperwood, aiding in the latter's incarceration as he had, had not helped his peace of mind. Butler knew that Cowperwood, outside of his liaison with Aileen, was no more guilty than scores of others who were out and walking around. Still he did not regret his own attitude. The thing that did weigh on him was the fact that from the time Cowperwood had been sentenced, and more particularly after the time he had cried on Aileen's shoulder in prison, she had turned on her father in an almost brutal way. Her attitude, unnatural as a child, was quite explicable as that of a tortured sweetheart. Cowperwood had told her that he thought Butler was using his influence to withhold a pardon for him, even though one were granted to Stener, whose life in prison he had been following with considerable interest; and this had enraged her beyond measure. Bonhag carried news of Stener's comforts and the manner in which his friends were looking after his future to Cowperwood, and from the outside Steger and Wingate, who were looking after Cowperwood's petition, informed him that they understood that the governor was not favorably inclined, and would have to be worked on.

Stener was sure to be pardoned out in the course of time—he not so sure; and the reason that Stener's pardon was delayed was on account of him. Aileen lost no chance of being practically insulting to her father, ignoring him on every occasion, refusing as often as possible to eat at the same table, and when she did, sitting next her mother in the place of Norah, with whom she managed to exchange. She refused to sing or play any more when he was present, and cut to the quick the large number of young political aspirants who came to the house, and whose presence in a way had been encouraged for her benefit. Old Butler realized, of course, what it was all about. He said nothing. He could not placate her. Her mother and brothers did not understand it at all at first. (Mrs. Butler never understood.) But not long after Cowperwood had gone to the penitentiary Callum and Owen became aware of what the trouble was in several ways, which complicated matters for Butler greatly. Once, when Owen was coming away from a reception at one of the houses where his growing financial importance made him welcome, he heard one of two men whom he knew casually, but who were not friends of his, say to the other, as they stood at the door adjusting their coats, "You saw where this fellow Cowperwood got four years, didn't you?"

"Yes," replied the other. "A clever devil that—wasn't he? I knew that girl he was in with, too—you know who I mean—Miss Butler—wasn't that her name?"

Owen, who was waiting for his hat some distance back in the hall, was not sure that he heard right or that the Miss Butler referred to was Aileen. He did not get the connection until the other guest, opening the door and stepping out, remarked: "Well, old Butler got even, apparently. They say he sent him up."

Owen's brow clouded. A hard, contentious look came in his eyes. He had much of his father's force. What in the devil were they talking about? What Miss Butler did they have in mind? Could this be Aileen or Norah, and how could Cowperwood come to be in with either of them? It could not possibly be Norah, he reflected; she was very much infatuated with a young man whom he knew, and was going to marry him. Aileen had been most friendly with the Cowperwoods, and had often spoken well of the financier. Could it be she? He could not believe it. He thought once of overtaking the two acquaintances and demanding to know what they meant, but when he came out on the step they were already some distance down the street and in the opposite direction from that in which he wished to go. He hesitated, and decided that he could look them up later if he chose. Meantime he proposed to ask his father about this and find out what he knew.

On demand, old Butler confessed at once, but insisted that his son keep silent about it. "He's in prison now," he explained, without telling Owen all the hell he himself had been through, "and he'll stay there if I have my way. No good 'll come of tellin' about it now. Yer mother don't know, and it's good that she doesn't. I'm not through with him yet, but let that stand."

"I wish I'd have known," said Owen, grimly. "I'd have shot the man down."

"Aisy, aisy," said Butler. "Yer own life's worth more than his, and ye'd only be draggin' the rest of yer family in the dirt with him. He's had somethin' to pay him for his dirty trick, and he'll have more. Just ye say nothin' to no one. Wait. He'll be wantin' to get out in a year or two. Say nothin' to her aither. Talkin' won't help there. She'll come to her sinses when he's been away long enough, I'm thinkin'."

Owen tried to be civil to his sister, but since he was a stickler for social perfection and advancement, and so eager to get up in the world himself, he could not understand how she could possibly have done any such thing. He resented bitterly the stumbling-block she had put in

745

his path. Now, among other things, his enemies would have this to throw in his face if they wanted to—and they would want to, trust life for that.

Callum reached his knowledge of the matter in quite another manner, but at about the same time. He was a member of a very distinguished athletic club which had an attractive building in the city, and a fine country club, where tennis, cricket, and lacrosse were played. It was in the club building in the city, where he went occasionally of a week-day evening to enjoy the swimming-pool and the Turkish bath connected with it, that he came into his first knowledge of the situation. Like all organizations of this character, the club was divided up into cliques and rings of the young bloods. Callum, like others, and because of his own and his father's prominence, had strong friends and enemies. It was rumored around this organization some time before Cowperwood went to jail that Aileen was connected with him in a clandestine manner, and that that was why he was going to prison. One of the young men who was exceedingly friendly to Callum came to him in the billiard-room one evening and said, "Say, Butler, you know I'm a good friend of yours, don't you?"

"Why, certainly, I know it," replied Callum, with that bonhomie which characterizes the feeling of young men who run together at the age of twenty-seven. "What's the matter?"

"Well, you know," said the young individual—whose name was Richard Pethick, and who had an insane desire to be associated with the best of the social element within his ken—looking at Callum with a look of almost strained affection, "I wouldn't come to you with any story that I thought would hurt your feelings or that you oughtn't to know about, but I do think you ought to know about this." He pulled at a high white collar which was choking his neck, and straightened his tie, in which was located a perfect emerald.

THE FINANCIER

"I know you wouldn't, Pethick," replied Callum, very much interested. "What is it? What's the point?"

"Well, I don't like to say anything, as much as I like you," replied Pethick, whose trousers were unduly narrow, after the mode of the season, "but that young Hibbs is saying things around here about your sister."

"What's that?" exclaimed Callum, straightening up in the noble fashion made and provided for all such cases. There is a standard of conduct which applies to every situation in all these would-be realms of perfection. They have a theory as to how one should conduct himself on each and every occasion—marriage, birth, death, adultery, family scandals, and so on—to say nothing of the ordinary polite occasions such as dinners, receptions, and the like. It is understood, Heaven knows on what authority, just how one must look and act. The eyebrows must be raised in a well-defined way, the face must blanch in a histrionic manner; one must under many circumstances look taut and dramatic, but always dignified and refined. On this occasion Callum did so on the instant.

"What is it he says about my sister? What right has he to mention her name here, anyhow? He doesn't know her."

"Now don't get mad, Callum; please don't, I beg you," pleaded Pethick, feeling himself to be the center of a most important event. Something really exciting was about to happen here, and he was the cause of it. A *distingué* row between men of real distinction. Oh, joy, oh, pride! what could be more important? He laid a restraining hand on Callum's arm, but the latter, half angrily, half histrionically, pushed it away.

"What was it he said?" he asked. "Tell me that. What did he say?"

Pethick affected to be greatly concerned lest he cause trouble between Callum and Hibbs. He protested that he did not want to, when he was dying to tell. "Why,

747

he's circulated the yarn that your sister had something to do with this man Cowperwood, and that that's why he's just gone to prison."

"What's that?" exclaimed Callum, losing the make-believe of the unimportant, and taking on the serious mien of some one who feels desperately. "He says that, does he? Where is he? I want to see if he'll say that to me."

Some of the grim fighting ability of his father showed in his slender, rather refined young face.

"Now, Callum," insisted Pethick, realizing the genuine storm he had raised, and being a little fearful of the result, "do be careful what you say. You mustn't have a row in here. It's against the rules. He may be drunk. It's just some foolish talk he's heard. Now for goodness' sake don't get so excited."

Callum's face was quite pale, and he was moving toward the old English grill-room, where Hibbs was supposed to be. The latter, Harry Hibbs, the son of a wooden-ware manufacturer, was consuming a brandy-and-soda with a friend of about his own age when Callum entered and called him.

"Oh, Hibbs!" he said.

Hibbs, hearing his voice and seeing him in the door, arose and came over. He was an interesting youth of the collegiate type, educated at Princeton, and idling rather easily in a position of his father's bestowal. He had heard the rumor concerning Aileen from various sources—other members of the club, for one—and had ventured to repeat it in Pethick's presence. There were other club-men drinking in the grill-room, and reading in the general lobby, which Pethick and Callum had crossed.

"What's that you were just saying about my sister?" asked Callum, grimly, looking Hibbs in the eye and shoving his ringed right hand in his coat pocket.

"Why—I—" hesitated Hibbs, who sensed trouble and

who was eager to avoid it. He was not exceptionally brave and looked it. His hair was straw-colored, his eyes blue, and his cheeks pink. "Why—nothing in particular. Who said I was talking about her?" He looked at Pethick, whom he knew to be the tale-bearer, and the latter exclaimed, excitedly:

"Now don't you try to deny it, Hibbs. You know I heard you?"

"Well, what did I say?" asked Hibbs, defiantly, who despised Pethick, and who now realized the mistake of ever having made friends with him.

"Well, what *did* you say?" interrupted Callum, grimly, transferring the conversation to himself. "That's just what I want to know."

"Why," stammered Hibbs, nervously, "I don't think I've said anything that anybody else hasn't said. I just repeated that some one said that your sister had been very friendly with Mr. Cowperwood. I didn't say any more than I have heard other people say around here."

"Oh, you didn't, did you?" exclaimed Callum, withdrawing his ringed hand from his pocket and slapping Hibbs in the face. He repeated the blow with his left hand, fiercely. "Perhaps that'll teach you to keep my sister's name out of your mouth, you pup!"

Hibbs's arms flew up. He was not without pugilistic training, and he struck back vigorously, striking Callum once in the chest and once in the neck. In an instant the two rooms were in an uproar. Tables and chairs were almost upset by the energy of men attempting to get to the scene of action. The two combatants were instantly separated; sides were taken by the friends of each, excited explanations attempted and defied. Callum was examining the knuckles of his left hand, which were cut from the blow he had delivered. He maintained a gentlemanly calm. Hibbs was very much flustered and excited. He maintained that Pethick had been eavesdropping and lying about him. The latter was protesting that he had done the only thing which an honorable friend could do. It was a nine days' wonder in the club, and was only kept out of the newspapers by the most strenuous efforts on the part of the friends of both parties. Callum was so outraged on discovering that there was some foundation for the rumor at the club in a general rumor which prevailed that he tendered his resignation, and never went there again. Pethick was in glory for several months, the center and retailer of a scandal. Callum went to Owen for an explanation, who gave him one quickly.

"The thing to do," he said, in conclusion, "is to hush this thing up. Say nothing. I wish to heaven you hadn't struck that fellow. It will only make more talk. She ought to leave this place; but she won't. She's struck on that fellow yet, and we can't tell Norah and mother. We will never hear the last of this, you and I—believe me."

"By damn, she ought to be made to go," exclaimed Callum.

"Well, she won't," replied Owen. "Father has tried making her, and she won't go. Just let things stand. He's in the penitentiary now, and that's probably the end of him. The public seem to think that father put him there, and that's something. Maybe we can persuade her to go after a while. I wish to God we had never had sight of that fellow. If ever he comes out, I've a good notion to kill him."

"Oh, I wouldn't do anything like that," replied Callum. "It's useless. It would only stir things up afresh. He's done for, anyhow. It's all over except the talk about it—but good God!"

They planned to urge Norah to marry as soon as possible. And as for their feelings toward Aileen, it was a very chilly atmosphere which Mrs. Butler contemplated from now on, much to her confusion, grief, and astonishment.

These occurrences left Aileen lonely and brooding; but she had Cowperwood for comfort. Her attitude toward her father did not help the situation any; and in this divided world Butler found himself all at sea as to what to think or what to do. He brooded deeply for months, finding no solution of the situation, and finally, in a form of religious despair, collapsed in his business chair, sitting at his desk. A lesion of the left ventricle was the immediate cause. They found him there the next morning, his hands folded in his lap, his head on his bosom, quite cold. His death could not have been laid to his grief over Aileen exactly, for he was a very large man—apoplectic and with sclerotic veins and arteries. For a great many years now he had taken very little exercise, and his digestion had been considerably impaired thereby. He was nearing seventy, and his time had been reached.

He was buried with honors out of St. Timothy's Church, the funeral attended by a large body of politicians and city officials, who discussed secretly among themselves whether the career of his daughter had anything to do with his end. All his good deeds were remembered, of course, and Mollenhauer and Simpson sent great floral emblems in remembrance. They were very sorry that he was gone, for they had been a cordial three. But gone he was, and that ended their interest in the matter. Butler had left all his property to his wife in one of the shortest wills ever recorded locally.

"I give and bequeath to my beloved wife, Norah, all my property of whatsoever kind to be disposed of as she may see fit."

There was no misconstruing this. A private paper drawn secretly for her sometime before by Butler, explained how the property should be disposed of by her at her death. It was Butler's real will masquerading as hers, and she would not have changed it for worlds; but he wanted her left in undisturbed possession of everything until she should die. Aileen's originally assigned portion had never been changed. According to her father's will, which no power under the sun could have made Mrs. Butler alter, she was left $250,000 to be paid at Mrs. Butler's death. Neither this fact nor any of the others contained in the paper were communicated by Mrs. Butler, who retained it to be left as her will. Aileen often wondered, but never sought to know, what had been left her. Nothing, she fancied—but felt that she could not help this.

Butler's death led at once to a great change in the temper of the home. After the funeral the family settled down to a seemingly peaceful continuance of the old life; but it was a matter of seeming merely. The situation stood with Callum and Owen manifesting a certain degree of contempt for Aileen, which she, understanding, reciprocated. She was very haughty. Owen had plans of forcing her to leave after Butler's death, but he finally asked himself what was the use. Mrs. Butler, who did not want to leave the old home, was very fond of Aileen, so therein lay a reason for letting her remain. Besides, any move to force her out would have entailed an explanation to her mother, which was not deemed advisable. Norah was to be married six months after her father died, and was in all probability to live in Trenton, where her husband's interests were located. Callum was thinking of getting married in order to relieve himself of the general odium of the situation. He was very fond of the daughter of a well-known flour manufacturer, with whom the Butlers were on social terms, and who reciprocated his affection. Owen himself was interested in Caroline Mollenhauer, whom he hoped some day to marry—as much for her prospective wealth as her affection, though he was quite fond of her. In the January following Butler's death, which occurred in August, Norah was married very quietly, and the following spring Callum embarked on a similar venture.

In the meanwhile, with Butler's death, the control of

the political situation had shifted considerably. A certain Tom Collins, formerly one of Butler's henchmen, but latterly a power in the First, Second, Third, and Fourth Wards, where he had numerous saloons and control of other forms of vice, appeared as a claimant for political recognition. Mollenhauer and Simpson had to consult him, as he could make very uncertain the disposition of some hundred and fifteen thousand votes, a large part of which were fraudulent, but which fact did not modify their deadly character on occasion. Mollenhauer and Simpson had to pay almost immediate attention to him in the disposition of certain favors; and, in the interest which his raw and forceful personality created, Butler and his enmities were forgotten. His sons disappeared as possible political factors, and were compelled to confine themselves to the street-railway and contracting business —as much of these as they had under their control. The pardon of Cowperwood and Stener, which Butler would have opposed, because by keeping Stener in he kept Cowperwood in, became a much easier matter. The scandal of the treasury defalcation was gradually dying down; the newspapers had ceased to refer to it in any way. Through Steger and Wingate, a large petition signed by all important financiers and brokers had been sent to the governor pointing out that Cowperwood's trial and conviction had been most unfair, and asking that he be pardoned. There was no need of any such effort, so far as Stener was concerned; whenever the time seemed ripe the politicians were quite ready to say to the governor that he ought to let him go. It was only because Butler had opposed Cowperwood's release that they had hesitated. It was really not possible to let out the one and ignore the other; and this petition, coupled with Butler's death, cleared the way very nicely.

Nevertheless, nothing was done until the March following Butler's death, when both Stener and Cowperwood had been incarcerated thirteen months—a length of time which seemed quite sufficient to appease the anger of the public at large. In this period Stener had undergone a considerable change physically and mentally. In spite of the fact that a number of the minor aldermen, who had profited in various ways by his largess, had called to see him, and that he had been given, as it were, almost the liberty of the place, and that his family had not been allowed to suffer, nevertheless he realized that his political and social days were over. Somebody might now occasionally send him a basket of fruit and assure him that he would not be compelled to suffer much longer; but when he did get out, he knew that he had nothing save his experience as an insurance agent and real-estate dealer to depend on. That had been precarious enough in the days when he was trying to get some small political foothold. How would it be when he was known only as the man who had looted the treasury of five hundred thousand dollars and been sent to the penitentiary for five years? Who would lend him the money wherewith to get a little start, even so much as four or five thousand dollars? The people who were calling to pay their respects now and then, and to assure him that he had been badly treated? Never. All of them could honestly claim that they had not so much to spare. If he had splendid security—yes; but if he had splendid security he would not need to go to them at all, and he had not. The man who would have actually helped him if he had only known was Frank A. Cowperwood. Stener could have confessed his mistake, as Cowperwood saw it, and Cowperwood would have given him the money gladly, without any thought of return. In his poor understanding of human nature, Stener considered that Cowperwood must be an enemy of his, and he would not have had either the courage or the business judgment to approach him.

During all this time, up to the day that he was discharged, Cowperwood had been working in his cell and slowly accumulating a little money through Wingate. He had paid Steger considerable sums from time to time, until that worthy finally decided that it would not be fair to take any more.

"If ever you get on your feet, Frank," he said, "you can remember me if you want to, but I don't think you'll want to. It's been nothing but lose, lose, lose for you through me. I'll undertake this matter of getting that appeal to the governor without any charge on my part. Anything I can do for you from now on is free gratis for nothing."

"Oh, don't talk nonsense, Harper," replied Cowperwood. "I don't know of anybody that could have done better with my case. Certainly there isn't anybody that I would have trusted as much. I don't like lawyers, you know."

"Yes—well," said Steger, "they've got nothing on financiers, so we'll call it even." And they shook hands.

So when it was finally decided to pardon Stener out—which was in the early part of March, 1873—Cowperwood's pardon was necessarily but gingerly included. A delegation, consisting of Strobik, Harmon, and Winpenny, representing, as it was intended to appear, the unanimous wishes of the council and the city administration, and speaking for Mollenhauer and Simpson, who had given their consent, visited the governor at Harrisburg and made the necessary formal representations which were intended to impress the public. At the same time, through the agency of Steger, Davison, and Walter Leigh, the appeal in behalf of Cowperwood was made. The governor, who had had instructions beforehand from sources quite superior to this committee, was very solemn about the whole procedure. He would take the matter under advisement. He would look into the history of the crimes and the records of the two men. He could make no promises—he would see. So in ten days, after allowing the petitions to gather considerable dust in one of his pigeonholes and doing absolutely nothing toward investigating anything, he issued two separate pardons in writing. One, as a matter of courtesy, he gave into the hands of Messrs. Strobik, Harmon, and Winpenny, to bear personally to Mr. Stener, as they desired that he should. The other, on Steger's request, he gave to him. The two committees which had called to receive them then departed; and the afternoon of the day on which the pardons were issued saw Strobik, Harmon, and Winpenny arrive in one group, and Steger, Wingate, and Walter Leigh in another, at the prison gate, but at different hours.

CHAPTER LXXIII

THIS matter of the pardon of Cowperwood, the exact time of it, was kept a secret from him, though the fact that he was to be pardoned soon, or that he had a very excellent chance of being, had not been denied—rather had been made much of from time to time. Wingate had kept him accurately informed as to the progress being made, as had Steger; but when it was actually ascertained, from the governor's private secretary, that a certain day would see the pardon handed over to them, Steger, Wingate, and Walter Leigh had agreed between themselves that they would say nothing, taking Cowperwood by surprise. They even went so far—that is, Steger and Wingate did—as to indicate to Cowperwood that there was some hitch to the proceedings and that he might not now get out so soon. Cowperwood was somewhat depressed, but properly stoical; he assured himself that he could wait, and that he would be all right sometime. He was rather surprised therefore, one Friday afternoon, to see Wingate, Steger, and Leigh appear at his cell door, accompanied by Warden Desmas. There had been a little tactical arrangement on the part of Steger and Leigh, which saw to it that the party which was taking out Stener should have proper leeway, should be gone, in fact, when they arrived.

Warden Desmas, to whom the pardon was submitted on their arrival, was quite pleased to think that Cowperwood should finally be going out—he admired him so much—and decided to come along to the cell, to see how he would take his liberation. The four thus arrived together, finding Cowperwood hard at work on his task of chair-caning. On the way Desmas commented on the fact that he had always been a model prisoner. "He kept a little garden out there in that yard of his," he confided to Walter Leigh, whom Steger introduced to him. "He had violets and pansies and geraniums out there, and they did very well, too."

Leigh smiled. It was like Cowperwood to be industrious and tasteful, even in prison. Such a man could not be conquered. "A very remarkable man, that," he remarked to Desmas.

"Very," replied the warden. "You can tell that by looking at him."

The four looked in through the barred door where he was working, without being observed, having come up quite silently.

"Hard at it, Frank?" asked Steger.

Cowperwood glanced over his shoulder and got up. He had been thinking, as always these days, of what he would do when he did get out. The death of Butler had improved matters much. His success with Wingate, in a small way, was a great aid. His wife had had time to become reconciled to the thought that he did not care to live with her any longer. Much lay before him, if he did not suffer some additional slap from fortune. Curiously, he had been feeling these days that he could not—that his period, his present period, at least, of storm and stress was over.

He smiled and nodded to Steger, Leigh, Wingate, and Warden Desmas. "What is this," he asked—"a political delegation?"

He had suspected something on the instant. All four smiled cheeringly, and Bonhag unlocked the door for the warden.

"Nothing very much, Frank," replied Steger, gleefully, "only you're a free man. You can gather up your traps and come right along, if you wish."

Cowperwood surveyed his friends with a level gaze.

He had not expected this so soon after what had been told him. He was not one to be very much interested in the practical joke or the surprise, but this pleased him— the sudden realization that he was free. Still, he had anticipated it so long that the charm of it had been discounted to a certain extent. He had been unhappy here, and he had not. The shame and humiliation of it, to begin with, had been much. Latterly, as he had become inured to it all, the sense of narrowness and humiliation had worn off. Only the consciousness of incarceration and delay irked him. Barring his intense desire for certain things—success and vindication, prin- cipally—he found that he could live in his narrow cell and be fairly comfortable. He had long since become used to the limy smell (used to defeat a more sickening one), and to the numerous rats which he quite regularly trapped. He had learned to take an interest in chair- caning, having become so proficient that he could seat twenty in a day if he chose, and in working in the little garden in spring, summer, and fall, which had been per- mitted him. Every evening he had studied the sky from his narrow yard, which resulted curiously in the gift in later years of a great reflecting telescope to a famous university. He had not looked upon himself as an ordinary prisoner, by any means—had not felt himself to be sufficiently pun- ished if a real crime had been involved. From Bonhag he had learned the history of many criminals here incar- cerated, from murderers up and down, and many had been pointed out to him from time to time. He had been escorted out into the general yard by Bonhag, had seen the general food of the place being prepared, had heard of Stener's modified life here, and so forth. It had finally struck him that it was not so bad, only that the delay to an individual like himself was wasteful. He could do so much now if he were out and did not have to fight court proceedings. Courts and jails! He shook his head when he thought of the waste involved in them.

"That's all right," he said, looking around him in an uncertain way. "I'm ready."

He stepped out into the hall, with scarcely a farewell glance, and to Bonhag, who was grieving greatly over the loss of so profitable a customer, he said: "I wish you would see that some of these things are sent over to my house, Walter. You're welcome to the chair, that clock, this mirror, those pictures—all of these things in fact, except my linen, razors, and so forth."

This last little act of beneficence soothed Bonhag's lacerated soul a little. They went out into the receiving overseer's office, where Cowperwood laid aside his prison suit and the soft shirt with a considerable sense of relief. The clog shoes had long since been parted with for a better pair of his own. He put on his well-preserved derby hat and his gray overcoat—the one he had worn the year before, on entering, and expressed himself as ready. At the entrance of the prison he turned and looked back—one last glance—at the iron door leading into the garden.

"You don't regret leaving that, do you, Frank?" asked Steger, curiously.

"I surely don't," replied Cowperwood. "It wasn't that I was thinking of. It was just the appearance of it, that's all."

In another minute they were at the outer gate, where Cowperwood shook the warden finally by the hand. He and Steger and Wingate and Leigh then entered a carriage outside the large, impressive, Gothic entrance; the gates locked behind them; and they drove away.

"Well, there's an end of that, Frank," observed Steger, gayly; "that will never bother you any more."

"Yes," replied Cowperwood. "It's worse to see it coming than going."

"It seems to me we ought to celebrate this occasion in some way," observed Walter Leigh. "It won't do just to take Frank home. Why don't we all go down to Green's? That's a good idea."

"I wish you wouldn't, Walter," replied Cowperwood, feelingly. "I'll get together with you all, later. Just now I'd like to go home and change these clothes."

He was thinking of Aileen and his children and his mother and father and of his whole future. Life was going to broaden out for him considerably from now on, he was sure of it. He had learned so much about taking care of himself in those thirteen months. He was going to see Aileen, and find how she felt about things in general, and then he was going to resume some such duties as he had had in his own concern, with Wingate & Co. He was going to secure a seat on 'change again, through his friends; and, to escape the effect of the prejudice of those who might care to do business with an ex-convict, he was going to act as general outside man, and floor man on 'change, for Wingate & Co. His practical control of that could not be publicly proved. Now for some important development in the market—some slump or something. He would show the world whether he was a failure or not.

They let him down in front of his wife's little cottage, and he entered briskly in the gathering gloom.

On September 18, 1873, at twelve-fifteen high noon of a brilliant autumn day, in the city of Philadelphia, one of the most startling financial tragedies that the world has ever seen had its commencement. The banking house of Jay Cooke & Co., the foremost financial organization of America, doing business at Number 114 South Third Street in Philadelphia, and with branches in New York, Washington, and London, closed its doors. Those who know anything about the financial crises of the United States know well the significance of the panic which followed. It is spoken of in all histories as the panic of 1873, and the wide-spread ruin and disaster which followed was practically unprecedented in American history.

At this time Frank Algernon Cowperwood was once more a broker—ostensibly a broker's agent—doing business in South Third Street, and representing Wingate & Co. on 'change. During the six months which had elapsed since he had emerged from the Eastern Penitentiary he had been quietly resuming financial, if not social, relations with those who had known him before.

Wingate & Co. were prospering, and had been for some time, and that gave him a good standing. Ostensibly he lived with his wife in the small house in North Twenty-first Street. In reality he occupied a bachelor apartment in North Fifteenth Street, to which his intended wife occasionally repaired. The difference between himself and his wife had now become a matter of common knowledge in the family, and, although there were some faint efforts made to smooth the matter over, no good came of it. He frankly told his parents that so far as he was concerned he was through with the old order of existence, and from now on the paths of himself and his wife would lie in different directions. The difficulties of the last two years which they had experienced had so inured his parents to expect the untoward and exceptional that, astonishing as this was, it did not shock them so much as it would have years before. They were too much frightened by life to quarrel with its weird developments. They could only hope and pray for the best.

The Butler family, on the other hand, what there was of it, had become indifferent to Aileen's conduct. She was ignored by her brothers and Norah, who had heard; and her mother was so taken up with her religious devotions and her brooding contemplation of her loss that she was not as active in her observation of Aileen's life as she might have been. Besides, Cowperwood and his mistress were more circumspect in their conduct than they had ever been before. Their movements were more carefully guarded, though the result was the same. Cowperwood was thinking of the West—of reaching some slight local standing here in Philadelphia, and then, with perhaps one hundred thousand dollars in capital, starting out into the boundless prairies of which he had heard so much—Chicago, Fargo, Duluth, Sioux City, places then heralded in Philadelphia and the East as coming centers of great life—and taking Aileen with him. The problem of marriage with her was insoluble unless Mrs. Cowperwood should formally agree to give him up—a possibility which was not manifest at this time. The only thing which he could see for it was for him to take Aileen away with him, and to trust to time and absence to modify his wife's point of view.

This particular panic, which was destined to mark a notable change in Cowperwood's career, was one of those peculiar things which spring naturally out of the optimism of the American people and the irrepressible progress of the country. It was the result, to be accurate, of the prestige and ambition of Jay Cooke, whose early training and subsequent success had all been acquired in Philadelphia, and who had since become the foremost financial figure of his day. It would be useless to attempt to trace here the rise of this man to distinction; it need only be said that by suggestions which he made and methods which he devised the Union government, in its darkest hours, was able to raise the money wherewith to continue the struggle against the South. After the Civil War this man, who had built up a tremendous banking business in Philadelphia, with great branches in New York and Washington, was at a loss for some time for some significant thing to do, some constructive work which would be worthy of his genius. The war was over; the only thing which remained was the finances of peace, and the greatest things in American financial enterprise were those related to the construction of transcontinental railway lines. The Union Pacific, authorized in 1860, was already building; the Northern Pacific and the Southern Pacific were already dreams in various pioneer minds. The great thing was to connect the Atlantic and the Pacific by steel, to bind up the territorially perfected and newly solidified Union, or to enter upon some vast project of mining, of which gold and silver were the most important. Actually railway-building was the most significant of all, and railroad stocks were far and away the most valuable and important on every exchange in America. Here in Philadelphia, New York Central, Rock Island, Wabash, Central Pacific, St. Paul, Hannibal & St. Joseph, Union Pacific, and Ohio & Mississippi were freely traded in. There were men who were getting rich and famous out of handling these things; and such towering figures as William H. Vanderbilt, Jay Gould, Daniel Drew, James Fish, and others in the East, and Fair, Crocker, W. R. Hearst, and Collis P. Huntington, in the West, were already raising their heads like vast mountains in connection with these enterprises. Among those who dreamed most ardently on this score was Jay Cooke, who without the wolfish cunning of a Gould or the practical knowledge of a Vanderbilt, was ambitious to thread the northern reaches of America with a band of steel which should be a permanent memorial to his name. The project which fascinated him most was one that related to the development of the territory then lying almost unexplored between the extreme shores of Lake Superior, where Duluth now stands, and that portion of the Pacific Ocean into which the Columbia River empties—the extreme northern one-third of the United States. Here, if a railroad were built, would spring up great cities and prosperous towns. There were, it was suspected, mines of various metals in the region of the Rockies which this railroad would traverse, and untold wealth to be reaped from the fertile corn and wheat lands. Products brought only so far east as Duluth could then be shipped to the Atlantic, *via* the Great Lakes and the Erie Canal, at a greatly reduced cost. It was a vision of empire, not unlike the Panama Canal project of the same period, and one that bade fair apparently to be as useful to humanity. It had aroused the interest and enthusiasm of Cooke.

Because of the fact that the government had made a grant of vast areas of land on either side of the proposed track to the corporation that should seriously undertake it and complete it within a reasonable number of years, and because of the opportunity it gave him of remaining a distinguished public figure, he had eventually shouldered the project. It was open to many objections and criticisms; but the genius which had been sufficient to finance the Civil War was considered sufficient to finance the Northern Pacific Railroad. Cooke undertook it with the idea of being able to put the merits of the proposition before the people direct—not through the agency of any great financial corporation—and of selling to the butcher, the baker, and the candlestick-maker the stock or shares that he wished to dispose of.

It was a brilliant chance. His genius had worked out the sale of great government loans during the Civil War to the people direct in this fashion. Why not Northern Pacific certificates? For several years he conducted a magnificent campaign, surveying the territory in question, organizing great railway-construction corps, building hundreds of miles of track under most trying conditions, and selling great blocks of his stock, on which interest of a certain percentage was guaranteed. If it had not been that he knew little of railroad-building, personally, and that the project was so vast that it could not well be encompassed by one man, even so great a man, it might have proved successful, as under subsequent management it did. However, hard times, the war between France and Germany, which tied up European capital for the time being and made it indifferent to American projects, envy, calumny, a certain percentage of mismanagement, all conspired to wreck it. On September 18, 1873, at twelve-fifteen noon, Jay Cooke & Co. failed for approximately eight million dollars and the Northern Pacific for all that had been invested in it—some fifty million dollars more.

One can imagine what the result was—the most important financier and the most distinguished railway enterprise collapsing at one and the same time. "A financial thunderclap in a clear sky," said the Philadelphia *Press*. "No one could have been more surprised," said the Philadelphia *Inquirer*, "if snow had fallen amid the sunshine of a summer noon." The public, which by Cooke's previous tremendous success had been lulled into believing him invincible, could not understand it. It was beyond belief. Jay Cooke fail? Impossible, or anything connected with him. Nevertheless, he had failed; and the New York Stock Exchange, after witnessing a number of crashes immediately afterward, closed for eight days. The Lake Shore Railroad failed to pay a call-loan of one million seven hundred and fifty thousand dollars; and the Union Trust Company, allied to the Vanderbilt interests, closed its doors after withstanding a prolonged run. The National Trust Company of New York had eight hundred thousand dollars of government securities in its vaults, but not a dollar could be borrowed upon them; and it suspended. Suspicion was universal, rumor affected every one.

In Philadelphia, when the news reached the stock exchange, it came first in the form of a brief despatch addressed to the stock board from the New York Stock Exchange—"Rumor on street of failure of Jay Cooke & Co. Answer." It was not believed, and so not replied to. Nothing was thought of it. The world of brokers, of whom Frank A. Cowperwood was one, paid scarcely any attention to it.

Cowperwood, however, who had followed the fortunes of Jay Cooke & Co. with considerable suspicion of its president's brilliant theory of vending his wares direct to the people—clergymen, grocers, etc.—was perhaps the only one who had suspicions. He had once written a brilliant criticism to some inquirer, in which he had said that no enterprise of such magnitude as the Northern Pacific had ever before been entirely dependent upon one house, or rather upon one man, and that he did not like it. "I am not sure that the lands through which the road runs are so unparalleled in climate, soil, timber, minerals, etc., as Mr. Cooke and his friends would have us believe. Neither do I think that the road can at present, or for many years to come, earn the interest which its great issues of stock call for. There is great danger and risk there."

So when the notice was posted, he looked at it, wondering what the effect would be if by any chance Jay Cooke & Co. should fail.

He was not long in wonder. A second despatch posted on 'change read: "New York, September 18th. Jay Cooke & Co. have suspended."

Cowperwood could not believe it. He was beside himself with the thought of a great opportunity. In company with every other broker, he hurried into Third Street and up to Number 114, where the famous old banking house was located, in order to be sure. Despite his natural dignity and reserve, he did not hesitate actually to run. If this were true, a great hour had struck. There would be wide-spread panic and disaster. There would be a terrific slump in prices of all stocks. He must be in the thick of it. Wingate must be on hand, and his two brothers. He must tell them how to sell and when and what to buy. Now was his great hour.

CHAPTER LXXIV

THE banking house of Jay Cooke & Co., in spite of its tremendous significance as a banking and promoting concern, was a most unpretentious affair, four stories and a half in height, of gray stone and red brick, sixty by one hundred in size, and most unsatisfactory as to its floor height and general air-space. It had never been deemed a handsome or comfortable banking house. Cowperwood had been there often. Wharf-rats as long as the forearm of a man crept up the culverted channels of Dock Street to run through the apartments at will. Scores of clerks worked under gas-jets, where light and air were not any too abundant, keeping track of the firm's vast accounts. It was next door to the Girard National Bank, where Cowperwood's friend Davison still flourished, and where the principal financial business of the street converged. As Cowperwood ran he met his brother Edward, who was coming to the stock exchange with some word for him from Wingate.

"Run and get Wingate and Joe," he said. "There's something big on this afternoon. Jay Cooke has failed."

Edward waited for no other word, but hurried off to get his brother and Wingate as directed.

Cowperwood reached Cooke & Co. among the earliest. To his utter astonishment, the solid brown-oak doors, with which he was familiar, were shut at twelve-fifteen of this bright noonday, and a notice posted on them, which he quickly read, ran:

September 18, 1873.

To the Public,—We regret to be obliged to announce that, owing to unexpected demands on us, our firm has been obliged to

suspend payment. In a few days we will be able to present a statement to our creditors, until which time we must ask for their patient
consideration. We believe our assets to be largely in excess of our
liabilities.

JAY COOKE & CO.

A magnificent gleam of triumph sprang into Cowperwood's eye. In company with many others he turned
and ran back toward the exchange, while a reporter, who
had come for information, knocked at the massive doors
of the banking house, and was told by a porter, who peered
out of a diamond-shaped aperture, that Jay Cooke had
gone home for the day and was not to be seen.

"Now," thought Cowperwood, to whom this panic
spelled opportunity, not ruin, "I'll get my innings. I'll
go short of this—of everything."

Before, when the panic following the Chicago fire had
occurred, he had been long—had been compelled to stay
long of many things in order to protect himself. To-day he
had nothing to speak of—perhaps a paltry seventy-five
thousand dollars which he had managed to scrape together.
Thank God! he had only the reputation of Wingate's
old house to lose, if he lost, which was nothing. With it
as a trading agency behind him—with it as an excuse for
his presence, his right to buy and sell—he had everything
to gain. Where many men were thinking of ruin, he was
thinking of success. He would have Wingate and his two
brothers under him to execute his orders exactly. He
could pick up a fourth and a fifth man if necessary. He
would give them orders to sell—everything—ten, fifteen,
twenty, thirty points off, if necessary, in order to trap the
unwary, depress the market, frighten the fearsome who
would think he was too daring; and then he would buy,
buy, buy, below these figures as much as possible, in order
to cover his sales and reap a profit. His instinct told him
how wide-spread and enduring this panic would be. The
Northern Pacific was a hundred-million-dollar venture. It
involved the savings of hundreds of thousands of people

—small bankers, tradesmen, preachers, lawyers, doctors, widows, institutions all over the land, and all resting on the faith and security of Jay Cooke. Once, not unlike the Chicago fire map, Cowperwood had seen a grand prospectus and map of the location of the Northern Pacific land-grant which Cooke had controlled, showing a vast stretch or belt of territory extending from Duluth—"The Zenith City of the Unsalted Seas," as Proctor Knott, speaking in the House of Representatives, had sarcastically called it—through the Rockies and the headwaters of the Missouri to the Pacific Ocean. He had seen how Cooke had ostensibly managed to get control of this government grant, containing millions upon millions of acres and extending fourteen hundred miles in length; but it was only a vision of empire. There might be silver and gold and copper mines there, if you would. The land was usable—would some day be usable. But what of it now? It would do to fire the imaginations of fools with —nothing more. It was inaccessible, and would remain so for years to come. No doubt thousands had subscribed to build this road; but, too, thousands would now fail if it had failed. Now the crash had come. The grief and the rage of the public would be intense. For days and days and weeks and months normal confidence and courage would be gone. This was Cowperwood's hour. This was his great moment. Like a wolf prowling under glittering, bitter stars in the night, he was looking down into the humble folds of simple men and seeing what their ignorance and their unsophistication would cost them. He hurried back to the exchange, the very same room in which only two years before he had fought his losing fight, and, finding that his partner and his brothers had not yet come, began to sell everything in sight. Pandemonium had broken loose. Boys and men were fairly tearing in from all sections with orders from panic-struck brokers to sell, sell, sell, and later with orders to buy; the various trading-posts were reeling, swirling masses of

brokers and their agents. Outside in the street, in front
of Jay Cooke & Co., Clark & Co., the Girard National
Bank, and other institutions, immense crowds were beginning to form. They were hurrying here to learn the
trouble, to withdraw their deposits, to protect their interests generally. A policeman arrested a boy for calling
out the failure of Jay Cooke & Co., but nevertheless the
news of the great disaster was spreading like wild-fire.

Among these panic-struck men Cowperwood was perfectly calm, deadly cold, the same Cowperwood who had
pegged solemnly at his ten chairs each day in prison,
who had baited his traps for rats, and worked in the
little garden allotted him in utter silence and loneliness.
Now he was vigorous and energetic. He had been just
sufficiently long on 'change once more to have made his
personality impressive and distinguished. He forced his
way into the center of swirling crowds of men already
shouting themselves hoarse, offering whatever was being
offered in quantities which were astonishing, and at
prices which allured the few who were anxious to make
money out of the tumbling prices to buy. New York
Central had been standing at $104\frac{7}{8}$ when the failure
was announced; Rhode Island at $108\frac{7}{8}$; Western Union
at $92\frac{1}{2}$; Wabash at $70\frac{1}{4}$; Panama at $117\frac{3}{8}$; Central
Pacific at $99\frac{5}{8}$; St. Paul at 51; Hannibal & St. Joseph
at 48; Northwestern at 63; Union Pacific at $26\frac{3}{4}$; Ohio
and Mississippi at $38\frac{3}{4}$. Cowperwood's house had
scarcely any of the stocks on hand. They were not
carrying them for any customers, and yet he sold, sold,
sold, to whoever would take, at prices which he felt
sure would inspire them.

"Five thousand of New York Central at ninety-nine,
ninety-eight, ninety-seven, ninety-six, ninety-five, ninety-
four, ninety-three, ninety-two, ninety-one, ninety, eighty-
nine," you might have heard him call; and when his sales
were not sufficiently brisk he would turn to something else
—Rock Island, Panama, Central Pacific, Western Union,

Northwestern, Union Pacific. He saw his brother and Wingate hurrying in, and stopped in his work long enough to instruct them. "Sell everything you can," he cautioned them quietly, "at fifteen points off if you have to —no lower than that—and buy all you can below it. Ed, you see if you cannot buy up some local street-railways at fifteen off. Joe, you stay near me and buy when I tell you."

All the while the secretary of the board, the thin, cadaverous Mr. Ammerman, was appearing on his little platform.

"E. W. Clark & Company," he announced, at one-thirty, "have just closed their doors."

"Tighe & Company," he called, at one-forty-five, "announce that they are compelled to suspend."

"The First National Bank of Philadelphia," he called, at two o'clock, "begs to state that it cannot at present meet its obligations."

After each announcement, always, as in the past, when the gong had compelled silence, the crowd broke into an ominous "Aw, aw, aw."

"Tighe & Company," thought Cowperwood, for a single second, when he heard it. "There's an end of him." And then he returned to his task.

When the time for closing came, his coat torn, his collar twisted loose, his necktie ripped, his hat lost, he emerged sane, quiet, steady-mannered.

"Well, Ed," he inquired, meeting his brother, "how'd you make out?"

The latter was equally torn, scratched, exhausted.

"I never saw such a place as this," he replied, tugging at his sleeves. "They almost tore my clothes off."

"Buy any local street-railways?"

"About four thousand shares."

"We'd better go down to Green's," Frank observed, speaking of the lobby of the principal hotel. "We're not through yet. There'll be more trading there."

He led the way to find Wingate and his brother Joe, and together they were off, figuring up some of the larger phases of their purchases and sales as they went.

The excitement did not end with the coming of the night. The crowd lingered in front of Jay Cooke & Co.'s on Third Street and in front of other institutions, waiting apparently for some development which would be favorable to them. For the initiated the center of debate and agitation was Green's Hotel, where on the evening of the eighteenth the lobby and corridors were crowded with bankers, brokers, and speculators. The stock exchange had practically adjourned to that hotel *en masse*. What of the morrow? Who would be the next to fail? From whence would money be forthcoming? These were the topics from each mind and upon each tongue. From New York was coming momentarily more news of disaster. Over there banks and trust companies were falling like trees in a hurricane. Cowperwood in his perambulations, seeing what he could see and hearing what he could hear, reaching understandings which were against the rules of the exchange, but which were nevertheless in accord with what every other person was doing, saw men known to him as agents of Mollenhauer and Simpson about, and congratulated himself that he would have something to collect from them before the week was over. He might not own a street-railway, but he would have the means to. He learned from hearsay, and information which had been received from New York and elsewhere, that things were as bad as they could be, and that there was no hope for those who expected a speedy return of normal conditions. No thought of retiring for the night entered until the last man was gone. It was then practically morning.

The next day was Friday, and suggested many ominous things. Would it be another Black Friday? Cowperwood was at his office before the street was fairly awake. He figured out his programme for the day to a nicety, feeling strangely different from the way he had felt two years before when the conditions were not dissimilar. Yesterday, in spite of the sudden onslaught, he had made one hundred and fifty thousand dollars, and he expected to make as much, if not more, to-day. There was no telling what he could make, he thought, if he could only keep his small organization in perfect trim and get his assistants to follow his orders exactly. Ruin for others began early with the suspension of Fisk & Hatch, Jay Cooke's faithful lieutenants during the Civil War. They had calls upon them for one million five hundred thousand dollars in the first fifteen minutes after opening the doors, and at once closed them again, the failure being ascribed to Collis P. Huntington's Central Pacific Railroad and the Chesapeake & Ohio. There was a long-continued run on the Fidelity Trust Company. News of these facts, and of failures in New York posted on 'change, strengthened the cause Cowperwood was so much interested in; for he was selling as high as he could and buying as low as he could on a constantly sinking scale. By twelve o'clock he figured with his assistants that he had cleared one hundred thousand dollars; and by three o'clock he had two hundred thousand dollars more. That afternoon between three and seven he spent adjusting his trades, and between seven and one in the morning, without anything to eat, in gathering as much additional information as he could and laying his plans for the future. Saturday morning came, and he repeated his performance of the day before, following it up with adjustments on Sunday and heavy trading on Monday. By Monday afternoon at three o'clock he figured that, all losses and uncertainties to one side, he was once more a millionaire, and that now his future lay clear and straight before him.

As he sat at his desk late that afternoon in his office looking out into Third Street, where a hurrying of brokers, messengers, and anxious depositors still maintained, he had the feeling that so far as Philadelphia and the life here was concerned, his day and its day with him was over. He did not care anything about the brokerage business any more. Failures such as this, and disasters such as the Chicago fire, that had overtaken him two years before, had cured him of all love of the stock exchange and all feeling for Philadelphia. He had been very unhappy here in spite of all his previous happiness; and his experience as a convict had made him, he could see quite plainly, unacceptable to the element he had once hoped to associate with. There was nothing else to do, now that he had re-established himself as a Philadelphia business man and been pardoned for an offense which he hoped to make people believe he had never committed, but to leave Philadelphia to seek a new world.

"If I get out of this safely," he said to himself, "this is the end. I am going West, and going into some other line of business." He thought of street-railways, land speculation, some great manufacturing project of some kind, even mining, on a legitimate basis. Anything, not to be a broker any more.

"I have had my lesson," he said to himself, finally getting up and preparing to leave. "I am as rich as I was, and only a little older. They caught me once, but they will not catch me again." He talked to Wingate about following up the campaign on the lines in which he had started, and he himself intended to follow them up with great energy; but all the while his mind was running with this one rich thought: "I am a millionaire. I am a free man. I am only thirty-six, and my future is all before me."

It was with this thought that he went to visit Aileen, and to plan for the future.

It was some six months later that a train, speeding through the mountains of Pennsylvania and over the plains of Ohio and Indiana, bore to Chicago and the

West the young financial aspirant who, in spite of youth and wealth and a notable vigor of body, was a solemn, conservative speculator as to what his future might be. The West held much. He had studied the receipts of the New York Clearing House recently and the disposition of bank-balances and the shipment of gold, and seen that vast quantities of the latter metal were going to Chicago. He understood finance accurately. The meaning of gold shipments was clear. Where money was going *trade was*—a thriving, developing life. He wished to see clearly for himself what this world had to offer. Two years later, after there had been the meteoric appearance of a young speculator in Duluth, and after Chicago had seen the tentative opening of a grain and commission company labeled Frank A. Cowperwood & Co., which ostensibly dealt in the great wheat crops of the West, a quiet divorce was granted Mrs. Frank A. Cowperwood in Philadelphia, because apparently she wished it. Time had not seemingly dealt badly with her. Her financial affairs, once so bad, were now apparently all straightened out, and she occupied in West Philadelphia, near one of her sisters, a new and interesting home which was fitted with all the comforts of an excellent middle-class residence. Mrs. Frank A. Cowperwood was now quite religious once more. The two children, Frank and Lillian, were in private schools, returning evenings to their mother. "Wash" Sims was once more the general negro factotum. Frequent visitors on Sundays were Mr. and Mrs. Henry Worthington Cowperwood, no longer distressed financially, but subdued and wearied, the wind completely gone from their once much-favored sails. Here, too, came Anna Adelaide Cowperwood on occasion, a clerk in the city water office, who speculated much as to the strange vicissitudes of life. She had great interest in her brother, who seemed destined by fate to play a conspicuous part in the world; but she could not understand him. Seeing that all those who were near to him in any way seemed to rise or fall with his prosperity, she did not understand how justice and morals were arranged in this world. There seemed to be certain general principles—or people assumed there were—but apparently there were exceptions. Assuredly her brother abided by no known rule, and yet he seemed to be doing fairly well once more. What did this mean? Mrs. Cowperwood, his former wife, condemned his actions, and yet accepted of his prosperity as her due. What were the ethics of that?

In another part of the city there had lived for some time, with her mother, Aileen Butler, who had long continued a relationship which to her seemed final and irretrievable. She had speculated much as to her past conduct and her future, and had rejoiced at Frank's sudden return to wealth and power. His every action was known to her, his present whereabouts and prospects. Not long after his wife's divorce, and after many trips to and from this new world in which he was now living, these two left Philadelphia one afternoon in the winter for good. Aileen explained to her mother, who was willing to go and live with Norah, that she had fallen in love with the former banker and wished to marry him. The old lady, gathering only a garbled version of it at first, consented. There was then their final departure, which ended forever for Aileen this long-continued relationship with this older world. Chicago was before her—a much more distinguished career, Frank told her, than ever they would have had in Philadelphia.

"Isn't it nice to be finally going?" she commented.

"It is advantageous, anyhow," he said.

CONCERNING MYCTEROPERCA BONACI

There is a certain fish whose scientific name is Mycteroperca Bonaci, and whose common name is Black Grouper,

THE FINANCIER

which is of considerable value as an afterthought in this connection, and which deserves much to be better known. It is a healthy creature, growing quite regularly to a weight of two hundred and fifty pounds, and living a comfortable, lengthy existence because of its very remarkable ability to adapt itself to conditions. That very subtle thing which we call the creative power, and which we endue with the spirit of the beatitudes, is supposed to build this mortal life in such fashion that only honesty and virtue shall prevail. Witness, then, the significant manner in which it has fashioned the black grouper. One might go far afield and gather less forceful indictments — the horrific spider spinning his trap for the unthinking fly; the lovely Drosera (Sundew) using its crimson calyx for a smothering-pit in which to seal and devour the victim of its beauty; the rainbow-colored jellyfish that spreads its prismed tentacles like streamers of great beauty, only to sting and torture all that falls within their radiant folds. Man himself is busy digging the pit and fashioning the snare, but he will not believe it. His feet are in the trap of circumstance; his eyes are on an illusion.

Mycteroperca moving in its dark world of green waters is as fine an illustration of the constructive genius of nature, which is not beatific, as any which the mind of man may discover. Its great superiority lies in an almost unbelievable power of simulation, which relates solely to the pigmentation of its skin. In electrical mechanics we pride ourselves on our ability to make over one brilliant scene into another in the twinkling of an eye, and flash before the gaze of an onlooker picture after picture, which appear and disappear as we look. The directive control of Mycteroperca over its appearance is much more significant. You cannot look at it long without feeling that you are witnessing something spectral and unnatural, so brilliant is its power to deceive. From being black it can become instantly white; from being an earth-colored brown it can fade into a delicious water-colored green. Its markings change as the clouds of the sky. One marvels at the variety and subtlety of its power.

Lying at the bottom of a bay, it can simulate the mud by which it is surrounded. Hidden in the folds of glorious leaves, it is of the same markings. Lurking in a flaw of light, it is like the light itself shining dimly in water. Its power to elude or strike unseen is of the greatest.

What would you say was the intention of the over-ruling, intelligent, constructive force which gives to Mycteroperca this ability? To fit it to be truthful? To permit it to present an unvarying appearance which all honest life-seeking fish may know? Or would you say that subtlety, chicanery, trickery, were here at work? An implement of illusion one might readily suspect it to be, a living lie, a creature whose business it is to appear what it is not, to simulate that with which it has nothing in common, to get its living by great subtlety, the power of its enemies to forfend against which is little. The indictment is fair.

Would you say in the face of this that a beatific, beneficent creative overruling power never wills that which is either tricky or deceptive? Or would you say that this material seeming in which we dwell is itself an illusion? If not, whence then the Ten Commandments and the illusion of justice? Why were the beatitudes dreamed and how do they avail?

THE MAGIC CRYSTAL

If you had been a mystic or a soothsayer or a member of that mysterious world which divines by incantations, dreams, the mystic bowl, or the crystal sphere, you might have looked into their mysterious depths at this time and foreseen a world of happenings which concerned these two, who were now apparently so fortunately placed. In the fumes of the witches' pot, or the depths of the radiant crystal, might have been revealed cities, cities, cities; a world of mansions, carriages, jewels, beauty; a vast metropolis outraged by the power of one man; a great State seething with indignation over a force it could not control; vast halls of priceless pictures; a palace unrivaled for its magnificence; a whole world reading with wonder, at times, of a given name.

And sorrow, sorrow, sorrow.

The three witches that hailed Macbeth upon the blasted heath might in turn have called to Cowperwood, "Hail to thee, Frank Cowperwood, master of a great railway system! Hail to thee, Frank Cowperwood, builder of a priceless mansion! Hail to thee, Frank Cowperwood, patron of arts and possessor of endless riches! Thou shalt be famed hereafter." But like the Weird Sisters, they would have lied, for in the glory was also the ashes of Dead Sea fruit—an understanding that could neither be inflamed by desire nor satisfied by luxury; a heart that was long since wearied by experience; a soul that was as bereft of illusion as a windless moon. And to Aileen, as to Macduff, they might have spoken a more pathetic promise, one that concerned hope and failure. To have and not to have! All the seeming, and yet the sorrow of not having! Brilliant society that shone in a mirage, yet locked its doors; love that eluded as a will-o'-the-wisp and died in the dark. "Hail to thee, Frank Cowperwood, master and no master, prince of a world of dreams whose reality was sorrow!" So might the witches have called, the bowl have danced with figures, the fumes with vision, and it would have been true. What wise man might not read from such a beginning, such an end?

THE END